Born in 1965, Jeremy Dronfield grew up in South Wales. He was educated (eventually) at the universities of Southampton and Cambridge, where he took degrees in Archaeology. This is his second novel.

Also by Jeremy Dronfield

The Locust Farm

RESURRECTING SALVADOR

Jeremy Dronfield

HEADLINE
FEATURE

First published in 1999
by HEADLINE BOOK PUBLISHING

A HEADLINE FEATURE softback

10 9 8 7 6 5 4 3 2

ISBN 0 7472 7314 6

Typeset by
Letterpart Limited, Reigate, Surrey

Printed and bound in Great Britain by
Mackays of Chatham PLC, Chatham, Kent

HEADLINE BOOK PUBLISHING
A division of Hodder Headline PLC
338 Euston Road
London NW1 3BH

For Kate again
and to the memory of
F.Z.

Information is not knowledge
Knowledge is not wisdom
Wisdom is not truth
Truth is not beauty
Beauty is not love
Love is not music
Music is THE BEST
(Frank Zappa, *Joe's Garage Act III*)

Like a cluster bomb, history split its seams and scattered its little bomblets of mayhem into all their lives; at so many times and places, and in so many ways, it is difficult to know where to begin. Begin at the beginning, you say. Skim your fingernail around the roll of tape, searching for the point where it catches and pulls, crumpling into a wrinkled ridge then peeling away with a rasp.

That's one way; the natural beginning, just waiting for you to find it.

Or pick a card; go on, any card. Look at it, memorise it, and put it back on top of the deck . . .

Or think of Salvador and dig deeper for a metaphor . . .

Skate the tip of your finger along the string, springing away as you pluck it: pluck and release, pluck and release – until the resonant harmonic is reached, hypersonic, oscillating through the cavities of the whole instrument . . .

And on a coda, of course, or perhaps a brief cadenza; that is how Salvador would have conceived of it.

Or . . .

Or it might simply begin on a blue summer's day in the long, green, rocky valley where orange roof-tops hung from the steep scarp and flurried down to huddle and bake in the bottom of the fold, where an impatient white river giggled between the piers of a long-legged stone bridge.

He presses his foot on the brake, and guides the little red Lotus to a gentle halt in a passing-place below an overhanging cliff.

Come on, he says. *Let's look.*

He doesn't bother to open the little door; the car's white carapace has been folded and stowed, so he simply – and with prehensile grace – pushes himself up onto the seat-back, swings his legs out and ejects himself onto the tarmac.

1

You're full of beans all of a sudden, she says with an indulgent smile, but he doesn't hear her; he has crossed the road, and the whine of a Citroën struggling up the hill in low gear drowns out her words. She gets out of the car (decorously using the door) and pauses for the passage of a second Citroën and a Mercedes van. She waits while they race past, horns shouting, skirmishing their way down towards the little town, then crosses the road to join him.

He is sitting on the low stone wall that fringes the narrow road, an insubstantial lip against the gaping drop to the valley floor. As she approaches cautiously (she hates heights), his eyes turn from the view and look up at her. *I said, you're full of beans all of a sudden.* Her smile is a little more fixed, a little less indulgent. He smiles back. *I never tire of your little colloquialisms. I seem to hear a new one every day.* He pats the warm wall and nods at the view. *Come and see. Sit by me and look – it's beautiful.* He finally notices the fearful expression in her face. *I can't*, she says. *I hate heights – But you're standing in the traffic*, he protests. *You'll get run down.* She shakes her head. *I think I'll go and sit back in the car.*

As she is about to move away, he catches hold of the hem of her skirt and tugs. Off balance, she squeals and stumbles forward a step; close enough for him to wrap an arm tightly around her thighs. He holds her there: she wriggles and pushes against his shoulder, her eyes closed tight and beginning to be tearful, but he notices that her mouth cannot help smiling a little; that there is an ecstasy of exhilaration mingled with the terror; danger viewed from safety. He hugs her closer to him, and her resistance begins to subside.

Look, he says. *Just open your eyes and take a look. You don't know what you're missing. – Seen it*, she says, shuddering. He laughs. *No, you haven't. Open your eyes. Go on, just a little peek. – I can't. – Yes, you can.* Her eyes flicker open – just momentarily, just long enough for the yawning, rock-toothed void to swoop in on her – then she closes them again. His strong arm clamped around her thighs makes her feel secure – she knows she won't fall – but her brain cannot encompass the breadth and depth of the drop: it spills over her synapses and sends tingling sparks of terror down to her nerve endings. Her knees are buckling, freezing. She wraps her arms around his head, stuck like a cat on a limb, unable to move.

Take me back, she begs. *Please.* The fear has outgrown the ecstasy, and he can see tears brimming through her knitted eyelids. He stands – slowly, awkwardly as she clings to him and squeaks in alarm at every movement – and shepherds her back across the road. As he helps her into the car, he feels a shiver rack her body. He crouches down beside her and looks into her face.

Are you okay? He rummages in the glove compartment and unearths a packet of tissues wrapped in cellophane. He tears one out and hands it to her. She dabs at her eyes and nods reluctantly, dutifully. *I will be.*

Satisfied and contrite in equal measure, he stands up and looks at the view once more.

I'm home, he whispers.

Or . . .

It might begin with that first entry in Lydia's little notebook. That's how she would have conceived of it. Left behind in that lonely room, scribing tiny writing onto the ruled page.

See through the tears into a dream, and watch the dream come real . . .
Buried . . .

Go on; imagine it one more time. Set your mind to work on the details, and maybe this time it will be true. Start with the physical sensations; think about each one individually, isolated.

Encased

Stripped

Bound

Ensheathed

Now suture them, blend them together, explore them as one . . . And here it comes; always returning to the claustrophobia; enclosed in shell-pink satin; not a fabric you would have chosen for yourself, but you do not imagine that you will get to exercise a choice in this. Underneath the satin is a layer of thin white plastic sheet cut from a giant roll (you can feel it crackle under the glossy fabric) – just in case, you understand; just in case: sometimes the burst and punctured dribble terrible liquors from their rents and orifices. Behind the plastic is wood: smooth oak, pale as bled flesh.

And what about sounds? Muffled, of course; all the high frequencies of ambient space peeled away as the vibrations struggle through the dense layers. Only the lower, lumpen, obdurate tones make it all the way to your sheathed ears. Muted, wordless voices. A solitary declamation; a rustling congregational reply. And soft music like air bellying a curtain in an open window. And then, out of the music, comes the *p . . . p . . . p . . .* Frozen feet; deadened footfalls of hard heels on cold stone . . . coming closer . . . and halting on the other side of the darkness.

Then a pause filled with breathless anticipation . . .

You can feel the sudden intakes of breath and the little stifled grunts, then you are rising – after so many silent hours of stillness, you are up and moving; sailing along with perfect grace, eased by a hundred solemn sidelong glances (a hundred? – just one would do); away from the mourning music, out of the shadows and into the light . . .

. . . People do not know this . . . you yourself did not know this until it happened to you – but you can sense this change; you can feel the shift, like strong sun on closed eyelids; you see it even through the tight cocoon of satin and oak . . .

The music recedes further; no more than a distant whisper now, and the footfalls crunch on gravel. A turn, a short, slow journey of gentle rises and falls, like a blunt-prowed barque over frozen ocean swells, and then a pause, and you are sinking . . . sinking . . . sinking . . .

A jolt, and your journey has reached its last pause, still washed with light; a pause that pulses with a single recitative voice, then you skate sideways and sink again – floating down like a feather, inch by inch, and come to rest at last. The slack straps tauten and slide out from under you, snapping out and trailing loose like streamers from a departing ship, and you are alone.

They are still there, the congregated presences, but you are alone in your deep earthen plot. The patter of stones and soil on the low roof above your chest finally blots out that last vestige of filtered, muffled light, and . . .

. . . And what if you could rise up now? What if you could drift out invisibly and look into their faces, what would you see? How many of them are there for you, and how do they feel? There is no way of knowing. But how otherwise can you know what your life is like; until it is finished? Like knitting up a garment, you cannot tell until the end whether your life will even fit you. Now, when it is finally over, it is too late; now, when at last people might look at you and judge whether your completed life is fit and suited to you, now you have no way of looking into their eyes and receiving their judgement: tears, indifference, satisfaction.

You cannot even look to see whether there is anyone there . . .

REUNION

Beth shivered; almost an ecstasy; a chill ripple that began under the hairs on the nape of her neck and spread quickly out across her shoulders, down to the small of her back, and pulsated through her midriff; from there, it hurried down her legs and buffeted against the tips of her toes in waves, making them tingle and go numb. She couldn't believe what she had just seen; couldn't believe what she heard – or rather, silently sensed – the vision say.

I would forgive you if only I could see you . . .

She shifted her position a little to the left; while the service was being read, the heels of her new black suede shoes – low though they were – had been slowly sinking into the soft turf, until the arches lay flat on the wet soil. She drew them out one by one, clenching the insoles with her numbed toes so that the shoes wouldn't depart her feet in the process. When she had finished her surreptitious manoeuvre and her shoes were beginning to mate all over again with fresh, virgin turf, she took a clumped white tissue from her bag and dabbed at her eyes. Not an out-of-place act here, but quite redundant. Her tears had been wept the morning after she heard the news – and would return again before too long, setting in for the duration like the December drizzle that drifted over the moors, softening its earth – but they would not come today; today her eyes were dry and dull as top-beach pebbles. She couldn't weep here; not when there was so much besides grief to keep her emotions dancing nervously from foot to foot. Dominant amongst them was the fear that had haunted her ever since she could remember – or at least since that tarnished silver summer seven years ago when she left the house one early morning and never went back; the fear that, sooner or later, she would be found out. If only she had been honest; if only she had stayed in touch,

6

things might never have turned out this way.

She finished nudging at her eyes and, crumpling the dry tissue in her fist, looked straight ahead of her, at the spot in mid-air where the apparition had hovered momentarily, gazing reproachfully at her, judging her, then dissipating to the cold, damp breeze with an audible sigh. Instead of recapturing the vision, she found herself looking across the little arena of grieving, straight into Audrey's face.

If anything, the sight jolted Beth even more than the ghost. She hadn't seen Audrey since... well, not since seven years ago. She had barely changed. (Beth managed to take in a few details before – sensing Audrey's gaze rising from the ground to meet hers – she hastily looked away.) Still as smart and slight and slim as ever: neat, narrow ankles rising out of neat, heeled shoes (hers didn't sink into the turf, Beth noted). Above the ankles was a pair of slim, flawlessly black-sheathed calves topped by perfect, lumpless knees. The hem of the black woollen coat above revealed exactly the amount of lower thigh that might be provocative in other circumstances but was just the hither side of discretion here. Even as a low-budget student, Audrey had always looked as though her clothes had been cut by sinful angels from magically blemish-proof, creaseless fabric. And her hair – then as now – was of such a rich, deep burnish that it could have been spun by gods from a mystical alloy of gold, copper and silk.

What an insufferably smug cow. Beth was surprised to find that, even in that brief glimpse, she loathed Audrey as much as she ever had. Beth – whose thighs and bottom and upper arms were beginning to accumulate fat in the way they had always threatened to – just knew that Audrey had never looked fat in anything... no, worse than that; had never even *worried* that she *might* look fat in anything she wore.

Something else that Beth had noticed, and which added an extra dimension to her discomfiture at seeing Audrey again, was that her eyes – even hooded, even cast solemnly down – looked just as supercilious, just as hotly wicked and coldly contemptuous as Beth remembered them.

This realisation tempered the guilt and shock instilled in her by the accusing ghost; the judgment had not been intended for her (at least not all of it). Seeing Audrey again reminded Beth of how it had really happened; reassured her that it had been Audrey, with her wickedness and her coldness – and above all, her legs – who had caused it all.

Yes, thought Beth with uneasy satisfaction, it had all been Audrey's fault.

Audrey shuddered; a brief ripple across the still surface of her composure. All through the ceremony (in the chill echo of the church and across the hummocky, windswept turf of the little graveyard and around the rectangular shaft in the black soil into which she had just watched Lydia's box recede forever), she had maintained a surface of marble smoothness and marble hardness. What had disturbed it had been raising her eyes (following the straps as they slid and scurried up the sides of the grave) and finding herself looking at a familiar pair of legs. Shapely legs; womanly legs. A little heavy in the calf, but still as shapely and womanly as they had ever been. She knew whose legs they were immediately; not only because of their shape, but also because of the little snicked, bobbly patch on the thick Lycra covering the inside right ankle. Beth always used to ride an old jalopy of a bike with a bent chain-guard that snatched and snagged at the ankle, giving every pair of tights that same rough patch. So, either Beth still owned that bike or the tights Audrey was gazing at now were over seven years old. Either could be true.

Having recognised the legs, Audrey wasn't taken by surprise when her gaze ascended to eye-level and found the face: still a pretty face with warm, melancholy eyes and full lips. What made Audrey shudder so suddenly was the clear impression of haunted huntedness in those eyes as they glanced evasively away. Guilt? Embarrassment? After all this time? All she had done was blab her mouth off because she was jealous. (Audrey wasn't meant to know, but he told her.) It hadn't come to anything, and anyway, they had all been jealous in their own way, even Audrey.

She knew whose fault it had really been, and it wasn't Beth's (well, not much, anyway); no, it all stemmed from the inadequately supported low-slung bosom of the shabby sack of flab who stood blubbering wetly into an embroidered handkerchief diagonally opposite her now (out of sight of Beth, who could hear the burbling whimpers but had not yet attached a name to them).

Rachel.

Rachel, Audrey noted, had definitely changed, or rather evolved: *her* legs (Audrey realised with a surprise that she had never seen Rachel out of doors in a skirt before), which had always been rather thick and shapeless, were now decidedly fat and shapeless. No, the deep purple crushed velvet skirt, long and baggy with ridiculous hippie tassels around the hem, was a severely ill-judged fashion choice. Audrey shuddered again. It was this monstrous blob, whose sentimentality was as glutinous and as larded as her body, who had introduced them to him in the first place.

Yes, Audrey thought, it was all Rachel's fault.

Rachel trembled; thick, racking sobs welled up under her ribs and bubbled up to her throat. She tried to stifle them by pressing her tongue hard against the roof of her mouth, but they kept leaking out through her nose with little whistling gasps and gobbets of liquid snot, both of which were caught and muffled in the thick pad of wadded handkerchief.

It had not escaped her notice that she was the only one crying, and that only made her cry all the more. Poor Lydia; to reach the end like this and have so little grief expended for you.

When Rachel had first heard the news, she was devastated. (This, at least, was how she remembered it now. In fact, her first response had been *Lydia who?* But that had only lasted a moment, and the unwelcome memory was already firmly repressed.) When the realisation of what had happened impacted on her, she had wished she could run all the way to Devon, just to be there. But she couldn't go anywhere; she was locked to a mound of concrete in a copse on the outskirts of Huntingdon, protecting the ancient woodland from the advancing by-pass. Desperate to be free, she tugged and hauled at her arm, which was inserted up to the bicep in a section of drainpipe set into the mound, her wrist securely cuffed deep inside. The Sheriff's men, who could easily have released her with their hammers, picks and pneumatic drills (indeed, they were there for that very purpose) seemed to feel that she deserved her plight, and stood back to enjoy the spectacle of her imploring, wailing struggle. Her left arm was bruised and grazed and bleeding, two shattered fingers hanging limp, when Clifford finally got her out. Word had filtered through to him, deep in the warren of tunnels under the hillside, and he had come to her aid (endangering the lives of his fellow tunnellers in the process) . . . Dear Clifford. Sweet Clifford; he stood beside her now, his gentle hand lightly clasping her bandaged arm.

Sensing that she was being watched, Rachel sniffled and looked up as the priest spoke the closing words of the service, and found Audrey's eyes looking at her. They lingered for a moment, then darted away towards the grave. Audrey was just as beautiful as ever; angelic, almost. But paler than she used to be; more solemn. Perhaps, Rachel thought charitably, perhaps Audrey did not weep for her friend because she was too deeply shocked. Audrey had been, after all, closer to Lydia than either she or Beth. Audrey and Lydia; Rachel and Beth, that was how she remembered it. In fact, it had been Lydia and Beth, Audrey and anyone who could be of use, and Rachel and nobody. Nevertheless, Rachel had loved them all like sisters; she was heartbroken when they parted, knowing that they might never see one another again . . . But now, here they were again; brought together by Lydia, as they had been in the beginning. It had all been—

9

. . . With a rush of nausea, Rachel caught herself forming the end of the sentence: *Lydia's fault.* Instantly, she deflected the blame and directed it towards its true owner.

Yes, she thought with grim satisfaction as she blew her nose, it was all my fault.

Before leaving the graveside, Beth waited her turn to take a little handful of the damp, loamy earth from the uncovered heap and let it fall into the grave. Unconsciously, she gripped the soil too tightly in her fingers and, instead of pattering softly on the coffin lid, the muddy clump hit the lacquered wood with a dull thud and stuck there, looking like a dog turd. After frowning miserably at it for a moment, she cast about for a more appropriate valediction. A little way off, lying forlornly on the grass between two headstones, was a fresh white lily, fallen from one of the bouquets. Beth picked it up and returned to the foot of the grave. Raising the flower to her lips, she lightly kissed its petals. *Goodbye, Lyd,* she whispered, and let it fall into the pit. It dropped lightly on to the coffin and, carried by its momentum and a cushion of air, skated along the top and came to rest beside the brass plaque engraved:

LYDIA ELAINE HUTTON DE LA SIMARDE
1969–1998

As she stood and watched, the remainder of the mourners passed by – Lydia's half-brother, Gabriel; Madame de La Simarde, her mother-in-law; a short, distinguished-looking man with combed-back hair; a middle-aged couple in antique mourning dress – more clumps and showers of soil fell and battered the flower, squashing down its cup of petals until it was half-buried. When the last of them had gone, Beth finally turned and walked away.

She had not gone far – indeed, she had barely reached the gravel path that wove erratically between the monuments and headstones – when all her senses were suddenly assailed by a shape looming up before her, as though it had risen like a wight out of the very ground of the churchyard. She sensed a blur of black satin and purple velvet, then the apparition engulfed her, clamping its strong arms around her neck and swamping her nostrils with a mixed odour of acrid, unwashed hair, musty cloth and sour flesh.

'Oh, Beth,' Rachel sobbed. '*Beth, Beth, Beth, Beth* . . .'

'Don't get snot on Beth's coat, there's a dear,' said a voice nearby. Beth, her cheeks squashed up into her eye sockets by the force of the embrace, squinted over Rachel's shoulder. Audrey was watching the scene, her expression hovering between amusement and disdain.

At last, just as Beth thought she would pass out from the combination of bodily smells and restricted oxygen, Rachel relaxed her grip and held her out at arm's length, gazing intensely into her face with pink, puffy, tear-lined eyes.

'Oh, Beth,' she whispered.

'Rachel,' said Beth weakly. She tried to smile, but all she could manage was a sad little twitch at one corner of her mouth.

'That was a beautiful gesture, Beth; the flower . . . Lydia would have been touched.'

Beth tried to smile again, and this time managed to twitch both corners. She turned to Audrey. 'Hello, Audrey,' she said, offering her hand.

Audrey glanced at the hand uncertainly; there were faint streaks of black mud across the palm, and some of the stuff had somehow wedged itself under the fingernails. The pause lengthened, and Beth was about to shamefully withdraw the soiled hand, when Audrey reached out and took it. Leaning forward, she laid her cheek lightly against Beth's and puffed a soft *mwah* into the air beside her ear.

'Well,' Beth began, but the word just hung in the air. She wished she could think of some suitable comment to sum everything up, or some excuse that would allow her to leave now. She had hoped to be able to attend the funeral quietly and anonymously (after all, she had never really known any of Lydia's family, either blood or in-law), then just depart immediately afterwards, go for her train and leave it all behind. She hadn't counted on meeting ghosts from the past. But even seeing Audrey on the other side of the grave had not altered her plan; so long as there was no eye-contact, there was no need to acknowledge each other's presence. But now, Rachel had tied an invisible cord around her and she could feel herself being drawn back in: Come in, Bethany Glaister, your game is up.

'Long time no see,' said Audrey, adding her own gentle tug on the cord.

'Well, we've all moved on, haven't we,' said Beth, resisting. 'We've got different lives. New lives. We're different people now.'

Audrey nodded. 'Moved on or passed on,' she said, glancing back at the grave, where two workmen were waiting for the last of the mourners to leave before filling it in. 'All nonsense really,' she added. 'People don't change. Circumstances change, but people never do.'

Beth gazed at her. 'No,' she said. '*You* certainly haven't changed.'

'I mean,' Audrey went on, 'just because someone gets older or fatter or . . . or *richer*—' a deeply felt bitterness pervaded this word '—doesn't mean they've changed inside.'

11

'People *do* change,' said Rachel feebly, but Audrey cut across her:

'Take you,' she said, looking at Beth. 'Your circumstances might have changed, but you still ride around on that old rust-heap of a bike.'

Beth stared at her. 'How on earth do you know that?' she demanded.

Audrey smiled, and her sudden, inexplicable surge of anger seemed to subside. 'It's a simple enough deduction,' she said. 'You always were sentimentally attached to it. People don't change; QED.'

Beth hesitated. Audrey was right in at least one respect: collectively, they hadn't changed at all; after seven years apart, seven years spent leading increasingly divergent lives, here they were within minutes of their reunion, already arguing. They had slipped back into their accustomed roles as though they had parted only yesterday: Audrey argumentative, Beth unable to resist rising to her, and Rachel trying to join in from the sidelines. Only one actor was missing from their little scene: the one who had brought them back together. As Beth remembered it, Lydia's part was usually to bash their heads together.

'Let's not argue,' said Beth. 'For Lydia's sake, let's not argue. Not today.' Now that she was inextricably roped in, she felt she might as well let herself be dragged along as well. 'I could do with a drink,' she said. 'It's not far down to the village. Shall we see if we can find a pub?'

Watch them walk away. You aren't really disappointed by them; after all, you would never have guessed that anyone would even come, would you? This is something you cannot understand: How did they know about you? Who told them? Could they have known simply by instinct?

You have your doubts about this; it seems deeply improbable . . .

But they came: that is the important thing. They came.

Whoever they were.

Madame Geneviève Louise Perez de La Simarde stood silently by the mirror-chrome prow of her Daimler – parked well away from the higgledy-piggledy vehicles on the swathe of grass that swooped down from the tor – and watched them walk out of the churchyard together: the dark, pretty girl with the fat, slatternly dumpling on one side of her and the spindly whore on the other. Not for the first time, she reflected on the wisdom of the matrimonial choice her son had made. Not that there was a wealth of promising material amongst them: no man would touch that diseased-looking slattern (she reminded Madame de La Simarde of the Basque peasant women who used to hawk trinkets in the villages near her great uncle's estate, only dirtier), and she shuddered with relief that he had had no connection with the skinny one: she might dress and comport herself with the superficial carapace of a stock-bred lady, but she had the eyes of a common whore. New money; Madame de La Simarde had sensed the smell of it in the very cut of the girl's clothes . . . The pretty one, though: the one who had dropped the flower into the grave; now, she might have made a better daughter-in-law than the highly-strung English mare she had been encumbered with. There was something in the warm, pale olive features of this young woman that implied the combination of the Latinate and the Frankish that was the hallmark of real breeding. Besides – and at least as important – she had the cut of hips and thighs that spoke of mothering.

Madame de La Simarde sighed. It was too late; always too late. It had become too late for her years ago, and now it was too late for the next generation. All her plans had failed in the face of advancing age and spring-trap death, and she felt a weight of *Weltschmerz*, a sadness for the world that was all the poorer for her failure . . .

She turned away from the churchyard and found Février waiting silently and patiently as ever, holding the car door open for her.

'So, Février,' she said. 'I am all alone at last. What do you think of it all?'

Février knew very well what she was thinking of; he had served her for fifty years, and he knew the fabric of her mind intimately. His own mind might not be all it had once been, but he could still sometimes deduce her thoughts before she had even begun thinking them (there weren't all that many of them, after all). He smiled slightly and inclined his head in a little bow to indicate that it was his honour to reply: 'I think, Madame, that the dark-haired young lady would have made an exquisite wife for my late master.'

Madame de La Simarde's face warmed a little. 'You continually astound me, Février. That is precisely what I was thinking.' Février inclined his head a little more to show the depth of his gratification. 'But it is too late,' she continued regretfully. 'There shall never be an heir now.'

Février raised his eyes and looked directly at her; a liberty which she would never have tolerated from any other servant. She gazed back at him; looked deep into his eyes. There was obviously something occurring in his mind that he did not dare put into words, and she probed his eyes, trying to catch hold of the thought . . .

Suddenly, her face brightened, and she smiled warmly, gratefully at him. 'Oh, Février,' she whispered. 'You are a marvel! Why did I not think of it?' She stepped briskly past him and settled herself into the back seat of the car. 'Come along!' she called. 'We must begin this instant!'

Février slammed the door after her and, suppressing a rare grin of excitement, walked around to the driver's side and climbed in.

'I never imagined Devon would be such a depressing place,' said Beth, looking out of the window at the bleak, damp street. She kept her voice low, so that the sparse scatter of locals wouldn't overhear. This wasn't the most hospitable pub she had ever been in. Out in the car park, Audrey's gleaming little Rover 200 had looked starkly, incongruously exuberant beside a weary-looking Sierra and a battered Datsun pick-up, which were the only other vehicles parked there. The moment they walked in through the door, the place had fallen suddenly silent and a dozen pairs of curious eyes – none of them female or under forty – had turned in their direction. Had she been on her own, Beth would have fled, but Audrey strode defiantly to the bar and ordered their drinks. Little by little, conversations resumed, the little groups of men turned in on themselves and, within ten minutes, the two young women were no more interesting or conspicuous than the wallpaper.

'It's not the place,' said Audrey. 'It's the weather. I was brought here on holiday once, when I was fourteen. We had weather like this then, and that was the middle of August. God knows, a funeral in December isn't going to make a place stand out in your mind as a holiday hot-spot.'

Beth shook her head. 'No,' she said. 'Still, it was a nice service.'

Audrey frowned. 'Why do people always say that? Funerals are rituals for disposing of dead bodies, for Christ's sake. How the hell can that ever be *nice*? People talk such crap.'

Beth looked at her in surprise, then smiled wanly. 'Well, you know what Oscar Wilde said about cynics.'

'Yes, and I also know what he said about surfaces.'

'That wasn't Oscar Wilde; that was Lady Bracknell.'

'What's the difference? Anyway, your darling Oscar said a lot of things, but you'd be a fool to live your life by them.'

Beth gave up the argument and went back to gazing out at the street. 'I know people who *enjoy* going to funerals,' she said. 'Some of the old folk in my mother's family, for instance. You'd think they'd dread any reminder of death at their age. But that's the Welsh for you. Celtic culture is incredibly morbid. They're obsessed with ghosts and spirits and crystal balls and things . . . Do you believe in ghosts?'

'Don't be ridiculous. Why, do you?'

'No, not really. It's just that, today, at the funeral, I . . .' She hesitated, and shook her head. 'Oh, never mind.'

Audrey gazed at her. 'So,' she said. 'Rachel's got herself a boyfriend at last.' She took a cigarette from a packet of Silk Cut Extra Mild, then offered the pack to Beth, who shook her head. 'Sure? Mmm, trying to give them up myself.' She lit up and blew a thin, precise jet of smoke towards the ceiling. 'At least, I assume it was a boyfriend,' she added. 'Either that or her laundry bag has sprouted legs and started following her about.'

Beth smiled reluctantly; after the altercation in the churchyard, she had resolved to ride out this encounter with Audrey good-naturedly, however argumentative or bitchy she was. 'He seemed nice enough,' she said non-committally.

Audrey snorted. 'He'd have to be. Did you see how much weight she's put on?'

Beth shifted self-consciously as the barb ricocheted off Rachel and embedded itself in her, just as Audrey had probably – at least subconsciously – intended it to. She inched the edges of her coat across her lap to give her thighs better concealment from scrutiny.

'Where have they got to, anyway?' she wondered. 'I thought they were meeting us here.'

'God knows,' said Audrey. 'Last I saw of them, they were shovelling themselves into their love-bus. Did you see the state of it? I doubt if it's seen an MOT certificate since Henry Ford's day. Probably couldn't start the wretched thing.' She took a long draw on her cigarette, gazing at Beth through the smoke. 'So, how about you?' she said, wafting the smoke away from her face, spinning the hazy blue ball into a vortex. 'How's life in the land of Glaister?'

Beth shrugged. 'I get by,' she said evasively. Meeting Audrey again was like meeting a stranger; but a stranger who felt entitled to probe into the private corners of her life. 'I get by,' she repeated.

'You don't sound too thrilled about it,' said Audrey. 'Any blokes in the picture?'

'I live with a guy called Iain.'

'And what does he do?'

'He's a writer.'

'Ah,' said Audrey, leaning forward. 'That sounds sexy. Has he written anything I would've read?'

Beth shook her head. 'I doubt it.'

'Well, what has he written?'

'Oh, little things.'

Audrey sighed. 'I think, in my next incarnation, I'll come back as a dentist . . . What *sort* of things?'

'He's had a couple of short stories published in *Granta*, that sort of thing. He's working on a novel at the moment.'

Audrey's shoulders slumped, like an athlete at the end of a long run. 'And how about you?' she went on doggedly. 'What do you do? Are you his muse?'

Beth smiled ruefully. 'Hardly. I'm a recruitment consultant. I'm a recruitment consultant and I live in Peterborough. End of story. How high can you aim with an English degree these days?' She winced inside as she said it; only a few days ago, Iain had chided her for using expressions like this: someone of twenty-nine, he said, should not be saying things like *these days*. It was a sign that you were letting senescence creep up on you; it was only a short stumble from *these days* to *in my day* and *when I was young*. When you reached that stage, he said, you had bought your ticket for the long and dreary minibus ride to senility. You might as well shoot yourself in the head. As though *he* could talk.

'Sounds okay to me,' said Audrey. 'Anyway, if it's any consolation, I never had you down as a career girl. I had you tagged for motherhood. Who else but you would have taken a job in the university crèche in their first term? I expected to find you married. Burgeoning brood of little Glaisters.'

Beth stared at her, trying to quell her emotions, knocked off keel by the irony that, although this was the bitchiest remark Audrey could possibly have made, she had no idea that it was anything other than a friendly gibe.

'No,' she said at last. 'No children.'

'Iain not keen on daddyhood?'

'You could say that.'

'I see.'

Do you? A brief, silent stare. 'What about you? Not children – I mean, what do you do for a living? Something well-paid, by the look of that car. And that outfit.'

Audrey ignored the compliment. 'Why do you assume I wouldn't have children?' she demanded.

'Because they'd get in the way,' said Beth simply.

Audrey nodded. 'That never stops people,' she said.

'Come on. The only way you'd have children is on toast.'

Audrey laughed. 'Okay, fair enough. No, no children.'

'So what do you do for a living? I'm sure it's something terribly glamorous.'

'Of course,' said Audrey, smiling archly. She sipped out the last drop of clear liquid from her glass and set it down in the middle of the table. 'Get me another drink and I'll tell you about it.'

Quiet time, he'd said. *Just taking meself upstairs, love, take the weight off me bunions. You'll be fine for an hour, won't you?* Huh. Maggie stood by the till and twizzled the balloon of a wine glass around a balled corner of towel. His bunions? What about her veins? Never a word about them. Truth was, he was a lazy, good-for-nothing layabout, and no mistake. She'd only married him because of the pub; she'd needed someone who knew what he was doing to help her run it after Dad died. And, of course, he was a handsome man back then, her George, even if knowing what he was doing had turned out to be mostly to do with how to let the wife take the strain. She'd have given him the boot, she reckoned, even now after nearly thirty years, if it wasn't for it being his name over the door these days. Where would she go, though? She'd spent her whole life behind this bar, right from when she'd been so small that Dad would sweep her up and plonk her down between the ash trays and the pump handles to be admired by the grizzled old regulars. *Ain't she a pretty little un now* . . . Being lifted up to feed sugar lumps to the brewer's drays in the cobbled alley . . . Then a big, black rush to the day she was swept off her feet less literally by Georgie the hired hand, when she was nearly thirty and thought she would stay on the shelf forever (not such a pretty un now) and lose the pub into the bargain. Handsome Georgie Peorgie of the flaming bunions and the chronic backache. Huh. All dismissed in a grunting exhalation.

Take them two, now – the pair sitting over by the window. Maggie would bet her last pound that *they*'d never been beholden to any no-hope malingerer of a man in their lives. She could tell at a glance (and she had barely taken her eyes off them since they came in, such a rare sight they were) that they were women in control, like the ones you saw on the telly and in magazines, with their dark, expensive clothes and their posh voices. What she would love to know, though, was what two such exotic specimens were doing down here?

One of them was getting up and coming over, carrying two empty glasses. Maggie stepped forward and pasted a thick smile across her features. 'What can I get you, my lover?' she asked.

17

The woman, who was the plumper and less smart – but in Maggie's opinion the prettier – of the two, put the empty glasses on the bar. 'A vodka and tonic, please, and er . . .' She cast her eyes back and forth along the breastwork of colourful, brightly lit pumps. 'Er, a half of Löwenbräu.'

'Business, is it?' said Maggie, taking a fresh glass and pressing it up against the Smirnoff optic.

'Sorry?'

'Down here on business?'

The woman shook her head sadly. 'No.'

Maggie smiled brightly. 'Holiday, then?'

'Funeral.'

'Oh . . . Oh, I see. That's sad. Family, was it?'

'Friend.'

Maggie sighed sympathetically. 'Young, were they? Terrible, that is, folks dying young, before their time.' She switched on the lager pump and spoke to the glass as it filled with yellow foam. 'Like that young girl, few weeks ago. Threw herself off a tower, they say, over in France. In all the papers it was. Consumed by grief was how they said it, an I don't doubt they're right, what with the life she had. That'll be two pounds twenty, please.'

The five-pound note sticking out like a flag between the young woman's fingers stopped travelling across the bar and hovered, trembling slightly. Maggie reached out a hand to receive it, but it retreated.

'She didn't jump,' said the young woman. 'It was an accident. And it was a window, not a tower.'

Maggie's brain went momentarily blank as she looked at the woman's face, her chest tightening with the dawning realisation of her blunder. 'You don't mean . . .' She gestured vaguely towards the outdoors, and then at the woman herself. 'Oh no . . . no. Oh, God love me, I'm awful sorry. I didn't realise, I thought they'd buried her weeks ago. Weeks ago.'

'There was an inquest. The funeral was this morning.'

'I'm ever so sorry. My George – that's my husband – he's always telling me, "Maggie," he says, "the way that tongue of yourn prattles on, you'll fall right over it one a these days." An e's right, I do . . . Now I think on it, I do remember someone sayin about a Simmard funeral the other day, but I wasn't takin no notice an it went clean out of my head. What must you think of me?'

The woman's smile was thin and artificial. 'Never mind,' she said. 'It doesn't matter.' She held out the five-pound note again, and Maggie took it. 'Do you know them well?' the woman asked tentatively. 'The family, I mean – the Simardes. I suppose they must be well known locally.'

'Weeell,' said Maggie judiciously, opening the till and fishing out change, 'not as much as you, I dare say, you bein a friend a theirs.'

'Oh, I hardly know them at all. I was just a friend of . . . well, the girl.'

Maggie pushed the till drawer closed. 'Well, I only know gossip, really, though they do say as a landlady gets to hear everything first. Though them as says it may be wrong, I s'pose, eh?' She laughed. 'Two pound eighty,' she added, placing a little column of coins into the woman's hand. 'Mind you, for all they're foreigners, there's been Simmards round here longer'n any living folks's memory. Fled away from Napoleon, though they've still got a place over in France that's identical to this one, right down to the wallpaper an furniture, they say. Home away from home, I s'pose. An their servants is all French – don't hire no locals cept old Joseph Ward who does the gardens for em.'

'They're not well liked, then?'

This woman was curious, all right; despite what she said, she must know the family well enough or she wouldn't be going to a family affair like a funeral, and Maggie wasn't going to be drawn into putting her foot in it again. 'Well, I wouldn't say that,' she said cautiously. 'Son was a famous musician, but he died, and now his young widow's gone too, so the old lady's on her own. She never did go out much – least not down this way – and now I s'pose she'll go out even less. Withdrawing, like. Her man comes in here sometimes. Butler sort of thing, or handyman or whatever. French, but nice enough with it, though a bit quiet for most people's liking. Funny name, an all – February, that's what e told me it means, an his sister's April. 'What happened to January an March?' I says to him – just joking, like – an e looks at me real serious an says, 'They're both dead.' I mean, what can you make of that? Was e joking or what?'

Despite his strangeness, Maggie had a soft spot for the dour Frenchman. His heavy accent reminded her of youthful afternoons at the cinema in Exeter, mooning over Yves Montand. For all that he must be near sixty, she often daydreamed, as she leaned on the bar and watched him sitting silently in the corner sipping his pint of bitter and sucking on his pipe, of eloping with him; running away to a foreign land to roam in a perpetual moonlit night. In her imagination, as she peeled twenty years off both of them, it seemed so vivid that she could hear the crickets and smell the honeysuckle and taste the rugged bristles on his coarse skin and . . . as if coalescing from her dreams, she could see him now, walking through the door, large as life. Her heart fluttered – half with emotion and half with alarm, as though her talk and her thoughts had conjured him out of the air.

'Speak of the Devil!' she exclaimed.

'Excuse me?' he said, frowning.

He was dressed in funeral clothes: an outlandish outfit which included an old-fashioned tail-coat and wing collar with a thin black tie clasped in place by a diamond-headed silver pin.

'I hardly recognised you,' Maggie lied. 'This young lady was just asking about your lot.'

Février raised his eyebrows; just fractionally, just the barest hint of interest cracking his impassive face. 'Was she now?' He turned to the young woman and, to Maggie's proprietorial rapture, bowed magnificently, clicking his heels. (More like German than French, she thought). '*Enchanté*, Mademoiselle Glaister,' he said, while the woman looked at him with undisguised astonishment. 'My mistress has commanded me to present her compliments and to invite you – and the other young lady of course—' he turned towards the window-seat, where the woman's friend was sitting, watching curiously, and directed another little bow towards her '—to dine with her this evening. If you would do her the honour of accepting, I am here to escort you.'

He concluded the invitation with another little bow from the waist that made Maggie's knees go weak. The woman's friend, obviously awash with curiosity now, came over to find out what was happening. To Maggie's amazement, the two women hesitated over the invitation, looking doubtfully at each other. That was style, Maggie thought; she would probably have embarrassed herself rigid, practically busting a gut in her eagerness to accept. Then again, she'd never get asked in the first place.

'What time?' asked the thin one.

'Excuse me?'

'Dinner. What time is it?'

'My mistress dines at nine o'clock, but if it would suit you, she would be pleased to receive you for afternoon tea. I can take you now.'

'Nine?' said the thin one, who was clearly tempted by the invitation. 'What do you think, Beth?'

Beth pursed her pretty lips. 'I don't know. I can't, really; I've got a train to catch.'

Février looked from one to the other of them. 'You have important business to return to?'

'No, said Beth. 'But I—'

'My mistress will provide you with a room.' There seemed to be no end to his mistress's hospitality. 'Your travel arrangements will be attended to in the morning, just as you wish.'

Beth shrugged, defeated. 'Audrey?'

Audrey grinned. 'Oh, I'm game for anything.' She looked at Février.

'I've got my own car. We'll follow you.'

'As you wish.' Février bowed one last time, turned smartly about, and left.

Beth watched him go despondently. 'Why on *earth* did we agree?' she moaned. 'A whole night?'

'Oh come on, don't be a spoilsport.'

Beth sighed. 'I'll have to phone Iain.'

'Go on, then. Tell him you're researching material for him. I'll wait in the car.'

Maggie directed Beth to the payphone at the end of the bar. Five minutes later, the women were gone, leaving Maggie with two untouched drinks and the quiet murmur of dull conversations around her. She sipped at the abandoned vodka and tonic and lapsed back into her daydreams.

THE CASTLE

P ause . . .

He stopped moving, and looked around again. The dank brown stretch of marsh on his right was thinning here, giving way to the blue-green surface of the lake. To his left, the forest was as dense and impenetrable as ever; thick grey trunks tightly packed, the narrow gaps choked with broad fans of bright green palm fronds. He turned around and looked back the way he had come; since leaving the tower five minutes ago, he had followed the rickety, rotten-looking wooden walkway across the lake-shore marshes, his skin creeping at every step as the gap narrowed between the path and the glowering forest, bringing him closer and closer to its overbearing shadows. He strained his ears, but all he could hear was the lapping lake-water and the guttural chorus of reptilian croaks and hisses, both growing louder, closer, more insistent, and the continual grunting creaks of the walkway beneath him.

Three more pauses, three more hesitant advances, and the trackway finally branched: one leg continued along the lake shore, threading its way through the thinning marsh which had now degenerated into wide pools of evil-looking water; puce, spotted with tufted clumps of reed. The other way swung suddenly left, climbed and plunged through a gap in the forest, disappearing under the black eaves.

Without hesitation, he chose the first way. A brief inspection, though, showed that the causeway – rotten and slimy and gnawed by the creatures that dwelt in that dark, desperate water – had collapsed along several metres of its length. So, he turned back again and, taking his courage in both hands, followed the way that led into the forest.

As soon as he passed between the gnarled pillars and the frond curtains, the watery sounds of the marsh vanished, and the oppressive air was filled with the distant whistles and chirrups of strange birds and – much closer – toadish burps and hiccups; all familiar yet not quite identifiable, all natural and yet somehow hostile.

A few steps in, the way was barred by a gate: head-high and made from split logs bound together with leather thongs, it was attached to its tree-bole frame by two rusting iron spikes hammered into bare patches cut in the bark. Presumably, the gate – along with the trackway he had followed through the marsh – had been constructed by the vanished folk who had once inhabited the abandoned and decrepit lake village he had passed a few minutes ago; the folk who (he now believed) had been driven out of their homes by the man who lived in the tower.

He pushed the gate, and it swung open with a damp, moss-softened creak. He was about to pass through when a huge, orange-backed bug – which he had taken for a bulbous nodule of fungus adhering to the bole on his left – split its shell and took flight, startled by his movement. Its wings thrummed loudly in his ears, making him flinch, and it fluttered momentarily in his face before rasping off into the trees. His heart pounded, and a sweat broke out on his brow. What had alarmed him about the bug – aside from the sudden flurrying – was the fleeting glimpse he had caught of its eyes: fat, shining white orbs protruding above heavy, claw-like mandibles, staring at him, scrutinising him.

Once inside, he found that the forest was not as dark as he had expected. The sunlight struggling feebly through the dense green canopy was mixed with a lava-red glow which seemed to leak from deep clefts striating parts of the forest floor, creating a dreamy luminosity of rubies and emeralds. There was a path winding away into the obscurity. Like the gate, it was constructed of split logs which had been pegged down in two parallel strands like rails, the gap filled with white stone-dust that had been tamped down like concrete and worn to concavity by the people who had once followed it in and out of the forest.

His progress became even slower now, pausing at every step to look around and listen. Carefully and fearfully, he made his way deeper and deeper into the forest. The path veered and forked like a maze, suddenly plunging down fissures and over ridges, tunnels carving through the massive trunks of ancient trees, disappearing into flowing bands of phosphorescently luminous blue water. Again and again, he found himself doubling back at dead-ends, going round in circles as the path split and parted, multiplied, wandered and converged. At last, though, just as he was considering fleeing back to the comparative tameness of the sunlit marshes, he noticed an overgrown path he was sure he hadn't yet tried. Feeling that he was on the brink of discovering the way through to the other side of the forest, he struck out along this new path.

A few paces further on, the trees opened out into a clearing, and the path dissolved into a grassy slope, on the peak of which was a magnificent totem pole, ten metres high and three metres across its girth, carved where it stood from the trunk of one of the forest's most massive trees. At its base, where the spreading roots formed the octopus tentacles of a vast, bulbous creature with huge, snarling fangs and painted green eyes, a semicircle of nine small standing stones had been set on the slope. Corresponding with the stones were nine tree-stumps. Closer examination showed that the top of each stump had been smoothed and engraved with geometric patterns and strange, indecipherable symbols; like horoscopes, he thought.

Nonplussed, he stood back and surveyed the grove. He decided to check his gear. He had been on this journey for some time, and his pack was growing full and heavy with the items he had found and picked up. There was a large iron key, some pieces of crystal, a brass telescope, an old gramophone record, a severed head, an iron hammer, a gold coin, a dagger, and a leather-bound book. He took out the book and opened it: its yellowed pages were covered with dense paragraphs of brown ink. He flipped through until he came to a page which teemed with intricate sketches resembling the designs engraved on the tree-stumps. There was also a diagram which appeared to be a plan of this very grove. Whoever this journal had belonged to had been here before him.

Putting the book away, he approached the nearest standing stone, and touched it. There was a deep rumbling from under the earth, and the stone began to sink into the ground. So, that was it: a lock; depress the stones in the right order, and the secret of the grove would be revealed. Lowering them in the wrong order, though, might trigger a trap . . .

He stood back and studied the stones for a minute, then decided to try the central one. He touched it, and watched with satisfaction as it too began to sink. Then, as soon as it had sunk to half its height and stopped, there was an explosion of noise behind his head: a piercing, ear-jangling screech that nearly made his skin tear itself from his body. The pointer raced away to the right as he jumped, and the scene before him began to spin wildly round and round . . .

His heart pounding and aching in his chest, he pushed back his chair and reached out towards the source of the sudden noise still screeching behind him. He paused for a moment to let his panic subside, then picked it up.

26

'Hello?' he said, a shade of irritation in his voice.

There was a pause. 'Hi,' she said hesitantly. 'It's me. You weren't busy, were you?'

He sighed. 'Oh, it's you. No, I wasn't busy.'

'Oh. You sound a bit pissed-off.'

'Pissed off? Me? You must be even more hugely mistaken than Max.'

There was an uncertain silence on the line, only interrupted by the bullfrog croaks and bird-whistles from the forest glade. 'Did he turn you down?' she asked.

'What do you think? Anyway, I wouldn't write for his jam-rag of a paper if he paid me.'

'You're too good for him,' she agreed. 'You'd be wasted.'

'Mmm . . .'

'Have you got very far today?'

He gazed at the screen. The forest was still whirling wildly, out of control. He rolled the mouse, bringing the cursor back to the centre of the screen, and the picture stopped rotating.

'Oh, you know . . .'

'How much?'

Beside the computer was a single sheet of A4 with six lines written on it, two of which had been viciously crossed out. 'Ten pages,' he said.

'Oh good. And you haven't been at that game?'

'Cross my heart and hope to have my balls chewed off . . . So, how did it go? Where are you, anyway? Shouldn't you be on your way back by now?'

'Well, yes. The thing is, there's been a bit of a change of plan. That's why I'm calling. I won't be back till tomorrow, babe.'

'Why?'

'Don't worry. I've got somewhere to stay.'

'But—'

'Look, my money's running out. I'll phone you again tomorrow, okay?'

'When—?'

'And keep writing. I love you. Bye.'

'I love you too,' he mumbled into the deaf silence.

He put the receiver down and picked up the sheet of paper. After looking miserably at it for a few moments, he replaced it in the shadows behind the towering bulk of the computer and returned to the forest.

The sun was breaking through the clouds when Audrey walked out into the car park. It glittered on the polished chrome of a pale blue Daimler limousine sitting on the potholed, hardcore-scattered expanse of wet mud. Its engine was purring quietly, and Février was sitting at the wheel, his face veiled by the dapple of reflections on the windscreen. He inclined his head politely towards her as she passed, and she smiled back.

She thumbed the button on the key fob, and the little Rover bleeped, winked and clunked its locks off. She climbed in, tossing her bag onto the back seat, and turned the key in the ignition.

Beth walked out of the pub with a deepening feeling of foreboding. Absolutely the last thing she wanted was to meet Madame de La Simarde (she had met her once, briefly, years ago, and once had been enough), let alone spend a whole night under her frightening roof. All she wanted was to be away from here; away from the funerary gloom and Audrey and Rachel and all the other ghosts of the past, especially the spectre of Lydia; to get home to Iain and their real-life, day-to-day heartaches and their familiar, comforting domesticity. Yet how could she have refused such an invitation? There was something irresistible in this man's demeanour; a manner that mimed subservience but simultaneously conveyed ineffable authority. At least, that was how it seemed to her; she hardly had the experience to cope with high-ranking servants of the old school, and she would scarcely dare refuse any offer of hospitality conveyed by such a commanding presence.

She was conscious of his gaze following her across the car park from behind the windscreen of the tall blue Daimler. She kept her eyes averted as she walked over to Audrey's car. She compounded her feelings of inadequacy when, hopping over a puddle to get to the car door, she skidded on the mud and almost fell; she just managed to grab the door handle and steady herself in time. She could sense his stern, contemptuous eyes on her as she climbed in, taking in every detail of her ill-bred clumsiness.

'Don't get too comfortable,' said Audrey as Beth settled herself into the seat and pulled the door shut. She was fiddling with the ignition key and pumping the accelerator pedal with her foot.

'What?'

'Slight hitch, I'm afraid.' She turned the key; the starter whined busily, but the engine just thrummed, chugged and died. She tried again doggedly, but still without success.

'What's the matter?'

'Buggered if I know, darling. I'm not a mechanic. Maybe it's all the wet weather.'

'It was fine earlier.'

Audrey turned the ignition off and gazed ironically at Beth. 'You don't say,' she muttered. 'Well, it's well and truly fucked now.'

There was a brisk *rat-a-tat* of knuckles on the window beside her, and Beth turned to see Février stooping towards her, his face barely a foot from hers on the other side of the glass. She flinched, and her heart leapt up in alarm. He made a winding gesture with his hand, and she looked helplessly at the interior of the door.

'That button there,' said Audrey.

Beth pressed a little black rocker switch on the arm-rest, and the window hummed down into the door.

'There is a problem?' he inquired.

'It won't start,' said Audrey, leaning across and turning on a dazzling, irresistible smile. 'You look like just the sort of chap who's a wizard with cars. If I pop the bonnet, would you care to take a look?'

Février resisted the irresistible smile. He looked down at his immaculate coat and stiff, snow-white shirt-front. 'Normally, of course, I would be privileged to offer what humble help I can, but as you can see, I am hardly dressed to the purpose. Also, I am no expert in these modern cars. There is a garage in the village. They will attend to it. In the meantime, I shall drive you.'

He opened Beth's door and stood back, making it clear, with due deference, that no disagreement would be brooked. He took Audrey's keys, saying that he would organise the car's collection, and offered to transfer their luggage. There wasn't much to transfer: all they had apart from their shoulder bags was a carry-case containing Audrey's laptop computer.

Février held the door open while they ensconced themselves in the

Daimler's broad back seat, Audrey sliding nimbly across the deep, yielding ivory leather and sitting elegantly, smiling to herself, while Beth plumped down reluctantly, embarrassed, awkwardly slumped like a sack of potatoes, her long, voluminous coat runkling under her legs and ballooning up beneath her chin. She made a futile effort to tame it, but only succeeded in hurting her shoulder as she hauled at its tails. She gave up and sat still, her bag cradled on her lap like a swaddled baby. If there was a knack to sitting stylishly in an elegant car, Beth certainly didn't possess it.

Audrey gazed around approvingly at the luxurious cocoon; the leather, pale and richly creased on the seats, taut and black on the steering wheel and handbrake lever, and the sweeping banks and panels of dark walnut polished to the texture of glass.

'Well, this is a turn-up,' said Beth as the door closed with a deep, quiet thump. 'Why on earth do you suppose she'd want to see *us*?'

'Can't imagine,' said Audrey. 'Friends of Lydia's, I suppose.'

Beth nodded, although this explanation hardly seemed adequate; why should Madame de La Simarde be remotely interested in any friends of Lydia's? Especially ones so distanced by time and divergence. (Beth was still young enough, she might have been consoled to realise, to think of seven years as a great chasm of separation and growing unfamiliarity.) What was more, Lydia's relationship with her mother-in-law could hardly have been, well, cordial.

'There weren't any children, were there?' she said.

'What?' said Audrey, glancing over her shoulder. There was a faint click and a hiss as the boot lid rose behind them and Février loaded in her carry-case. 'What children?'

'Lydia and Salvador. They never had children, did they?'

'No idea. Didn't see any at the funeral, but then I suppose they wouldn't necessarily be there, would they.' She looked over her shoulder again. 'What's he doing?' The boot was still open and, from the sounds resonating through the bodywork, Février seemed to be moving things about, rummaging through heavy objects. 'What's she like, this woman? Her chauffeur's certainly a strange one. D'you think he dresses like Neville Chamberlain all the time?'

Beth shrugged and shook her head. *Chauffeur*; Février seemed more like a manservant than a chauffeur. (Hadn't that woman just now said he was a butler?) A manservant; it was strange that such an antiquated term popped into her head, but it seemed apposite; there was an ancientness (in her mind, she found herself spelling it *auntientness*, the very word imbued with its own meaning), an antiquity in his deportment and demeanour for which the common words of service — chauffeur, butler, valet — antique as they were, felt too modern.

'Did you never meet her?' she asked in answer to Audrey's first question.

'No. Did you?'

'Only the once. Back at the beginning. Remember when she came to visit Salvador, and he disappeared? That weekend. That was when he and Lydia were . . .' She fumbled for a phrase to express the love, the almost obsessive cleaving that had come about during that spring term, '. . . first getting together,' she finished feebly. 'I shouldn't think she'd remember me, though.'

'She might. Anyway, I shouldn't worry too much; there are bound to be lots of other people there.'

The boot lid closed with a soft thump, and Février came round to the driver's door. He coiled himself into his seat and, half-turning towards them, said: 'Ladies,' and gave a small bow from the shoulders. Then he started the engine and began to guide the long, broad expanse of the bonnet across the car park towards the exit.

Nobody spoke as the car hummed along the narrow road that wound its way out of Wheddend and up onto the moor. Even Audrey, Beth could sense, was a little intimidated by this man, and neither of them quite had the nerve to slide the glass screen across and shut him out. Even though, by some arcane, manservantly sleight or craft, Février somehow contrived to surround himself now with an aura of near-invisibility, to efface his own presence, there was just enough left to stop both their mouths. Then again, perhaps no such inexplicable explanation was required of their silence; Beth, at least, was quite glad of the opportunity to stop talking, to shrink back from the compulsion to pick at scabs. And so she sat and tried to concentrate on watching the damp, drear scenery roll by.

The bright interlude hadn't lasted long, and bulbous grey clouds were lowering over the moor again; except in the north, where a triangle of blue framed the grey granite fist of the tor punching up through the rolling green. Beside the road, a small gathering of Dartmoor ponies stood and cropped the grass; as the car passed, one of them – a hazelnut-brown mare – looked up and seemed to gaze straight into Beth's eyes. She smiled back, and the mare tossed her head and moved away. They passed a bus stop, where an olive-green bus with a broad yellow stripe down its side was standing empty, its driver reading a newspaper spread out over the steering wheel, and then, just beyond the bus stop, the church where Lydia's funeral had taken place. The grave would be filled in by now, thought Beth, and Lydia would be alone under the weight of plum-pudding black moorland soil . . . She didn't want to think about that, so instead she considered the church itself: a squat Norman block gathering its trees and graves about it like a nest. Wheddend itself had had no church, and yet there was one here, with not a house to be seen for miles around. Drawn up on the verge, by the church's dry-stone wall, was the luridly painted hulk of Rachel and Clifford's Volkswagen camper. As they passed, she twisted in her seat, but could see no sign of them. She turned to Audrey, who just shrugged and pulled a face: *Don't ask me.*

Just in front of the lych-gate, the road forked and they cut away to the left, sweeping down off the moor-top and into a wooded valley, the grass verges rising up on either side into steep, overgrown earthen banks, tall trees huddling close and arching over to form a filigree tunnel. The tunnel continued for about a mile, sometimes following the contour of the valley's side, sometimes winding and swooping down with sudden steepness until, without warning, the trees gave way, the banks receded, and a vista opened up; the valley spread before them, a broad cleft artfully landscaped with trees, streams and a lake. At its centre, like a fairy-tale castle, were the clustered witch's-hat turrets of a French château. Or a perfect simulacrum of one, dark and heavy in Dartmoor granite. A cacophony of images crowded out of the pages of childhood stories and danced in Beth's mind as she looked: she thought of the Count of Monte Cristo and the Prisoner of Zenda; she even thought of Chitty Chitty Bang Bang and the castle of Vulgaria – from up here, with the car's silent tyres on the smooth road, they could almost be flying, soaring down to circle the pointed, fishscale-tiled cones; they would land on the wide expanse of mown grass by the lake, to be greeted by a throng of liberated children, and they would find that, really, this place was not at all like the image that had leapt first into her mind and which she was still trying to squash as she fantasised the car into flight: with the gloom of foreboding and under the thickening charcoal of the lowering sky, the edifice below made her think ineluctably of Castle Dracula.

As she shivered under her thick coat, the view was suddenly snatched away; the forest rose up again on both sides and enclosed the car, but this time there was none of the dappling effect of the fretwork of branches, none of the tinted shade; only a deepening, darkening gloom. Off to the side, the ranked trunks receded into a haze, a dour, creeping grey-brown darkness, the mulchy forest floor still and lifeless, pervaded by a primal, amorphous dread. She tried to imagine how Lydia must have felt, travelling down this road after Salvador's funeral, utterly alone and coming to spend the short remainder of her days here. Of course, as Beth knew well enough, Salvador had been buried in France, and Lydia too had died there, but there was no room in her mind at the moment for such pedantry; this corner of the world drew gloomy thoughts to it like flies to a flypaper.

At the bottom of the hill, the road broadened and forked again; a wide-splayed fork in the crook of which stood a bulky granite gatehouse straddling a high, arched gateway. The building mimicked the château in miniature, with a small false turret at each corner, narrow lancet windows and cruciform arrow-slits on either side of the gateway. The car slowed and passed under the arch, emerging like a ghost train out of the wild woodland into a man-made imitation of wilderness: here, the trees – tall elms, thickset horse-chestnuts and broad-boled oaks – were spaced out with casually artful randomness, breaking away to open grass as the drive curved around the almost perfectly oval lake. Not a glimpse was to be had of the château; beyond the lake, the trees sprang up again, slender limes marshalled into neatly spaced rows on either side, alternating with tall, smooth-sided bell-shapes of box and privet. Then the drive turned a corner, and there it was, rising up from a flat, semicircular apron of crushed quartz fringed with grass like green baize; a rearing façade of dark, smooth-cut granite framed between twin, splay-footed round towers. It looked different close-to, Beth thought as the car crunched a wide arc across the raked quartz and rolled slowly under another mansard-roofed archway in the centre of the façade; it didn't loom quite as much as she had expected, its proportions broad rather than high, rescued from squatness by the steep, sharp points of the two towers.

They emerged in a courtyard, where the car finally rolled to a stop. Février got out and opened the doors for them. 'My mistress will receive you in the Music Room,' he said. 'If you will excuse me.' Then, to their astonishment, with a further bow but not another word of explanation, he got back into the car and drove away through another archway at the opposite end of the courtyard.

Audrey and Beth stared at the rear end of the Daimler as it disappeared, then looked at each other, bewildered and disorientated.

'That is one weird guy,' said Audrey. 'And this is one weird place.'

'What do we do now?' Beth demanded helplessly, a plaintive, childlike tone creeping into her voice.

Audrey shrugged. 'Your guess is as good as mine.'

They looked around them. The courtyard was trapezoid in shape, with two wings running back from the corner towers at the front, converging gradually until they ended, one truncated, and the other abutting a third tower, taller and fatter than the other two. Between the two wing-tips was the small rear gatehouse through which the car had gone, and a low stone balustrade which gave a glimpse of hedged parterres beyond. Inside the court, the architecture – apart from the towers – was of pale yellow sandstone; perhaps an attempt by the builder to lighten the oppressive sensation of enclosure. An attempt that patently hadn't worked. The right-hand wing was fronted by stacked, open galleries; three storeys faced with arches that halved in width as they rose, so that the ground floor had three wide openings, the first floor six and the top floor twelve narrow arches with smooth piers and elaborately carves spandrels, looking to Beth as though it had been forcibly and reluctantly expatriated from its proper home in Florence or Rome. The left-hand wing was square-set and pierced by regular rows of high windows. (The two were known, respectively, as the Italian Wing and the Old Wing. Both, of course, had been built at the same time, but the nomenclature had been transliterated along with the architecture itself from the French original.) In Italy or Spain, or even France, filled with bright, liquidescent light, the galleried wing might have had beauty, but here, grey-washed with the weak light of a winter afternoon amongst the ankles of Dartmoor, it glowered sullenly; the entire courtyard's precisely framed spaces and light-bowls lurked with bleak shadows, a rhombus of dark foreboding pent-up and pinioned by the sharp points of the three towers.

Of course, Beth didn't think any of this at the time; all she knew was that it scared the shit out of her. She looked at Audrey. 'What shall we do?' she repeated.

Audrey looked around her and finally settled on the Old Wing. Beside the spot where the car had deposited them was a broad sweep of shallow steps leading up to a wide, porticoed doorway. The double doors were closed, but their top halves were glazed. Audrey went up the steps and peered in, cupping her hands on either side of her face. She tried one of the big, polished brass handles. It turned, and there was a deep, echoing *cdnk* and a rattle of glass as the door opened. She turned back to Beth. 'Try in here, I suppose.'

Beth stayed where she was at the foot of the steps, suddenly rooted to the spot. A little girl again, trespassing where she oughtn't to be; a holiday memory from Cheshire flooded into her mind, of herself and Sandra Whitmore setting out tremulously to explore Mendacre Farm, the abandoned and reputedly haunted huddle of tumble-down buildings on the far side of the railway line that ran by Mendacre Spinney. They would never have willingly gone there, but they had been goaded beyond endurance by the taunts of Paul and Darren Cheeseman (Too scary for *girls*). As they approached the grime-blinded windows of the old farmhouse, the stories of dread and fear that had accreted on the husk of the place – murder, suicide, strange disappearances – crowded in on them, vivid and bloody, and they ran away, squealing and clutching each other's hands, before they had advanced even half-way across the farmyard.

She felt it again; that in-too-deep trespass sensation; the trembling knees and clogged feet, stomach lurching and neck almost swivelling off its moorings as wide eyes tried to cover every possible direction of attack. Only the pallid ghosts of those feelings, but enough to hold her rooted.

'You have a look,' she said. 'I'll wait here.'

Audrey paused, her fingers resting on the handle of the half-open door. 'What? Come on, this must be the way.'

With a quick glance to either side, as though expecting someone to leap out of nowhere and arrest or assault her, Beth started reluctantly up the steps.

The door opened on to a vestibule lined with fern-filled jardinières, fronds drooping and brown-curl-edged. Set into each marbled side wall was a low stone cistern with a gargoyled water-spout; unidentifiable carnivorous faces dribbling brown water from stubs of corroded lead piping. There was another glass-panelled door directly opposite the entrance, leading into a vast hallway. As they crossed the threshold, their heels click-clacked loudly on the black and white chessboard tiles, echoing off bare granite walls decorated with rayed suns and fans of daggers, swords and halberds. Between the stone pillars lurked suits of armour and huge, shadowy paintings. There were two doors of blank, iron-studded oak, one on either side of a great, gaping fireplace. Unconsciously moving closer together, Beth and Audrey ignored the doors and walked to the far end of the hall, where the granite gave way to the white marble of a great spiral staircase. They had seen spiral stairs in their time, but none like this: twenty feet in diameter, with wide, shallow steps fanning out from a central pillar that was as thick as a tree-trunk but utterly smooth, with no discernible joints. The uncarpeted, wear-lapped steps swept down and spilled out like a breaking wave into the fringe of the hall. At the foot of the stairs, two corridors led away to left and right.

What they had seen in the inside did nothing to quell the apprehension Beth had felt before entering. The schizoid chaos of styles – the Victorian conservatory gentility of the vestibule, the montages of vicious ironmongery in the medieval hall, and then the classical grandeur of the marble staircase – hinted at a designing mind which was not so much quixotically eclectic as downright demented.

'Where—' Beth hesitated, startled by the loud echoes of her voice. She lowered it to a hoarse, intruder's whisper: 'Where now?'

'This way,' said Février.

Beth's heart tried to leap out through her ribs as she spun round and stepped backwards in fright. (Even in her alarm, though, she was gratified to notice that Audrey also flinched and gave a little gasp, although that might have had more to do with Beth treading on her foot.) He had materialised behind them so suddenly and silently that he might have been propelled up through the floor on a stage trap; all that was missing was a thunderclap and a puff of smoke.

Audrey regained her composure quickly and followed him as he strode off down the right-hand corridor, Beth tagging along reluctantly. In the corridor, the style changed again: parquet flooring and panelled wainscotting with foliage-patterned wallpaper above and deep, wide windows looking out over the castle grounds. At the end of the corridor, Février opened a pair of double doors and ushered them through.

The Music Room appeared to be a combination of library, drawing room and conservatoire. On one side, the wall was lined from floor to high ceiling with bookcases, flanking an ornate fireplace the same size as the doorway they came in through; opposite was a row of three tall french windows facing on to a terrace. The furniture in between – a collection of fat-backed sofas and bow-legged chairs and tables – was oriented to provide a view of the far corner, where the room bellied out to fill the bottom storey of the large corner tower. The floor here was raised, and occupied by a grand piano and a forest of wooden chairs and music stands. Near the foot of the short flight of steps leading up to the low platform, two small sofas had been ranged before a low circular table. There were two figures there, diminished to dolls'-house size by the scale of the room: a middle-aged maid was transferring the paraphernalia of afternoon tea – silver-spouted pots, jugs, bowls, spoons, knives, cups, plates and platters – from a huge tray and laying them out on the table, under the sharp gaze and syncopated staccato stream of instructions and reprimands, in French, from a tiny woman in a black dress with a cowl neck. The mistress of the house. She was sitting opposite the sofas, on a curious seat like a long, low stool, framed by a rising, ruched-silk screen set against the wall behind, giving her an air of enthronement. Beth was immediately put in mind of Lady Catherine de Bourgh, and felt more nervous than ever.

'Madame,' said Février loudly as they entered.

That was all; no introductions, no announcement of names, just the one word, but accompanied by a clicked-heel bow of a magnificence that surpassed all his previous effacements. There seemed to be a protocol at work here that none of Beth's literary dredgings of country-house manners could prepare her for; perhaps, she thought, this was the modern way or the French way, or perhaps a form that had evolved entirely independently of fashion and was peculiar to this one household. She glanced at Audrey to see how she was taking it, and was disconcerted to see a barely concealed expression of amusement behind the polite mask. But then, perhaps that was the best attitude to take; to be Elizabeth Bennet to Madame de La Simarde's Lady Catherine.

Février stepped aside to let them pass, and they walked the length of the room while she gazed at them in silence, leaving off her supervision of the maid to study her visitors as they approached. As they came closer, Beth noticed inconsequentially that the seat she was sitting on was the exact twin of the stool which stood before the enormous ebony piano on the platform.

'I welcome you,' she said in a voice that was full and deep but edged with harshness, like the moorland granite from which her castle was built. 'It is our misfortune that we meet only on such a sad day. Lydia was a much beloved daughter-in-law. She will be deeply missed.'

Her accent, again rather like her home, was a curious mixture; the vowels and intonation were pure English gentry, but many of the consonants – some savoured richly while others were elided altogether – exuded French. She spoke her lament with every outward appearance of sincerity, but there was a hollowness somewhere behind the eyes that made Beth feel that if the sentiment was genuine, it was not very deeply felt.

'Février, take the young ladies' coats so that they may sit.'

This also seemed to be part of the protocol, with no suggestion that he might have been remiss in not relieving them of their outdoor layers before presenting them. Beth gave up her coat with reluctance; the small fire that had been lit in the huge fireplace was completely inadequate, and the room was only a little warmer than outdoors.

'You are a little later than expected,' Madame de La Simarde said as they sat down, one on each of the sofas.

'I had a little difficulty in locating them, Madame,' said Février, who was standing by with their coats draped over one arm, waiting to be dismissed.

Madame de La Simarde stared sternly at her guests. 'No matter,' she said. 'Tea, I am afraid, has followed your example. It is also a little late.' She glanced at the maid, who was pouring hot water into the teapot from a chased silver urn. 'Do you not find,' she went on, 'that as one grows older, *some* servants seem to become more of a hindrance than a help.'

The maid blanched and concentrated all the more intently on making the tea.

'Oh, absolutely,' said Audrey, smiling. 'I've often said it myself.'

'But of course, you are young yet,' said Madame de La Simarde, apparently not hearing her. 'Age will come, though, it most certainly shall. The secret is to wear it well, like finely cut clothes. Take Février here, for example. Tell me, how old do you suppose he is?' She peered sardonically while Beth and Audrey shrugged and shook their heads in embarrassed unison and Février stood mutely to attention. 'Fifty-five, perhaps?' she prompted. 'A little older? Sixty?' She turned to the maid, who had finished filling the teapot and was laying out a salver of cakes. 'Avril, tell the young ladies your brother's age.'

The maid, who was not young herself, straightened up, one hand going instinctively to rub at the small of her back. She glanced timorously at her mistress, then with a hint of fearful pride at Février. 'He is seventy-six years old, Madame.'

'Do you hear that? Seventy-six! And yet you have never seen a finer figure of a man in his prime.' She gazed with admiration at her manservant for a few moments while Beth forced an awkward smile and Audrey murmured, 'Extraordinary'. 'Thank you, Février,' she said at last. 'You may go. You also, Avril – if we require any further disarray and incompetence, we can endeavour to supply it for ourselves.'

There was no trace of humour or irony in her voice, and Avril turned away with her eyes cast down. As she passed, though, she shot a glance at the two visitors and, as it flicked past and settled momentarily on Beth, she thought she saw an expression there of . . . what? Sympathy, she would have guessed, or even pity. But before she had time to probe the look any further, Avril was gone, following her brother out of the room. The door closed with a soft click, and they were alone.

'Now,' said Madame de La Simarde, pouring tea into three cups. 'Names.'

'I beg your pardon?' said Audrey, who was not used to being addressed like a corralled miscreant.

'On a first acquaintance, it is customary for there to be a mutual furnishing of names.' She smiled with condescending indulgence. 'You know who *I* am, of course. Of you I know little, other than that you were close friends of my dear daughter-in-law.'

She placed a cup of tea on Beth's portion of the table and trained her gaze on her. Beth felt Elizabeth Bennet begin to crumble inside her. 'Er, Bethany Glaister,' she said, as though offering an apology. It seemed such an insufficient explanation of her identity and excuse for her presence here (But she had been *invited*, she told herself in vain) that she felt compelled to go on: 'We met once before, Madame.' Madame de La Simarde showed no sign of recognising the prior acquaintance. 'In Cambridge,' Beth added. The inscrutable gaze went on. 'You wouldn't remember me, I suppose,' she concluded lamely. Just how many people – impressive, important, remarkable people – must this woman have met in her life? Of course she wouldn't remember.

Madame de La Simarde's eyes glazed over for a moment, as if in extreme boredom, then cleared. 'We spoke,' she said. 'Your mother lived in Wales, and your late father was a writer ... No, a poet. You were studying English Literature, and were composing a piece of work on Oscar Wilde.'

'Oh,' said Beth. 'You do remember.'

'You told me that you intended to achieve an upper second-class degree.'

Beth's cheeks flushed, and she avoided Audrey's eyes. 'Um, well, I don't think I said I intended, not as such. I sort of hoped I would.'

Madame de La Simarde frowned at her. 'Hoped? Whatever would be the use of that? If you desire to achieve something, you must *intend*. Hope is for the weather and playing the lottery; achievement is won by will alone. Tell me; did you achieve the class of degree you "hoped" for?'

Beth flushed deeper, growing quite hot despite the chill of the room. 'No,' she mumbled, almost inaudibly.

'Precisely.' Madame de La Simarde sipped her tea. 'My father was Castilian, a very determined race; our family motto (it was in Latin, so I shall translate for you) was *The arrow shot highest by the tautest string flies farthest.* You, child, shot low and weakened your bow by stringing it with hope.'

Trussed, judged and dismissed, Beth stared in dismay into her teacup while Madame de La Simarde turned her attention to Audrey. The last trace of Elizabeth Bennet's spirit dissipated and departed; her head filled with the beginnings of tart rejoinders (*Madame, forgive me, but I . . .*) which tailed away lamely to nothing. Perhaps she should simply get up and leave, but even had she possessed the courage, she had nowhere to go. She tried to console herself by waiting for Audrey to undergo her customary embarrassment at having to introduce herself as Audrey Shufflebotham.

'You, I am certain,' Madame de La Simarde was saying to her, 'I have never met.'

Audrey was looking quite inordinately comfortable, and even a little smug. 'Quite correct,' she said. 'My name is Audrey Quintard.'

Beth started, and her cup rattled in its saucer. She stared at Audrey. *Quintard?* . . . Good God, so she *had* married him, despite everything. When had that come about? More to the point, *how?* Talk about achieving by firmness of intention. The way she bounced a glance at Beth as she pronounced the name suggested that their disagreement had not been forgotten; no wonder she had looked so smug. God, if only she knew . . .

The interview (or lecture – it certainly wasn't like any social conversation Beth had ever had) dragged on for eleven, twenty-three, thirty-two, forty minutes, according to Beth's occasional surreptitious consultations of her watch. They were told a little of the history of the Château and of the Simarde family, and a great deal about

Salvador (a genius and last of a great ancestral line, painted in hues that didn't quite harmonise with their own memories of him). He had given a great many of his finest performance in this very room. That, they were told, with a nod towards a guitar on a stand beside the piano, was one of his concert instruments. A Torres; ancient and priceless and the finest ever made. They heard relatively little about Lydia: a dear, dear daughter-in-law, almost a real daughter, but talked of with a dry-eyed composure that hardly seemed right for the day of her funeral. Madame de La Simarde finally drew the audience to a close by rising from her seat and pinching the thick gilded cord of a bell-pull beside the silk screen.

'You are tired, of course,' she said as she pulled the cord. 'You have had long journeys and a distressing experience.' For a moment, Beth wasn't sure whether she was referring to the funeral or this visit, but Madame de La Simarde went on: 'Grief drains the emotions and wearies the body in a way that physical work never can. You shall be summoned for dinner,' she went on without a pause. 'In the meantime, you may occupy yourselves as you wish. There are many pleasant walks around the grounds, or you may prefer to use the library. There is a good musical collection here' – she indicated the high banks of shelves – 'and an excellent general collection in the Green Library. Février will guide you if necessary.'

Audrey smiled politely. (She and their host had been getting on like a house on fire; Audrey evidently recognised a sage of her own craft when she met one, and there had been clear admiration in her eyes several times as she listened to the hectoring flow.) She cleared her throat. 'Er, I wonder ... I had a bag with me, in the boot of the car ...? I thought I might do some work.'

The relationship faltered; Madame de La Simarde looked at her with a momentary mixture of distaste and bewilderment, as though the query were not merely obtuse but also rather impertinent. 'You will find that your luggage has been transferred to your room,' she said.

Audrey coloured. 'Oh, right. Thanks.'

The door opened at the far end of the room, and the maid appeared again.

'Avril, show the young ladies to their rooms. Provide them with anything they require.'

'Yes, Madame.'

Madame de La Simarde then rattled off a stream of quick French, which was accompanied by a nervous choreography of nods, head-shakes and bobs, and a volley of *Oui, Madame* and *Non, Madame*. Then, turning back to her guests, she said, 'Dinner is pheasant. I trust that is agreeable,' and they were dismissed.

L ydia's room. She had been given Lydia's room.

When Avril had left, Beth sat down on the hard wooden chair by the window, still wearing her coat (she had asked for it back on the pretext that there were some items she needed in the pockets). Despite the advancing front of crackling warmth billowing from the fire, she felt chilled to the core. There was a thin strand of icy air streaming in through a crack under the lower sash, and she held her finger in the flow, as if to confirm that the cold did not come entirely from inside her.

The window faced east, looking out across the lawns and the drive, towards the glowering shadows of the moors, framed above by the deepening, darkening sky and below by the fringe of the trees in the park. This must be a pleasant room on a summer morning, catching bright rays from the rising sun, and Beth tried to concentrate on this thought, but it just made the room's hostile, sullen oppressiveness in the depths of an overcast winter's afternoon seem all the more depressing. How many hours must Lydia have endured, cut off from her friends and her meagre, distant family, sitting here in this chair, gazing out at this desolate view, wondering where life had gone. It must have been even worse here than in France; here she must have felt the proximity of the people she knew and the world they inhabited. To be a prisoner (for that was how her life looked to Beth) and still be able to perceive the outside of the cage; that must be the worst fate of all.

Suddenly, shockingly, with a rush of insight as powerful as that she had experienced earlier that day when she saw the apparition at the grave-side, Beth saw her own life in a different cast: watched over

41

silently and invisibly by Lydia. She felt Lydia's envious presence in all the nooks and corners of her life during the past seven years, and the thought made her want to cry; cry for the depths of Lydia's loneliness and her own wilful indifference to it.

She stood up and pulled the coat more tightly around herself. Clamping its front under her crossed arms, hugging herself for comfort, she began to wander restlessly around the room, trying to shake off Lydia's ghost. But it followed her; wherever she turned, Lydia haunted every corner: every inch of polished floor and Persian rug she had stood on; the bed where she had slept; every piece of furniture she had touched; the walls she must have hopelessly gazed at for hour upon dreary hour... All of these things were Lydia – touched by her presence – and yet not her; there was not a single stick or stitch or fibre or hue that had been brought into this place by her. She had come into this room, lived in its space, then departed, leaving nothing visible behind her to alter it.

The weight of sadness that settled on Beth's shoulders was too great for her to bear, and she longed to lay her hands upon something of Lydia's; something of her own that would contain her pure essence. She stopped in the middle of the hearth rug, oblivious to the intense heat surrounding her, and wondered: there must be *something* here; some small item at least must have been left behind. She stood still, glancing around the room, from the wardrobe to the bed to the tall chiffonier to the washstand... Then, responding to an impulse, she went straight to the bedside table. Sitting down on the edge of the bed, she opened the drawers one by one, starting from the top.

The first two were empty: apart from their embossed floral lining papers, all they contained was an aroma of aged, dusty wood and stale lavender. But, as she slid open the third drawer, her heart leapt; here already was a little piece of Lydia. Lying face-down in the bottom of the drawer was a postcard. It was unwritten, but Beth knew right away that it must belong to Lydia, who had always been an obsessive sender and receiver of postcards. Her room in Cambridge had been virtually wallpapered with them: some from friends, but most from her half-brother, Gabriel, who was a courier for a tour operator and pandered fondly to Lydia's passion by sending her these flimsy little rectangles of sunshine. From Bali to Zanzibar and from Alice Springs to New York, the mosaic had covered her pinboard by the end of her second term, then rapidly spilled over onto her walls, desk and wardrobe. Friends would ask her if she had ever been to these places herself, and she would always say that she didn't need to; she could simply lie on her little bed and look at the postcards, and be transported to all the corners of the world in her imagination. Beth and Audrey, though, who knew Lydia better than anyone else, were aware that, in truth, she desperately yearned to go to these faraway places, but was kept bound within Britain by a pathological terror of flying and of the sea. Beth was sure that it had been this thwarted desire for exotic places that had attracted her to Salvador: whereas for the others it had always been his beauty or his convoluted psyche or – above all – his music, for Lydia it was his foreignness and his vast archive of traveller's tales. How, though, he had managed to coax her to France was beyond Beth's imagination. Marriage must have changed her.

Beth took the postcard out of the drawer and turned it over. The picture was a striking one: dark grey against an implausibly cobalt sky was a stone tower: almost Tolkienesque; tall and thin and pointed as a needle, set upon a broad stone dais. There were no people in the photograph, nor any other indication of scale, so as far as Beth could tell, the tower might be as tall as Pisa or as small as a pillar-box. She turned the card over again and read the legend: *Lanterne des Morts. Cimetière de Gondecourt, XIIIème siècle.*

She recognised the name: it was the village near the Simarde estate in France . . . *Lantern of the Dead* . . . The words made her go cold; why this grim image? Why this postcard? Why here, why *now*, on this day of all days? For a fleeting moment, in her susceptible state, a horrible, fantastic notion sped across her mind: this was a message from Lydia, from beyond death: *This is the place.* This *is where I died*, the picture was telling her. *They're lying to you.* The thought was briefly lit up by a hideous, superstitious luminosity before fleeing again into the shadows at the back of her mind. No, she reasoned, this tower had nothing to do with Lydia's fall. The version she had heard was officially endorsed: Lydia had fallen to her death from a window in the derelict old château on the Simarde estate. She was rushed to hospital, but despite a long operation, the cranial trauma was too severe, and she died on the operating table. This morbid postcard had nothing to do with the story, and it was only the sickening spin of chance that had placed it here for Beth to find. Only partially convinced by her own rationalisation, she laid the postcard on top of the bedside table and had another look in the drawer. The only other item was a small key, two inches long and purple-brown with slow, finger-smoothed dust, abraded to bright metal along the edges of its claw-like wards. As she held it up to the weakening light, her imagination spiralled out again, and she picked up the postcard: *This was the key to the tower!* . . . She had a vague mental image of an ancient door creaking open into an interior of glowing gothic darkness, pregnant with sinister secrets . . .

Again, she caught herself. This was getting silly; the atmosphere of this gloomy castle had infiltrated her mind and was breeding thoughts

43

which belonged in a cheap thriller or – worse – in one of those ridiculous adventure games Iain was always playing when he was supposed to be writing.

Anyway, the key was too small to be a door-key. It must fit some other, smaller lock; perhaps a box or a chest or a drawer. It wasn't connected with the tower at all.

When she had settled down, steadying and studying herself, she concluded that her flights of imagination were caused by nothing more than guilt at the tragic loneliness of Lydia's death and the last few years of her life. Clutching the key and the postcard to her chest as though they were remnants of Lydia herself, she lay back on the pillows and closed her eyes. At last, she felt the tears returning; they gathered in her chest and rushed up her throat, leaking out of her in stifled, gasping sobs. She rolled over onto her side and curled herself into a ball, shaking with the force of her weeping. Slowly, quietly, she drifted into sleep, and as the feeble daylight shrank away to darkness, her crying smoothed and shallowed into a gentle ebb of dreaming breath.

Finding Salvador

1

Spool backwards, watching it all blur by . . . and *stop*. Forward a little, and . . . *stop*.

Ainsw—

Whoa, that looked familiar . . . Peter stopped his bike by the kerb and peered up at the street sign, bolted to the wall about eight feet up, barely lit by the weak leakage from a too-distant street lamp . . . Ainsworth Street . . . He consulted the fading, blurring biro inscription on the heel of his thumb again. Close, but no cigar; no, he definitely wanted Ainsworth *Cottages*. As unlikely as the address sounded in the middle of a city, the smudges of blue ink did not resemble *Street* at all. He looked despondently up and down the long, interminably straight terrace of small houses, and felt – not for the first time – the sensation of having wandered into a different town. This was certainly not the Cambridge with which he was so intimately familiar; since cycling across Parker's Piece and under the tent of rainy light shining down on Reality Checkpoint, he had considered the resonance of such a sinister name being attached so firmly to an innocent lamp standard. It marked the southern boundary of University and Town, collegiate and municipal; more than a difference between cultures or modes of life, it felt like the portal between dimensions of existence. Peter's perception of this unconformity was the reverse of that implied by the name of the Checkpoint; for him, the reality, all that was solid and tangible and meaningful – in a sense, all that truly *existed* – was *inside* the invisible perimeter. It was invested in the ancient, carbon-stained stone and the winding streets and the arched windows and the smell of books and ancient wood; it was even in the newer presences of concrete and plate glass and nests of humming computers. It certainly wasn't out here in the orderliness of planned, uniform streets of uniform houses, where even the student dwellings reeked of the artificial, brick-built imaginary world of industry and commerce, where the trains bound out for King's Lynn clattered along beyond the back fences.

After a moment's consideration, he kicked off from the kerb and carried on pedalling along Ainsworth Street, wavering erratically to avoid the worst of the puddle-filled potholes. After a hundred yards of houses had reeled repetitively past, he came to the end of the street, where it branched and was blocked by a cluster of tubbed shrubs. Still no sign of Ainsworth Cottages. He turned round and began pedalling back the way he had come.

About half-way along the street, he encountered another cyclist coming the other way: a girl in a yellow rain-cape, riding quickly and confidently on a fragile-looking racer, snicking and shimmying her skinny front wheel deftly between the ruts as though their pattern was imprinted in her mind like a map. He squeezed his brakes and brought the bike juddering to a halt. 'Excuse me?' he called querulously. She whisked past him, then there was an answering squeal of brakes and she paused, looking back at him over her shoulder. Peter smiled politely. 'I say, excuse me, could you direct me to Ainsworth Cottages? I'm afraid I've got myself rather lost.'

She peered at him through thick, round glasses speckled with droplets of water. She had a round face with a large, shapeless nose, all framed and squeezed to plumpness by the tightly tied hood of her cape.

'Did you say Ainsworth Cottages?' she asked.

'Please tell me you know it. I can't continue this hopeless quest all night.'

Her cape fanned upwards as she pointed in the direction she was heading. 'It's this way,' she said. 'On the right.'

'Oh, glory!' he cried, turning his bike around in the middle of the road. 'Now, where precisely?'

She hesitated, twisting round in her saddle and peering harder, trying to make out his face in the gloom and drizzle. 'Actually,' she admitted, 'I'm going there myself. Follow me. I'll show you.' She seemed satisfied that he meant her no harm, and smiled at him before kicking off and swishing away down the road ahead.

A little further on, she swung abruptly right and headed into a narrow gap – barely six feet wide – between two houses. He had passed this gap twice before and ignored it, taking it for an access way to some back-alley or lock-up garage huddled in the lee of the railway embankment. As he followed the girl, though, he discovered that the alleyway opened out into a muddy, gravelled lane, which in turn opened out as if by magic into what appeared to be a clearing in the middle of a thickety copse of hawthorn and horse-chestnut. At the far end, the rusty back end of a Sherpa van protruded from a nook amongst the bushes, and on the right stood a row of three low, two-storey cottages. Yellow light leaking from their small, square windows lit the scene, and its warmth, along with the banks of foliage bordering the walls and creeping up to their roofs, made them look as though they were set into the earth itself, like a row of little hobbit-holes.

The girl got off her bike outside the end cottage – illuminated in every one of its four windows and emanating a muffled thudding of loud music – and began uncoiling a length of chain and a padlock from under the saddle.

'I suppose you've come for the party,' she said, lashing her bike to a rotten-looking, lichen-green fence post.

He dismounted beside her and began looking for a place to park his own bike. 'Indeed,' he said, scanning the gloomy undergrowth. 'Dionysos has crooked a finger in my direction and I am powerless to resist. Anything besides temptation . . .'

There was no more fencing to be seen, so Peter leaned his bike carefully against the sturdy-looking outer branches of a hawthorn bush. It stood just long enough for him to be satisfied and step away, then it collapsed into the bush, showering him with spray from the whiplashing, water-laden branches and flinging a bottle of green Chartreuse out of its basket and into the undergrowth.

'Shitty, *shitty WANK!*' he muttered furiously, crouching down and peering into the bush.

The girl looked at him without even a flicker of amusement, only deep concern. 'Do you want a hand?' she asked.

'Several,' he said, grunting as he fumbled about inside the bush. 'Any but my own.' His delicate hands skittered amongst the prickly twigs and the sodden mulch of dead leaves, searching for the precious bottle. At last, he found it and edged back out of the sharp, showering foliage, holding the bottle up in one wet, muddy hand and hauling his bike out with the other. It came free with a tearing, snapping wrench and flung another cloud of droplets at him.

He felt close to tears as he gazed down at himself. 'I can't go in looking like this,' he moaned. 'My carnation! Just *look* at my carnation!' He had devoted a whole hour of tender care to choosing and colouring it, and now it drooped, limp and battered, from his buttonhole.

The girl gazed sympathetically at him. 'Here, let me help,' she said, rummaging under her voluminous cape for a tissue.

'People will think I'm a postgraduate,' he complained miserably as she began dabbing specks and streaks of mud from his hands and face.

She smiled. 'No, they won't. Now, keep still – you've got a bit of leaf about to go in your eye.'

Peter gazed into her plump, plain face as she cleaned him down. 'I love you,' he said. 'You and I shall be married before the week is out.'

She giggled shyly and went on dabbing and wiping at his soft skin.

Beth stood by the table in the small kitchen and surveyed the neat rows of bottles, cartons and cans uncertainly.

'Is there enough here, do you think?' she asked.

Audrey turned away from the small mirror which hung from the wall between the overflowing patchwork of the pinboard and the control panel of the Baby Belling. She tutted. 'Of course there is. Most of them will bring their own, you know.'

'Hmm, I suppose . . . I was just thinking we could've done with more orange juice and stuff. Some of Rachel's friends don't drink.'

'Oh, you do surprise me . . . Actually, I *am* surprised – I wasn't aware the Frump From The Dump *had* any friends.'

Beth glared sternly at her. 'I hope you're not going to pick on her this evening. You promised you'd—'

'No, Mum,' said Audrey wearily, turning back to the mirror. 'Don't worry, I've got bigger plans than Rachel-baiting.' She pressed her bright pink lips together and examined their gloss. 'Anyway,' she added, 'there's plenty of water in the tap if they're so bloody puritanical.'

'I don't understand why you can't just make an effort to get on with her. I mean, we're stuck together after all, and I know *she* likes *you*.'

'Well, I wish she wouldn't – it's rather tiresome, and God knows I give her little enough reason to.'

A young man – one of the first arrivals, who had turned up on the doorstep promptly at eight – wandered in from the adjoining living room. He had bright, ferociously cropped ginger hair that jarred with long, limp limbs which gave him the appearance of wilting, like an unappealing breed of orchid left out in scorching sunlight. 'We've had a vote,' he said. 'We think it's our duty as early guests to get this party run up for take-off before the less committed revellers get here. How about it? Any danger of excessive volumes of alcohol heading our way?'

'Of course,' said Beth, reddening slightly. 'Sorry, Rob. It's all here.' She hefted two six-packs of inexpensive lager off the table and passed it to him. 'Take that to start with and tell them there's more in here when they want it.'

Rob tucked the cans awkwardly under one arm and, grinning slyly at her and quickly scanning the selection, reached out and whisked up a half-bottle of vodka. 'Light the blue touch-paper and stand well back,' he said, heading back towards the living room.

'And put some music on!' she called after him. He waved the vodka bottle in acknowledgement and disappeared. '*He* didn't bring his own,' she whispered to Audrey as the sound of the cans being planked down on the living room floor heralded the growth of chatter from a quiet flutter to a lively jabber punctuated with loud exclamations. 'Nor did any of them. I *knew* we should've got more.' She gazed at the array, noticeably diminished by the disappearance of the cans and the vodka. 'I'm hopeless at this sort of thing. I haven't had a party since I was eight. I don't know the grown-up rules.'

Audrey laughed. 'There aren't any. Just relax and be the birthday girl.' She lowered her voice: 'This lot are just the liggers. Real party people won't arrive till at least nine.'

In ones and twos, the early arrivals wandered in and out of the kitchen, and the place began to come alive with the sound of chatter, clinking cans and cracking, fizzing beer cans. As Beth patrolled nervously from kitchen to living room to hallway and back again, trying hard to host and coax the gathering, she sensed the tension breaking and dissipating. As loud, insistent music burst from the stereo (Abba, of all things – who on earth did *that* belong to?), the slightly staid, awkward gathering evolved suddenly into a party.

An hour later, the music had swollen and sprouted tendrils that crept through all the rooms, up the stairs, and infiltrated every vibratable atom in the house, and along these feelers the party itself expanded, as the guests began to move out from the hub and find their own spaces to talk, drink, huddle, and intimately insinuate themselves with each other; the gaps left in the central pool of the living room between the hardened dancers and those who couldn't or wouldn't conjoin them-selves into couples were periodically replenished by new arrivals.

At eight-thirty, Beth took her first sip of lager – daintily decanted into a glass – and was chided by Audrey for behaving like a maiden aunt (*Would she prefer a nice cup of Darjeeling, perhaps?*). She made a conscious decision to let go and enjoy herself for once; to fracture Audrey's neatly constructed little vision of her. *You're twenty, for God's sake*, she told herself. *Twenty today. Act it.* Trying not to gag, she drank down the lager as fast as she could and opened another can.

By nine-thirty, she was swimming deep, dancing in the middle of a crush of people, an open can in one hand, a cigarette weaving smoke strands behind the other. Opposite her was a tall man with a heavy jaw and dark eyes (*Hi, I'm Danny. Wanna dance?*), who claimed to be doing a PhD on Dark Matter in the Universe. Her sudden rapture was already beginning to flag; the mixture of bitter drink and dense smoke, stewed by over-enthusiastic dancing, was starting to make her feel queasy, and the loud music and confinement were closing in oppressively on her senses. Also, Danny was trying to get too close too quickly. He seemed to be under the impression that the cosmic tone and slightly sinister-sounding title of his subject somehow made it sexy, and he tried to explain it to her at intervals as they danced, taking advantage of the noise to lean close. Each time, he came closer and retreated less, until his lips brushed against her hair and his nose nuzzled her earlobe. When Beth realised that she was slowly and unconsciously reversing through the crowd, trying to retreat from his invasion of her space, and had crossed more than six feet of congested carpet in this manner, she decided that enough was enough. Claiming a need for the toilet, she broke off from him and made her escape.

In the relative calm quiet and clear atmosphere of the hall, she found Audrey sitting on the stairs. Like Beth, she had a drink – a bottle of red wine – in one hand and a cigarette in the other. Beth went and stood by the banister. 'Not enjoying yourself?' she asked.

Audrey shook her head. 'I'm having a great time. Just came out to get some fresh air and wait for someone *interesting* to show up.'

'There are interesting people here,' Beth ventured, snaking her body against the rail to allow a swaying couple to pass.

Audrey squeezed herself to one side as the couple stepped with drunken delicacy around her. She glared resentfully at their legs as they passed. 'Are there?' she said. 'Then you'd better introduce them to me, cause *I* haven't met any.' She sipped her wine, sucked on her cigarette and smiled. 'They're all so incredibly fucking *shallow* – all they want to talk about is their essays or their colleges or their bloody *rowing* teams, for Christ's sake.'

'You should've been born twenty years earlier,' Beth grinned. 'Should've been a flower-power student.'

'I can't *stand* boaties. Who the hell would get up at six in the middle of January to go and sit in the fucking river? Other than the fucking criminally unhinged.'

Beth nodded. 'Have you se—'

'And they think they're so sodding macho for it. Arseholes . . . What did you say?'

'I was going to say, have you seen any sign of Rachel?'

Audrey sneered. 'Talking of interesting people . . . No, I haven't.'

'Funny,' said Beth, looking at her watch. 'She should be back by now.'

As she spoke, there was a loud hammering on the little front door; three heavy, urgent thumps that made the nine little panes of bottle-glass rattle audibly, even above the pounding music from the living room. Beyond the glass, a blur of yellow loomed up. Just as Beth was about to step across and open the door – wondering how they were going to accommodate any more people in the tiny house – a key grated in the lock and the door flew in. The blur of yellow turned into a flurry of rain-cape accompanied by a tall man in an old-fashioned ensemble which looked more appropriate to a grouse moor than a student party.

'I'm dreadfully sorry,' he was saying to the rain-cape. 'I had no idea you actually *lived* here.'

'Rachel!' Beth cried. 'Where the hell have you been?'

'Go and get yourself a drink,' Rachel said to the man. 'The bathroom's upstairs on the right if you want to, er, freshen up a bit.'

The man nodded graciously and gave an elegant little bow which, whilst directed at Rachel, somehow managed to encompass all three of them in its genteel aura. Then he turned and disappeared into the living room.

Beth closed the door behind him, and the music sank to a pervasive thumping. As she turned back, she noticed that Audrey's eyes, which had been alternately alive with fiery irritation and dull with disappointment at the company fate had offered her for the evening, were now faraway, gazing thoughtfully at the blank face of the living-room door.

'What happened to you?' Beth demanded. 'We were getting worried. And who's your friend?'

'Sorry,' said Rachel, unstringing the tight hood of her cape and pulling it up over her head. 'The talk went on and on, and then some of us went for a pizza.' She hung the cape hastily on the least encumbered of an already overburdened row of hooks beside the front door, and turned to Beth and Audrey. Her eyes were alight with excitement. 'I've got news!' she said. 'It's so exciting!'

Beth glanced in surprise from Rachel to the living-room door. 'What . . .?'

Rachel frowned, then shook her head impatiently. 'No, not him,' she said. (She tried to sound nonchalantly dismissive, but her cheeks coloured pink.) 'No, I've heard a rumour.'

Audrey's attention wandered back to her friends, and the impatience returned to her face. 'God,' she said sarcastically. 'We're absolutely breathless. What rumour?'

'Go on, you'll never guess . . .'

Audrey sighed visibly. She got up from her perch on the stairs and went to the living-room door. 'I can't stand the excitement. I'm going back to the party.'

'No, wait,' Rachel pleaded. 'Let me tell you.'

Audrey let go of the door handle. 'Okay, tell us your big news,' she said resignedly.

'You'll never guess,' Rachel said, 'who's been made a fellow of Wolfburne...'

Audrey and Beth waited for enlightenment while Rachel eyed them both eagerly. Audrey shrugged. 'Simon Le Bon? Colonel Gaddafi? Jim Davidson? Do we really care?'

Rachel paused, squeezing one last drop of suspense from the moment. '*Salvador de La Simarde!*' she said with breathless awe.

Audrey's eyes widened in amazement; she came closer and laid a tremulous hand on Rachel's sleeve. 'Not... not *the* Salvador de La Simarde?'

Rachel beamed with pleasure. 'Yes!' she yelped.

'Really?'

'Honestly!'

Audrey removed her hand and gazed stonily at her. 'Who the *fuck*,' she demanded, 'is Salvador de La Simarde?'

Rachel's face fell. She stood squirming under the cruelty of Audrey's sneer for a moment, then turned and fled up the stairs towards her room.

'Rachel!' Beth called uselessly after her. She turned to Audrey. 'There was no need to be like that,' she said.

'I can't help it. She just... I don't know.' Audrey mimed claws down a blackboard. 'She *grates* on me... Anyway, let's get back to the party and root out these interesting people – we're missing the prime of the evening.'

She opened the door, and the palpable tangle of noise burgeoned out into their faces. Laughing and forgetting about Rachel, they linked arms and wove their way into the throng.

2

The rain had stopped during the night, and the clouds had gathered up their skirts and rolled away towards the coast. The sun was rising and turning the pearl-grey winter sky to pale pinks and blues as Peter emerged from the warren of back-streets and nosed his bike out on to Mill Road. The long, narrow thoroughfare, which would be bustling and choked with Saturday traffic in a few hours' time, was all but deserted. The pavements were empty except for the flutter of wind-blown litter, and the shops were shut up and blank-eyed; all except the newsagent opposite, where a yellow light burned behind the poster-patterned glass and a short Asian woman in a sari was setting out a splayed *Express* sign on the pavement. Peter smiled cheerfully at her and rode on.

When he reached the sprawling crossroads at Parker's Piece, the lights were red, but there wasn't a whisper of traffic in the post-dawn hush. He jumped the lights, pedalled quickly across, bumped up the kerb on the far corner and, weaving nimbly between the lines of railings, set out across the open park, humming a melody of vapoured breath into the air as he went; as he passed Reality Checkpoint, he was grinning into the chill slipstream.

It had been a rather splendid party, after all, in spite of his misgivings, and he congratulated himself on his finer, sharper instincts having overcome his grosser prejudices. Not that it had started well; aside from the tussle with the dripping hawthorn bush, the company had at first seemed every bit as dull and colourless as he had imagined. But – and this was a crucial *but* – it was a *girls'* party, and Wolfburne girls at that: none of your Newnham nonsense – Roedean spewings with their scrubbed cheeks and buck teeth – but three-to-two state-school pieces, sharp and well turned-out, with just enough newly discovered class consciousness to find his brand of Wildean (No, perhaps not Wildean after all, he corrected himself, not if he could help it), his . . . well, yes, damn it, it never did any harm to set them a challenge – to find his Wildean aura of decadent, sophisticated refinement fascinatingly exotic. Within an hour, overcoming the damp indignity of his arrival, he had established his court in the cramped hallway, and had them dancing in his palm till well after the red-rimmed eye of two in the morning.

And he had claimed a prize for his efforts; she had been a sweet one, that, and one of the hostesses to boot; sidling up to him in a quiet corner as he was draping his scarf around his neck. He had taken her hand and pressed its soft knuckles to his lips, and she had smiled hazily up at him. *Don't go*, she whispered. *It's early yet.* Sweet, delicious lie; how could he resist?

It had been ruinously late then, but it felt abominably early when, a bare few hours later, she chivvied him out of her bed and into his cold clothes. Not that he cared; despite the chill and the sleepless ache in his head, he was still smiling as he cleared Parker's Piece, bumped down the kerb of Regent Street and cycled off towards his college. He would be seeing her again if he had anything to do with it, even if he couldn't remember her name.

When Beth finally dragged herself out of bed, a tangle of jellied limbs and disparate, flitting aches and pains, it was after ten-thirty. She had been woken by the mixed, pleasant sensations of bright sun warming her bare legs where the duvet had fallen away, and a winter-cold draught that chilled their shaded surfaces. She had lain there enjoying it despite the ache of dehydration in her skull until the sharp pain of overhydration in her bladder forced her out.

She was seized by a fuzzy giddiness as she stood up, and she stumbled her way across the landing to the bathroom. Fortunately, it was unoccupied (rare treat) and she locked herself in gratefully, sniffing the air; concealing itself unsuccessfully behind the usual fug of soaps, perfumes, cleansers and Harpic was an intrusive, unwelcome, acid smell. She soon tracked it down to the corner by the window: an ejectamentum of bitty, liquid vomit that had missed the toilet and was lurking in a slowly drying puddle on the curled corner of the linoleum. Her body shuddered and her stomach convulsed, threatening to add to the congealed spoor. Holding her breath, she peed as quickly as she could, then washed her hands and face, feeling slightly better as the steamy water and the soap-scent drove away the stink of the puddle.

She gazed at herself blearily in the mirror as she rinsed her hands. *Chronological age*, she murmured, *twenty years and one day. Physical age . . . Anybody's guess. Cut off her leg and count the rings . . .* She tied the belt of her dressing gown tightly around herself, winced as the knot bit into her tender stomach, and loosened it again. Then she padded down the stairs, picking her way carefully between the litter of crushed cans, upturned glasses and empty bottles. In the hall, she stooped (reining in another lurch from her stomach) and harvested the post from the doormat. Electricity bill, phone bill, letter for Rachel, two letters for Audrey, and three postcards from Thailand. Still no sign of a birthday card from her mother. Sighing, she laid the postcards on top of the book-case beside the door, alongside the two from Hong Kong and Burma, and took the other post with her.

In the kitchen, she found Audrey and Rachel already up and dressed, both in unconscionably good moods, and each in her own way making the morning hellish. Rachel had the vacuum cleaner running at a skull-splitting volume, and appeared to be hoovering the laundry. 'Tissue got in the wash,' she shouted above the diabolical racket. It had been a communal black wash, and *somebody's* tissue (Rachel glared surreptitiously but without real malice at Audrey) had infiltrated it, splitting itself into a thousand soggy pellets which adhered diligently and tenaciously to every single square inch of every single garment, drying to a greyish snowflake frosting which Rachel was removing with the vacuum cleaner's curtain brush.

Beth put her hands over her ringing ears. 'D'you *have* to do that now?' she shouted weakly.

Rachel beamed. 'Pardon?'

'I said *stop it*, before my head explodes.'

Rachel switched off the vacuum, and the painful screaming whined away to silence. 'Sorry, I can't hear you,' she said.

'Thank you,' said Beth, sitting at the table and rubbing her temples. 'Peace at last.'

'Someone got a sore head?' said Audrey.

'Ng.' Beth stroked her temples. Out of the corner of her eye, she noticed Rachel reaching for the vacuum cleaner's ON button. 'Switch that thing on again and I'll stab you in the kidneys with a steak knife,' she warned.

Audrey was busy in the corner, burning bread. She liked to imagine she was making toast, but really she was just burning bread, expressing some deep-seated, latent partiality for inflicting physical torture. She liked it well done, she said. The toast would pop up, honey-brown and eager to be eaten, but Audrey, without so much as glancing at it, would bang it back down into the inferno and leave it there, trapped between the red-hot griddles until every delicate bubble and every frail strand of golden crust withered to black and died in a curl of acrid blue smoke. Only then were its mortal remains considered ready for her plate.

This morning's victims were just reaching the end of their cremation as Beth sat down. The bitter smoke stung her nostrils and made her stomach churn. (At least they didn't have to suffer the blattering accompaniment of the smoke alarm any more, not since Beth had removed its battery and hidden it in a drawer.) She waited until Audrey had sat down and was just about to take an unbuttered corner of charcoal between her teeth.

'There's sick all on the bathroom floor,' she said with vengeance in her heart. 'A really smelly one.'

Audrey's mouth hesitated for a moment, then, unfazed, bit into the carbonised slice. 'I mow,' she mumbled around a mouthful of ashes. She chewed and swallowed. 'I saw it.'

'Well, you could've bloody well cleared it up.'

'Did you?'

'No.'

'Well then. Whose is it, anyway?' Audrey glanced at Rachel, who was silently brushing the laundry.

'Don't look at me,' she said. 'I didn't even drink.'

Audrey took another bite. 'Don't worry,' she said to Beth, one hand decorously in front of her mouth. 'I'll shee to it later.'

Beth looked at her in astonishment. 'You?'

'Why not?'

'Well . . .'

Audrey smiled. 'It's the least I can do. I mean, you're the birthday girl.'

Beth's look of surprise changed to one of suspicion. 'You're in an awfully good mood this morning,' she said sullenly. 'Considering the amount of wine you put away.'

Audrey's smile broadened, and she put down her toast. 'I've every reason to be,' she said. 'This time yesterday, I was a hopeless, clueless child, with no rudder to guide me, no star to follow into the world. In other words, zippity-squelch career prospects. Today, though, all is clear. I can see my future, and it's golden – fortune stretching out in front of me like a . . . like a . . .'

'Big long stretching thing?' suggested Beth impatiently.

'Exactly.'

'How come?'

Audrey pulled her chair forward and laid her forearms on the table. 'Well, you know that guy at the party last night? The one Rachel brought with her?'

'You mean Peter?' said Rachel, glancing up from her brushing.

'I mean Peter. Well, you'll never guess who he is. Peter *Quintard*. His father's chairman of Quintard Rayner – you know, the publishers. His uncle's the managing director. You know, I *thought* I'd seen him before, when he came in. Short Lorna pointed him out to me in the Mill last term. She was at school with his sister.'

Beth frowned. 'What's all this got to do with you?'

Audrey rolled her eyes impatiently. 'Don't you see? It's my break! You know I want to work in publishing. If anyone can get me in, he can.'

'What makes you think he'd be interested in getting you in?' said Beth.

Audrey looked knowingly at her. 'Oh, he'll be interested all right,' she said complacently. 'Don't you worry about that.'

Rachel, brushing at a velvet skirt that belonged to Audrey, glanced up. 'He said he wanted to marry me,' she said quietly. Audrey turned to look at her, an expression of astonishment turning to derision so quickly that Rachel's cheeks reddened in shame. 'He was only teasing,' she added.

The derisive snort that Beth could sense forming up in Audrey's nostrils readjusted itself and came out as a contented sigh; she really was in a good mood. 'So,' she continued, 'I think I'll be seeing more of the divine Peter in the near future. Don't be surprised if there's an engagement ring on my finger before the end of the year.' She fanned out her elegant, unadorned fingers so that they could both imagine this golden future event.

56

Beth gazed at her. 'You really are a mercenary bitch, Audrey,' she said, without much malice.

'Thank you. I try.'

'Just don't be too confident, that's all. He might fall in love with somebody else. *You* might.'

'No chance. I know my man, dear. He'll get me in, so long as I let him get in me.'

Rachel huffed, and picked irritably at a stubborn white fleck on the hem of the skirt.

'Oh dear,' said Audrey. 'Do I detect disapproval from the hairy armpit camp?'

Rachel kept her eyes down, concentrating on picking off bits of tissue like fleas. 'It's no better than prostitution,' she muttered. 'No wonder men treat women the way they do. You're pandering to their power.'

'Rachel,' said Audrey, 'most of publishing is *run* by women. I just don't think I'll get very far if I hang about waiting for a well-connected lesbian to take a fancy to me.'

Rachel glared at her. 'Why do I get the feeling you're missing the point? You're colluding with masculine power structures, prostituting yourself. Why can't you get where you want to go on your own merits?'

Audrey smiled and stretched her lithe body languorously. 'Merits? My dear, that's exactly what I *am* doing.'

Rachel stood up, going red in the face. 'It's women like you that . . . that . . .'

'Women like me that what? Actually get what they want?'

Speechless, Rachel flung the skirt back into the laundry basket and stormed out of the kitchen while Audrey gazed calmly after her.

'You really are the limit,' said Beth. 'Do you know that?'

Audrey shook her head. 'She's just jealous. Did you hear her – *He asked me to marry him*. She'd do the same if she had the looks. Wouldn't you?'

'If *I* had the looks?'

'You know what I mean. Would you?'

'What, screw my way into a career? Well, frankly, no. No, I wouldn't.'

'Come on, don't say *you're* going to go all *Spare Rib* and judgmental on me.'

'I'm not judging you. Just be careful, that's all. He might not be quite what you imagine.'

Audrey's eyes narrowed. 'Do you know something I don't?' she asked. 'You do, don't you – come on what is it?

'Nothing. I don't know anything about him. But neither do you. I mean . . .' She groped around for an objection, however spurious, and found one in the memory of his manner and the green carnation in his lapel. 'He could be gay for all you know. Aren't you jumping the gun?'

Audrey laughed. 'Oh, I don't think so. I know enough to be going on with. Like I said, I know my man.'

They put off the tidying-up for as long as possible. By late afternoon, though, they could stand it no more, and set to with grim determination.

'What do you make of it?' asked Rachel, holding open a bin-liner while Beth moved around the room tossing in empty cans, bottles and the contents of overspilling ash trays. Audrey was upstairs, surprising them both by keeping her promise to clean the bathroom.

'Oh, I wouldn't take her too seriously,' said Beth.

'She seemed to mean it, though.'

Beth shrugged. 'Maybe. But she doesn't know anything about him, least of all whether he'll be interested in her.' Even as she said it, she knew better; she knew Audrey's character and knew the effect she had on men. 'Don't let her wind you up like that – you know it only entertains her.'

'I know, I know,' Rachel muttered. 'I suppose you're right, but it's not so much whether she'll *do* the things she says as the attitude behind it all.' She shook a cluster of cans and cigarette ends down to the bottom of the bag. 'Maybe I wouldn't react quite so much if I felt she liked me at all,' she added with doubtful logic.

Beth recognised the invitation to protest that, no, of course Audrey liked her *really*, deep down, but she couldn't be bothered to say it; she still felt hung-over and depressed, and just wanted to get the tidying-up over as quickly as possible so that she could go to her room for some peace and solitude. She wasn't in the mood for Rachel's insecurities, so she just mumbled an indeterminate 'Hmmm.'

Rachel was undeterred. 'Would you let a man . . . well, you know. Just like that?'

'Me? Just like what?'

'Well, *using* your body. Just so you'd get some favour in return.'

Beth shook her head. 'No, of course not.'

Rachel hesitated. 'Last night, at the party . . .' her voice trailed away uncertainly.

'Mm?'

'Well . . .'

Beth looked at her; something was obviously bothering her, something more than Audrey's personal morals. But she didn't get a chance to find out what it was: Rachel was interrupted by the sound of the front door jumping off its latch and swinging violently against the wall.

A voice muttered *Bugger*, then the hall light clicked on and the voice called out: 'It's me! Come out, come out wherever you are!'

'Lyd!' cried Beth, and rushed out to the hall. Lydia was standing on the threshold, looking like an angelic visitation, haloed by a circlet of orange street-light as she shed her wings (hauled off the straps of her towering rucksack). At the sight of Beth, she let the rucksack topple to the floor and flung out her arms. As they collided and enfolded each other, she murmured happily, 'Ah, who is this come to greet me? Brush the snowflakes from my eyes so I might see. Ah, my own long-lost child!' She held Beth at arms' length for a moment, then hugged her again. 'What a welcome! I should go away more often. How was the party? God, I was so sorry to miss it. I got you a present.' With the front door still wide open and a frosty breeze flowing round her, Lydia opened the lid of her rucksack and rummaged inside. 'Dirty knickers ... clean socks ... walking boots ... camera ... Ah, here it is!' She drew out a gift-wrapped package and handed it to Beth. 'It's the new Wilde biog,' she said. 'The Ellmann one you were on about. I picked it up in York. You haven't already got it, have you?'

Beth tore off the wrapping paper. 'Oh, thank you, Lyd.' She kissed Lydia on both cheeks and began shepherding her into the sitting room, carrying her rucksack for her and swinging the front door shut with her foot. 'We're still in a mess,' she said. 'It was a bit of a riot. We've only just got round to cleaning up.'

Lydia glanced around the dishevelled room. 'Looks exactly the same as when I left,' she said. Rachel was standing in the middle of the room, looking shy, the bin-liner still trailing from one hand. 'Hi, Rachel,' said Lydia, smiling. She gave her a brief squeeze, then retreated to the sofa and slumped down on it. 'So,' she said. 'Tell me all the gory details. Where's Aud? Don't tell me she's defected to Newnham?'

'She's in the bathroom,' said Rachel. 'Swabbing up sick.'

Lydia raised her eyebrows in surprise. 'Oh. Well, I was nearly right.'

Rachel went to the kitchen to make tea, coming back from time to time to stand in the doorway and listen and laugh at Lydia's traveller's tales. She had only been away for a fortnight, walking the Pennines on a field trip for her course, but they had missed her sorely. Her presence lent a warmth to the house that went out like a snuffed flame when she was away. She was a bringer of laughter, a settler of disputes, a core of happy strength, dismantling the pecking order by sheer good will.

Audrey, who had finished her cleaning duties long ago and had been sitting in her room, plotting her infiltration of the Quintard publishing empire, came down to say hello, drawn by the warm susurrus of laughter rippling up the stairs. For the first time in two weeks, she made no acid gibes at Rachel's expense, but talked and listened and laughed with the rest of them.

3

The chattering and catching up went on long into the evening, helped along by half a bottle of red wine left over from the party and a ham-and-mushroom pizza that arrived on the back of a moped. It was nearly eleven when Beth, aching and weak with the fatigue still hanging over her from the night before, reluctantly extricated herself from the gathering and went upstairs to bed.

She was about to get undressed when her eyes fell on the book lying on the corner of her desk; a thick, green-spined block resting on a rumpled cushion of purple wrapping-paper. She picked it up and ran her fingertip over the raised gold lettering of the title. She had coveted this book for months, standing in Heffers and poring over the photographs in an agony of indecision: fifteen pounds was a lot of money, and Beth was obsessively careful with the dregs of cash left over after rent, food, college charges and the lists of books she had no choice but to buy. Then her second year had started and thoughts of Oscar had all but drowned in a vortex of Tennyson and Dryden, Shakespeare and Dickens, structure, post-structure and close-reading of countless antique texts. She had forgotten about the book, not even aware that the paperback edition had come out during the previous term. Trust Lydia to remember.

She sat down at her desk and opened the book at the first chapter, already considering ways of pressing it into service; perhaps the ore of a dissertation might be mined out of its pages.

Tappity-tap. 'It's only me,' said a voice outside her door.

She looked up. 'Come in.'

'I saw your light on,' said Lydia, opening the door. 'I'm not disturbing, am I?' She glanced at the towers of textbooks and filled sheets of ruled A4 on the desk. 'Back to the grindstone?'

Beth shook her head. 'Not tonight. I was just having a look at my present.' She held up the book. 'Thanks again, Lyd. It was brilliant of you.'

Lydia brushed away the thanks with a wave of her hand as she closed the door and sat down on the end of the bed, but she couldn't disguise a small smile of satisfaction. 'So,' she said, 'what's this new boyfriend of Audrey's really like?'

'Boyfriend?' Beth was nonplussed for a moment. 'Oh, him. Future boyfriend, you mean. Pardon me – future *husband*.'

Lydia grinned. 'Audrey's a laugh,' she said. 'So serious. So determined.'

'Oh, it's been Lurve City here this weekend – Let's All Go Cow-Eyed Over Great Men Junction. One of Rachel's heroes has been given a fellowship at Wolfburne. You can virtually see the froth of excitement coming out of her pores.'

'Rachel?' said Lydia. 'Little Rachel? I didn't think she had heroes – only heroines.'

'This is different. This is one of her *musicians*. Salvador something. Guitarist.'

Lydia raised her eyebrows. 'Spanish?'

'French, I think. I'd never heard of him, either. He was a world-famous child prodigy in the Seventies, apparently. Went off the rails for a while. Bit like a guitar-playing Nigel Kennedy, I suppose, but without the comeback. Anyway, Rachel's been doing a lot of dreamy staring into space since she heard about it.'

'Maybe she should take a leaf out of Audrey's book,' Lydia mused. 'I mean go for it. At least this Salvador sounds more interesting than Audrey's publishing tycoon.'

They discussed Audrey's career plans and her proposed means of achieving them for a few minutes, finding that neither of them had much of an opinion either way, except for a certain tacit admiration for Audrey's sheer, uncowable confidence. The conversation lulled then as each of them wandered for a while in their own thoughts.

'Beth,' said Lydia eventually.

'What?'

Lydia hesitated, then shook her head. 'Nothing ... So, have you fallen in love while I've been away?'

'Ha. Fat chance. How about you?'

Lydia pulled a face. 'Maybe I'd fall in love properly if I thought anyone would have me.'

It was said in perfect seriousness, but you could never tell with Lydia. 'You know,' said Beth, 'you're my best friend, but sometimes I just don't understand you. You say things like that and half the time I think you're kidding and half the time I almost think you mean it.'

Lydia's lips stretched wide, spreading out to their accustomed laughing grin, but at the last moment they faltered and turned inside out. Tears spilt out of her eyes; she bowed her head, and a choking sob burst out of her.

'Lydia!' Beth gasped, horrified. 'Lydia, for God's sake, what's the matter?'

Lydia's cheeks were running wet now, and her voice came out

weakly, pinioned between her sobs and her efforts to stifle them. 'Nothing,' she gulped. 'Just overtired and overstressed.'

Beth didn't know what to do; it was like being a child and seeing one of your parents break down in front of you. Lydia didn't cry; she was a tower of resilient good humour, and Beth felt childishly helpless in the face of her sudden, inexplicable tears. Instinctively, she went to the bed and sat beside her, laying one hand tentatively around her shoulders while the other hovered uncertainly in mid-air. 'What is it? Tell me.'

'Don't know,' said Lydia. She rubbed away the tears with the back of her hand, but they kept on flowing.

'Talk to me, Lydia,' Beth pleaded. 'Something's happened. Tell me about it.'

Lydia's sobs became worse, and she could hardly speak. 'I . . .' she began. 'I'm . . . so . . . alone . . . All the . . . time.'

'Alone? What d'you mean?'

She wiped futilely at the tears again. 'I've got nobody. Nobody wants me.'

Then Beth remembered . . . 'Didn't it work out with Stephen?' she asked gently.

Lydia's eyes closed tightly, and she shook her head. Beth sighed. Stephen Rae was on Lydia's course; a compact, razor-jawed package of self-assurance with whom Lydia had enjoyed several well-reported, closely analysed but ultimately inconclusive flirtatious episodes outside lecture rooms and in the college bar. Beth and Lydia between them had predicted that the tentative feelers of flirtation might easily swell and burgeon into full-blown sexual revelry along the Pennine Way. But their last conversation on the subject had been way back before Christmas; since then, there had been no more quickly snatched tingles to report, and Beth had forgotten all about razor-jawed Stephen. Until now, she assumed that Lydia had put him back on the shelf as well.

'He got off with Sarah on the second night,' Lydia moaned. 'The second bloody night!' She put her hands over her face and mumbled into her palms. 'You should've seen them, Beth – you couldn't have poked a blade of grass between them the whole two weeks; Sarah going round looking like the cat who's got the cream, the custard and the whole sodding trifle. *And* she had to tell me all the details, like I was her special confidante or something. Insensitive bitch.'

Beth gazed down at Lydia's hands, writhing around each other in her lap. The nail on the left index finger had a little dint in it, which she had been picking at while she spoke, until a tiny, curled white whisker of nail-edge stood out. She put the nail in her mouth and gripped the sliver between her teeth, twisting her finger viciously so that the tip of the nail tore across, yanking with it a fragment of the surrounding flesh. Beth winced as the crooked crescent came loose and was spat out, flying off into the shadows beyond the circle of lamp light, while Lydia went on chewing at the ragged fringe left behind.

'Here,' said Beth, taking a clean tissue from the breast pocket of her shirt and holding it out, bunched like a desiccated flower, in front of Lydia's face.

Lydia took it and wiped her eyes, then blew her nose. 'Nobody ever wants me,' she whispered. 'Nobody ever will.'

'That's nonsense,' said Beth, desperately trying to regain solid ground as they slid deeper and deeper into the quagmire of self-loathing. 'You've got everything – looks, personality... everything. I bet there are guys all over Cambridge, crying themselves to sleep over you at this very minute.' She flailed about her mind, ransacking it for something concrete with which to substantiate her assertion. 'I mean, look at Richard,' she concluded.

As soon as she'd said it, she could have bitten off her tongue. It was hardly the best example to give: Richard Gannet from Magdalene, also known as Mister Curly Wurly. He had pursued Lydia with thick-skinned devotion for two whole terms, protesting his peculiarly deranged brand of undying love. An admirer was one thing – a romantic, flattering, arousing thing – but a frog-eyed, obsessive, unearthly stalker was something else.

Lydia stared. 'That *freak*?' she spat. 'Is that the best I'm ever going to do?'

Beth shook her head. She would never have mentioned Richard had she not been so caught off balance. Since adolescence, as she had grown familiar with the social map of her gender, she had become skilled in dealing with the petty, temporary but still always racking despairs of emotional frustration, but now she was at a loss. That the poison should show itself bubbling malevolently in Lydia's blood was unimaginable; Lydia was as sturdy as cast-iron, as resilient as a rubber ball, as bright and full of promise as all the colours of the rainbow. Had Beth ever thought deeply about it, she might have realised that cast iron can be as brittle as puddle-ice, that rubber melts so easily, and that the colours of the rainbow do not inhere in themselves, but are only the refraction of other light. Even now, she could not reason it out; all she knew was that there must be something here much deeper than a transient unrequited passion for lovely Stephen Rae and his razor-jaw.

Lydia's words crept out again, timidly, hesitantly: 'Sometimes,' she said. 'Sometimes, there's this dream... I imagine...'

She got no further; her lips trembled again, and the words were drowned in a renewed flood of tears. This time, Beth overcame her hesitancy and flung both her arms around her friend, squeezing her close, feeling the hot gasps of breath on her neck and the cold slick of tears on her chin. As the sobs went on, she stroked her shoulders and rocked her gently back and forth until, at last, the crying began to ebb and grow quiet.

4

There was a vast, dusty plain, flat as a paved floor, and from it rose two towers. That much she could tell; there may have been more towers, but from where she was, she could only see two. Her cell was below ground, but if she stood on tip-toe on the edge of her bed, she could see out between the bars of the tiny window. There, across the flat expanse of dust, she could see one of the towers: tall, cylindrical and thin, with a pointed tip. It was made of silver, polished so highly it reflected the landscape all around it; and, in the centre of the reflection, distorted by the tower's curvature, was a mirror-image of the second tower, the tower in which she was imprisoned.

Every so often, people would walk past her window; a flitter of feet and ankles. None of the people ever noticed her; they were always too busy talking amongst themselves and too intent on making for the silver mirror tower to notice the small, insignificant face peering up at them through the bars. Most were strangers, but some were known to her; craning her neck as her toes teetered on the edge of the bed, she stared up at the familiar faces: there were her friends – all of them ignored her and walked on by – and there was her dead mother, then her father and step-mother – they ignored her, too. She cried out to them, begging them to release her, or at least speak to her, but still they walked by. There was Stephen, arm in arm with Sarah, then came Audrey, deep in conversation with Rachel. Then, most agonising of all, came Beth. She was walking with Gabriel and another man she couldn't see properly and didn't recognise. They were laughing together, taking no notice of the cries coming from the barred window by their feet, cries that grew louder and more despairing until she thought her lungs would burst

—and she jerked upright, panting and sweating, in the darkness, the thin, hoarse ghosts of her cries still struggling in her throat.

After a minute or two, she calmed down, her heart and breathing subsiding to a steady rhythm. The room was a well of shadowy shapes, picked out by the orange glow of the single street-lamp in the lane outside. Her own room, which was at the back of the house, was much darker than this, and she wondered in those first few moments of waking panic where she was.

She looked back at the bed: Beth was lying beside her, one arm curled under her head, breathing deeply. It had happened without being talked of; they had simply lain down together in the bed and fallen asleep in each other's arms. Still fully clothed, they must have become unbearably hot, because the duvet had been kicked off and was lying in a heap on the floor. The radiator had long since grown cold, though, and the winter chill had crept in and filled the room. She swung her legs off the bed and gathered up the duvet. As she flung it out like a sail over Beth, it whipped past her face, and she caught a scent from it; a smell of bodily warmth. She pulled a corner up to her nostrils and inhaled. It smelt of Beth; a fresh scent of her body, mingled with the smells of her perfume, her deodorant, her shampoo . . . and something else. She inhaled deeper . . . The other scent was elusive but vaguely familiar; it seemed to hint at togetherness; warmth and security weaving themselves into the cotton.

She straightened the duvet, smoothing it over Beth's shoulder, then slithered back in, snuggling close. Beth sighed in her sleep and curled an arm over to receive her.

She settled down and closed her eyes, thinking about the dream; the old, familiar dream. Her mind wandered on, and she imagined herself dead, another familiar dream. Would anyone notice then? She could picture the darkness and the closeness inside the coffin. Again, all there was of the people around was their footsteps. She rose out and looked into their faces, searching for sorrow . . .

She turned on to her side, squeezing Beth's arm to her . . . The pillow had that same smell . . . Within a few minutes, she was asleep again. This time, her dream was full of inexplicable colour . . . and music. Beautiful music . . .

They never mentioned that night. When Beth woke the next morning, Lydia was gone. She wondered if she had dreamed it all, but her rumpled, slept-in clothes and the glistening arc of a solitary blonde hair curving across the pillow told her she hadn't.

They never mentioned that night, and Lydia never mentioned the tower dream. From that day onwards, as it had been before, Lydia kept her private griefs locked in their cell beneath the glittering tower.

As far as Beth could tell, the momentary outburst had been driven out by the second dream, the one which rang with music and radiated bright colours; the one Lydia did tell her about, the one which, Beth would one day say to her, came true.

The Not-Quite Great Uncles

What force of nature determines the happiness of love?

Once upon a time in England, there were two sisters: Ruth and Verena. Verena certainly never had what you could call a happy love life. In fact, she may have set some sort of record for romantic misfortune. Between 1939 and 1945, she became engaged, in succession, to six different men: one for each year of the War. Each and every one of them, with a kind of grim inevitability, was snatched away by death before Verena could get him up the aisle. What made this sad succession so terrible – or comical if you were one of the sisters' crueller neighbours – was that not a single one of the doomed fiancés saw active service. They weren't even in the armed forces. When Ruth got engaged in December 1939 to Joe Hutton, a Lance Bombardier in the Royal Artillery, Verena wondered aloud whether it was wise to love a man who might be dead within the year. Verena, more wisely, chose Frank Westerbrook, a train driver who had no intention of joining up and whose reserved occupation kept him safe from conscription. A month before their wedding, Frank was struggling to free up a seized coupling when his locomotive – whose brake he hadn't set properly – started to move. He was crushed like a fly between the buffers of the loco and its tender, and died a week later in hospital. Verena was prostrated with grief, but a year later had recovered enough to agree to marry forty-one year-old Ernest Winterflood, who taught Science at the local grammar school. As well as being a keen biologist, he was also an enthusiastic motorist. One Saturday afternoon, he took Verena for a drive in his Austin Chummy, using up his last two gallons of pre-ration petrol. A swerving, screeching encounter with a bread van just outside Bishop's Stortford led to a ditch, with the Austin's wheels spinning away their momentum and Ernest lying beneath, his neck broken. Verena was

66

thrown clear by the impact and was led away from the scene with just a bruise on her upper arm and mud-stains on her dress.

Do people learn from history? No, they usually find that if they keep banging their heads against a wall for long enough, it eventually stops hurting.

In the years that followed, Verena stuck by her judicious theory and turned down many proposals from soldiers. She had had enough heartbreak, and she wasn't going out of her way to invite any more. Her next intended was Frank Warren, who was bracketed by a stick of German bombs on his way to the Anderson shelter. Frank left no earthly trace other than the splintered remains of the walking stick he carried to excuse his un-uniformed status. Eddie Tooey succumbed to heart failure (a pronounced murmur having kept him safe from active service). Verena was evasive about how number five died. Nobody ever met him, and all that has been handed down is the name Albert and a vague rumour about drowning. Thereafter, it was Hitler's Flying V-Weapons one, Verena nil.

Meanwhile, Joe Hutton went through (it seems) nearly every campaign the British Army fought in North Africa and Europe, and came home a Battery Sergeant Major with a titfull of medals (as Dad said) and not so much as a scratch on his rather ruddy skin. The week after VE Day, Ruth gave birth to Anthony, who grew up to be my father. Verena, who played safe, had a dresser drawer containing a little pile of tissue-wrapped engagement rings as her spoils of war.

I sometimes wonder whether I ought to feel haunted by the spectres of those six men who never quite became Great Uncles. But I don't. There isn't enough room for them.

D *on't go . . .*
The words lurched slurred and breathless out of Beth's mouth as she tumbled suddenly out of sleep like a struggling cat ejected from an upturned sack.

She sat up on the bed and pressed her fingers into her sticky eyes, then wiped away the smear of dribble from the corner of her mouth. Her sinuses were sore, and her senses were fuzzy and dulled. It took several moments for her to realise what was causing the stinging above the roof of her mouth: gradually, she noticed a strong smell of acrid smoke permeating the darkness.

She shuffled hastily off the bed and trod blindly across the room towards where she thought the door must be, holding out probing fingers ahead of her. After three short, staggering steps, her fingertips bumped against the corner of a picture frame; simultaneously, her knee barked painfully against the edge of something hard and heavy and sharp. She shrieked silently and hobbled to one side, fingertips scanning the wallpaper until she reached the door in the corner of the room. It seemed to take an age of fumbling to find the light switch; the curious, antique design of the castle placed it – and the handle of the door beside it – a clear foot higher than she was used to, giving her the disturbing sensation that she was shrinking, Alice-like, into an invisible looking-glass world. At last her fingers found a cold, bulbous lump on the wall and dragged the heavy bakelite switch downwards. It made a thick, audible *ctchunk*, and the room leapt in on her, bathed in yellowish light.

The air was hazed grey with smoke . . . Fire . . . *Fire!* Her heart thumping in syncopated time with the throbbing pain in her knee, she hauled the door open and rushed through.

And stopped dead . . .

She had braced herself to meet an inferno: she had expected the corridor to be choked with thick smoke, to hear the distant rumbling crackle of the advancing fire and voices raised in warning and alarm . . . And there was nothing except the lingering, acrid reek in her nostrils and the flailing panic in her chest. The corridor, though dark, was silent and clear; the door to Audrey's room across the way gazed calmly, blankly back at her, its bottom edge leaking light into the shadowy carpet.

She stood there for a while, frowning and glancing up and down the long, gloomy corridor, then turned and went back inside. There was still a haze of smoke in the room. Although her head ached from daytime sleep, she was wide awake now, and it only took her a moment to track down the source of the smoke: a hot coal had fallen from the overladen fire and rolled to the lip of the grate, where it had burned a yellow-fringed arc of black in the edge of the Persian hearth rug. Seizing one of her shoes, Beth batted the coal back into the grate and beat out the bright embers still clinging to the rug and the polished wood below. When they were all dead and black, she went to the window and slid up the sash. The trickle of bitterly cold air became a billowing breeze and began to dissipate the smoky sourness in the room. Then, still holding her shoe by its heel, she slumped back on her haunches, leaning back against the bed and resting her forehead on her uninjured knee.

'I want to go home,' she murmured into the warm woollen fabric of her skirt. 'Please let me go home now.'

She had dreamed of the last time she had seen Lydia. They had stood on Garret Hostel bridge, leaning on the rail and watching the first of the summer morning punts skimming under the willow curtain opposite Trinity; looking but not seeing; too absorbed in their own private drama. Only, in the dream, it was Beth rather than Lydia who was marrying him, and it was Lydia who wanted to leave the tryst-place . . .

Saving Salvador

1

He looked out with unaided eyes at the slightly hazy view. He hardly ever wore his glasses. It had nothing to do with vanity; he simply preferred the way the world looked without them. When he did wear them – to pore over a close-printed score, for example – they always bore a thin film of grease and dust. The crystal-sharp sight that burst in through clean lenses was more than he could stand. He preferred the world obscured or slightly out of focus.

The court was clearing now; the puddles and trickles of students disgorged from the staircases around the cobble-gridded rectangle of velvet lawns had slowly dissipated through the high arch beside the porter's lodge, draining out of the quad and into the bicycle-bustle rapids of Trinity Street. Now the court echoed emptiness from its high Georgian windows, its flower beds and the blank ashlar rear-end of the chapel. Only a few, infrequent figures could be seen now, appearing from their lettered mouseholes and moving about, not staying out in the cold open air for long, but retracing their steps or hurrying on to other mouseholes. A charcoal-suited porter stopped and stooped by the shallow fountain pool which stood at the intersection of the two main paths and picked an empty crisp packet from the rim of the water, pinching it fastidiously between two extended fingers. Holding it out at arm's length like a dripping pennant, he made his way back towards the gateway and dropped it into a litter bin, then disappeared into the two-bar electric warmth of the lodge. From the opposite corner of the court, a tall, willowy young man wearing a college scarf (black with bold purple and yellow bands) and carrying a bulging, sausage-shaped Nike bag, came darting out of F staircase and scampered across the open space, skipping over the corners of the rectangular lawns as he went, like a charging warhorse instinctively dodging the bodies of the fallen. Then he was gone, vanishing into the shadows under the archway, leaving the court empty and sullen behind him.

Salvador sat by the window of his sitting room and watched the scene below, smiling vaguely at the young man's prancing performance. He had been here, sitting in the window seat, for nearly two hours now. Rising early (he found it difficult to luxuriate in sleep on the ancient, mallow-soggy biscuit the college called a bed, and always woke with an aching back), he had made himself a big pot of coffee and settled down by the window with a manuscript book open on his knees, intending to sketch out an orchestration that had been playing itself out in his mind for several days. He was now on his second pot, and the wide page of faintly ruled staves was still blank.

It had been a mistake to sit by the window; he couldn't resist looking out. Salvador gazed through windows the way other people watched television: sitting for hours at a time, absorbed in the world unfolding on the other side of the glass. Conversely, he looked at television the way other people looked out of their windows; glances snatched in passing, or occasional consultations to see what the cultural weather was doing. It was a question of where one stood in relation to reality. For Salvador, the world of performance was the world he had been inducted into, and what went on behind the curved oblong glass in the corner was mundane and familiar (he had put on his world-face and stepped out into it often enough in his life), whereas the world that enacted itself beyond whatever window he found himself in front of had the perfume of strangeness; exotic and entrancing. And so it was this morning, as he sat and gazed and neglected the preparation for the sequel to his inaugural performance.

There had been another window-gazing gloomy morning just like this; barely more than a year ago, but already a world away. From four floors up, he had spent the morning watching the rain-soaked yellow cabs cluster at the lights by the news-stand on the corner with its wall of front pages drooping with damp while the shingle of umbrellas waltzed in contraflow patterns around it.

That window-gazing morning in another world had, in effect, been the cause of this one. It was the morning his Uncle Valéry came to call. Uncle Valéry was, according to family whispering, Something High Up in the French Embassy in Washington (the fact that nobody seemed to know quite what or exactly how high up implied the further titillating conclusion that it was Something Secret). He was in town on a visit to the United Nations. That was as much as he would admit to (something to do with the Security Council, perhaps?), and Salvador wasn't about to probe any deeper; Uncle Valéry had the sort of bastion charisma that made people reluctant to ask him impertinent questions, which, when you thought about it, was probably a basic job requirement for people who were High Up and Something Secret. Anyway, Salvador was more curious about how he had found out his address, or even that he was living in New York at all, than he was about Valéry's political activities. But no answers were likely to be had, so he just sat sullenly and gazed out of the window while his uncle prowled slowly about the apartment, absorbing its every shoddy detail, from the bathroom ceiling that resembled rancid, yellowing Christmas-cake icing thickly dusted with black pepper, to the damp, scraped and peeling wallpaper in the hallway and the stained floor-boards which neither Salvador nor his landlord (responsibility had been a matter for dispute since he moved in) had bothered to cover with carpet. Uncle Valéry finished his tour standing on the rag rug in front of the blocked-off fireplace. He aimed an unblinking, inscrutable, but not entirely unfriendly stare at Salvador's window-silhouetted profile.

'How do you pay for this?' he asked, with a slight inflection on the last word and a minute corner-eye glance at the apartment, hinting at the depth of his distaste for such unspeakable squalor.

Salvador looked away from the window for a moment. Uncle Valéry was, like his sister – Salvador's mother – slight, wiry and very short (his eyes barely came level with the mantelpiece above the high fireplace), but, also like her, managed with easy grace to intimidate just about every person he met; an effect which had something, Salvador reasoned, to do with an innate belief – no, a firm, unwavering *knowledge* of natural superiority. Valéry's black hair was swept back and greying a little at the temples; he wore a long, double-breasted coat as black and smooth as his hair, and there was a splash of burgundy silk scarf at his throat. Salvador half-expected there to be a vast, silent bodyguard stationed at the door, sharp suit bulging with muscular eloquence while his master toyed charmingly with the helpless, floundering victim. There would be a brisk snap of fingers (*Giuseppe, show him what happens to dishonourable men who don't respect their mothers*) and an infinitesimal nod, then Giuseppe would step forward, accompanied by the soft snick of an opening razor. But there was no bodyguard, only a small, immaculately wrapped package of easy authority standing quietly on the rag rug, waiting for his question to be answered.

'It's not expensive,' Salvador replied, speaking English in defiance of Valéry's French.

Valéry smiled. 'You have begun to acquire an American accent,' he said pleasantly, following his nephew into English and making his defiance look petty and childish. 'You know, for one whose life has been devoted to pleasure rather than hard work, you do not seem to be surrounding yourself with comfort.'

72

For all the leisurely insults loaded into this observation, it was undeniably true about the apartment; it was cheap by Village standards, but even so it bit deep into the erratic trickle of royalties he still received from his recordings, and most of what was left – supplemented by occasional income from playing with pick-up bands in the jazz lounges and with Village bar bands – went on bills and food. There was almost nothing left for pleasure; sometimes he bought a record or a new set of guitar strings, but that was about all.

'Do you have that insured?' asked Valéry. He nodded towards the corner furthest from the window, where Salvador's Torres stood clasped by the rubber-tipped fingers of a chromed guitar stand. 'I don't imagine you play it often. It should be in a museum.'

Salvador stared at his uncle; the implication was as clear as a slap in the face. 'You think I'd destroy it to cash in the insurance?' he said. 'Do you have any idea what that guitar means to me?'

Uncle Valéry's gaze didn't flinch or fade. 'Is it insured?' he repeated.

Salvador wavered. 'I can't afford insurance,' he said feebly. 'Mother probably still has it covered. That would be just like her – she wouldn't let a thing like *that* lapse.'

Valéry draped his black kid-leather gloves over the back of one hand and stroked the fingers flat with his palm. 'Your family,' he began, 'by which I mean your mother, of course, would like to know how long you propose to keep up this pretence.'

Salvador, bored with the conversation and wishing his uncle would get to the point quickly and leave, went back to looking out of the window. The rain was easing off and the umbrellas were beginning to fold. 'What pretence?' he murmured wearily.

'Don't add obtuseness to your repertoire of pretension; you are not a stupid boy.'

'I'm not a boy at all,' Salvador replied absently, his attention diverted by something going on directly beneath his window. It seemed that Giuseppe had not been an idle fancy after all; there he was, as large as life (certainly every bit as large as Salvador's imagination of him), standing beside a long black Mercedes which was pulled up illegally by the kerb. A policeman appeared to be explaining – with a lot of chin-jutting and nightstick-pointing – about city parking restrictions, and, in return, Giuseppe seemed to be explaining – with icy, menacing calm – about diplomatic immunity. The policeman didn't seem to realise the danger he was in; *Watch out!* Salvador wanted to shout to him. *Watch out for his razor!*

'You think you are a man, perhaps?' Uncle Valéry was saying. 'Then perhaps you can tell me what kind of a man it is who walks away from his family responsibilities without telling his poor mother where he is.

73

Without even saying goodbye to her.'

Salvador sneered at the window pane. 'My *poor mother* could have found me easily enough if she'd wanted to . . . Oh, I'll bet she's still got the precious Torres covered, but she couldn't care less about her only son.' He turned away from the window to see the effect his words were having on Valéry, and was startled to find his uncle standing right beside him; he hadn't even heard him move. 'Do you know what she did to me once?' he asked, covering over his startlement with words. 'Yes, you probably do – there were enough people there to witness it. You might even have been there yourself; I don't remember. I was fourteen years old, and she humiliated me in front of a roomful of the most important people you could imagine.'

'I was there. I saw. It was pitiable.'

'She couldn't care less if I died.'

Uncle Valéry smiled a warm, comforting, conciliatory smile and rested a hand on Salvador's shoulder. Salvador was mollified by the gesture, which he shouldn't have been; he should have kept an eye on the other hand, which swept out of nowhere and slashed the expensive kid leather gloves across his face. 'Don't you ever,' said his uncle with a reptilian hiss, '*ever* say such a thing about your mother again.' He straightened up and smoothed the gloves over his hand again while Salvador smarted and tried to stop his eyes watering. 'If you had the slightest idea of the sacrifices she has made for you, the lengths she went to to make you what you are – or were – or what it cost her to bear you . . . I was there, you know, when you were born, just as I was there when your brother died. I saw it all, so don't tell me she doesn't care.'

'Okay, so she *cares*,' said Salvador, spitting as much sarcastic venom into the words as he dared. 'What am I supposed to do about it? I'm too old to be her performing monkey now.'

Valéry's thick black eyebrows arched upwards. 'Performing monkey? Is that how you saw yourself? The world saw you as a prodigy. A genius even.'

'Performing monkey,' Salvador repeated emphatically. He got up from his window seat and picked up a pack of Marlboro and a book of matches from his decrepit table.

'When did you acquire that habit?' asked his uncle, watching him light a cigarette.

Salvador drew on the smoke and tossed the dead match onto the table top. 'About the same time I stopped being a performing monkey.'

'I see . . . Is this conversation going to remain mired in childish jabber, or can we talk like adults?'

Salvador snorted smoke and grinned in spite of his sore cheek. 'Talk if you like. I'm not stopping you. Just do me the common courtesy of getting to the point and fucking off. I've got things to do.'

Uncle Valéry looked around the room, as though choosing somewhere to sit down. He appeared to change his mind, though, and remained standing. 'I have a proposal for you,' he said.

Salvador smiled. 'But you know I can't marry you, Uncle Valéry, we're related.'

Valéry stared calmly at him. 'Very well,' he said quietly, and, picking up his briefcase, he began to head for the door.

Salvador sighed. 'Okay, okay,' he said. 'Tell me your precious proposal.'

Valéry paused, then came back. He set his briefcase on the table, his hands laid upon its top edge as though it were a lectern. He gazed at his nephew with a mixture of sternness and wan weariness. 'You understand that I would not be doing this were it not for my concern for my sister.'

'Well, that goes without saying, doesn't it.'

'No, it evidently does not. I say it because I have no wish to add to the disgustingly excessive quotient of self-centredness that you already possess.'

Salvador took the insult with equanimity; he was, to his surprise, beginning to enjoy the situation; being in a position where his mother had (however indirectly) to persuade him to do anything was entirely new to him. Besides, for all his outward apathy, he was actually quite intrigued; was Uncle Valéry going to attempt to recruit him as a secret agent?

'Cambridge University,' said Valéry cryptically, snapping open the clasp of his briefcase. 'I take it you have heard of the place?'

Salvador tilted his head to the side and smiled sarcastically. 'Where?' he said.

'Don't be pert. There is only so much insolence I will take from you. Your mother would not tolerate it.' He took a thin sheaf of close-typed green papers out of the briefcase and leafed through them before handing them over. 'Wolfburne College is inviting applications for the Hunt Fellowship in Creative Arts,' he explained. 'Music will be their preference, I think. It is not a research post; rather they seek a kind of artist in residence. You will be expected to give performances organised by the college and do a little teaching. In return for this light burden, you will be provided with rooms and dining in the college, and a modest stipend of six thousand pounds, to which your mother, when I have spoken to her, will add a further twenty. With your continuing royalties, small though they are, you will be adequately comfortable. A sinecure, in effect.'

Twenty-six thousand pounds? He did some rapid mental exchange-rate calculations and squinted at the papers (putting on his glasses would indicate too much interest in the offer). There was a page headed *Further Particulars* and, despite what Valéry said, an application form with large blank spaces for *Previous Research* and *Proposed Research*. 'You seem very certain that I'd get it,' he said. 'What if they turned me down? Not that I'm going to apply – why should I? I'm happy here.'

Valéry cast his sceptical eyes around the room once more. 'Oh, you shall get it,' he said. 'Trust me for that. With your family and your fame behind you, how can you fail?'

The policeman had given up his attempt to ticket the Mercedes, and the long black car was still sitting undisturbed by the kerb. Salvador looked down from his window and watched as Giuseppe opened the door for Uncle Valéry. The visit had concluded with no undertaking on Salvador's part to collude with his uncle's proposition, but somehow he knew he would eventually; once his family knew where he was, they would become a virtually irresistible force, and he doubted he had the energy any longer to play the part of the immovable object. Besides, he was sick of New York – or at least sick of his part in its pantomime; the bands he sessioned with were going nowhere, and the ones he tried to create were riven by arguments and petty jealousies. Perhaps he might benefit from a change of environment, a change of the figures and faces and incidents that drifted past his window.

The journey from that window to this had been a quarter-globe of distance and a whole universe of outlook; the ancient court on one side and, if he went through to look out of his bedroom window, the sluggish green-brown river kempt by the stone walls of New Court on the far bank. A world away from the bustle and near-anarchy of the city streets, to an existence stitched and pleated by a seemingly endless rote of arcane and idiosyncratic rule and custom. On his first night at Formal Hall (here, eating was apparently called 'Hall', and the formally begowned college halled its way through five formal courses on Wednesdays and Fridays), he found that, on the clash of a small gong, the fellows processed to Hall in strict order of seniority, the most recently elected proceeding last. Not only did even the youngest of them know the full order in its every detail, they also appeared to care deeply and jealously that it was rigidly and solemnly adhered to; even the young man last in line before Salvador (who, he had been told in tones of gleeful horror by the Bursar, was a researcher in Social and Political Sciences and *virtually an anarchist*) snapped to attention with Pavlovian obedience at the sound of the gong and sought his correct place in the line, flicking specks of scurf from the dangling sleeves of his impeccably pressed gown.

76

So antique and creaking did the place seem, that Salvador had been very surprised to learn that, amongst the Cambridge colleges, Wolfburne was regarded as something of a subversive. Being neither the oldest of the colleges (it was founded in 1668 by a former Cromwellian general turned royalist silk and slave merchant) nor the youngest; neither the biggest and richest nor the smallest and poorest, its distinction lay in its comparative radicalism: one of the first male colleges to admit women (doing so as soon as they were granted leave to take the University's degrees), it had pursued the co-educational policy enthusiastically until, by the 1980s, female undergraduates outnumbered the males by five to four. (Though the fact that their representation at High Table was as conservatively minimal as at any other college sometimes made Salvador wonder about the fellows' motives in this policy.) It was similarly radical in its approach to class versus academic distinction, and outstripped King's in its pruning and deconstruction of Old School connections, seeking and gathering from the cream of the country's comprehensives and grammars until state-school entrants outnumbered their independent counterparts three to two and Wolfburne's record for teaching and postgraduate research stood ace-high in the international deck.

So, there had to be a reason for the college's adherence to other traditions; it must be either a show of sheer cultural flair or some desperate psychology that lay behind the ferociously pedantic clinging to the skirts of protocol and ritual practice. Being a wayward child of bastioned tradition himself, Salvador would have been interested to find out, but he had so little opportunity; aside from Hall (where the conversations were mostly as lame and mundane as any that could be had by crossing the road and entering any one of the town's thousand pubs), he had barely spoken to anyone in the three weeks since his arrival: but then he had come late in the term – sorry, *full* term, which was different from term – so perhaps he had missed out on some vital initiation. His inaugural performance had been given in the college chapel: a recital of pieces by Tárrega and Sor, attended by a smattering of fellows, some appreciative music enthusiasts from outside the college and several partially bored students arrayed in the choir stalls. The recital had required no rehearsal; the pieces were as ineradicably ingrained into his fingers as the patterns of whorls and creases that made up their prints. The Torres (for old times' sake, he chose it over the more sensible Fleta) sang delightedly in the high vaults of the chapel, seeming overjoyed after its long and dangerous exile in the city of endless restlessness, and his audience was eventually, unconditionally charmed. This ritual completed, however, his duties as Hunt Fellow seemed to vanish into the ether like spent notes. Apart from one hour a week tutoring the college's solitary guitar student, there was no timetabled call upon his time. Even performances, in all aspects of their scheduling, programming and frequency (or infrequency) were left entirely up to him. Nobody ever made their way across the court towards his staircase (except the elderly and semi-defunct Classics professor who lived above and an Acoustics PhD who occupied the rooms below). Nobody ever knocked on his door, even though it was always exposed (he had not acquired the knack of the twin layers of door yet, and his oak was permanently wedged open).

After only seven weeks, Salvador was utterly bored. And utterly lonely; so lonely that he even began to miss his mother. She would love it here, he thought. She would be utterly delighted by the intricate protocol woven into the college's fabric.

Despite Uncle Valéry's parting exhortation to write to her without delay and apologise for his behaviour, he had not contacted her from that day to this. Even if it cost him the promised supplement to his stipend, he could not bring himself to inscribe a single page to her, much less apologise. He was all too familiar with the performance that passed for apology in the *famille* de La Simarde; abject, pitiable prostration, followed by a long period of taciturn opprobrium which would, if danced upon with the appropriate amount of fawning attendance, slowly evolve into chastening forgiveness. He couldn't stomach going through all that, not any more. The money came anyway: every Thursday, a pale blue envelope appeared in his pigeon-hole in the porter's lodge, postmarked either Chasseneuil or Devon & Exeter, containing a cheque; no note, of course, no word of communication, just the promised money.

And so he sat, empty manuscript book across his knees, the new compositions and arrangements that had begun to coalesce in his head above the Arctic Circle as the 747 carried him across the time zones neglected; he sat and watched through his window.

And then it all changed, and nothing was ever the same again.

He didn't notice whether she came into the court through the archway or from one of the staircases, so he didn't know whether she was an indigene of the college or an outsider; she just seemed to materialise by the fountain. He didn't take much notice of her at first; just a dumpy girl in spectacles with scraped-back hair, a bundle of yellow rain-cape over one arm and the strap of a small, bright blue rucksack over the other. Then she did something interesting; quite startling, in fact: she looked straight up at his window. He recoiled from the glass in shock, like an escaping prisoner caught in a search-light. When he peeped out again, she was glancing furtively about the court and – yes, how extraordinary! – walking towards his staircase.

Had she been looking at his window? It was difficult to be certain without his glasses; perhaps she was Mr Acoustic's girlfriend (but he spent every day and every evening at his laboratory, and was rumoured in any case to be homosexual), or a tutee of the creaking professor upstairs (but he hadn't had any tutees for decades, it was said). He waited . . .

And then it came, the *thud-ud* of knuckles on his door. With a tremor of desperate excitement fluttering in his stomach, he got up from his window seat and went to answer it. The door opened on a round, plump and coarsely featured face, beaming up at him, blushing furious pink blotches from neck to temples.

'Hello,' he said, smiling politely. The little rosebud mouth, which was the face's only pretty feature (actually, it was disconcertingly pretty in amongst the crude clay) twitched and trembled inarticulately. 'What can I do for you?' he prompted.

'I . . .' she stammered. 'You . . .'

She didn't get any further; the pinkness drained away to ghastly cheese-rind white, her eyeballs rolled upwards in their orbits, and, with a gurgling sigh, she slithered forward spastically and measured out her length (short, squat) in a heap of crumpled yellow rain-cape and bright blue rucksack across the threshold of the room.

Salvador stared down at her in horror. Was she ill, or simply insane? What on God's earth had made her come and have a seizure in *his* doorway? Whatever the reasons, he decided he had better not leave her there; the strangled, drowsy moans bubbling out of her throat suggested that she was having difficulty breathing. After an unsuccessful attempt to pick her up (she was as limp and intractable as a rubber sack full of sand), he hooked his hands under her double-knit-lagged armpits and dragged her across the room towards the sofa, where he hauled her into a sitting position, adjusting bits of her – an arm here, leg across that way, head back – until she was sufficiently balanced for him to let go of her and stand back.

After a moment's dithering hesitation, he went to the kitchen and filled a glass with water. When he returned, she was beginning to stir, eyelids fluttering half-open, limbs twitching. He waited for her eyes to open properly, and held out the glass.

'Here,' he said.

She stared blankly at him. Her skin-tone had shifted from the rind to the inner cheese: a camembert, colour of parchment, texture of wet dough. There was a thin strand of dribble seeping from the corner of her mouth, which she wiped away with a baggy sleeve. 'Did I faint?' she asked weakly. 'Oh God . . .'

'Have a sip of this,' he said. 'You'll feel better.'

She took the glass and held it between both her palms, glancing at it as though uncertain what to do with it. 'Oh God,' she said. 'Oh God . . . It's so embarrassing . . . I could die . . .' At last, she took a sip of water.

'Any better?' he asked, and she nodded. 'Are you unwell?'

She shook her head. 'Sorry. I'm so sorry.' She drained the glass and held it out to him. 'Thank you. I'm better now.'

He took the glass and went to the kitchen to refill it. He came back to find her on her feet, retrieving her rucksack and cape from the doorway. 'Sit down,' he said. 'Have another drink of water.'

She stood there, awash with shame, clutching her possessions to her chest. 'I'm so sorry,' she said again. 'I've never done that before. I was just so . . . so . . . you know.' Her eyes wandered around the room with hunted desperation, and fell on one of his guitars – the pale-bodied Fleta – which was reclining in a deep wing-back armchair beside the fireplace.

'Sit here,' he said, and yanked the guitar out of its seat. (Was it his imagination, or did her breath catch and her eyes widen as his fingers seized the instrument by its slender wooden neck and it gave out a quiet, concussive open chord?) He placed it on its stand and held out a hand towards the vacated armchair. She sat down obediently, still hugging her rucksack and cape, and took the refilled glass from his hand.

'Now, tell me what I can do for you,' he said. 'I don't have many visitors,' he added.

She dived into her rucksack and, her face beginning to suffuse with fuchsia again, dredged out two items: a cassette wrapped in cellophane and still bearing its Heffers' price label, and a stapled sheaf of ruled A4 covered with neat, rotund handwriting. 'Can I have your autograph?' she said, adding, almost without a pause: 'And could I read you my essay?'

2

Eight weeks and counting. Boredom was doing terrible things to his brain.

There was nothing to look at outside either of his windows this evening: the court was deserted, and the river was a well of impenetrable darkness. He tried looking into the television instead, but there were only soap operas and sport there. Instead of switching it off, though, he left *EastEnders* to play itself through in the background with the sound muted.

He picked up his Les Paul and plugged its coiled liquorice umbilicus into the amplifier. Sitting down on the edge of the sofa, he curled his fingers around the guitar's neck, forming elaborate, silent chords while the amplifier hummed softly and his right hand hovered, restlessly waiting for a chord-shape it felt like sounding. He wasn't in the mood. He put down the Les Paul, hovered a moment over the Fleta, then picked up the Torres. He cradled its fat, feather-light body on his thigh and went through the same miming motions. He could hear the chords in his head as his fingertips sculpted them – coy minors, deep barred majors, sevenths, suspensions and rich, augmented formations riffled out as arpeggios or sonorous six-string crashes, travelling a closed placental loop between hand and brain with no movement of air particles or ear drum . . . He wasn't in the mood for the Torres either, and the fingers of his right hand rested idly on the mute soundboard. He set it back on its stand, and sat down at his desk, where his manuscript book lay open, its staves crawling with urgent, black-inked dots, beams and curlicues. He could hear this music inside his head, too, as his eyes tracked the pulse of the bars across the paper until they ended abruptly at an unwritten coda on page four.

Would it be possible, he wondered, to compose a piece that emptied out his head; to write something that he couldn't hear, that so transgressed the boundaries of his native language that the little musicians inside his brain would be unable to speak it? Dissonant and xenochronous; reproducible perhaps with the fingers but not with the inner ear . . . He tore a page from the middle of the book and took up his pen. In dense India black, he marked a time-signature on each of the eight staves: 4/4 at the top, base time; then 3/4, a deviation; then a layer of 5/4, the beginnings of confusion; then the raging hordes of xenochrony, 7/8, 5/16, 13/8 . . . And the keys: F-sharp major, C major, B-flat minor, piling up in a conflict of dissonance. Then came the notes themselves: syncopated groups of triplets, quintuplets, septuplets, inscribed on the staves in parallel so that no individual line had the chance to form its own independent melodic identity . . .

When he had filled the page, and each staff contained at least three bars, he finally dared to look at the thing as a score, as a coherent whole. And he had done it! This was music; notated and underpinned by a rhythmic and harmonic logic (a perverse logic, perhaps, but a logic all the same), and he couldn't hear it! The little musicians were utterly stumped: apart from the odd sporadic, incoherent yelp, they stared at the sheet in silent stupefaction and couldn't play it.

As a composition, though, it was a piece of shit; a piece of calculated theory, probably unplayable by anybody living, and almost certainly unlistenable. The delirium of his achievement folded in on itself; he crumpled the paper into a ball and tossed it in the waste-paper bin. Then he put on his jacket and went out into the night in search of a drink and some sane company.

Bridge Street was alive with headlights and pubgoers. Late workers were queuing in the bus shelters outside St John's. Feeling city-invisible, he crossed the road and headed towards the Baron of Beef. He didn't make it, though; passing the Mitre, he paused in the pool of light and conviviality that spread out onto the pavement from its windows, nostrils inhaling the warm, vegetal pungency of beer. Here.

The Mitre's front room, warmed by the smoke of a half-built log fire, was full up with mid-week drinkers and the lingering smell of bar meals, so he went through to the back, where it was quieter and darker, lit by flickering electric candles that cast an orange gloom on the unpolished wood and rough nicotine-brown walls. He bought half a pint of Stella Artois from a muscular T-shirt behind the bar and found an unoccupied two-stool table by the cigarette machine. Before sitting down, he fed two pound coins and a fifty into the machine and wrenched a depleted pack of Marlboro out of its wooden drawer. A previous occupant had left a copy of the *Independent* on the table, along with an empty crisp packet and a half-pint glass with a wilted lemon slice and some chunks of melting ice in the bottom. Feeling suddenly lonely and exposed, Salvador unfolded the newspaper and pretended to read it while he listened to the fragmented conversations going on around him and stole occasional peeks at the people they belonged to. There was a group of men and women – office workers, by the look and sound of them – around the table to his left. They sat with sexes mixed but conversations segregated, talking across each other: the men were re-enacting dialogue from a sitcom he had never seen, while the women discussed the difficult pregnancy of someone they worked with.

The table on his right was much more interesting to look at – four young women – but frustratingly harder to listen to; their table was further away and their voices were swamped by the rising volume of the office workers' intercutting, competing conversations. They were clearly undergraduates: even if he hadn't been told this by the green rucksack propped against a table leg and the Wolfburne scarf draped over the back of a chair, its end trailing on the dusty floorboards, he could certainly have divined it from their appearance. Students, he had learned, marked themselves out from their chronological peers by sustaining the tense pink varnish of adolescence long past the moment when the chrysalis should have cracked and adults should have emerged; like teenage people painted onto full-grown adult blanks.

And he ought to know; he had stayed like that himself for ten years now.

Two of the student girl-women were facing him, and he studied them first. The one on the left caught his attention; she was simultaneously thrust forward into the arena of startling visual presence by the brightness, tightness and fullness of her blue sweater, and sucked back into the shadows by her own darkness: in full sunshine, her hair, which was cut in a long, artless and tousled bob, would reveal its blurred rosewood palette of rich browns and reds, but in the dim light of electric candles, it was ebony black. Her eyes were large and had lids that slanted down at the corners, giving her face a look of sadness; even when she smiled, which she often did, the smile had a strange, fey melancholy look. Her small mouth was the shape of a musical note; like the oval bead of a quaver snipped from its stalk, and when she parted her lips to speak, they formed a perfect, pink-rimmed semi-breve. The friend sitting on her left also wore her hair in a bob, but neater, straighter, and thick, buttery blonde. She was smaller and slighter than the others: pretty and delicate, a porcelain orchid. She alone had discarded the teenage chrysalis: it was partly in her face – sharp, high cheekbones and an alert, knowing look in her almond eyes – and partly in her clothes – she wore a short skirt and sheer flesh-coloured tights, while her friends clothed their legs either in jeans or thick black schoolgirl tights. Had he seen her alone, he would have made many wrong guesses before suggesting doubtfully that she might be a student.

By all laws of fairness and averages, the other two girls – the two he couldn't see properly – should be as plain as brick walls. He continued his study clockwise. The back view of the girl nearest to him didn't suggest plainness. Her thick, heavy hair was gathered into a pony-tail, held in place by a deep-green ruffled velvet band. It was a paler blonde; mixed strands of silver tarnish and gold that glittered and shimmered as she moved her head, the pony-tail rolling lazily and lapping at the sail-taut cotton of her pink T-shirt. He could tell little else about her, other than how lithely thin she was, like a willow-wand; he imagined he could almost enclose her waist between his hands – just there, just above the runkled, belt-gathered waistband of her jeans. He felt it would crush his heart to find that her face wasn't equally beautiful; to see her turn, and find that she had a hideous nose, or mean little eyes, or big buck teeth.

As he looked at the fourth member of the group, he experienced a sudden lurch of recognition. He had thought she seemed familiar: blonde hair again, but another shade paler, almost colourless, scraped up into a sort of top-knot like a wilting lily; a half-profile of plump, pink cheeks and gold-rimmed spectacles. She was the very same girl who, only last week, had swooned into his sitting room and then read her incomprehensible and faintly embarrassing essay to him. The music student. His number-one fan. What was her name? Ruth or Rebecca – one of those biblical R-names . . .

'. . . so why shouldn't you write about it?' she was saying, becoming audible now that the office workers had left.

There was a murmur of noncommittal responses, then the slight, womanly orchid gestured with her cigarette. 'Because it's using one art-form to describe another,' she said authoritatively. Her voice was deep, with a chainsaw rasp in its lower register. If she was an orchid, it was one wrought from steel and diamond. 'Think about it. Say you want to, I don't know, say you want to talk about the way Joyce made up composite words. You can just *quote* those words themselves.'

'Using the same medium they're made of,' said the dark girl, supporting the argument with apparent reluctance. 'But surely you can—'

'Using the same medium. Exactly. You can *say* "scrotumtightening", for example. Imagine if you wanted to do the same thing, but you had to describe the words without actually quoting them. That's what writing about music is like . . .'

'But—'

'Using one art-form to describe another, incompatible one. What was it someone said – Writing about music is like dancing about architecture. Who said that?' They all shook their heads. 'Whoever it was, they were right. It's nonsensical, a pointless exercise. Why not just listen to the music? Forster said that music . . .'

Why not? he thought; he already knew one of them, and they were talking about his subject. He folded the newspaper and put it down . . .

'Mind if I join you?'

Salvador, half-way out of his seat, looked up in dismay and found Daniel Lloyd-Jones, Wolfburne's elderly Director of Studies, bearing down on him with a pint of bitter in one hand, an overstuffed ring-binder under his arm, and a vulpine grin all over his face. Without waiting for a reply, he hooked the spare stool out with his foot and lowered his long, thick-middled body onto it, placing his burdens on the tiny, overcrowded table. 'Weren't thinking of leaving, were you?'

Salvador sat down again. 'No,' he said. 'Just getting comfortable. These stools . . .'

Lloyd-Jones laughed; a loud, high-pitched *HA*! that made heads turn at neighbouring tables. 'Give the old posterior rather a battering, don't they? But I should have thought your fresh young buns ought to be relatively unscathed; rather more resilient than my slack old arse, eh?'

He took a vile, tar-encrusted briar pipe out of his jacket pocket and parked its well-chewed stem between his yellow teeth, then began his perpetual, distracted ritual of searching about his person for tobacco and matches. 'So,' he said, the empty pipe jerking up and down as he spoke, 'what's a physically fit young blood doing drinking alone on a weekday evening? When he could be improving his mind or sowing his oats? Eh?'

Salvador frowned and glanced about for a moment before realising that Lloyd-Jones was referring to him. (He had travelled the world and attuned his ear to many strange manglings of English, but he still found that the language retained the power to disorientate him: Daniel Lloyd-Jones's *faux*-gentry pronunciation and antique turn of phrase was an especially intriguing specimen.) 'I was a little bored in my rooms,' he said with a shrug. 'What about you?'

'Celebration, my fine European Apollo!' Lloyd-Jones finally located a box of Swan matches and laid it on top of his binder. It immediately slid off onto the floor. 'I may count myself saved,' he said, stooping to retrieve them. 'Though not in the evangelical sense. This evening has witnessed an extraordinary meeting of the McGill management committee. A most extraordinary meeting indeed.' (As well as his post at Wolfburne, Lloyd-Jones held a chair in the McGill Institute of Musicology; thus, despite all contrary evidence, he seemed to regard Salvador as a natural collegiate ally.) 'Those arse-stuffed, wet-eared little swine have been trying to unseat me.'

'Pardon?'

'Turn me emeritus, put me out to grass – bloody retire me! *Me!* With a bark of triumph, he produced a plastic pouch of tobacco from his inside pocket and began stuffing his pipe. 'By God, though, I've turned their little conspiracy tonight, you see if I haven't. Sent the buggers bootless home and weather-beaten back. *HA!*'

Salvador smiled, despite himself. In spite of his colleagues' opinion of him as an unreasoning – possibly even psychotically deranged – old buffoon who held the Institute back by pretending never to have heard of any composer after Mahler and who attracted allegations of sexual harassment from his female students (and some dark muttering from males) like a magnet attracts pins, Salvador couldn't help quite liking Daniel Lloyd-Jones. Perhaps because, as a newcomer, he hadn't yet stumbled into the indiscriminate glare of the old man's paranoid fantasies. Perhaps it was also because Salvador had known many more monstrous personalities in his lifetime, some of them in his own family. Not now, though, not this evening . . .

'Can I get you another?' Lloyd-Jones asked, lighting his pipe and noticing that Salvador's glass was almost empty.

Salvador saw his chance. 'No thank you, Daniel. I ought to be leaving now.'

'Nonsense! You wouldn't deny an old fellow company in the hour of his victory, would you? Same again?' He seized Salvador's glass and eyed its pale dregs suspiciously. 'Lager, is it?' he said with distaste. 'Overpriced fizzy pop. So be it.' And he stalked off towards the bar while Salvador's heart slumped.

Audrey sipped her vodka-and-orange. 'Bugger that,' she said. 'Did you hear the latest about Helen?'

'Which one?' asked Lydia.

'Middleton, of course. Had an abortion.'

'I didn't even know she was pregnant,' said Lydia. 'Are you sure?'

'Where did you get that from?' Beth added sceptically.

'Miranda Fuller. It's gospel. She got herself up the duff at Christmas, apparently. She was last seen on Friday, singing the Black Psalm and going off to have it plucked and flushed.'

Lydia pulled a face. '*Singing the Black Psalm?*'

Audrey shrugged. 'Sorry. Those Victorians get to you every time. Crying into her tea at the Copper Kettle, if you prefer. Red in the face and awash with snot . . . *Helen Middleton*, though. You can hardly believe it, can you? I mean, the big deal she makes about being a Catholic.'

'They're not all as devout as you,' said Beth sardonically. 'Some of them even use contraception.'

'*I* use contraception. That's half the point. What I mean is, Helen goes to Mass and everything – I haven't been since I was about twelve.'

'But you're anti-abortion,' said Lydia.

Audrey's cheeks flushed. 'That's got nothing to do with religion,' she insisted. 'You know that perfectly well. It's because . . . well, because I—'

'Because you've never got pregnant,' said Rachel irritably. 'Why won't you accept that a woman should have control over her own body?'

'I do, absolutely. But I mean, accidental pregnancy – *excuse me?* I don't buy it. Control implies responsibility – contraception's so reliable, I don't believe *any* pregnancy is *ever* wholly accidental.'

'That's crap,' said Rachel. 'But even if you were right, even if some poor, damaged woman gets herself pregnant on purpose and then regrets it, should a child really have to pay the price for the mistake?'

'What, by being killed, you mean?'

'You know what Rachel means,' said Beth. 'Being brought up by a mother who doesn't want you. What a miserable life.'

All three of them gazed at Audrey, each suspecting that if the worst

86

ever did happen to her, she would be at the nearest clinic in seconds flat, trampling her way to the front of the queue. Rachel, trembling with anger, voiced the suspicion, and added: 'I'm surprised it hasn't happened already, considering the way you put yourself about.'

Audrey lit a cigarette and gazed levelly at Rachel through the smoke. 'It won't happen,' she said. 'I'm too careful. And you can comfort yourself with the thought that it'd never happen to you, either.'

Rachel balked. 'What's that supposed to mean?'

'No man's that desperate,' Audrey murmured.

'Do you know who the father is?' asked Lydia brightly, trying to stem the breach before Rachel could rise to Audrey's remark.

'Helen's lover?' said Audrey. 'No. If you believe the kinder rumours, it's Eden Campbell, but the crueller souls are pointing the finger at Donald Maitland.'

'Her tutor?' said Lydia. 'That's sick.'

'Sick but alarmingly plausible, if you think about it. She has got a thing about older men. Comes from sucking up to God, I suppose.'

While Beth and Lydia steered the conversation towards safer ground, Audrey looked across at Rachel: her cheeks were mottled pink, and her fingers, gripping a glass of milky ginger ale, were shaking. However much she told herself that she disliked Rachel for her self-righteous and wholly theoretical received opinions, she always felt uneasy in the aftermath of a confrontation. Rachel was such a soft target, so easy to pulverise. Audrey could feel the tinge of guilt creeping over her now; a little emotional flat spot, like the small, whispering pang of regret she sometimes felt in the dissipating wash after orgasm.

If Rachel's hands trembled and her cheeks bloomed with a rush of blood, though, it was not Audrey's doing. She had just glanced round at the sound of a loud, familiar *HA!* And noticed who was sitting at the next table. Her throat tightened, and she leaned towards Beth. '*It's him!*' she hissed excitedly. '*It's him!*'

'Who?' said Beth, alarmed. 'Where?'

'Salvador de La Simarde!' Rachel whispered. 'Over there!'

'Where?'

'With Lloyd-Jones.'

Rachel, not daring to turn round, watched Beth's face turn from bafflement to intrigue as her eyes scoured the room, skipped over Daniel Lloyd-Jones and settled finally on Salvador. Had she been more perceptive, Rachel might have noticed Beth's pupils dilate slightly and her breathing catch as her eyes focused.

'That's *him?*' she whispered. 'He's . . .' She had been about to say *lovely*, but it hardly seemed to do justice. Rachel had told them at tedious length about his talents, his career and his aristocratic background, but she had never once described the man himself. In place of the inbred, prognathous gangle of precocity flabbing into early middle age that Beth had abstractedly imagined, she found herself gazing at a ... *sullied angel* was the phrase that jumped into her momentarily addled brain. He was tall and wiry, with a dark, loose fringe of curls that had gone uncut just a little too long, almost veiling his wide, boylike eyes. His hands, at the ends of long, lean wrists coated with a translucent film of fine black hair, were not as she would have imagined musician's hands. Instead of thin, gracile wands, he had fingers like a manual worker; thick and coarse, contrasting sharply with the rest of his body, but still graceful in their movement. She imagined the worked-in strength there must be in those fingers, and sighed.

Intrigued, Audrey and Lydia leaned in towards the hushed, excited confabulation. 'What's up?' asked Lydia.

Beth gathered herself in. 'Rachel's just seen Salvador,' she said quietly. 'Behind you. *Don't look now!*

'What's he like?' Lydia demanded, trying to steal a surreptitious peek over her shoulder. 'Is he nice?'

Beth could virtually hear Audrey's lust-glands beginning to squirt their chemicals into her bloodstream as she looked. 'Oh, he's nice all right,' she said.

Lydia tried again to see the object of their attention, but couldn't even get a glimpse without turning right around. With her elbow, she nudged the shoulder of her jacket off the back of the chair. It fell to the floor, carrying her scarf with it. As she twisted round to gather them up, she stole a glance at the neighbouring table, and found herself looking straight into his eyes. He smiled at her. She smiled back. She hurriedly rearranged her belongings, then turned away.

'What d'you reckon?' Beth asked.

Lydia shrugged. 'Not bad,' she said, pulling a face as they all looked at her incredulously. 'Not bad,' she repeated. 'What d'you expect me to say?'

The laws of fairness and averages hung rent in tatters. She was beautiful. Imperfections were there – an upper lip that protruded just a fraction too much, and a nose that could have had just the tiniest bit more definition – but these were the kind of flaws that only added to beauty, he thought. And there was a kind of marish pride in her startlingly incongruous dark eyes and the cast of her mouth that lent her English paleness an hispanic aura. As she turned away, he sat staring stupidly at her back, struck dumb. Had he been told that most men's appraisal of her looks was usually *Not bad* or *Quite attractive*, he would either have reeled at their mastery of understatement or laughed at their idiocy. One smile from her, he was sure, could knock him sideways.

Her friends were leaning into a huddle over the centre of their table, whispering to each other. From time to time, the slight, womanly one and the dark-haired one shot glances at him; glances that were veiled in casual furtiveness (he might not have even noticed at any other time) but tricked out with amusement. They must be able to see the dumb ox look on his face, and they were laughing at him. He sighed and smiled politely back at them.

'You just wait,' Lloyd-Jones was saying complacently. 'I can hear the sound of dot-matrix printers churning out resignation letters as we speak.' He slurped a mouthful of foam from his second pint and smirked.

'Sorry?' said Salvador, disoriented as the words cut in on his reverie.

'I said that there shall be unseasonal snow in Cambridge by morning, and the snow shall be a flurry of resignation letters.'

'Pardon? Who's resigning?'

Lloyd-Jones frowned at him. 'I say, I do believe you haven't been listening to a word I've been saying.'

'Sorry, I was just thinking.'

'Well, don't. It's a most unappealing habit in the young. The lonely wandering ground of the mind is for the old and infirm. Tell me what thoughts you could be having that are more fascinating than my famous victory over the plaster gnomes of the Institute?'

'Oh, just things.'

'Just things, eh? Well, in that case I shall begin again . . .'

'It's all right,' said Audrey. 'He's not looking . . . What d'you suppose a little peach like him is doing drinking with an old fart like Lloyd-Jones? They can't be friends, surely.' She looked at Rachel with unprecedented respect. 'I'd no idea you could be such a dark horse. You've certainly kept him under wraps. And you say you've been in his *rooms*?'

Despite the imputation of impure motives, Rachel was delighted with their reaction. Except Lydia; she didn't seem particularly impressed. But Beth and Audrey . . . Wait until they heard him play! 'Well,' she said, feeling that she had better repudiate the manner of intimacy that Audrey seemed to be implying. 'It was just a scholarly visit. I wanted his opinion of my essay.' She thought it best not to mention the autographed cassette.

'What essay?' said Beth. 'I didn't think you had essays.'

'Of course I do. It's for Fiona Gale. It's on the Modernist movement and the male orgasm.'

Beth almost spat her lager out on the table. '*What?*'

Rachel looked nonplussed. 'Surely you've heard the debate?' They all stared at her in disbelief, shaking their heads. 'Well,' she said, 'the basis of the argument is that the structure of composition in Romanticism and Modernism is based on male sexuality and the desire to expedite climax. All those huge, resolute crescendos. They reflect the tumult of the male orgasm. Women tend to prefer Minimalist forms, because they involve prolonged repetition; stable and sensitive, without any big, thrashing climaxes.'

There was a long pause. 'I see,' said Beth. She and Audrey and Lydia glanced uncomfortably at each other. Poor Rachel.

'Well,' said Audrey, recovering quickly, 'it shows a bit more front than I'd have credited you with.'

Praise and approval from Audrey's ungenerous lips – however dubious their connotations – were rare as swallows in winter. Rachel felt a rush of pleasure so intense that her cheeks turned scarlet again and a sharp tingle shivered her spine. Audrey, watching her squirm with delight, was satisfied. She regretted having been so spiteful earlier. After all, it might be worth keeping in with Rachel if she could fish up such choice acquaintances. Perhaps, if Rachel's hook were somehow baited just a little more, Audrey might be able to take over the reel and have him flopping and gasping on the bank before too long. (In a temporary delirium, she forgot all about Peter Quintard.)

Lydia was looking at her watch. 'Hadn't we better be going?' she suggested. 'We don't want to miss the start of the film.'

Oh Jesus, God, no – they were leaving! They were pushing back their chairs and standing up, pulling on their coats and jackets and gathering up their belongings. The one glimmer of pleasurable company he had seen in months, and they were moving out of his reach while he sat with his ankle caught in a snare. In his heart, the tolerant fondness he had harboured for eccentric old Daniel Lloyd-Jones turned to loathing and resentment; why couldn't the insane old bastard just shut up and leave him alone?

Rachel decided she needed the toilet. Audrey – rather surprisingly, since she had only drunk one vodka and usually had a bladder as elastically capacious as a balloon – followed her.

Rachel came out of the cubicle to find her in front of the mirror, touching up her lipstick. While she washed and dried her hands, Rachel watched in the mirror, fascinated by the artisanship of the process: the smooth, quick precision with which the soap-soft finger of pillar-box red was drawn around the stretched, rigid O; lips coming together, soft and pliant, rolling against each other for a moment like seals in the surf, then an O again, delicately blotted with a single gossamer ply teased from a white tissue. Rachel – aside from an obligatory child-hood romp with her younger sister through their mother's dressing table – had never worn make-up, and she sometimes wondered where you went to acquire such skills. Even the choice of materials seemed so daunting. On occasions, carried by an impulse, she had made her way determinedly to the cosmetics department at Boots, only to find herself floundering amongst the perfumed counters. The bewildering array of brands – many of them horrifically expensive for what you seemed to get – was the first problem. Then there were all the different kinds of materials: foundations, lipsticks, lip-liners, eye-liners, and all the other mystifying tubes, sticks, brushes, compacts and applicators. Even if you got past that obstacle, there were all the ranks and columns of colours and shades, and the constantly hovering received understanding that choosing the wrong shades (dictated by the myste-rious, unknowable forces of fashion and skin and hair colouring) could be a mistake of the direst proportions. Where did women like Audrey learn how to cope? Was it something that your mother was supposed to tell you about when your periods started, along with the facts of life and where to buy sanitary paraphernalia? Her own mother had been distressingly lax in both departments. Perhaps they covered it in state school curricula; a non-examined supplementary course like sex educa-tion that you did alongside O-Levels. Personal Grooming Studies. Optional, parental consent required. Not at Rachel's school, though. They hadn't even had sex education (even biology had been a bit evasive about human reproduction). It must be a state-school thing: Lydia and Beth were both quietly acquainted with the art's arcane skills and materials, even though neither of them practised it as regularly as Audrey. So, alone and unguided in Boots, Rachel invariably kept her money in her purse and went unpainted.

Audrey noticed that she was being watched. She peeled the tissue from her lips and offered a brightly drawn, appeasing smile. 'Would you like some?' she asked.

Rachel frowned. 'What?'

Audrey held up the lipstick. 'You can have some if you like.'

Rachel grinned gauchely. 'Oh, I don't think so . . . I wouldn't—'

'Oh, of course you would. Even Andrea Dworkin puts on a bit of lippy from time to time.' Suppressing the disturbing mental image this evoked, Audrey glanced doubtfully at the colour of the lipstick in comparison with Rachel's rather pasty complexion. She put the lid back on and riffled through her make-up bag until she found a paler, fleshy pink shade. She pulled off the cap and held it poised. 'Here.

Now, open wide...' Rachel hesitated, then opened her mouth as though she were at the dentist's. Audrey patted her chin with a forefinger. 'Less teeth, more lips,' she said. Rachel relaxed her jaw slightly and pushed out her lips. 'That's better... You know, you've got nice lips.' She began to paint a pink line around their rim. 'Rachel, I'm sorry I snapped at you earlier. I don't really think about you like that. I was only teasing. I just think you could... well, take a bit more care over your appearance. It never does any harm, you know, and I'm sure it would give you more confidence... There... Now, just let me blot you...'

Rachel looked in the mirror, and was astonished at the transformation. Her lips, which had always seemed no more than uninteresting, functional pads of flesh, had suddenly become adornments, teeming with latent subliminal signals. She had once read that painting the lips had originated with Roman prostitutes, amongst whom it symbolised proficiency in particular services (Like a sort of advanced Girl Guide badge – First Aid, Camping, Pet Care, Needlecraft, Fellatio.)

Audrey looked critically at her handiwork, and reached into her make-up bag again. 'I think we need a little touch of eye-liner, don't you?'

Beth and Lydia waited on the pavement outside the pub.

'Not bad?' Beth was saying. 'I still can't believe I heard you say that. Tell me I imagined it.'

Lydia laughed. 'So he's not my type. Each to their own, Beth.'

'He's better looking than Stephen Rae.'

Lydia's smile froze. 'Is he? Well, I wouldn't know.'

Damn. Probably not such a good idea to mention Stephen Rae. Lydia had rallied tremendously after her heartbreak on the Pennine Way, but Beth had never looked at her in quite the same way since. She could see a brittleness under the skin and a friable quality in her voice (even in a welter of joy) that she realised had been there all along, but which she had never noticed before.

'I'd never have thought Rachel could be such a dark horse,' Beth said, changing tack. 'I wonder if she's got designs on him.'

She and Lydia looked at each other for a moment, tantalised by the thought, then shook their heads in unison; they were kind enough not to laugh, though, even in her absence.

'I think he's her Arthur more than her Lancelot,' said Lydia.

'Ready, children?' said Audrey, materialising beside them.

'You two took your time,' said Beth. She glanced at Rachel, then glanced again, then stared. She looked odd; a peculiar, unusual brightness in her eyes. For one short, bizarre moment, Beth wondered if she had been in the toilet popping pills. She might have been less surprised by that than the truth. She peered closer in the dim street light.

Lydia noticed it too. 'Rachel, are you wearing make-up?'

Audrey spoke for her. 'I've decided to appoint myself Rachel's personal makeover consultant. Don't you think she looks good?'

Rachel looked at them shyly, anticipating laughter, a nervous smile twitching her glossy lips. They made polite, approving noises while Audrey looked on with a mixture of satisfaction and critical appraisal.

Lydia smiled. 'I think you look terrific, Rachel.'

As they walked on, Audrey fell in beside Rachel. 'I think we'll have a go at your hair tomorrow,' she said, glancing at the limp top-knot. 'I'm sure I can do *something* with it.'

'. . . and from that day onwards, I had the old bugger wheezing his bloody accordion right under my window every blasted evening. Every time I went down to complain . . .'

Lloyd-Jones' monologue wandered in and out of focus as Salvador sat with his chin cupped in one palm, twisting the rim of his glass with the other.

'. . . So, in the end I broke camp and stole away to the Latin Quarter . . .'

Rebecca and her friend came out of the women's toilet. The other two had already left. He watched with dismal, thwarted eagerness as they walked across the room without so much as glancing in his direction, disappeared through the passage that led to the front bar and slipped irrevocably out of his life. In a town of so many students, what would be his chances of bumping into them again? And he was sure he wouldn't have the nerve to actually track them down, even if he could remember Rebecca's surname. (Or was it Rachel? . . . Ruth?)

'. . . went and got himself killed in a mountaineering accident. Damn silly pastime at his age. Barely recognisable, they tell me. Did you ever meet him?'

'Sorry? Meet who?'

'Have you got cloth ears? Mathieu Querelle. Finest musicologist the Sorbonne ever had. And they had some good ones.'

Salvador sipped his beer. 'Yes, I met him once. My mother knew him.' He had to think of something, and quick.

Lloyd-Jones shook his head sadly. 'Terrible loss. Finest they ever had. He was behind the Ensemble des Anciens, you know. I had the honour of attending one of their rather rare performances, shortly before he—'

'Daniel,' said Salvador, desperation finally overcoming his weary, worn-out manners. 'I don't mean to be rude, but I've just remembered something. A phone call – I'm expecting a phone call.'

'But you haven't finished your—'

'I've really got to go. I may have missed it already. Thank you for the drink. Goodnight.'

Lloyd-Jones watched him go, his eyes narrowing suspiciously. Why should the mention of Mathieu Querelle produce such an extraordinary reaction? After a few moments' contemplation, he opened his ring-binder and leafed through to a page covered in bunched, erratic scrawls connected by a network of arrows, brackets and boxes. In a clear space at the bottom, he wrote:

Salv. de la S. ← ?(Sorbonne?)? → Mat. Querelle

He took a sip of beer and stared at the page, pursing his lips and trying to puzzle out how this surprising new piece fitted into the jigsaw. He would have to keep his eyes and ears open around this strange young man in future. And his mouth shut. Staring into space, he began to go over every word they had exchanged, looking for clues and (cursing himself) any damaging remarks he might have let slip.

The picturegoers filed into the long, tunnel-shaped foyer of the Arts Cinema, several of them glancing curiously at the three women arguing amongst themselves in the corner by the back entrance to Eaden Lilley.

'It's not my fault,' said Beth indignantly.

Audrey stared at her. 'I said *I'd* get the shopping in if *you* went for the tickets.'

'No you didn't. You said you'd get the shopping *and* the tickets. Why would I go out specially when you were going out anyway?'

'You said you'd be passing on your way back from the library.'

'No, that was *Tuesday*. I said I wouldn't be able to get them that day because I'd be *in* the library.'

'Bull*shit!*' said Audrey. 'I remember it clearly. *You* said—'

'Look, does it matter?' said Rachel, frantically trying to douse the crackling tinder. 'It was a misunderstanding. It wasn't anybody's fault. Anyway, we might still get in.'

At that moment, Lydia emerged from the tunnel, elbowing and twisting her way through the crush. She shook her head. 'Sold out,' she said despondently.

'Well, that does it,' Audrey fumed, glaring at Beth.

'Let's have a vote,' said Lydia, forestalling a second round. 'Home or back to the pub?'

Beth and Rachel voted for home. Lydia herself would have quite liked another drink, but as the contents of her wallet added up to exactly twenty-nine pence, an old dry-cleaning ticket and some pellets of grey fluff, she reluctantly voted for home as well. 'What about you, Aud?' she asked.

Audrey huffed. 'Do I have much choice? Come on, let's go.'

He was too late; by the time he got out onto the street, they had gone.

Instead of heading back to Wolfburne, he strolled disconsolately through the town, hands in pockets, gazing into darkened shop windows. At the entrance to Market Passage, he paused a moment, considering the queue for the cinema and wondering whether to join it. He rejected the idea and walked on.

As he approached the corner where Sidney Street widened and Market Street branched off, he heard a man's voice shouting furiously somewhere up ahead, words blurred with echoes from the shop-fronts. At the corner, he paused, scanning the passers-by for the source of the disturbance. In the shadows on the opposite corner, between the bus shelter and the bicycle-festooned railings of the Holy Trinity church, a short, wiry man was standing, gesticulating wildly and shouting a stream of bilious rage at someone sitting on a bench in front of him.

'*Why d'yer ave ter wind me up, eh?*' he was yelling. '*DON'T focken wind me UP!*'

Salvador walked closer. The recipient of the man's fury was a young woman, who sat on the bench with her head bowed and her hands meekly folded on her knees. Every so often, she raised her head a little and seemed to mumble something in reply; something conciliatory which only seemed to make him more angry.

'*Alf a focken HOUR I was waiten there like a focken prick, an where was you? Focken pissen about up ERE!*' Mumble, mumble, mu— '*On the focken CORNER I said! Are yer deaf or focken stupid or what?*' He went to cuff the woman on the side of the head; she shied away, and he seized her hair. '*Yer know what your trouble is, don't yer?*' he screamed into her face. '*Yer focken AVE ter wind me UP! Yer always focken do!*'

The passers-by, Salvador noted, carried on passing by, describing a wider and wider arc around the scene, keeping their eyes averted. Nobody intervened. Salvador walked across the road towards the couple.

'*Yer stupid, d'yer know that? D'yer know ow focken pigshit focken STUPID yer ARE?*'

'Excuse me . . .'

Mumble, mumble, mum— '*NO! THAT bloody corner, yer stupid cow! Not—*'

'*Excuse me.*'

'. . . Oo the fock are you?' The man's eye-level barely came up to

95

Salvador's chin, but there wasn't the least modulation of the aggression in his face or tone as he turned and glared up at him. His face, like his body, was small, narrow and sinewy, and he had a wispy black moustache that twisted with his sneering lips. 'Keep out of it, mate,' he warned.

Despite the rising constriction of fear in his throat, Salvador persisted. 'I think the young lady would like you to stop shouting at her.'

'*What?*' The man let go of the woman's hair and tapped his nose. '*Keep THIS out,*' he shouted, and prodded Salvador hard in the chest. '*Or I'll focken FLATTEN it!*'

'But can't you see how upset she is? You're making her cry.' Salvador glanced down at the woman, but she wasn't crying; from behind the curtain of dishevelled hair, which she was making no attempt to straighten, she stared into space with dry, dead-fish eyes. He stepped towards her, holding out a hand, but the man moved quickly, stepping between them and shoving him in the chest with both hands, making him wheeze and stagger back.

'*Whaddyer think yer doin, eh? Keep yer focken ands off er!*' He advanced on Salvador, poking and shoving him in the chest and shoulders. '*What's your focken game, eh?*'

'Get your hands off me!'

'*Tappen other fellers' birds? Wanna focken fight for er, do yer? Come on!*' He shoved again, hard.

'*I said get your filthy hands off me!*'

The man's small, bone-hard fist whipped out like a snake's tongue and snapped against Salvador's cheek like a hammer. His vision blurred, and he lost his balance. As he fell backwards and crashed to the pavement, he thought he heard a woman's voice; distant, echoing, screeching out his name. There was a sound of running feet, then the back of his head hit the concrete, catapulting his eyeballs out of their sockets and onto his chest, where they rolled about, half-blind, sending back incoherent signals to his jarred brain for a few moments before shutting down completely.

3

There was a deep, mechanical clunk followed by a sustained electronic screech that echoed harshly in the bare room.

'Interview with Lee Roberts. Officers present: Sergeant Whiteley and WPC Brand. Time is ten fifty-seven p.m ... Now, Lee, d'you want to tell us what happened?'

Lee stared truculently across the table at the two officers. He looked as though he was having some difficulty focusing; aside from his torn T-shirt, grazed knuckles and a cut, distended upper lip that gave his moustache a startling resemblance to a partially bloated earwig, his left eye was swollen and rimmed with red-tinged puce.

'Are you sure you wouldn't like a solicitor present?' asked Sergeant Whiteley.

'No, I aven't bloody done notten.' His voice was slurred by his puffed lip, hissing around the exposed teeth.

'Then tell us what happened.'

Lee glared. 'Give us a fag an I might.'

WPC Brand glanced at the sergeant, then pushed a packet of Benson & Hedges across the table. Lee fumbled a cigarette out, having difficulty with his tightly bandaged knuckles. He leaned forward while the policewoman lit it for him, then slouched back in his chair.

'Come on, Lee – we haven't got all night. What happened?'

'I dunno. Look at the state a me. Whaddyer focken *think* appened?'

'We want to hear what *you* think happened. Perhaps you could tell us why a respectable fellow of Wolfburne College would pick on Lee Roberts, having an innocent evening out with his girlfriend.'

'I dunno. E was a focken eadcase – poken is nose in, tryner put is mitts on me bird.'

'He tried to assault your girlfriend?' the sergeant asked. Lee didn't reply. 'Did he attack you?'

Lee grunted. 'Yeah. Focken eadcase.'

Sergeant Whiteley laid a manila folder on the table. 'We've got two statements here from witnesses who say you were having a violent row with your girlfriend and when Mr Simarde intervened, you punched him. What d'you say to that?'

'It's bollocks. I never touched er.'

'But you did punch *him*?'

'*E* started it! E got what was comen.'

'Did you punch him?'

'E coulder bin some bloody pervert for all I knew – tryner put is ands on *my* bird!'

'Did you punch him? Yes or no?'

'Focken ell. *Yeah, I focken punched im!*'

'Thank you. Now tell us what happened next.'

Salvador lay on his back on the plastic-covered mattress, eyes closed against the harsh ceiling light. The cell was overheated, and he was sweating uncomfortably. He slid his arm under his neck, trying to take the weight off the back of his head, but nothing seemed to ease the throbbing. He could only distract himself from it by concentrating on the sharp pain in his left cheekbone.

His memory of what had happened was vague. He remembered the confrontation, and the punch in the face, and he could still feel the nauseating thud as his head hit the pavement. Then everything shifted into a dreamy haze, and the next thing he remembered clearly was sitting in the back of a police car, holding on to his head and moaning in agony.

The slick of sweat was gluing his shirt to his back, clammy and slippery on the smooth plastic. He rolled awkwardly onto his side and groaned miserably. What if the College heard about this? Would he lose his fellowship? What on earth would he do then? Loathsome as the place might be, he needed the money.

The eye-slot in the door snapped open; a pair of eyes and a nose appeared. 'Come on,' said a brisk voice. 'FME's here. Let's get that head seen to.'

Lydia walked back across the foyer and sat down on the hard plastic chair, sighing and looking at her watch.

'Well?' said Beth.

'They haven't interviewed her yet. We could be here all night at this rate.'

'What about Salvador?'

'He's got to be seen by a doctor before they can talk to him. Head injury.'

Beth nodded. 'Poor guy . . .'

Lydia glanced at her and smiled. 'Poor Rachel,' she added. 'I still can't believe it . . . I did really see what I think I saw, didn't I? I mean, it wasn't some kind of hallucination?'

Beth shook her head. She could hardly believe it either. Not of Rachel. They had been on their way to collect their bikes, which were chained to the church railings. Emerging from Market Passage, they heard the sounds of a fracas coming from the opposite side of the road. They hesitated; there was a fight obviously about to break out, and the two antagonists were squaring up right in front of where their bikes were parked. Audrey took a few steps forward to get a closer look, then stopped and turned back. 'It's him,' she said excitedly. 'I'm sure it's him!' Beth and Lydia knew immediately who she meant – they recognised him by his lime green jacket and his dark curls – but before they could get their minds into gear and even begin to wonder what to do, the little shouting man in the T-shirt lashed out. His fist slammed right into Salvador's face, and he went over backwards like a bowling pin, landing heavily on the ground. That was when the stark, staring impossible happened. Rachel, who had been standing shocked to silence and immobility at Beth's elbow, opened her small, newly lipsticked mouth and let out a dervish scream: '*SALVADOR!*' Before they could stop her, she shot across the road like a terrier after a rabbit. Salvador's attacker was stooping over him, fists clenched, shouting obscenities and swinging back his foot to kick his supine, buckled-up victim in the ribs. He never got a chance to complete his swing; the heavy wooden butt of Rachel's umbrella, arcing out like a cavalry sabre propelled at full-blooded charge velocity, sliced into the side of his head and sent him spinning. As he staggered, trying to regain his balance, Rachel squared up and hit him again; a hard quarter-staff jab in the stomach. He doubled over, retching. Rachel dropped the bent, broken umbrella and seized him by the hair, propelling him across the pavement and slamming him face-first into the church railings. He tried to struggle, but every movement entangled him deeper in the dense nest of bicycle frames, until he was trapped like a fly in a web. Lydia, Audrey and Beth, who had stayed rooted and gaping at the extraordinary, unbelievable brawl, finally regained the use of their legs and ran across the road. Beth and Audrey grabbed Rachel by the shoulders (she was spitting and muttering incoherently and still raining weakening blows on the man's back) and tried to restrain her, while Lydia went to Salvador. She crouched down beside him and raised his head. The curls at the back were sticky with blood, and his eyelids were flickering alarmingly. 'Are you okay?' she asked. She uncoiled her college scarf, rolled it up and placed it under his head. 'Can you hear me?' she asked. His eyes opened, and as they focused on her face, she smiled with relief. 'I think he's okay,' she called out . . .

Audrey came back into the foyer carrying a tray with three plastic cups of tea. 'What's the latest?' she asked as she handed them round.

'Rachel hasn't been interviewed yet,' said Lydia. 'And Salvador's waiting for medical attention.'

Audrey sat down and crossed her legs. 'You know, I'm never going to look at Rachel in quite the same light again.' She blew gently on her scalding tea. 'It's certainly been more exciting than the cinema.'

'There,' said the doctor as she finished applying the dressing. 'I think you'll live. Although you might lose a few of those pretty curls when that dressing comes off.' She examined his eyes again, pulling down his lower lids with her thumb and squinting through an ophthalmoscope.

'Can he be interviewed yet?' asked the custody sergeant, who thought she was taking rather longer than was really necessary over the examination.

'Yes,' she said, switching off the scope. 'There's no conclusion.

Nevertheless, the moment you've finished with him, I want him straight down to Addenbrooke's for an x-ray.' She smiled at Salvador. 'Just a precaution,' she added.

She quizzed him briefly about arrangements for registering with a GP, and gave him the phone number and address of her practice. Then, with just a shade of reluctance (or so the sergeant suspected), she packed her bag and left.

'Right, son,' he said. 'Let's get your side of the story.'

In Cell C-7, Rachel sat on the hard bed and stared dizzily at the floor. It was more than an hour since the affray, but her limbs still trembled with thrills of exhilaration that rippled through her like liquid electricity. The knuckles of both hands were pink and scuffed where she had thrashed wildly at the man's horrible, bullying back, and Audrey's eye-liner was smeared around her eyes, dissolved and spread by her tears of rage and her attempts to dash them away. The sight of that vile, bullying, braying man's fist hitting Salvador's face had spiked and jolted her heart like an electroconvulsive shock, and she had run across the road with protective vengeance seething in every cell of her body. The moment her first blow sliced home, the rage hit boiling point and transformed into a kind of riotous joy, a perverse exultation. Each subsequent blow was a greater and greater thrill; by the time Audrey and Beth pulled her back, she was gibbering and frothing like a wild animal with the smell of blood in its nostrils. And then had come a succession of smaller, subsiding thrills at the hands of a series of incredulous police officers: being bundled into the police car, having her belongings confiscated and bagged, her fingerprints and mug-shots taken, and finally being led along the shiny grey corridor and hearing the resonant clang of the cell door closing behind her.

A prisoner! All her life had been a different kind of prison: a flat, featureless plateau of unevents. At school, she had never received so much as a single line or a solitary minute of detention. And here she was – here she *was* ... Just wait until she got a chance to tell them the details. (It was clear, in spite of what witnesses might tell them, that they believed Salvador must have beaten the man up, and that she had merely helped stick the boot in.) Just wait until she told them ...

She started at the sound of the eye-slot flicking back. There was a jangle of keys as the door was unlocked and swung open. The custody sergeant stood in the doorway.

'Wouldn't believe it to look at her, would you?' he said over his shoulder to the WPC standing behind him.

Rachel peered curiously at him, discomfited at being talked about as though she were a retard. 'Wouldn't think what?'

The sergeant grinned. 'Lindy here's just been talking to your boy-friend.' (*Boyfriend?*) He shook his head. 'Nice educated girl like you, going round beating up innocent scaffolders. What's the world coming to?'

Her balloon sagged slightly as a little jet of air squeaked out. Her moment had been stolen. They knew already, and apparently believed. She perked up, however, when they led her out of the cell and she saw the little blackboard fixed to the wall beside the door. Chalked on it were the words *R. BUTLER – G.B.H.*... Rachel Butler, late of St Jude's School for Girls, lamb-shy flute student at Wolfburne College, Cambridge, turned inflicter of Grievous Bodily Harm. On a scaffolder (presumed likely wolf-whistler). Avenger of the fine and brittle against the coarse and hard, of the beautiful against the ugly, protector of the vulnerable against the bullying oppressor. She was Diana, Nemesis and Apollo all rolled into one. From now on, there would be no more Ms Nice-Girl. She was Superwoman.

Squaring her shoulders, head held high, she followed the blue uniforms back down the shining corridor towards her destiny.

If it hadn't been for the stinging from her knee and the cold creeping across the floor and gathering around her, Beth might have drifted back into her dream; instead, she floated on the surface of it, dipping her fingers in, trying to hear the sound of Lydia's voice and see the details of her face.

She was suddenly yanked out of herself by a soft rapping of fingernails on the door and a voice calling her name. She stood up hastily, straightening her skirt and coat (she still hadn't taken it off).

'Come in,' she called. The door opened, and Audrey's face appeared from behind it. 'Oh, it's you,' said Beth, her body slumping with relief.

'No need to sound so disappointed.' Audrey stepped into the room, pushing the door to behind her. 'I just came to see if you were okay. I heard your door go, and . . . Well, actually, I was bored to tears, to be perfectly honest. There's only one book in English in my room: *The Hound of the Baskervilles*. I'd have to be a bloody sight boreder to read *that* in *this* house, I can tell you.' She paused. 'Why's the window open?' she asked, then sniffed the air. 'Have you been having a bonfire or something?'

Beth showed her the burnt rug. 'I feel awful,' she said. 'God knows how I'm going to explain this to Madame de La Simarde.'

'It's that maid's fault,' said Audrey. 'She did the same with mine; she's built it too high.'

To Beth's surprise, Audrey took the poker and tongs and, kneeling down on the hearth rug, set about expertly relaying the fire, removing the excess coals and raking out the ash. Beth sat down on the end of the bed and watched her.

'Any sign of Rachel yet?'

Audrey shook her head. 'Not that I know of.'

'Aren't you concerned?'

'Hardly. Remember, this is Rachel we're talking about. Rachel always turns up, like the proverbial you-know-what.'

'I suppose she's got Clifford.'

Audrey sniggered. 'Exactly. They're probably hugging trees somewhere, I should imagine.' She finished laying the coals and stood up. 'D'you want to close that window now? It's freezing.'

Beth got up and slid the sash down, damming the flow of moorland cold. As she turned back to the room, Audrey frowned at her legs; an astonished gaze that climbed upwards, taking in the rumpled coat and disarrayed hair.

'What the hell have you been *doing* in here, Beth? You look like you've been in a fight.'

'I fell asleep, and then I couldn't find the light switch. I whacked myself on that thing.' Beth pointed at her assailant, revealed now as a Singer sewing-table, its ornate cast-iron legs bristling with vicious-looking curlicues. She sat down again on the bed and examined her knee. 'These tights are ruined,' she moaned, picking helplessly at the gaping hole; an oval of bloodstained pale flesh stark against the deep black. 'I can't go down to dinner in these. I look a fright.'

'No spares?'

Beth frowned at Audrey. 'Well, no – I was expecting to be back in Peterborough by tonight.' She sighed. 'I'll have to do without.'

Audrey pulled a face. 'Bare legs? With that skirt? No way. I'll get you sorted out.' Without giving Beth a chance to protest, she strode to the door. 'Back in a minute,' she said, and was gone.

Left alone again, Beth took a tissue from her coat pocket and, wetting it with her tongue, began tentatively dabbing and swabbing the wound. Once the blood had been cleaned away, it didn't look too bad; just a little graze.

'Audrey to the rescue,' said Audrey triumphantly, coming back in. She held out a neat wad of folded black nylon bound in thin white card. 'Brand new. Untouched by human thighs.'

Beth took the packet and looked at the label doubtfully. 'Stockings?' she said querulously.

'Don't worry – they're hold-ups. No need for rigging.'

Beth glanced up at her. That wasn't what concerned her. 'Yes,' she said. 'I mean, no . . . But, well, *stockings*?'

Audrey's face fell. 'Sorry,' she said sullenly. 'I'll take them back if they're no good.'

Beth instantly felt ashamed of her ingratitude. 'No, Audrey,' she said hastily. 'No, they're fine, honestly . . . Thanks. They're great.'

Audrey nodded curtly and turned away, absorbing herself in examining a painting of foxhounds that hung above the mantelpiece. Beth peeled off her tights and tossed them into a corner, then unwrapped the stockings. They were flimsy and filmy; gossamer-thin compared with the sturdy Lycra she was used to, and the broad bands of lace at their tops made them seem ludicrously fanciful. To judge from her manner, Audrey must wear this sort of thing all the time. Beth had worn stockings on probably fewer than half-a-dozen occasions in her whole life, and then as behind-closed-doors costumery rather than clothing.

'How long have we got?' she asked as she drew the stockings on.

Audrey had moved on, and was scrutinising a painting on the wall above the sewing-table – the one whose frame Beth had encountered in the dark just as her knee collided with the table's leg. It depicted a stag hunt captured in the momentary lull between the hunter drawing down his aim on the stag and the blast of the gun. Audrey was looking closely at the stag, whose blank eyes gazed beyond the hunter and out of the frame at the viewer.

'Hm?' she said.

'How long have we got?'

Audrey sighed. 'Who can tell? Any of us could go at any time. You've only got to look at Lydia to see that.'

Beth frowned. 'What? I meant, how long have we got before dinner?'

Audrey turned away from the painting and smiled bleakly. 'Of course you did . . . There, that's better,' she said, looking approvingly at Beth's newly sheathed legs. 'Nine o'clock, apparently. Don't you remember? They do things old-style in this castle. Or maybe it's continental style, I don't know. Dinner and then to bed. Ruinously unhealthy.'

'Do you always carry spare stockings with you?' Beth asked.

Audrey smiled. 'Of course. You never know when you're going to get a ladder.'

'All the time with these things, I should think.'

'I answered one of those questionnaire things once. You know, for the *Guardian*, where they ask you what objects you always carry with you. I put: stockings, clean knickers and a condom.'

Beth glanced at her. 'You haven't changed at all, have you?'

'No. If you recall, that's exactly the point I was making earlier. None of us do, dear.'

Beth nodded. 'I suppose so . . . So, you married Peter after all.'

'Of course. I said I'd have him, didn't I, right from the start.'

'But I thought you broke up.'

104

'We got back together. It was May week . . . Of course, you weren't there, were you? You'd done your disappearing act . . . What *did* happen to you? You walk out of the last but one Tripos paper, and by the time I get home you've vanished, never to return.'

Beth reddened. 'Well, I sort of . . . you know, had a bit of a breakdown. Exam pressure. You remember how bad it was. I came back and resat them later.'

Audrey gazed at her, as though waiting for more, but no more was forthcoming. 'Well, anyway,' she went on, 'it seemed Peter couldn't get me out of his system. He came to the Wolfburne ball – looking for me, I'm sure, although he swore he wasn't. The rest was inevitable.'

'And did you get your glittering career?'

Audrey smiled. 'I think this might turn into a sit-down-and-have-a-fag story. Do you mind?'

Beth shook her head, and Audrey disappeared to her room a second time, returning a few moments later with a packet of Silk Cut and her lighter. She pulled a chair up beside the fire and lit a cigarette.

'Did Peter get you your career?' Beth repeated when Audrey had settled herself.

She took a long drag, hollowing her cheeks and stretching her jaw. 'Oh, in absolute spades, darling,' she said, breathing smoke. 'I knew what I was about, choosing Peter. Gerald – that's Peter's father – was a real sweetie, lovely man. He gave me a job straight away, in—'

Beth interrupted: 'Did you sleep with him as well?'

'Who, *Gerald*?' The cigarette dangled from Audrey's shocked mouth. 'Beth, what sort of person do you take me for?'

'Okay, just checking.' Beth noted that Audrey didn't actually deny the charge. In the peculiar and convoluted moral code by which Audrey lived, outright lies were avoided whenever possible (a fastidiousness Beth attributed to her Catholic upbringing), but the truth could always be deviously circumvented. Indignant shock didn't necessarily mean outraged innocence with Audrey. Beth thought it entirely plausible that Audrey might sleep with her father-in-law, but she let it pass. 'Carry on,' she said.

Audrey stared at her for a moment, then flicked a bead of ash into the fire and went on with her story. 'Gerald put me in as assistant to one of Quintard's fiction editors. I was good at my job – really good, but the connection still had its uses in the accelerated promotion stakes. After a few months, Gerald persuaded the board to give me a full editorship. They were launching a new imprint called Red Garter.' Audrey grinned. 'You can imagine; erotic fiction for women. Anyway, they gave it to me to run. I made the best of it, but it never really worked out all that well, because we got so few usable submissions.

Most of them were drippy romances that were about as erotic as a wet haddock. People didn't seem to realise that putting in a member or a honeypot every chapter doesn't make a love story into erotica. Aside from that, we'd get stuff so pornographic you'd need asbestos gloves on just to handle the manuscripts. Real nasties. Paedophilia even. Anyway, once you'd weeded all the dross and the unprintable filth out of the slush pile, there wasn't all that much left that passed the Wetness Test. We had a handful of regular authors, but—'

'Wait a minute,' Beth interrupted. 'The Wetness Test?'

'Excitability ratings. My assistant and I graded the books according to the degree of w—'

Beth held up a hand. 'Okay, I think I get the picture.'

'Anyway, after about a year of trying to expand our list by bowdlerising the filth and spicing up the more passable romances, I decided I'd had enough. I resigned.'

Beth smiled. 'You know, I can imagine you doing that job. It must have suited you. Remember when we filled in those careers forms at Cambridge, saying what jobs we'd like to do? I wouldn't have been surprised if you'd put 'Pornographer'. Why on earth did you resign? And what did Peter's father think?'

Audrey paused, uncertain whether Beth's friendly teasing was really all that friendly. 'Who cares what he thought? He offered me Orb – you know Orb; quite a nice literary list, but I turned it down. I split up with Peter at about the same time. Actually, he left me, so I think I was within my rights leaving his family firm. I wasn't that bothered; I'd established my own network by then, so I didn't need the Quintards any more. I was bored with publishing, so I took a job with the BBC: producer's-assistant-come-production-manager. Last year, I set up my own production company – ClearCut Films. We make documentaries and travel programmes.'

'Really?'

'Most of them go to Channel 4. We've got a crew out in Rwanda at this very moment, in fact, doing a film on the aftermath. We tried to get Benedict Allen to present it, sort of combine reportage with exploring, but he turned it down.'

Beth nodded dumbly as Audrey went on talking about past, present and future projects. Mentally, she measured the gulf between Audrey's life and her own: she talked so casually about things – script editing, shooting schedules, the problems of insuring mortgage-value cameras for filming in Namibia and Colombia, syndication deals – things that were so far beyond Beth's sphere of experience they were almost mythic; a world away from recruiting clerical staff for Peterborough building societies.

'So,' said Audrey, 'tell me more about the state of the nation of Glaister.'

'What? Oh, you've already heard all there is to know. I can't believe how dull my life seems compared with yours.'

'Nonsense. You've barely told me anything about Iain. Tell me the secrets of successful relationships.'

'There aren't any. Just choose somebody you like.'

'And you like Iain?'

'Yes, I liked him as soon as I met him.'

'But did you love him?'

'I still do.'

'So what's the problem?'

Beth frowned. 'Problem? There isn't a problem.'

'Yes there is; there's always a problem. Tell me about it.'

Beth sighed and stared down at her lap. She seemed to have spent her life listening patiently to other people's problems; and having listened so much, she sensed the degradation, the humiliation of exposing those damp, fungus-ridden little secret corners. But she also felt the insidious desire to talk, to scrutinise herself and be scrutinised, if only to find out whether her worries were real and normal or whether she was just going slowly mad. So why not talk to Audrey; someone who knew her well and whom she would probably never see again after tomorrow; someone, moreover, who would be sufficiently uninterested to refrain from offering unwanted advice.

'Is it to do with his novel?' Audrey prompted.

'I don't know, really. I suppose so.'

'It usually is with writers. They're a bloody peculiar breed.'

'He's having trouble writing it, but he won't admit it. I see him struggling, and I can see he hates being dependent on me, but whenever I try to talk about it, he thinks I'm putting him under unreasonable pressure or making ultimatums. I'm interfering with the artistic flow, except the trouble is, there *isn't* any flow. He's hardly written a word in months that hasn't ended up in the bin.'

'It's all perfectly normal. Take it from me; I've known plenty of writers. You have to be patient.'

'Oh, I've got plenty of patience. Audrey, I'd wait till the end of the earth for him. He's the one who's losing it.' She paused. 'And now he's started with these funny little obsessions.'

'Obsessions?'

'Little things. Nothing really awful, but I worry. Like the smells, for example. One night, we were in bed, and he started sniffing – really frantically, like a dog after a bone. I asked him what was the matter, and he said he could smell sweetcorn. "Sweetcorn?" I said, and he said,

"Can't you smell it?" I said I couldn't, but he kept sniffing, saying the bed smelt like a tin of Jolly Green Giant had been emptied in it. I mean, *sweet*corn? Then, another time, we were having a cup of tea with some chocolate biscuits. He started making this funny face and glaring at the biscuit he'd half-eaten. "This biscuit tastes of mushrooms," he said.'

'Weird,' said Audrey approvingly.

'I know. There are other things, too. The other day, we were in Sainsbury's, and the woman on the checkout forgot to give us our three pence for re-using our carrier bags. Iain didn't say anything until we were out in the car park, then he got really worked up about it. He said it had happened before, and he reckoned there was a conspiracy – Sainsbury's were telling their employees not to hand out people's carrier-bag pennies unless they were asked, and they must be making a fortune by keeping the pennies and then writing them off against tax. He worked himself up into a fury about it. Before I could stop him, he was marching back to the shop and demanding to see the manager. I could've died, it was so embarrassing, everyone was staring at us while he shouted at this woman behind the customer-service desk.'

'Weird,' said Audrey again. 'But I've heard plenty weirder.'

'I mean, I love him to bits, and none of it is that serious, but . . .'

'It'll sort itself out. It's frustration; once he gets his teeth back into writing, he'll be happy again. At least he's stayed with you.'

Beth nodded. 'I know. He's always good to me. Cooks for me, does the washing, everything.' She smiled; now that she had spoken it, she felt happier about it. Audrey's unfazed reaction made her wonder whether she had been worrying for no reason. What must her relationship with Peter have been like?

'. . . You said you split up with Peter . . .'

She left the question unasked, so that Audrey could choose not to answer it. She needn't have bothered with such delicacy; Audrey was plainly itching to fill in the details. All that had been required was a mutual exchange of intimacy.

'Sexual incompatibility,' she said with relish.

'Sorry?'

'Peter, in a rare moment of personal honesty, decided he was homosexual. After spending most of his life pretending to the world he had more camp than the boy scouts, he finally realised it was true. He left me for a management consultant called Adam who had a flat in Notting Hill and a line in coy sophistication. They met on an outward-bound management course in the Lake District. Something to do with sharing a one-man tent in the middle of a snow storm lit a spark which, so far as I know, is still burning to this day.' She smiled.

108

'Outward-bound. How appropriate.'

Beth gaped, her brain catching up slowly. 'Peter was *gay*?'

'Queer as a three-pound note, darling.'

'Good God . . . I suppose he always was a bit . . . How did you cope? What did his family think?'

'His family? Well, they went totally crazy-apeshit. Myself, I didn't give much of a toss; I was too busy realising I was gay too.'

Audrey gazed steadily at Beth while she spoke, enjoying watching her jaw slam into her lap. She had been looking forward to this moment all afternoon; the effect was almost as entertaining as when she had told her parents.

'*You*?' Beth gabbled. 'You're a . . .' She lowered her voice. 'A lesbian?'

Audrey smirked. 'There's no need to whisper; I shouldn't think we're being bugged. Actually, I'm more bi than gay. I still sleep with men. Hence the handiness of condoms.'

Beth stared at the floor, writhing in embarrassment. Audrey, a lesbian? It was inconceivable. 'How did you . . . you know, find out?'

Audrey tossed her cigarette end into the fire, where it ejaculated a little spurt of purple flame before wrinkling to black. She shrugged. 'Most people say they always knew, deep down, right from when they were children. Knew they were different. I had no idea. Although I suppose I've always gone for a certain kind of man – you know, something a bit feminine about them.'

'Like Peter.'

Audrey snorted. 'Not really. Peter had a contrived effeminacy; camp isn't the same thing as femininity. Underneath, he was as big and muscular as they come. No, Peter was just career advancement.'

'So how . . .?'

'I discovered completely by accident. It was the day after Peter had decided to lay his big gay revelation on me. We'd had a blazing row about it the night before, and I stormed out of the house the next morning without bothering to wake him up. It was on my mind all day at work; I was still running Red Garter then, and everything I read kept reminding me of it. We had some proofs to collate; a rush job for the next day. Marina – that was my assistant – Marina and I stayed late to finish it. It was pretty obvious I didn't have my mind on my work. Anyway, I was in no mood to go home to Peter, so we went for a drink. I told her all about it – God knows why, I'm not usually one for pouring out my troubles. She was well-known around Quintard as the firm's pet lesbian – not butch, though; strictly catwalk. Anyway, I suppose I thought she'd understand.' Audrey paused and smiled. 'Funny – I asked her the exact same question you just asked me: how did she discover she was gay? She said the question assumed that she'd unearthed her sexuality under a bush or something. 'How did *you* discover you were straight?' she asked me. 'How did you discover you had two legs and a head?' That made me think. Anyway, I still didn't fancy going home, so we went back to her flat and ended up drinking Bailey's until midnight. To this day, I don't quite understand how it happened, but one thing, as is one thing's wont, led to another . . . It was an eye-opener, I can tell you. You could say I did discover my sexuality under a bush.' She smirked. 'In a manner of speaking.'

'Did you ever . . .'

'Did I ever what?'

Beth wanted to ask: had she ever felt any attraction to women before, but it seemed such a crass question when what she had in mind was, had Audrey ever found *her* attractive; after all, they had shared a house for two years. In and out of each other's rooms, sharing a bathroom, seeing each other undressed or half-dressed. Thinking about all those times now, she felt a deep unease creep into her. She had never thought of herself as homophobic; it was just that she didn't like the idea of . . . well, being taken unawares. Being fancied when her fancy-defences were down.

'Nothing,' she said at last, hiding her shameful thoughts. 'It doesn't matter.' She looked at her watch. 'Had we better be getting ready for dinner?'

Knowing Salvador

1

Salvador sat on the Master's voluptuous blue sofa and gazed drowsily out at the sun-dappling willow boughs, criss-crossed from time to time by the colourful tops of passing punt poles. The sounds of the river – the watery clunks of poles hitting the hard bottom, the low boom of punts colliding, and the susurrus of shouts – drifted in under the half-raised sash.

His head still hurt. The tight bandages made it worse, but he didn't dare remove them in case his brain fell out. Secretly, he thought the bandages made him look a little bit heroic, the white band aslant across his brow; all it needed was a seep of blood at the temple and a gold-braided standard, and he would resemble the last man standing after a battle. But by God it hurt; a thick knot of throbbing that shot sharp arcs of pain up over the dome of his skull and into the sensitive places behind his eyes. He closed them, just listening to the soothing sounds, and waited for the Master.

That morning, the first after his night in the town, he had woken feeling as though his head had been hacked off with a cleaver, given several hours in a spin dryer at top speed, then clumsily glued back on. He wouldn't be setting foot outside his rooms for at least a fortnight. After swallowing a small palmful of aspirin, he felt just about well enough to try and have breakfast. A shambling exploration of the fridge and cupboards revealed the extent of his breakfast-making potential: no coffee, no tea, a pink carton with about half a cupful of deceased, sludgefied milk, and three slices of bread (including crusts) with spots of turquoise mould growing on it.

An hour later, his stomach griping with hunger, he was in a queue at Sainsbury's in Sidney Street with a basket of fresh groceries, ignoring the stares and glances that probed around his flamboyantly injured head. Returning to the college, he stopped at the Porter's Lodge and emptied out his pigeonhole. (*Bin in the wars ave we, sir?* Said Cyril, the head porter, causing several loitering undergraduates to turn and stare at him.) There were three envelopes. The first was from his mother, containing a cheque (still no letter). The second was from Classic Lotus Ltd of Newmarket, who were delighted to inform him that the 1964 Elan he had picked out six weeks ago in a delirium of temporarily moneyed self-indulgence had completed its restoration programme and road tests, and was ready for collection; subject to payment of an outstanding final balance of £6,479.49 inc. VAT. The letter did not induce quite the rush of excitement it would had it arrived a day earlier, but still his heart leapt up and leaked a trickle of adrenalin into his blood. The third envelope diluted it; it was unstamped and bore the college crest. He tore it open and found a small sheet of similarly crested notepaper.

Dear Salvador,
  Heard about your little contretemps last night.
  Would you care to pop up and see me? I shall be in the Lodge between 3
and 4 p.m. today.
  With regards,
  Mic. J.

His innards slumped. Behind this diminutive, disingenuously informal signature loomed the towering (in every sense of the word) figure of Sir Michael Jacobs, Master of Wolfburne. This was it. He couldn't claim not to have foreseen it. He would be stripped of his fellowship and ejected from the college. What would his mother say? She would certainly break her silence for something like this. And Uncle Valéry . . . Against this, the feeling of the little red Lotus slipping beyond his financial grasp seemed quite insignificant.

At four minutes to three, he crossed Monck's Court in the direction of the Master's Lodge. The defence cobbled together and rehearsed in his mind seemed to consist of little more than semi-hysterical protestations of innocence: he had been set upon by a vicious thug, his arrest had been a mistake. But whenever he came to the cause of his alleged attacker's injuries (he had been told about them, but hadn't seen them himself), he was at a loss. The police had told him virtually nothing: they locked him up, interviewed him briefly, locked him up again, then, with no word of explanation, released him. The only clear memory he had of the time between the man's fist laying him out and being loaded into a police van seemed like a dream: he had imagined that the girl from the back room of the Mitre – the beautiful thin girl with the thick

112

blonde pony-tail – was stooping over him, cradling his head in her hand, a look of deep concern in her eyes. He had mumbled incoherently at the vision, and she had smiled reassuringly at him; the warm, gorgeous smile he remembered from the pub . . .

At the Lodge, he was greeted by a housemaid in a blue nylon smock, who ushered him upstairs to the sitting room and brought him a cup of coffee and two chocolate digestives on a willow-pattern plate. The Master would be up soon, she said.

He looked disconsolately at his watch. It was twenty-five to four. He had drunk the coffee, eaten a biscuit, glanced at all the portraits of former masters, browsed the scatter of books and magazines on the vast coffee table, eaten the other biscuit, and reclined on the sofa with his eyes closed, trying to will the pain out of his skull.

Finally, at quarter to four, he heard a door open downstairs. There was a mixed mumbling of voices in the hall that went on for some minutes, then the sound of the front door closing, followed by brisk, heavy footfalls on the stairs.

'There you are!' boomed a voice from the open door, full of surprise, as though he had been hiding up here. Sir Michael was an immense man: six and a half feet tall and proportionately broad. He had a leonine head of silver-grey hair and a flat, slablike face that reminded Salvador of the stone heads on Easter Island. This afternoon, his alarming magnitude was accentuated by the broad black beetle-wings of academical dress. 'Am I late?' he asked, striding into the centre of the room and fanning Salvador – who had begun to rise to his feet – back into his seat. 'Are you being looked after?' He spotted the empty cup and plate, and stalked back to the door. Leaning out, he shouted: '*Belinda!* . . . *BELINDA!* . . . Ah, there you are. Fresh coffee, please, and two cups.' He came back into the room, hauling the voluminous gown off his shoulders and flinging it into a chair. 'Viva,' he explained. 'Doctoral candidate. She put forward one or two slightly attenuated interpretations of the foundation of Weimar, but I think we shall be recommending a pass.' He sat down heavily opposite Salvador and crossed his needlecord-barked tree-trunk legs. 'How's the old noggin?' he asked, peering at the bandage. 'All the King's horses and all the King's men, eh?'

'Oh, it's getting a little better.'

'Good, good . . . Now, the reas—'

'Master,' Salvador interrupted, pre-empting the preamble to his dismissal. He was sure the dismissal would be very polite and conducted with English cordiality, but he would prefer to get it over with as quickly as possible. 'Master, I—'

'Michael,' said the Master. 'Professor in the lecture room, Sir Michael in Whitehall, and Master in committee. You know, as dear as those honorifics may have been bought, I rather relish these rare occasions when I can sit in my favourite armchair in my sitting room and just be plain old Michael Jacobs again . . .' He smiled. 'Sorry, you were saying . . .?'

The man exuded bonhomie, but there was a distinctly bogus ring in his call for informality. Salvador preferred it if authority figures stuck by their authority instead of putting on this false matiness. '. . . Er,' he began, 'I was going to say that it wasn't my fault. The fight, that is. I was attacked, you see. The police released me without charge.' He leaned forward. 'Look, I can't afford to lose this fellowship. I've incurred certain . . . financial obligations. If I lose my stipend, I shall—'

The Master grunted urgently and held up a hand the size of a flag. 'Wait, wait, wait,' he barked. 'I feel you are about to dig yourself into a very eggy hole indeed. I have no wish to be privy to your private financial dealings, however shady and intriguing they may be.'

'They aren't *shady*. They're just—'

'Good! Tell me no more!' He rubbed his chin. 'Am I correct in inferring that you believe your position here to be in jeopardy because of your, ah, arrest?'

Salvador stared dumbly and nodded.

The Master laughed; a long, loud, rich rumble that vibrated the windows. 'Priceless!' he chuckled. 'It's quite delightful to meet someone who has seen so much of the world and yet remains so unworldly. Dear, dear Salvador; you would have to do rather worse evil than this to scupper a Wolfburne fellowship. Actually, I think you'll find yourself elevated a trifle in the fellows' esteem. Wolfburne has a somewhat egregious – though fundamentally honourable – tradition of street fighting. Oh, yes. It goes back to the Jesus Green Massacre of 1832. Thirty-seven of this college's undergraduates took on a gang of townsmen in a dispute over fishing rights. It took the combined proctors of Wolfburne, Magdalene, St John's and Sidney Sussex, plus a contingent of the local militia to break up the fight. Of course, the protagonists were rusticated for two terms – another college would probably have sent them down – but they began a tradition that has been tacitly admired throughout the University, and has been sustained by a pretty regular string of bruised knuckles, busted noses and broken jaws ever since. It's gone rather quiet lately, but I'm glad that at least one of our members is inclined to uphold it . . . You may not believe it to look at me now, but I made my own small contribution to the tradition when I was an undergraduate.'

114

Looking at the huge hands and imagining the steam-hammers that would result when they were bunched into fists, Salvador had no difficulty at all in believing it completely. Suddenly, he had found himself tossed abruptly from one tortuous corner to another: from protesting his innocence of any gratuitous involvement in disreputable brawling, to avoiding any embarrassing admission of the true, feeble extent of his involvement.

'Anyway,' the Master went on as the housemaid came in with a tray of coffee and more digestives, 'I didn't ask you here just to talk about punch-ups ... Thank you, Belinda ... My daughter is getting married in July, as you might have heard. The wedding will take place in the college chapel. Now, as you may be aware, Lady Jacobs, my wife, is a very great admirer of your playing. She has asked me to ask you if you would do us the honour of playing at the wedding.'

He walked back across Monck's Court feeling morally better than he had an hour earlier, but physically worse. The stress of the afternoon had added unimagined new aching layers to his scintillated cranium. Little multicoloured darts of pain flickered about at the rim of his vision, melting in and out of the band of deep purple haze that was growing there.

When he passed under the archway that connected Monck's Court and First Court and saw her standing there, outside the entrance to D staircase, he thought he was imagining her. When he came closer, walking in the shaded path around the fringe of the court, and she didn't fade away, didn't shimmer and vanish, he knew she was real.

Lydia watched as Rachel fussed with the bouquet of cornflowers and sweet-williams she had bought from the market (99p a bunch or £1.50 for two), picking off browned leaves and folding back the thick swaddle of damp paper. She smiled fondly. 'They're not going to get any better, you know. They need resuscitation, not arranging.'

Rachel looked at her, then back at the flowers. 'D'you think they're no good? It was all they had left.'

'They're lovely, Rachel, but they'll be dead if they don't get in some water soon.'

Rachel nodded glumly. 'Look, I'm going to go up and knock again. He might be in. He might not have heard.'

'Okay.'

'Will you hold them?'

Lydia accepted the soggy bundle, surprised at how heavy it was, and cradled it in her arms, holding it away from the front of her shirt like a baby with a full nappy. Rachel was sweet. She had rescued this man from a beating, and now she was bringing him presents. *He* ought to be bringing *her* flowers. If they had known how long they would be standing here, they could have waited for Beth and Audrey to get back from their lecture and brought them along. They would have leapt at it; they fancied the pants off him, although Lydia couldn't quite see why. He was pretty enough, but . . . well, just *but*. Poor Rachel. She obviously saw him in a silvery aura of innocent, childlike hero-worship. Maybe it was just as well they had come alone; Rachel wouldn't get a look-in if Beth and Audrey were there.

. . . If he ever showed up. She looked again at the trickle of people coming in through the gatehouse, but he wasn't among them. She was about to call up to Rachel and suggest that they call it a day when she sensed that someone was coming up behind her.

'Hello,' said a soft voice.

She turned round, and almost dropped the bouquet in alarm at the sight of him; he had come so closely so quietly, and his bruised face was dreadfully pallid below the swathe of bandage.

'*There* you are,' she said, recovering her breath quickly and laughing to cover her shock. He gazed blankly down at her. 'Oh, sorry,' she said, beginning to gabble. 'Lydia Hutton, I'm a friend of Rachel's, we sort of met last night, but you could hardly say we were properly intro-duced . . .' She adjusted her grip on the flowers and, after wiping her damp hand on her jeans, held it out to him.

He took her hand and gripped it lightly. 'Lydia,' he murmured. He held on for a long time, looking unfocused.

'Yes,' she said. 'Lydia . . . Oh, what am I doing? These are for you.'

Her hand wriggled out of his, and she held out the flowers. He blinked at them for a few moments, then took them. At last, he smiled. 'You were there,' he said, looking at her face. 'I saw you. You saved me.'

'Well, sort of. Actually, it was Rachel who saw him off, we couldn't believe our eyes.' She leaned in through the entrance. '*Rachel!*' she called. '*Rachel! He's here!*'

Rachel. *That* was it. There was a patter of quick feet on the stone steps, and Rachel appeared. Her Superwoman transformation hadn't lasted long; as soon as she saw him, she began to go pink and mute.

'Hello, Rachel,' he said. 'Are you . . . all . . .' His voice fell away to an incoherent mumble; his eyes dulled and deadened, and he staggered on buckling legs. The bouquet fell from his fingers and hit the ground with a wet thump.

Lydia jumped forward and threw an arm round him. 'Rachel, help!' she gasped, struggling to support his slackening weight.

He wasn't heavy, and between the two of them they managed to help him up the stairs to his rooms. They laid him on a sofa, and

Lydia watched over him while Rachel ran to call a doctor. She sat beside him on a footstool and held his hand. What rough hands they seemed; quite out of keeping with his long, slim body. Not as she (like Beth before her) would have imagined musician's hands. The fingers were thick and blunt, with calloused tips. Even limp, they hinted at tremendous strength. At first, he lay worryingly still, making tiny squeaking noises in his throat. But as she watched, his eyelids began to flicker open and showed signs of focusing, and his breathing gradually steadied. His fingers squeezed her hand. They *were* strong; but gentle.

'Still in there, are you?' she asked, and he smiled.

He raised himself up a little on the cushions, so that he could look around. He peered at the room: at the walls, the furniture, his guitars, but kept returning to Lydia's face.

'Who are you?' he whispered.

Oh dear . . . 'I'm Lydia,' she said patiently, squeezing his hand. 'Rachel's friend.'

He smiled again. 'I know you're Lydia,' he said. 'But who are you? Why do you keep coming into my sight?'

'I don't know. Why do you keep keeling over in front of me?'

His eyes narrowed, peering up at her. 'You're the most . . . You're beautiful, like an angel.'

She snorted. 'And you're delirious.'

'Maybe. I don't think so.'

His voice was like his fingers; strong, slightly coarse, but gentle. There was hardly a trace of an accent; perhaps a slight hint of French heightening the vowels.

'You speak English very well,' she remarked, feeling foolish even as she said it.

He smiled. 'I hope so. I started learning when I was six. I learned Italian, as the language of music, Spanish, as the language of the guitar and my ancestors, and English as the language that crosses all borders. And German, for no reason that I can recall.' He looked at her. 'Do you want to hear a story?' He smiled, and closed his eyes for a moment. 'When I was thirteen,' he said, opening them again, 'I played a season of summer concerts with the Nordische Ensemble in Salzburg. I remember it especially because it was the first time I had spent any length of time out of my mother's supervision.' He smiled. 'I was very closely guarded.'

'You shouldn't talk,' she said, but without conviction. Part of her was concerned that he shouldn't tire himself, nor pay her any more startling and misguided compliments. But there was another part of her – the hungry part that hoarded all those flimsy little rectangles clipped from the world – that had been snagged by the mention of Salzburg.

'It's only a little story.' He closed his eyes again, concentrating on the memory. 'We were given a week's holiday, and the orchestra manager – his name was Dietrich, and he was also the ensemble's oboe player – took me and some of the ensemble members to stay at his house in the Alps. It was the most beautiful place you ever saw; perched on top of a forested scarp at the mouth of a great rocky gorge. Every evening before sunset, while the women teased me and the men tried to get me to drink schnapps and kir, Dietrich would take his oboe and go down the hill to practise in the open air. One evening, there was a telephone call for him – an urgent call – and I was sent to fetch him. As I walked down the slope, I thought I could hear a whispering in the trees; faint and musical, floating in the air. Every time I thought I had hold of it, it vanished. When I got to the mouth of the gorge, the sound was submerged by the noise of the rushing river. The water was foaming and ice-green and ice-cold. It was melt-water from the snow higher up the mountain; it would freeze you to death in a minute if you fell in, and it cooled the air in the gorge as it passed. There was no sign of Dietrich, so I began to walk along the footpath that followed the river into the gorge. As I walked the musical sound returned. It was fuller now, with discernible notes and echoes of notes that danced in and out of the gaps in the noise of the water. It made your spine shiver to hear it. As I walked further, the music became louder, but its echoes shifted and leapt over the rock walls so that you couldn't tell where it came from. It seemed to surround you: one moment ahead, the next above the far side of the river, the very next right behind you, and all the while haunting and beautiful.' His closed eyelids squeezed tighter for a moment, as though holding back tears, but then he opened them and looked at her. 'I remembered that just now. You made me think about it. Your face, to me, is just like the sound of that music.'

As they cycled side by side across Parker's Piece, Lydia barely listened to Rachel's prattling about the likely efficacy or insufficiency of the doctor's verdict (a prescription for painkillers and an order to rest); Rachel's voice went *mwah blarble mwah mwah blah* beside her and the bicycle wheels hissed on the tarmac; everything else was just fuzz. Nearing the far corner of the park, she almost mowed down a pushchair containing twin toddlers – only Rachel's warning shriek and the young mother's dextrous steering prevented their transformation into toddler pâté with tangled pushchair and bicycle garnish – and still she didn't quite come out of herself. She was elsewhere, thinking about an Alpine gorge and the haunting, limpid notes of an oboe tripping and slipping among the evening rocks and trees.

That evening, she confided his words to Beth. (Rachel had gone to bed early, tired out by all the excitement, and Audrey was out, supposedly spinning her web of enticement for Peter Quintard.) Beth listened and said nothing, but she smiled and sighed in all the right places. When asked, she said No, he didn't sound as though he was delirious or gibbering, and Yes, it was perfectly believable that someone might feel that about someone like Lydia, and Wasn't it ironic that when at last it happened – a bruised, beautiful man with his bruised, beautiful words – it had to come without any reciprocal attraction.

Lydia half-smiled at that, remembering her dismissive, perfunctory verdict, and wondered aloud to Beth whether she had been too harsh. Privately, she wondered if she had just said it as an evasion, a deflection. She wasn't going to stick her fingers in the trap again only to have them sliced off.

She decided to wait and see.

Thinks

A late bath, water foaming, steam dripping on the puckered glass behind the drawn blind. Staring at the ribbed curl of the shower hose and the ribbed curl of toes resting between the taps.

Every day beyond the front door is a gauntlet-run of looks. Looks that glance, gaze, stare. She is conscious of them all the time: glances that zing harmlessly off her armour, stares and gazes that grope, fondle and penetrate. And each of them has the same clammy-fingered morbidity. Never interest, never fondness, love or even, God forbid, eroticism. Just prurient curiosity, like looking into the innards of a rotting corpse; dirty and hostile, sometimes fearful; waiting for her to return the look, shy away; and then to pounce. The looks are sometimes furtive, but never secret or veiled; always bold with the strength of invulnerability. Her hide has grown thick and calloused, like overworked fingertips, but not yet thick enough. It can never be thick enough.

She knows that others feel this way. Beth for instance. But Beth sometimes receives looks she likes: gazes and glances that are invited, enticed and welcomed; good gazes. Audrey, Beth has said privately, welcomes all looks from all sources; feeds on them like life-supporting nourishment. So Beth says. Never fears the predation, because she is the greater predator. If the looks ever dry up, Audrey will probably enter a twilight; she will probably go about naked, wearing signs saying

119

PAY ATTENTION. HERE ARE MY TITS, HERE IS MY ARSE, THIGHS HERE . . . That's what Beth says. But Lydia knows better; Lydia knows a secret about Audrey that nobody else knows; even Audrey doesn't know she knows it.

She discovered it in Smith's, by the magazine racks. She wasn't surprised to see her there; Audrey is the only one in the house who is a regular magazine reader. Glossies, that none of the others can afford to buy. But something in her posture – something secretive – and the look of apprehensive concentration as she examined an article, made Lydia hold back and hide. After Audrey had gone off to buy the magazine, Lydia sneaked over to the shelf and picked out another copy. It was *Company*. Audrey took *Elle*, sometimes *Vogue*, and occasionally slummed it with *Marie Claire*. *Cosmopolitan* was simply too low-rent, while *Company* was absolutely beyond the pale. What had made her look at it; buy it, even? Lydia looked at the cover stories. IS YOUR MAN A LOVE-CHEAT? 10 WAYS TO TELL . . . Hmmm, unlikely . . . GETTING IT RIGHT IN BED . . . Hardly . . . ARE YOU A CRYPTO-LESBIAN? . . . Very improbable . . . ABORTION: WE DISCUSS THE ISSUES . . . Finally, YOU ARE SEXY: WE TELL YOU THE 20 SECRETS OF FEELING GOOD ABOUT YOUR LOOKS.

As the months passed, and Audrey showed no sign of being pregnant, cheated-on or a crypto-lesbian, Lydia came to realise that her seamless, boundless confidence, like her clothes and hair, was drawn from the glossy pages of magazines . . .

Water growing tepid, soap-slick eating away the banks of foam. *You're beautiful*, his voice says in her head. She tries to recall what an oboe sounds like, but all she can conjure up is a clarinet. She cloaks it in rocks and pine-blanketed mountain slopes far away, and she can understand why it maintains such a grip in his memory, among all the sights he must have seen. She recalls his look, and compares it with all the others. His eyes bright and lazy with delirium. Something different there, something weak and plaintive. And his words. Seeing that sound in her face.

She yanks the plug out by its chain and stands up, reaching for a towel, humming a little tune.

Imagines

The chalk-dry bullet sticks like glue to his tongue and soft palate, secreting a hint of bitterness. He tosses back half a tumbler of water, sluicing away the pill, but not the taste, which lingers insolubly in the back of his mouth.

What is she doing now? What is she thinking? What *did* she think?

She didn't react much: paused, hesitated, smiled politely. Withdrew her hand from his. He apologised for offending her, she told him not to, said it was a nice story.

A nice story. She will never, if he has anything to do with it, find out how *nice* a story it was. He thinks of his long, deep memory as an ocean; plumbable, explorable. Some memories, though, are piled up so high that they jut permanently above the blue surface; stone-hard, immovable islands and part-inundated atolls. That evening in the gorge is one. There is a terrible, haunting beauty in it... His message was urgent, so he marched on through the gorge, pausing at intervals to listen to the sound. He was definitely getting closer. Then, just as it seemed to be echoing right inside his skull and up and down his tingling spine, it stopped. He turned a corner, and halted. There was Dietrich; he was standing against the fading light, high on an outcrop of rock. One arm held his oboe aloft, the other was crooked, pointing at the side of his head. There was something small and black held there. Salvador stood, entranced; the silhouette man seemed unreal; even when the shot kicked out and bounced *crack-ack-ack-ack* around the gorge, he didn't move a muscle. Only when the oboe came tumbling down the slope and landed at his feet did he come to his senses. Dietrich crumpled, twisted and fell sideways. Salvador's cry of horror was swamped by the crashing of the ice-green water as it received the falling body.

Why *that* memory?

She's probably asleep by now, as I should be. To sleep, to dream of her. He wonders if she is dreaming of him, but thinks it somehow unlikely. She must be so used to such attentions; these little promissory avowals of love. Must receive them all the time, and from men stronger than him, men with unbandaged, unbruised heads who didn't collapse like wilted flowers in front of her.

His head thumps more painfully than ever as the blood of shame rushes upwards to his neck and face at the memory.

He only has one thing to offer, only one thing of value. He swallows another pill and, despite the pain, sits down on his sofa with the light, slender Torres cradled in his lap. He begins carving hesitant chords on the fingerboard, enticing them gently out of the strings. He thinks about her name, and has an idea. The scales and chord-shapes evolve and out of them grows a melody, which develops into a passage, which grows variation and counterpoint until it becomes music, whole and rounded and new.

And the pain has gone away, soothed out of his nerves by the concerted forces of pills and rippled strings. He plays the short piece again and again, modifying a chord here, adding a triplet there, until he is sure that every note is engraved in his fingertips' memory. Only then does he go to bed, where he sleeps deeply and dreams long dreams of quiet.

2

Lydia scurried down the stairs, drawn by the sound of the letterbox flap clattering and the soft, fluttering thuds of post flopping onto the doormat. She scooped up the items and stood in the hall, sorting them. They were all for her. There were two postcards from Gabriel – Alice Springs and Ayers Rock – a glossy envelope she didn't need to open because its invitation to apply for a Barclaycard was printed on the outside, and lastly – oddly – a large, board-backed manila envelope with *Please do not bend* printed in bold red letters on the front. She frowned at it; her name and address were written in an upright, elegant hand with graceful curves and subtle curlicues.

She took it through to the sitting room and sat down on the sofa. Rachel was there, cleaning her flute. She had spread a duster on the carpet in front of the fireplace, and the flute's dismantled silver sections were laid out on it like museum bones. She looked up as Lydia came in, smiled, and went back to rubbing the flute's mouthpiece with silver polish.

Lydia set aside her postcards and peeled back the flap of the stiff envelope. She inserted two fingers and drew out the contents: three leaves of thick, ivory-coloured paper. Sheet music. The complex notation was neatly hand-drawn with a fine-nib pen in night-dark black ink. It was beautiful to look at, but completely meaningless to her. Written at the top of the first sheet in fine strokes of the same black ink were the words *Prélude. Evening Whispers Echoed.* Below that: *by Salvador de La Simarde*. She frowned at it. Why on earth should he send her unintelligible sheet music?

Nearly three weeks had passed since the fracas in Market Street and the hot, confusing afternoon that followed it; three weeks in which everything had seemed to return to normality: the perpetual cycle of lectures, essays, tutorials, revision, and more lectures. Rachel had gone back to see him regularly (accompanied on a few occasions by curious, lust-struck Beth and Audrey) and came back with reports of his improving health, which Lydia received with modulated and slightly abstracted gratification. She had also reported, in sly confidence, that he always asked after Lydia and wanted to know why she never came to visit. He had a gift for her, he said, but would say no more. Lydia suggested to Rachel that it mightn't be such a wise idea for under-graduates to cultivate friendship with a college fellow. Mightn't there be some rule against it?

The truth was she had never been back to visit him because she was afraid to. She had thought often about what he had said to her that afternoon, and was disturbed by her reaction to it – a yearning to hear it again, and to hear more. With him, she had felt she was closer than she had ever been to the exhilarating otherness of the wide world, and he had a way of speaking its otherness (or perhaps she had a way of hearing it from his lips) that brought it to her more vividly than all the postcards and books ever printed and all the television programmes ever filmed. If she saw him again, she knew she would want him and his exotic worldliness to be her own. And what chance did she stand? She had been burnt once by Stephen; with Beth and Audrey eyeing Salvador seductively from the sidelines, she would surely be edged off the stage into the pit yet again. She couldn't compete with them. It was possible – probable, no, virtually certain – that Beth would back off and allow her a clear run, but Audrey wouldn't.

She turned over the heavy leaves of paper and gazed at the notes: some bare and isolated, others clustered or stacked, tied together with beams and arcs. She wished she could read it. She understood the title: Evening Whispers Echoed; but that was all. She listened for sounds from the kitchen, but it was silent. The others must be out or shut away with their work. 'Rachel,' she said. 'Can you make any sense of this?'

Rachel, who had been watching her surreptitiously, put down the mouthpiece, wiped the traces of polish from her fingers, and took the top sheet of the expensive-looking paper, holding it carefully by its edges. She glanced over it. 'His gift!' she exclaimed. 'This is it! He's composed you a piece of music!'

'But I can't read it,' said Lydia plaintively, feeling churlish and ungrateful even as she said it; that whether she could decipher the code might not be the point. She had watched delight unfold like a flag in Rachel's face, and looked for a stripe, a star, a single thread of jealousy; but there was none. Even so, she thought it best to include Rachel in the gift; let Salvador speak through her. 'What do you make of it?' she asked. 'Is it good?'

Rachel's eyes ran quickly over the notes. 'Well, it's a solo piece. Polyphonic – presumably for guitar . . .' She was silent for a few moments, aside from intermittent, soft little sing-song hums in her throat. 'Seems like a nice tune,' she said after a while. 'I can't really tell without hearing it properly. I don't quite have that gift. I can read a piece like this off the page and get the gist, but I can't really hear it the way some people can.' She frowned at the sheet, eyes darting back and forth, then a sudden beam of delight flooded out of her face. 'Oh, that's *lovely!*' she said. 'That's so sweet, and so clever!'

'What is?'

Rachel jumped up from the hearth rug and sat beside Lydia on the sofa. 'See this?' she said, pointing a stained finger at two little hash marks at the beginning of the first pair of coupled staves. 'At first glance, that ought to mean it's in the key of G-major,' Rachel explained. 'But it's not. See these chords—' She pointed to several places on the page where notes were stacked up; three, four or five little ovals at a time piled on top of each other. '—You can seek out the tonic, dominant and sub-dominant by the way they're linked. This is the tonic here – the keynote chord, if you like – and it's a C.'

Lydia waited. 'Which means . . .?'

'It means it's modal. Modes are evolved from ancient Greek scales. You have a scale like a normal scale, but the keynote is shifted, so it has a different sound, a different . . . well, flavour.' She tapped the sheet of paper and chuckled with delight. 'This is in the Lydian mode. The *Lydian!* Isn't that lovely?'

Lydia smiled, but not with the delight that Rachel seemed to expect her to feel. She gazed at the myriad black marks on the paper and wondered at the hours of laborious care that must have gone into marking them – every tiny, perfect oval, blacked-in or hollow, every curve and line and whisker immaculate and regular. All those hours, all that tense curation. She imagined she repeated dips of nib into ink, and the false starts smirched and blotted and discarded. All those other hours, the hours that had gone into its composition, were closed to her, and she wished she could appreciate the thing more deeply than as merely a beautiful but meaningless pattern of jet-black marks on ivory paper.

'Will you play it for me?' she asked.

Rachel looked doubtful. 'I don't know . . .'

'You *can* play it, surely? I mean, it doesn't look that difficult.'

'Well, it's for guitar – I can't play the chords and stuff on the flute . . . Anyway, that's not the point. He'll want to play it for you himself, I'm sure.'

Lydia munched her lips in frustration at the tantalising, inaudible dots. 'I want to hear it now,' she said.

Rachel hesitated. 'Well, okay, I'll have a go. But I can't do it justice. Don't be disappointed if it doesn't sound too good.'

She rubbed off the last of the polish and reassembled her flute, slotting the sections into each other and testing the action of the keys. Then, with the music propped up on the mantelpiece, she set her lips to the mouthpiece. 'I'll do what I can with the chords,' she said, lowering the instrument for a moment and skimming the page one last time.

'Okay.'

As the first low, sibilant note hummed from the flute, Lydia sat back and closed her eyes. The first note, sustained a moment, tripped suddenly down the scale; before hitting bottom, it climbed back up in short, trilling leaps. By the end of the second bar, she found herself in the gorge, listening to distant notes echoing.

Rachel stumbled at the bottom of the page, caught in a tangle of difficult chords. She paused and went back, picking her way through, finding improvised monophonic handles on each stack of notes; the bare, rocky vertebrae of the structure. She didn't stumble again; finding a logic in the chord sequences, she tip-toed through them on the teetering moment as they occurred.

Lydia heard the suggested chords in her head; they rang out in the gorge, bursting round her like crashing water, with the melody weaving between them like a ribbon path . . .

Hears

The tune repeats, circles back, then leaps onwards to a coda and ends in a welter of chords that skip up the fretboard then wind their way rapidly back down and die away in a chorded, ringing harmonic.

. . . She keeps her eyes closed until the last subliminal vibration has faded away to silence, then opens them. He seems far away, lost, eyes still closed, hearing the perfect silence, cradling the hollow, musical wood.

At last, he looks at her; shy. 'What do you think?' he asks.

What *does* she think? That she is on the brink of the gorge, about to fall and be swept away in the boiling green water?

'Play it again,' she says.

This time, she keeps her eyes open; watchful, gaze kept on the brink; not so that she might keep herself from falling (it is too late and too inevitable to be staved off), but so that she might see herself fall, keep track of when it happened. How it happened. To *whom* it happened? She watches his fingers grip and press and pluck and stroke the image into her head; she watches his face pushing the fingers into their graceful, tortuous, killing forms; a little frown, lips pushed forward then retreating and bunching, parting, cheek muscles tightening over bone cliffs and hollowing, eyebrows inching together and rising like meeting waves, eyelids opening and closing, drooping drowsily.

In the silence after, he asks again. 'What do you think?' Tentative, anxious. This is for her. This *is* her, in his head.

She doesn't reply in words. She rises from her chair and crosses the room; such a small space, and yet it seems such a long walk, tense with imagining. His fingers rest on the taut, mute strings, and her fingers reach out and rest on his.

Her price. A hundred hours of joyful toil. Her recompense. A question.

Later, she said: 'Tell me about New York.'

'What about it?'

'Everything about it.'

And every occasion after; *Tell me* . . . He told her everything there was to tell, but she never seemed quite satisfied. There was always more.

The Poem

My friend told me this story.

She was on a train, going home to Wales. At some point in the journey, she found herself sitting opposite a handsome older man who had a line in shy charm and easy conversation. Before she knew it, she was drawn into his sweet web, enthralled and flattered by his words. As the train left Bath, however, he fell silent and began writing in a small notebook. One just like this.

'What are you writing?' she asked.

'Oh, just thoughts,' he replied.

She left him to concentrate on his thoughts, noticing that, as he wrote, he glanced up from time to time and smiled shyly at her.

He got off the train at Bristol. As he stood up, gathering his belongings, he hesitated. Appearing to come to a decision, he tore a page out of his notebook.

'I wouldn't normally do this, but . . .' And, blushing scarlet, he folded the page and put it in her hand. Then he turned away and was gone.

Intrigued, she opened the page. Inside was a poem. It was titled with her name, and rhapsodised about how the many facets of her beauty had smitten his heart. It wasn't the first poem she had had written about her (her father had been a poet), but she was enraptured. Also near heartbroken that she would never see him again. She read the poem over and over; so intently that she almost missed her stop.

It wasn't until she arrived home that she noticed the phone number written on the back. In the midst of the welter of harmonious chimes ringing in her head, there was a sudden, dissonant clang.

She read the poem again.

And again. Her literary faculties began kicking into gear.

. . . He was eclectic, she'd give him that. She identified phrases and images from Yeats, Shelley, and even Pope. What was more, she realised that the phonic structure allowed the physical descriptive details of the poem's object to be tailored quite easily to meet any case. *Dark* could become *gold*, *ebony* could become *silver*, *before me* could become *beside me* . . . and so on, throughout the four short stanzas. Any combination, and no disruption of the rhythm or even the rhyme.

Git.

She looked at the number again, considered for a moment, then went to the phone.

Rarely in her life did she ever derive such satisfaction from a simple phone call.

There was more talk than food. Madame de La Simarde, Audrey observed later, didn't just hold forth; she held fifth, sixth, seventh and eighth. Had there been printed menus that night, they might have looked something like this:

9 p.m.
Dinner

Aperitif
(Pineau rouge)
Tour of recent family portraits

Entrée
(Mushroom bisque)
The Simarde dynasty: an introduction
The Last Marquis & The Revolution

Main course
(Roast pheasant with seasonal vegetables)
Philippe-France de La Simarde: Soldier of the Empire

Dessert
(Tarte Tatin – Lydia's favourite)
Salvador: A Gift from God

Coffee
(Viciously strong in thimble-size cups of paper-thin porcelain)
Vague metaphysical ramblings on Resurrection and Providence

12 a.m.
To bed, with leadenly laden stomach and head buzzing with caffeine and a
daunting web of ancestral history

The two guests kept quiet most of the time, letting their hostess do
nearly all the talking (as though they had any choice). Audrey
prompted from time to time with polite questions.

During a pause between courses, Madame de La Simarde deviated
temporarily from her own family's heritage and delved into that of her
servants. 'Février,' she said, looking at her manservant with an expression that could almost pass for fondness, 'has a *very* intriguing history.
Is that not true, Février?'

Février was busy clearing away the remains of the soup course. Beth
thought she saw the servant's impassive mask slip for a moment. He
was leaning down beside her to take away her half-empty bowl, and she
noticed his jaw slacken ever so slightly; there was a momentary catch in
his breathing, and the bowl clattered maladroitly against the neat row
of silver cutlery. He recovered quickly, scooping up the bowl and
laying it in the crook of his elbow alongside the others he had
gathered.

He inclined his head deferentially. 'If you say so, Madame.'

'I do say so. Tell the young ladies about your siblings.'

'My . . .? Ah, yes. Of course, Madame.' He turned to address the
guests. 'We were all named after months of the year. I had brothers
called Janvier and Mars, and my sisters were Avril, Mai, Juin and Juillet.
Mai and Juin died as infants. Mars and Juillet were *Maquis* – resisters –
in the War and were killed. My elder brother Janvier went into the
family business and died in the line of work. Avril and I are the last of
our family.'

'As I am of mine,' said Madame de La Simarde. 'Février's "family
business", as he is pleased to call it, was at least as notable as his
parents' eccentric choice of names for their offspring. Février comes
from the Île de Ré and a long line of wreckers.'

'Wreckers?' said Audrey, glancing up at Février and picturing a yard
full of deceased cars.

'Wreckers,' repeated Madame de La Simarde. '*Naufrageurs*. Under
French law, you see, people dwelling on the coast were entitled to a
share in any flotsam washed up on their stretch of shoreline after a

shipwreck. Some enterprising families took this legal right to its logical limit and pursued it as a trade. The Île de Ré was particularly notorious for its *naufrageurs*, who used all manner of cunning tricks with lanterns and such to lure ships onto the rocks. Some grew quite rich on the spoils they gathered.'

'Many paid a high price for their riches,' said Février. 'It was a perilous trade, and honourable for its danger.'

He set the dirty dishes on a sideboard, from where Avril collected them and took them away, returning with the main course, which Février proceeded to serve. Meanwhile, Madame resumed her lecture on the history of the Simardes, moving on to the foundation of the Devon estate. It had been designed and built by Philippe-France de La Simarde after the Napoleonic Wars, as an exact replica of the original at Gondecourt. Philippe-France had been a colonel in Napoleon's army, captured by the British in Spain and incarcerated as a parole prisoner on an estate near the new Dartmoor prison. He fell in love simultaneously with the county and the daughter of the British Trade Minister, who was both lord of the manor and Philippe-France's extremely hospitable gaoler. After the war, Philippe-France married his lover and bought a tract of land next door to his former prison. There he set about recreating the exact twin of his ancient family estate. A fortunate project, since the original burnt down a few years after final completion of the replica. Since then, the Gondecourt estate had been re-centred on a smaller mansion built in the style of a château.

Audrey only half-listened to this story. Beth noticed that she spent most of the remainder of dinner gazing at Février with a thoughtful expression on her face. Probably thinking about the wreckers of the Île de Whatsit and wondering if there was a programme in it. Audrey had never been one to let an opportunity pass by unscrutinised, and Beth could almost hear her calculating brain ticking over and her antennae twitching. She sat up and paid attention, though, when Madame de La Simarde returned to the passing of the final generation and speculated on the future of the family estates.

'Poor Lydia,' Audrey murmured. 'The tragedy is, out of the four of us, I always thought she'd be the most perfect mother.' She smiled. 'After Beth here, of course.'

Beth looked sharply at her. *Was* it possible she had some notion of what she was saying? She couldn't, surely; she hadn't been there.

'Did they try to have children?' Audrey asked.

Madame de La Simarde fixed a softened gaze on Beth, as though recognising the look she had given Audrey. 'Of course,' she said. 'What married couple with such a responsibility to posterity would not? Unfortunately, my son made a ... I hesitate to say it ... an unhappy choice of wife in that regard. My daughter-in-law proved to be barren. Infertile, as one says today.'

'Oh,' said Audrey, looking down at her plate. 'I see.'

'I have not given up hope, however,' said Madame de La Simarde. She directed a little conciliatory smile at Beth. 'Oh yes, hope and prayer may serve in those rare times when determination fails. They have served me well in the past, and they may do so again. Where my strength of will did not suffice, prayer brought back my Salvador, resurrected. It has happened once before, and I pray that we might yet receive salvation before I am dead and it is too late.'

Audrey and Beth exchanged glances across the table.

'Salvador resurrected?' said Audrey doubtfully, unsure whether she had heard right.

Madame de La Simarde gazed proudly, defiantly (and stone-cold soberly) back at her. 'Indeed,' she said. 'Some may choose to call it by another name, but I know it was resurrection. He went away from me,' she added, even more confusingly, 'but he came back on the wings of an angel . . . I see your looks, both of you. You think I am old and mad and rambling. You are young yet; what have you seen of life or death or the unguessed will that lies behind them? This family is ancient beyond your comprehension. Do not imagine it has survived the turmoil of centuries by accident. It is favoured by Providence and buttressed by the supreme will of Man. The will has not expired, and Providence may yet resume its title and provide . . . We shall see, we shall see . . .'

There are times when the pleasure of being out in the world is so intense that I yearn to be home.

Losing Salvador

1

It was one of those times. With him, it was always one of those times.

The engine roared and whirred. Behind their heads, the cathedral tower dipped below the shallow horizon. The fenland wind whipping over the windscreen tugged at Lydia's hair, working its fingers into the roots and drawing it out behind like winnowing porpoise tails. It tugged also at Salvador's curls, combing them back and tickling the fresh pink scar tissue on the back of his skull.

He was healed and whole. Over a month had passed since the Market Street fracas; Lydia had brought about the last phase of his rehabilitation, and the Lotus marked its completion.

He had walked whistling into the Porter's Lodge that morning to find another letter from Classic Lotus. They respectfully reminded him that his car was ready for collection, and they mentioned again the payment outstanding. If he had decided not to have the car, would he be so kind as to inform them, in which case they would refund some of the money he had already paid and find another buyer. He rushed immediately to the nearest phone and made two calls: one, anxious, to Classic Lotus, and another, teasing and evasive, to Lydia, asking her to meet him at Drummer Street bus station in an hour.

The Elan was waiting when they got to Newmarket: a flame-red scarab with a sleek, ribbed ivory knapsack on its back, pulled up to the kerb outside the showroom between a plum-coloured Europa and a banana-yellow Super Seven. Salvador, incoherent with excitement, walked round and round it several times, stroking his fingers along its wings and bonnet, before opening its door reverently and sliding into the driver's seat to gaze in wonder at the ranks of chrome-bezelled dials and switches on the walnut dashboard. He switched on the ignition and turned over the engine, sighing rapturously as it burst open its throat and roared on the first spin of the starter. He sat hunched over the lacquered wheel, grinning like a child, and played with the switches; turning on the wipers, making the faired-in bug-eye headlamps go up and down. Then, with help from Lydia and the Classic Lotus manager, he undid the catches and folded down the ivory hood.

Eventually, reluctantly, he allowed himself to be led indoors (with many backward glances) to pay over what he owed. He waited impatiently while the paperwork was processed, then the keys were formally handed over, along with a facsimile of the 1964 Owner's Manual, a complimentary bottle of Turtle Wax polish and a valeting kit.

Lydia was waiting in the car, and he paused on the forecourt, gazing at her and the Lotus and grinning like an idiot. For once, he wished he had his glasses; he could scrub them to crystal clarity and look unblinking at this sight for all eternity. A month ago, it had seemed he was doomed to spend his life on an endless plateau of boredom, with his music as the only relief. Now, he could scarcely cope with the surfeit of happiness that throbbed inside him.

After a few moments, he came to; he tossed his free gifts into the boot and hopped into the driving seat, settling comfortably into the runkled black leather.

'Okay,' he said. 'Let's drive.'

He drove cautiously at first. The engine grumbled impatiently in low gear, but he guided the long, frighteningly vulnerable pill of glossy red glass-fibre warily through the streets of Newmarket, slowing to a crawl to pass between parked cars and oncoming traffic. Lorries, vans and even other cars seemed to tower with predatory malice over the low-slung Lotus, eyeing the perfection of its shining scarlet with malign envy.

Lydia teased him about his caution, and he laughed. 'It reminds me of when I first learned to drive,' he said, raising his voice above the juddering traffic. 'Only a lot more crowded. Février taught me at Gondecourt – first around the estate, then out on the roads.'

'Who's Février?' Lydia asked.

'An old family retainer, you might say. Sort of a manservant, you know? Bit of a genius with cars. He was the only person my mother would trust to teach me. She was nervous of letting her son and cars mix with each other. I suppose, after . . . Oh, which way?'

'Which way what?'

They were coming to a roundabout. Salvador pointed at the sign as they pulled up. 'Which way shall we go? The choice is yours.'

Lydia looked at the sign and considered the choices. It offered the

A45, either on to Bury St Edmunds or back to Cambridge, and the A142 to Ely. She frowned and tapped her fingers on her knees. 'Eeny, meeny, miney, mo—'

A horn parped behind them. 'Quick, choose!' he urged, glancing in the mirror at the impatient build-up of traffic.

'Ely,' she said at random. 'Straight on.'

Salvador gunned the engine and let in the clutch. The little car leapt forward like a hare, coursing round the roundabout with its engine screaming and hurtling off up the wide fenland road.

With the traffic left behind and none in front, Salvador gave the engine its head, sending it racing up through the gears, cycling from guttural roar to banshee wail and back again. Beside him, Lydia's heart raced with it as the fields and hedges whipped by, grey tarmac whirling into a blur less than two feet below her exposed shoulder. She looked across at him and saw a face lost in rapture.

Of course, she knew what he was up to; knew full well what was streaming through his unconscious; better than he did, probably. With his fingers gripping the wheel and gearstick, outstretched feet dancing lightly on the pedals, he was making love to her through the car; caressing her, gripping her, urging her and himself on, fucking her with a welter of spinning shafts and plunging, oil-drenched pistons. The Lotus was her embodied. She turned her face towards the fields and put her hand to her mouth, concealing her smile.

She could hardly blame him, after all; they had been seeing each other for over a week now. In secret; both afraid of what the College would make of their relationship, snatching every moment they could, cramming a month's worth of romance into eight days, and this, she realised now, was the closest they had come to sex. It wasn't that he didn't want it (he obviously did, but was too gentle to push or cajole), nor that she didn't; nor was she prudish or missish or even unusually sparing in giving herself up to pleasure. She had wanted him that very first day, when the notes of his playing were dying in the air; she stilled his fingers and kissed him, but that was all. Somehow it hadn't gone further; he had filled her up with his music, filled her up with his experience of the world outside her confining seas, but hadn't filled her up with himself. She hadn't let him do that; she hadn't been quite convinced by him, couldn't quite believe that such a strong avowal of love (or even of lust) could be so sharply focused on her. But then, just now, she had seen him looking at his new car, and saw in his face a look of childlike awe mingled with adult desire, and recognised in it the look he had worn when he looked at her that first day and every day since. Why had she not noticed it before? It was so obvious. Did she really harbour such loathing for herself that she was unable to filter out the slurry of unwanted, predatory, hostile, contemptuous looks and see the truth?

Tonight, she decided, tonight she would risk all and offer herself to him.

If they made it home in one piece. '*Slow down a bit*,' she shouted above the engine-roaring, wind-rushing noise as they passed a convoy of caravans and hurtled on past Soham. *Pleasure me slowly and long*, she thought.

He nodded and eased back to seventy-five, then seventy, then sixty-five, and settled in behind a silver Audi.

It was one of those times.

He pulled up outside an alley in Ainsworth Street and fiddled nervously with the gearstick while the engine idled. He was reluctant to leave her; the short hours till evening seemed unbearably long from this end. He should ask her.

'Thank you,' she said, as though he had given her a lift. She saw the look. 'It's not long. You've got things to do. You said.'

'I know. I don't want to do them. I want to be with you.'

She put a hand on his cheek and turned his face towards her; kissed him, holding his mouth a long time against hers. 'So do I,' she said.

'We could go away.' He flushed, and had no idea how inexpressibly charming his awkwardness was. 'For the weekend, I mean. To the seaside?'

She gazed at him for a long time, smiling. She forestalled his gabbling retraction by kissing him again. 'I'll bring my bucket and spade,' she said.

It was that easy. He would go off and pack a few things, and be back to collect her in an hour. She stood on the pavement and watched him roar away down the street, hand waving in the air, then turned and hurried away along the alley.

She might have lingered longer, waiting to watch him out of sight. She might have, if she had had any suspicion that it would be the last she would see of him.

2

'Thank you, Cyril. Ask her to wait. I shall be down directly.'

Cyril stared at the receiver as though it were a talking snake. He had been a porter at Wolfburne for nigh on twenty years, and he had never known the Master come down from his Lodge and meet a visitor at the gate. Except the Queen, of course, but that was different. The Master simply *never* came down.

'The Master will be down directly,' he said, half to himself.

The lady took it as though she expected nothing less. She gave a perfunctory nod and turned away from the counter. Cyril pretended to go back to sorting keys, keeping a discreet watch on her from behind the door of the key cupboard. She walked out of the Lodge (one of the few people, he noticed, who didn't have to duck under the low stone arch of the doorway) and stood in the great gatehouse passageway. She might only be small, Cyril supposed, but she had an imperious poise about her that made the Queen look like a charlady.

He had seen it all now: through the window, he could see across the quad to the entrance to Monck's Court. The Master didn't just come, he came hurrying as though he was late for an appointment. Cyril felt a pall of shame for the dignity of the College, mingled with an inbred, professional pang of gossipy curiosity; in the end, his shame was the greater, and he lost himself inside the great gatefold of the key cupboard so that he wouldn't have to see any more.

'Madame,' said the Master. 'It is an honour and a pleasure to meet you at last.'

'Master,' she said, and offered him her hand, palm down. To his surprise, he found himself taking it in his huge paw and bowing like a courtier to kiss the tiny olive knuckles.

'Welcome to Wolfburne College, Madame.' He hesitated. 'Can I offer you some refreshment? My Lodge is—'

'I have come to visit my son,' she said, 'but I cannot find him. I have been told that he has no classes today, and yet he is not in his rooms.'

'I see,' said Sir Michael. 'I take it he was expecting you?'

'No, he was not. Nevertheless, I had not imagined that he would be given to wandering away from the College like this.'

The Master smiled ingratiatingly. 'Madame, Cambridge colleges are no longer monastic institutions. Fellows and students are quite at liberty to come and go as they choose within the confines of their academic duties.'

Her dark eyes looked up at him, boring into him. 'Then it is a change for the worse. I hesitate to say this,' she said, and didn't hesitate at all: 'Your servants are most reprehensibly given to gossip.' She glanced back towards the Porter's Lodge. 'Now, I am aware that this is a malaise that afflicts all servants, of whatever class, but one must take steps to ensure that the habit of passing on tittle-tattle does not stretch to repeating it to visitors.'

Sir Michael frowned, and followed her glance. 'Tittle-tattle?' he repeated.

'When I inquired of your head porter concerning my son's whereabouts, his impudent assistant offered a remark from which one would infer that Salvador is out with a young girl.' She paused. 'An *undergraduate*. I seek your assurance as Master that this cannot be true.'

Sir Michael coughed discreetly into his fist. 'Well, Madame, I'm afraid I can neither confirm nor deny it. I have heard a *rumour* that Salvador has become friendly with a number of female undergraduates of this College. I'm sure it would all be above board. A platonic circle of disciples, if you will. Admirers. I had not received any intelligence that he was, er, *going out* with any particular one of them.'

'Then your porters evidently know better than you. The implications of that man's remark were quite unequivocal. My question to you is this: What action do you propose to take?'

'Action? Well, I suppose I could speak to him and ask him for the truth. But Madame—'

'If it is true, then I want it stopped. Do you not have rules about such behaviour?'

'Of course. Normally, a ... *liaison*, a relationship of the nature you describe between a fellow and an undergraduate would be a disciplinary matter, but in Salvador's case ... He has virtually no teaching duties, he is not a provider of pastoral care, nor does he have any influence upon the academic careers of our students. There is no potential for abuse, you see, so we would probably turn a blind eye so long as there were no complaint from the student.'

'*I* am complaining, Master. I repeat, I want this thing stopped.'

'Very well. Just as you wish.' Sir Michael was looking over her shoulder, towards the gates, as though seeking an escape route. 'Ah,' he said. 'Speak of the Devil and he appears. This is one of the young ladies in question. You can find out the truth for yourself.'

The last she saw of him.

Almost.

Lydia rushed about her room, disgorging the contents of her wardrobe and drawers onto the bed, wrestling shirts, skirts, trousers and dresses from their hangers and holding them up in front of the mirror. She gradually sorted them into a pile of Possibles and an untidy strew of No-Ways. She began to pick carefully through the Possibles once more, then gave up and just stuffed things at random into a bag, wadding them in with handfuls of underwear and her one and only swimsuit, two summers old and never yet worn.

She sat on the edge of the bed for a few minutes to collect her thoughts and her breath, then got up and went out onto the landing. She was the only one in, and the house hummed with the others' absence. Feeling as though she was being watched, she crept across the landing and slipped into Audrey's room. Compared with Lydia's and Beth's, it was immaculately neat; shoes lined up with regimental precision beneath a clothes rail filled with cellophane-sheathed garments arranged by colour; no stray sock-toes or bra-straps peeping from the closed drawers; no cultigens of fungi growing in old coffee cups by the ranked ring-binders on the desk. Lydia tip-toed over to the bedside table and opened the drawer. And surprise-surprise, there they were. Three packets, would you believe. She wouldn't miss just one.

She was too excited to wait in the sitting room, so she sat with her bag at the foot of the stairs, jiggling her nervous energy out through tapping toes. Through the panes of knobbled glass in the door, she would see his shape before he even got up the path; she would be on her feet and out of the door before he even knocked.

Excitement carried her through the first half-hour. Impatience got her through the next. Then a mixture of anxiety, disappointment and sinking inevitability set in and she lost track of time. She didn't see his shape through the door. Didn't get to it before he could knock, because he didn't knock. He just appeared there in the darkening hall; she raised her head from her cupped palms and there he was, looking at her.

'Where've you *been*?' she demanded. 'It's been *hours*.'

He didn't reply; just stood and looked. Then he turned away.

'Don't I get an explanation?' she asked. 'Salvador? *Salvador!*'

He turned back to her. He seemed about to speak when suddenly the door crashed inwards and obliterated him; it swung into his back and splintered his body into a million glittering sparks.

'*SALVADOR!*' she screamed. She leapt forward off the stairs and tried to throw her arms around his shadow, but he was gone; her fingers butted against the opening door, and she yelped in pain.

'Lydia! What's going on?' Beth stood on the threshold, door key in hand, looking in horror at the wailing Lydia. 'What's happened?'

Lydia sucked her fingers and stared in horror at Beth. 'He was here,' she said. 'Right there, where you're standing.'

'Who?'

'Salvador.'

'*Salvador?*'

Lydia nodded frantically, tears starting to trickle out of her eyes. 'He was supposed to come, and then he didn't, and then he just appeared and, and *vanished* . . . He was a *ghost*, Beth! Christ, something's happened to him.' She saw the speeding red Lotus in her mind. 'Oh God, he's dead, he's dead, he's—'

'Lydia!' Beth took hold of her shoulders and shook her. 'You're hysterical. Calm down. He's not dead – I saw him just now.'

'When?'

'I don't know. An hour or two. Tell me what's been going on.'

Lydia began to explain, increasingly incoherently, what had happened since that morning, and Beth gradually realised that she must have been sitting there on the stairs, getting more and more over-wrought and tired, for over three hours.

'What's happened to him, Beth? It's happened again, hasn't it? Why can't anything go right for me? Why do the bastards always dump me?'

Beth tried to lead her into the sitting room, but she wouldn't come, so they sat down together on the hall floor. 'I don't think he's dumped you,' she said. 'I think he got sidetracked.'

'*Side*tracked?'

'You'll never guess who showed up at Wolfburne this afternoon – his mother.'

Lydia frowned at the wall, trying to comprehend. 'Mother? . . . Why? He didn't say she was visiting.'

'I don't think he knew . . . You should've seen his face when he came through the gates and saw her there.'

'How do you know all this?'

Beth smiled. 'I made the mistake of being in the wrong place at the wrong time. Giant Jacobs was talking to her, and of course he recognised me and called me over . . . She gave me a right grilling, I can tell you. All about who I was and what I did and what my relationship with Salvador was.' She glanced at Lydia. 'I don't envy you,' she said. 'She's only about two feet tall, but she scared the living daylights out of me. One of those *No girl is good enough for my little boy* types. I'd avoid her if I were you.'

'So where is he now? Why hasn't he let me know?'

'He's probably in shock. Or being given a good caning by his mama, or both more than likely. The last I saw of them, they were going off towards his rooms, leaving poor old Jacobs looking like one of the Queen's corgis had just widdled on his shoes.' She patted Lydia on the knee. 'Shame about your weekend, though. I expect he'll be in touch once he's got rid of her. Like I said, you're best steering clear.'

Lydia followed Beth's advice; she lay low in the house for the whole of the following week. There was one tense moment on the Sunday morning, when Madame de La Simarde came to call. Beth answered the door to her and, despite her quavering heart, held her ground stoutly, claiming that Lydia was not at home and not expected back that day. In a sense, it was true. Lydia didn't seem quite at home all that week, spending most of her time lying on her bed or walking around the house in a daze. Then, at the end of the week, the rumours seeped through. Beth couldn't hold them back forever, and wasn't surprised when Audrey let slip the news of Salvador's disappearance.

The last anyone had seen of him, apparently, had been at Wednesday's Formal Hall, when he had sat with his mother, looking cowed; he was very quiet, and red about the eyes. Madame de La Simarde left the following day. Beth, Audrey and Rachel went to his rooms (ostensibly on Lydia's behalf, but driven more by their own curious agendas). He wasn't there; his oak was closed, and remained so the next day, and the next. They asked around, but nobody had seen him. One of the porters told them that the Lotus hadn't been seen in the Fellows' car park since Thursday.

The exams came and went. May Week came and went. The summer vacation came and set in. And still a part of Lydia waited for him to return. She didn't go home for the summer, because she had no home to go to. Every so often, she would traipse to New Court and look up at the blank windows of his rooms, wondering what had gone wrong.

October brought the new term, and there was still no sign of him returning. As the four women entered their final year, their workloads grew heavier, and Lydia began to forget the beautiful Salvador. She no longer went to look up at his rooms. She didn't go near the College if she could help it. Just as she had wondered where Salvador had gone (into the tooth-fairy oblivion of beings that had never really existed), her friends wondered where the Lydia they knew had gone, and cursed Salvador for stealing her away and leaving behind this lifeless husk.

THE DARK MIDDLE

In the dark middle, there was a dreamlessness; as she tracked the first angle of the night (how much: – a parsec, a quadrant, a segment?), she did so in the timeless, spaceless instantaneity of deep sleep, the anaesthetic blackness that leaks in as pre-sleep dream-thoughts haze and blur and fade away.

Then it came; with the long, slow blink of unconsciousness, she was there; the lights snapped on and the tower leapt out in front of her. She dreamed it into being, and the dream instantaneously imploded; self-destructing, flinging her out like a catapulted stone into the quiet of waking night – gasping – pillow squeezed between white-knuckled fingers – heart sprinting – a fragment of an instant of sleep spiralling in on her, telescoping her brain—

'Shit,' she whispered. 'Shit' – the soft syllable sighed out with the outrush of breath, a perfect, voiceless epithet of shock.

Beth switched on the lamp. There was a familiar gull-wing of chrome and black leatherette beside the glass pitcher on the bedside table, which turned out to be her watch. She tilted the face and peered at it. Twenty to one. Only twenty-five minutes had passed since she had parted from Audrey in the corridor; only fifteen since laying her head down on the pillow and switching off the lamp.

She turned onto her back and lay with her eyes open, fixed on the ceiling rosette, listening to the turbid silences of the castle. Those closest, most audible, were the house-silences; the silences of wood and plaster and soft furnishings and drapery, and of sleeping breath and empty rooms. Further afield was the silence of the staircase, cold and plangent; this was where house-silences became castle-silences – the ghost-silences of stairwells and turrets and deep, dark cellars. Silences she didn't want to dwell on, so she probed further. Beyond the thick stone walls and thin window panes were the chittering, braying silences of the distant woods and, further still, another layer; the blank, stony moor-silence. She reached the grave-silence, and recoiled. Echoes of a distant, half-forgotten childhood chant began to circulate slowly in her head . . .

> *Far away,*
> *In a dark, dark wood, there was a dark, dark house,*
> *And in the dark, dark house, there was a dark, dark room,*
> *And in the dark, dark room, there was a dark, dark cupboard,*
> *And in the dark, dark cupboard, there was a dark, dark shelf,*
> *And on the dark, dark shelf, there was a dark, dark box,*
> *And in the dark, dark box, there was a . . .*

A what? What came next? A dark, dark book? A dark, dark severed head? A ghost? She went through the chant again (it worked best, she remembered, if you imagined it in trembling Caledonian, like Fraser from *Dad's Army*), but each time she came to the dark, dark house, she saw it as the pencil-point tower in Lydia's postcard, and the dark, dark box kept conjuring itself up as the chest, the case, the box or whatever kind of container it was whose lock fitted the spindly crab-claw key . . .

> *. . . and in the dark, dark box, there was . . .*

There was what? What had Lydia (for there was no doubt in her mind that the key belonged to Lydia) placed in the box? And where *was* the dark, dark box? In a dark, dark cupboard, presumably. But in which of the castle's brooding host of dark, dark rooms did the dark, dark cupboard and its dark, dark secret lurk?

. . . Surely, it ought to be here, right here in Lydia's room.

Beth threw back the blankets and climbed out of bed. The fire had almost died now – just a smattering of red embers amongst the withered bank of grey powder – and the room was cold; chill air curled around her bare legs and up under the loose skirt of her borrowed cambric nightdress. She padded across and stood on the hearthrug in the weakening aura of warmth while she decided where to begin exploring. After a few moments' thought, she started with the chiffonier. It was shoulder-high, with six deep, bow-fronted drawers. Mouse-quiet, she pulled out the top drawer and looked inside. Empty. So was the next one, and the next. Nothing. She slid the last drawer right off its runners and set it on the floor, leaning it against the end of the bed. The other five followed quickly, and she crouched down and peered into the empty ribcage of slats and stringers, reaching an arm in and feeling around for a false bottom or back.

Leaving the drawers where they were, she started on the wardrobe, a great, double-doored armoire the size of a rhinoceros's sarcophagus. She swung the doors open; inside the cavern, her solitary black coat hung like a limp bat from the brass rail. Below, there was a bank of eight small drawers, and on the right a column of six deep shelf compartments rising to the roof of the wardrobe. The eight drawers soon joined the others on the floor, stacked in careful, teetering towers. Another peering, groping examination showed that they concealed nothing below or behind other than fluff and a thin carpet of ancient, powdery sawdust. She probed all the empty shelves except the highest, which was out of her reach. She carried a chair over from the sewing-table and climbed up on it, but, with a sigh of inevitable disappointment, found the last shelf as bare as the others; likewise the dust-desert that lay beyond the armoire's carved, finialled pediment.

The sewing-table was next; its three tiny drawers yielded the only artefacts of habitation she had found so far – rainbow coils of silk thread, a scree of silver bobbins, together with a jumble of needles, threaders, quilters and a host of other, unidentifiable machine attachments – but not a hint of the dark, dark box.

All that was left now was the marble-topped washstand, which had no drawers or doors, and the bedside cabinet, where the postcard and the crab-key itself had been found. Its drawers joined the others, but the whereabouts of the dark, dark box remained an elusively, infuriatingly dark, dark secret.

The only thing left to do would be to hack holes in the walls or prise up the floorboards. It *must* be here. In her mind, the box was beginning to assume Lost-Ark significance, and lateness, tiredness and futility were not going to stop her until she had raked out and scoured every nook and corner of the room.

Start with the obvious: a loose floorboard. Still stealing as silently as a mouse, she set about replacing the drawers. They wouldn't go. No matter how she jiggled and shifted them, not a single one of them would go back in its slot. Each one had been hand-crafted to fit perfectly in its space with less than a hair's-breadth to spare; each was invisibly unique and none were interchangeable. Deciding to deal with the drawers later, she stacked them on the bed. With the floor cleared, she rolled back all the rugs and crawled about, digging her fingernails into the cracks between the polished boards, ignoring the pain from her grazed knee. It was no use; they were all nailed down and solid as paving slabs; there wasn't a creak, squeak or budge between any of them.

She sat back on her haunches and let despondency wash over her.

146

There was nothing of Lydia here. In a creep of cold sweat, she looked around her and saw the state of the room. Had she gone insane? Rugs rolled up and dragged from the floor, furniture pulled to pieces and piled higgledy-piggledy on the rumpled bed; she could hardly have burgled the room more thoroughly had she been a frantic addict, told that there was a stash of her favourite substance concealed somewhere in it. And for what? A mythic box of secrets conjured up in the thrice-heated cauldron of her own ridiculous imagination. Why must a key necessarily have a lock? The crab-claw was probably just one of the great diaspora of keys that lurk clunking about in odds-and-ends tins, in the backs of cupboards, on shelves, in drawers, amidst the swarf and oil of garage floors; widower keys, surviving long after the passing of their lock wives.

And now how long was it going to take her to put it all back; all those wretchedly idiosyncratic drawers ... She went to the bedside cabinet and looked at her watch: one minute to one. Then, more to punish herself with her own stupidity than out of any lingering hope, she decided to look in the one place that remained untouched: behind the paintings. *Look at yourself*, she murmured as she lifted them one by one off their hooks and leaned them against the wall. *You're a mad, deranged bitch. What the hell do you think you're doing?* ... With an effort, she lifted down the largest, heaviest canvas.

And there it was, right before her eyes: wallpaper, three blur-edged rectangles of wallpaper, the blue brighter and paler than the rest, the gold curlicues still with a nascent glister. No secret hiding place, though. Damn.

Then, two things happened simultaneously: one passed unnoticed (her watch's minute-hand flicking on to one o'clock); the other she might have given almost anything not to have noticed. Somewhere behind her, so close it could have been in the room with her, there was a heart-rending, keening scream.

Beth's heart twisted in fright, and she dropped the painting; it glanced off the edge of the sewing-table and crashed to the floor as she spun round, crying out: 'Lydia!' She stared, goggle-eyed with horror, as the scream died away to a hoarse gurgle, then silence.

There was nobody there.

A vixen. It must have been a vixen crying, out in the park. These windows were so thin that any sound close by in the stillness could carry through them as clearly as through empty space. She had heard vixens crying before, and they sounded just like that. Just for an instant, though, Beth had believed utterly and ineffably in the existence of ghosts. That cry, high-pitched and hollow, was harrowed out by such an ache of terrible sorrow that, in the silence of the night, it seemed it could hardly have come from any living person . . .

She was just calming herself (not very successfully) with the vixen explanation when the cry came again, fainter, further off; this time, it definitely didn't come from within the room, but it didn't come from outside either; its edges and echoes were hemmed in and muted, as though it came from somewhere deep inside the house.

The warmth of exhilaration had evaporated from her body, and she felt the chill of the room snapping at her toes and chewing into her torso, its teeth sharpened by the awful horror of that distant wail. She wanted to lock the door and dive into bed, burrowing in, pulling the thick, heavy layers of sheets and blankets up over her head and hiding like a child. But there was a problem: aside from the cold, there was another sensation growing in her body; a tickling itch in her lower abdomen that told her she badly – really quite desperately – needed to go to the toilet.

Slowly, silently, she opened the door. The passage was in darkness; she stood and tilted her head in the direction of the landing and staircase, holding her breath and listening, but there wasn't a sound to be heard from the sleeping house. In the other direction, a long, dark way away, where the bathroom was, there was a tall window which cast a pool of silver moonlight onto the walls and floor. She walked quickly along the soft carpet, heading for the light, feeling the age-warped boards rise and fall under the balls of her feet, darkness plucking at the back of her billowing nightdress.

In the windowless bathroom, the light from the full, round moon that seemed to float right outside the corridor window was so bright that she left the light off and the door open while she sat down on the stone-cold seat and peed. Somehow she felt that, if she closed and locked the door, she might never have the courage to open it again and take flight back to the sanctuary of her room. No wonder people used to have chamber pots in houses like this, she thought; discreetly tucked under the bed, fire-warmed to welcome the squatting bottom; what a sensible idea . . . And then it struck her, perhaps because she pictured a pot peeking out from under the fringe of the valance: when she had spun round in alarm at the sound of that wail, and then when she stood juggling the desire to hide under the bedclothes against the pleas of her bladder, she had seen it but not registered it: the boneyard of piled drawers hadn't been there any more: not on the bed, not on the floor, not anywhere. As though, while her back was turned, as she lifted down the paintings, the drawers had taken themselves up and, without a sound, flown back into their sockets . . . She shook her head, but couldn't drive out the image; the drawers definitely hadn't been there.

Back out in the passage, it was still sleep-silent, and curiously warm; she no longer felt the deep bone-cold hugging her. She hovered uncertainly for a few moments outside the bathroom: her room was only twenty yards away, a dull yellow glow coming from the open door. Dare she go back in, though; could she handle it if the drawers really had put themselves away? If they had, then she would know there were ghosts. She considered going and knocking on Audrey's door and seeking sanctuary for the night; it was slightly nearer, and she could get to it without having to see into her own room. Audrey would be scathing – maybe even angry – but that would be better than going back to the ghosts.

She took one step along the corridor, then stopped, statue-still. Somebody was coming out of her room: a shadow, followed by the figure of a woman, young and slight, in a white nightdress identical to the one she herself was wearing. For a moment, she thought it was Audrey, and she almost called out, but the hair was wrong; pale blonde and grotesquely cropped, standing up in uneven tufts and spikes. Beth stopped breathing, and stared. The woman paused outside the bedroom door, just as Beth had done a few minutes earlier, glancing furtively up and down the passage. For one full second, she looked straight at Beth; the light was too dim to make out the details of the woman's face – except for the eyes, which seemed to shine with an almost animal terror – before she turned away and started creeping quickly towards the staircase.

The seconds passed, and Beth's breathing cut back in with a hiss. 'Lydia?' she whispered, but the woman had disappeared into the shadows.

Beth paced quickly along the corridor to her bedroom door (strange how warm she suddenly felt) and looked in. The drawers were there, stacked on the bed just as she had left them, and the wardrobe door was still gaping. That meant (her mind wrestled frantically with the logic) that she wasn't dreaming . . . Unless she had dreamt ransacking her room, in which case she was still dreaming. But what about the drawers putting themselves away? If she had dreamt that, had she dreamt going to the toilet? But if she had dreamt that, then she must have dreamt seeing the ghostly woman coming out of her room, in which case she must still be dreaming now. In which case . . .

In which case, there was only one way to be sure: follow the woman and find out if she was real.

Seized by a rush of unreasoning, inquisitive courage, she ran swiftly and silently along the passage until she came to the wide archway that led onto the great spiral staircase. The light was good here; a glazed dome at the head of the shaft let the pearlescent moonlight flood in, helter-skeltering down the white marble steps and glinting on the alert aquiline faces of the busts in their alcoves. She paused, listening for the sound of footfalls on marble. She thought she could hear them, faint and distant; soft, quick paps of bare feet, but she couldn't tell whether they came from above or below, or whether the sound was really just the blood pattering in her ears.

She decided to go down.

The air was still warm, but the marble was cold under her feet as she slipped lightly from step to step, outstretched fingers tracing the curve of the wall, round and round, down and down, past archways – pausing and listening at each one – until she stood on the lip of the breaking marble wave above the yawning cavern of the hall. The great fire was still glowing in its grate, and the chessboard tiles, the stone pillars and the suits of armour were licked and lapped by its faint orange light. Slower now, as the brief blush of fearlessness ebbed away, she descended the last few steps. As she crossed the hall towards the vestibule, she felt the presence of the armoured knights growing; invisible, watchful eyes stared out from behind spiked visor grilles, and mailed gauntlets tightened on the hilts of their swords, inching the broad, glittering blades out of their scabbards.

The vestibule door was locked and bolted, and the iron-studded oak doors on either side of the fireplace were too fearsome (and too well-guarded by the silent knights) even to try.

Then she heard it again, behind her, clear and present – *fa-fa-fa-fa* – bare feet falling on carpet, running now – *fa-fa-fa-fa – pap-pap-pap* – out of the carpeted corridor and onto the tiles of the hall. She turned quickly and saw the woman – the same woman, nightdress flowing behind her – running for her life across the hall and vanishing into the right-hand corridor, in the direction of the Music Room. Without pausing this time, Beth took off in pursuit, flying heedlessly past the knights, who snarled and creaked their armour menacingly at her, and down the corridor. The Music Room door was wide open, but when she rushed through and skidded to a halt on the carpet, the woman had gone, and the vast room was still and silent and dark; the furniture lurked in deep wells and impenetrable thickets of shadow, and the air hung dense and palpable. There was only one way out: one of the french windows was open, and the edges of the long, heavy curtains curled over and bellied slightly in the faint breath of incoming breeze. Hands held out in front of her, sensing the imminence of barked shins and stubbed toes, she picked her way blindly between the chairs and tables, and eventually arrived, miraculously unscathed, at the open window. She parted the curtains and stepped out onto the terrace. Even out here, she still felt quite warm; the only sensation of cold came from her feet on the gritty stone slabs. She looked around the moonlit garden ... And there was the woman; flying out across the lawn towards the trees and the lake. Suddenly, she stumbled and fell sprawling on the grass. Beth ran across the terrace towards the steps that led down to the lawn, but the woman had already scrambled to her feet: she turned round and, to Beth's astonishment, cried out in a voice cracked and shrill with fear and hatred: 'Stop following me! Leave me alone!' Then, inexplicably, she screamed, '*I won't do it! I won't!*' Beth froze, stricken with shock and confusion, half-way down the steps. Then the woman turned on her heels and took off again; in a twinkling, she had disappeared round the corner of the balustraded wall surrounding the raised parterre. Beth was about to set out again in pursuit when she sensed that there was someone behind her, running across the terrace. Before she could turn to look, the rushing figure went past her in a blur; she was shoved aside and lost her balance; as she fell, she heard a grunted curse, and the figure was gone. She didn't feel herself hitting the ground; the next thing she knew, she was lying on the grass, cold dew soaking into the back of her nightdress, gazing dreamily up at the pointed peak of the great corner tower. Then a third figure drifted into the fringe of her vision: Madame de La Simarde, dressed all in black, with a bright silver chain at her throat, came to the top of the terrace steps and stood gazing out across the lawn. Then Beth's eyes fogged over and the tower, the Old Wing and Madame de La Simarde all blurred and faded away to black.

The tower was empty. Purged. Cleansed. He had turned the key, pressed the button, and set the rotating globes in motion. The time-space continuum shivered and a great gash opened up in its fabric, sucking the tower's evil occupants into a QuickTime vortex of annihilation and oblivion.

For nine days he had struggled against the forces of evil – wandering, puzzling, fighting, searching, advancing, falling back – and now it was over; the discs had been ransacked for every last intricate megabyte of 2-D scenery and every point-and-click mystery. All was laid bare; the land was liberated and the tower was empty.

Like his brain, he thought. He pulled down the Apple menu and extracted the little calculator. £34.99 divided by nine days and an average of (he pursed his lips and estimated) say nine hours per day. That came to £3.89 a day or 43p per hour of engrossment. Not bad value, he thought, compared with a trip to the cinema or the cost of a book. A hardback book, anyway.

If only. Somewhere inside his empty-feeling brain, that book was lurking. Once, it had shouted and clamoured to be let out, to be released from its prison of nebulous thought and set in solid Stylewriter print so that it could evolve to the pinnacle of stiff pages bound in boards. Now it no longer clamoured, but skulked. Thoughts had been diverted and re-routed to avoid the streets it inhabited, which became dusty and decayed and choked with garbage and fallen masonry; impassable now to all but the most determined efforts of regeneration. It was no longer a place for the curious to stroll; the buildings were decrepit and rotten, and the population was sullen and hostile. Iain's half-hearted attempts to draw them out of their ghetto to the sunlit uplands were doomed; it would take more than a few scribbled lines. It would take a whole-hearted, gargantuan effort, complete with sincere, timetabled pledges and a fundamental change of attitude. As none of this seemed to be forthcoming, they would stay in their slums, thank you very much, consoling themselves that they might have other selves, living in a parallel brain whose owner was more serious, more committed, who would draw them out carefully and lovingly and place them in print in the tangible world.

It shouldn't be this hard, he had reasoned, so why was it? He had effortlessly filled page after page with his short stories. Some of them had been good enough to not only be published in prestigious periodicals, but to be praised. Two of them had even been anthologised. But you couldn't live by short stories. They might occasionally put bread on the table and petrol in the car, but they couldn't turn the car into a BMW or park it on the generous driveway of an expensive house. Agents and publishers wouldn't touch them unless they were offered by established authors. They couldn't be summed up (they said) in a single blurb; they carried no clear identity, no easily grasped marketing handle; the market was too small, and so they didn't sell. There had been writers before him who had made lucrative livings from short stories, but Iain would not be one of them; he hadn't the stamina or the patience for the long, slow climb. His course was clear; what he needed to do was buy the big lottery ticket, to stand up in the stirrups and lunge for the brass ring. He needed to write a full-length novel. The Long Story that would earn Big Money. An agent, an advance that would buy the BMW, royalties that would pay for the expensive house. Fame. Notoriety. Tax-deductible foreign holidays.

Straight away, he had run into a big problem. It wasn't a lack of ideas; he had ideas all right, an embarrassingly large and fecund population of them. Nor was the problem his recently discovered love of computer games. As much as Beth might abominate and anathematise them as harpies that sucked greedily on his time and energy, games were not the problem.

No, the problem was him. For years, he had written stories. Just stories; that was all they were to him as a child, transmuting into something called *short* stories as he grew into an adult. His stories were good. Some were even brilliant, but he never knew why they were always short. He told himself that he relished the constraints of ten pages, twenty pages, fifty pages at most – three, ten, twenty thousand words with no pointless characters, no irrelevant digressions, no extraneous lyrical flows. His stories were spare, spartan, deceptively simple, and usually written in the vernacular. (The editor who anthologised him compared him to 'an intoxicating *mélange* of Hemingway and

Lardner, cast in an utterly modern mould'.) It was only now, as he surveyed the box-files fat with notes and his pitiably thin sheaf of attempted chapters, that he knew where the problem lay. Perhaps he had known it before but had laced it over with plausible lies. Whatever. Now there was no mistaking the dull, ugly truth. The reason his flair for storytelling had seized up and busted in the face of a large project was obvious and predictable: he had a cripplingly short attention span. He couldn't hold all the pieces in his hands at once so that they became facets of the same thing. One item might attract him and hold his interest, but his mind went numb when he tried to assemble it with others, retaining the clarity of their details so they could be interlaced into a cohesive whole.

His answer to the problem was to deny its existence, first pressing on doggedly, then telling himself that the story simply needed more time to gestate. Computer adventures were helpful in filling the vacuum left behind. Especially helpful now that there was a new problem, bred of the first: he had lost confidence in his ability to write. In crossing the river from the village-studded polder plain of short stories and trying to scale the citadel of the novel, he had unwittingly demolished his bridges and shot holes in his boats. He now found himself wandering on the shoreline, surveying the wreckage. There was no vessel to carry him back out of this purgatory, and despondency was growing day by day. Unable to advance, unable (and indeed still unwilling) to retreat, playing games provided a lateral escape route.

He had ideas; he had a story – many stories in fact – and he had characters and snatches of dialogue and situations, a chronology, a beginning and an ending. Ideas piled upon each other in writhing heaps until he couldn't cope with them. And now, in his struggle to pin them down, he found that he was no longer capable of inscribing a single sentence, a single phrase, that did not embarrass and shame him with its tawdriness, its banality or its overworked pretension.

Game over.

When the conflagration on screen had faded to black and the credits had rolled, he quit the program and shut down the computer. What now? Have another go on the treadmill, he supposed. Lying to Beth; that had been the first time. Usually, she was there to witness his sloth; even when she was out at work all day he couldn't pretend, because there were no new words to show her when she came home. When she had phoned this afternoon, though, he had seen the night and day before her return stretching before him, and had fooled himself that he would get something done in time. He had better get started.

He took a fat yellow folder down from the shelf and opened it. Inside were some of his notes; page upon page of urgent writing, some small and dense, some bold and chaotic, with chronological charts and sketched flow-diagrams and lists of facts. It was the disarrayed blueprint of the novel that lived in his head but could not be brought out into orderly pages of narrative. It really shouldn't be so difficult; after all, the story was a true one, it had been known to him since childhood and had grown year by year as his knowledge increased. He didn't have to worry about the details, because they were there in his grandfather's diary and reams of documents obtained from the Public Record Office and the Ministry of Defence; he didn't have to worry about the background, because it was there in a dozen history books, all lined up on his shelf.

He laid the folder aside, picked up a pen and paper and sat down in an armchair. (He never wrote straight to computer; the temptation to slip into the Finder and blip open a game was too strong.) After staring at the blank page for a while, he went and made a jug of coffee. Sitting down again with a full, hot mug balanced beside him, he lit a cigarette and exhaled a long, smoky sigh. His pen hovered, then wrote at the top of the page:

Sergeant Urbanski's Journey

Brief, he thought. Just a sketch-story. No reader, no critical eye peeping over your shoulder. Brief and quick, like tearing off a plaster. Don't go for effect, go from the gut . . .

He took another long drag of smoke, his pen hesitated for a moment, then plunged through the gate. The nib ran wriggling back and forth across the page and made it, gasping and trembling, to the end of the third line, paused momentarily, then lunged on again. The words burst out of him in an ecstatic rush; he had poured lines of ink across three and a half pages before coming up to gasp for air and smoke, a long finger of disregarded ash hanging precariously from his cigarette. With an inward yelp of joy, he realised what was happening. He was about to stop and scan over what he had written, but something prevented him. *No*, it said, *don't stop. Keep going.* And, stubbing out his cigarette, lighting another and taking a swig of coffee, he wrote on into the deepening night.

Finally, at around two in the morning, his synapses buzzing with an electric concoction of caffeine, nicotine and adrenalin, he wrote the final sentence. His head flopped back on the cushions, and the pen slipped from his fingers, landing with a clattery splash in the half-empty mug of coffee (his third) that stood on the carpet at his feet.

For a full ten minutes he reclined, eyes closed, letting the excitement fizz down to something like calm. It had been a sort of dementia, and now, in its cooling aftermath, he had to force himself to shuffle the sheets of scribbled paper into order and read what he had written.

Not bad in itself, he decided, once he had amended it, crossing out a line here, a paragraph there, sprinkling the prose with alternative words. Not bad, but not *right*; it was a short story, but it wasn't a Short Story (Iain knew the difference, which was why he had been so good at the art). He had pushed himself off from the shore, but instead of sailing back to the banks of home, he was now floundering in mid-stream. What he had poured into these pages was, could be, should be the foundation of his novel, but it was incomplete, gapped, no symmetry, no point, no . . .

No anything, he concluded. It was a simple odyssey, and he had had enough of simple; he wanted complex. Time and life didn't work like a story: they didn't start in one place, move along and stop. The present moved forward into the future carrying the past with it. It was like music; the repetition of themes with variations; consonant chords piled up, implying the topmost melody.

Still, he had some words on paper; ten pages, just as he had told Beth. He slid a paperclip over one corner and tossed the bundle onto his desk, noticing with a sad satisfaction that it was just heavy enough not to flutter and swoop to the floor. At least he would now be able to begin playing his new game tomorrow, secure in the knowledge that he had a whole sheaf of new words to show her when she returned.

He crushed out his last cigarette, turned off the reading lamp, and made his way to bed.

156

One of the problems, one of the *many* problems (and not one of the biggest – but wasn't it always those footling little trip-wire problems that caused the big, bad dynamite problems to blow up in your face with such ferocity?), one of the many, many problems in Audrey's marriage to Peter had been the night terrors. She had suffered from them as a child, scaring her parents half to death on several occasions, but in her late teens they became less frequent until, when she grew up and went away to university, they stopped. Every night she slept soundly, undisturbed by the nocturnal horror; the suffocation and gut-wrenching screams. Then she married Peter. Their first home was a rented, furnished two-bedroom terrace in Blackheath. On their first night in the house, Peter was torn violently from a gentle dream of sleepily cavorting hermaphrodites by a soul-harrowing fusillade of horror-movie screams. His new wife was sitting bolt-upright, gasping with terror, clawing frantically at the air, as though fighting off a monstrous assailant. It took an hour of gentle coaxing to persuade her that she was safe (safe, at least, from imminent murder), and even then, the light stayed on until dawn while they held each other in mutually assured fearfulness.

A year later, they moved into their second house, a three-bedroom detached in Highgate, bought with a hefty deposit and a twenty-year mortgage. The night terrors continued; if anything, they became more frequent. Eventually, at Peter's tentative suggestion, they moved into separate bedrooms. He couldn't take the stress of pulse-quickening wrecked nights any longer. Audrey would lie awake in her single bed in the spare room, staring into the darkness and wondering what had brought the terrors back. It couldn't be anxiety about her career, which was galloping with effortless velocity, leaping nimbly over easy promotional jumps; indeed, Peter's father had been so delighted at the vindication of his judgement in placing his untried daughter-in-law so high in the firm that he had contributed substantially towards the purchase of their new house (they couldn't have afforded to be detached in Highgate by themselves for a while yet), and even bought them a second car... No, everything she had planned was working itself through like a dream (*hah*, she thought); better even than her most optimistic estimations. The problem, she had been forced to conclude, was Peter himself. Having separate rooms threw stark, merciless light on the real problem: they found the arrangement congenial because it circumvented the embarrassment of their non-existent sex life, which had fallen irretrievably to pieces within a few months of marriage. They liked each other well enough (when they weren't arguing), but, for reasons she couldn't yet put her finger on, they deeply, fundamentally failed to harbour any sexual desire for each other. The return of the terrors hadn't helped; she could never quite shake off the feeling that Peter himself was the nightmare presence that was trying to kill her.

A few years later, after their acrimonious split, she got her break in television. One of her first jobs was as producer's assistant on a documentary about sleep disorders. She had been fascinated, and quite heartened, to learn that her affliction (*sleep paralysis*, the psychologist they interviewed called it) was really quite common, and had an historic, mythic depth: in the Middle Ages, it had bred the succubus myth, and it probably (in the psychologist's opinion) lay behind modern claims of abduction by aliens. The reports were so similar; and so very similar to Audrey's own nocturnal terrors.

The pattern was always the same. She would wake in the night; or, rather, she would dream that she had woken. The room was utterly dark, a thick, inky blackness; either there was no light or she had gone blind. She was lying on her back, and she couldn't move, couldn't breathe; a heavy, immovable dead weight lay on her chest, squeezing her lungs and pinning her to the mattress. But that wasn't the worst part. The worst part was that, somewhere in the room, lurking in the darkness, watching her, was an indescribable, malignant, malevolent presence. She tried to struggle, but the weight was too heavy; she tried to gasp for breath, but her lungs were being crushed out of her. And now the presence began to move towards the bed. Closer and closer it crept, until it loomed over her. Invisible fingers reached out of the darkness and began to close around her throat...

—and with a gargantuan convulsion of desperate strength, she wrenched herself out of the spectre's grasp and screamed for all she

158

was worth, gulping down breath and shrieking and shrieking until her throat was ravaged and sore, and then she was out of bed, with one frantic need driving her; to reach the light switch; to blast the room with light and annihilate the murderous presence before it could catch her again. Head down, leading with her clenched fists, she rushed across the room, sobbing with fright, crashing into furniture that shouldn't have been there, and reached the wall. She fumbled for the switch, groping with outstretched palms over the wallpaper. It wasn't there! They had taken away the switch! Now she was doomed; if she didn't get the light on quickly, the presence would find her and get her. Suddenly, just as she sensed its claws closing in behind her, her hand stumbled on a cold, globular protuberance, and she wept with relief. The room filled with light, and the presence was killed, obliterated, vanished, leaving behind just a dissipating aura of fear.

. . . For several moments, she stood with her damp forehead resting on the wall, her suppliant fingers still cupping the bulbous bakelite light-switch, recovering her breath and finally realising where she was . . . A strange place; sleeping in a strange place had brought it on, she knew. Eventually, she let go of the switch, straightened up and turned to face the room. A strange room in the strangest of houses, with . . . stranger still, the bedroom door wide open and – she gasped and almost screamed again – a body sprawled on the rug at the foot of the bed; a woman in a white nightdress, limbs flailed out and twisted as though she had fallen from a great height.

Not dead; only sleeping, but sleeping the still, deep, drowning sleep of the dead.

'Beth!' Audrey knelt down and leaned over her. 'Beth!' Beth's eyelids flickered and twitched as Audrey slipped a hand under her neck and raised her head, but still she didn't wake up. Audrey tried patting her cheeks; lightly at first, then tapping and finally slapping them audibly. At that, Beth's eyes sprang open suddenly and stared wildly up at her. 'It's not me!' she gasped. 'I won't do it!'

'Do what?' said Audrey, startled. 'Beth, it's only me. You were dreaming.'

Beth stared and blinked, focusing gradually. 'Dreaming?' she slurred groggily.

'Dreaming,' Audrey said firmly. 'And sleepwalking, by the look of it.'

'Where am I?'

'In my bedroom. You've been sleepwalking.'

Beth closed her eyes, then opened them again. 'I was in the garden.

There was somebody ... I was running away, and they chased me ...
Or was I chasing?'

'It was just a dream,' Audrey repeated, helping Beth to her feet. 'It must be the night for nightmares.' She sat Beth down on the edge of the bed and looked at her, frowning. 'How on earth did you get into that state?'

Beth looked down at herself. The white nightdress was torn across one shoulder; two of its little buttons were missing, and the front hung open. She drew the edges together at her throat and looked at her feet. The soles and the clefts between her toes were encrusted with grey grime and her ankles were speckled with dried splashes of orange mud. 'I don't know,' she said.

'Tell me what happened. What you remember ...'

Beth told her everything: from waking up and strip-searching her room to the moment she blacked out beneath the terrace steps. She frowned in concentration as she tried to mentally glue the disjointed moments together: the two screams, the disappearance of the drawers, going to the toilet, seeing the woman coming out of her room; and once again, she tried to work out logically which parts were real and which she must have dreamed.

Audrey tried to help her. 'When you heard the scream and turned around, the drawers weren't there?'

Beth shrugged hopelessly. 'I don't think so. But I only noticed later.'

'And then they came back?'

'Yes, after I saw the woman coming out of my room.'

'The woman, yes ... And you thought she was Lydia?'

'I don't know. Yes ... I didn't really see her face – I just sort of felt it was her.'

'I think it was all a dream,' Audrey concluded, although she couldn't quite keep the tone of doubt out of her voice; she was still shaking from her own nightmare and the shock of finding Beth in her room. 'The whole thing,' she added, for emphasis. 'All just dreams.'

Beth looked down at her feet. 'Then how did this happen?'

'You walked in your sleep. It's been known to happen.'

Far from calming down, Beth became even more agitated. 'Not to me,' she insisted. 'I've never sleptw— sleepwalked. Never in my life.'

Audrey couldn't think of anything more to say, and so they fell silent, listening to the erratic paddering of their own hearts and the lurking whispers of the castle creeping in through the open bedroom door.

Suddenly, Beth broke the silence. 'Will you go and look?' she asked, looking pleadingly at Audrey.

'What? Look at what?'

'My room . . . I just need to know . . .'

Audrey understood. '. . . If the drawers are out?' Beth nodded. Audrey glanced uneasily at the open door. 'Can't you go yourself?'

Beth shook her head and looked even more desperate. With a sigh, Audrey walked over to the door and peered out into the corridor. She could see the yellow glow of lamplight from Beth's room. Lydia's room . . . Her heart beginning to race faster, she went to step across the threshold, but the gloom clutched at her legs and clogged her feet. She struggled against the fear for several moments, then stepped backwards, closed the door and locked it.

'I can't,' she said.

'But I don't want to go back in there on my own,' Beth whined, becoming a helpless child again.

Audrey felt a brief shiver of irritation at Beth's pathetic tone, but she understood; there was something out there, in the corridor, in Lydia's old room, that was almost palpably forbidding; however much she might tell herself that they had put it there, a demon compounded of their own superstitious night-fear, she could no more make herself go into that room than make herself fly from the battlements.

'You can share my bed if you like,' she said at last. 'It's not quite king-size, but it's easily big enough for two.' Seeing a doubtful expression steal across Beth's face, she felt another tremor of irritation. 'Don't worry,' she said wearily. 'I won't pounce on you. I'm not in the mood, and besides, you're not my type.'

She unstacked the landslide of heavy, feather-filled pillows until she had uncovered the long, fat bolster. Then she pulled back the bed-clothes and laid the bolster down the middle of the bed. 'There,' she said, rearranging the pillows. 'That should keep your virtue intact. You take that side.'

After they had settled down between the stiff linen sheets, Beth gazed across the undulating landscape of pillows at Audrey's face, nestled in the folds of white. Audrey smiled back, and Beth felt comforted by her strength. She was seeing a new side to Audrey; as ready to smile as sneer. And then there were the little acts of kindess; first the stockings and now this. Beth chided herself for her lack of gratitude, and wondered where this new warmth had come from. Perhaps it was coming to terms with . . . well . . .

'Aud . . .'

'What?'

'. . . Er, just out of curiosity, what is your type?'

Audrey sighed. 'Oh, I don't know. Not you . . . Shall I put the light out?'

'. . . Okay.'

In the darkness – a snug, companionable darkness now – Audrey turned over and settled into her own thoughts. Beth was so coyly fascinated by her sexuality. So many were. *My type . . .* She could hardly say what it was; she would never admit the fact to Beth, but she had only experienced two women, and they had been as different from each other as they could possibly be. Marina had been the first, the seducer; olive-skinned, elfin and boylike, with adolescent breasts and narrow hips. A series of abortive, fumbling failures, which she preferred to forget, had come afterwards, but then, last summer, she had met Ursula. Ursula was Danish and a script editor, and had come looking for work with ClearCut Films. She was as magnificently different from Marina as lust from love; a junoesque valkyrie with warm, pale, welcoming thighs and breasts like ripe cantaloupes . . . No, Audrey's type, if she had one at all, could only be defined by what it excluded, and it most certainly excluded friends. Exploring the erotic possibilities of the female form was still an adventure; sensual intimacy was one thing, but emotional intimacy was something she might never be able to handle with a woman. With men, you knew the rules of engagement and emotional play-off, but with women, well, she wasn't sure she wanted to be understood and second-guessed; men always had that tentative nervousness in the face of her emotions that allowed her to keep something back that was inviolably her own. That was the soft pith at the core of power, she supposed, and she was loath to give it up.

Beth lay quietly, listening to her heart slowing and her breathing shallowing out. It was strange, sharing a bed with another woman. She had only done it once before, and what intrigued her about it was the quiet and stillness. Sometimes, sleeping next to Iain was like sharing a bed with a menagerie of woodland creatures. After they had kissed goodnight, he would roll over and yawn, braying out the racking exhalation with a noise like a deer bellowing from a mountain-top. Then, while he wandered in his dreams, he would emit little squeaks, squawks and chirrups, twitching like a puppy, while she lay awake listening and waiting for his most alarming lycanthropic transformation: as his dreams turned frantic, he would grind his teeth and squeal like a wild boar, floundering across the bed towards her, and try to burrow his head under her pillow. Sometimes he lost control of his breathing, which was truly frightening. She had to wake him up then. It's *in-out-in-out*, she told him. Not *in-in-in-in . . . squeak-squeak-BLEARRGHH!* His final animal impersonation, though, the one that wiped away the distress of the others and made her heart crumple with tenderness, was the one he always did in the mornings, when he dragged himself out of bed and wallowed about the flat with the fingers of sleep still fondling his brain: curled up on the sofa, he would gaze timidly over his coffee mug at her while she got ready for work, his bush-baby eyes wide with wonder at the brashness of the waking world.

Other men she had slept with had been noisy, but none had ranged as widely through the forests of the night as Iain did . . . Women were so much quieter . . . She wondered again at how much Audrey had changed, and decided that now might be the only opportunity she would ever get to unburden herself.

'Audrey?' she whispered. '. . . Are you awake?'

'Hmm . . . Only just.'

'Do you remember Ainsworth? Our house?'

'Of course.'

'We had some good times there, didn't we? I mean, sometimes we did, the four of us.'

'Mmm, if you say so.'

'. . . Do you remember my big birthday party?'

'Of course I do. I could hardly forget; that was when I first met Peter, remember.'

Beth paused. 'Peter, yes . . . Audrey, I don't know quite how to put this, but I slept with him that night.' There; it was out. She sensed Audrey turning over to face her, and gabbled defensively. 'I didn't do it deliberately – I mean, I had no idea you were interested or I wouldn't have, you know I wouldn't . . .'

There was a peculiar liquid burbling sound from Audrey's side of the bed. Surprised, Beth realised that she was laughing quietly.

'I wondered if you'd ever get around to confessing.'

Beth raised herself up on her elbow. 'You mean you *knew*?'

'Uh-huh. Peter told me.'

'*Peter?* When?'

'Oh, after we'd been going out for quite a while. He suspected I was . . . well, seeing someone else. I think he thought I'd be jealous. Realise how desirable he was.'

'. . . Oh. Were you? Jealous, I mean.'

'No, but I thought you might be.'

'Me?'

'Weren't you?'

'Hardly. I only slept with him once. And I was pissed.'

Audrey paused, and Beth could tell she was smiling, even in the dark. 'What was he like?' she asked. 'A good performance?'

Beth hesitated.

'Well?'

'He was rubbish,' said Beth, grinning, and she heard a giggle bubble out of Audrey. 'Really useless,' she added.

Audrey turned onto her back, and the bed shook gently with her silent laughter. 'Oh God, Beth,' she breathed. 'I have missed you.'

Changing Salvador

1

Salvador sat by his bedroom window and waited patiently. For a boy of his age, he was very good at waiting. In a life which looked from the outside as though it was composed of light and music and adulation, Salvador seemed in fact to have spent more time waiting than anything else: waiting in airport lounges, railway stations and taxi ranks, waiting in dressing rooms, rehearsal rooms and in the dimly lit backstage corridors of concert halls and provincial theatres; always waiting for something to begin. The performances themselves, when viewed through the prism of memory, seemed like brief, luminescent beads strung out on a single long strand of abeyance.

And so he waited. He sat on his practice chair and gazed out of the window at the gravelled apron below, where his mother's Mercedes was parked. Février had folded the top down for her, so she should certainly be leaving soon. She was driving to Limoges to inspect samples of the new dinner service – one hundred and twenty pieces of fine bone china – which had been specially commissioned for next month's grand party. It was to be a joint celebration of Madame de La Simarde's fiftieth birthday and the fifth anniversary of Salvador's first public performance. Thirty carefully selected guests had been invited for an evening of fine food, fireworks and music, the centrepiece of which was to be Salvador's solo recital of an expanded version of that first professional programme.

He heard his mother's heels clack on the marble floor of the landing, and looked back over his shoulder as the bedroom door opened briskly, accompanied by a sharp, perfunctory rap of knuckles on the panel. She stood silently on the threshold for a few moments, gazing at him with obvious pleasure, then her eyes narrowed as she glanced first at his music stand with its unopened books, then at his guitars resting idly on their frames in the corner of the room.

165

'Have you been practising?' she asked, a tone of suspicion in her voice.

He lowered his eyes. 'No, Maman,' he said quietly. 'Not today.' His mother frowned deeply, and he added: 'I know the pieces, Maman. I could play them blindfolded.'

She sucked her cheeks in and looked sternly at him. 'You can never have too much practice, Salvador,' she said.

'I know, Maman,' he conceded, even though it was palpably untrue; it was only too easy to have too much practice. More than once he had practised and practised a piece until he was note-perfect – more than note-perfect – and the result was usually the same; loss of effort, loss of pain, a mechanical performance stripped of feeling. But it was no use trying to explain this to his mother; she would only interpret it as yet another excuse for sloth.

Her expression softened slightly. 'How high do your aspirations reach, my son?'

'Mother,' he replied automatically, 'they reach to the very highest.'

'Then you must practise, practise, practise! The great Salvador practised for eight hours a day, every single day of his life. You have his genius, but it is nothing without practice.'

'I understand, Maman.'

She looked at her watch. 'I shall be leaving soon,' she said. 'I should be back by six. Avril has instructions to prepare dinner for half-past seven. Now, you be a good boy and practise those pieces this afternoon. Do not let Salvador be ashamed of you.'

'Okay,' he murmured. He noticed her posture stiffen and her lips compress into a thin, stern line. 'Yes, Maman,' he corrected himself.

She stared at him for several moments. 'I cannot begin to imagine where you acquire these slovenly expressions,' she said. 'Do not use them, do you hear?'

'Very well, Maman.'

The hard line softened to a fond smile and, with a lingering gaze, she slowly turned away and closed the door behind her.

On the landing, she paused, listening to the light wooden clunks as Salvador picked up his practice instrument and sat down with it. There were several wowing, staccato twangs as the instrument was summoned into tune (new strings settling in, she guessed), then the scales began, rippling up and down with light, easy fluidity. Satisfied, she smiled and continued down the stairs.

As soon as he heard her footsteps receding, Salvador stopped his scales and gazed despondently at the open folios on the music stand in front of him. It was true; he could play the pieces blindfolded. Every last semi-quaver was ingrained in his ear and his fingertips. He believed he could play his way flawlessly through the whole fifty-minute recital without even being consciously aware of playing at all, let alone seeing the notes or the movement of his fingers on the strings. He decided to prove it to himself right now, in the minutes of waiting still left before his mother finally departed. With the great Salvador looking approvingly over his shoulder, he closed the book and adjusted his posture, then splayed the fingers of his left hand to form the opening notes of the first piece.

As they emerged, his mind immediately diverged from the task of conscious guidance and wandered away, settling after a few moments on the memory of the last time his mother had allowed him to abandon his practising and accompany her on one of her trips out. Only an afternoon's shopping in Angoulême, but it had turned out to be a red-letter day in Salvador's interior calendar; more deeply engraved than his first public performance, and not only because it was more recent.

They left the Mercedes parked beside the town ramparts in the shadow of the covered market, and strolled through the narrow, rising streets to the Place de Marengo, where they had lunch in a brasserie overlooking the church. Salvador was gazing out of the window, watching the silt-grey pigeons swooping and fluttering and fussing around the church spire, his forgotten café-au-lait going cold by his elbow, when his mother stood up suddenly, closing her clutch-bag with a loud *snap*.

There was no leisurely lingering with Madame de La Simarde, no decadent, slothful relishing of inaction in the middle of the day; for her, a shopping trip meant that you ate your lunch, then went promptly to the shops you needed to visit, made your purchases, and went home. Today, there were two visits to be made. The first – and the only one which required Salvador's presence – was to Monsieur Duprée's small but elegant shop in the Rue des Postes.

'Come along, Salvo,' she said briskly, tapping the tiny glass face of her watch with a fingernail. 'Two o'clock.'

Jean-Baptiste Duprée had had a chequered career, but nobody knew much, if anything, about it. They did, however, suspect. The fingernails of the curious picked and poked at the edges of his armour, but uncovered nothing to confirm their suspicions. It had begun, according to local mythology, with the fall of France in 1940. Precisely how the coming of the new regime had affected him was unknown, and he tended to become extremely vague when questioned on the subject.

His defensive reticence had led to whispered rumours that he had been a collaborator. It was said that he had once been a promising player of the *cor anglais*, but had vanished from his home village, somewhere up north, shortly after the Germans rolled in, and had returned in the spring of 1945 a broken man, prematurely aged and walking with a stick. He polished, packed and sold his precious instrument, and used the money (it was said) to move to Angoulême, where he established his little emporium. For the past thirty years, he had passed his days standing motionless, with vacant, watery eyes, behind the glass counter cabinet with its stock of strings, resin blocks, tuning forks, pitch pipes, mouthpieces, metronomes and all manner of musical paraphernalia, his slightened body framed by the ranks of instruments pegged to the walls around him: glints of polished brass and silver pipework dominated by the dark russets of fat-bodied cellos, violas and violins. Some days, he would stand there for hours at a time, only moving to close up the shop at midday and reopen at two. On the occasions (never more than two or three times a day) when the *pang* of the bell above the door announced the arrival of a rare customer, he would leap into motion as though electrified, transformed from a sagging mannequin into an attentive, punctilious one-man hive of solicitude.

Not this afternoon, though. This afternoon, as chance would have it, when Salvador and his mother opened the door and stepped into the cramped little shop with its genteel aroma of metal polish and age-ripened wood, Monsieur Duprée was nowhere to be seen. Madame de La Simarde glanced at her son in surprise, then approached the counter and peered over, as though expecting to find the proprietor stretched out on the floor behind it, the accumulated weariness of his perpetual vigil having finally taken its inevitable toll. But there was still no sign of him. Still too surprised to be irritated by this lack of service, Madame de La Simarde cleared her throat with unaccustomed timidity and rapped lightly on the glass counter.

In the back room of the shop, Monsieur Duprée was torn from his reverie by the sudden sound. For the past hour, he had been gazing with faraway eyes into the open instrument case on the table in front of him. Lying inside the case was the long, slender, intricately worked form of a *cor anglais*. He had not willingly laid eyes on one since ... well, more years than he cared to remember. It had been mistakenly delivered by his supplier that morning (the order had been for an oboe for a customer in La Rochefoucauld), and he had received a terrible jolt on opening the packing crate and finding the one instrument he had always steadfastly refused to stock nestled in amongst the plastic sheeting and wood shavings. It was like finding the decaying corpse of an old friend.

168

He looked up, startled by the sound from the front of the shop. 'Monsieur Duprée!' called a voice. Mortified, he leapt up from his chair and hurried along the passage. He had recognised that voice immediately. Although Madame de La Simarde's custom was not the most rewarding from a purely pecuniary point of view (her son's concert instrument – an exquisite 1960 model by Ignacio Fleta which complemented delightfully the family's priceless Torres – had been purchased from a dealer in Paris), the value of the prestige of such a connection was beyond price. She regularly travelled the sixty kilometres to Angoulême – rather than going to Limoges, which was much nearer Gondecourt – especially to patronise his shop. He found favour with her because of his adherence to old ways: he kept a wide stock of traditional accessories, and eschewed the electric instruments from which his competitors were making their fortunes.

'Please forgive me, Madame,' he murmured breathlessly, trying desperately to sustain an air of decorum in spite of the sweat breaking out on his forehead. 'I was attending to important administrative business.' He produced an enormous cotton handkerchief from the breast pocket of his jacket and dabbed delicately at his brow.

'Strings,' said Madame de La Simarde curtly, her impatience aroused at last.

'Excuse me?' said Monsieur Duprée.

'My son requires strings.'

'Aaah!' said Monsieur Duprée, beginning to regain his composure. 'Then the young gentleman has come to the right place!' He put the handkerchief away with a flourish and strode (or at least made a passable imitation of a stride in the confined space) to a rosewood cabinet in the corner and began sweeping open its mosaic of tiny drawers one by one. 'The usual order?' he asked over his shoulder, riffling through the rows of square wax-paper envelopes with his fingertips.

Madame de La Simarde glanced at Salvador. 'Yes please,' he said.

Monsieur Duprée nodded in satisfaction and selected two large handfuls of envelopes from six different drawers, carried them back to the counter and spread them out like playing cards. 'Four sets of gut,' he said, starting to sort them into piles, 'and twelve of nylon. All, however, of the very finest quality.'

Salvador watched abstractedly as his strings were sorted, only half-listening to the shopkeeper's attempts to make conversation with his mother. His attention wandered, and he gazed around the shop at the instruments on display.

And that was when it happened; in later years, he would always trace the key-change in his life back to Monsieur Duprée's little shop, to that moment when, glancing idly around, his eyes suddenly lighted on a splash of discordantly bright colour coming from an open case lying on the floor beside the little door panel which led to the window display. Disregarded by the two adults, he walked up to it and looked in over the raised lid of the case. It was oblong and shallow, unlike anything he had ever seen; a little like the shape of a clarinet case, but much, much bigger. It was lined with a vivid orange plush material and, resting in this luxuriant bed was an instrument that looked as though it came from an alien world. In many respects it resembled a guitar; it had a head and a neck, a fretboard and a body with a tailpiece and bridge; its body even had the familiar hourglass shape of a guitar (albeit with a chunk bitten out of one edge where it joined the neck), but every other feature screamed in raucous mockery of his instrument's traditional form. The neck was slimmer, the machine heads and tuning keys were chromed and stuck out from the glossy black head like antennae, the strings were of shining steel and were filament-fine, and the body was small, slim as a book and covered in bizarre features – knobs, switches and strange metal plates set beneath the strings. And then there was the colour; a bright sunburst splashed across the body, gradated from pale yellow in the centre through brilliant orange to a deep blood red at the edges. At the top of the head, the name *Gibson* was inlaid in simple, slanted mother-of-pearl letters.

He had seen photographs, of course; occasional fleeting glimpses in magazines left lying around in airport lounges, but he had never in his life seen one of these things for real. As he stood there, hypnotised, taking in every detail of its form, he felt that, despite its gaudy, almost grotesque appearance, it was the most startling, ravishing, desirable object he had ever seen.

Slowly, dimly, he became aware of two human presences, one on either side of him, and he was caught in the frothing wash of signals emanating from each of them: from his mother swelled wave upon wave of mounting disapproval and distaste which crumbled and swallowed Monsieur Duprée's frantic air of abject apology.

At last, Madame de La Simarde found her voice. 'What,' she whispered with the quiet malevolence of a cobra's hiss, 'is this?'

Salvador, still consumed by rapture, smiled. 'It's an electric guitar, Maman.'

She tore her eyes away from the instrument and stared at him. 'I can see that, you obtuse child. What I want to know is what this ... *abomination* is doing *here*.'

She looked at Monsieur Duprée, who melted visibly, wringing his hands and trying to mould his face into an emollient smile.

'Madame,' he stammered, then the words came tumbling out, barely coherent: 'Madame, please excuse me – my business, you understand – I cannot apologise enough, but you *must* try to understand, please – I must try to move with the times – I do assure you of how grateful I am – honoured indeed – to have your esteemed, your noble custom, but my customers are too few – there aren't enough to pay my bills. I just thought – and I do beg Madame's pardon once again – I would not have left this out had I known Madame and her brilliant prodigy would be calling – it is just an experiment, you see . . .' He tailed off, staring desperately at the open case, not daring to look Madame de La Simarde in the eye.

She waited silently, and when it seemed certain that the outpouring would not resume, she turned to Salvador. 'Collect your strings,' she said blankly. While he went to the counter and gathered up the paper packets, she looked coldly at the deflated, defeated proprietor. 'You may prepare your bill and send it to me directly,' she said.

Monsieur Duprée nodded dumbly. Madame de La Simarde had not paid her bill for nearly a year and a half, but it would not take long to itemise.

'Come along, Salvador. We are leaving.' As Salvador held the door open for her, she turned back and glanced at the gaudy monstrosity lying in its case. 'If we return—' a slight but perceptible emphasis on *if* – 'I shall not be anticipating any further unpleasant surprises.'

Monsieur Duprée, delighted by the implication that her custom was not utterly lost to him, assured her fulsomely that there would be none, and that this aberration would be banished from his shop as quickly as lay within his power. After they had gone and he had closed the door quietly behind them, he laid a hand over his palpitating chest and wiped the sweat from his brow. It always took him a little while to get over a visit from Madame de La Simarde; this time it would take rather longer than usual.

(Monsieur Duprée did not lose Madame de La Simarde's custom; indeed, she was such a creature of habit that her patronage quickly and quietly returned to normal. However, Monsieur Duprée's plan for modernising his range of stock would never come to fruition. When he finally went bankrupt some years later, Madame de La Simarde's account – still unpaid – would be only one of many burdens on his business.)

—A car door slammed, interrupting Salvador's train of thought. His fingers, which were in the middle of a complicated run from the bottom to the top of the fretboard, faltered and stumbled.

He looked up and found, to his surprise, that he had played all the way through to the closing passage of the second movement. The little recording device which seemed to exist in his brain, listening carefully and faithfully to every nuance of his performance even when his conscious mind was wandering elsewhere, provided him with a clear playback of snatches of the past few minutes. He closed his eyes and listened to the interior sounds; as he had suspected, the well-worn path along the staves had been trodden mechanically – like an especially unimaginative automaton. He sounded like a fairground barrel-organ.

He put his guitar back on its frame and stood up to look out of the window. His mother's car had started up and was half-way to the gates, where Février was waiting to swing them closed behind her. He was alone at last. He sat down on the edge of his bed and tried to still the incipient tremble of excitement at what was about to happen; his fingers were perspiring and tingling, and his chest was throbbing. With a final glance out of the window to check that his mother was definitely gone (she was – the gates were closed and Février was walking away across the lawn towards the arboretum and the lake), he rose and went over to the towering stereo system which loomed – all bright brushed aluminium panels and dark walnut casings – in the far corner of the room, and switched it on.

That afternoon in Monsieur Duprée's shop, that burning bright splash of glitz in the brown corner had planted a tiny spore of yearning inside him, and in the dank darkness at the back of his mind, the spore had mushroomed into an obsession. At first, he had been overwhelmed by a desire to taste the sound such an instrument might make. For all its strangeness, it was after all the bastard progeny of his own instrument, and he was so attuned to the structure and resonances of guitars that he could make a vague, intuitive guess as to what it might sound like, but he had never heard one played except in overheard fragments of pop songs in which it was hard to tell what instruments were making what sounds.

Then had come another unexpected pivotal moment. A few weeks after his first encounter with the Gibson, he was in New York. Backstage at Carnegie Hall, while his mother was off somewhere having an argument with his tour manager, Salvador got talking with Krstov Velecky, a Czech violinist who was playing in the programme. Krstov was at least a year younger than Salvador, but he had not been shielded nearly as much from the diabolical blandishments of modern music. He found it hilarious that Salvador, a son of the Free West, should be so ignorant of rock and roll; the very score from which capitalism was played.

'You never heard of Cream?' he asked incredulously, but the name elicited only blank incomprehension.

Salvador shook his head. 'No. Who is he?'

Krstov roared with laughter. 'Not a he,' he said. 'Cream is a group. Or it was a group. English. Few years ago. Eric Clapton?'

'I think I've heard the name somewhere. He is a guitarist?' Salvador asked tentatively.

Krstov rolled his eyes and shook his head in disbelief. 'Listen,' he said, tucking his violin under his chin and poising his bow. 'This is called "Sunshine Of Your Love".' He played the riff, watching Salvador's face for a reaction. 'You never heard that?' he asked, stopping after a few bars.

'No.'

'It sounds better with a rock group. Listen to this.' Again, Krstov played several bars: flickering low notes cut up by wailing highs.

Salvador smiled. 'I like that tune,' he said. 'What is that called?'

' "Layla".' Suddenly, Krstov's eyes widened. 'Jimi Hendrix,' he said anxiously. 'Please tell me you know Jimi Hendrix.' He stared at Salvador. 'You don't? You think you are player of guitar and you don't know Jimi Hendrix? Man, I—'

Before he could go any further, Krstov was interrupted by the stage manager giving him his five-minute call. As he walked away, he turned back to Salvador. 'As they say in my country, you are in need of re-education, my friend,' he said. 'Don't worry. I will see to it.'

The following afternoon, Salvador was alone in the sitting room of the hotel suite, stringing his Fleta, when a flat, square package was delivered, wrapped in brown paper with a Macy's label attached. Taped to the front of the package was a blue envelope with his name on it. Inside was a note written in a neat but barely decipherable hand:

Not the rivs I play you but ver important leson One. Listen ver carfuly –
Jimi is God.
Krstov.

He opened the package and found a record; an album that had – to him – two fantastically novel features: a fold-out sleeve containing two LPs, and a cover design consisting of a sea of naked women, their skin strangely tinged with a greenish-tainted sepia, their bodies wallowing in the slopes of a fisheye lens. In the bottom right-hand corner was a legend in austere white capitals: THE JIMI HENDRIX EXPERIENCE: ELECTRIC LADYLAND.

Salvador felt his knees weaken as he gazed at the record, glancing nervously at the door, then he hurried into his bedroom and hastily shoved the record under the bed, along with the ripped packaging and Krstov's note. It wasn't the cover design that alarmed him and made

173

him fear for his mother's reaction should she catch him in possession of it (although that was bad enough) so much as its clear, frank statement that it contained *pop* music.

To his frustration, he had no means of listening to it; the only piece of equipment he carried on tour with him was his portable Uher tape recorder. During the weeks that followed, as the concert itinerary wove across the United States and back to Europe, he received two more flat packages from Krstov. They were always wrapped in brown paper, and were always handed to him personally by hotel staff when his mother was not present. (Madame de La Simarde's reputation was widely known, and even someone as bullish as Krstov was inclined to be discreet.) In addition to the Jimi Hendrix record, there was one by the other group Krstov had mentioned, Cream, and another by someone called Frank Zappa. It was entitled *Zoot Allures*, and the note accompanying it exhorted him to pay special attention to the title track and another piece called 'Black Napkins': *This guy is extrodinry cool*, it said; *This is his newst albm. Perhaps youl dream that one day you play guitar this wel.*

For five weeks, the records inhabited a burrow at the very bottom of his suitcase, while Salvador yearned to be home, in the fragile privacy of his room, so that he could begin to delve into the wicked world of the electric guitar.

While the hi-fi hummed softly, he got down on his knees and groped about in the dust under his bed. The archetypal hiding place. Where most boys of his age kept dirty magazines, though, Salvador kept something much more powerful, with far greater potential for danger and shame.

They were pushed right to the back, and he had to lie flat and stretch to reach them. He emerged a few moments later, clutching his secret treasure: three small plastic cases, unmarked except for their Memorex logos and the letters *A*, *B* and *C*. Records were too difficult to hide. At the first opportunity, he had transferred their contents to cassette and thrown them away, leaving the tapes unlabelled (he had memorised the track listings by this time, anyway). He still hadn't heard them. While they recorded, he had kept the volume turned to zero and his ear pressed to the door, listening out for the approaching clack of footsteps on the landing.

He chose tape *A* and inserted it in the tape deck. Even alone in the house (aside from Avril, who didn't hear too well and would be in the kitchen anyway), he still didn't dare play the tape out loud. He plugged his headphones in and clamped them firmly over his ears before lying down on the bed. When he was comfortable, he reached out and

174

pressed PLAY, then settled down to find out at last what this Jimi Hendrix could do.

The music – loud, raucous, sinuous and sensuous – burst into his brain and whirled around like a tornado. He listened, eyes closed, to the long succession of tracks, his heart almost breaking with disappointment. The surreal electric beauty he had expected to find wasn't here at all; instead there was just cacophonous wailing, grinding and squealing. As the last seconds of 'Voodoo Child (Slight Return)' faded to silence, he knew at last that there was nothing but brambles outside the confining castle walls. He felt he wanted to die, but not without taking vengeance on Krstov for telling him such foul, cruel lies.

He ejected the tape and glared furiously at it. The only thing that prevented him hurling it in the bin was fear of its being discovered there. On an impulse, he replaced it in the tape deck and made himself listen to it again. The more he suffered, he reasoned, the less easily fooled he would be in future.

He hated it less the second time. It still sounded like the aural equivalent of a medieval vision of hell, but the guitar playing was interesting. Interesting in the way the midst of a battlefield was interesting: loud, messy and hellish, but morbidly compelling. The technique was untutored and ragged, but this Hendrix managed to wring some extraordinary, nightmarish sounds and figures from his instrument. Wagnerian hysteria as imagined by an hispanic Edgard Varèse on drugs; that was the closest he could come to describing it.

The third time he listened, he finally got the point. He had been listening with the wrong ears, looking for the wrong things. He should have remembered the revelation in Monsieur Duprée's shop and been properly prepared. He had been blind to the obvious: this music was *meant* to be primitive; it was *meant* to startle and shock. Once he had leapt that simple but invisible hurdle, he found he could switch off his intellect and listen with his heart and gut. The third slight return to the voodoo howls and growls that closed the record made him weep tears of joy.

Initiated now, he carried on with his adventure. He listened to the Cream tape next. It was good, but seemed to lack an indefinable edge that was present in the Hendrix. Eager to go on sampling this strange new world, he switched Cream off half-way through and tried the Frank Zappa.

Here, he leapt right up to the pinnacle. Here, at last, was exactly the thing he had been looking for all along. This man had the same native, violent understanding of the guitar as Hendrix, but he also closed an impossible loop, plugging into the bowels of classical tradition. He had a savagery of temperament, but he understood dissonance and polyrhythms and modes and sophisticated time signatures. Salvador shuttled the tape back and forth, listening to 'Black Napkins', 'Friendly Little Finger' and 'Zoot Allures' over and over, by turns laughing and crying.

And as he listened, he knew one thing: one day, *he* would play like this.

2

He kept getting the feeling he was being followed, but the only thing trailing him was fear. At every corner and in every doorway, he stopped and listened, but there were no sounds at all. No footfalls, no breathing other than his own. They would all be asleep. Even Février, unlikely as it might seem, had to sleep.

He left the shadows of the last outbuilding and set out across the moonlit lawn. He skirted the foot of the mausoleum hill; although it made the distance longer, the steep slope would have been treacherous in the dark. Two hundred metres further on, when the great dome-shaped hill stood between him and the house, he switched on his torch and picked his way towards the tangled fringe of the forest that enclosed the ruins of the Old Château. He had never been here at night before. The overhanging branches and fronds were clotted with deep shadow and lurked with an unseen dread emanating palpably from the husk lying at the forest's heart. The moonlight leaked weakly through the thick canopy, and even the probing finger of torchlight seemed to falter and dim. There was sound here: a continuous blanket of cricket-scritches that reverberated inside his skull. Head swivelling, nervously owl-like, trying to cover every possible direction of attack, he walked up and down under the forest's eaves. It all looked so different at night, and he missed the entrance twice. He found it on the third pass – a moss-clothed stone gate pillar next to a small fig bush. Between was an opening which led to a narrow trodden path. He hesitated a moment, then stepped through and let the forest engulf him.

There was no reason to be fearful here, he told himself. This was the ancient home of his ancestors; one day it would belong to him and he would be its master. But he remembered something his father had said: Philippe de La Simarde had taken a different view from that of his wife, who perceived history – past and future – in terms of triumph and mastery. Salvador's father had always spoken of his ancestry as something immanently powerful to which he was in thrall – an aggregate weight of generations of which he was not the representative but merely the servant, weak and timid and surveilled. Salvador felt their presence here: he was trespassing on their ground, creeping in their ghost gardens with unworthy intent. If he had thought more carefully, he might have chosen a different hiding place for his smuggled goods.

He counted the paces in from the gate pillar – six short steps – and turned left. There, shying back from the yellow torchlight, was a ragged stump of overgrown stone wall; the remains of an ancient gatekeeper's lodge. He set down the torch and, kneeling precariously on the wobbling stones, reached into the bushes on the far side. He fumbled about, thorns and brambles scratching at his knuckles, then his fingers found the rough, crackled vinyl. He felt his way along the edge of the object until he found the plastic handle. He gripped it firmly and pulled. It seemed lighter than it had been that afternoon, when he had carried it up the hill from Gondecourt (creeping out of the post office and making his furtive, darting way through the woods and fields), and it came up from its secret nest with ease. His night-fears ebbed as he looked at the long black case. He should have taken it and hurried back to the house, but the temptation to gloat over his prize was too great to resist. He set it on the wall, undid the glittering clasps, and raised the lid.

At first, he felt a jolt of nightmarish horror, realising that he had been found out and foiled, perhaps even by the ghost ancestors who ruled this place. Inside the case was a bed of green velveteen with a concave guitar-shape, but no guitar. His sanity teetering on the brink, he shone the torch inside and felt into every corner, as though the instrument might be concealing itself there, as petrified as him.

Then the momentarily mad spiralled into whirling insanity. Somewhere behind him, he heard a thin, tinny open chord.

'You are looking for this?'

As he spun round, the torch caught on one of the metal clasps, sending itself and the case clattering over the wall into the bushes. He cried out in anguish and shrank back from the voice, trying to make himself invisible. Suddenly, there didn't seem to be enough darkness.

There on the path, standing in a thin shaft of moonlight, was a girl. She was small and thin – a child, perhaps two or three years younger than him. Her feet were bare, and she wore only a thin white nightdress. Her hair was pale blonde; the colour of tarnished silver in the moonlight. Cradled in her arms, solid and heavy and bright, was his guitar.

'Look what a pretty thing I've found,' she murmured, and stroked a fingernail across the strings. 'How quiet it whispers.'

'Who are you?' he demanded. 'What are you doing here?'

'I knew you would come for it. I watched you hide it. I wanted to know what was inside the long box that was so secret. And what a pretty thing it is!'

'Who are you?' he repeated. 'Where do you come from? This is private property.' He felt foolish even as he said it; here he was, stealing about amidst the graves of the centuries-dead, and telling a ghost-girl it was private property.

'I live there,' she said.

She raised a hand to point vaguely away into the forest blackness, but the guitar was too heavy for her to hold in one hand. It slipped from her grasp and fell with a thud onto the soft earth. She yelped and leapt back from it as Salvador ran forward to grab his precious instrument. He stared at her, still too frightened to be angry. 'Where?' he asked.

With her hands free, she pointed more precisely. 'There,' she said.

He peered into the darkness, then stared at her in disbelief, his fear growing even greater. 'In the *Old Château*?' he whispered.

She laughed. 'Of course not. Only dead people live *there*.'

'Then where?'

'Beyond. It doesn't have a name.' She frowned. 'Perhaps it has a name. I don't know it, though.'

His panic subsided slightly. 'Do *you* have a name?'

She shook her head. 'I don't exist, so I don't have to have a name.'

'Don't exist?'

'That's what Uncle says. *You are a figment of someone else's imagination. Go away.* So I don't need a name.'

'But people must call you something.'

'There is only Uncle. He just calls me *you*. Or sometimes *girl*.'

Salvador yearned to put his guitar back in its case and flee, but he didn't dare turn his back on this bizarre, unearthly waif. He felt she might turn into a monster if he took his eyes off her. He might have been less frightened of her if she had shown even the slightest sign of being afraid of him. But she didn't; she walked right up to him now and stroked the strings of his guitar again. She seemed enchanted by its soft, thin ringing. It was then, as she stood so close he could feel her breath on the back of his hand, that he noticed the human smell of her and his fear receded. He would have expected her to smell of lilies or roses or of nothing; instead, she smelled of unwashed child flesh, a little like slightly soured milk.

'Why does it sing so quiet?' she asked, looking up at him. He could see now what extraordinary eyes she had: large and wide-set, with deep, black, dark-adapted centres. He also sensed the budding nubs of womanhood under the thin nightdress.

The back of his neck prickled with heat, and he took a step back, clutching the neck of the guitar. 'It needs an amplifier,' he said. 'It's electric.'

'Oh.'

'Who *are* you?' he persisted. 'Does this uncle of yours know you're wandering in the forest in the middle of the night nearly . . . with no clothes on?'

She smiled and walked a little way along the path, circled a tree and came back. 'I have clothes on,' she said, looking down at her night-dress. 'I could ask you the same. What are *you* doing in my forest so late? But I know the answer already: *seeking secret treasures.*'

'*Your* forest? I—'

'*Sshh!*' She raised a hand and glanced over her shoulder, as though hearing a call, but all Salvador could hear was the crickets and the owls. 'I have to leave now,' she said, and began to walk away.

He started after her, then hesitated. 'Don't go! I want—'

She turned round, and carried on walking backwards. 'Don't be afraid,' she said. 'I won't tell about your secret.'

'Come back!'

But she was gone; she retreated from the pool of moonlight and shimmered away into the shadows. Her voice came back to him from the darkness, far away: 'Not a soul,' it said, and he heard no more.

He jerked upright in his seat, stumbling from sleep.

'Sir?'

He looked up and saw a face hovering above him, brightly coloured with deep orange tan and fire-engine lipstick.

'Hnh?'

The face smiled; a wide, smooth grin. 'Sorry to wake you up, but we'll be landing in a few minutes.'

The speaker above his head hissed. 'Ladies and gentlemen,' said a male voice. 'This is Captain Donahue. We will be arriving in Sydney in approximately seven minutes: eleven-fifty-eight, local time. The weather on the east coast is clear and sunny, with a temperature of twenty-nine degrees and a slight sea breeze. On behalf of my crew, I hope you have had a pleasant flight and wish you a safe onward journey. Thank you.'

'There,' said the stewardess. 'That proves it.' She smiled again and leaned closer, pushing a thick waft of *Opium* into his face. 'You'll need to fasten your seatbelt,' she said, and moved on up the aisle.

He fumbled sleepily with the straps. One had worked its way under his legs and the other had entangled itself in his neighbour's armrest.

He clasped the ends together and looked out across the wing. Clutched between the glaring aluminium skin and the sky was a triangle of deeper blue, flecked with white, and a slivered arc of glittering, shimmering city. The plane banked suddenly and the wing rose, sweeping away the earth and flooding the window with sky.

So that was it. To have come back after all this time. Now he knew why her face had hit him so startlingly between the eyes. She had reminded him of the nameless moonlight girl. He had forgotten all about her. She had been there all the time, haunting the dark recesses of his mind, overshadowed by what had happened shortly after that night in the forest.

The plane rolled back slowly, the wing levelling off. The ocean had gone, and the city was rising up, its glitter resolving into buildings, roads and crawling cars.

He wondered where she was, what she was doing, whether she was thinking of him.

She was, though she didn't know it. At the very moment the 747's tyres sank down and touched Sydney's concrete, a solar night and half a world away, Lydia was dreaming of him. She saw him in the midst of a night-dark forest, pursuing a white-clothed figure along moonlit paths. The figure was her. She wanted to stop and let him catch her, but her feet would not let her; they just kept carrying her along, faster and faster, until his cries were left far behind.

She whimpered in her sleep and rolled over, sliding gradually into a dreamless, painless black hollow.

By morning, the dream was erased, and she began learning not to think of him at all.

THE SNOW CASTLE

Casualty List

People I have lost. Line them up and call the roll of souls.

6 almost-Great-Uncles	(various causes)
1 Grandmother, paternal	(cancer of the womb)
1 Grandfather, paternal	(heart attack)
1 Grandmother, maternal	(still with us in body, though not in mind)
1 Grandfather, maternal	(lung cancer)
1 Great Aunt	(stroke)
1 Mother	(breast cancer)
1 Father	(road accident)
1 Step-Mother	(murdered, in my dreams)

They have all expended too much grief on each other to have any to spare for me.

She was so pale; so white and translucent, she seemed to emanate light. One small foot flat on the rug, the other on points, toes curled under. White nightdress gathering light from the glittering window and radiating it; thin folds of cotton full of light and the soft shadow of the slight form underneath. There was a truth in her poise; an honesty in the purity of her paleness; an unfleshed opinion, unsubstance which could stream unhindered through a needle's eye.

. . . For a few moments, Beth believed she might still be asleep; still wandering in the dream of the woman in white . . . Then, Audrey turned away from the window and gazed at her. For the first time ever, she noticed how insubstantial Audrey was; in that undefended moment of aloneness, she saw the gracility of her body and the attenuated delicacy of her face, like thin, translucent porcelain. Just in that one moment, between *She's still sleeping* and *Ah, you're awake.* Then she smiled, her eyes veiling themselves over with a mesh of immanent strength.

'Come and look,' she said.

Beth rubbed the sticky beads of sleep from the corners of her eyes and pushed back the bedclothes. A fire had been kindled in the grate, but the air felt cold around her calves after the deep, heavy heat of the bed. Walking on the balls of her feet to keep the sensitive insteps off the icy boards, Beth crossed the room and joined Audrey on the rug by the window. Peering out through the frosted panes, she saw the reason for the brilliance of the morning light. The window overlooked the courtyard, and from tower to tower, from the fan of steps below to the ridged roof of the Italian Wing opposite, the whole castle was clothed in deep snow. It cloaked, mantled and capped the towers and clung to the piers of the arched galleries. And still it fell; fat, cottony flakes drifting and swirling, blurring against the rhombus of grey sky above the castle's roofs.

'I was about to wake you,' said Audrey, her voice hushed as though the falling flakes might hear her and stop frolicking. 'I wanted you to see it now, while it's still like this.'

'It's beautiful,' Beth murmured.

'It is, isn't it? . . . You won't see a sight like this often in your mortal life.'

They watched in silence, feeling like children on the very fringes of the world, peering into a magical kingdom.

Beth shivered. 'I've gone all goose-bumpy,' she said, rubbing her arms. Audrey didn't seem to feel the cold at all, and stayed where she was while Beth turned reluctantly away from the window and went to crouch down in front of the fire. When she had warmed herself through, she left Audrey to get dressed and went down the corridor to the bathroom.

She rotated the industrial-scale polished brass taps and, while the deep, narrow bath began to fill with a combined Niagara of scalding and icy waters, billowing smoky steam, she lifted the toilet lid and peered apprehensively inside. The water in the bowl was crystal clear, even though she was sure she hadn't flushed it last night. Perhaps that had been a dream, too.

The bath filled rapidly; by the time she had undressed, the swirling water was beginning to lap at the lip below the rim. She turned the taps off, tested the temperature, and climbed in. She lay back for a while, listening to the gurgle of water in the overflow pipe and letting the warmth seep into her, then lifted her legs one by one and began soaping away the night's sleepwalking grime.

Half an hour later, her skin steeped to pale pink and tingling against the brush of the soft cotton nightdress, she padded back along the corridor to Audrey's room.

Audrey was dressed and made-up, and was standing in front of the window again, looking out at the snow while she brushed her hair. She turned round as Beth came in. 'Ah,' she said, noticing the soggy clump of white cotton in Beth's hand. 'You've encountered Personal Hygiene Dilemma Number One.'

Beth unfolded the washed-wet knickers and frowned at them. 'I gave them a wash through. They'll be dry in an hour if I put them in front of the fire. I'll have to do without them for a bit.'

'I'd have given you a liner if you'd asked.'

'I didn't know you had any.'

'Well, you didn't ask.'

Beth shrugged and carried a chair over to the hearth-rug. 'Actually, I think I'd prefer clean to lined,' she said, draping the damp little triangle over the chair-back. '. . . Aud, I know this might sound daft, but have

184

you been to the toilet this morning?'

'Yes, why?'

'Was there a wee already in there?'

Audrey laughed. 'In the bowl or on the floor? I can't say I noticed. No, I don't think so. Why?'

'Oh, just something I must've dreamt.' She looked around and sighed. 'Better get dressed, I suppose.' She glanced uncertainly at the door, thinking of her clothes, still where she had taken them off last night. In that room. 'Er, this is going to sound even dafter, but will you come with me?'

Audrey smiled indulgently. The snow seemed to have put her in an extraordinarily good mood. 'Come on,' she said. 'I'll hold your hand.'

Beth's watch was still ticking on the bedside table. Her skirt and blouse were still neatly folded on the chair by the window. The curtains were still drawn. The hearth rug still had a little black-edged bite out of one side. The bedclothes were thrown back, as though the occupant had got up hurriedly. Gone to the toilet. Back in a few moments . . .

And that was all there was to show that anyone had been here. The paintings hung on their hooks, the wardrobe door was closed, and the multitude of drawers nestled, unopened, in their proper places.

Beth stared dumbly at the room while Audrey wandered about peering at things like a detective looking for clues. 'You're sure you took *all* the drawers out?' she asked. Beth nodded, and Audrey looked satisfied. 'Well, there you go – you did dream it.' She opened one of the drawers in the chiffonier and looked inside.

'I *must* have,' Beth murmured. 'But it was so *real* . . . Maybe they've been put back.'

'Who by? Elves?'

'Avril or someone.'

Audrey slid open another drawer. 'They were all empty, you said?'

'Every one of them. It seemed so cruel, like they couldn't wait to obliterate every last trace of Lydia.'

Audrey beckoned. 'You *did* dream it. Come here . . .'

Beth joined her in front of the chiffonier. She stared into the open bottom drawer, her jaw going slack.

'I think we've found a solution to our little underwear dilemma,' said Audrey.

The drawer was full – bulging, brim-full – of women's underpants: cotton briefs, lace-trimmed panties, silk french knickers; all neatly folded and piled in rows; two rows white, one shell-pink, one sky-blue, one black.

Audrey opened the next drawer up. 'Bras and camis,' she said, and opened the next. 'Socks and tights . . . Scarves . . . T-shirts and tops . . . More T-shirts . . . Oh, and one empty one.'

'Lydia's,' Beth whispered. She lifted up the sleeve of a fuchsia T-shirt, stroking the soft fabric between finger and thumb, then let it fall again. In her memory, she usually pictured Lydia in a pink T-shirt. Lying on the sun-dried grass of Laundress Green, her thick metallic hair spilling out amongst the stalks or flowing over her cradling hand . . .

'Well, waste not, want not,' said Audrey.

'What?'

Audrey knelt down and began picking about in the knicker-drawer. 'Our need is the greater. As you said, better clean than lined.'

'But you can't!' Beth protested, aghast. 'They're Lydia's!'

Audrey paused and glanced up at her. 'Come off it, Beth. Look at them – these are all brand new. They've never been worn.' She picked out a pair of black panties and held them up for inspection.

'They're still Lydia's.'

'I doubt if she even saw them, let alone touched them. Beth, not everyone spends Sunday washing out the same sad pairs of pants they've had for years. Some people are so rich they probably don't wear the same pair twice. I've known people like that. Lydia was that rich.'

Beth still looked doubtful. 'They're still hers,' she repeated. 'Whether she wore them or not.'

'Oh, for God's sake, Beth, don't be so sensitive. So superstitious. I doubt if Lydia's soul resides in a pair of M&S skimpies. Here . . .' She pulled out two pairs of plain briefs, one black, one white, and tossed them at Beth, who caught them awkwardly in her arms. 'It's just a shame the bras are the wrong size,' Audrey went on. 'Too big for me, too small for you, I'd guess. Still, there are plenty of tights if you're still feeling squeamish about stockings.' She pushed the drawers closed and stood up. 'I'll leave you to your modesty, then. I'm going to see if I can hunt down some breakfast.'

Beth walked along the corridor towards the stairs, spiritually and physically uneasy in her burgled underwear. Lydia had evidently stayed as skinny as ever. At twenty, she had hovered on the threshold between size eight and ten, whereas Beth had been ten creeping in the direction of twelve. In the past few years, her hips had completed that stage of their outward journey, and were entrenched at twelve. Soon, she suspected, they would up and continue marching with smug confidence towards fourteen. Lydia's little pants weren't exactly uncomfortable, but they were decidedly snug.

She paused at the foot of the stairs, glancing about and wondering where to go. The hall, though still gloomy, war far less scary with the morning snow-light filtering in through the glazed vestibule doors. Even the armoured nights seemed docile and almost benign, snoozing quietly behind their visors.

Cocking her head and listening, she heard a sound of clinking china and metal clashing lightly on metal. It came from the right-hand corridor, in the opposite direction from the Music Room. She remembered that this was the corridor the ghostly-wild dream-girl had run from in her desperate flight. The memory, though it seemed insubstantial now and as fleeting as the girl herself, made her nervous as she followed the sounds, peeping cautiously through open doors into ante-rooms, drawing rooms and parlours. The last door on the right gave onto a small room (*small*, she thought sardonically; her and Iain's little flat would fit into it nearly twice over) with a long, polished mahogany dining-table in the centre and two sideboards beneath the windows, laden with plates, napkins, cutlery and bright silver domes. Audrey was there, alone, coffee cup in one hand and a cigarette in the other. She was working her way along the right-hand sideboard, lifting the lids of tureens and salvers one by one.

She glanced up as Beth came in. 'There's no kedgeree,' she said, raising the dome of a particularly huge tureen, peeping underneath and replacing it. 'My first real country-house breakfast, and there's no kedgeree. Or devilled kidneys.'

Beth poured herself a cup of tea and took two croissants from a piled salver. 'And you can thank your lucky stars,' she said, sitting at the table. 'Have you ever had it? Rice and fish for breakfast . . . I had it once at my cousin's. Delusions of grandeur, that branch of the family. I nearly yugged it all up in the garden.'

Audrey gave up the search and sat at the table with her pot of coffee and her cigarette. 'I'm not that hungry anyway,' she said.

Beth tore open a croissant, hesitated a moment, then buttered it. It was a cold day, after all; she'd need some fats. 'What's the plan?' she asked. 'What shall we do?'

'Hm . . . Well, assuming the local bumpkins have put my car right, we should be away by about . . .' She looked at her watch. 'Oh, midday at the latest, I should think. I'll drop you at Exeter station. Does that suit?'

'Thanks. What about the weather?'

Audrey got up and went to the window. The snow had stopped falling now, and the clouds were thinning, but it was at least a couple of feet deep where it had drifted beneath the window.

'No problem,' she said. 'I've driven on snow before. Anyway, it won't be as bad once we're down off the moors.'

Beth nodded. 'Audrey, we . . .' She hesitated.

Audrey waited. '. . . What?' she said at last.

'Oh nothing.' Beth stirred a dribble of milk into her tea.

We should keep in touch. She had caught herself on the brink of saying it; funny how the human mind was littered with all the trite little stock expressions, and offered them up at appropriate moments – even when you didn't want them – like an over-attentive waiter. One for every occasion, but especially for meeting and parting, for tacking together the parted ribbons of separate lives. *How are you? What have you been doing all these years? Do call if you're in the area. We must keep in touch.* Part of her had almost meant it. She had discovered an affection for Audrey that had taken her by surprise. Either Audrey had changed (in the unfrightening light of day, Beth wasn't so sure about this) or she herself had changed. Or perhaps it was just circumstance and heightened sentiment. Perhaps the affection wasn't for Audrey, but for what she represented; a scrap of the distant past; the time when everything worked and was new. Whatever; it wouldn't work now. There was too much hurt hidden there, poking up through the surface like the bones of bodies buried in windblown dunes. Too many bad spirits and malignant memories. She would prefer to keep this weekend in her pocket; a single memory of closure; the moment she finally said goodbye and resumed the long business of forgetting.

Audrey had caught her unspoken mood, if not its meaning. 'Actually,' she said, 'I'll be sorry to leave this place, won't you?'

Beth looked around the walls. 'No, I won't.'

'I mean, I'm desperately sorry about Lydia and everything, of course I am, and I wish the circumstances were different, but this place is just . . . out of this world.'

Beth nodded. Out of this world; that was it exactly. Exactly what had gone wrong for Lydia: she had been plucked out of the world and made to live confined in this nether-land of dead ancestors who weren't even her ancestors . . . And *Sorry about Lydia and everything?* What everything? There was no everything; there was just Lydia, dead. Bracketed in Audrey's mind with a nonexistent everything that reduced her importance to a mere constituent of itself.

'The sooner I get out of here the better,' she said, putting down her half-eaten croissant and slumping back in her chair.

Just then, they became aware that they were being watched. They looked up, and found the maid standing unobtrusively in the doorway. Beth flushed, hoping her last words hadn't been overheard, but Audrey just smiled with perfect condescension.

'Good morning, Avril,' she said. 'Where's your mistress this morning? We were expecting to breakfast *en famille.*'

Beth flinched inside at the insensitivity of this remark; if there was one thing this chilly house conspicuously lacked now, it was a family.

Avril bobbed a little curtsy and advanced into the room. 'Madame takes breakfast at seven o'clock,' she explained. 'She did not wish her guests to be disturbed so early.'

'Very considerate,' said Audrey. 'Is there any news of my car? We'd like to be away before the end of the morning.'

'I do not know, Madame. Février has attended to it.' She looked uncomfortable. Timid creature, she had probably only come to clear away the breakfast things, and hadn't bargained for the visitors still being there, let alone having to answer their questions. 'Madame de La Simarde will be in the Blue Morning Room when you have finished your breakfast,' she added with an effort, then curtsied and began to back out of the room.

'Wait a minute,' said Audrey, glancing at Beth. 'Where's the Blue Morning Room?'

'Ah, it is next to the Green Parlour.'

Audrey rolled her eyes. 'And the Green parlour is . . .?'

'It is next to the Music Room, Madame.'

'The Music Room?'

'Yes, Madame. That is—'

'Okay, okay. We know where the Music Room is.' She gazed at Avril for a moment, relishing her next words before uttering them. 'You may go now.'

'Thank you, Madame.'

When she had left, Audrey poured herself a second cup of coffee and lit another cigarette. 'Why do they assume that the layout is so self-evident? *Next to the Green Parlour?* I mean, *what?*'

Beth smiled. 'You really get a kick out of bullying the servants, don't you? I think you were born into the wrong age and . . .' She was about to say *and class*, but stopped herself; Audrey wouldn't take kindly to being reminded of her origins, nor of the fact that Beth knew about them. She stirred her cooling tea and said instead: 'Maybe it should've been you that married Salvador.'

Audrey pulled a face. '*Me?*'

Beth looked steadily at her. 'You fancied him enough.'

'. . . Well, maybe enough for . . . No, not enough to marry him . . .' She took a mouthful of coffee and stubbed out her half-smoked cigarette. 'Come on, eat up. We'd better be going and saying our goodbyes.'

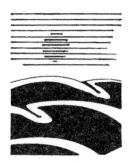

As they walked along the corridor, Beth wondered what had become of Rachel. Typically slow, she had slipped a day behind everyone else.

Farewell. Farewell until I see you reborn . . .

Rachel crouched at the foot of the rocky tor and spoke low into the cool, moist air. One by one, she received the objects Clifford passed down to her and laid them out on a flat shelf of stone.

A granite pebble.
I shall know you in earth and in stone
A twig of hawthorn
I shall know you in the roots of the earth and in all things living
Intertwined sprigs of berry-clustered holly and mistletoe
I shall know you in death and in birth
A twenty-pence coin
I shall know you in riches and in the love of giving
I shall know you each apart and both together, always and everywhere . . .

When the offerings were laid and the words spoken, she unwrapped her flute from its velvet shroud and put it to her lips. Starting softly, she whispered a trail of notes from its hollow silver, sometimes sparse, sometimes flurrying. It was a tune she hadn't played in years – Clifford had never heard it before – but she remembered every note. Its composer had called it *Evening Whispers Echoed*, and Rachel was now the only person living who knew it and understood its significance.

This – all of this – had come as a double-barrelled shock to her. The others – Beth and Audrey – had known about his death for a long time. Read it in the papers, probably. But for Rachel, it was as though they had both been snuffed out simultaneously. Which, in a sense, they had: only existing in her mind these seven years, their death and its news were one and the same thing.

She concluded her little ceremony and stood up, Clifford's hand at her elbow helping her overcome the cold-induced stiffness in her knees. For a while they stood and contemplated the arrangement of offerings on the gritty stone altar, and the towering tor and the emptiness of the moor, and Rachel thought a last goodbye to the two people she had loved most and known least.

After a while, she sighed and took Clifford's hand. It was getting late, and the light was beginning to fail; while a suitable place had been easy enough to find – the tor had beckoned like a beacon – gathering the proper items had taken a lot of walking and poking about in the hedgerows and copses that clung about the shoulders of the moor near the church.

'Come on,' she said. 'They'll be wondering where we've got to.'

They walked down the long, shallow slope towards the church where Lydia's mortal remains lay under the wet black soil and where their painted home was still parked aslant on the grass verge.

The old VW started first time, as it nearly always did. In a previous incarnation more earthly than those that Rachel had come to believe in, Clifford had been a motor mechanic (though one wouldn't think it to look at his spindly frame and long, delicate, almost dainty fingers), and he lavished the same kind of fond and painstaking care on the VW's engine as Rachel did on her precious silver flute.

The camper burbled smoothly down the hill into the village. Clifford brought it to a halt at a T-junction, waiting while a small train of cars churned impatiently on the main street. They had been forced to a crawl by a tow-truck negotiating its way carefully around a pair of bollards to make the turn-off. As it turned, passing the camper and beginning to grind and wheeze its way up the hill, Clifford looked at the car it was towing: a shiny green hatchback with its front wheels clamped to the truck's tail in an attitude of supplication. If he hadn't known better, he would have sworn it was the same car he'd seen a few hours ago at the church; the snazzy little Rover belonging to Rachel's snooty friend. He craned his neck and looked at the number plate, but only got a few letters before it was out of sight. However, he did spot a blue strip sticker in the rear window with BURRELL ROVER and a London phone number . . . It *was* her car.

He pointed it out to Rachel, who twisted round in her seat to peer after the receding rear end. 'I wonder what's happened. Can we follow it?' she asked.

He grunted. 'Not really,' he said. There was a car behind them, gunning its engine impatiently, and the roads were too narrow and the junction too tight for the ungainly VW to execute a smart U-turn. The car behind parped its horn, and Clifford let in the clutch, swinging left in the direction the tow-truck had come from.

'They might be in the pub still,' said Rachel without much conviction. 'Wherever it is,' she added with even less.

Like Beth and Audrey before them, they found that the little village only had one pub. They parked the van in the car park and went in. There was no sign of the two friends, and the surly landlord wasn't eager to help. (Maggie had gone upstairs soon after Beth and Audrey had left, her veins screaming blue murder. She told George that if he didn't go down and take over, she'd give him something to make him think a bunion was a birthday present.) He looked at their unkempt hair and ragbag clothes with undisguised distaste and answered Rachel's questions with hostile, monosyllabic grunts. No, he hadn't seen any women in his pub. Yes, he was sure. No, he didn't recognise the sketchy descriptions she offered. Yes, a broken-down car had been towed away from the car park. No, he didn't know who it belonged to.

Back outside, they stood in the car park for a few minutes, wondering what to do next. Rachel looked about at the hedges, the muddy ground, the trees, the houses across the street, as though expecting to detect a clue or pick up a scent.

'I know!' she said at last, clapping her hands. 'We'll try the garage! They're probably there.'

They embarked again and retraced the route taken by the truck, turning off the main street and heading back up the hill. But there was no garage on that road, and they were out of the village in no time, heading back towards the moor. They backtracked and scoured the streets. Eventually, at the far end of the village, they found it: a bare and potholed forecourt with two battered pumps and some dilapidated, dusty-windowed buildings decorated with discoloured adverts for spark plugs, Simoniz and Michelin tyres. Rachel got out and went to a shed-like lean-to at the side, where there was a door marked RECEPTION in scratched hand-painted letters. After a few minutes, she came out again, looking even more bewildered than when she went in. She climbed back into her seat.

'Any luck?' Clifford asked.

'Strange,' she said. 'It was their truck all right, but he didn't know where it was going. Not back here, apparently.' She turned and looked at Clifford. 'I don't understand. What can have happened to them?'

Choosing Salvador

1

It was Christmas Eve, and Rachel was alone at number 3 Ainsworth Cottages. The others had gone home for the holiday. Even Lydia had found a family to stay with: Gabriel had recently got married and had curtailed his travelling for a while. To mark the beginning of his new life as a family man, he had invited his step-sister to spend Christmas with him and his brand-new wife in Yorkshire.

Rachel didn't mind being alone; she was alone inside her head most of the time anyway. She could have gone home if she had wanted to. Instead, she had opted to save her soul by volunteering over the holiday at the homeless shelter on Chesterton Road and playing in the seasonal concerts at St Edward's church. Among her small concessions to self-indulgence, she had bought a little tree and a box of tinsel from the hardware shop at the end of the street and set it up in the sitting-room window. At its feet was a small pile of presents, some wrapped by herself for herself, but most sent by her parents.

A glass of wine partially mulled in front of the gas fire and Bach's Magnificat on the turntable. Perfect. She was standing in front of the tree and wondering whether she ought to put some lights on it (if she hurried, she could just make it to the shops before they closed) when there was a glass-rattling knock on the door. She flinched, spluttering tepid spiced wine, and looked at her watch. It was far too early for Henny to be calling; St Edward's wasn't for another three hours. She put her glass down and crept out into the hall, leaving the light off. There was a tall, distorted man-shape beyond the panes in the door, silhouetted by the lane's solitary lamp. Its arm reached out and knocked again, and there was a short, muffled coughing sound. Whoever it was must be aware that someone was at home; if they couldn't hear the sound of Bach (which she now realised was rather loud), they would have seen the light on in the sitting room. She braced herself and went to the door, putting the chain on before opening it; just enough to peep out, ready to slam it shut again if necessary. There was a man standing on the path. He was tall, with shaggy, curly hair that straggled over the collar of his shapeless overcoat and a beard that looked as though it had been half chewed away by rats. He looked like one of the denizens of the hostel, but what on earth was he doing here? Might he have been following her? She peered at him, trying to place him. There was something vaguely familiar about him, but the part of his face that wasn't hidden behind the unkempt beard was obscured by shadow.

He cleared his throat, making that hoarse coughing sound again. 'Hello,' he said.

Another pang of familiarity. 'Hello,' she said automatically. 'Er, what can I do for you? The hostel's not full already, is it? I can give you an address if you . . .'

She tailed off. He was laughing at her; at least, his shoulders were shaking, and she assumed he was laughing. 'You don't recognise me, do you?' he said. 'It's me, Rachel.'

She frowned and peered closer, trying to penetrate the shadows. 'Sal . . . No. *Salvador*. It's you!'

She saw an arc of white teeth amongst the beard. 'You're not going to pass out on me again, are you?' he said. 'I don't think I could catch you through this door.'

'What are you going to do now?' she asked. 'Resume your fellowship?'

He looked down at his mug of coffee and shrugged. Seeing him in the light, she realised how misled she had been by his beard and uncut hair; instead of the rags her prejudiced imagination had dressed him in, the clothes he was wearing – a baggy herringbone coat over a thick sweater and jeans – were clean and kempt. Wherever he had been sleeping in the past eight months, it clearly hadn't been under hedgerows.

'I don't know,' he said. 'I doubt they'd have me back after this long.'

'Nonsense. Of course they would. This is Cambridge, remember. Lydia's tutor disappeared for nearly a year once. Everyone assumed he was doing fieldwork in Bali, but it turned out he was pursuing his ex-wife around the West Midlands, trying to get custody of their children. They took him back without a word.'

Salvador smiled, but couldn't conceal the pall of anxiety in his face at the mention of Lydia. 'I don't know,' he repeated. 'Maybe I don't want to come back.'

'Then why are you here?'

He put his mug down on the floor and looked frankly at her. 'Isn't it obvious?' he asked.

Nine months ago, she would have been nervous in his presence, and flustered by his look, but not any more. She gazed steadily back at him. 'If you've come looking for Lydia, she's not here.'

He looked down. 'I guessed that. Where is she?'

'I doubt if she'd want to see you even if she was. You should think yourself lucky you found me here and not Beth. I saved you from a beating once before; I'm not so sure I'd do it again. If it weren't for the fact that I feel this is all my fault, I'd—'

'Why would *Beth* want to beat me?'

'Because Lydia's our friend, and she'd be too gentle to beat you herself.'

He stared at the carpet. 'I see.'

'You broke her heart, Salvador.'

He looked up again. 'Did I?' He sounded almost pleased with himself; he recognised the tone himself, and backtracked before Rachel could pounce: 'I mean, I never dared hope she cared for me that much.'

'Cared for you? She loved you, Salvador. And you deserted her.'

'Do you imagine I'm proud of that? You've got no idea what my life has been like. When my mother came . . . I just had to go. I went out of my mind for a little while.'

'No idea what *your* life has been like? Can you imagine what Lydia's life was like after you disappeared? You never even phoned or wrote. You might have been dead for all she knew.' She paused, and her tone softened slightly. 'Where did you go?'

He shrugged. 'I drove around the country for a while. When I'd spent nearly all my money, I left the car at Heathrow and got on a flight to Australia.'

'Australia? Why?'

'An old friend lives there. We were child prodigies together. Performing monkeys, as I used to say.' He smiled. 'It was like those Vietnam veterans with messed-up heads huddling together in the forest because nobody else understands them. I thought Krstov would understand. He's done very nicely for himself. He teaches violin at a school in Melbourne. Married now, with two little children, and very happy. He put me up for a few months. We played some recitals together, with me on piano. I got a few things straight in my mind, then I felt I was ready to come back. That and I think Valeria wanted her life and her husband back. Whatever, I got on a plane and here I am.'

Rachel waited for him to go on, but he seemed to think he had provided enough of an explanation. 'And you thought you'd waltz back and take up with Lydia where you left off?'

'No, I'm not stupid. I know what I did to her, and I'm sorry. I just hoped she might . . .' He shrugged.

'. . . Forgive you? I wouldn't bank on it . . .' She gazed at Salvador; defensive of Lydia as she might be, she couldn't help feeling for him. 'It's no good telling me you're sorry. Tell her. And make sure you mean it.'

His eyes lit up. 'You'll tell me where I can find her?'

She gazed at him in silence for a long time. 'I shouldn't,' she said at last. 'I *ought* to tell you to go to hell and never bother her again. I expect that's what Gabriel will do . . .' She went over to the table and wrote something on a slip of paper. Before handing it over, she took a long look at him. 'I'd have a haircut and get rid of that horrid beard if I were you. I don't think cavemen are quite Lydia's taste.' She laughed. 'Listen to me – I sound like Audrey all of a sudden. Audrey thinks I'm a sentimental drip, and maybe she's right.' She held out the slip of paper. 'This is the address. I know I'll live to regret it, but I think you should have one last chance. Both of you.'

2

If Gabriel had been in a better mood, things might have worked out very differently. As it was, there was almost a fight in the street.

It hadn't been a good Christmas in the Huttons' fledgeling household. In his years of travelling, Gabriel had experienced many different Christmases: from Times Square to Bondi Beach to carousals in the expatriate communities of countries where Christmas didn't officially exist. The British domestic family Christmas, though, was just a foggy memory; from abroad, his home thoughts had slowly transformed it into a thing of Dickensian goodwill. Over the past few days, though, the cosy image had been dismembered log by log and chestnut by chestnut, and he was not a happy man. His ill-humour had begun before the season had even got into full swing, mostly because of Helen. He was finding out things about his new wife that he would have preferred to remain hidden. Most upsetting of all was an incomprehensible and almost instantaneous dislike of Lydia. Torn between the two women, he found himself instinctively siding with his step-sister; not at all good for marital harmony, this led to a semi-private argument on Christmas Eve which Helen concluded by implying that his *obsession* with Lydia couldn't be entirely explained by brotherly loyalty. She stormed off, leaving this hideous accusation hanging in the air, and spent the night at her parents' house. She returned the next day, contrite and determined to make the best of the limited Christmas spirit, and with her mother and father in tow. She cooked a passable lunch, and things seemed to settle nicely back on track, despite the fact that her present to Gabriel was an entirely inexplicable Black & Decker drill (he was useless at handiwork). His mother turned up after lunch; she drank four glasses of red wine, laughed at the drill, and, unable to resist Lydia's presence, immediately resumed her stepmother persona. Gabriel now found himself defending Lydia from two sides whilst simultaneously fending off his mother's snide attacks on Helen's housekeeping. The house had five bedrooms, so when the guests showed no inclination to leave that evening, he felt he had no option but to invite them to stay over. All of them accepted. By lunch time on Boxing Day, he had had enough. Lydia had hidden herself away in her room, and he felt the need to escape as well. Pleading the garage's sudden and desperate need for shelving, he picked up his present and made a dash for the front door. It was a mistake. An hour later, with extraordinary skill, he had bored a total of three wonky holes in the garage wall and somehow managed to break the drill. Instead of whirring busily, it just gave out a plaintive wailing and emitted little wisps of acrid smoke.

It wasn't the best time for another unwelcome visitor to call. At first, under the impression that the man was just some innocent friend of Lydia's from college, Gabriel tried his best to quell his temper and be polite. He went indoors and called Lydia down from her room. As soon as he saw the expression on her face as she looked at the man, he realised his mistake. Frustrated, bored, homebound, angry and with his one matrimonial Christmas present lying dead on the garage floor, something snapped inside him. He took a swing.

'You *cunt!*' he roared.

'*Gabriel! NO!*' Lydia hurled herself at his back, trying to restrain his fist as it arced out. Gabriel lost his balance; his punch whisked past Salvador's head and he toppled over, landing face-down in the flower bed with Lydia on top of him. She scrambled to her feet, and Salvador stepped forward to help her. Seeing this, Gabriel was up in a flash and ready to have another go. This time, Lydia stepped between them. She put her arms around Gabriel to restrain him.

'Don't,' she pleaded. 'Leave him, please.'

'*Cunt!*' he growled over her shoulder. 'I ought to pull your fucking *head* off.'

'I know,' said Salvador. 'I wouldn't blame you if you did.'

'Wouldn't you? Oh, *wouldn't* you?' Gabriel struggled, but Lydia tightened her grip. 'Let me at him, Lyd. I'll show the bastard he can't mess around with my family.'

'Stop it, Gabriel!' She held him even tighter, eyes closed. 'I know you're angry, but you're just hurting me even more with this.' Feeling him relax, she loosened her grip and held him at arms' length. 'Go indoors, Gabriel. I'll deal with this.'

He didn't take his eyes off Salvador. 'No,' he snarled. 'I'm not leaving you alone with this poncy strip of shit.'

Lydia glanced at Salvador, then smiled warmly at her brother. 'Gabriel, *go*,' she said softly, and rubbed his chest. 'I'll be okay . . . Please?'

Eventually, Gabriel was persuaded to leave them alone. He gave Salvador one last venomous look, then went inside and closed the front door. He found the others watching the scene through the sitting-room window. Helen turned and gazed at him as he came in. She didn't say anything; she was wearing that expression again; the one she had worn on Christmas Eve. She shook her head contemptuously and went out to the kitchen.

'Nice-looking boy,' his mother said, turning away from the window. 'Who'd have thought it, little Lydia . . .?'

He leaned close to her, his mouth almost brushing her nose. 'Mum,' he whispered, 'why don't you just fuck off and die.'

'I'm sorry,' he said. 'I think I've ruined your Christmas.'

'Don't flatter yourself. It was already ruined.' She looked back at the house and saw the sitting-room curtains twitch. 'Come on,' she said, going out through the gate. 'There's too much of an audience here.'

They walked along the street until they came to a children's playground. It was deserted apart from two young mothers loading their toddlers onto the baby swings. Lydia sat down on the roundabout and watched them.

'Why do you have that effect?' she asked absently.

'What effect? Making people angry?'

'Men,' she murmured. 'That too. No, I was thinking more of your effect on women. What is it that makes them want to protect you? Like Rachel . . .' She grinned involuntarily at the memory, then quickly hardened her face again.

'I saw her. She told me where I could find you.'

'Did she now. I think I'll be picking a few bones with Rachel.' She glanced up. 'Sit down, for Christ's sake – you're making me nervous hovering like that.'

He sat down next to her on the roundabout and fingered the chipped yellow paint on the steel handrail between them. 'It wasn't her fault,' he said.

198

'I know. She couldn't resist . . . You know, I should've let Gabriel thump you really.'

'You should,' he agreed. Suddenly, he got up again and knelt on the tarmac in front of her. 'Here,' he said, pointing to his cheekbone. 'You thump me.'

'Don't be ridiculous.'

'I mean it,' he said. 'I'm offering you revenge. Here's my face; go on, hit it.'

In spite of herself, she laughed. 'Get up, you fool.' He didn't move; just knelt there smiling that smile of his. 'You realise,' she said, 'if Gabriel hadn't been in such a foul mood, I probably wouldn't be sitting here talking to you. I'd've just gone back indoors, he'd've told you where to go, and that would've been that. If he hadn't gone to hit you . . .' She looked at him and sighed. 'My bag was all packed, Salvador. I was so excited. I sat in the hall and waited for you for three hours, and you never came. I thought something awful had happened to you.'

He got up off his knees and sat down on the roundabout again. 'It had. My mother happened to me.'

'What's that supposed to mean?'

'I hope for your sake you never find out.'

'Don't play games with me, Salvador. You owe me an explanation.'

'I'm not playing games. My mother forbade me to see you. She told me she had instructed Sir Michael that my fellowship was to be terminated if I carried on seeing you . . . I argued with her. For the first time in my life, I actually stood up to her. I said I had never wanted the fellowship in the first place; that I would give it up tomorrow and go if it weren't for wanting to be there for you. She said terrible things about you then; things I can't bear to think about, let alone repeat. I said even worse things back. She is immensely strong, immensely powerful, but I know how she can be hurt. She did something she had never done before – perhaps because she never needed to before – she struck me. Slapped me across the face. I realised then how wrong I was to be scared of her; her power over me was an illusion. I mean, anyone can hit, can't they?'

Lydia looked at him and knew he was lying, but only to himself. He was scared still; there was a plaintive tone in the question; a tone that begged her to tell him he shouldn't be. How could anyone be that frightened of their own mother? 'What did you do when she hit you?' she asked gently. When he didn't reply, she answered herself: 'You hit her back, didn't you?'

He nodded. 'She's so strong inside. After a while you don't see how small she is. She fell over and hit her head. She was standing in the middle of the room, near the table. When she fell down – when I *knocked* her down, she hit her head on the corner. I panicked and ran away. I thought I had killed her. I'm not proud of myself for what I did to her. I'm even more ashamed of what I did to you.'

'You could've contacted me. You could've phoned.'

'I did. I tried.'

'What do you mean, you *tried?*'

'I called your house before I left Cambridge. They said you didn't want to speak to me, which seemed reasonable. Didn't they tell you?'

'Who? Who's *they?*'

'I think it was Audrey, but I'm not sure. It might have been the other one . . . Beth?'

Lydia stared. All this time she had been blaming everything on Salvador, and all the time there had been this knife stuck unseen and unfelt between her shoulder blades.

'I'm sure they were just trying to protect you,' he suggested. 'Who can blame them, in the circumstances.'

A bitter breeze was beginning to stir the air in the playground, and tiny beads of reluctant snow were starting to whirl. Lydia was wearing the clothes she had come to the door in – a thin cardigan over a T-shirt – and Salvador noticed that she was shivering; deep shudders that started in her stomach and juddered up through her body. He took off his overcoat and wrapped it round her shoulders, coiling his arms around her to fold it closed at the front.

'So,' he said, sitting back and looking about him at the playground and the back gardens. 'This is the real Sheffield.'

'I don't know. Is there any other kind?'

'It's one of those places I only remember as a date on a tour schedule. I played here once at the . . . I can't remember what the theatre was called.'

She shrugged inside the voluminous coat. 'The Crucible?'

He shook his head. 'Possibly. It was a long time ago, and it wasn't a regular venue. That was at the height of my monkey fame.'

'Your what fame?'

'Never mind. You grew up here?'

'Some of the time. My dad brought me here to live after Mum died. He married Susan and exposed me to nine years of living hell. For three of those years, I didn't even have him to run to, after he died. Gabriel was the only one who kept me sane.' She glanced at Salvador. 'Don't judge him by what you saw just now. He's the closest I've got to real family. He sees himself as my protector, and he *has* protected me. From his own mother, mostly. And his wife.'

A silence descended and settled on them like the thickening snow crystals that were gathering on their clothes and hair. They both knew that there was only one thing left to say, and neither wanted to be the one to say it; him to beg it or her to offer or deny it. Eventually, Salvador begged it.

'So,' he began tentatively. 'Will you . . . I mean, can you . . . Lydia, I want you to come back with me.'

She looked at him and smiled. 'Won't you lose your fellowship?'

'I don't care.'

'Why should I come with you?'

'Because I love you. Love always deserves a second chance.'

'And a third and a fourth, no doubt. That's very pretty, Salvador.' She leaned towards him and brushed her cold lips against his, watching his face. He closed his eyes, and she followed him into the kiss, pressing hard. Her fingers combed through his curls, finding the uneven patch of scar tissue. Then she released him. 'No,' she said. 'I don't think I should come with you. It's too dangerous.' She stood up and unwrapped herself from his coat. 'Here. You'll be needing it for the drive home. I imagine it's pretty cold in that car. I presume you've still got that little red mean machine?'

'You won't come?'

'No, Salvador.'

He could see the pain this was causing her, but he couldn't let go. 'But I love you,' he persisted.

'No, you don't.'

'I *do!*' He took a step towards her.

'Stop. Don't touch me.' There were tears in her eyes. 'Go, Salvador. Leave.' She held the coat out again. 'Here, take it.'

He gazed bleakly at it. 'Keep it,' he said. 'I don't want it. It smells of you now. If I'm leaving without you, I don't want to take your ghost with me.'

Lydia stepped up to the porch, the coat hung over one shoulder. They had parted at the garden gate. Salvador had kept his dignity if not his coat; he had spared her the pain of any more last-ditch begging and pleading. He had simply pointed out the Lotus – parked fifty yards away down the car-crowded avenue – and said he would wait. Ten minutes; and if she didn't come, he would leave and never bother her again. She just wanted to know one thing: where had he been all this time? He told her about his stay in Australia, and she nodded, satisfied. Ten minutes, he reminded her. Think it over and know that I love you. It's impossible, she said. It's over, Salvador.

Helen's mother let her back into the house, eyeing her curiously. In the living room, the television was turned up loud, and the family – minus

201

Gabriel – were staring at it as though their lives depended on it, an almost visible atmosphere of tension gripping the air between them.

'He's in the garage if you want him,' said Helen, tight-lipped. 'Sulking.'

Susan stared at Helen, but said nothing. She stared at Lydia, and her eyes welled with contempt.

The kitchen was strewn like a battlefield with the abandoned detritus of a large-scale family lunch. A gravy-smeared plate lay broken on the floor, shards kicked into a corner by the bin. The connecting door to the garage was closed, and Lydia could almost feel the echoes of its slamming still reverberating off the melamine surfaces. She opened it and went down the steps. Gabriel was bent over the work bench, his new drill in bits before him. He looked up as Lydia came in. His expression of frozen anger melted slightly.

'You're back, then,' he said, forcing a smile.

'I am,' she replied.

'Give him the elbow, did you?'

She sighed. 'Gabriel, what's it like having a family?'

'Family?' He glanced towards the door. 'Not my family, are they.'

'Helen is. Susan certainly is. And Helen's family is your family now.'

'I suppose.'

'What's it like?'

He snorted. 'I think you can guess.' He held up a piece of the drill – a barrel-shaped thing bound in coils of fine copper wire – and swept a hand over the bench to indicate the other dismantled components and the buckled plastic casing. 'That's my Christmas,' he said, and sighed. 'I've made a big mistake, Lyd. I don't want congealed custard and relatives and – Christ – *hours and hours* of Last Of The Fucking Summer Wine. For God's sake, put me in a crate and send me back to Bondi. I want to scorch my skin and ride the surf and eat freshly caught tuna steaks griddled on the beach while the Pacific dries on my back. *That's* Christmas.'

He sighed again and went back to fiddling with the now irreparably dismembered drill. Lydia watched him for a few moments, then went back into the house. She went up to her room and sat on her bed with the coat folded in her arms. She held it up to her nose and inhaled. *It smells of you now*, she whispered.

Salvador looked at his watch. The ten minutes were up, and she hadn't come. It had been a desperate offer; one that only came true in films. He turned the key and the engine shouted into life. He pushed the stick into first and let off the handbrake.

As he pulled away, there was a loud bang that echoed through the car's bodywork. For a moment, he thought he must have misjudged the turn and glanced the wing off the car parked in front. But the bang had come from the back. As he stamped on the brake and the car jolted to a halt, the nearside door was flung open and something large and dark flew past his head.

'It's no good – it doesn't suit me.'

She swung a bag in; it loped over the back of the seats and landed on top of the coat. Then she slid into the passenger seat and slammed the door.

He stared at her. 'Lydia . . .'

'They aren't my family,' she said, grinning wildly. 'I want my own.'

'You came.'

'I left Gabriel a note.' She met his gaze – too astonished yet to show rapture – and pointed towards the street. 'Drive,' she said. 'Quick, before I change my mind.'

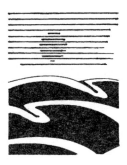

Février always polished the silverware by candlelight; there was no light like it for reflecting and blooming on the pale metal. Using a soft cloth draped loosely over his fingers, he buffed the stem of the last candlestick, whipping the cloth back and forth with brisk movements, so that it rippled and cracked like a wind-blown flag. When every millimetre of the chased silver glowed, he stood the candlestick alongside its many siblings, cousins and other, more distant relatives, on the square of green baize he had laid out on the pitted surface of the pantry table. He pushed the lid back on the tin of Duraglit and brushed the mound of damp, dirtied cotton wads into the wastebasket. Cleaning the silver was so much easier these days. Easier, cleaner and quicker, and the silver seemed shinier for it. It shouldn't be this way. Cleaning silver should be a craft; the way it had been when he was a boy. Had it not been for the fact that he hated the job – a loathing bound up with a deep-dug shard of quiet shame, which was in turn tied to the memory of uniform buttons – had he not hated the job, he might have responded more to the little pang of guilt that pinched his soul every time he unlidded the lazy Duraglit and applied its raw, simple chemicals to the ancient silverware. Those long memories didn't dim like silver. The growing forgetfulness of age was treacherous; eating away at recent, needed memory while deeper pictures remained as fresh as ever; fresher and clearer as each year passed, in fact.

The last piece of silver was different from the rest. It was the most precious; so precious that it was never displayed. It lived – with an aura of immanence that made the biomorphism seem almost literal – in a leather-bound box inside a locked rosewood cabinet built especially for it which stood under a full-length portrait of the late Monsieur de La Simarde in Madame's boudoir. In fact, it had two cabinets: one here, and one at Gondecourt. Whenever Madame travelled between the two estates, the leather box went with her. It sat on the table now, in front of him. He paused, then slipped the heavy japanned clasp and lifted the lid. The precious object nestled inside on a bed of rumpled crimson velvet. Unlike some of the family silver, much of which was ancient plate, this piece was young and solid and priceless. And it was to be polished the old way, with the old materials.

He slipped his fingers into the box and lifted it out, hefting it in his hand for a few moments, relishing its weight and smoothness and the soft sheen of candlelight on its surface. He laid it on the baize and set about lining up his collection of elderly tubs, pots and cloths.

He was about to begin when he was interrupted by a loud, musical jangling behind him. He turned round and looked up at the bell board. In the middle of the lower row, one of the fist-sized brass bells was dancing back and forth on its spiral iron spring. The Blue Morning Room. He rose and untied the strings of his apron, hanging it on the back of the door and putting on his black morning coat. He snuffed out the candles and opened the curtains, then stopped momentarily in his sitting room to check his appearance in front of the mirror – shooting his cuffs, straightening his collar and smoothing down his thinning hair – before making his way up the back stairs.

He knew what this call would be about, and he was well prepared.

A dark flicker snagged at the corner of Geneviève de La Simarde's eye, and she looked towards the window. A robin had alighted on the meniscus of snow on the sill, a smear of brown and scarlet against the white. He seemed to be peering at her through the glass, head cocked to one side. It reminded her of something; something long ago.

Another winter; an older, younger winter, and a greater, deeper, colder snow which muted and muffled and froze the whole land. Under its white carapace, behind the chokers of frost that closed in on every window, within its stone-coldness, the Château was blood-warm with the great mounds of split logs and coal that blazed in every gaping fireplace. Warm also with the lives of a whole family. Old Monsieur de La Simarde was away at Gondecourt, overseeing preparations for the coming summer; the estate had been used as a rest station for American pilots – amongst other things – and had been left in a shocking state. He had taken Philippe with him: young Philippe, the priceless and newly husbanded heir. Even in their absence, the house felt full. There was Madame de La Simarde, her daughters Sylvie and Alexandre, together with their husbands and broods of children. Geneviève was the newest addition to the family, and the most carefully chosen, and in her belly, warmest of all in the warm heart of this frozen land, nestled a pulsing bud of life, placed there by Philippe, a bud that would soon become the next newcomer; the most keenly awaited. Geneviève could feel his greatness, and had already chosen a great name from the ranks of her father's Castilian ancestors . . .

. . . No, that wasn't it. There was another winter; even older, even younger. She had been just a visitor then, a guest; a distant Iberian cousin, waiting out the tense, uncertain years of the Civil War. Overlooked, patronised, her small years condescended to by all the family, even the servants. A hanger-on; a refugee. It snowed that winter, too. In a desperate attempt to make her mark, she tried to ingratiate herself with young Philippe, seven years her elder, by gathering a hoard of snowballs in the corner of the courtyard and pelting him with them as he crossed on the way to his lessons in the Italian Wing. Fury was a reaction she could tolerate so long as it got her noticed. She was thrashed raw that night. The punishment, and the fact that Madame de La Simarde herself administered it, reassured her that she existed, and that her status was perhaps higher than she had estimated. When at last she returned home, she carried inside her an invisible padlock that clasped her soul to the memory of Philippe's earnest, adolescent sternness and the glow of warmth inside his magical English Snow Castle. One day, she confided to herself, the Snow Castle would be hers and she would rule it from gatehouse to turret-top, filling it once more with the greatness that had originally bred it. Its proud family would be *her* family.

And what had it come to? She had imagined a power that was shaded and implicit, and all the more potent for it. Ruling from behind Philippe's throne, and, when Philippe eventually passed on, from above and behind her sons. Becoming the singular locus of power, a sonless matriarch, a blank final page, had never been part of her plan.

The robin seemed to sense a threat – perhaps a shadow moving on the surface of his glossy bead eye, a scent caught on the frigid air – and with a flurry of wings and a puff of snow crystals, he leapt off the sill and went flapping across the lumpy white landscape of the parterre and came to rest on the balustrade on the far side, a tiny brown dot on the ridge of snow.

Geneviève turned back to the room and her guests, who were sitting together on the sofa, deep in whispered confabulation. It was pleasing to have guests again. Guests who had known Salvador. She would not let them leave without a sharp, deep-gouging ache of reluctance. The Château was colder now; colder and empty as a shell, but she gave silent thanks for the snow that hemmed them in.

'You can come with me,' Audrey murmured. 'I'll drop you at King's

Cross. The trains are bound to be running up there. If not, you can stay over and I'll drive you up to Peterborough tomorrow.'

'Or Iain could come down and collect me,' Beth suggested. 'From London.'

'Fine. Whatever.'

'This is really good of you, Aud.'

'Don't mention it.'

Beth glanced at Madame de La Simarde. She was sitting, thin legs daintily aslant, in a cabriole chair with embroidered upholstery of a pastel-pale blue that matched the blue of the room. She seemed different this morning; a shade less haughty, several tones quieter, less inclined to meet their eyes with flinchless hauteur. She hadn't spoken much. She had asked them if they had slept well (Perfectly, they both lied) and told them that she had telephoned to inquire about train times. She regretted to have to report that no trains were running that day, because of the snow. The moorland roads would be terribly dangerous, she said, but she would have Février drive them to Whed-dend in the Land Rover, where Mrs Quintard's car would no doubt be ready for collection. The roads from there would certainly have been cleared and gritted or salted or whatever it was they did to icy roads. She rang for Février and then grew gradually quiet, withdrawing into herself, as though preoccupied, while they conferred in low murmurs. And now, looking at her, Beth understood why she had sent for them and had them stay the night. Beth had misjudged her; mistaken her ossified, mannered detachment for emotional coldness. It was only now, in the cold morning, with her guests about to depart and almost certainly never return, that she began to feel the loss of the last vestige of her close kin. From this moment, she would live utterly alone in her vast castle, amidst the bare, bitter warren of tall, blank, unlived-in rooms, corridor upon corridor of them echoing her loneliness. Beth pitied her. All her riches, all her power, and all the great webs of lineage had come to this: an old lady sitting alone in the nascent eternity of a frozen December morning. Perhaps she really had loved Lydia after all, in her own autistic way; a surrogate daughter as a substitute for her lost son.

The door opened, and Février appeared. His dress was only slightly different from yesterday's funeral weeds. He still wore the black tail-coat, but the wing collar and black tie had been replaced by a soft grey gilet and an ivory stock, making him look like an unwigged, monochromed Regency footman.

Madame de La Simarde looked up from her contemplation of the fire. 'Février,' she said. 'There you are. Have you telephoned the garage this morning?'

'I have, Madame.'

'And what is the news? Has Mrs Quintard's car been repaired?'

Février inclined his head regretfully. 'Unfortunately not,' he said. 'There has been a delay.'

Audrey rose impatiently from her seat. 'What delay?' she demanded.

Prompted by a slight nod from Madame de La Simarde, Février turned and addressed Audrey directly. 'A replacement part is required. They do not have it.'

Audrey sighed. 'Typical. What part?'

A tiny trace of uncharacteristic panic fluttered briefly in his eyes. 'Forgive me, I do not know. It is something to do with the electronic ignition. I do not know modern cars well.'

'So how long is it going to take?'

'A new part has been ordered. I am told it will be there before this afternoon.'

'And then how long?'

'I am assured that it will be very quick. No more than thirty minutes.'

Audrey had heard garage talk before, and wasn't easily fobbed off. 'Where's your phone?' she demanded. 'I'll speak to them myself.'

'Please,' said Madame de La Simarde. 'Allow me to speak with them. They will listen to me.' She looked sternly at Février. 'If there is laxness in their attitude, I shall extirpate it. I shall *not* have my guests inconvenienced.'

The terrace outside the Music Room was partly sheltered from the wind by trellises, and the snow was thinner here; only an inch or two deep on the paving stones. It creaked and sifted under Beth's feet as she walked to the steps and looked down at the thickly blanketed lawn. A trail of broad, chunky boot-prints led down the steps and across the virgin white expanse, curving away and disappearing round the corner of the parterre. Any footprints that lay under the snow would be undiscoverable now, and she would never know whether her nocturnal chase had been a dream or not. Though of course it must have been a dream; or at least a very vivid sleepwalking episode. All the evidence pointed to it. The drawers, for instance. And a ghostly waif wandering the corridors? She was a victim of too much literature; Castle Dracula, Lady Catherine de Bourgh, and then Charlotte Brontë reaching up out of her psyche and filling her head with nonsense about mad Mrs Rochester imprisoned in her attic.

Ridiculous. From the safety of daylight, she smiled at her foolishness and hugged her coat around herself.

'*Bugger . . .*'

The exclamation slipped through a gap in the slackening wind and drifted up to the terrace. Beth frowned and went down the steps, following the trail of prints, stepping in them to keep the snow from inundating her dainty, ridiculously impractical shoes. Rounding the high balustraded wall, she found Audrey standing in the centre of the lawn in the middle of a web of irritably criss-crossing, circling footprints. She was staring at something held in her left hand, jabbing at it with a gloved finger and muttering under her breath. She looked up as Beth approached. 'I can't get a bloody signal anywhere,' she said, poking the mobile phone a couple more times and holding it to her ear. 'When I think of the amount of money this wretched thing costs me . . .' She glanced down and noticed Beth's shoes, flecked with snow and inelegantly straddling her own deep boot-prints. 'You should've borrowed some wellies,' she said. 'You're going to ruin those shoes.'

'Who are you phoning? The garage?'

'Huh! *If* I knew the number. *If* this bastard son-of-a-bitch piece of plastic trash actually *worked*.'

'Why don't you use the proper phone?'

Audrey paused and looked up doubtfully at the castle. 'I don't know. I'd rather not. Anyway, it seems to be hidden away somewhere; I haven't spotted it.'

'It's in a little room off the hall. Sort of an office. They've even got a fax.'

'How did you stumble across that?'

'I didn't. I asked. I had to phone Iain.'

'Oh . . .'

'Who were you phoning that's so secret, then?'

'Oh, just my researcher. I wanted to see if she could find anything out about these wrecker folk.'

Beth smiled; she had been right. 'No weekend rest for telejournalists, eh?'

'Damn right. Not if I've got anything to do with it. Weekends are for wimps.'

'Why not just speak to Février if you're so interested? At least use the phone indoors.'

Audrey shook her head. 'I think this one needs careful handling. I don't want to speak to him unless I'm sure there's a film in it. It'd help if there was some sort of angle, something contemporary to tie it in with. Maybe if another oil tanker went down, or there was another Zeebrugge. I'll get Suzi to look into it before I approach Master Février.'

Beth inclined her head and peered sardonically at her. 'Don't tell me you're *scared* of him?'

Audrey balked. 'Scared? Of course not. He's an odd bod, though. Hidden depths . . . Did you notice the way he flinched when Madame mentioned his past? Almost threw your soup in your lap. I'd swear he thought she was referring to something other than his shady family business.'

'Such as?'

'I don't know. That's what I need to be careful of.' She tapped the phone's snub aerial against her chin. 'Didn't he say his brother and sister were in the Resistance?'

'Yes. Killed, he said.'

'Well, there's a possibility. You don't think he could have been a collaborator, do you? Hey, maybe *he* dobbed them in to the Nazis. Maybe he *was* a Nazi. Some French people were, you know.'

Beth looked sceptically at her. 'I think the cold's starting to affect your brain.'

Audrey shrugged. 'Instinct coupled with imaginative speculation followed up by rigorous investigation; that's what documentary television's all about. There's *something* fishy in that man's past, and I don't mean living by the sea. I can smell it, but I need something more solid to go on before I give him any hint that I might be interested in dipping my shrimping net into it.'

'Very sensible. Shall we go in now? I'm frozen.'

Audrey shook her head. 'You go in if you like.' She looked at the phone cupped in her hand. 'I'm going to have one last try. I'll see if I can get a signal up on that hill.'

Beth retraced the trail of boot-prints back to the castle. At the top of the terrace steps, she turned and looked back. Audrey, an insubstantial dark sliver against the white, was striding purposefully towards the wooded hill that overlooked the estate. Beth shook her head and went back indoors.

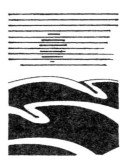

Another bluebottle was buzzing and thumping against the kitchen window. Monsieur Duprée had never seen such tenacious flies. Certainly not at this time of year. They were unswattable; each one had to be laboriously beaten to death with the rolled-up week-old copy of *Charente Libre* he kept wedged behind the fridge. Apart from himself, the flies were the only inhabitants of this building who refused to relinquish life with no more than an easy, weary sigh. The block stood on the fringe of Angoulême's *Centre Commercial* – hazed hectares of bleached concrete superstores – and inside it, unseen from outside, was the waiting room at the end of human life. They drifted in here, the relationless scrag-end of the town's elderly, installed the knick-knack remnants of their lives, sat down in front of their television sets and waited to die.

Monsieur Duprée chased the bluebottle up the pane and stunned it on the third *thwack*. It fell onto the sill, where it skidded and buzzed fitfully amongst the dried-up husks of its kin. He raised the newspaper once more and delivered the *coup de grâce*, fanning up a cloud of dust and fly corpses that showered and settled on the floor around the tartan toes of his Charentais *pantoufles*.

Jean-Baptiste Duprée wasn't ready to die yet. He didn't feel old enough. At twenty-five, when he emerged at war's end, he had looked closer to forty. At forty, he looked sixty and walked with a stoop. Then a strange cryogenic process seemed to set in. At sixty, he still looked sixty. At seventy, he *still* looked sixty. Now, at seventy-eight, his appearance had still not entered its fourth score. Losing the shop had been a tonic in disguise, he was certain; all that worry gone, no more need to talk to people or pretend, and with a secret store of francs salted away to eke out his old age. And now he had a Project to keep

211

him going. He was writing down the true story of his life. Not that he thought anyone would read it; he just felt happier knowing that a written record would live on after him. Nobody had ever told him to his face that they suspected him of collaboration, so he had never had a chance to contradict the whispered rumours he had overheard. He had never been forced to lie. It wouldn't have done any good anyway: *Qui s'excuse s'accuse*, his conscience told him. The truth would out after his death.

He looked up from the fly-speckled linoleum and sniffed the air. There was a smell coming, seeping into the apartment. Why hadn't he noticed it before? The cold weather, probably. The smell reached into his nostrils and tickled an unpleasant memory. He knew that smell as well as the odour of his own feet. Another one must have shuffled across the waiting room and out of the exit. That would explain the unseasonable flies and the relentless, twenty-four-hour TV mumble from Madame Butain's apartment during the past... how long? Six weeks? Jesus and Mary, no wonder there was a smell.

He tried telephoning the warden, but she was out (as usual), so he called the hospital instead. Then he put on his shoes and overcoat and went out for a walk.

A cold December wind was blowing in over the ramparts and raising short-lived dust-devils in the centre of town. Everyone was at lunch, sealed in behind half-drawn shutters, and the Rue des Postes was deserted. Monsieur Duprée hadn't set foot in this street since drawing down the blinds on his last day of no-trade, nearly seventeen years ago. It had been semi-pedestrianised, and the shop-fronts were brighter. That aside, the narrow, sun-shaded street had changed remarkably little.

He walked half-way along and stopped outside his old shop. He was surprised and strangely disconcerted to find that the old façade had been preserved, albeit with the woodwork of the door and window frame painted sunflower yellow. It was now a clothes shop: where the regimented lines of dark viols had once hung, there were now racks of T-shirts and sweaters; a display of winter knitwear filled the window which had once bristled with glittering brass and black woodwind. The glass, which had once borne the genteel announcement *J.-B. Duprée, Instruments de Musique: Vente, Achat, Réparation. Partitions, Cordes et Tous les Accessoires*, in florid, hand-painted black and gold, now had a bold blue sticker proclaiming *FAÇONNABLE JEANS*.

Good luck to them. In retrospect, he recognised how much he had hated the place. It had forced him into a mould he didn't fit. He had no idea what had guided his footsteps here after so many years. Death, perhaps; he had expected to find the past dead and dusted over, and so feel more alive himself. But the past wasn't dead; it was visible under the surface, like pigs' trotters in aspic. Death didn't come to the past, only to people, and he could sense its presence behind his back and smell its decay in his nostrils. It had seeped off Madame Butain as she slowly liquefied in her armchair, and crept through walls and windows into his apartment. The smell had brought back memories; and such memories as could curl and dry up the soul. Bodies strewn and putrefying by the roadside like rag bundles. The liquor stink was always mingled in his memory with the odours of diesel fumes and pigshit and, over it all, burnt cordite. He thought of the dried-up fly corpses on his window sill, and felt sick.

When he returned home, there was an ambulance parked outside the building. People in overalls and white face-masks were carrying a stretcher out through the door. The stretcher had a long black plastic bag on it. Monsieur Duprée didn't look any closer; he could imagine what was in it. The hallway and stairs reeked with a thick, heavy scent of spices. Madame Butain's front door was open, and a man with a canister on his back was spritzing the spice smell around the walls while others carried out more plastic bags; these smaller and hinting at the shapes of cushions, curtains and bric-à-brac, all now ineradicably impregnated with Madame Butain's decomposed aura.

Monsieur Duprée went into his apartment and closed the door. Without taking off his coat, he sat down at the kitchen table and shuffled through the pile of close-written sheets of paper. He took a fresh sheet and wrote at the top: *Chapitre 4. Les Chemins de la Paix...* *Les chemins de la paix, les chemins de la guerre*; it was strange how such phrases stuck in one's mind... He paused a while, gazing at the blank page, remembering, then put down his pen. It was no good; he had to get rid of those flies.

He unrolled the newspaper and swept the corpses onto it. When every last one was gathered up, he scrunched it into a ball and pushed it into the bin. Then he sat down and took up his pen again.

And still couldn't write. Whenever he looked at the page, he saw the face of Madame de La Simarde, staring at him with imperious disapproval. This happened to him from time to time: faces from the past – usually the long, deep past – faces he had forgotten, floating up from nowhere and imprinting themselves behind his eyes, as clear as if they were standing in front of him; faces of the dead and the living, of enemies, persecutors and friends, and those he had never even met other than as corpses. It was a function of growing old, he guessed; the brain could only hold so much past. Like a cesspit, unpleasant leakage was inevitable if too much was piped in. These faces were a sign, a warning that his memory had reached its limit. But why Madame de La Simarde? He looked at the title of his new chapter and thought he could guess: it was partly revisiting the shop; there was also the fact that, like him, her family was whispered about simply because they had been in the wrong place at the wrong time and kept quiet about it. He was also reminded that, of all the ways to war and peace, the only one he had not trodden had been the one to freedom, the one to England.

He made up his mind quickly, recapturing the decisiveness of his youth. Less than two hours later, he was at the station, booking a ticket on the TGV. He would have to dig deep into the secret store to pay for this journey, but what did it matter? He would be dead soon enough, and his francs would be no use to him after that. Best to spend them on making that journey at last.

What was more, he reasoned as the train whispered away from the station and set its wedge nose to the north, there was at least one family there on whose acquaintance he could call in need. Perhaps, should he find himself in that part of the country, he should call on them anyway, need or not, and pay his respects. He had, after all, always been fond of young Salvador. He wondered again why he had thought of them so suddenly after all these years.

He closed his eyes and sat back in his seat. These modern trains were so comfortable. Within a few moments, he was asleep.

Back in his apartment, in the kitchen waste-bin, pressed up against some Camembert rind and a stale end of bread, the unread, week-old copy of *Charente Libre* was unscrunching itself stiffly. Specked with crushed flies and sandwiched between reports of the mayoral elections and yet another fatal accident on the N10, was a headline which had leapt off the page and into Monsieur Duprée's brain without brushing against his preoccupied conscious mind. *Famille de La Simarde*, it read, *deuxième tragédie.*

Sergeant Urbanski's Journey

It was a long journey, the one to war. For many of those who fought, the journey went far beyond the bounds of their experience or even imagination of distance. Few men, though, travelled as far as my grandfather. Hardly any, I think, circumnavigated the entire globe only to end up in the wrong place at the wrong time and fighting, it has to be said, the wrong war.

And, I must record for the sake of his memory, with the wrong rank. Sergeant Jan Urbanski was born into the officer class; he attended the Academy at Krakow and passed out into a prestigious regiment of light cavalry. By the age of twenty-two, he had hopped nimbly up to the rank of Captain, with a whole company under his command, an entire magnificent company of the bravest, finest, noblest cavalry in the world. The year following this posting, his proud company spent four weeks in training under the supervision of a visiting British officer from a sister cavalry regiment; a training that consisted of riding around the country-side on bicycles with slitted cardboard boxes over their heads and broomsticks attached to the handlebars, learning battlefield tactics to prepare them for the arrival of the armoured cars and light tanks that would soon be replacing their horses. The training was to have lasted six weeks, but was interrupted a fortnight before the arrival of the new vehicles, and was never resumed. Events had overtaken them; the Germans had invaded.

The advance was so fierce and so quick that there was no hope of the armoured vehicles being delivered in time for the defence, so Captain Urbanski's regiment had to make do with its horses. Much as they loved and respected these animals, many men muttered that they would do just as well with the cardboard boxes and broom handles; they had heard of the quality of the German panzers, the self-propelled assault guns, and the fanatical panzer-grenadiers who accompanied them, and they knew they hadn't a hope in battle.

Urbanski's regiment was billeted in the centre of Warsaw. When they went out to man the defences in the outer suburbs, they left their horses in the stables. His regiment was not one of those that rode into heroic, legendary suicide, charging the German armour on horseback. Many, though, wished later that they might have gone that way rather than in the more prosaic but not much slower massacre amongst the streets of exploding, collapsing buildings. By the last day of the battle, only seven men were left of Urbanski's company: himself, two sergeants, one corporal and three troopers. That night, as the Germans closed in to snuff out the last remaining pockets of resistance, he led his survivors back into the city. The horses had fared even worse than the men; the barracks district had been devastated by shells and bombs, and in the remains of the stables only three horses were still alive and unharmed.

They felt ashamed, saving themselves while their comrades were still fighting, but my grandfather said to them: *There is nothing left here to defend. The city is dying. Listen.* And they listened; the crumping, blasting, whining, roaring of incoming mortar bombs and heavy shells, and the pathetic, intermittent crackle of small-arms firing in reply. *We will return,* he said. *One day, we will return. Be sure of that.*

So, the seven men and their three horses, with as much food, fodder and ammunition as they could scavenge and carry, and with boots, hoofs and loose equipment muffled with strips of blanket, began to pick their way between the mounds of rubble, out of the city centre and through the eastern suburbs. Much of the night was spent carefully scouting and probing the German lines until, dangerously close to dawn, they found a way out under an unguarded bridge, ducking low and paddling along the edge of the river. They followed its course for a mile, then struck out into the depths of a thick forest. By the time they reached its heart, Warsaw was dead. The dive-bombers were gone, the guns were silent, and a mournful pall of grimy black smoke smeared the morning sky above the ruined city.

There was no time for reflection or regret; now that the city had fallen, the invaders would be quick to consolidate their victory. Soon, the whole country would be seething and crawling with them.

After they had fed their horses, the seven men sat down and tried to forge a plan. Going east was quickly ruled out; falling into the hands of the Russians was as dreadful as handing themselves over to the Germans. North was a possibility; even if Danzig had already fallen, they might find passage from one of the smaller villages. If they could get to Sweden, then they could be in England within a matter of weeks. But what if they failed? What if they were trapped with their backs to the sea? Then there was south. That was a blank, a mystery. Aside from Urbanski, all came from uneducated peasant families; they had never travelled, and had only the vaguest notions of what lay beyond their country's borders. All they knew about the south was that there were many different countries that spread out for hundreds, maybe thousands of miles. They turned to their captain for guidance, and he proposed a plan: they would head east. This would allow them to stay ahead of the German forces and also enable them to hear word – if word came – of any possibility of escape across the Baltic. Then, before reaching the Russian border, they would strike south, staying inside Poland for as long as possible. They would skirt the Ukraine and strike across Rumania to the Black Sea, and then ... where? The map grew greyer. They pinned their hopes on one of the distant British outposts: Cairo or north-west India, a distance unimaginable even to Urbanski.

And so they set off, seven cavalrymen, unhorsed, reduced to foot soldiers with their small train of pack-animals. Behind them, the German tanks spread out, eating up their homeland in an unrelenting, rolling wave.

The crisis came ten miles short of the Russian border, in the Pripet Marshes. They had heard rumours in the towns of Polish soldiers escaping north to Sweden, but there was chaos everywhere; nobody really knew what was happening, and the rumours contradicted each other. Urbanski didn't believe them, but some of his men were swayed. Corporal Lasek and Troopers Skop and Zwolanski wanted to change the plan and go north. After a hot-tempered argument, the dissenters persuaded Sergeant Burzawa and Trooper Ploszewski to their side. Only Sergeant Dyrda refused to budge, his dyed-in loyalty to his captain reinforced by an instinctive mistrust of rumours. He insisted that he and the captain would take two of the horses; theirs would be the longer journey, after all. But, as he went to redistribute the animals' loads, there was a rattle of bolts and three rifles pointed at him. *Not so quick*, said Corporal Lasek. *There's five of us, remember.* Dyrda reacted swiftly and angrily; he seized the barrel of Lasek's rifle and swung it aside, at the same time bringing his revolver to bear on the corporal's face. *Shoot your old sergeant, would you? How many times have I saved your worthless lives, eh? Well, I'm finished with you. If you want to go and commit suicide, go ahead, but me and the Captain take two horses.* They glared at him for several moments, then their rifles wavered and lowered, their mutiny cowed.

Looks like we're on our own, sir, said the sergeant as they watched the shamed soldiers walk away towards the north. *Scum. The Russians are coming – they'll scoop them up even if the Germans don't.*

Captain Urbanski shook his head and, without a word, and for reasons he was never quite able to explain, he took out his knife and cut the insignia and pips from his uniform. *Now*, he said, letting them fall to the ground, *now we are equal. No more 'sir'. We are both sergeants; brothers.* Sergeant Dyrda seemed to understand the gesture. He nodded solemnly and, taking the reins of one of the horses, began to walk south. Sergeant Urbanski took the reins of the other and followed.

Two weeks later, they crossed the Rumanian border at midnight. The supplies they had brought with them from Warsaw had dwindled almost to nothing, and they began to ride their unburdened horses more often. As they descended from the Carpathian Mountains, they began to hunt and forage for food and fodder in the wide Danube valley, and they did indeed become like brothers. Sergeant Dyrda eventually overcame his embarrassment, and learnt to address his former captain as 'Jan' or simply 'brother'. They discarded their uniforms in favour of peasant clothes, but kept their weapons.

After three more weeks, they had crossed the Ukraine, and stood on the shore of the Black Sea near Odessa, gazing out across its flecked grey surface. Where now? they wondered.

Where now, indeed. Laid out across my knee as I write, I have *The Mitchell Beazley New Concise Atlas of the Earth*. Its newness is long gone, its dust-cover ragged and torn, its spine broken and coming apart. It was given to me by my parents for my ninth birthday. One Sunday afternoon, I took it round to my grandparents' house and persuaded my grandfather to mark out in its maps the route of his great journey, telling me the story as he went. I can still see him, sitting close to me at the small fold-down dining table, the skin sagging on his age-worn cheeks, exuding an aroma of pipe-tobacco ancientness, as he chose from the selection of coloured felt-tip pens I had brought with me and began to trace out the route he and Sergeant Dyrda had trodden, lifetime-long ago, speaking a deep rumble of Polish-inflected, exotic-sounding place-names interweaved with brain-tingling adventures. It became a regular ritual, this tracing of his long walk to war, and each time I learnt more. Whether his reticence was worn down by my eagerness, or he remembered more, or the story simply grew elaborate in the telling, as stories will, I do not know. Some things, though, were brought out from behind a veil of censorship as I grew older. In a region labelled TALIMUPENDI, east of the Hindu-Kush, he put a blue cross to mark the place where the second of their horses died in the bitter mountain winter. It was only on the umpteenth telling that I learnt that, in a desperation of wasteland hunger, they shot the horse and ate what they could of it, then walked on with frozen joints of horsemeat hanging from their packs.

They couldn't get to Cairo, and the green line he drew on the map meanders its way around the Caspian Sea, crossing the outlying provinces of the Soviet empire until it reaches Peshawar. Here, they were turned back at the border by a British officer to whom they presented themselves as refugees. Only Urbanski spoke any English, and that badly, and their papers had long been lost or destroyed. In despair, they turned north-eastwards. From here on, the green line strikes out, studded with many different coloured crosses and dated dots marking encounters with Chinese soldiers, Siberian provincial apparatchiks, tribesmen of the hills, desert and tundra, until it eventually ends at a tiny place called Ulja. From there, a dotted line crosses the Sea of Okhotsk to the fantastically named Sredinnyj Chrebet. At last, at Petropavlovsk, in the spring of 1941, a year and a half after leaving the borders of their homeland, they gained passage to Alaska on a Canadian fishing boat. Finally, even though their journey was only half-way through, Sergeants Urbanski and Dyrda felt that they had reached an ending – an end of fear and flight. A US government official in Anchorage accepted them as refugees. The line continues on a new map, this time in blue. They were put on a train south, winding down the west coast to California, where, to their surprise, they were confined in an internment camp. Six months they spent there, until my grandfather read a news cutting about whole divisions of Polish expatriate soldiers being raised in Britain. *That is where we should be*, he said to Sergeant Dyrda one evening over their tin plates of bean stew. After negotiating their way through a labyrinthine bureaucracy (my grandfather's English improving quickly and immeasurably), they were granted deportation to Britain. Thus began the second great leg of their journey, as long as the first, but, give or take the perils of a U-boat-infested Atlantic, less fearful and certainly less arduous.

They reached Scotland on 27 March 1942. Two and a half years and some fifteen thousand miles lay behind them; now, only a few fingers' breadth of map-flat land and sea separated them from their homeland. Then the fear returned. *What if they don't accept us?* they worried, remembering the British officer at Peshawar. At this point in the story, my grandfather's eyes would twinkle. *Imagine our fear*, he would say. *We had to be screened by Intelligence, you see, to make sure we weren't spies. We were marched into an office at Polish Brigade HQ, and who do you suppose we saw, sitting there behind the desk?* Even though I had heard the story a dozen times, his excitement stopped my breath. *Colonel Kaczmarek!* he would exclaim. *Our old CO!*

Naturally, he was delighted to see them; they were the first survivors of his regiment he had seen since escaping through Finland. No, he had heard nothing; not a single word of news about any of his men until now.

Of course, I always wanted Grampa to go on with his story – the most exciting bit, the War, was yet to come – but he always refused. *There's your happy ending*, he said. *Be pleased with it*. When I was eighteen, shortly before his second heart attack carried him out of my life forever, he told me the rest of the story. By then, I had gleaned much of the big picture from history books, and I had some inkling of why he was so reluctant to relive his part in it.

In short, he was betrayed; he and his comrades were betrayed by events, by their adoptive country and, finally, by history.

Catalogue of Betrayal

Item. Sergeants Urbanski and Dyrda were accepted into the 1st Polish Independent Parachute Brigade Group. Trained by the British to the same élite standard as other airborne units, they were placed under the control of their own exiled government, with the promise that their role would be to fight for their homeland. When the time was right, they would be dropped near Warsaw (Warsaw! My grandfather's blood thrilled when he heard it) to help the underground Polish Home Army rise up and drive out the Germans.

You can read the rest, as I did, in the history books. The plan never happened; the British Army had its own war to fight, and it wasn't about to let a valuable resource be thrown into somebody else's conflict. Besides, in the late summer of 1944, the Allies had a New Plan; a bold and eager plan to follow Overlord and end the War before Christmas. The British wrested back control of the Polish brigade, and recast the fate of its men forever. The plan was given the name Market Garden, and the Poles' part in it was to be dropped south of the Lower Rhine to help the 1st British Airborne Division in its attempt to capture the Arnhem bridge. The rest of the story was a miserable trail of bad faith and betrayals imposed or discovered.

Item. The Poles were dropped near Driel on the fifth day of the operation, delayed by bad weather in England. The German defenders at Arnhem were ready for them, and filled the descending clouds of parachutists with gunfire, killing and wounding many of them.

Item. Because of the delay, the British airborne troops north of the river were slowly crumpling under the weight of assaults from the two SS panzer divisions whose presence the allied planners had known of but refused to believe in. All that remained was a ragged, dogged perimeter clinging to the bank of the Rhine around Oosterbeek, west of Arnhem. The ferry point where the Poles were to cross and join them was now outside the perimeter, unprotected and covered by batteries of German guns.

The British commanders decided that the crossing would go ahead anyway. Under cover of darkness, of course, which would make all the difference.

Item. First shock. On the first night in Driel, my grandfather's company commander called him away from his guard position. One of the SS prisoners captured in Driel church earlier that day was asking to see a Captain Jan Urbanski. The company commander was bewildered: nobody in the Brigade knew of his former rank (remembering his oath of blood brotherhood to Sergeant Dyrda, he had forgone a commission and begged Colonel Kaczmarek to keep quiet about it). He was taken to the church's crypt, where he met the enemy soldier; an SS Unteroffizier in a wrecked uniform, with a bloody bandage covering half his face. He was dying, they said; a grenade blast had caught him in the head during a skirmish that afternoon. Urbanski didn't recognise him until he spoke – *Forgive me, my captain,* he said in a weak whisper – then the remains of the face stirred a memory; he had last seen it over the barrel of a rifle five years before. *Corporal Lasek?* he said in disbelief. He listened to the halting story in silence; the walk to the Baltic, the skirmish with German troops near Gdynia, capture and imprisonment, and then the offer; join up and escape the death camps. The others had refused, but he had taken his chance and sworn his oath of blood loyalty to Hitler.

My grandfather walked away from the church in shocked silence and returned to his post. Behind him, SS Unteroffizier Lasek died raving his guilt and shame in the damp crypt.

Item. Second shock. Urbanski's platoon was in the first wave to cross the river. The small rubber boats supplied were inadequate, the current was too strong, the British had not seen fit to train the Polish paratroopers in riverborne assault, and the wide strip of water was covered by a dense array of German weapons. Moreover, the security of darkness was torn apart by a carnival umbrella of arcing flares. Many died in the black waters, shredded by machine-gun fire or drowned as their little boats floundered and drifted. Sergeant Dyrda was one of them. His long journey came to an end there in mid-stream, his boat swallowed up in the fountainous explosion of a mortar bomb. His body was washed away and never found. It distressed my grandfather for the rest of his life that, by the time he heard of Dyrda's loss, his brain was too battered by other shocks for this new one to have its proper effect.

Item. An act of heroism. On the afternoon of their second day north of

221

the river, the section of the Oosterbeek perimeter into which the survivors of Urbanski's platoon had been slotted was selected by the Germans for an armoured assault. A cobbled-together force of eight tanks and self-propelled guns, supported by SS panzer-grenadiers probed the line, laying down a barrage as they rolled along the road towards my grandfather's slit-trench. Lining the road nearby were three 6-pounder anti-tank guns. A single round from the lead tank – an elderly Mark IV – destroyed the first gun and laid waste to its crew, while machine-gun fire from the second tank – a massive, lumbering Tiger – seared through the crew of another gun, killing them all. The last 6-pounder was commanded by Lance Corporal Hart, a former draper's assistant from Nottingham. He laid his gun calmly and quickly, and fired. The Mark IV's turret exploded and burned. Hart's second shell disabled the Tiger, and his third destroyed a StuG that was following close behind. Still the tanks ploughed on. Just as his loader was sliding in a fourth shell, a round from another StuG smashed into Hart's gun, hurling up a fountain of earth, metal and flesh. The tanks resumed their advance. The infantrymen, who were busy pouring suppression fire at the panzer-grenadiers, were amazed to see one of the gunners' bodies stir, draw itself into a crouch and begin crawling painfully across the road towards the surviving, crewless gun, leaving a trail of blood in its wake. It was Lance Corporal Hart. Despite his wounds, he succeeded in laying the gun and firing off a round left in the breech by the dead crew. A fourth tank burst and flamed. He tried to load another shell as the remaining tanks carried on advancing, tracks squealing and grinding as they swerved around their crippled brothers to get a clear shot at him, but he was too weakened by his wounds. My grandfather had seen enough; he scuttled out of his trench and across the road, spraying a magazine of Sten bullets towards the enemy positions as he ran. He was followed a moment later by the English private who had been sharing his trench. The private sat on the gun's trail to steady it while Hart aimed and Urbanski loaded. Two more tanks were immobilised before the survivors turned and fled back to their own lines, followed by the grenadiers. Lance Corporal Hart remained crouched over the gun as they moved away, as though aiming a parting shot. Urbanski touched his shoulder . . . then his face . . . There was no response; he was dead.

Item. An act of shame. After nine days of slaughter, the remnants of 1st Airborne Division and 1st Polish Brigade were evacuated back across the river to safety. The attempt to capture the Arnhem bridge had failed.

Someone had to be blamed for the failure, but who should it be? The planners who overstretched their resources and ignored intelligence reports in their determination to believe it would be a pushover? The commanders in the field, perhaps, who let XXX Corps' advance halt just short and failed to relieve the Arnhem force? The Airborne Corps Commander, who took up thirty-eight precious gliders transporting his HQ to Holland when he could have organised affairs more effectively from England? Of course not; it was quite clear to everyone that blame attached fairly, squarely and unequivocally to the Polish Brigade. Not all the blame, naturally – after all, these were the British, who, as everyone knows, have a natural sense of fair play. It was absolutely fair that the Brigade's commander, General Sosabowski, who had had the temerity to warn the British commanders to expect heavy German resistance and to criticise them afterwards for ignoring him, should be dismissed in disgrace from his command.

Item. The destruction of the tanks was witnessed by a major from Divisional HQ, who took the men's names and told the two survivors he was going to put in a citation for the Victoria Cross for all three of them. He survived the evacuation and honoured his word. At the Arnhem investiture, Lance Corporal Hart's widow received his posthumous VC. Private Drake was there, too; even though his citation had been amended at Corps level to a more realistic Distinguished Service Order, he was pleased with his medal. Sergeant Urbanski was not present at the investiture; by the time the citation was passed on from Army Group HQ, his name had quietly vanished from it. On 17 October 1944, Army Group Commander Field Marshal Montgomery, the author of Market Garden, had written to Field Marshal Sir Alan Brooke: 'Polish Para Brigade fought very badly and the men showed no keenness to fight if it meant risking their own lives.' The lack of bravery awards rather proved his point.

Item. After the evacuation, the Poles were marched south to Nijmegen (while the surviving British paratroopers were taken by lorry) and spent time on garrison duty in the city (while their British comrades were flown home to a heroes' welcome).

My grandfather's last military duty came after VE Day, when his Brigade was sent to Germany as part of the allied occupation force. He never made it to his homeland. The Home Army had risen unaided and had withered and perished while the Polish Brigade was fighting at Arnhem. His long journey reached its ebb there, just two hundred miles away from the Polish border, which was now effectively a provincial border of the Soviet Union. When it was all over, he returned to Peterborough, where he had been billeted before Arnhem, and spent thirty years grinding away his spirit in the brickfields. No employer would give a Pole any better work, and the historical revisionists were too late in coming to his aid.

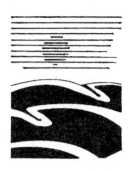

Not entirely purged, then... He was back in the forest, and this time it was for real; the canopy arching over his head seethed with solid, three-dimensional creatures. And now the enemy soldiers were after him; tracking, flanking, closing in. He could hear the *schicca-schicca* of their helicopters and the growls of the dogs and... yes, there it was, the jangling alarm bells that meant they had pinpointed him on their scanners. He leapt up from the undergrowth and ran, crashing through the bushes, leaping a stream and lumbering like a bear up a steep, tree-strewn scarp.

They were waiting for him; a semicircle of troops like standing stones, automatic weapons levelled at his body. The alarm bells were deafening now. He stumbled to a halt, choking for breath. The sergeant walked forward and placed a pistol to his head. Just before pulling the trigger, he leaned forward and whispered into his cowering ear, the voice breaking through the pulsing alarm: 'There's no escape from here, Joe. Now answer that fucking phone.'

He clawed his way out of bed and lumbered, half-blind, up the steep slope to the living room. It took him several moments to decide which of the erratically lurching objects on the desk was making the pulsating, ear-shredding racket: his numb fingers slithered over the printer and the computer, knocked the mouse and keyboard off the desk, and finally grappled the phone off the hook. The noise stopped, and he sighed into the mouthpiece.

'Hlugh,' he slurred.

'Hello?' said a strangely familiar voice. 'Iain? It's me.'

Me? '... Oh, yeah. Hi.'

'Did I get you out of bed by any chance?'

He rubbed his sticky eyes. 'Hmm.'

'Iain, it's nearly eleven o'clock! What are you like?'

'I's up late. I's writing.'

'Oh . . .' She sounded mollified, and well she might: it had reached the stage where he might be excused anything short of rape and murder if it meant getting some writing done. 'Good. Is it going well?'

'Mm. S'a'right.'

'Only alright?'

'No, it's okay.' He looked at the scrawled pages lying on the desk, and his heart sank. He knew, somehow could tell just from the shape of the writing, that it would be shit. Unstructured, rambling babble. 'Where the hell are you, anyway?' he demanded.

'At the Château. The Simarde place.'

'*Château?*' He was still dreaming. 'In *France?*'

'No, silly, the one in Devon. Look, I'm—'

'I thought their château was in France.'

'They've got two. Listen—'

'Two?' One château might be considered a tragedy . . . No, that was wrong. He scratched his head. 'Why have they got two?'

'Oh, it's a long story. We had this lecture about it over dinner last night. *This* château is a copy of the original at a place called Gondecourt that burned down.'

'Oh. I thought you said they had two. How can they have two if one burned down?'

'They've still got the estate and a house and . . . Oh, it's too complicated and you're obviously half asleep. Listen, I just called to say I'll be a bit late back. There are no trains because of the snow. Audrey's going to give me a lift as soon as her car's fixed . . . Hello? Are you still there? . . . Iain?'

'. . . What? Yeah, still here. Say that name again.'

'What name? Audrey?'

'No, the name of the château place. The other one.'

'Gondecourt?'

'That's the one.' He stared at the desktop and mouthed the word. *Gondecourt.*

'What about it?'

'I dunno. Is it famous?'

'Not that I know of. Why?'

He rubbed his eyes again and yawned. 'Dunno . . . What're they like, these people? They looking after my pumpkin alright?'

'Fine. I'll call you again if there's any more news. D'you want to take down the number here in case you need to phone me?'

He scribbled the number on the back of an old receipt and attached it to one of the blobs of Blu-Tack that surrounded the plastic rim of the computer monitor. 'There,' he said. 'Fixed in stone.'

'Okay. See you later tonight, I hope. Love you.'

'Love you too. See you.'

Click.

He sat back in the chair and rolled the word *Gondecourt* around his brain, bouncing it off all the departments he could think of to see if it stuck to anything. If the place wasn't famous, why did the name seem so familiar? *Gondecourt* deflected suddenly and collided with another phrase from the scrambled conversation: *no trains because of the snow.*

He went to the window and parted the curtains. The bright sunlight made him blink and squint . . .

Snow? What snow?

An hour later, nicotined, coffeed and with a stomach full of bran flakes, he felt almost (but not quite) reattached to the waking world. Ready enough, at least, to cope with reading over Sergeant Urbanski's Journey.

Actually, it wasn't nearly as bad as he had expected. In a way, he was quite pleased at the way the structure fractured in the second half. He hovered a while over the death of Corporal Lasek, wondering whether it ought to be itemised as a shock or a betrayal. A discovery, perhaps. What was it when you found that one of your . . . Then he remembered.

The name that had been bouncing around his head finally hit a pigeonhole and slotted home. *Gondecourt, Château de.* He *had* heard of it before, and he thought he knew where.

He put his story down and went to the crowded bookshelf above the desk. The reference wasn't where you would expect to find it. He ran a finger along the spines until he came to a thick, black-jacketed volume entitled *The Waffen-SS on the Eastern Front.* He took it down and leafed through to the index.

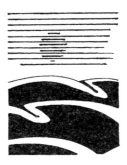

Beth trudged up the spiral staircase alone, ignoring the stares of the marble heads. There would be no home-going today after all. The part for Audrey's car – despite Madame de La Simarde's intervention – had not arrived at the garage. Audrey had fumed for a while, insisting that Février should drive her to the garage so that she could deal with the incompetent swines herself. It would be useless, he assured her; the part had not arrived because the supplier had closed for the day, and there was nothing they could do about that. Try another supplier, she suggested impatiently. The garage had already tried; they were all closed. After that, Audrey seemed to resign herself to being stranded. The last Beth saw of her, she was heading for the hills again to have one more go at contacting her researcher.

Back in Lydia's room once more, Beth found that the bed had been made, a fire lit and a fresh pitcher of water placed on the bedside table. She sat on the bed and looked around, willing the room to be different from yesterday, from last night. The snow-reflected light made it brighter, and the fire crackled furiously, but the room still felt chilly. Audrey's room seemed to warm through nicely with a fire in the grate, but this one seemed impervious to the flames, as though there were something inherent in its walls and furniture that repelled heat. Or removed it, like a black hole. Danny, she remembered, had gone on a lot about black holes. And dark matter and antimatter. That had been her stated reason for dumping him; he was so boring. He had gone off the rails a bit after that, she was told, but she had been too busy going off the rails herself to notice. A black hole, he said, was a collapsed star, a clump of matter so dense that a teaspoonful would weigh millions of tons. (She could sympathise; she felt a bit like that herself sometimes.) Gravity so strong that it sucked in light and heat.

Something dark was here. Something . . .

She jumped off the bed and knelt down in front of the fire. Holding her hair back from the flames, she craned her neck and peered up into the broad chimney. And there it was, nestling in a hidden alcove where her dream had failed to find it.

Black holes, coincidentally, were on Audrey's mind at that moment, too. This whole castle was like a black hole, with the moor as its event horizon; sucking in modern technology and killing it. First her car, then her phone (she still hadn't got a signal, even from the top of the highest scalable hill), and now her power adaptor. She crouched beside the skirting board with the chunky black plug dangling uselessly from her hand, defeated by the antique five-amp socket. She glowered at it, but no effort of will or cunning would make the thick brass prongs fit into those three tiny round holes.

She would have to do the best she could on batteries. She should get at least four or five hours out of the two she had with her, assuming whatever time-warp forces were operating here hadn't sucked the sap out of them. She abandoned the adaptor and lifted the lid of her PowerBook. Holding her breath, she pressed the startup button. The disk drive whirred and rattled, the smiley face appeared, and the little jigsaw pieces began to line up at the bottom of the screen. She sighed with relief and sat down. Lying ready on the desktop was a file labelled *Ideas 11-98*. She opened it, scrolled to the end, and had got as far as typing 'Ile de Rey (??): WREC—' when there was a frantic knocking on the door. Before she even had a chance to look up or say 'Come in', the door was flung open and Beth appeared, pink-cheeked and breathless with excitement.

'I've found her!' she cried. 'I've found her!'

'Found who?' Audrey asked, but Beth had already gone, leaving the door wide open. '*Found who?*' she shouted.

There was no reply. She put the computer to sleep and went out into the corridor. She found Beth in her room, kneeling on the hearth rug with a small wooden chest set on the floor beside her.

She looked up as Audrey came in. 'This is it!' she said. 'I've found Lydia.'

Perverting Salvador

1

Salvador felt well pleased with himself in the weeks following his night in the forest. He sometimes wondered about the nameless barefoot girl, but his mind was too full to give her much thought; she receded into dreamspace while he was engrossed in exploring his secret prize. He had plenty of opportunity during those weeks. His mother went out often, busying herself with arrangements for the *Petite Fête de Musique*, as she called it. On days when she did not go out, he waited patiently for night to fall, then took his new guitar from its hiding place under his bed and experimented quietly while the house slept.

The first difficulty he had to overcome was how to hold it. The insubstantial size and very substantial weight of its solid body made it impossible to cradle easily on the left thigh in the manner bred into him. Since first seeing the Gibson in Monsieur Duprée's shop, he had developed supernatural antennae which homed in on pictures of electric guitars and electric guitarists. They nearly always played standing up; if they sat down, they held the instrument on their right thigh, close to the hip. He tried both postures (his cheap Japanese Gibson replica came with a free strap) and found both equally uncomfortable. He persevered, though, and slowly grew accustomed to the strange feel. The fingering also felt peculiar. The fine steel strings were slacker and lower on the fingerboard than he was used to; they felt sloppy and imprecise. This was cured easily enough by purchasing some heavier gauge strings and raising the bridge a few millimetres. There was nothing he could do, though, about the sound the guitar made. He had assumed that the grinding, howling, piercing sonorities he had heard in his little tape collection somehow inhered in the electrified instrument, but they did not. When he first plugged the guitar into his hi-fi (using a special adaptor he had bought), the sound that came out was as clean and pure and bland as clear glass. At first he thought it might be the fault of the cheap guitar, but listening carefully to the tapes confirmed that those sounds came from playing very, *very* loud; driving the amplifier until its innards burned. He tried it just once. When he was absolutely certain that nobody else was in the house, he turned the hi-fi up full. Immediately he understood why players wielded their guitars like weapons; he felt its power without even playing a note. The speakers hummed palpably, and just moving his fingers onto the strings to form a chord-shape produced sounds like furniture being moved in the next room. When he played the chord – just with the gentlest stroke of a fingernail – the distorted, jangling *boom* that burst out of the speakers rattled the window panes and shook the floor beneath his feet. Interesting as an instrument of sonic warfare, but actually playing at such a volume was clearly impractical. There had to be an easier way.

Something he had noticed in photographs was the little boxes electric guitarists often had at their feet: tiny devices covered with knobs and switches into which the instrument's lead was plugged. These boxes must surely have something to do with the sounds he heard. Looking at his prize (he liked to stand it next to his other guitars and admire its audacity), he realised that it was, in effect, a musical quadriplegic. Immanent power it might have, but out of its nest of cables and gadgets it was mute and helpless.

One day – specifically, one rainy day far in the future, in a Los Angeles music store – he would find himself thankful for these early handicaps. It was early one Monday morning, and there was only one other customer in the store. He stood with the proprietor over by the drum kits and listened to Salvador sampling a fantastically expensive Gretsch White Falcon. Sitting on a Fender Twin amplifier, his foot joggling a wah-wah pedal, he played through a long, complicated piece he had recently finished transcribing to paper from a Frank Zappa record. When he had finished and was returning the guitar into the anxious hands of the proprietor, the other customer came over to compliment him on his playing. He introduced himself as Vinnie and asked if Salvador was interested in auditioning for a group. He wrote a Hollywood address on the back of an empty Winston pack and said to be there by eight that night if he was interested.

He was interested. He had never been in a group. The address turned out to be a suite of luxurious rehearsal rooms. At one end of the largest room, on a dais, enough equipment had been set up for a band of at least eight pieces. There were banks of synthesisers, two drum kits, enough percussion for an orchestra, guitars, basses, and a dockyard skyline of microphone booms. Around the room, standing in groups or disconsolate lines, were dozens of would-be band members. Salvador found himself on the fringe of a cluster of guitar players at the back of the room. They all seemed to know each other, and he felt very alone. Still, he settled down to wait his turn and watch what happened. On the stage, separated by a palpable aura of casual self-importance, were the current members of the band. There was one man who was obviously in charge. He had his back to the room, and all Salvador could see of him was a green T-shirt and a short tousle of thick, dark hair. It was the turn of one of the hopeful keyboard players, and it wasn't going well. He had been offered a piece of sheet music to play from; he obviously couldn't read it, but was trying desperately to bluff his way through. While he watched the painful humiliation that resulted, Salvador realised he had been noticed. Vinnie left his drum riser, crossed the stage and whispered in the bandmaster's ear, pointing at Salvador. The man's head turned to look, and Salvador almost choked. It was *him*.

The keyboard player was dismissed, and Salvador, numb with shock, was called up onto the stage. *Take a seat*, he was told. When he was plugged in and tuned up, the bandmaster sat down opposite him. *Can you read?* he asked, settling his own guitar on his lap. *Uh-huh. Well, what's more important is, can you play?* Without warning, and without giving Salvador a chance to reply, he reeled off four bars of intricate pentatonic figures pulsing with difficult, unusual rhythms. *Play that*, he instructed. Salvador hesitated a moment, then replicated the passage; but where the bandmaster had played with a pick and produced his runs of rapid notes by hammering on and pulling off with his left hand, Salvador picked each tiny note cleanly and individually with his right. The man's eyebrows rose fractionally, but he seemed otherwise unimpressed. *Close*, he said. *Now play it reggae.* Salvador's brain boggled, but he tried it anyway, fading out the first beat of each bar. Next he was presented with a more complex piece in mixolydian mode. *Play that. Only, when I make this sign . . . switch to seven-eight.* Salvador became so absorbed in trying to follow the bandmaster's instructions he didn't notice how quiet the room became, as every pair of eyes and ears fixed themselves on his audition.

After a few more exercises, he was sent away with the verdict that his playing was 'interesting', and heard nothing more for two months. Then a call came from the bandmaster, asking him to attend a second audition. This time, he was the only auditionee. Over the course of three hours, he was handed scores to read, listened to tapes, and was put through tests that scoured out every last ounce of his imagination and technical skill. In his young life, he had played every composition ever written for classical guitar, with some of the world's most eminent orchestras and conductors. Never, though, had he experienced anything like the challenge to his talents he underwent in those three hours.

He went away exhausted and still with no firm promises. Another three months went by, then he got another call. Would he be ready to go into rehearsal the following week?

He was in. In the long run, it mattered little that he was out again less than three months later (he was just too intense and serious to be roadable, the bandmaster decided eventually); what mattered was that music lived for him again. He was pushed out to limits he had never imagined before, walking on the rim of the universe, seeing sound-shapes that should not logically exist. From the very first moment, he knew he could never go back to the tiny, inert space he had once inhabited except as a visitor.

That was all far in the future. Alone in his bedroom, he struggled with limitations, not limits; the limitations of volume and poor equipment and the tight hobble of his classical tutoring. One day he would be grateful, for the result of the struggle was a unique style of playing; unique and sufficiently interesting to catch the attention of Frank Zappa's drummer. Now, though, it was all just too frustrating.

Particularly frustrating because, during the days when she was at home, his mother shortened the hobble by insisting that he practise incessantly. With a fortnight to go before the *Petite Fête*, she suspended his daily lessons and made him redouble his efforts. His performance, she insisted, was to be not one millimetre short of divine perfection. She recited the guest list to him to emphasise the importance of practice. Were one to plant a bomb under the house, he thought, one could deprive Europe at a single stroke of some of its most eminent cultural figureheads. Salvador was planning a much less violent rebellion. In the middle of the programme, he had secretly inserted Villa-Lobos' Prelude No 2 in E-major. His mother was not enthusiastic about Villa-Lobos; as a Brazilian, he was not a true European, and his compositions spoke too much of the twentieth century. She especially loathed his Prelude No 2 because of the laconic negro cadences she detected in its main phrases. Imagine her reaction, he thought, when it popped its insolent head above the parapet between Schubert and Tárrega. He would pay for it later, but it would be worth the price to see her fume impotently while trying to maintain her composure in front of her august guests. She would be enraged, but would be unable to say a word, because Andrés Segovia, the most highly honoured guest of all, had been a personal friend of Villa-Lobos. It was a flawless plan.

On the evening of the *Fête*, Salvador stood with his mother and Uncle Valéry in the hall and greeted the guests as they arrived. All of them knew Madame de La Simarde of old, and all arrived with obedient promptness at eight o'clock. They were ushered into the Red Drawing Room and served apéritifs. When Salvador had received anniversary congratulations and compliments from each one of them, he was sent away to ensure that all was in order in the Green Salon, where his performance would be given.

The Green Salon was a less impressive venue than the Music Room in the Château (upon which it had been modelled in miniature), but still magnificent. It had been decorated for the occasion with silk and cloth-of-gold drapery hung between the pilasters, picked out in panels in the national colours of Spain, Italy, Germany, Austria and France, to represent the confluence of European music in the evening's programme. The electric lights had been switched off, and the room was lit by candles, clustered in groups of five to mark Salvador's five years of concert performances and the five decades of Madame de La Simarde's life. There were twenty-six clusters, representing the twenty-six generations of the de La Simarde family. That made a total of one hundred and thirty candles, signifying the years of union between the houses of Perez and de La Simarde. One end of the room had been cleared of furniture: here, Salvador's chair and footstool had been set up and his Torres, newly strung and bedded-in, waited silently on its stand.

The corner adjacent to the improvised stage had been mysteriously curtained off. He asked Février – who had been dispatched to attend to any problems with the furnishings and decorations – what was behind the curtain.

Février shook his head. 'I do not know, sir. I think Madame may be planning some surprise. A gift of some kind.'

Salvador longed to peep behind the curtain, but didn't get a chance; the doors opened and Madame de La Simarde entered. She glanced about, checking that every detail was just right, then signalled to Avril that the guests were to be escorted through.

The programme for the evening was this: a formal greeting by Madame de La Simarde, followed by a short recital of works by Sor. Then would come dinner and, afterwards, the main body of Salvador's performance. The first part of the evening went well. His playing was sublime, despite over-rehearsal and an unnerving front row made up of his mother, the Director of the Viennese State Opera, his former tutor Abel Carlevaro (whose Uruguayan birth Madame had always graciously overlooked) and – guest of honour – Andrés Segovia. Over dinner (of which Salvador was only allowed two small courses, lest the rigours of digestion interfere with his concentration), Segovia complimented him warmly on his interpretation of the *Grand Solo*, quizzed him on the relative merits of Fleta and Torres, and asked him why there were no works by Villa-Lobos on the programme. Salvador blushed and looked down at his empty plate, saying nothing.

He had been having second thoughts about his little act of subversion, but the Master's words gave him courage. He played the rebellious Prelude with high-strung zest. As its last pert chord faded out and applause welled into the vacuum, he looked to see his mother's reaction. To his disappointment, she gave none: her face in the candlelight was utterly unmoved; not even a hint of disapproval in her stare. The applause ebbed away, and he began the next piece.

The recital moved on. Février, moving silently and invisibly, opened the terrace windows one by one. The warm, narcotic night air rolled gently in and shimmered the candle flames, dancing them like iridescent marionettes to the notes from Salvador's guitar. The reason soon became clear: as the music reached its final climax, fireworks burst and sparkled above the night-blue lake, punctuating Tárrega's chords with crackles, spits and booms.

The guests rose to their feet as one, applauding passionately, tossing *bravos* and calling for an encore. Madame de La Simarde rose from her seat and stood beside her son, acknowledging her share of the adulation. When the guests eventually grew quiet and resumed their seats, she addressed them.

'Ladies and gentlemen,' she said. 'Thank you. You shall have your encore in a moment. First, I wish to say a few words. First of all, thank you for coming to my little *fête*, my little *soirée*. As you know, today marks the end of my first half-century on this earth. The true celebration, however, is for my son and the gift that he has displayed for you this evening.' Another patter of applause and more cries of *bravo*.

Madame de La Simarde glanced at Salvador and went on: 'Any mother will tell you what a difficult thing it is to bring up a son. The material one has to work with can seem so unpromising, yet it is provided by God, and with good breeding, care, and above all vigilance, the difficulties of nature can be overcome and the best made of what is provided. As you can see, I have not done too badly.'

A ripple of polite laughter, slightly bemused; Madame de La Simarde making a *joke*?

'I had thought not to say these words to you, but Salvador has given me a little sign this evening that he would like me to. Salvador, the second in a line of great musicians to bear that name, has truly been a gift from God. But boys, however well bred, however extraordinary, however well tutored and cared for, will be boys. Boy, in short, have a compulsion to masturbate.'

Salvador almost dropped his guitar. He stared in horror at his mother. The silence deepened; except for one or two guests who had drunk too much and snorted convulsively, the assembly froze and gazed in stupefaction at their hostess, hoping they had heard wrongly.

'My son,' she continued, 'is no exception. He shares the weakness of his kind. He does not control his basest urges, and has made a whore of his divine gift . . . Février, the curtain.'

Février went to the corner of the room and drew back the velvet curtain. There, standing in its open case like a corpse at a wake, was Salvador's electric guitar. In the glow of the candles, its bordello reds and oranges did indeed look pornographic beside the ascetic modesty of the Torres.

'This . . . I hesitate to call it an instrument. This . . . *thing*, this travesty, this obscene parody of the finest musical instrument on God's earth, is the secret slut upon which my son chooses to expend and pervert his precious talent. There, I have decided that his encore for you this evening will be to learn a lesson in true value. You, ladies and gentlemen, shall be his esteemed witnesses.'

She seized the electric guitar from its case and propped it against the wall. Then she called Février forward. To everybody's alarm, he bore in his hand a heavy woodman's axe. Without speaking or showing any sign of emotion, he prised the Torres from his young master's fingers and placed it on its stand. Then he stationed himself beside the two guitars and waited.

'Now, Salvador,' said his mother. 'You have the opportunity to exercise free will. The choice is absolutely your own. I cannot advise you. Which shall it be: your muse or your whore? Choose.'

Salvador looked about him in shame and despair, faces blurring as his eyes stung with tears. Février, impassive; his mother, imperious, but with a taint of pain in her eyes; his tutor and the Austrian opera director appalled; and Segovia. He didn't dare look at Segovia. The Master was known to abhor the electric guitar only slightly less intensely than did Madame de La Simarde. His gaze fixed on his two instruments: the priceless Torres and the five-hundred-franc Gibson replica. How had he been discovered? Somebody must have informed on him, but who? The barefoot girl? Almost blind now with weeping, he lunged forward and made his choice, hugging the instrument to his body.

'Very well,' said his mother. 'You have chosen. There is no going back from this point; remember that.'

She nodded solemnly at Février. He raised the axe and swung. There was a tremendous crash as the blade bit into the wood, sending it cartwheeling to the floor, splintering and smashing, strings breaking with sharp bullet-cracks and sad twangs. He raised the axe again and sliced the body in two. The bridge and tailpiece buckled and stuck out like broken bones. A third stroke reduced what remained to matchwood. The pickups dangled from a single chunk of painted mahogany, entangled in a mess of wires. One gold plastic volume knob flew off and rolled across the floor, coming to rest by Salvador's feet.

As he stared down at the wreckage, he felt his mother's hand on his shoulder.

'In my heart,' she said softly. 'I knew you would choose well. The blood that flows in your veins ordained it.' He wiped the tears from his eyes and stared at her. 'Salvador is proud of you,' she said. 'You shall shame him no longer. You are forgiven, my son.' She held out her arms and smiled. 'Now you may embrace me.'

He stood motionless while she put her arms about him. As they closed behind his back, he began to yield, leaning towards her, sensing the softness of her under the shell; the softness that could be felt but not seen, that he had known as a tiny child. Finally, he sank into her. The Torres fell to the floor, and he flung his arms around her and sobbed.

When children grow up, they don't outgrow their parents; it is parents who shrink and recede from their children.

It all depends on your perspective, of course.

2

Salvador didn't resign his fellowship; nor, as Rachel had predicted, was he forcibly parted from it. Most people seemed to have hardly noticed his absence. Sir Michael called him to the Master's Lodge a few days after his return and gave him half an hour of vague, allusive waffle about propriety and pastoral care, a rag-bag homily stitched together with references to some unspecified misdemeanour and slightly toadyish inquiries about his mother's good health. He told Salvador – for no actual stated reason – the story of a colleague, a professor at Oxford, who had been suspended from his post and then sacked for conducting a series of *intimate relationships* with undergraduates in his department. Salvador nodded in all the right places, and said very little.

The solution was simple: secrecy. And when he said secret, he told her, he meant *totally* secret. Not even her friends should know. That's impossible, she said. It's essential, he replied. *Nobody* must know about us.

So, officially, not even her friends – not even Beth – knew about Lydia and Salvador. Unofficially, though, they guessed. Not even Rachel was that naïve. But they never mentioned it, itch to as they might. Six blind eyes were turned, three curiosities stoppered and suppressed.

It was a recipe for disaster, and each of them knew it, deep down, but still they kept their mouths shut. It was easier that way. As far as they were concerned, Lydia was still single, but happy with it now.

As they breasted the rise of the New Year and started down the home slope of their final year, they paired off:

Audrey with Peter. Poor man couldn't resist her charms. They hit a crisis patch late in the Easter term, and separated for a while, but they were destined to be together. Audrey willed it, and it was inevitable.

Beth with Danny. Her birthday-party astrophysicist. They met again in the library tea-room. He re-introduced himself, and after much persuasion, she agreed to go out with him. He was sweet, but rather dull.

Rachel with Jesus. Since her charity work at Christmas, her relationship with the Messiah had grown passionate, although her friends suspected that she was just compensating.

In a sense, they were all compensating. They felt happy enough (a state they would one day learn was the best most human souls could hope for). Inwardly, though, they all envied the relationship Lydia wasn't having with Salvador.

3

He wasn't sleeping. His back was turned to her, but she could tell he was awake by the lightness and shallowness of his breathing. His black hair and the white sheet gave his skin a pallor: the off-white tint of cut beechwood that comes to olive skin kept too long indoors. Even Australia had failed to breathe a tan onto him. Taut and smooth as a filled sail over the light muscles of his back and shoulders. Her own skin still fizzed with the touch of it.

It had come at last. *He* had come at last, clenched tight between her whiter thighs. His ineptitude had taken her by surprise. Looking at the supple, wiry sinews of his hands, she had imagined he would play her body expertly and magnificently, like a musical instrument; fingering, stopping and plucking her strings with sublime, passionate skill, chords ringing in her brain. Salvador and his Human Guitar. (After all, a cliché might become a cliché because of its truth.) But he was startlingly inexperienced, and his touch was untutored. Strangely, this excited her more than she could have imagined; for all his lack of finesse, he was both enthusiastic and patient, raw and tender, keen to try new flavours. When she came, she pulled at his hair and pressed down his face, wanting to eat him alive. She fucked him quickly and greedily, and afterwards was delirious and exhausted and just a little bit ashamed of herself.

But what did he feel? She didn't ask, and he didn't tell her. What was he thinking, lying there, pretending to be asleep? Guilt and shame? Was he thinking about his mother? Or what the Master might say if he could see?

She pushed back the sheet and slipped close to him, pressing herself spoonwise into his back, crooking her legs into his. He twisted his head round on the pillow and looked at her. She couldn't tell whether he was smiling or just grimacing at the effort of trying to see her face.

'Tell me what you're thinking,' she said.

Now he smiled, and she knew he hadn't been smiling before. 'Why do women ask men that? What does it matter what I'm thinking?'

She put an arm around him and squeezed his chest. 'It's a prompt. You're supposed to say you were thinking about how good the sex was or how wonderful I am and how much you adore me.'

'Oh. Well, that's exactly what I was thinking of.'

'Which?'

'All three.'

She pinched his nipple, and he yelped. 'Liar,' she said. 'What were you really thinking about?'

'Honestly?'

'Honestly.'

'I was wondering whether I should re-string my Fleta now or leave it another week.'

She gazed at his face for a few moments, then sighed and rolled away from him. 'I wish I was surprised, but I'm not. You could at least *try* not to be predictable.'

He turned over and followed her across the bed. 'Those things are still true, even if I wasn't thinking them at that moment.' He reached out a finger to trace the line of the crevice between her upper arm and lolling breast. 'You asked for honesty,' he said.

She scoffed. 'Honesty isn't in your dictionary. If it was—'

She was interrupted by the muffled sound of knocking on the door. They frowned at each other in silence for a moment, then he got out of bed and reached for his dressing gown.

She watched him pull it on, noticing with a little tug of desire that his cock wobbled stiffly through the opening at the front. 'Don't let anyone see you, for God's sake,' she giggled as he poked it back under cover. 'Bring that baby back to me while it's still warm.'

He went through to the sitting room while she waited, holding her breath. When several minutes had passed and he didn't return, she got out of bed and followed him, wrapping a sheet around herself and peeping cautiously through the crack of the bedroom door.

He was alone, standing by the window. She opened the door wide and stepped into the room. 'Coast clear?' she asked.

He nodded. 'No one there.'

She joined him at the window, hiding behind him and trying to peer over his shoulder at the courtyard below. As she peeped, she slipped an exploratory hand under his dressing gown. Soft. Damn.

Before she had a chance to rectify this, he turned and hustled her away from the window. 'What are you doing?' he whispered urgently. 'What if someone sees you?'

'There's nobody about,' she protested, not letting go of his handle. *He* might panic, but *it* knew when to have a good time.

He reached back and hurriedly pulled the curtains closed, just as she whipped away the belt of his dressing gown.

'I want to give you a gift,' he said.

'A gift?'

'Well, call it a souvenir if you like.'

He reached up to the mantelpiece and took down a small white envelope. For one horrible moment, she thought he was going to pay her. But when he opened the flap and turned the envelope upside-down over the coffee table, all that fell out was three thin discoids of what looked like translucent brown plastic.

'They're guitar picks,' he said.

She peered sardonically at him. 'You're going to give me a plectrum? Wow.'

He shook his head. 'Not just any plectrum. These are hand-made. They're very special to me. Before I settled in New York, I spent some time in Tahiti. I met a man there who lived on the beach, carving things from tortoiseshell. Desmond. He was about the happiest man I ever met. His life was so simple, just sitting there all day with his carving-block between his knees, listening to the sea rolling on the sand and chatting and bartering with anyone who stopped by. He used only shell from tortoises who had died from natural causes, and the tortoises there lived a *long* time.' Salvador held up one of the little discoids. 'This pick is ancient. It was riding around on the back of a tortoise while America was still being hacked out of the wilderness and the British Empire was in its prime ... I bought ten of Desmod's picks. I gave him a bottle of whisky and eight dollars. Some wore out from playing, and I lost a few. I've only got these three left now. Call me a fool, but I treasure them. They remind me of how happy Desmond was with his life, and how much I envied him his simplicity.' He held out the pick. 'I want you to have this one.'

She took the thumbnail-size sliver and held it up to the light. It was wax-smooth and paper-thin. On an impulse, she put it to her lips and licked it. 'I can taste the sea-salt,' she said. 'And you.'

'Never show it to anyone,' he said. 'But of course, you know that.'

'Yes, I know that.'

She slipped it into her pocket and stood up. 'I'd better be going,' she said.

He didn't seem to hear her. He was fingering one of the tortoise-shell picks and gazing into some far distance that didn't include her. 'Incidentally,' he said at last. 'It was Frank Zappa.'

She frowned. 'Pardon?'

'That first evening, when I first saw you. The four of you were arguing about writing and music. Using one art form to describe another. Someone had said that writing about music was like dancing about architecture, and you were trying to remember where the quote came from. Well, it was Frank Zappa.'

She smiled. 'That was *ages* ago. What made you think of that? Anyway, it wasn't—'

'I worshipped him,' he went on. 'Did I ever tell you I was in his group? It was only for a short while. He fired me. He was very nice about it: he said he liked my playing, and I did great eyebrows, but I just wasn't roadable. I guess I was a little tightly strung.'

'*Highly* strung,' she corrected.

'Right. Anyway, that was just before I went to Tahiti.' He came out of his dream and looked at her. 'Must you go?'

She nodded. 'It's dark out. No one will see me. That courtyard's lit like a crypt.'

'Shall I drive you home?'

She shook her head. 'Better not.'

'When . . .?'

'I'll come again tomorrow. Keep yourself warm for me. Goodnight, Salvador.'

The Paradox Cup

For my third birthday, my father gave me a teacup and saucer. He called it the Paradox Cup. The saucer, which was red with a yellow stripe, had Noddy and Big Ears chasing each other around the rim. The little blue cup had writing outside and in. By the time I was old enough to read the writing, my father was dead and gone, and I was never able to separate the words from the inexplicable fact of his disappearance.

In lettering he must have painted himself (it didn't sound like something that would come from Noddy), the outside of the cup read, *What is written inside the cup is true.* Inside, it said, *What is written outside the cup is false.*

I still have the cup, and the inscription still seems as slippery as it ever did. There have been times in my life, however, when its mocking little paradox has seemed a perfect reflection of what was happening in my head. Perhaps that is what my father intended. Perhaps he felt that way himself. Perhaps the little cup caused it all.

243

4

This was no time for shirking, Beth told herself. Work, work, work! Easter term was waning, and the vacation was looming. The catapult strings would tauten, stretch and suddenly fling her into the minefield midst of final exams.

Right now, at this moment, she should be upstairs, locked in her room like a good girl. There should be books, there should be lecture notes. A mug of coffee at her elbow, a revision timetable imprinted in her brain, and diligence in her soul.

That was where she should be. Not vegging out on the sofa in front of Ruth Rendell repeats, with men on her mind and chocolate biscuits piling up in her stomach. She was hypnotised by the conviction that the actor who played Inspector Wexford looked *exactly* like Danny, given a haircut and another thirty years' ageing. Even the accent was similar – a sort of unplaceable, soft country burr. She pictured herself still with him when he was padded and softened and greyed like that, and the thought made her nauseous. What else might give? Some things just couldn't get any worse. *By the length of a man's rod shall ye know him, and by his wielding of it shall he be judged.* If there was a supplementary Part II paper on Danny's shortcomings (literal or otherwise), she'd be up for a First.

The front door opened and closed, and there was a sound of shoes scuffing on the mat. Beth switched the television off and listened, thankful for a distraction that wasn't of her own making.

'Who dat out dere?' she called.

'Who dat in dere saying who dat out dere?' came the reply. Lydia appeared in the doorway. 'Hi,' she said. 'All alone?'

'Apparently. Good trip?'

'Fair. Bloody train was late.'

'And how was Sheffield?'

Lydia took off her jacket and collapsed into an armchair. 'Oh, not bad. I made my peace with Gabriel. He and Helen have had a bit of a reconciliation since Christmas. She's agreed to go to Thailand with him at Easter, and he's agreed to try line dancing.'

'Line dancing?'

Lydia smirked. 'It's her life. Poor Gabriel. I can't quite see it somehow.' She looked around the room and sighed. 'Where is everybody?'

'Rachel's at church. Audrey's been out all day.'

'With Peter?'

'I imagine.'

'How about you? Not seeing Danny?'

Beth prickled with anger. 'We're not joined at the hip,' she snapped. Lydia blanched, and Beth felt ashamed of herself. 'Sorry,' she said. 'I decided to stay in and do some revision.' Her cheeks flushed with guilty blood.

The telephone sang out, and Beth reached across and grabbed it gratefully.

'Hello? . . . No, she isn't. Can I give her a—. . . Oh, hello, Peter . . . No, it's Beth . . . Fine, thank you. Listen, I'll get her to ring you as soon as she . . . Yes, okay . . . Bye.'

'That was Peter,' she said, hanging up.

'Hmm. Audrey's not out with him, then?'

'No. He hasn't seen her since before the weekend.'

'Oh dear.' Lydia grinned. 'You don't think she's looking for better offers, do you?'

Beth shook her head. 'Audrey? Who knows?'

They were about to go their separate ways to bed when Audrey blustered in, pink-cheeked with night chill and, Beth sensed, an inordinate quotient of glee.

'Where have you been all day?' she asked. 'Peter phoned.'

That brought her up short. Her face fell. 'Oh. Did he say anything?'

'Only that he hadn't seen you since Friday and could you call him.'

'Right. Fine.'

'Where *have* you been?' Lydia asked. 'Somewhere good, by the look of that grin.'

'Hi, Lyd. Good weekend?' She went on without waiting for a reply: 'Certainly not. I've been sweating in the UL all day. I've got essays to write. No time for lurv on the express to success, darling.'

Beth snorted. 'The UL? Till this time?'

Audrey flushed. 'Who the fuck d'you two think you are? My dad? I bumped into Sue and Tim. We went for a drink. Satisfied? Now, if it's okay with you, I'll be getting to bed.'

As she picked up her bag and headed for the stairs, Beth and Lydia looked at each other. It wasn't quite like Audrey to tell such spectacularly blatant lies. Usually, ultimately, she just didn't care enough. Beth wished that, just occasionally in her life, she could have a mere tenth of that ability.

5

Salvador parked the Lotus in the amputated butt-end of Chesterton Road and walked around to the park. In the shadow of the church steeple, tucked away in the corner of the park, was a children's play area. She was there before him. Her bike was parked up against the see-saw, and she was sitting on a swing, nudging herself gently back and forth with her foot. She looked alone and vulnerable against the deserted space of grassland, as she did in the world.

She was gazing down at the ground, daydreaming. She took so long to notice him approaching that he mistook her mood for sullenness, and was surprised when at last she saw him and leapt off the swing, running to him and hurling herself at him, wrapping her arms and legs around his body. She covered his face with kisses, squeezed him hard, then dropped to her feet.

He laughed self-consciously and looked around to make sure no hidden watchers had materialised from the turf. There was no need; this park, situated outside the reality boundary and hemmed in by the houses and thundering traffic of Elizabeth Way, belonged exclusively to local dog-walkers and skateboarders. Nobody from the University ever came here.

'It's like Sheffield all over again,' he said, looking at the playground furniture. 'Except the weather and the welcome are warmer. This time you're glad to see me.'

She hugged him again. 'I was glad to see you then ... *Ooh, you're so cuddly. I can't let you go.* I was, really.' Eventually, she relinquished her grip and led him by the hand back to the swings. 'Gabriel sends his regards, by the way,' she said, resuming her seat.

'His *regards*?'

'He said to tell you he's sorry for trying to beat the crap out of you. His words.'

'You didn't tell him about us, did you?'

'No, he just assumed.'

'Oh. Well, tell him his apology is accepted. Also tell him there's nothing going on between us.'

Lydia braked her swing and gazed at him. 'Do we *have* to keep it quite so secret? I seem to be the only person I know who has a good relationship, and I can't even tell anyone about it. I mean, Audrey and Beth—'

'Especially them! You can't tell them!'

'I think they've probably guessed.'

'Well, they can guess all they like. You are not to tell them. Can you really trust their loyalty that much? I don't think so. It's just too juicy a piece of gossip. They would tell someone, and before you know it, the whole College knows about us.'

'Okay, okay. Keep your wig on. I won't tell.' She began swinging to and fro again. 'Anyway, it wouldn't be very nice, rubbing their noses in it.'

'Pardon?' His command of English was almost native, but sometimes these little anglicisms slipped by him.

'Me being so happy while they're so miserable.'

He sat on the spare swing and set it in motion, following her rhythm. In response, she swung faster and higher, kicking out her legs until the chains buckled and whip-cracked. Their swings met at the top of a stroke, and in the momentary, weightless pause, he asked, 'Why are they so miserable?'

She fell away, accelerating, and they met again, two beats later, in mid-swing. 'Man trouble,' she said, and hurtled on past.

'What do you mean?'

'I . . .' She was panting, incoherent with effort. 'I feel . . . sick.' She stopped kicking her legs, and let the swing slow gradually, shallowing to a halt while Salvador carried on whisking back and forth; this was a new experience for him, and he was enjoying himself. Lydia was red in the face, but grinning. 'Bad boyfriend choices,' she said when she had got her breath back. 'Not the happiest pair of love-bunnies at the moment, I'm afraid. Audrey's split up with Peter, and I think Beth's on the brink of finishing with Danny.'

Salvador, on a fast backward downstroke, dug his heel into the ground, gouging a furrow in the bed of mulch and bringing his swing to a juddering, swerving halt.

'They're splitting up too?' he said.

'I wouldn't be surprised. She's been getting really snappish lately. Bad tempered. She avoids him when he phones. She says she's busy working for exams, but I've seen her. She just sits around all day watching television.'

'And Audrey?'

'Oh, she's even deeper. She puts on that fey *What, me? Depressed?* thing she does, but she can't stand Peter's name being mentioned.

There's something going on there, but she won't talk about it. Neither of them will.'

He nodded silently and gazed down at the ground. Eventually, he looked up at her. 'Lydia,' he said. 'I love you. You know that, don't you?'

She smiled and squeezed his hand. He was gripping the chain, and the links bit into his palm. 'Of course,' she said. 'I'm here, aren't I?'

He nodded. 'Lydia, there's something I've got to tell you.'

'Oh God, don't say that. I've always dreaded someone looking all earnestly at me and saying that.'

'I may have to go away for a while.'

'Go away? When? Where? You're not going to do your disappearing act again?'

'No, of course not. But it's important. It concerns you. I want to know that, when all this is over – when we're not part of this ridiculous system any more, when we can do as we please and not be secret – I... Will you marry me?'

She stared at him, speechless, for a long while, her expression impaled between amusement and shock. How do you deal with an irresistible offer shot through with unreality? Later – much, much later – when she tried to explain her decision to herself, she felt it was like being mired in poverty and having someone say *Here is ten million pounds. Because such riches are beyond both your experience and your imagination, there is some risk attached. We cannot specify what that risk is, exactly, but your life could be destroyed. Will you accept the money?*

'Yes,' said the poverty in her, using her voice. 'Yes, I will.'

He sighed deeply. 'Thank God. We don't have to plan it, not yet – I just need to know that, at the end, it will have all been worthwhile.'

'Of course it's worthwhile. You know how I feel. Now tell me why you have to go away.'

He took a pale blue envelope out of his jacket pocket and handed it to her. It was addressed to him, and bore a blue *Prioritaire* sticker. 'Read this,' he said, handing it to her.

She took out the letter and unfolded it; a single sheet of crested notepaper with three short paragraphs of fine copperplate. 'It's in French,' she said.

'From my mother. She sends me a cheque every fortnight, but this is the first time she's ever included a letter.' He watched her for a moment as she peered at the writing. 'I can translate for you if you like.'

'No,' she said. 'I can cope ... *My Dear Son*,' she read aloud.

He snorted. 'That's me.'

'*I* ... Oh, stuck already.'

'*I trust.* That's a rather antique way of expressing it, but that's my mother for you.'

248

'*I trust . . . that this communication finds you healthy and . . . working . . .?*'

'*. . .as befits your talents.*'

Lydia smiled. '*I can vouch for that . . . I have received recently a letter from my cousin Albert, who has some exciting news. He has found in Barcelona a merchant—*'

'*Dealer* is closer. Your French is really good.'

'I read it better than I speak it . . . *a dealer who possesses a Torres which is the . . .* something something . . . *you already own.*'

'*The exact twin.* You know my Torres. It's one of a special series made by Antonio de Torres Jurado between 1878 and 1882. He was the greatest luthier who ever lived, and many claim this series of guitars are the finest he ever made. Most are believed lost. It seems cousin Albert has discovered one.'

Lydia went on reading: '*He wishes to know whether we would like to buy the instrument. He will . . . make it assured?*'

'*Secure it.*'

'*. . .On our behalf. I have told him that my son must see the instrument and approve it. One will not go to Spain. Albert will make to have it brought to Gondecourt for you.*'

She looked up from the letter. 'That's kind of them. When will you go?'

'I don't know if I shall.'

'Why not?'

He took the letter back and stared suspiciously at it. 'She has some ulterior motive. Why would I go to Gondecourt to inspect this guitar when I could easier fly to Barcelona? Or it could be shipped here.' He gave the letter back to Lydia. 'Read on.'

'*Do you know, Salvador, it is ten years since you have been at Gondecourt?* You haven't been home in ten years? . . . *The estate misses its heir.*'

'Ha. The *estate* misses its heir! She does not, apparently.'

'Of course she does. That's what she means.'

He grunted. 'Read over the letter again. Do you notice anything amiss?'

Puzzled, Lydia pored over the words. At last, she realised what he meant. 'She calls you *vous.* I didn't notice.'

'Every French-speaking mother on this planet addresses her child as *tu.* But not my mother. She last called me *tu* when I was five years old. Never again after. Oh, she has her reasons, but . . .' he hesitated. 'If I go to Gondecourt – *if* I go – it shall only be with you to accompany me.'

It took several moments for the implications of this assertion to sink in. 'Salvador, I can't! She's the cause of all this . . .' She gestured around her at the park. 'This *sneaking about.* If she *meets* me . . .'

'She won't know. She never met you before, she doesn't even know your name. We'll tell her you work in a bank or something. We met at a concert.'

Lydia frowned as though she were in pain. Couldn't he see what he was asking of her? 'My exams,' she objected desperately. 'I can't go away.'

'It would only be for a few days in the vacation. You can work extra hard before and after. Take books with you. You won't miss much.'

'I will. I'll flunk out, Salvador.'

'Of course you won't. Anyway, what's the point of a geography degree if you've seen nothing of the world? Look on it as extra revision. What do you call it? Fieldwork.'

She sighed. 'You're not going to give up, are you?'

'If I've inherited nothing else from her, I've got my mother's stubbornness.'

'It's no use. I still can't go.'

'Why? What other reason could there be?'

'Why? Why d'you think I've never been abroad? Salvador, I'm scared of flying.'

'That doesn't matter. So are lots of people . . .' He saw the horror in her face, and relented. 'Okay, so we'll drive.'

'I'm scared of boats as well. Ferries. They give me the horrors.'

Salvador's shoulders sagged. 'Then I shan't go. The Torres can stay in Barcelona and the estate can go on missing me.'

'I'm sorry.' She reached out and stroked his cheek. 'Don't sulk, Salvador. It's not attractive, even in you.'

He brushed her hand away. 'I'm not sulking. Merely stating a fact. If I go to see my mother, then it is only with my future wife to accompany me. Can't you see what this means to me?'

She looked at him and saw. What she saw was the same childlike fear she had sensed in Sheffield. She saw the little boy looking out from behind his eyes, and knew she could never willingly refuse him anything. The question was whether her fear was greater than his. Or her courage. Air or sea, flight or floating made no difference; it was height that slimed her brain and petrified her body. Either way, she pictured herself locked into an inescapable tin capsule, floating above a yawning void, held there only by the tenuous abstraction of physics. Air flow, pressure and lift . . . *upthrust is equal to the weight of water displaced* . . . How could you be sure that any of that really *worked?* It was all abstract, all just words and equations.

She looked at him again, deep into those big, childlike eyes, and knew where his courage and desire stood relative to hers.

'I'll need a passport,' she said.

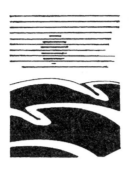

And in the dark, dark room, there was a dark, dark chimney,
And in the dark, dark chimney, there was a dark, dark box,
And in the dark, dark box, there was a ghost.

It was like a miniature pirate's chest, made of some dark, stained wood bound with iron straps. In its chimney alcove, it had been quite safe from the flames, but its outward-facing end bore a thin coating of soot. Before laying it on the rug, Beth wiped the soot off with a tissue, studying the box as she cleaned it. It had an ornate iron escutcheon, browned with age, which was engraved with a flowery monogram (either *VA* or *AV*). The keyhole looked just the right size to take a small, claw-warded key.

'How do you know it's hers?' Audrey asked.

Beth fingered the key, holding it up and brushing the pocket-warmed iron across her lips. She touched it with the tip of her tongue, and tasted the sourness of corrosion and the salt of use. 'I just know,' she said quietly.

Audrey knelt down on the rug and looked impatiently at her. 'Well? Aren't you going to open it?' Beth hesitated, fingering the key uncertainly. 'I'll open it if you're scared.'

Beth looked at her. 'No, I'm not scared. Why would I be scared?'

'Well, if a pair of panties can give you the heebie-jeebies, this . . .' Audrey touched the box and assumed an expression of foreboding. 'Who knows?'

It was true: Beth was scared of what the box might hold, but she was damned if she was going to be made fun of. She slipped the key into the lock and twisted. It turned easily, there was a tiny *clack*, and the lid twitched slightly as the catch released.

As Beth raised the lid, a thick odour of ancient, dusty wood and stale smoke rose from the box.

'What's in it?' asked Audrey, shifting around on the rug to see inside.

The interior of the box was small – less room than a shoe-box – and there wasn't much in it. Beth reached in and took out three small notebooks: two were leather-bound and bore the Simarde family crest; the other was older, cheaper, bent and dog-eared. She opened one of them at random and felt a stab of pain at the sight of Lydia's tiny, meandering hand. She closed it quickly and passed it to Audrey. 'Diaries,' she said. Underneath the notebooks were some letters, still in their envelopes. 'These must be from Gabriel,' she murmured, seeing the Sheffield postmark. 'Look; she never even opened them.' Underneath the letters was a bundle of postcards, tied with a green ribbon. At first, Beth thought they too must be from Gabriel, but when she untied the ribbon, she found views of Dartmoor, Gondecourt and the Val de Vienne. The topmost one showed a row of grey-faced, terracotta-capped houses straggling down a narrow, sun-scorched lane. She turned it over. *Dear Beth*, she read, feeling a sharp stab in her chest, *Returned now and settling in nicely. S's mother still a total sweetie. Wish you could see us here. Big love and hugs, all forgiven, Lydia xx*. It was dated July 1991.

Audrey read over her shoulder. 'She sounds happy enough,' she said. 'Why didn't she send it?'

'I don't know.'

'What does she mean, "all forgiven"?'

Beth sighed. 'We had a row, the very last time I saw her. The day I left Cambridge. I told her she shouldn't marry Salvador.'

'Why?'

'I told her he wasn't trustworthy.' She glanced at Audrey, and her cheeks coloured. 'Well, he wasn't, was he? I told her . . . Well, that's all. I said she was a gullible fool. Naïve and gullible.'

'Oh. I see.'

Beth picked up the next card – a view of a long stone bridge decked with flags. *Dear Beth*, it said, *I can see this bridge from where I'm sitting. Don't worry about me. Assume you will have heard by now. Don't worry – I'm fine. Yours as ever, Lydia xx*. This one was dated July 1997, almost exactly the mid-point, Beth realised, between Salvador's death and her own.

There were over thirty cards in all, arranged geographically rather than chronologically (how like Lydia). A few of the earlier ones were addressed to Rachel or Audrey, but all the rest were written to Beth.

'That's it,' said Beth sadly, as though she had been hoping for more. 'All there is left of her.'

'What's that?' Audrey asked, peering into the box.

There was something wedged into the joint in one corner. Beth got a fingernail under it and prised it out. It was a small, egg-shaped sliver of translucent tortoiseshell. A plectrum.

'Salvador,' said Audrey. She took the plectrum from Beth's fingers and scrutinised it, holding it up to the light. 'Is this all she kept of him?'

Beth looked at her. 'Maybe it was all he ever gave her,' she said, suddenly angry. 'Apart from grief.'

'Well, quite.' Audrey tossed the plectrum and the unopened letters back into the chest, but kept the notebooks. 'Dare we read these, do you think?'

Beth suddenly saw a vision of Lydia lying naked on a slab, herself and Audrey standing on either side with greedy, inquisitive scalpels poised. She brushed the vision away and sighed. 'I don't see why not.'

Rachel was at a loss. She simply didn't know what to do: her instincts were pulling her one way, and Clifford was pushing her the other.

Waking up to snow hadn't been a good start. They had driven back up to the moortop for the night, and had woken to find the VW half-buried. The snow had drifted up to the windows and over the roof on one side, and engulfed the camper up to its axles on the other. When they had eventually dug it out, using aluminium dinner plates as shovels, it refused to start. Clifford fiddled and poked about in the VW's rear end, gradually dismantling the ignition and fuel systems with frozen fingers, accumulating a spreading pile of greasy black bits and pieces on the compacted snow. Finally, just as he was losing the last traces of feeling in his fingers, he located the trouble: somehow, moisture had found its way into the carburettor and frozen, blocking the fuel feed to the engine. By the time he had removed the ice, reassembled the engine and started it (with frequent hand-warming breaks), mid-day had come and gone.

He was all for moving on: getting away from this Arctic hell-hole and heading east. Could they drive in these conditions? Rachel asked. He was pretty sure he could. Anyway, they had to make a move, he said; God knew what might have been happening at the site while they had been away. They ought to have set out yesterday, instead of chasing round looking for her friends.

They nearly had their first ever argument then. Rachel was still aching inside from the funeral, whilst Clifford's reawakening fingers were throbbing with intermittent hammer blows of pain. Both of them were irritable.

'I doubt if they're making much progress in this weather,' said Rachel, thinking of the road contractors. 'Do we have to leave?'

'I'd rather,' he said, sucking his fingers one by one. 'Anyway, your friends are probably back in London by now, toasting their capitalist toes in front of the fire while we're stuck out here in this.'

She gazed around at the white wasteland, scarred black by the granite of the tor and the church. 'I don't know,' she said. 'I think they're still here. I can sense it.'

Clifford grinned in spite of the pain. 'Who d'you think you are? Obi-Wan Kenobi? *I sense a disturbance in the Force, Luke. A presence I haven't felt since—*'

'Stop it,' she scolded, punching him on the arm. She laughed, though, and they knew they weren't going to argue. 'You know I can sense these things. Wasn't I right about Stack?'

'Mmm. I guess.'

'I *felt* he was still in there, and he was. If we'd followed what the others said, he'd have been buried alive.' She looked about again and inhaled the cold air. 'I just *know* Beth and Audrey are still here. Can't we have just one more try at finding them?'

What I Once Believed

These are some of the things I believed when I was a child.

—That dogs were boys and cats were girls.
—That there were two crimes the police could arrest you for:
1) Driving your car in a wobbly way; 2) Weeing on the pavement.
—That Father Christmas ate the tangerines and mince pies I put out
for him.
—That babies came out of their mothers' bottoms, covered in poo.
—That my mum and dad would always be there.
—That grown-ups were wise and kind and basically decent.

It seems odd that, of all our beliefs, it is always the most fantastically
inaccurate that are the longest and hardest to unlearn.

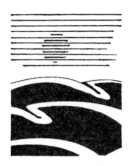

'I had one of these,' said Beth.

Only two of the notebooks turned out to be diaries. The third – the cheap, dog-eared jotter – Lydia had kept as a sort of commonplace book.

Audrey looked up from her perusal of the diaries.

'I started it in my first year at Cambridge,' Beth explained. 'I showed it to Lydia once. I can't believe she copied me. She's even given it the same title, more or less. *Things I Once Believed.*'

'People's greatest desires are usually shaped by what other people have got,' said Audrey with the conviction of somebody who had seen a great deal of people's desires. She looked pointedly at Beth for a moment, then said: 'She looked up to you. I can't imagine why, when she had me as a role model.'

Beth smiled and riffled through the pages. 'She was a better writer than me . . . She seems to have kept at it for longer, too. I gave up on it after a few weeks. I ran out of thoughts.'

Audrey closed the second diary and held it out. 'Swap?'

Beth relinquished the notebook, but seemed reluctant to take the diary. She held it gingerly, turning it over and over, scrutinising the spine, tracing the embossed crest with a fingernail: everything bar opening it.

Audrey wasn't reading either; the notebook lay on her lap, and she was staring vacantly into space, head cocked to one side as though listening to some elusive sound.

Beth indicated the diary. 'Is there anything about wh—'

'*Ssh!*' Audrey held up a hand. She frowned and craned her neck, trying to catch hold of whatever sound it was that nagged at her. Suddenly, she leapt to her feet. '*My phone!*' she yelped.

She ran from the room, across the corridor, and skeltered to a halt in her own room. Her coat was where she had left it; flung across the foot of the bed, emitting a faint, muffled chirruping. She wrestled with it, ransacking the pockets, getting entangled in its folds in her haste. At last, in an ecstasy of panic, expecting it to go silent at the very last moment, she hauled the phone out of its burrow and fumbled with the mouthpiece.

'Hello? Suzi? You got through! . . . Oh, hello . . . Yes, it is . . . Yes, she is. Hold on a moment, please.'

Beth was still gazing uncertainly at the unopened diary when Audrey came back and held the phone out to her.

'It's for you,' she said.

Beth eyed it, bewildered. 'For me? Who is it?' She took the phone and held it to her ear. It was no bigger than a bar of soap, and she found herself squidging her mouth to one side to meet the mouthpiece. 'Hello?' she said warily.

'Hi, babe.'

'Iain! How did you get this number?'

There was a hollow, hissing pause. 'It was on the pinboard in the kitchen. I tried the other number. There was no answer.'

'Oh. Oh, I see.' She remembered now; tracking the number down and never having the courage to use it.

'You don't sound surprised.'

'Don't I?' Beth frowned. There was a suspicious tone in Iain's voice. 'What's the matter, hon? Writing not going well?'

'Oh, the writing's just zippety-doo-dah, sweet thing.'

'Good . . . Um, is something the matter? You realise how expensive it is, calling a mobile number.' She avoided Audrey's eye as she said this, turning her shoulder to hem herself in with the phone.

'I just called to say I love you. Is there anything wrong with that?'

'No. That's sweet.'

'Actually, I didn't. I just called to say I remembered where I'd heard of Gondecourt.' His tone changed to one of excitement as he said this, and Beth felt the chill warming out of her. She liked it when his enthusiasm was aroused.

'Oh?' she said. 'Where?'

'I've just got back from Vince's. The reference I had was a bit thin, so I've borrowed some books.' He paused. 'Are you ready for this? It appears the Château de Gondecourt had a pretty chequered career during the war. From 1940 to '42 it played host to a number of meetings between Vichy ministers and their German opposites. Pétain is known to have holidayed there at least once. In 1942, the estate was commandeered and used by the Gestapo. There was a lot of resistance in the region, so they set up a special HQ there.'

Beth glanced over her shoulder at Audrey and thought of Février.

'It gets worse,' Iain went on. 'From December 1942, part of the estate was given over to a rest and reorientation facility for *Einsatzgruppe* officers.'

'What officers?'

'*Einsatzgruppe*. You know about the Waffen-SS? Well, these lads make the SS look like a boy scouts' jamboree. They weren't combat troops. Their training was in racial theory and extermination methods. They were used on the Eastern Front. Their job was to follow in the wake of the advancing army and root out the racially inferior populations ready for ethnic Germans to move in.'

Beth almost gagged. 'Are you sure it's the same place?'

'Château de Gondecourt. Known locally as the Black Château. More properly called the Château de La Simarde. It's here in black and white.'

'Is there anything about the family?'

'Were they involved, you mean? I don't think so; no more than by implication. It's all a bit vague. Most of them fled in 1940, and the rest seem to have cleared out in '42. Two of them – it doesn't give any names – were tried for collaboration in 1947 and acquitted, although one of their servants was imprisoned for the heinous crime against humanity of screwing one of the *Einsatzgruppe* officers and having his baby. They trumped up some spurious evidence of her identifying Maquis members to the Gestapo, and she was done for.' There was a pause. 'Christ, she was only fifteen at the time. Talk about projecting collective guilt.'

'Does it give a name for her?' Beth held her breath and listened to the sound of books being moved about. Avril would be about the right age to be that girl.

'Yes, here it is. Yvette Butain. Scullery maid of some sort. Imprisoned for six years and disowned by the noble family. What a bunch of charmers.'

Beth started breathing again. If Avril wasn't implicated, then it seemed somehow more likely that her brother was also innocent. 'Is there anything else?' she asked.

'No. That's about all. I just thought you might be interested . . . So, shall I see you back this evening?'

'Sorry, babe. Audrey's car's still not fixed. We're going to be stuck here another night.'

Another long pause. 'Oh. Right. Still snowing?'

'It's stopped now, but the trains still aren't running.'

'I see. Typical, eh? Give me a call if there's any news, and give Audrey my best.'

'Okay. Bye, babe.'

'Bye.'

Beth studied the phone. 'How d'you switch it off?'

'Here.' Audrey took it back and pressed a button. She dialled and held it hopefully to her ear. Her expression transformed instantly into rage. 'Bastard! I don't believe it – dead as a fucking doornail! How did *he* get through?' She glared furiously at it, then pitched it across the room. It bounced off the washstand and fell with a loud clatter onto the floorboards. Beth watched in dismay as she sank down on the rug and buried her face in her hands.

Iain sat with the receiver cradled in his lap, staring out at the dry, snowless street and cloudless sky. He was thinking of the friends he had known at university. Like Beth, he had lost touch with them over the years, and he imagined meeting them all again after such a long separation. He imagined the drinking, the reminiscing, the laughter. More than that, he imagined the illusion of irresponsible youth recaptured and the feeling of sharing something unique; a set of experiences which formed the core of one's being. The intimacy and the exhilaration of discovery. Most of all, returning to the thought again and again in a tightening spiral, he imagined meeting Carenza again. At the very centre of that core of intense bright light lay that one weekend in Brighton. A single forty-eight-hour bead at the nether end of a thirteen-year thread, yet its heat still leaked constantly into his fantasies; the smell of salt and the sight of a flat sea through a window could constrict his breathing and stir up an erection. If he were to meet her again, far from home, how much would newly built affections count for? An ice cube in a boiling pan. Beth must have had experiences like that. He knew she had had lovers, as everyone had; and like everyone, they would still live in her imagination. What if one of them were there? Surely the deceased Lydia's circle of friends had extended beyond just Beth and Audrey.

He put the phone back on the hook and walked to the window. Like stinging nettles, suspicion sends out rhizomes, burrowing fast through the soil, springing up with prodigal tenacity; before you know it, the forest floor is choked with cloying, venomous green.

The broken-down car. The snow. No trains. The ringing phone that nobody answered. Her surprise at his finding the mobile number flowered late into startlement, then horror. She had rallied quickly, but he wasn't fooled by her show of interest in his little investigation. Another night away, another night re-awakening these hot, irresponsible years. He saw the future, and it was him, still alone, still waiting for the phone call that said she was never coming back.

He couldn't wait that long; he had to know now.

He picked up the phone again and dialled 1471. The digitised voice at the other end recited the last caller's number and told him that the call was made at 10:52. (Its tone was disapproving, as though it knew damn well he had been asleep, and what a shameless, slothful bed-slug he habitually was.) The number given matched the one Blu-tacked to the monitor. Strike one. Next he called Directory Enquiries and got the same number again. Strike two. So at least she was where she said she was. He tried calling the number again. It rang and rang, but there was still no answer. No ball.

Sky blue ... How did you find out about the weather? The BBC? Was there some national meteorological office somewhere? He hit on a simpler solution: the horse's mouth. He noted down the appropriate STD codes and began generating random numbers. The first got him through to an insurance office in Exeter and a receptionist called Mandy. Could she help him settle a bet? he asked. Was there snow on the ground? Mandy, amused and surprisingly eager to oblige, went to look. No, she reported, there wasn't any snow. Her friend Natasha said some had fallen during the night but hadn't settled. He thanked her and hung up.

Snow falling but not settling. Except in a certain somebody's devious mind; enough to provide an idea for an alibi.

He decided to check further. The next random number threw up a grumpy-sounding man in Okehampton who was on shifts and didn't give a flying toss what the weather was doing. Two more numbers were non-existent, but the next gave him a bakery in Tavistock. Oh yes, they'd had a bit of snow in the night – just a sprinkling, mind. Heavier on the moors. They'd missed a delivery because of it.

Hmm. Was that a strike or a no-ball?

Finally, he tried Rail Enquiries and asked about trains to the West Country. Yes, sir, they were all running. What destination did he require? Yes, absolutely certain; no services had been interrupted.

A home run. Got you, Beth Glaister. Lying, scheming ... *screwing* bitch.

One last test. He dialled Audrey's mobile number again. *Switched off or out of range.* What a surprise.

He sat and stared at the air for a few minutes, churning with powerless rage, then he got up, went through to the bedroom and dragged a travel bag down from the top of the wardrobe. It didn't take long to pack; he was on the road within fifteen minutes, heading west.

Audrey's despair only lasted a minute or two. Eventually, she looked up and found Beth watching her with concern in her eyes. She smiled sardonically, then got up off the floor and went to retrieve the phone. 'Don't worry about me,' she said, looking it over to check it wasn't broken. 'It'd take more than a poxy lump of plastic to beat me . . . What did Iain want?'

Beth wasn't quite sure. On the face of it, he was eager to pass on the fruits of his research, but she couldn't evade the nagging feeling that he was actually checking up on her. Keeping tabs. *Why?*

She suppressed the thought and repeated the gist of what he had told her. Audrey was agog. 'I *knew* there was something suss. I'll *bet* that Février knows more than a thing or two about it . . . He's a demon little researcher, your Iain. Tell him if his novel doesn't work out, there's always a job for him with me.'

'I'll mention it.'

Audrey looked at Lydia's chest and surveyed the scatter of notebooks and postcards on the rug. 'I wonder if she knew anything about the history she married into. It's always the women, isn't it, bearing the brunt.' She glanced at Beth and smiled self-consciously. 'Listen to me. I sound like Rachel.'

She picked up the commonplace book and opened it. Then she lay down on the bed, her head cradled in one hand, and began reading. Beth, following suit, lay down beside her and opened the diary.

Resurrecting Salvador

1

'I can't see what all the fuss was about,' said Lydia. 'I think she's absolutely charming.'

'Charming, yes ... Just as the cobra's gaze charms the cornered mouse.'

She ignored him. 'A bit stiff and formal,' she conceded. 'A bit *proper*. But then, that's the aristocracy for you.'

'Huh. My family hasn't been aristocracy since 1790.'

'Oh, Salvador, you know perfectly well what I mean; aristocracy in all but title.'

He grunted, but said nothing. It was the second day of their visit; an unseasonably scorching, breezeless afternoon, too hot to drive out, but too bright to loiter in the cool darkness indoors. Avril had made them a small picnic, which they took to the lake. They ate brie and golden apples and drank chilled white Chinon, dangling their bare feet in the cool water, where waterboatmen chased and great blue dragonflies hovered and darted among the reeds like iridescent flying needles. After they had eaten, Salvador lay back on the grass and closed his eyes against the sun while Lydia sat under the shade of her wide-brimmed hat and breathed in the view like rich oxygen.

A terrible nausea of fear had paralysed her before and during the Channel crossing – worse than any conventional sea-sickness could have been. She had sat in the cafeteria, as far from the windows as she could get, with her eyes closed, almost catatonic with fright. She couldn't escape the vision of the cumbersome ferry floating on a membrane, thin as clingfilm, above a dark, dizzying void. After that, this hot, bright vale of green and gold seemed like the very incarnation of paradise.

Beyond the sunspot-glittering glass oval of the lake was a pale, shorn grass slope, studded with elm and sycamore and oak, rising up to the rim of the forest that blanketed the distant hills. The afternoon sunlight struck so richly on the forest canopy that, even from here, every bulge and wrinkle of its massed foliage stood out in deep relief, like green-gold cauliflower heads, and she felt she could almost touch its texture and taste its greenness. It felt like a benediction; a grace and reward for overcoming the ordeal, and she wished she could rub off some of this feeling onto Salvador.

Why was he so down? And why so truculent and evasive with his mother? She understood how difficult his relationship with her had been in the past, but surely he ought to be able to put it all behind him. He had cajoled, persuaded, and finally blackmailed Lydia into making this journey with him, but as soon as they had sighted the thickening blue sliver of French soil from the top deck of the ferry (she had gone up there to look at the water and try to convince herself of its substance), his mood had seemed to change; a quietude which deep-ened to sullen taciturnity as they drove through the Pas de Calais. Although with every mile south he seemed to be coming home – his accent grew a distinct Gallic tinge, he fell into using French phrases more often, and even, she thought, started to *look* more French – yet he seemed to be enacting the journey as a pilgrimage of penance, a martyrdom, rather than a homecoming. And so they went slowly, meandering down the D-roads, with many detours and two overnight stops, as if to postpone the journey's end as long as possible. He rallied for a short while on the last day. They had reached l'Isle Jourdain, and he pulled the car over to look at the view. As he looked down into the deep Vienne valley, a spark had lit in his eyes – although she was too busy coping with her vertigo and his teasing to appreciate it – as though he felt the pull of home. It didn't last; he didn't quite go back to his former sullenness, but his brief good mood evolved into a sort of fey fatalism, which was even more unnerving. His moods infected her and, as they covered the last winding fifty kilometres, she grew as nervous of reaching the Château de La Simarde and meeting its black-widow matriarch as she had been about crossing the sea.

And all the worrying had been wasted; Madame de La Simarde had been charm and hospitality personified. (Her warmth didn't even fade when Salvador tested the guitar that had been shipped all the way from Barcelona at great expense and pronounced it a clumsy fake.) Lydia wondered why he had so mortified himself. She supposed it must be awkward to be reunited after so long and hurtful a rift, but, in common with all those who have no family of their own, Lydia couldn't understand why he would not allow himself to be closer to his; to love them, be close to them, and think himself lucky to have them.

She dabbled her toes in the water. 'Shall we go for a walk?' she suggested.

'It's too hot,' he said, eyes still closed. 'You go, I'll stay here.'

She sighed and plucked a long, stiff stalk of grass from the bank. Holding it between forefinger and thumb, she tickled his cheek with its tip. He twitched, and she withdrew it. She paused, counting to ten, then tickled his ear. He raised a hand to brush away the irritation, but still didn't open his eyes. She waited while he settled down again and, smiling to herself, brushed the stalk lightly over the back of his hand and down between his fingers; as his hand flinched and turned, she withdrew the stalk and traced a slow line across his neck. He opened his eyes and sat up.

'What's the matter?' she asked, hiding her instrument of torment.

He frowned, rubbing his neck. 'A very persistent fly,' he said, blinking in the sunlight.

She tried not to grin. 'Well, what d'you expect, near water? How about that walk – we can get away from the insects.'

He lay back and closed his eyes again. 'No thanks. It's gone now.'

She leaned over and kissed him on the forehead. 'I'm going,' she said, standing up and straightening her skirt. 'I'm bored. Don't go to sleep, or you'll frazzle. Here . . .' She took off her hat and laid it over his face. 'I won't be gone long.'

He adjusted the hat, and spoke from beneath its straw dome. 'Don't go far,' he said. 'And don't go near the Old Château.' (He knew how curious she was about it.) 'It's not safe.'

'I won't,' she said, slipping her damp feet into her shoes.

He watched her walk away; a dappled silhouette receding through the open weave of straw. Then he closed his eyes again.

He was happy; happy that Lydia felt welcome here, even if he didn't; happy that she had fulfilled her desire to see a foreign land; happy at how beautiful she looked in its light; and happiest of all that she was his. The apprehension that had grown inside him like a malignant cancer at the imminence of his reunion with his mother – so long deferred, but closing in on him with looming, inevitable momentum – had almost crippled him. How would his mother – so deeply and sorely aggrieved by his neglect, even though she had brought it on herself – how would she treat him? And what would be her reaction to Lydia? She had no family – in either the literal or social sense – no connections, no lineage. She had charm and beauty and intelligence in abundance, but those qualities would be worthless in his mother's eyes if there was no blood or background or breeding. But then, miracle of confounding miracles, she had welcomed Lydia like a beloved niece; even when Salvador hinted at their plan to marry, no cracks appeared in the (to his eyes) faked civility. Perhaps he might have misjudged her, although he doubted it (history was against this interpretation) or, more plausibly, perhaps the nature of his revolt and the tenacious duration of his exile had shaken her; as her only child, he might have made her realise what was really important in life. Perhaps she had learned a lesson; that ancestry and family status were less important than familial love.

Pleased with this thought, he drifted off into a shallow, sun-baked snooze.

A light, warm breeze was beginning to breathe across the slopes as Lydia breasted the last few yards of the steep hill and paused to look at the view. The spreading boughs of the ancient sycamore cast dappled emerald shade over the pillared façade of the old mausoleum, rippling over the white stone as the moving air tickled the leaves. There would be a storm before nightfall, Madame de La Simarde had said; its first harbinger could already be seen in a line of smudged grey on the distant horizon.

The mausoleum, bearing the dead weight of its occupants' heavenward aspirations, stood on the highest point in the grounds, from which the whole estate could be seen. Away to the right, she could see back to the lake, and Salvador lying on its near bank, a tiny, dark smear partly obscured by a strand of reeds at the water's edge: beyond, the road emerged from the trees and threaded around the lake to the New House and its scatter of outbuildings. There, the road branched and continued curving out of sight, swallowed up by the thick rug of woodland that occupied the southern quarter of the park. Hardly anyone ever used that stretch of road any more, and its gravel was mottled with grass and weeds. Walking around to the far side of the mausoleum, she could see where the road found its way out of the woods and wound on, a frayed ribbon barely distinguishable from the unkempt grass, towards its final destination. After the order of the northern part of the estate, it was like looking at the second part of a Then and Now pairing. The shrubs and hedges lining the route, which had once been marvels of extravagant topiary, were shapeless and overgrown from more than a century of neglect, and the gardens had become rank tangles of unplanned trees thick with creeping undergrowth. In the middle of all this feral wilderness, still huge, still magnificent in decay, were the scarred and broken bones of the Old Château. Its roofs and pinnacles were gone, and the three great towers gaped at the sky like crooked-lipped mouths.

Don't go near the Old Château. It's not safe . . . Yes, but in what way? Surely, any other family would have demolished it and started afresh, but not this one. After they finally abandoned it, its remains had stood mouldering as the generations passed; unerased, but hidden from view.

She realised, looking around again at the panorama, that the estate had been reordered so that its old hub would be kept out of sight, screened by hills and smothered under wild woodland. Up here, by the mausoleum, was the only place from which it could be seen, unless one happened to stumble unsuspecting out of the woods and find oneself under its very walls.

Don't go near the Old Château. It's not safe . . . Couldn't she even take a closer look? She needn't actually go inside . . .

As she suspected, the Château couldn't be seen from down here; it had sunk from view before she even reached the foot of the hill, disappearing behind the screen of trees that jostled with the clumps and disordered ranks of distended privet hedges. It wasn't easy to get closer, either. The ragged road, which had once been a smooth, metalled carriageway, was blocked by a fallen tree. Its thick trunk was shrouded with creepers and flanked on all sides by thickets of hawthorn carpeted with dense nests of brambles. She tried a few times to pick a way round it, but the undergrowth kept rising against her, the brambles rasping viciously at her bare legs. She backed off and decided to skirt around in search of another way. It looked as though nobody had been here since the Château had been abandoned; as she walked on, she could see no sign of any path, nor even any thinning of the humid, insect-humming undergrowth. She couldn't even tell whether she was getting any closer. She was on the brink of giving up when she came across a tall, truncated trunk that was not a natural part of the forest; it was so patched with yellow lichen and green moss, and so deeply embraced by the fruit-heavy foliage of a vast fig bush that she almost missed it; only its square shape and the cracked and pock-marked stone globe that perched on its top spoiled its disguise as the broken body of a dead tree. She brushed aside the fig fronds, exposing the rusted juts of hinge pins set in the greened stone and, beside the pillar, on the far side of the bush, a trodden path leading into the forest. Her heart bumped with excitement and, glancing back over her shoulder as though entering a den of forbidden delights, she pushed past the gentle, yielding leaves and stepped onto the path.

It wasn't well worn – the brambles and nettles encroached at every step, and she had to stoop under overhanging branches spun with traceries of spider-web strands – but whoever it was who trod this way must come just often enough to prevent the forest swallowing it up and erasing it altogether.

And now she could see the Château. Only in glimpses – snatches of its dark bulk in rare lacunae between the webs of leaves and branches, a presence more often sensed than actually seen, but it was there, close and almost palpable. She picked up a stick – a forked wand of young willow – and used it to slash and beat her way through the blockages in the path and sweep away the spider-strands from in front of her face. After a while, she began to realise that the meandering path wasn't carrying her any closer to the Château; in fact, it seemed to be leading her past it. With a sinking sensation, she pressed on. Suddenly, the path veered away to the left, wove between a stand of great elms, and ended; the forest fell away as abruptly as if it had been mown down by a giant scythe, and she found herself standing amongst a scatter of red poppies on the edge of an open field of ploughed brown earth that rolled away into the broad valley.

In the near corner of the field, just a few yards away from her, stood an elderly tractor: its tyres were grey and cracked, the dull red paintwork was dented and spotted with rust, but its engine was rumbling steadily and a haze of blue smoke chuffed and burbled from the exhaust stack. Behind it, a man was bent over a yellow, box-like contraption – also battered and rusty – that was hitched to the back. He was short and thickset, with bright blue trousers pulled up over the almost spherical bulge of his midriff, tethered by leather-fobbed braces. His elbows worked back and forth as he tinkered with the machine's coupling. As Lydia watched, he stood back, gave the yellow cowling a thunderous, reverberating wallop with the head of a heavy spanner, and turned away from it. As he turned, she glimpsed his round face, as brown and crinkled as the ploughed field that he worked, topped by a deformed and greasy flat cap. His eyes passed over Lydia, standing silently at the forest's mouth, as though she weren't there. Then, as he was about to step up and climb back into the tractor's seat, he froze; he turned back slowly, his bright little eyes widening, and stared at her; his hand crept up and dragged the cap off his head, and he held it to his chest, his rotund, cheerful face sagging in awful, abject dismay.

'Bonjour,' she called out.

He went on staring at her, saying nothing, for several long moments. 'Bonjour,' he said at last, his voice hoarse and barely audible.

Her stock of O-Level French (grade A), which had lain neglected and corroding at the back of her brain since school, had been renovated and extended by Salvador, and she felt confident enough to try and converse with the strange little man. After all, he might know how to get to the Château.

'It's hot, isn't it?' she ventured. He took a step closer, peering at her, his cap still screwed up in his fist. 'Too hot for work,' she added, gesturing at the tractor.

He took another step forward, and stopped. 'You're real?' he murmured. At least, that was what she thought he said: *T'es vraie?* She smiled encouragingly, even though she was beginning to feel slightly uneasy; it would be just her luck to stumble upon the local simpleton. Or lunatic. She wondered whether she ought to slip back quietly into the forest and make a run for it, before he overcame his confusion and made a move. Suddenly, she felt very far from home, and dreadfully alone. Then, as though a veil had been lifted, his shiny brown face cleared, and he wiped his eyes on the back of his oily hand. 'I know you,' he said, adjusting his address to a polite *vous: Je vous connais.* 'Yes, I know you. You are the new Mademoiselle... Please, pardon me. I thought you were...' He spread out his hands helplessly, apologetically. 'I mean I thought I was in a dream.'

'No,' she said. 'I am real.'

He looked shrewdly at her. 'You have wandered a long way all alone, haven't you?' He must have noticed the look of alarm appear in her face, because he added: 'Don't be afraid, pretty Mademoiselle. Old Gianou may be ugly, but he isn't a monster... I say you must be alone because nobody of the family would walk that path with you.' He nodded towards the forest behind her. 'You are searching for the Old Château, am I right?'

She nodded. 'I can't find it. The path...' She shrugged.

'My forest path doesn't go to it – it goes from here—' he indicated his field '—to the estate. The Old Château – there's no need for a path.'

'No need?'

His face crinkled and twinkled with amusement, and he looked away to his right. She followed his gaze: in the corner of the field, there was a break in the forest curtain; beyond it was a stretch of open, uncluttered pasture, and, rising out of the long grass, the high, tumbling, roofless façade of the Château's main wing, bookended by its truncated towers.

'The Old Château,' Gianou chuckled. 'It's a sorry sight now, but in its day it was magnificent.'

Many would say it still was magnificent; like a crippled and blinded giant, or the fossilised bones of a great dinosaur. She looked at Gianou again, from the grubby cap (which had now found its way back onto his shiny, hairless head) to the blue cuffs of his trousers that gaped like drain-chutes several inches above the tops of his scuffed and broken boots.

'Do you work on the estate?' she asked.

'Work on it?' He grinned and tapped a thick finger against his temple. 'You might say old Gianou is part of the estate. My grand-father was gamekeeper. His grandfather was a hall servant, and before him, his grandfather was valet to the last Marquis de La Simarde. Seven generations, and I'm still here, working their fields and guarding the ruins of the great Château.'

'Guarding it?'

He nodded gravely. 'I guard against the ghosts that live in there, to make sure they remain sleeping. I stop them from getting out.' He looked at her and hesitated, his brown cheeks reddening to russet. 'Just now, when I saw you standing there . . .'

'You thought I was a ghost?'

He nodded. '*She has escaped*, I thought. *It is she – little Violina has escaped* . . . You look very like her.'

'Who is Violina?'

'Her real name was Victoria. She had a very sad life. She was the daughter of an English earl. The last Marquis, to whom the earl was indebted, forced her into a marriage with his grandson. These great families, they did things like that in those days. Some still do.'

Lydia tried to recall the family history that Madame de La Simarde had told her, but very little of it stuck in her memory; it was all so complicated, with its myriad filigree branches, and she had stumbled blindly amongst the strange names and floundered between the overlapping generations. The last Marquis, though, she did remember something about. He had managed to retain his title, his château and his head throughout the Revolution by ceding most of his lands and wealth to the state and forswearing his descendants' right to primogeniture. This last was the severest blow, because it meant that his title would die with him. During the remainder of his long life, through the turmoils of the Terror, the Napoleonic Wars, the reinstallation of the Bourbons, the collapse of the Empire, and all the ensuing confusion in the government and at court, he clawed back his lands and his riches, and negotiated a series of propitious marriages for his children and grandchildren. He died in 1842, a very old and – as Madame de La Simarde told it – triumphant man, having restored the fortunes of his lineage to a higher plane of wealth and status than it had occupied even before the Revolution. He had even succeeded – his last act on earth – in regaining primogeniture by devising some maddeningly complex system of wills and transactions to evade the Napoleonic Code. But, the failure that crowned his triumph with thorns, he was never able to restore the title of Marquis to his line.

'Why was she called Violina?' Lydia asked.

Gianou smiled sadly. 'The Marquis's grandson didn't want to marry her any more than she wanted to marry him. He treated her very cruelly. He beat her, and humiliated her in front of the whole household by bringing his mistresses openly to the Château. She bore him a son, Edouard, and she loved the child with all her heart. But her husband, egged on by the Marquis, declared that she was mentally deranged and unfit to be a mother. He had the infant taken away from her. Being cut off from her child broke her mind, and she really did become deranged. Her husband had her locked in a room in the Old Wing. Up there...' He pointed to the rows of empty, sky-blue windows in the broken façade of the Château. 'She was a prisoner. In the night, the servants could hear her crying for her lost child. They called her Violina, because the sound of her weeping was like sad music – beautiful and tragic at the same time. It broke your heart to hear it.'

Lydia looked at Gianou, and saw that his eyes were glistening with gathering tears. 'Finally,' he went on, 'Violina went completely mad. One night, she escaped from her prison and stole into the room next to her husband's, where little Edouard slept beside the maidservant who nursed him. While she gazed at her son lying asleep in his crib, the maidservant woke and cried out at the sight of the madwoman. Violina seized the baby's bottle from the dresser and broke it, and stabbed the maid in the heart. But her cries had already woken the child's father in the next room, and he came out, roaring drunk, and saw what had happened. Violina snatched the baby up in her arms – blankets and all – and ran for her life. Her husband roused the servants, and they pursued her through the Château. They cornered her like a rat in the top of the great tower – that one, there. She knew that if they caught her she would never see her child again, so, with one last wail of despair, with the infant still clutched in her arms, she flung herself from the window. Afterwards, when they took baby Edouard from under her broken body, he was completely unmarked, but quite, quite dead.' Gianou looked at Lydia, and his eyes were bright. 'She still walks here now. Some nights, I still hear the music of her weeping.'

Lydia sighed. 'That's the saddest story I ever heard.'

The old man smiled. 'And I thought you... You are her to the life. Take care of yourself, pretty Mademoiselle, and I trust your story will be a happier one. Good day to you.'

Lydia, gazing at the Château and lost in thought, barely registered his words. When at last she turned to acknowledge his parting, he had already mounted his tractor and was guiding it down the corduroy furrows towards the valley. Beyond, the storm-front smear on the horizon had thickened and darkened to the colour of grey clay. The breeze that bruited its advance was rising, whispering in the trees, flapping her dress around her legs and drawing loose strands of hair across her eyes. She turned away from it, skirting the unploughed lip of the field, and walked towards the ruined Château.

It seemed odd that the wilderness had not colonised this space; she supposed Gianou and his ancestors had kept it clear for reasons of their own, although they had made no attempt to preserve its original state. The lawn, which had once been manicured to bowling-green smoothness, had run wild with rough, dry pasture grass that tickled her ankles and calves as she walked; the topiaried shrubs had been pulled up or cut down long ago, and the unpruned rose bushes had run rampant, filling the feral garden with their scent. At the far end, the ground rose up in a steep, straight bank, in the centre of which – just discernible under an overgrowth of deep grass and weeds – was a short flight of four stone steps flanked by crumbling balustrades with mottled acorn finials. Lydia walked up the steps and found herself on a broad terrace, whose flag paving still showed in patches where the dense turf, studded like a plum pudding with crushed roof slates, had not yet crept. Ivy, rising up from trunks as thick as her arm, had spread tendrils over the whole face of the building, sparse and thin as capillaries on the stone of the upper storeys, dense and choking around the three enormous arched french windows that faced onto the terrace. Two of the windows were completely blank, but the third still bore the remains of its glazed doors, one hanging paintless and rotten from rusted hinges, fragments of glass still clinging to the desiccated mullions; its twin, growing a rash of discoid fungi, lay on the ground in a bed of rich green grass, being slowly sucked into the earth along with the fragments of slate. Beside the corroded brass handle, a powder-grey lizard sat warming itself in the sun. As she approached, it slowly turned its head, sensing her presence with little flickers of its hair-thin tongue; at last, when she came within a few feet, it tensed its long body, flicked its tail and darted away into the grass.

She stood on the threshold of the central french window and peered cautiously inside. The sunlight poured in through the open roof high above, broken only by the sparse rib-stubs of charred wooden joists, but the air inside met her skin with a damp, chilly touch, flavoured with the odours of vegetation and mouldered wood. The upper storeys had been burnt out, but the ground floor must have been untouched by the flames; instead, its boards had been left to the slower combustion of decomposition. They were dark and greasy with moss, and holed in places, but they looked sturdy enough. Lydia stepped forward cautiously, probing the boards with her willow stick, keeping her weight on the back foot, but they held firm. She began to step more confidently, avoiding the broken areas, and as she moved deeper inside, she felt the damp, cold air close in behind her.

The space she was in had once been a grand public room; vast and high, bowing outwards to take up the ground storey of the great corner tower. Now, trees thrust their fingers in through the end windows, and creepers grew across the walls, where the bared brick still showed patches of plaster and scraps of mildewed wallpaper. The room had never been cleared out, not even in the first exodus following the fire: the furniture and fittings had been left where they were, steeped in damp, slowly reducing to decaying heaps of colourless drapery and rotten timber. Here and there, a recognisable shape protruded from the litter: a rusted iron fire-dog, a chair leg, an oval table with two collapsed legs. Lydia lingered a while, trying to imagine the room as it had once been, but she couldn't bring it to life; if any ghosts did dwell here, they were mute and invisible, shy of her presence.

At the inner end of the room, the interior wall had collapsed. She picked and slithered her way over the rubble of bricks and crumbled plaster, and found herself in a small side-chamber. Its heavy oak door still hung, frozen by swollen rust to its hinges, wedged open by the same floor-litter of slate, broken glass and disarticulated furniture. The doorway led into a great hall. Built all of stone, the hall still retained most of its high, vaulted ceiling. The chessboard tiles on the floor were cracked and discoloured and coated with a film of stagnant water and green slime. To the left was a vestibule, denuded of its doors, and to the right was a massive spiral staircase, its white marble just discernible in patches between the scorch-blackening and the thick mulch of dead leaves that carpeted the steps.

After a moment's indecision, she elected to explore the staircase. Using her stick to drag aside the thick cobweb curtains that drooped between the wall and the pillar, she climbed slowly up the slippery steps.

He woke from a sleep's-edge dream of falling; his body lurching, legs kicking out. The straw hat fell from his face, and the sunlight slapped him hard across the eyes.

He sat up and rested his head between his knees, opening his eyes by degrees and trying to bring his watch into focus, blinking at its leaping face and invisible hands. After several blinks, he managed to assemble enough clues to deduce that it was gone four o'clock . . . He clambered to his feet and stretched, but instead of snapping back into poised alertness, his muscles sagged and felt hollow with weariness . . . Four o'clock? She had been gone for . . . He gave up the calculation without even attempting it; it was a long time, that was certain. Where could she possibly have gone? He puzzled for a few moments – Back to the house? Down to the village? – then heard himself warning, *Don't go near the Old Château*, and he knew, with a sickening jolt in his stomach, exactly where she had gone.

He muttered under his breath as he marched across the grass, cursing her wilfulness, her furtiveness, and his own carelessness. He went up the hill at a lumbering run, and was breathing hard as he stood beside the mausoleum and looked down on the Old Château. It didn't seem to have changed at all during the decade since he had last seen it, and a tendril of panic crept up his throat as he stared down at the broken walls and the strangling collar of the forest, and imagined Lydia blundering about inside amongst the invisible death-traps: the teetering blocks of loose masonry, the rotten floorboards that looked solid but would give way like pond-ice if you stepped on them, staircases that leapt into yawning voids; and he breathed an imprecation against his ancestors who, in their insufferable vanity and superstition, had refused to do what any sane family would have done long ago: razed the wretched hulk to the ground and buried its memory forever.

He called out her name, cupping his hands round his mouth and shouting at the top of his voice, then cocked his ears to listen for a reply. He called twice, but the only sound he heard was the rising wind rustling the leaves of the sycamore above him. Reluctantly, he set off down the hill, heading straight for the gap by the stone pillar. He knew the forest track from his own childhood episodes of furtive wilful curiosity, and from later, when it had become a useful route for smuggling forbidden treasures. He stopped twice to call her name again: once at the foot of the hill, and again at the fringe of the forest. Then, holding aside the fig leaves, he stepped past the pillar and into the woods.

A treasure chest! Lydia crouched down on her haunches beneath the chimney breast and leaned into the fireplace. Steadying herself with her shoulder against the blackened brickwork, she managed to wriggle both hands around the wooden box and lever it out of its alcove hiding place.

She had been wrong about all the upper storeys being completely destroyed; the first floor was gone, but as she climbed the spiral stairs, she had come to an archway which had once led to the rooms on the second floor. The landing, which lay above the hall, was stone-floored and intact. The interior walls at this level were little more than lowered stumps, and the whole hollow, skeletal shell of the Old Wing stretched out in both directions, the pale column of the staircase shaft rising two more storeys, its higher archways no more than gaping holes staring into the void. Beyond the landing, part of the corridor and one of the bedrooms still had some of their flooring. Tentatively, she climbed over the remains of the partition wall and lowered herself onto the bare boards of the bedroom. The floor only survived on the near side, forming a platform about eight feet by twelve. As she edged around, keeping close to the wall, she marvelled at her own bravery; the way the exploring fever had overwhelmed her crippling vertigo. She even dared to peer over the ragged, splintered edge into the room far below, recognising it as the grand drawing room through which she had entered the Château. Passing the bare window with its fenestration of ivy, she glanced out at the view over the fields, then, with a tingle of relief, reached the fireplace and stepped onto the solid stone grate. It was then, crouching down on this eyrie of safety, trying to control the inrush of emotions – terror and awe at her own daring, combined with a growing realisation of what she had done and how much harder it would be to get back down – it was then that she had noticed the box nestling in its hiding place.

She laid it down on the stone slabs. It was heavier than it looked; although it was only small – no bigger than a shoebox, really – it was made from solid wood and bound with thick iron straps, like a midget pirate's chest. The straps and lock were thinly patinated with orange rust, but the dark wood was clean and smooth, as though it had been placed there only last week instead of more than a century ago. There was even a key protruding from the lock. She gripped it between her fingertips and tried to twist it, but it was stuck fast. It wasn't rusted, but the ancient wards had seized from disuse. She examined the chest minutely; and the more she looked, the more convinced she became that it had belonged to Violina-Victoria. The lock's shield-shaped escutcheon had some engraving on it, illegible under the powdery rust. She spat on her finger and rubbed at it until the hair-fine lines stood out: there was a coat of arms and, below, a monogram of florid, nested letters. Peering closer, she disentangled an A in the centre, and overlaid on it a . . . a V! Victoria! She was sure of it. So, had this room – she gazed around with renewed fascination at the tumbled walls and the blank, ivy-choked window – had this been the room in which she was imprisoned, from which the haunting, tragic music of her weeping had crept out and permeated the halls and corridors of the Château? She shivered, and felt certain that it was; here, she could almost hear the whispering of the ghosts and feel their jostling presence.

Suddenly, she wanted desperately to leave; in a flash of insight, she saw the enormity, the folly of what she had done; as her defences caved in, the ghosts leapt up and wailed horribly in her ears, and the vertiginous void below swirled around her precarious perch. Trembling, clutching the precious box in her arms, she stood up and began to inch her way back across the floorboard platform towards the wall and the landing beyond.

274

Creak. She paused half-way across, then took another step. *Crack.* She paused again. Before, on her way out towards the fireplace, she had felt the weakened boards give slightly beneath her feet, but had paid no attention: now, perhaps it was the extra weight of the chest or the effect of her whiplashed nerves; now, she could actually hear them. They groaned and crackled dryly at every movement like a galleon in a storm. She clutched the chest tighter and carried on. She was still far from safety when: *Crrr-crck-ack!* She closed her eyes tightly and braced herself for the fall . . . When she opened them again, they were blurry with tears of fright, but she was still there, the floor still holding her weight. She couldn't make herself go on, and it was too far back to the fireplace. The deep, low embrasure of the window, however, was only a few feet away . . . She hefted the box in her hands and, grunting with effort, tossed it onto the ledge. *Crrr-k-k* . . . and silence. Then, with a titanic, desperate effort of will, she flung herself after it – one step, *crr-ga-gack!* As the boards began to break – two steps, *sssh-crrr-nch!* – and one last leap as the joists belched dust and collapsed beneath her feet, crumbling and clattering into the rubble far below. The rough, gritty stone of the window ledge scraped at her forearms and knocked the breath out of her body as she belly-flopped onto it, struggling against gravity that hauled at her legs, her fingers clutching at the crumbling mortar, feet scrambling for a toe-hold.

He stood on the threshold and peered in. It had all changed since the last time he was here: one whole corner of the Music Room had collapsed, exposing the ante-room and the hallway beyond. Before, there had been a doorway in that corner, leading to an impassable corridor whose floor had all rotted away. Back then, if you wanted – if you dared – to venture further into the Château, you had to climb out of the window at the far end and crawl on your belly under the bushes, wriggling over the banks of mossy rubble until you reached the raised parterre; then, you could clamber up onto the balustrade and get in through the . . .

He started at a sudden soft clattering sound, like gravel falling over stone. It had come from above him; above and to the right.

'Lydia?' he called. He held his breath and listened. Could he hear a faint sound of whimpering? 'Lydia, is that you?'

There was a pause, then a thin voice filtered down in reply: 'Salvador?'

'I'm here! Where are you?'

'I don't know . . . Help me, please . . .'

She couldn't sleep: every time she closed her eyes, she saw herself there again and felt the crippling terror. He was sleeping soundly enough, the marble-smooth bulb of his shoulder rising and falling steadily, the dark, tousled back of his head nestled deep in the pillow beside her. On their first night here, she had been surprised (having anticipated single, separate rooms) to find that his mother not only didn't mind them sharing, but actually seemed to expect them to. Ironic that here, close to the very cause of their enforced secrecy, they could be together openly at last, even if it did mean lying about who she was. But then, she had grown so adept at lies and secrecy and evasion in recent months that it had become second nature; a compulsion to creep furtively. Like this afternoon.

It had taken him almost an hour to help her down. When he climbed to the top of the mountain-range of rubble in the corner of the Music Room and looked back, squinting against the sun that streamed in through the rows of empty windows, he saw her there, curled up and rigid with fear, clinging like a barnacle to the window ledge. *How the hell did you get up there?* he demanded. *I'm stuck,* she bleated, almost laughing with relief at the sound of his voice. There was a great breach in the floor beneath the window, so in the end he had to go and find a long ladder (stealing it quietly from one of the estate's more remote outbuildings and carrying it with difficulty through the tangled forest), and coax her down like a stranded cat from a tree. She insisted on bringing the wooden chest with her, which made the task more difficult still.

As they trudged back across the park, the storm-armies finally rolled up the valley and broke over the estate, moaning and rumbling, lashing the trees with an artillery of wind, breaking off fans of twig-borne leaves and blustering them through the air like tattered flags, while fat grapeshot rain battered down the grass. They crept in through the back door after hiding the chest in the boot of the car. Luckily, they were so soaked and dishevelled that Madame de La Simarde, who met them in the hall, failed to notice the scratches on Lydia's shins, the moss-stains on her dress, and her scuffed shoes. She would have been furious, Salvador said, if she knew they had been to the Old Château.

Later, after they had both bathed, they lingered in their bedroom, drying and dressing and winding down. Lydia stood by the window, towelling her hair and gazing out through the rain-spattered window. She asked him why, in all the accounts of his ancestry, she had never heard the story of Victoria-Violina and her baby. To her surprise, he laughed and asked where she had heard *that*. She told him about the strange earth-brown man and his tractor.

'Gianou!' he laughed. 'Old Gianou! God, is he still here?'

'He said I looked like her.'

Salvador shook his head. 'It's just a fairy tale. Violina never existed; she's an invention. All old families have these folk-tales attached to them.' He came and joined her by the window, putting his arm around her waist. 'It's like ivy growing on a house; it's inevitable, and people get so used to it being there that they start thinking of it as part of the actual structure. It's a pity the tales are so much more appealing than the true history. Little Violina was always one of my favourites.'

And that had been it: Violina pruned from the family tree and dispatched, cast into the mulch-tub of myth...

... Lydia slipped out of bed and walked over to the window. The storm, which had squatted over the estate for most of the evening, emptying itself of wind and water, was drawing away now; the rain had thinned to a light spatter, and a band of clear blue-black dusted with bright stars was growing on the horizon. Silhouetted against it, she could see the mausoleum hill. Around her, the house was still and silent, and she thought of ships sailing through the dark hours of sleep... No, a house at night was not at all like a ship, when you thought about it. Or if it was, it was a pilotless ship, cast adrift amongst the shoals and reefs – or a lifeless cryo-ship hissing across the void, electric with the dreams of its sleepers. And in its path, unseen, stood jagged rocks or an uncharted moon...

... 'Jean-Louis Honoré de La Simarde was the last Marquis,' said Salvador, his fingertip hovering over the yellow parchment page.

They were sitting in the small library, cooled by their storm-soaking and cleansed of the Château dust by their baths. On a book-stand in front of them, Salvador had placed an ancient, leather-bound tome, opening it to a page bearing an illuminated, hand-drawn tree showing the Simarde lineage's last aristocratic sprigs. He handled the book with a fastidious care that she felt was open to interpretation; his mother would undoubtedly have taken it for due reverence, but to Lydia it looked more like revulsion, as though he were touching something toxic or infectious.

'I was made to learn this before I could even read it,' he said. He laid a sheet of paper over the page and closed his eyes, reciting the ancestral litany from memory: 'Jean-Louis 1750-1842: last-Marquis-saviour-and-restorer-of-the-estate: married-1779-Marie-Alexis-daughter-of-Vicomte-de-Malvin-three-children-two-sons – eldest Philippe-France 1781-1864: soldier-of-the-Emperor-and-founder-of-the-English-estate: married-1815-Lady-Caroline-Lambert-daughter-of-British-Trade-Minister-two-children-both-sons – eldest Louis-Philippe 1816-1867: early-life-of-dissipation-came-close-to-breaking-the-estate-but-later-reformed: married-1847-Irma-Constanza-Perez-first-cousin-of-Alberto-Carlos-Barón-de-Perez-Verdad-six-children-one-son – Philippe-

Charles 1860-1921 . . .' He opened his eyes, and went on in the same recitative monotone: 'No-mention-of-English-Victoria–Note-also-how-women-only-valued-by-whose-daughter-they-were-and-how-many-sons-they-bred.'

Lydia laughed and forgot that there was room in there – between Louis-Philippe's majority and his marriage to Irma-Constanza in 1847 – for a couple of little ghosts: a first wife and another eldest son, both deceased, both erased, never making it to the hallowed, buttery parchment. She also forget the chest with its monogrammed escutcheon . . .

. . . Now she remembered, in the quiet of the night. And she remembered old Gianou's voice and the words he used: *Her weeping broke your heart*; not *they say* or *it is told*; he said that her weeping *broke your heart* . . . and *You look very like her* . . . His words seemed to imply that not only had she lived, but that he had known her, had been there. It could almost be true: with his rich brown, furrowed face set with sharp, bright eyes and his thick fingers like oak-roots, he seemed like a blue-trousered Bombadil, born out of the bones of the earth, as old as the mountains but younger than the grass. She wouldn't be surprised to see him under the starlight, prancing over the hilltops, tending the stories and dreams that grew there.

She could almost believe in it. Certainly, whatever the book of lineage said, she still believed his story of little Violina and her lost child.

In her room across the landing, Geneviève was also lying awake, as she always did. She barely ever slept; did not seem to require sleep the way ordinary human beings did. In over thirty years, she had never slipped out of consciousness for more than two or three hours at once. At one time, in the midst of loss and despair, her wakefulness had been a torture, but she had later learned to regard it as a privilege. It was then, during the night hours, when the ether was clear of interference, that she thought her clearest thoughts. Wakefulness also allowed her to be vigilant.

There had been a night, for instance, many years ago, when she had heard Salvador creeping from his room at midnight. She got out of bed and watched from her window as he stole from shadow to shadow and crossed the lawn towards the Old Château. What on earth could he be up to? She waited, and an hour later saw him return with a long black case. The next day, while he was at his lessons, she searched his room and found the smuggled case hidden under his bed. When she looked inside, she felt sick with anger; the betrayal of the noble values she had instilled in him was almost more than she could bear. In the wide-awake nights that followed, she cursed herself bitterly. She had not worked hard enough. Somewhere, at some point, her moral vigilance had lapsed. Outraged though she was, she left the obscene thing in its hiding place and kept quiet about it. He must be given the chance to confess and repent of his own free will. Perfect absolution could only come from purging one's own soul. The namesake that was also his conscience would turn him from this path. But he refused to be turned; he went on concealing his corruption under a bland mask of obeisance, as though nothing were amiss in his soul. And so, reluctantly, she was forced to reveal him. His defiance in playing that degenerate little Prelude was the final provocation, and she exposed him without compunction.

She would never understand why the effect of that night had not lasted. Not only did his contrition and reformation not endure; it collapsed spectacularly only a few years later. She could never quite reason it out. Later, though, only very recently, she had begun to recognise that there was a pattern. Somewhere inside him was a demon, and that demon took the form of an insatiable hunger. Once he had sampled something forbidden, he could not be made to let go; he had to keep hold of it and bite ever deeper into it. In a way – a reluctant, grudging way – she had to admire his tenacity. If only she had recognised that demon early enough, she could have choked it before it had a chance to flourish. At the very least, she could have channelled and cultivated it to good, noble purposes.

And now his hunger was for women; like his father before him. In retrospect, she was surprised it had taken him so long to discover this breed of lust. This Lydia claimed she worked for an insurance broker. They had met at one of Salvador's public performances. On the face of it, it seemed plausible enough – she looked just the sort of etiolated plant that might grow in the confines of an office – but the lie, or rather the telling of it, was just so shamefacedly transparent. If this girl was not the same student with whom he had become infatuated last year, then she was certainly a lily scooped from the same pond. Moreover, it seemed that slaking his lust on her was not enough; he apparently intended to make this common little English slut his bride.

What was Geneviève to do about it? Why, nothing of course. Twelve months ago, such a plan would have appalled her, and she would have forbidden it, unleashing a volley of threats. Now, although it still appalled her – made her feel giddy with nausea – she would have to let it happen. Salvador was right; she had learned a lesson. The very same lesson Salvador's ancestors had learned, each in their own way. She had learned the value of expediency. She could not stop him without breaking the line apart forever, and the line was pre-eminent.

The only course of action was inaction; to wait for the generations to turn. When they did, Geneviève would be waiting, ready to carry the line onward, with the wisdom of her former mistakes to guide her.

In the silence of the night, she prayed that this Lydia, whatever her infinite flaws, might at least be possessed of a fertile womb.

2

She still didn't understand. She wanted an explanation, and he decided to offer her one. *Put your shoes on,* he said. *It's a long walk.*

'Now tell me, my son; do you know what the nature of genius is?'

Salvador gazed uncomprehendingly at the engraved patterns on the charcoal-grey marble. He knew that they were writing, but deciphering them was a skill he was only just beginning to acquire; beyond the ability to identify a few individual letters and the long, sinuous form of his own name, he could not read. He glanced up at his mother; her physical stature was diminutive, but to him she loomed like a giant: in only three-quarters of a decade, he would surpass her height, and would eventually tower head, shoulders and upper bicep above her, but he would always perceive her as she was now; a colossal pillar of watchful sternness, always looking down upon him.

'No, Maman,' he said quietly.

He hadn't understood more than half the words that formed the question, let alone the question itself, but his bare few years of life had taught him that it would not be wise to admit this. Even so, he could tell that the question was important; an important question on an important occasion. He had sensed the gravity of the day from the moment he woke. During breakfast, then while Avril helped him to dress, and all the way down the hill from the estate, through the village of Gondecourt and up the path leading to the cemetery, his mother had been distant, quiet, uncommunicative. Several times during the long walk, he had reached up instinctively and tried to insinuate his hand into hers. But instead of enfolding it or allowing it to grasp and hold on to a single finger as usually happened when they walked about together, her hand shied away from his; each time his fingers found her palm, it retreated. He had kept glancing up at her as they walked, looking for a reason for her hand's unusual behaviour, but there was no sign, no expression in her face. He had searched there for anger, and searched his memory for any unconscious misdemeanour he might have committed to induce it, but there was nothing there;

nothing that he was capable of discerning, anyway.

And now this strange place, this incomprehensible question.

'No,' he repeated helplessly. Confused, he forgot wisdom: 'I don't understand,' he said. The words were out before he realised what he was saying.

She looked at his face. 'Salvador,' she said, more gently than he expected, 'never let me hear you use that expression again: *I do not understand* is a marriage of words that has no legitimacy in this family. Not in me, nor in your father, nor in you. There is only *I understand* and *I shall* *understand*. The only thing that is beyond our comprehension is the mind of God.' She paused. 'And even that, I believe, may be deduced if one listens carefully enough.' She glanced at the crucified Christ cast in bronze above the entrance to a nearby tomb and surreptitiously crossed herself as she said it. (It was a gesture that would remain in Salvador's memory for the rest of his life; as though God were the only person whose difference of opinion might be accorded respect.)

Salvador nodded obligingly. 'I see, Maman.'

'So, would you care to rephrase what you said just now?'

He frowned in concentration, trying to recall what he had said; his words seemed tossed and scattered in the stream of his mother's speech, and he felt himself sinking below the lapping surface. With his mouth going dry, he tried tentatively: 'I *shall* understand?'

He was rewarded with a smile; a rare smile warmed by the satisfaction in her eyes. He did not dare relax, though; he knew that this warmth could dissipate in an instant and crackle with hard, cold icicles of disapproval if he faltered now.

'Good,' she said. 'Only with a little more conviction in future, I think . . . And *what* shall you understand?'

His eyes widened and his heart froze as the rushing water began to close over his head. 'I—' he began, and stuttered to a halt. He had been about to say *I don't know*, but the negative touched off a shrill klaxon in his head. 'I . . .' he began again timidly. 'I shall know . . .'

It was a desperate guess, and his mother gazed doubtfully at him for a precarious moment. Then she smiled again. 'Indeed,' she said. 'You shall know and you shall understand what you know.' She paused reflectively. 'Language is very important, Salvador. Next year . . . well, perhaps the year after – soon, however, you will begin your English lessons. English is a fine, strong language. It distinguishes between *will* and *shall*; a distinction between desire on the one hand and firm intent on the other, or between intent and tenacious determination. It is a mark of the doggedness of their race; their determination to succeed. The blood of the Lionheart flows in the veins of your father's line, my son – it is a blood that conquers. That is why we are a *shall* family.'

Salvador was beginning to feel safer now; he had heard his mother talk about blood and ancientness and conquering many times before, and the litany of determination was as familiar to him as his nursery rhymes. The local children of his age learnt the names of the trees and of the birds and flowers and insects of the fields and hedgerows; Salvador learnt the names of his ancestors, English, French, German and Spanish, their lands and estates, their titles, conquests and creations.

'Maman,' he ventured. 'Why have we come to this place?'

Gathering her skirt decorously about her knees, Geneviève crouched down in front of her son so that she could look directly into his eyes, and at last she took his small hand in hers. 'My son,' she began, and he was shocked to see tears in her eyes, 'I have decided that the time has come . . . There is someone here whom you must meet: someone who can help you to understand the nature of genius.'

For one moment – just one brief, elusive moment as he glanced nervously beyond her shoulder, he thought he caught a glimpse of somebody; two people – a man and a woman – standing some distance away between the ranks of white stone tombs. The man, whose face seemed as close and distinct as his mother's, stared imploringly at him, as though trying to communicate. But when Salvador blinked and looked again, the man and woman had both vanished, and only his mother's face was there. Her hands were on his shoulders, gently but firmly, turning him round to face the most momentous meeting of his life.

'And who did you meet?' asked Lydia. She looked back at Salvador; he was standing, statue-still, on the threshold of the cemetery, framed between the high wrought-iron gates. His eyes were gazing, unblinking, into the distance. She went to him and touched his arm. 'Salvador?' she said softly, but he didn't seem to hear her. 'Who did you meet?'

He was silent for a few moments, then: 'Whom,' he said quietly, still gazing ahead. '*Whom* did I meet . . . English is a fine language, but the natives corrupt it terribly.'

She laughed. 'Pedantry isn't your style, Salvador.' She squeezed his arm. 'I want to hear the rest of the story.'

He looked at her; life and sensation seemed to seep back into his eyes as she smiled at him, and he smiled back. 'Come on,' he said, pointing towards the tall, spindle-thin stone tower in the centre of the cemetery. 'It's just down there, beyond the *Lanterne*.'

This place was unlike any burial ground Lydia had seen at home: the village churchyard in Hampshire where her mother lay, or the municipal cemetery in Sheffield that contained her father's and grandfather's graves; in those places, death was a return to the earth, sleeping beneath the ill-kempt grass and the greening, lichen-patched stones, mortal remnants melting into the roots of sighing, bowing, ancient trees. Death cycling into life. *Pagan*, she thought suddenly; a pagan way of death compared with this high Catholic order of grandeur. Here, death was monumental; circumscribed by high stone walls and set out in rows of slabs and pitch-roofed charnel houses set four-square in a grid of dry, dusty gravel paths. Not a tree in sight, not a shred of grass, not a patch of weed to be nourished by the liquor of organic sleep; no greens or browns or hummocky turf; only white stone, black marble and hard corners. Here, there appeared to be no *Rest in Peace*, only the anguish of *Regrets Eternels* and the imploring of *Priez Pour Lui*. Some spartan stones bore only a name, a set of dates and a cross; others, more ostentatiously, had large iron or bronze crucifixes bolted to them. Again and again, she read the same inscription – often in flowery enamel plaques with gold borders: *Retourné à Dieu*, and she knew it was a lie; this place was not about return or renewal or regeneration; it was a place of preservation, where the immutability of stone and steel and enamel stood for a futile longing to keep the dead in the architecture of the living, to deny the fragility of the organism and its eventual, inevitable decay amidst a welter of eternal regret. But organic decay could not be evaded entirely, even here: unreplenished wire wreath-frames hanging from the walls of tombs looked like empty lobster-pots, with blackened, seaweed-like strands of dead vegetation hanging from them, and wilting bouquets stood grieving on many of the grave-slabs. Some mourners had tried to avoid even this acknowledgement of natural decay by making their memorial tributes in the form of vases of artificial roses with plastic stems and fabric petals, or even knick-knack-shelf ceramic bowls with china flowers, placed amongst the petrified forests of little, free-standing marble plaques inscribed with *À Notre Oncle, Regrets* or *Souvenir*, like stone birthday cards or a sideboard display of family photographs.

Please, Lydia thought as she walked through this petrous, ferrous city of the dead, *please don't ever put me here. Let me be buried in brown earth and green grass. Preferably beneath the branches of a big shady tree in an untended corner. And let me be forgotten.*

As they rounded the broad circular dais from which the Lantern of the Dead raised its thin, stony finger, they came to a row of tombs that were larger than the rest. (Most tombs in the cemetery, she couldn't help disrespectfully thinking, were about the size and shape of allotment huts or outdoor privies, whereas these were more like comfortably-sized garden sheds.) In the centre, dominating all around it, stood the largest tomb of all (a well-to-do greenhouse, she thought): it was built of ash-white ashlar with a classical portico. Inscribed on the pediment above the entrance in large Roman capitals was the legend:

FAMILLE DE LA SIMARDE

The entrance itself consisted of an elaborate double-door of black wrought iron with large glazed panels and an enamelled family crest worked into the metal filigree. As they came closer, she could see that the door enclosed a gloomy vestibule which took up the front quarter of the building.

'Here we are,' said Salvador. 'The family tomb.' He was trying to speak lightly, but Lydia could see the tension in his eyes. He took a small key on a thin silver chain from his pocket and slotted it into the lock. 'They stopped using the old mausoleum around 1890. For some reason, my great-grandmother took against the idea of having the dead so close to the house. Nobody knows why. Nobody will talk about it. Avril once told me . . . Well, never mind what, it's all old fairy stories. She – my great-grandmother, that is – made her husband have this tomb built and promise never to use the estate for burials again. The family have been buried here ever since. My great-grandmother herself was the first and my father was the last.'

Lydia expected the iron gates to creak and squeal eerily, but they swung open silently on well-oiled hinges. The three walls of the vestibule, from ground to ceiling, were made up of rectangular stone plaques engraved with names, dates, extracts of verse and, on many of them, a small, gilt-framed oval photograph of the occupant; an album of the dead souls interred beyond the back wall. Towards the bottom were rows of blank plaques; it was these that disturbed Lydia the most; like empty boxes on a form waiting to be filled in.

'Only room for a couple more generations,' said Salvador quietly. 'We shall be amongst the last, you and I.'

Lydia shivered. 'Don't talk like that,' she said irritably. 'It's not funny.'

'I know. Do you see me smiling?'

She looked at him; no, there was no flicker of a smile on his lips, and no trace of irony in his eyes. She gazed at the names and the years and the fading, yellowing photographs, feeling a horror creeping over her skin. 'I don't want to be buried in there,' she said suddenly, earnestly. 'Not ever.'

'But you're one of the family,' he protested mildly, as though she had timorously refused a place at the dinner table. 'Or you will be soon. You and I and our heirs; we'll all end up here eventually.'

She stared at him for a few moments, then went hurriedly out through the gates and across the path to where the sunshine poured living warmth onto her face. She sat down on the edge of the Lantern's dais and rubbed her eyes. After a minute or two, Salvador came and sat down close beside her. There was silence for a while, then he spoke softly: 'Sorry.'

There was no reply; Lydia just kept gazing into the distance, towards the woods and fields on the far side of the valley.

'I'm sorry,' he repeated. 'I didn't mean to upset you. If it's any consolation, I dislike it probably as much as you do.' This time, her eyes flickered a little in response. 'I expect,' he went on, 'I mean, by the time we ... you know, when we ... my mother won't be here any longer, so it won't matter where ...'

'Stop it,' she said, closing her eyes tightly. 'Can we please just not talk about it?'

He nodded. 'Okay.'

'Why is your family so obsessed with dead ancestors? I mean, it's interesting and everything, but you ... well, you can take it too far. I want to be a living person, not some sort of ... of *trainee forebear*. I don't want my plot marked out before I've even lived.'

He smiled apologetically. 'I understand,' he said. 'I really do understand. We shall never speak of it again.'

'Not until we're old and grey.'

'And wrinkled,' he added.

'As prunes,' she said, squeezing his arm and smiling at last. 'Now, why don't you tell me the rest of the story. I mean, that's what you brought me here for, isn't it.'

He balked. 'Oh. I don't know. Maybe we should save it for another time.'

'Save it? But you've dragged me all the way up here just to tell it! You can't leave me dangling now – I want to hear the end; who you met here.'

He hesitated; telling this story had not merely been the reason for embarking on the long walk from the estate to the cemetery; it was actually the main purpose in bringing her with him to France. He had reasoned that it was only here, where it had happened, that she – and indeed he himself, perhaps, with her help – might learn to truly understand him.

'I'm not sure you'll want to hear it now,' he said.

'Don't be silly. Of course I do. Who did you meet?'

'Well ...' He took a deep breath and folded his hands in his lap. 'I suppose you could say I met myself ...'

... You shall understand ...

285

'But there's nobody there,' he protested.

'Look closer. Here.'

The gates had opened silently, and he stood tinily, tremblingly in their maw as though they might gobble him up at any moment. He looked closer.

The fresh, unfaded eyes glazed calmly back at him from under the convex oval of glass. He could feel the cloying water of incomprehension rising again: he tried to wiggle away, but the hands on his shoulders clamped like steel, fingers closing in like clothes-pegs, hanging him out in the cold wind.

The patterns of gold-lined grooves in the black marble shifted uncertainly on the surface of his brain, until one of them locked suddenly onto the familiar template imprinted there:

'Salvador!' he cried.

The grip on his shoulders moved, and he sensed his mother's head dipping down close beside him. 'Very good,' her voice said softly in his ear. 'Can you read the other words, my son?'

He didn't need to; he looked at the face again: the eyes, below a lick of black fringe, were still gazing coolly into his. He knew that face as well as he knew his own, and when he looked closer at the eyes and mouth, he thought he could see something there; an uncertainty, a tremor of fear that struck a harmonic note, resonating in his own heart.

At last, his mother's fingers loosened enough to allow him to turn around and look at her. Her eyes – so close to his that he could make out the tiny crinkles and pinprick white dots in the skin beneath the lashes, and the concentric lattices of jade in the brown glaze of her irises – her eyes were different now; the sadness had gone and they were alight with excitement. They fluttered momentarily as some strands of her black hair drifted across their lids, lifted by the growing cold breeze. The last time he had seen her face this close, this excited, was when she was reassuring him in the strange studio, whispering words of encouragement as she posed him for the photograph . . .

And now he was drowning; just three tiny words choked out of his throat as he went under: 'Maman, it's me . . .'

'*C'est moi* . . . That's all I could say.'

Lydia stared at the plaque – the last but one in the descending sequence – wondering that she hadn't noticed it before. To the incurious glance, it looked no different from the others – black marble engraved with gold-inlaid, oblique, sans-serif letters, a small oval monochrome photograph beside – but she felt that *this* . . . well, surely *something* should have leapt out and struck her sharply on both cheeks. It said:

ICI REPOSE

SALVADOR HONORÉ FRANÇOIS PHILIPPE DE LA SIMARDE

Below had been added:

LA MUSIQUE DORT AVEC LUI

She looked back at him, to see the expression on his face, but he was gone; for a moment she thought he had vanished into the air, but then she spotted him sitting once more on the steps of the dais below the tower.

'I don't understand,' she said, and he laughed – a short, hollow *ha*. 'It's you. As a little boy. There's a photograph and everything.'

He shook his head. 'I did say you could say I met myself. Look again at the dates.'

She looked; in between the name and the epitaph, where her disbelieving eyes had barely glanced before, was inscribed:

NÉ LE 13 FÉVRIER 1947 RECUEILLÉ PAR DIEU LE 20 AVRIL 1958

'1958,' she read out loud. 'That's before you were born.'

'Me and yet not me,' he smiled.

'I still don't understand. What does it mean?'

'My alter-ego, my nemesis, my progenitor, prototype, prefigurement, mentor, my inspiration, my tormentor. Down the years, I've come up with a lot of words, trying to capture what he has been to me. In the end, he is Salvador: Salvador the First, Salvador the Archetype. First, last and always. The nature of genius in a marble plaque.'

Now Lydia understood, but she still couldn't believe it. 'You're telling me,' she said warily, as though she might be missing some crucial clue, 'that your parents had a child before you, and when he died they gave you his name?'

'His name exactly. The bearer of those names – Salvador Honoré François Philippe – was destined for greatness, you see.'

'And your mother brought you here . . . when you were *five* . . .'

'Or thereabouts – I can't remember exactly. Yes, she brought me to

287

meet him. That was how she put it. I expected to meet a living person, but instead I met a dead boy who had my face and my name.'

Lydia was appalled. 'That's an *awful* thing to do to a child. Who knows what kind of harm you could do.'

Salvador looked at her. 'You think I've been harmed?' He shrugged. 'Maybe so. It certainly had an effect, I can tell you that.'

'An *effect*? I'm surprised you came out of it with your sanity. I still can't believe any mother could *do* that.'

'Well, you don't know my family, and you don't know my mother. You have to understand her. She comes from an ancient family, full of greatness, and in marrying my father she renewed an old union with a line as august and ancient as her own. She believed from childhood that she was destined to breed a greatness – breed it, you understand, not *be* it – breed a greatness that would surpass all that had gone before. It didn't matter to her what sphere it was in, although it pleased her that it turned out to be music, because it was one of her loves. He grew into a musician of extraordinary talent. Of course, with his Spanish heritage, his instrument had to be the guitar, and he played it like angels were dancing on the tips of his fingers. But then, just as her child was on the threshold of conquering the world with his powers, he was snatched away from her on the wing of a Citroën DS. He was walking out of the gatehouse on his way to Gondecourt when this car swept in and hit him. He might have survived, but he was flung back against the gatehouse wall so violently that his skull broke like an egg. It turned out that the car was being driven by a young conductor who was coming to visit my mother. She had written to him about putting on a debut concert for her son.'

'Oh my God,' said Lydia. 'How could you live with yourself after that?'

'He didn't. He died in a car accident himself a few years later. He was drunk, apparently, and drove his car off a bridge into the Loire. It was said he turned to drink after the decline of his career. My mother is a powerful woman; she has powerful connections. She made sure he never worked in music again. She destroyed his career as surely as he had destroyed her precious boy. Like I said, you have to understand her. She was devastated. Avril told me how hard and stern she became afterwards, even though part of her was dying inside. She tried to have another child to replace him, but she seemed to be barren, even though she was still fairly young. Years went by. They didn't have much in the way of treatment in those days. She and my father visited the best clinics in Europe, but in the end all she was left with was the potions and unguents of old wives and witches, and the power of prayer. My mother has never been a particularly devout woman, but she wore her knees to the bone and burned candles in every church from here to Angoulême, praying for the soul of her Salvador to be returned to her womb, promising a greatness that would be a glory to God. And then one day, it happened. One night, in the middle of winter, Avril was summoned to her bedroom by frenzied ringing. She found Madame in a sweating, breathless ecstasy. She had received a visitation of angels, she said, who stood in an arc of golden light around her bed and promised her a child to replace the one taken from her. Sure enough, a few weeks later, she found that she was carrying me . . . Me and yet not me. Him and yet not him. So, what other name should she choose? It was more than a mere reincarnation as far as she was concerned; it was a resurrection!'

Lydia shook her head. 'I still can't believe . . . I mean . . .'

'At least it meant I was guaranteed love and care, even if I had to wear somebody else's skin.'

'I can't believe you can be so philosophical about it.'

He smiled. 'Well, that wasn't what did the damage. I haven't told you the rest of the story yet. Many years later, I found out something about the original Salvador that changed everything.' He stood up and held a hand out to her. 'If we go back to the house, I'll tell you about it.'

3

The room was smaller than the one they shared, its furniture crowded and competing for space; yet, rather than feeling cosy, it had the reverend, untouchable aura of a shrine or a museum. Which, in effect, it was; cleaned and dusted regularly, but never aired or rearranged. In one rare corner of uncluttered space beside the small single bed stood a straight-backed chair, with a canted footstool and a delicate rosewood music-stand arranged in front of it. To one side, a child-size guitar rested on a wooden frame. In an alcove next to the fireplace was a towering stack-up hi-fi and shelf upon shelf of records and tapes. In the other fireside alcove was a bookcase overflowing with bound volumes of sheet music.

'Preserved just as I left it, after all these years,' said Salvador, and he sighed. 'Actually, not as I left it. More as I should have left it, according to my mother. I'm not the only one commemorated here. I inherited this bedroom, along with everything else, from Salvador. He haunted me here and everywhere. My life's purpose was to live up to his standards, and I was never quite good enough. When I sat here and practised, I sensed his impatience with my efforts. When I neglected my practice, I sensed his disapproval. When I did well, pushing back the limits of my talent, he smiled condescendingly at my modest achievements. If I ever appeared to deviate from my duty to greatness, my mother was always there to remind me of whose shoes I had been honoured to step into.'

He ran a finger across the thin spines of the record sleeves. 'All traces of contamination and evil influence rooted out now,' he murmured. His finger hopped down a shelf and skimmed along a row of cassettes. 'All traces bar one, apparently,' he said, sliding one of the little plastic boxes out and handing it to Lydia.

She looked at the cassette. She recognised the cover from Rachel's record collection: it showed a twelve-year-old Salvador sitting on a low stone wall in a garden, frowning in concentration as he played – or pretended to play for the camera – his prized and famous Torres. It was only now, though, that Lydia recognised the background: a sweep of green lawn rising up to a steep hill. Looking closer, she could just make out the out-of-focus façade of the mausoleum in the top left corner, in the gaps between the bold white lettering of the title.

'You look sweet,' she said.

'Me and yet not me,' said Salvador, taking the cassette back. 'And in more ways than one.' He flipped open the case and took out an unlabelled Memorex cassette. 'My mother has a dozen copies of this record – vinyl and cassette. She would never think to look inside this one.'

'Why? What is it?'

'Just what it says, from a certain point of view: a recording of the great Salvador de La Simarde playing pieces by Fernando Sor.' He switched on the hi-fi and slotted the cassette into the tape deck. 'But not quite,' he added. 'The original of this was made on an old Grundig reel-to-reel. This is a copy I made in secret. The sound quality isn't too great.'

'Why in secret?'

'It contains . . . well, you'll see what it contains.' He pushed the door of the tape deck closed. 'This,' he said in a hushed voice, 'is the *truly* great Salvador – the original Salvador, the Salvador who extended the bounds of genius, in whose shadow I lived and in whose image I was moulded. This is gold and diamonds – the only recording ever made . . . Sit down – make yourself comfortable and listen.'

Lydia sat on the end of the bed and waited while Salvador paused ceremoniously before pressing PLAY and turning up the volume.

There was a long, soft hissing, then a loud *click-clunk*; the hissing redoubled and there was a noise of chair legs scraping on floorboards against a background of intermittent coughs and murmuring voices.

The noises faded away gradually, there was a pause, then the first chord rang out, loud and raucous, and dissolved at once into a pitter-pattering cadence of rapid notes.

It was a short piece – six or seven minutes at most – and Lydia never once took her eyes off Salvador's face as it played. He sat on the hard, stern chair and stared at the floor, his face expressionless except for almost imperceptible twitchings that rippled the muscles of his lips, cheeks and eyelids in time with the music.

The last notes faded away to a silence that was immediately swamped by a clatter of enthusiastic applause and bravos from the small, invisible audience. Salvador reached up and clicked off the tape. 'That,' he said quietly, '—or rather the legend of it – was what I was made to live up to all through my childhood.'

Lydia would never have claimed to have a very sophisticated ear for music; she was no connoisseur of the subtler nuances of style and expression, but even she could tell that there was something in the playing that was not quite right. There were no wrong notes as such, and the playing was exuberant, but there were several thudding near-misses, and the whole was interlaced with crude mechanical buzzes, squeaks and rattles of strings on frets that were absent from her Salvador's playing. If this was the sound of genius, then it was immature, unschooled, unrefined genius.

'How old was he?' she asked.

Salvador shrugged. 'I don't know. Eight, perhaps. Nine, ten ... It hardly matters. I discovered this recording by accident when I was fifteen, and it nearly destroyed me. All my life, I had been living with the ghost of a sublime genius haunting me, looking down at my clumsy efforts, sighing over my incompetences, impatient with my struggle to live up to him. And then I stumbled upon the very voice of that ghost genius speaking through that tape. The model I had been encouraged – no, forced – to regard as divine turned out to be no more than a shabby fake.'

Lydia looked helplessly at him. 'He might just have been having an off-day,' she suggested desperately.

Salvador shook his head. 'The playing is quite advanced, but the technique is crude, the feeling for rhythm and harmony and expression is not there.' He ejected the tape and held it in his hands. 'I was better than this when I was seven years old!' he hissed. 'When my fingers could barely reach across the fretboard of this baby instrument here! Nobody – not the greatest tutors the world has ever known – not Carlevaro or Segovia – could have turned this Salvador into a guitarist.' He sat down again, holding up the tape. 'I listened to this recording over and over again, trying to puzzle out the lies my mother told me, trying to make excuses for his bad playing – his age, for example. But there was no escaping the truth: He had no *gift*. None whatever. He could have practised for all eternity, and he would never have been a *tenth* of the musician I became.'

His face was mottled with anger, but he collected himself and went on more quietly: 'It became unbearable. In the three years that followed, I couldn't bring myself to tell my mother that I had learned the truth – she must have suppressed it in herself or never been aware of it – whatever, I couldn't shatter her precious dream of him as it had been shattered for me, even when she continued to reproach me with his memory. She still does it. Last summer, when she came to Cambridge and I ran away, she did it. She said I was neglecting my music. She said Salvador, in his infinite superiority, would be looking down at me from Heaven with shame in his eyes. She cursed the God who had taken him away and put me in his place. Even then I couldn't tell her, and so I struck her. I could easier hit her, knock her down, even kill her, than tell her that Salvador was no more than a cosseted, talentless brat. I hit her and ran away.'

Lydia looked at the pain in his face, and understood at last. 'I always thought there was more to it than you told me,' she said.

'It was like being forced to relive a part of my life I thought I'd escaped. She drove me away the first time when I was only eighteen. Before I left here, her last words to me were "You have failed me." Well, I could stand that, but she added: "You have failed, my son." ' He smiled wanly. 'I think that's what she actually said, but at the time I didn't hear that quiet little comma. What I heard was "You have failed my son." '

'How?' asked Lydia. 'How had you failed?'

'I allowed myself to become polluted.' He forced a grin. 'Rock and roll was my downfall. In my mother's eyes, it was the ultimate betrayal of Salvador's memory, but I had discovered a new universe, and I couldn't learn to live in both. Not at that age, anyway. I had to explore this new universe, so I cut all my ties and departed.'

THE TOWER

*G*o *wherever you wish*, she had said.

If only it were that simple. Over lunch, Madame de La Simarde had reiterated her apologies for the enforced extension of their stay, and expressed regret that there was so little here for the entertainment of young people. Her manner had warmed since yesterday, and she seemed particularly concerned that Beth was unhappy being here. Beth, alarmed at being singled out, protested incoherently: No, not at all, completely the wrong impression. The Château was really fascinating – you know, the architecture and everything, and the history. Madame de La Simarde smiled approvingly and invited her to explore; to regard the Château as her own.

A short while later, Beth stood alone in her room, gazing down at a postcard peeping out from under the valance. Their little read-in had been interrupted by the call to lunch: hearing footsteps approaching along the corridor, she and Audrey had quickly bundled Lydia's artefacts – chest, notebooks, postcards and all – under the bed. While they had lain together, sharing Lydia's remnants, it had seemed almost like having her back, reconstituted from dry bones. But the gap between *almost* and *actually* was too painful; Beth, at least, had been *almost* grateful for the interruption.

She picked up the stray postcard. It showed a view of a château very like this one; the Château de La Rochefoucauld, according to the caption on the back. Lydia had dated it 15th April 1991 and written, *Dear Beth, Not the Simarde seat but similar. Are you surprised? – I've made it! I'm over the sea!!! Even more surprising – we're going to be married!!!! Wish I could see the look on your face when you read this. Can you imagine me as Lady of the Manor?! Can't wait to see you. Keep revising. Love, Lyd.xxxx.*

This was one postcard Lydia must have known she couldn't send even before she wrote it. Their wretched, oh-so-precious pact of *no-tell* had still been in force, and that little piece of news had lain dormant between them; sprung at last when it was too late. Wrong time, wrong place, wrong person.

She didn't want to think about that. She pushed the card back under the bed and went out into the corridor. She thought of looking in on Audrey, but just as her hand hovered over the door handle, her instinct told her not to. Audrey was busy. *Busy* was very important to Audrey. Instead, she walked along the corridor towards the stairs. At the end, she paused and looked back. Audrey's door, and her own, had receded into a row of doors, all identical, all closed.

Go wherever you wish. If only. *Regard it as your own.* In another life, perhaps. She went down the stairs and investigated the first storey. Another long corridor, virtually identical to the one above; more rows of closed doors. The trodden path of Sunday afternoon gawps round stately homes was missing: the roped-off corridors and staircases – *Private* – and selected doors wedged wide open – *Come in here. Look around. Wouldn't you like to OWN this?* An artifice of casual artefacts hinting at occupancy. *Don't touch that, you naughty girl.* There was no careful choreography of liberties and limits; no ropes; no limits except absolute ones. Doors closed, blank, susurrating like cell membranes with whispered rumours of what lay behind. Beth didn't have the courage to seize a handle and punch a hole in the membrane, and so she wandered the corridors, hearing the whispers and searching in vain for an open invitation. After a while, the corridors began closing in on her; whispers crept under the doors, snaked across the carpet and swirled about her ankles. Glass display-cases full of trophy wildlife creaked and cracked and snarled as she passed, and invisible watchers sneaked up behind her to blow cold breath into the nape of her neck. She walked faster and faster, until she was running. She helter-skeltered down the staircase, clattered across the hall, through the vestibule, and came to a halt at the top of the courtyard steps, gulping down cold, clear air.

Stupid idiot bitch. Audrey wouldn't have done that. Audrey would have just gone where she pleased. Audrey had no qualms about opening doors; she would have just turned handles and walked right in. Unintimidated; anywhere. But then Audrey didn't sense the vacuum that could lurk behind closed doors, the loss that lived in the unoccupied spaces.

For more than a year now, Iain had been trying to persuade her that they had outgrown their little flat. He needed *space* to write. He even found a house they could afford. She went with him to look at it. It was a pleasant enough three-bedroom terrace, light and warm, but the thought of living there made her skin crawl. It had rooms they wouldn't use; too many lifeless spaces behind blank doors. She liked the flat: bedroom, bathroom, kitchen, living room; two lives could warm and animate every part of it. Nothing was unused. They argued ferociously about it. That night, she dreamed that extraneous bits of her body were being cut away – a little toe, left hand, a breast, a leg – piece by piece, until she was just a brain in a jar. She was disturbed by how much she liked the feeling of being discorporated. She told him about the dream, and he said she ought to talk to someone. Wisely, she didn't tell him *who* had been doing the cutting. Had she admitted that, he might have left her.

The courtyard was quiet and echo-brittle. Paths had been swept and trodden through the snow, like tendons connecting the castle's limbs. When she had got her breath back, she crossed the court and stood in the arched cloister of the Italian Wing, so that she could look back and hold the bulk of the Old Wing in a single belittling gaze. It was here, in the far corner, half-concealed in overarching shadows, that she at last discovered an open door.

A low, arched door, half open, beckoning to her. She approached it cautiously and peeped through. Beyond lay a room with a high, fan-vaulted ceiling and bare alabaster walls dappled faintly with coloured gemstone light. She pushed the door a little wider, and saw a high stained-glass window above a small altar draped with red and white cloth and bearing a simple gold crucifix. Seated on a low stool before it, looking up at the window-lit wall, was Madame de La Simarde. She appeared deep in thought, but not praying. Instinctively, Beth began to retreat, but Madame de La Simarde had heard the creak of the door, and looked round.

'Come in,' she said, her face warming as she recognised Beth. 'Sit down beside me.'

Beth was snared. That's what you got for poking your nose into private corners. She approached the altar and lowered herself onto a second stool. It was upholstered in red velvet and was surprisingly comfortable.

'I come in here often,' said Madame de La Simarde. 'To pray, or just to remember.' She looked up at the window. 'Did I tell you that I was married in here? No. It was not the most august place for a wedding. My mother was married in Seville Cathedral, and my mother-in-law in the Church of St Sebastian in Vienna. But there was a war. We were little more than refugees. At that altar I made my vows, pledging my body as a vessel to carry precious cargo forward into the future, and my soul as its steward.' She paused and sighed. 'Every person who was present at that wedding is now dead, except me. The vessel has foundered, the cargo smashed and lost amongst the rocks, and I am left to wander on the shoreline, waiting for the tide to wash in and claim me.' She looked at Beth and smiled stoically. 'None shall come after me.'

'Is there no other family?' Beth asked.

'Oh, there is always other family.'

'Then surely things can carry on. Someone will take over.'

Madame de La Simarde shook her head sadly. 'They cannot. The design of the Last Marquis, forced upon him by the Revolutionary Code, depended upon the existence of an heir of the de La Simarde line. Without such an heir, the stratagem collapses. This estate may remain inviolate, but the French estates, which constitute the true core of the line, shall not. They shall be broken up and distributed among the lesser branches of the Marquis's descendants. When the legal vultures have finished filling their bellies, all that will be left will be broken bones; trampled and worthless. What has taken centuries to build can be reduced to rubble in a moment. And I, with all my grand ambitions, have been the author of it.'

Beth sensed an invitation to protest. 'You can't blame yourself,' she said. 'Parents may be responsible for what they do to their children, but they aren't responsible for what their children ultimately do to themselves.'

Madame de La Simarde smiled. 'Wise words for one so young.'

They were. Where had *that* little speech come from? Beth shrugged. 'I'm not so young as all that. I've seen a few things. Lived a little.' She looked up at the rosette in the stained-glass window, then down at the spartan little altar. 'Were Lydia and Salvador married here?' she asked.

'In this chapel? Yes, they were. On that very spot, where you are sitting. Like my own wedding, it seemed such a small occasion. So few people. Perhaps, in retrospect, one may see that as symbolic . . .' She took several long, slow breaths, then asked: 'Did you know Salvador well?'

Beth hesitated. 'I . . . Well, I *knew* him. Whether I knew him well . . .'

'You have no children of your own, yet you may imagine how a mother feels about her son. Especially such a son as Salvador. It is my belief that some people have a greatness which surpasses earthly bounds. It invests all that they touch. This, I believe, is what we understand as immortality. Even when they die, there is something of them that does not leave this earth. More than memory; something that is quite tangible. Salvador had that quality, as did his father. They are still here, all three of them. Sons and husbands, husbands and sons. Be wary of them, for they may steal your soul . . . Tell me, Bethany, do you intend to have children?'

Beth's skull jarred: why did people *always* have to ask that, and why did she never have the courage to tell the truth? 'Um, well,' she said, 'maybe one day. Who knows?'

'You shall know. Believe me, you shall know. When I first saw you, I could tell you were a mother.'

Beth blanched. 'Could you?'

'Of course.' Geneviève stretched out a wrinkled, bony hand and touched Beth's belly. 'It is in here. You cannot escape it if you have it. It radiates from the face. You are destined to mother children, and deep inside you know it.'

Beth looked down at the hand. 'Do I? Yes, I suppose I do.'

'You see?' Geneviève withdrew her hand and smiled beatifically. 'I knew it. One day, and perhaps sooner than you imagine.'

Beth stared at the altar and said nothing; there was nothing to say.

Greenilocks and the Five Bears

Long ago, in a vague land far away, there was a Princess who lived in a silver castle. Unusually – for this is a fairy tale – the Princess wasn't beautiful. In fact, she was rather plain, with a pug nose and eyebrows that met in the middle. However, she had the most marvellous flowing hair that was as green as emeralds. Her father, the King, called her Princess Greenilocks. Not a very romantic name, but better than Princess Hilda, which was the name she had been born with.

The King had one abiding passion: truffles. He loved eating them (sliced on roasted guinea-fowl was best) and Princess Greenilocks loved searching them out for him. For this purpose, she kept a fat pig called Nigel, who only had three legs but was the best truffle-hunter in the kingdom. On the first Monday of every month, Greenilocks would tie a length of red ribbon to Nigel's collar and let him lead her through the Great Forest. Nigel was a very well-behaved pig, and he never tried to gobble up the truffles he sniffed out before Greenilocks could get them into her basket, as many a less well-bred truffle-pig would.

One day, they hunted deep into the forest. It must have been near the end of the truffle season, because by afternoon there were only five truffles gathered in the basket. 'Oh dear, Nigel,' said Greenilocks sadly. 'Only five today. Still, the King will be pleased. I bet the other truffle-hunters haven't found any.' Nigel agreed, nodding his great pink head and grunting happily. And so they decided to give up the hunt and head back to the castle.

They had wandered far and wide in the forest since morning, and they soon realised that they were lost. They followed strange paths that seemed to go round and round in circles. Nigel, loping along on his three legs, soon began to grow tired, and Princess Greenilocks started to become frightened of the darkening forest. They were close to despair when they came across a cave. Sitting at its mouth, basking in the last rays of the afternoon sun, was a great brown bear. Although she was fearful of his sharp claws and terrible teeth, Greenilocks approached him.

'Mr Bear,' she said, 'good day to you. My name is Princess Greenilocks, and this is my pig, Nigel. We live in the silver castle beneath the mountains.'

'I know of it,' said the bear. 'And I have heard of you, Princess. What can I do for you on this fine afternoon?'

'Oh, Mr Bear, we are lost. Please tell us the way back to the castle.'

The bear smiled, showing his big yellow fangs. 'Of course, Princess,' he said. 'But what will you do for me in return?' He sniffed the air. 'I know – give me one of those delicious truffles I can smell in your basket.'

Greenilocks was reluctant, but fair was fair and she handed over one of her rare and precious truffles. The uncouth bear gobbled it right down in one go, without even wiping off the soil, then smacked his slobbery lips.

'Follow this path until you come to a stream,' he said. 'Then turn right. Good day to you.' And, with that, he shambled back into his cave.

Greenilocks and Nigel followed the bear's directions. Soon, however, they found themselves at the mouth of another cave, where there was another great brown bear, standing there with his colossal paws on his hips, for all the world as though he was waiting for them.

'Oh, Mr Bear,' said Greenilocks, 'please tell us the way back to the castle. Another bear told us, but we've got lost again.'

'Oh dear,' said the bear, scratching the side of his nose with a claw the size of a kitchen knife. 'Give me one of your delicious truffles and I shall tell you the way.'

Once again Greenilocks obliged, and once again she and Nigel set off, following the bear's directions.

Neither Greenilocks nor her pig had ever heard of *déjà vu*, but if they had, that is exactly what they would have called it when they came upon yet another cave guarded by yet another brown bear. After the expenditure of another precious truffle, they set out again, only to come upon *another* cave and *another* bear.

If there was one thing bears knew, it was that princesses never learn.

At the fifth cave, though, Greenilocks was becoming more than a little fed up. She only had one truffle left, and there was still no sign of the castle. 'Oh, Mr Bear,' she said, a little irritably, 'please tell us the way back to the castle.'

Like the other before him, the bear reared up to his full height, sticking out his huge furry belly and brandishing knife-like claws that protruded from paws the size of roast hams. 'Certainly, Princess,' he growled. 'Give me one of your delicious truff—'

'No!' said Greenilocks angrily. 'I've only got one left!'

'Give it to me!' the bear demanded.

Greenilocks stood her ground. 'No,' she said. 'It's for the King, and you shan't have it.'

'Then I shall eat *you*! And your fat pig!' The bear showed his huge fangs and roared so loudly that the ground shook.

'Wait!' cried Greenilocks as he bore down on her. 'I know a secret about bears.'

The bear paused. 'What?' he said, laughing contemptuously. 'What could a plain little princess possibly know about bears, the kings of the forest?'

Greenilocks looked up at the great bear defiantly. 'I know why you're so aggressive, for one thing. I know why you go about waving your claws and flashing your fangs, frightening defenceless princesses and stealing their truffles.'

The great brown bear frowned. '*Why?* Because we're the kings of the forest, that's why, and we can do as we please.'

Greenilocks shook her emerald tresses. 'Wrong,' she said. 'It's because you can't get proper erections.'

'*What?*' bellowed the bear.

'Look.' From under her skirts, Greenilocks produced her pocket-sized *Encyclopaedia of Zoology*, and opened it at the page headed 'Bears, great brown'. ' "Bears",' she read aloud, ' "are the only animals in the whole of the animal kingdom that have a strip of bone in the penis." ' She held up the book and showed him the diagram. 'See? That's what all the noise and bullying are about: you have to have a bone in your willy, otherwise you couldn't get it up.'

Nigel, who didn't have a bone in his willy, sniggered. The bear let out a deafening bellow of rage, and with a swooshing swipe of his terrible claws, knocked Nigel's head clean off. It bowled away into the trees, and his porky three-legged body slumped into a heap. Then the bear turned and reared up at Greenilocks, waving his bloody claws, saliva dripping from his fangs. In that terrifying moment, a plan formed in Greenilocks' clever head. A cunning and subtle plan that would get her past the bear unharmed and see her safely to the castle. However, cunning plans take time and effort to put into action, and this one would necessitate sacrificing the last of her truffles. Instead, she just whisked her trusty Magnum from under her skirts and shot him in the guts. Three bullets: Wham! Wham! Wham! As she stepped over his squealing, slowly dying body, she congratulated herself. Now she and the King would at least have one of the precious morsels for their tea.

Eventually, with help from a friendly doe, she found her way back to the castle. Although she missed Nigel, and never went truffle-hunting again, she lived happily ever after.

... And she was never again bothered by bears.

Wedding Salvador

1

Beth studied her reflection in the glass, but all she could see was a face-shaped coalescence of indistinct shadows, blurred by the racing tunnel wall and haloed by the glare of the carriage lights. She had a feeling, though, that even the clearest, brightest looking-glass in the world wouldn't illuminate the strange things going on behind her shadowed eyes. What was she even doing here? And where was she going, apart from mad?

Beth was up, dressed and out of the house before any of the others were even awake. She put on her clothes like an automaton, then packed her bag: pen, spare pen, back-up spare pen, and an extra pen just in case, cigarettes, matches, a spiral-bound jotter crammed with notes for last-minute revision, the copy of *Oscar Wilde* Lydia had given her (curled now and dog-eared) as a distraction from useless last-minute revision, and the little cloth Snoopy that had seen her through every exam since mock O-Levels, whispering up answers from his hiding place in her pocket. Lastly, she went to the bathroom and packed the plastic jar of paracetamol.

She wandered into the kitchen in a daze, but the thought of eating breakfast made her gut-sick. Instead, she poured out a glass of Audrey's grapefruit juice, sipped reluctantly at it like medicine, and left it unfinished on the table. Shoes. Bag. Door – *click*. Fresh air.

It had rained during the night, and the world was wet and summer-morning chilly, a bleached and hazy sun promising a stifling midday heat. Leaving her bike chained to the fence, she walked out along the lane, leaving Ainsworth Cottages sleeping under its counterpane of damp, mossy slates.

She had over two hours to kill, so she took a long, ambling detour along Fen Causeway to Newnham Terrace, then up Silver Street and around the back of the Anchor to Laundress Green. She sat on the low brick wall above the tumbling weir and watched the white-shirted chauffeurs at Scudamore's getting the punts ready for the day's trade, dragging the long chains rasping out of the rows of eyelets, laying out poles and paddles and plastic cushions. When she tired of watching them, she swung her legs over the wall and stared down between her feet at the water frothing out through the arches, hypnotised by the flow of webbed yellow spume. She lit a cigarette and tracked the path of the spent match tumbling in the water . . .

The last-but-one day. Tomorrow would be the last day of exams, the last day of being a student and, *de facto*, the last day of childhood. Tomorrow, or on Monday, or after the May Ball (no one had told her when to expect the precise moment to fall), she would be outside: extramuralised, de-institutionalised, out of the nest and alone in the world. And she still had no idea how to cope: where to go, what to do. And carrying *this* around inside her . . .

When she tossed her last cigarette end into the water and walked on, it was ten past nine; only twenty minutes to go. Audrey would already be there, exuding a quiet, nonchalant confidence amidst the nervous chatter and smoking her head off . . .

At Silver Street, instead of heading towards the town, she went back over the bridge and ambled along the Backs . . .

It wasn't enough time; she could feel the pull of the examination hall – a tightening knot of urgent fear and loathing in her stomach – but she needed more time to think.

The remaining minutes were whittled away, but no productive thoughts came to her. When she reached Garret Hostel Lane, it was twenty-past nine. As she topped the steep brow of the footbridge, she saw a cyclist coming racing around the corner of Trinity Hall and heading up the slope towards her. She caught a flicker of billowing white shirt and fanned, flowing blonde hair, then there was a screech of brakes.

'Beth!'

Beth lifted her eyes from the ground and focused. 'Oh, hi, Lyd.'

Lydia's beam of summer bonhomie crinkled into a frown. 'Haven't you got an exam this morning? We were all wondering where you'd got to – you were out before any of us were up.'

'I fancied a walk. Anyway, *you* were out till after I was down. Where were you?'

Lydia's delighted smile returned, full force, itching with excitement. 'Oh, Beth, you'll never guess what . . .' She hesitated and munched her lips uncertainly. 'Oh, it can't do any harm now. We've decided finally – we're getting married!'

The blow hit Beth square between the eyes, and she stammered: 'What?'

'Salvador and I have been seeing each other all along! We're getting married! Isn't it wonderful? It's all arranged. I've got my last exam on Friday morning, then we're going down to his family's place in Devon, and we're going to have our wedding in the chapel on the estate.' She grasped Beth's hand. 'Will you come? It's only going to be closest of close friends – just you and Gabriel if I can get in touch with him in time, and Salvador's mother of course, and . . . oh, please say you'll come!'

Beth stared at her. 'I . . . I don't know what to say.'

'Congratulate me, Beth! You don't look very pleased.' She squeezed Beth's hand. '*Please* say you'll come. I know it's short notice, but—'

'It's not that.'

Lydia's smile began to sag. 'Then what? Beth, I can't believe you're not happy for me.'

'I am . . . That is, I . . .' Beth closed her eyes and sighed. 'Listen, Lyd, I don't think you should marry him.'

Lydia laughed. 'What? Why?'

'Call it a premonition if you like. I don't want you to marry him. Don't do it, Lyd.'

Lydia looked narrowly at her. 'I don't believe it,' she murmured. 'You're jealous.'

'No!' Beth gripped Lydia's hand in both of hers. 'Lydia, I love you more than anyone in the world, and I want you to be happy . . . But you can't marry him.'

'Why not? . . . Beth, why can't I marry him? Tell me . . .'

Beth stared at the question paper, trying to bring the words into focus, but they wouldn't come . . .

By the time she finally wandered into the examination hall, numb and dazed, she was catastrophically late; the exam had been in progress for half an hour, and heads turned to stare at her as the invigilator – a nice lady who took one look at her face and didn't scold her – guided her to an empty desk. Audrey was there, on the far side of the room, craning her neck and staring with the others.

The words washed about on the white paper. She stared, trying to squeeze sense out of them.

University of Cambridge
ENGLISH TRIPOS Part II
Wednesday 29 May 1991
Paper 7(a)

THE HISTORY AND THEORY OF LITERARY
CRITICISM
Duration: The rest of your waking life.

Answer **three** *questions chosen freely from anywhere
in the paper.*

Although **Sections A** *and* **B** *are arranged chronologically, both offer opportunities to humiliate yourself
with your ignorance of subjects falling outside these
Sections.*

*No critic should be made the central subject of more
than* **one** *answer.*

Do **not** *use the same material twice,* **either** *in this
paper* **or** *in the examination as a whole. Believe us, we
will notice if you do.*

All questions carry equal marks.

He slept with Audrey.

SECTION A

1   It's not true. It's a lie. Discuss.
2   Consider the implications of Question 1.
Conclusion: It's not a lie. Why would I make
something like that up?
3   But you know what Audrey's like. She must have
seduced him.
4   Discuss sexual morality and gender, with
reference to the concept of seduction in the Victorian
novel. Oh, for Christ's sake, this isn't the nineteenth
century – nobody seduces anyone.
5   People like Audrey do – they take advantage.
6   No they don't. They just fuck each other.
7   Go blank and silent for a while. I don't care. It
was only Audrey. I love him.

SECTION B

8   How much does the truth cost? Discuss until your
heart bleeds into your brain and you choke on your
own grief.

She opened the first of her three answer booklets and stared at the
ruled blue lines. Selecting a black biro from her little collection, she

306

wrote in the centre of the page in tiny letters: *Why?* In the second booklet, she wrote *What's it for?* And in the third, *Bugger it all to hell.* Then she closed the books, wrote her name neatly on the front of each, and secured them together with the treasury tag provided. She placed them neatly on her desk, stood up and, to the accompaniment of a silent chorus of curiously swivelling heads, collected her bag from the snowdrift of rucksacks, plastic carriers, holdalls and briefcases beside the door and walked out into the cool, quiet corridor. She was outside in the hot, close sunshine and away before the startled invigilator had time to follow her.

She walked straight to Drummer Street and caught a bus to the station, where she spent the last red margin of her overdraft on a one-way ticket. From King's Cross, it was a short underground scuttle to Paddington and, by early afternoon, she was on the Intercity, heading west.

It was only as the train plunged into the Severn tunnel that she began to realise what she had done.

9   The candidate's mind is
    a)   parboiled
    b)   tormented
    c)   going nowhere
    d)   dangerously disturbed
    e)   about to explode
    [*Choose at least two options. Use more than one book if necessary.*]

There was a brief premonition of brightness behind the glass, then the train shot out of the tunnel, shouting down its own demented echoes. The window filled with the green of embankments, the big white signboard with its red dragon and *Croeso y Cymru* flicked by, then the ground fell away and the Caldicot Level spread itself out to the south. The train raced on; past Undy and Magor, skirting the high fences of Llanwern steelworks; and began to slow as the eastern shoulder of Newport rose and fell outside the window. She already felt the weary ache of a long day done, but it wasn't over yet; today, this day of all days, she had the whole of the rest of her life lying in front of her. To be completed by tea-time. *Your time is up; stop writing now, please. Make sure that your name and purpose are written clearly on each book and that any actions by which you do not wish to be judged have been clearly crossed out.*

She watched vacantly as the brown blancmange mud of the Usk slipped by beneath the iron parapet of the bridge. As the liver-coloured walls of the castle ruins that clung tenaciously to the river bank rose, hemmed in by the road bridge, the railway and the roundabout, she stood up and walked along to the end of the carriage. She leaned against the bulkhead, her hip bumping rhythmically against its yellow plastic as the wheels hissed and clacked over the last set of points.

The train jolted to a halt, the doors swung out, and Beth became invisible, sluiced out with the tide of alighting passengers, carried anonymously across the grey beach of the platform and through the ticket hall, to be deposited on the pavement outside as the wave dispersed towards the taxi rank and the subway.

I'm Bethany Glaister, she thought. *And I'm coming home.*

The bus carved its way out of Newport and shunted up the dual carriageway through Malpas, jerking and lurching at each set of traffic lights. At the last set, on the edge of Cwmbran's outermost sprawl, where the road bottlenecked and divided, the bus no longer wound through the pre-new-town village of Llantarnam as it had done when she was a child; instead, it swung left and sped along the new, wide, clean and utterly bleak Gehenna of Cwmbran Drive. It had been conceived as an artery, feeding vitality out of Cwmbran to Newport and the northern valleys and bringing back nutrients. Instead, it seemed more like a brutal thoracic incision that bled a gore of warehouses and DIY superstores and corrugated brown industrial units onto the flanking fields. Worse than this, the new road had obliterated the stretch of canal that had once plied the same route and in whose leafy umbrage Beth had once played.

She had taken this same journey a dozen times in the last three years: once each way at the weekend bookends of her vacations. Each time, she had noted the incremental changes – the house-line that had crept a tiny bit further up the quilted green velvet of the mountainside, the bright white and steel of the new Sainsbury's store that had stolen across the road from the town centre and dumped itself down on the ground where the shambling Victorian buildings of the Electricity Board had once stood – but it was only now that the cumulative effect of all the small changes impacted on her.

McDonald's (whatever happened to the Great British Burger?) and Sainsbury's (remember Fine Fare and International?) and neat little yellow Bustlers (instead of big old ratty red buses) and Thornton's truffles (sherbet bonbons weighed into paper at two ounces or a quarter) and B&Q (dingy little hardware shops with brown-coated assistants) and Mondeos and Peugeots and Renaults and new roads; paved pavements torn up and replaced with a sludge of sad, sticky tarmac. She was too young for this to be happening. Her childhood was becoming invisible. The present was eating up her past and vomiting it out in a homogeneous, predigested mush.

10 Discuss the contention that the candidate's age and condition can be described as one or all of the following:
 f) six and a half
 g) twenty-one
 h) over seventy

At the town centre bus station, she switched to another Bustler for the short hop across rail and river to Llanyrafon. Watching the bright buses circulate around the station's giant roundabout, she found herself envying the new crop of children for whom these little sunshine-yellow Noddy vehicles would one day be vague childhood memories rather than upstart bastard usurpers. Every act of vandalism a stored-up memory.

As the Bustler thrummed down the long slope away from the railway bridge, she noted that the swings and towering steel slide had been removed from the park. Another limb hacked off. She got off at Llanyrafon shops and walked across the car park towards the sheltered little parade, remembering that the big, uneven square of newer, blacker tarmac in the corner had once been a raised hide-and-seek garden. How could things change so much so quickly?

Instead of taking the short-cut round the back of the Crow's Nest and up Mill Lane, she skirted the shops and took the long way round, via Llanyrafon Way. She felt an urge to close the loop.

Here was a haven, preserved in the leached shades of an old transparency blown up to three dimensions. Beyond the chain-link fence and the grass of the playing field, where the climbing frames and the concrete stepping-stones still sat, the school hadn't changed at all. There were still bright paintings in the windows of the Infants classes, and the Junior block, unaltered, unextended, unmodernised, still looked as orange-brick fresh as its imprint in her mind. It was afternoon break, and the children were teeming in the playground. From this distance, if she didn't look too carefully, they might even be the same children, and she could almost see herself amongst them . . . Thankfully not; she couldn't decide which threshold was worse to teeter on: the void that gaped in front of her or the path that loomed in front of these children. The treacherous leap off the last headland of fourth-year Juniors onto the jagged rocks of secondary school, and the causeway of exams that led across the narrow isthmus to sixth form, then another leap, greater, even more death-defying, out of the sanctuary of home altogether, to hack and slash her way to the cold sweat of the examination hall behind Corpus Christi. She had struggled along the path that lay in front of some of these children, and where had it brought her? Back here, that was where; trying to recede into a ghost past that she wouldn't go back to for real at any price. And as she gazed at the milling mass of children, she could feel it all beginning again inside her; the ratchet clicking on, rotating, resetting itself to zero . . .

She turned away from the fence and ran across the road. She darted left into Liswerry Drive and didn't stop running until she reached the top of the hill. She sat down on a low garden wall for a while to claw back her breath and let the breeze carry the slick of sweat off her face, then walked on.

The short spoke of Rhodri Place projected from Liswerry Drive and cut across the hillside. The short, narrow path between the front gardens of the cut-and-fill terrace was like a trench, filled with afternoon heat. Windows were open and billowing with breeze-fluttered curtains, blinds and nets, but the gardens were quiet and deserted. Except for one on the corner, where an old lady in a violet sun dress and gold sandals was poking the whining snout of an electric strimmer around her rose bushes. Beth hurried on before she was recognised and trapped. The gate of number fourteen squealed open under her hand, and she climbed up the short flight of steps to the porch (almost the only one, she realised, that hadn't been replaced by a uPVC extension). There was a key in her bag, but she knocked anyway; whenever she had been away for more than a month or two, it stopped feeling like her home, and letting herself in didn't seem right.

There was no answer. She knocked again and waited. She was about to fish out her key when the lock rattled and the door opened.

'Sorry, I was out in the back gar—'

'Hello, Mum.'

'—den . . . What on earth are you doing here?'

'Aren't you pleased to see me?'

Horrified would be closer to the mark. 'You've got exams! Why are you here?'

'Not any more I haven't.'

Rosie stood aside automatically as Beth stepped into the hall, inhaling the familiar mixture of smells: Air du Temps and cigarette smoke on a background of Mr Sheen.

'You mean they're over?' She stayed where she was, holding the knob of the open door. 'I thought—'

'Yes, a cup of tea would be nice, thank you,' said Beth, beaming pleasantly at her mother. Her smile lasted about three seconds;

310

suddenly, uncontrollably, she burst into tears. She dropped her bag and sat down heavily on the bottom stair, buried her face in her hands, and cried like a baby.

2

She had married him because he was a poet, and had stayed with him because he turned out to be prosaic. After he was killed in a way that was neither poetic nor particularly prosaic – his ageing Austin A40 crushed like an egg by an even more dilapidated and brakeless juggernaut carrying a load of caustic soda from Ellesmere Port to Sheffield – Rosie Glaister put the house in Sandbach on the market and took three-year-old Bethany back to her home town. She hadn't been back in fifteen years, and when she arrived she found that her childhood hadn't been merely nibbled and chewed and eaten away; it had been massacred wholesale, flung into a ditch and built over. She decided to settle anyway, taking a part-time job in the office at Girling and a council flat in Southville, a sprawl built over the fields where her older sister had once ridden horses. When Bethany was five, they moved to Llanyrafon, a corporation-planned suburban utopia laid out over the hilly acres where her past had contained only a riverside farm and a water mill. The proceeds from the sale of the house in Cheshire had come through, and she bought an ex-corporation house high on the hill; from the front bedroom windows, you could see the mountain and dream that nothing had changed. She had brought a lot of her husband's family heirlooms with her from Cheshire, and recreated his presence in the new house, so that his daughter might at least have a phantom father. When Beth scored a string of faultless bullseyes in her A-Levels and followed her father to university, Rosie felt that the circle had closed itself and that the struggle had been worthwhile.

But now, for some disastrous reason she couldn't begin to understand, it looked as though the circle was breaking itself apart. She barely recognised the wretched heap of wreckage crying into a mug of hot, sweet tea, slumped in the armchair her husband used to sit in to think up his poetry. (In fact, Philip Glaister had spent most of those drowsy evenings daydreaming of Sylvia, the barmaid at the Bell in Middlewich, but Rosie wasn't to know about that.)

She sat at the end of the sofa, leaning towards her daughter, wretchedly unable to make the hurt – whatever it was – go away.

'What's the matter, sweetheart?' she pleaded. 'How can I help if you won't tell me?'

Beth shook her head. 'You can't help. Not now – it's too late.'

'. . . Your exams aren't over at all, are they? You said Thursday in your letter . . .' Beth shook her head again. 'Oh dear lord. You won't get into trouble, will you? What about your degree?'

'I don't care. I don't want it.'

'Oh, come on, that's just silly talk. Of course you want it.'

'I don't.'

'Yes, you do. Look how hard you've worked . . .' She looked shrewdly at Beth. 'Is it boyfriend trouble? Have you fallen out with Danny?'

Beth blew her nose. 'Hardly. I split up with Danny weeks ago, Mum.'

'Oh . . . He seemed so nice.'

'You never met him.'

'No, but—'

'Look, it's nothing to do with Danny, okay?'

'All right, darling, all right . . . Is it the exams, then? You've always been so good with exams.'

'Tripos is a bit different from A-Levels.'

'Of course it is. I expect there's a lot of pressure, but you're such a strong girl.' She laughed; a forced little chuckle. 'I was talking to Irene the other day, and I said to her, my Beth's—'

'Pregnant.'

'—done so well for herself, I can hardly . . . Pardon?'

'I'm pregnant, Mum.'

They stared at each other across a gulf of silence susurrating with tension and the distant whine of Irene Ashby's strimmer. Rosie's hands began to tremble, and her limbs went numb; like every daughter's mother, she had imagined this scene a thousand times, but she had always managed to recast it as a happy announcement, an occasion for hugs and congratulations. Beth's degree. Beth's career. Beth's fiancé. Beth's wedding. *Then* Beth's baby; that was the order it was supposed to come in.

'Oh dear, no,' she murmured. 'Does Danny know?'

Beth dug her fingertips into her eyes. 'Danny, Danny, Danny,' she wailed. 'Why should he know? It's none of his business.'

'Of course it is – if you're carrying his chi—'

'Will you shut up about Danny! He doesn't know, and he's never going to!'

With that, Beth jumped out of her chair and stormed out of the room, slamming the door behind her and thundering up the stairs. Rosie stared at the door, in a stupor. When she heard the bedroom door slam, she slumped back on the sofa, sighing and reflecting that some things, after all, never changed.

312

The role of mothers, their purpose in life, is to always, always, without exception, say the wrong thing.

3

The wedding took place, but not quite as planned. It was several weeks later than intended, and not one of Lydia's friends or relatives was there.

Gabriel and Helen were on holiday. Beth was off the list, even had she been around to invite. It would take Lydia a long time to forgive her for what she had said. When she confronted Salvador with Beth's allegation, he denied it. He seemed genuinely hurt, and so she believed him; Beth *was* just jealous. Of course, Audrey couldn't be invited; it would be so embarrassing. And Rachel, well, it would be awkward having just her; they would have to lie and make excuses for the others' absence, and that would spoil the event. So, they invited nobody.

They were married, as they had planned, in the Château chapel. Madame de La Simarde was there. She had startled Salvador by agreeing readily to a small wedding, and she stood curiously unmoved throughout the ceremony. The priest from Wheddend Church, who had an ecumenical bent and didn't object to the Catholic liturgy, officiated. Finally, the household servants made up the small congregation; Février and Avril standing together at the back of the chapel, coming forward at the end to sign as witnesses.

Madame de La Simarde offered the newlyweds a honeymoon: anywhere in the world for as long as they desired, and she would pay. She wanted them to feel encouraged to indulge themselves carnally; that way, Salvador might wear down his urges and drift back to music, and Lydia might be quickly impregnated. At Lydia's request, however, Salvador declined the offer politely. Instead, they chose a room in the Italian Wing with a four-poster bed and a view over the lake, and spent three weeks exploring Dartmoor. Lydia was enchanted by the Château. With the memory of the ruin at Gondecourt still sharp in her mind, it seemed quite magical: the dead shell reconstituted and resurrected. She

314

retraced the route of her furtive exploration, marvelling at every fresh detail restored: the Music Room, the hallway, the great staircase. She climbed up the stairs and located Violina's room on the second floor. Philippe-France de La Simarde had been truly obsessive in his replication of the original: the fireplace was identical, and even the little hiding place in the chimney had been reproduced. She visited that room often. She would stand by the ivyless window and listen to the ghosts of the other place. Surrounded by whole walls and furniture, the story of Violina became so vivid that she could almost see her: right there, on the chair between the window and the fireplace.

At the end of those three weeks, their honeymoon was over. They didn't move on, but their stay somehow stopped feeling like a holiday. They went out less and less, and what trips they made weren't holidayish. In August, they drove up to Cambridge for Lydia's graduation. None of her friends were there: she was Social Sciences, and Arts graduands were to be processed separately. While there, Salvador formally resigned his fellowship and arranged for his belongings to be moved to Devon. They returned via London, where Salvador had a meeting with Mark Stabile, an old acquaintance from America. He was setting up a recording studio in London, and Salvador was considering investing in the project. The meeting was inconclusive, and they returned to the Château with their lives still undecided.

The future's months peeled away slowly: Christmas came and went. Then, one morning in February, Madame de La Simarde asked Salvador to come to the Music Room. She wished to talk.

She began by asking him if he had enough money. She was still providing him with his stipendiary 'supplement', only now he had no expenses to cover. Yes, he had plenty of money. Did he have any immediate or long-term plans? Was he, for example, intending to resume his musical career? He bristled slightly at the inflection she placed on the word *musical*: she tolerated the presence of his electric instruments in the Château, but made no pretence of approving of them; he had to keep them in the Italian Wing, well away from her sight and hearing. He prevaricated: it was a possibility, he said. And Lydia? She was looking for a job. Unfortunately, there didn't seem to be much demand for geography graduates. Perhaps, he suggested, a little assistance from an influential relative would help.

He opened the piano and pressed out a sequence of soft, random jazz chords, just to be provocative. 'What do you think?' he asked. 'I'm sure you still have some strings you can pull. I was thinking perhaps the Foreign Office. Uncle Valéry used to have a lot of friends there.'

His mother was silent for a long while. When she spoke, she sounded unusually tentative: 'Do you not wish to begin a family?'

Salvador turned away from the keyboard and laughed. 'Me? A family? Good God, no.'

'You seem very decided. Does Lydia have an opinion on the matter? Have you discussed it?'

He was nonplussed. 'Well, not really.'

'Perhaps you should, rather than making decisions on your wife's behalf.'

He smiled wryly at her. 'Papa wouldn't have dared do that to you, would he, Maman?'

She ignored him. 'Talk to her. I shall be leaving for Gondecourt on Friday. You are aware of what date falls next week?'

He looked down at the carpet. 'Yes, Maman.'

'I see in your face that you would not wish to accompany me.'

'No, Maman.'

'Very well. I shall pardon you this once, but upon one condition. When I return next month, you shall have talked to your wife and reached a decision. I cannot see the two of you aimless like this. You are cluttering up my home.'

Madame de La Simarde took her servants with her to Gondecourt. Joseph, the gardener, came in from Wheddend each day and kept the ancient, ramshackle heating system ticking over, but aside from that, they had to fend for themselves. They had the run of seventy-nine rooms above and below stairs, and they made full use of it. Their *real* honeymoon started here. They hatched a challenge for themselves: to have sex in every single room, from bedroom to kitchen and from cellar to turret-top. If they did it twice a day (three times a day on weekends), they could just about reach their target by the time Salvador's mother returned. They started enthusiastically, and by the end of the first week had sampled a fair slice of the Château and a stimulating range of surfaces, from tasselled cushions to stove-warmed flagstones, and from heaped silk and satin drapery to rough oak tables. After nineteen rooms in eight days, Salvador's testicles started to feel like they had been bounced off the walls, and only the challenge was keeping him going. The pace flagged, and they turned to other diversions, returning to copulation whenever they felt up to it. Salvador drove them around in the vintage cars from his grandfather's collection. Those that were suitable went out on the road, while others they just took for spins around the estate. Mark Stabile was invited for a weekend, and he brought with him an entourage of musicians and record company hangers-on. Speakers were set up in the galleries, and the courtyard was flooded with music. They danced under the cold moonlight and went to bed with the owls.

One evening, when his mother's return was imminent, Salvador finally got around to doing as she had ordered: he brought up the subject of children. Lydia astonished him by leaping enthusiastically on the idea the moment he trundled it past her.

'But you're only twenty-one years old!' he protested.

'Twenty-two in April.'

'Big difference. What about a job, a career? Don't you want to live a bit first?'

She pointed out that, while she might be twenty-one, he was thirty, and it might not do to wait *too* long. And anyway, what was so terrific about a career? Had *his* career fulfilled him? Besides, there was nothing to stop her getting a job if she wanted one; there was such a thing as childminders. The more she thought about it, the more she warmed to it. Her *own family*; it was what she had been yearning for all these years.

When she put it that way, he had to agree. Somehow, having a child (*children*, she corrected) and their own home, away from here, would finally close the loop of independence from his mother that he had been assiduously but unsuccessfully building around himself since he was eighteen.

When Madame de La Simarde returned at the end of March and was told of their revised intentions, she was enraptured. Perhaps Salvador had chosen his wife with a modicum of wisdom after all. She went to the chapel and knelt before the altar. She lit a candle and prayed, handing up to God a list of instructions: That her daughter-in-law's womb be fertile and impregnated without delay; That the first-born child be a boy; And that he bear in the greatest proportion the divinely gifted genes of his paternal line.

Preparations were set in train. She (not Lydia) selected a room in the Old Wing for her grandson's nursery (the one Salvador and his ancestors had been raised in was unsuitable, because it was too far away from her apartments and had no adjoining room for a nurse or nanny), and had it decorated and furnished in a suitably edifying style. Once that was completed, she began consulting London agencies for suitable qualified, experienced and socially acceptable care staff.

A month passed and there was no happy announcement. Two months, three, four, five, and still nothing happened. Hedon was gradually squeezed out of their sex-life and replaced by charts and calendars and temperatures. They came in from the wild uplands of sensual abandon and took seats in the stuffy waiting-room of *trying for a baby*. (Whenever he heard that phrase, Salvador got a mental image of a fairground grabber-crane game.) But try as they might, Lydia's womb remained obstinately closed for business; dusty blinds drawn down and no tenant in residence. The atmosphere in the Château grew palpably tense as time passed by.

After nine months, Madame de La Simarde decided that enough was more than a feast. She took out a lease on a flat in London and scoured Harley Street for the best infertility specialist she could find. Salvador and Lydia, deciding that acquiescence was the better part of discretion, moved to the city and began a long, slow process of dehumanisation: a series of samples, examinations and tests which reduced their human personalities to sets of malfunctioning reproductive machinery. When the final results of the tests were established, everyone was surprised. Salvador's semen was apparently chock-full of healthy, well-adjusted sperm, while Lydia's internal equipment could have been a showroom example. The doctor suggested that their problem must have a psychological cause, and recommended a colleague who specialised in just the sort of therapy they required. They declined, with thanks, and he sent them away with the recommendation that they just stop worrying about it. If they did that, then everything would work out.

Everything did not work out. During her time in London, Lydia had experienced a drastic change of heart. She no longer dreamed of babies; instead, she had nightmares of monsters. Inevitably, they had become acquainted with several other infertile couples, and Lydia had been struck by their combination of wild optimism and bitter sadness. Their psychological defence against their problem seemed to be obsessive assault, like an indefatigable besieging army. Some had been trying for years. They were obsessed with their infertility, obsessed with the arsenal of possible cures, obsessed with their utterly consuming *need* for a baby. And they all shared the absolute conviction that the perfect family they yearned for could only be achieved by producing a baby from their own bodies. Fostering or adopting somebody else's was not even an issue. Listening to them talk, she realised that she didn't share their sentiments at all. Taking down her pants and spreading her legs for the endoscope, seeing her innards on the screen, poring through luridly illustrated magazines, she found herself more and more repelled by the biological baseness of fertilisation and pregnancy. Babies no longer made her mind swirl with a mélange of ga-ga sweetness, teddy bears and balloon wallpaper; they made her think of blood and seed pods and mucous membranes. The idea of a baby *growing inside her body* no longer seemed sublime and semi-magical; instead, it made her think of the *Alien*.

She didn't want to have a baby any more. At least, not one of her own, not yet. Salvador agreed, and they went back to Devon with a sense of relief, like people stepping out of a delirium. They told his mother they would keep trying, and Lydia resumed taking her pills.

The effect on Geneviève wasn't particularly noticeable at first. She grew rather quiet, and took to visiting the new nursery to gaze into the

318

empty cot. She also spent a lot of time in the Music Room, listening to Salvador's records and poring through albums of family photographs, coming back again and again to the pictures of her two sons. At night, her long, lonely waking hours were filled with the echoes of Salvador's music and the struggle to make sense of what was happening. Were they telling her the truth? *Was* there a physical problem? If so, it couldn't be with Salvador. His father had never had a problem with virility; indeed, his lack of problems in that regard had in itself been a problem on occasions. Lydia was an unknown quantity; there could easily be a problem there. But what if they *were* telling the truth? The implications of that didn't bear thinking about, but she couldn't help herself; she thought about them anyway. If there was no physical problem, then something much more serious was implied. She, Geneviève de La Simarde, had somehow erred; her children's barrenness was a judgement upon her. She went to the chapel and knelt before the altar and asked for guidance, but God was silent. Day after day, the silence went on; she was forsaken. Then, in the humid stillness of a summer night, she had a vision. It came to her just like the vision that had heralded the resurrection of Salvador, in a dazzling light that filled the room. Instead of angels, though, she saw all of her family: her husband, her mother and father, François de La Simarde, all the men and women who had fought for the survival of this great line, back to the Last Marquis and beyond; all crowded around her bed, staring down at her with contempt while she clutched at the sheets and cowered. Then the congregation parted and a small figure came forward. She cried out in joy and relief as she recognised her son: her first-born; her gift from God; her one true Salvador. He climbed up onto her bed and spoke to her.

> *Your first chance was life,*
> *And you failed it.*
> *Your second chance was resurrection,*
> *And you failed it.*
> *Your third chance was duty,*
> *And you failed it.*
> *Your fourth chance is love.*
> *Your fifth chance is yet to come.*
> *Your last chance shall be death.*

As he spoke, the figures faded away one by one. Then, with the last word, Salvador too shimmered and vanished, and she was alone.

She remembered his words forever after. She took one of his photographs from the album and wrote them on the back. *Life,*

Resurrection, Duty, Love became a mantra. Life, Resurrection, Duty, Love. And Death. *Your fourth chance is love.* She had no doubt what was meant by the words. *This* was her fourth chance, and in impatiently pressing her son to produce the next generation, she had come perilously close to failing again. Her fourth chance was to make good her third failure.

4

Geneviève de La Simarde did not believe in coincidence; like luck and hope, it was an artificial construct conceived by weak personalities to absolve themselves from responsibility, duty and discomfiting truth. So, when she received a letter a few days after her vision, she recognised it for what it was: an opportunity.

Salvador was summoned to the Music Room for another discussion of the future. He had noticed that his mother seemed to be more like her old self during these past few days, and he was wary. This time, there was no talk of children. She began by showing a token interest in his studio project (he had finally decided to proceed with the venture, and had been spending a lot of time in London recently, helping with the design and the selection of stock instruments). Then she produced the letter.

'This has come from Bernhard Stracher,' she said. 'Do you remember Bernhard?'

Of course he did; Bernhard was a composer and concert promoter, and for two years had been Salvador's personal tour manager. He had finally been driven off by the strain of constantly having to compete with Madame de La Simarde over boundaries of responsibility. He had always been particularly fond of Salvador, however, and the sentiment was mutual.

'How is he?' asked Salvador.

'Very well, it appears. He has married recently; for, I believe, the *third* time.' She permitted herself a little smile at this. 'His new wife is a cellist with the London Symphony Orchestra. Bernhard believes she has the talent to be a soloist. He is organising something he calls a *showcase* for her at the Bitburg Festival in September.'

'He's still in the business, then?'

'Oh yes.' She consulted the letter again. 'His reason for writing to me – and you may laugh at this – is to inquire whether you are still *in the business*, as you put it.'

'Why might I laugh at that?'

320

She gazed at him. 'He has followed your career, Salvador, and has heard of your involvement in pop groups. He asks whether you still play *real music*. Do not get angry; those are his words, not mine, and I think there is a little irony in them. It seems he admires the orchestral compositions of that alarming man whose pop group you joined . . .' She scanned the letter again, searching for the name.

'You mean Zappa?'

'Him. It appears the Festival is to feature a performance of some of his works by a German ensemble, and it was this that made Bernhard think of you. He has been looking again at some of the pieces you composed when you were under his care, and says how struck he has been by their quality.'

'Really? I've always thought they were childish daubs.'

'Well, he does not.'

Salvador folded his arms and looked shrewdly at her. 'Maman, where is this leading?'

She frowned. 'Leading?'

'I sense an impending Big Question.'

'There is no big question. I merely intended to ask what you wish me to tell Bernhard when I reply to his letter. Shall I tell him that you still play, or shall I tell him that you no longer wish to be a part of his world?'

Salvador considered the question. In truth, he didn't really play any more: it had been two years since he had done anything other than toy with never-to-be-finished experimental compositions, and even longer since he had played with other musicians. When he thought about it like that, he realised how much he missed it. Running a studio was all very well, but . . .

'Tell him I still play,' he said. 'Also tell him those pieces of mine he has are garbage. I did some much better ones after that. If you wait a little, I'll give you copies to send with your letter.'

It all started well. Bernhard wrote back, fizzing with enthusiasm for the selection of new Etudes and Preludes. They showed, he said, that Salvador's boyhood genius had matured just as it had always promised. These pieces were *true originals*. He rhapsodised at length about the delights that might be had from hearing Salvador himself actually *play* these masterpieces. He never saw the best piece, though. Despite Lydia's pleading, Salvador didn't send *Evening Whispers Echoed*. That one, he insisted, was strictly private. Outwardly, he maintained a distinctly laconic attitude to his concession to the musical world that claimed to love him. Inwardly, though, he felt a tingle of gratification at Bernhard's praise. He read through the pieces himself, studying their smallest details, standing back and viewing their structure, and had to conclude that, in fact, they really were rather good. Without quite being aware of what he was doing, he had attempted to marry the flavours and tonality of the classical music drip-fed into his veins since birth with the modernist complexities he had discovered during his years in outer darkness. This had led to a thwarting of traditional forms of *theme one, variation, theme two, restatement of theme, variation, recombination,* in which the music was perpetually dragged back to its origins. He had tried to make compositions that grew like stories, starting at one point and moving constantly forward, every phrase an unfolding of new thoughts. A music that was like life itself. Without realising it, he had achieved a form and flavour that was uniquely his, that owed no homage to the dead.

In late August, Bernhard wrote to him again, this time with a proposition. Although it was too late now for Bitburg, he was on the organising committee for another similar festival, to be held in Milan the following May. The draft programme for the penultimate day of the festival was currently being finalised. Sonja Sacher would be performing again, and there would be another selection of pieces by Zappa played by the same German ensemble. In between, there was a slot of approximately fifty minutes remaining to be filled. Would Salvador, by any chance, be willing to give a recital? Bernhard had taken the liberty of showing the new compositions to the committee, and they were keen.

Salvador didn't even need to consider: he telephoned Bernhard immediately and agreed to play. The prospect of airing his works side by side with music by the man who was the closest thing he had ever had to a hero was too much to resist. To his mother's unsuspecting delight (she hadn't heard any of the pieces, and was unable to read the manuscripts), he shut himself away with his instruments and immersed himself in refining and practising his pieces. For a few months, it seemed to Madame de La Simarde almost as though the old days had come back.

Then two things happened; things which made it clear that the old days were gone, and would never come back.

On Tuesday 7 December 1993, Salvador heard a piece of news that knocked the breath out of his body. Three days previously, at his home in Los Angeles, Frank Zappa had died. Salvador hadn't even known he had been ill. Apparently, it had been common knowledge for the past two years, so why had nobody told him about it? How had he managed not to hear?

He spent two whole weeks shut away in his practice room, listening to his Zappa records, his guitars standing untouched around him. Suddenly, there was a hole in the centre of his universe. He sensed the music slowly leaking out through the hole, and black thoughts seeping in to take its place. When he had listened to every last note on every last record several times over, he felt a little calmer, and set about plugging the hole. The *ass*hole; the place where broken hearts belonged. He picked up his guitars again and resumed playing. Out of the remnants of his grief he built a new composition and dedicated it to the memory of the great bandmaster. When he played it for Lydia, she declared it the best piece of music he had ever made.

The other thing that happened came in April. Final arrangements for the Milan Festival were under way. A programme of pieces had been submitted and approved by the committee; travel tickets and hotels had been booked. Lydia had promised to go with him, braving the Channel again for his sake. Then, with only a week to go, bending like a spoon under the constant pressure of gentle pestering, he decided to let his mother hear what he was planning to play.

She hadn't heard a single note of his programme. Her vision of the original Salvador had shaken her badly; since that night, she had been uncharacteristically reticent; even diffident in the presence of her son. The unaccustomed absence of hectoring dictatorship had disorientated him; first encouraging his secrecy, then leading him to spring the whole spectacle upon her in one performance.

He set up his instruments in the Music Room. Even with assistance from Lydia and Février, it took half a morning to carry the equipment across from his Secret Compositional Research Laboratory (as Lydia called it) in the Italian Wing. When everything was ready, Madame de La Simarde was summoned from her apartments. She came, all nervous excitement and expectant awe. When she walked into the room, she stopped dead and stared at the little stage at the far end. The grand piano had been pushed back against the curved wall of the tower to make way for a tall amplifier. Beside it was a rack of black boxes covered with knobs and winking starship lights. A spaghetti-strew of wires connected this construction with another box on the floor in front of Salvador's chair. To one side, lined up on stands, were his guitars: a recently acquired Aria Knight Warrior in black, bought for its multiple coil-taps and Kahler tremolo; his Gibson Les Paul, identical to the one he had met in Monsieur Duprée's shop twenty years ago (he had tracked one down in a Soho shop and spent half a year's stipend on it); and finally, his Fleta. Even this had not been spared the virus of electrification: a tiny clip-on transducer had been attached to its soundboard, trailing a thread-thin wire.

He watched as his mother recovered partial control of her limbs and walked, zombie-slow, to the seat set out for her, where Lydia was already waiting. Then, when he was satisfied that all was ready, he picked up the Fleta and sat down on his chair.

The recital lasted forty-five minutes, and Madame de La Simarde maintained a remarkable degree of composure throughout. She didn't cover her ears or scream or flee from the room; she simply sat with a fixed nightmare stare on her face. In fact, the sounds that came out of the towering black amplifier were not entirely displeasing; certainly nowhere near the unspeakable hideousness she had expected. The notes, especially those produced by the Fleta, filtered through chorus, phase and delay effects, took on layers of richness that were quite astonishing: at times, it seemed as though the timbral harmonics of a small orchestra were haunting the interstices of the instrument's tone. Given time – given a very great deal of time – she might *almost* have grown to like the tonal qualities Salvador had discovered. She could never, though, regard the shapes described by these sounds as anything other than hideous and sickening. Her son's pieces were composed of uncomfortable metres and weird, alien polyphonies which were as far removed from the sublime symmetry of Sor or Tárrega as the Pit was from Heaven.

She clapped mechanically at the end of each piece, and when the performance was over, she rose from her seat and left the room in stunned silence. She went across to the chapel, stood before the altar and demanded to know what was happening: Was this a test, or was God simply mocking her? She received no answer, and concluded that it must be a test. She had been told not to forsake her son, but to love him, and she had responded by giving him no *guidance*. What she had just been shown was the result of her neglect. Something had to be done to rectify her mistake.

From the chapel, she went to the parterre and walked up and down between the flower beds, discussing the problem with herself and trying to calm down. Was she, perhaps, making a mistake about this music? She quickly dismissed the notion. Bernhard was a good promoter, but she had no faith in his artistic tastes. Nor was there anyone on the Milan committee whose judgement she would trust. Had Segovia – or any of the great men with whom Salvador had once associated – heard his performance this afternoon, they would have been as appalled as she; it was not music, it was merely dissonance and cacophony. Adolescent masturbation once more, but in public. If he were allowed to replicate this in Milan, he would be humiliated and disgraced. And if he were humiliated and disgraced, then so would she and the whole house of de La Simarde. She had to prevent it, but she must at the same time be diplomatic. *Your fourth chance is love*, she whispered to the roses.

When she returned to the Music Room, she found Salvador and Lydia deep in conversation. The electronic monsters were still switched on and idling, emitting a faint hum. She apologised for her sudden exit; she had been simply overwhelmed by what she had heard. Salvador braced himself and asked for her honest opinion. She hesitated a moment, then said the music was very nice. Unfortunately, that alerted him right away; Geneviève de La Simarde *never* described *anything* as 'very nice'. Like or dislike, her opinions were always expressed in a tumble of florid adjectives. He pressed her further: What had she *really* thought? Surely the music was not to her taste?

'I think you over-estimate my conservatism,' she said. 'I am not quite such a *stick-in-the-mud*.' She smiled self-consciously, belying her own assertion; as though using a colloquialism were akin to wearing clown's shoes.

'Then tell me your opinion. I want to know exactly what you think.'

She sat down on a sofa and folded her hands in her lap, as if to give the question the full weight of her considered judgement. 'These were all your own compositions?' she asked. He nodded, and she thought some more. 'I believe,' she said at last, 'that what I have heard this afternoon shows that you have great potential as a composer.'

He glanced at Lydia. 'Potential?'

'*Great* potential. A promise that your skill in creation will eventually match your genius for interpreting the works of others.'

He jumped to his feet. 'Potential? Promise? I've been working on these pieces . . . for *years*, some of them.'

She gazed up at him, and her eyes beamed with good intentions. 'Time is important,' she said, 'but the equation is not so simple. Perhaps I must take a portion of the blame for this. I have encouraged you to believe that time invested may be reaped measure for measure. This is true when one is practising one's craft, but not necessarily so when *art* is the subject. *Creation.* There, time spent in contemplation may result in inspiration. However, great art will not come from working hard and long. Contemplate; grow as a man. You shall find that, as you achieve greater maturity, so your capacity to create will become greater. I know this is true, because I see the promise in what you have just played.'

Salvador took a deep breath and snorted. 'So, I've been wasting my time.'

'I did not say that.'

'Then what? Get to the point, for Christ's sake.'

Madame de La Simarde wondered how long she could keep this up.

325

She was unaccustomed to being addressed in this abrupt, insolent manner, especially by a boy on whom she had lavished such care; a boy who repaid all that she had done for him by vomiting up such indescribably ugly noise and insulting his betters by calling it music.

'All I wish to suggest,' she went on, suppressing her anger, 'is that you might reconsider your programme for the Festival; that it might be judicious to put your compositions aside – not all of them – and perform some classical pieces. I am sure you could manage to rehearse in the time available. Works of truly great art; works which the audience will know. Do not forget that you have been away for a long time. Your first duty must be to restore the standing you once had, and you shall not achieve that by playing a programme consisting entirely of ill-conceived, immature compositions.'

'Ill-conceived,' he murmured, and smiled. 'You know, I find myself wondering what Salvador would have done in this situation.'

Lydia stiffened. She had been listening with a growing sense of foreboding, wondering when the spectre of Salvador the First would rise between them. She took a step towards him and touched his sleeve. 'Salvador,' she whispered. 'Don't. Can't we talk about this another time?'

Madame de La Simarde looked at her. 'Your wife has a conciliatory bent. I have remarked it in her.' Her gaze returned to her son. 'Well, I have tried conciliation. You have replied with petulance. Salvador . . . My son . . .' Her eyes glazed over, as though she were trying to catch an elusive thought. 'Love,' she murmured, and her eyes came back to life. She stood up and touched his chest. 'My son is in you,' she said. 'You know what he would think and what he would have you do.'

'Play Tárrega, perhaps? Sor, Giulani, Schubert, Falla, Turina? Heaven forbid – Villa-Lobos even?'

'Yes, yes, all of these. Even Villa-Lobos. If God gave my Salvador a genius, it was to judge between great art and mediocrity.'

Salvador laughed. 'To judge it, perhaps. Anything but *play* it.'

She stared at him. 'I beg your pardon?'

Lydia gripped his arm and tried to turn him towards her. 'Salvador,' she pleaded. 'Stop it.' She looked imploringly at Madame de La Simarde. 'Can't you leave him alone? You're making him say things. He doesn't mean it.'

'My sons do not say things they do not mean. Explain yourself, Salvador.'

His anger finally peaked. He pushed Lydia aside and stooped over his mother. For a moment, she thought he would strike her again, and her face twisted with a mixture of alarm and defiance. But he just huffed and snarled furiously for a few breaths, then turned away. 'Dead people, dead people,' he fumed. 'Why does it always have to be dead people with you? Dead composers, dead sons, dead ancestors. Is it because they can be controlled? Show you anything – a piece of music, a piece of writing, a piece of human behaviour or emotion – and you go, What a piece of shit! This was done by some *alive* person. Bring on the dead – they know what's good! No fucking around now – gimme that dead-person music . . . I've had enough of it, Maman. Salvador is dead. I'm alive, I'm creating things, and he's just a bunch of bones in a tomb.'

Her face coiled down in fury, and she sprang. 'How *dare* you speak his name with such filth in your mouth! Had it not been for his genius, you would have been *nothing*. While he lived in you, you had something; now there is just common ugliness.' She seized his hands and held them up. '*His* genius animated these fingers. There is nothing of your own in here!'

Salvador stared down at her, horrified, for a few long heartbeats. Then he wrenched his fingers from her grasp and stormed across the room towards the stage. His guitars and amplifier clanged and boomed as he shoved them aside. Single-handedly, he hauled the piano away from the wall and rested one hand on its rim.

Too late, Lydia saw what he was doing. She watched in horror as his free hand scythed out and swept away the prop. The lid fell and drowned her scream in a single, colossal eighty eight-note open chord.

The vibrations were still echoing around inside the piano's ebony body when she ran up onto the stage. Salvador was lying on the boards, curled into a ball, face twisted in agony. One hand was clamped under his armpit, and the sleeve of his shirt was already blackening with blood.

She squatted down and tried to cradle him in her arms, but he kept writhing and twisting out of her grasp. She looked back at his mother, who just stood and stared. '*Call an ambulance!*' she screamed, but Madame de La Simarde just continued staring blankly back at her. 'What are you waiting for? *Call a fucking ambulance!*'

5

The surgeon, having done his best with Salvador's hand, now did his best to answer the women's questions. He assured Lydia that, although he had lost a lot of blood and did indeed look very ill, he would certainly recover. Madame de La Simarde's questions were harder to answer. Being something of an amateur musician himself, he knew a little of what might be expected. In his humble opinion, it seemed improbable that Salvador would ever play again. Had it been his *right* hand, it might have been easier. He had done his best to repair the damage, but there were limits to medical science and human physiology. The index finger was only broken, but the third and fourth digits had been very badly crushed: the bones were shattered, and there was a great deal of damage to the muscles and tendons. The fingers had been repaired and set with the utmost care, but the patient was unlikely to ever regain the degree of dexterity he had once had, even with prolonged physiotherapy. As for the middle finger, they would have to wait and see. It had taken remarkably well, considering the circumstances. Prognosis was problematic. They would just have to wait and see.

Wait and see. Demand, plead and threaten as much as she liked, Madame de La Simarde could get no better than that from any of the surgeons she consulted.

Salvador knew better. Sitting up in his hospital bed, he looked down at the swaddle of bandages at the end of his arm, two purple fingertips protruding, striated with black stitches, and he knew it was over.

His memory was shot through with thick patches of haze. What he remembered most was the noise. Lydia and his mother screaming and shouting, his own moans; the rending, splintering cacophony as Février tore apart the innards of the piano with a poker, searching for the severed middle finger. Then there was the noise of the siren and the noise of the pain yelling in his hand . . . then nothing.

News had spread quickly. The bedside table was a forest of cards. From Lydia, from Bernhard, from Krstov, from people he hadn't met in years. There was even one from Sir Michael Jacobs. Nothing from Maman, though. This time, she had no words to pass on from Salvador; no dead-person judgements to give him. He looked at his hand from the outside; coldly, as though it belonged to somebody else, and he sensed it from the inside, probing into the nerve endings. Over. Finished. There was no music left in there; dead-person or otherwise, it had all gone. If only he could crush it out of his head as well, he might be able to rest.

When he came out of hospital, he found the Château in a state of upheaval. Madame de La Simarde had decided that the household would move to Gondecourt. Since the duration of their stay would be indefinite, the move involved more preparation than usual. Things had to be packed, furniture, paintings and drapery had to be put under wraps, arrangements had to be made with the part-time outdoor staff. Salvador asked why they were moving. Lydia told him that his mother had decreed it for the sake of better air and better medical attention. This was only half-true. Madame de La Simarde had decided not to voice the belief that, if he were ever to recover the use of his gift, it would be by living in closer proximity to its source.

Salvador went along with the move; he didn't have the energy to argue. He did, however, insist on two conditions: that his Lotus be transported out to Gondecourt, and that every last item of musical equipment be left behind.

Madame de La Simarde complied with the first condition, but not the second. She made a show of agreeing, then ordered Février to pack the guitars in secret. She knew her son's mind better than he knew it himself: she wanted to be able, when he eventually began to recover his senses, to produce the instruments he would inevitably need.

They were never asked for, never touched. At Gondecourt, Salvador withdrew into himself. He spoke to Lydia, but hardly at all to his mother. After a while, even his conversations with Lydia grew fewer and less. He read a lot, and spent hours just sitting in a chair, staring at his claw-crooked hand. The fingers, even months after their crushing and severing, were stiff as shoe leather and dry twigs; when he tried to move them, all his crippled hand could manage was a spastic spider-crawl across his lap. A therapist came each day and made him do exercises, but he knew it was useless. He sat and stared, sat and stared, and thought about the enormity of what he had done. Such new notes as came into his head were drowned out by the inculcated old melodies of the Salvador time. He tried to think them out, but they wouldn't go; he tried to write them out, but they wouldn't go. The only thing he could do was *drive* them out.

6

What happened was well documented, but ambiguous enough to give the world grist for speculation. Madame de La Simarde was not forthcoming, either in confirming or refuting the rumours. She attended the inquest veiled in black, gave her evidence, and spoke to no one. Her daughter-in-law, also veiled, did the same. The evidence heard was as follows.

At approximately 10:20 a.m. on Monday 13 February 1995, Février Moreau, a domestic servant employed by the family, witnessed

Monsieur de La Simarde leaving the estate in his Lotus Elan. He thought nothing of it; it was nearly ten months since his accident, and his hand had healed sufficiently for him to drive without difficulty. In fact, he often went out driving. Monsieur Moreau had noticed nothing peculiar in Monsieur de La Simarde's behaviour that morning; nor had Madame Geneviève de La Simarde, his mother; nor had Madame Lydia de La Simarde, his wife. There had been no note; indeed, no communication of any kind.

Between approximately 11:00 and 11:10 a.m., several motorists witnessed a red sports car with a British registration plate driving erratically on the D 951 between Confolens and St Claud. It was going extremely fast and overtaking recklessly. Shortly after, at 11:27 a.m., gendarmes witnessed a vehicle of the same description on the D 12 in the Forêt de la Braconne. They recorded a speed in excess of 140 kilometres per hour and set off in pursuit. They followed the car for some distance, signalling for it to stop, but lost sight of it in the lanes near Champniers. The third and final recorded sighting of the vehicle was at the junction of the N 10 and N 141 near Angoulême. Again, it was travelling at extreme speed: estimates varied between 120 and 160 kilometres per hour. Several witnesses saw the little red car weaving between fast-moving traffic on the slip-road joining the westbound N 141. The driver appeared to lose control, and the car veered onto the main carriageway. It clipped the side of a lorry and went spinning across the central barrier into the path of an oncoming truck. The car came to rest on its back, very badly crushed. Its soft roof was completely flattened. Paramedics arrived on the scene within ten minutes, but the driver was found to be already dead. (The written evidence submitted to the court by the hospital but not read out loud stated that the body was decapitated.) The driver, formally identified as Salvador Honoré François Philippe de La Simarde, had no traces of alcohol or drugs in his bloodstream. Several witnesses, including the two lorry drivers, had been treated for shock, but none were seriously injured.

Despite rumours of suicide that had been circulating in the press, the verdict of the inquest was accidental death caused by reckless driving.

The funeral service was held in the chapel of the Château de Méringat, a little toy château on the Vienne which had once been a part of the de La Simarde estates. It poured with rain, and the overflow of mourners who could not fit into the chapel stood with heads bowed under umbrellas on the gravelled courtyard. Valéry de Perez, uncle of the deceased, read the eulogy and assumed the role of chief mourner. His sister, Madame Geneviève de La Simarde, although present in body, was absent in sense. Seeming almost as dead as the dead themselves, she processed behind the coffin from the chapel to the car and, nineteen kilometres later, from the car to the heart of Gondecourt cemetery. There, Salvador the Second was interred in the family tomb beside his brother and his ancestors. When the ceremony was over, Valéry had to lead her away; left to herself, she might have stood there for all eternity, staring, staring, staring . . .

Equally staring, equally idiotised, was Lydia. She did not go to the funeral. Instead, she sat at the table in the great humid kitchen with Avril, who had been ordered to stay behind to look after her. That morning, she had suddenly decided that she couldn't go; she couldn't bear to see him put into that heartless block of stone. There had been no argument: Madame de La Simarde had not (for once) had the will, nor Valéry the heart, to force her to attend. The argument that might otherwise have taken place was instead split into little packets of bitter, snide recrimination and scattered across the years that were to come.

A week or two after the funeral, Lydia finally felt ready to confide her feelings to her notebook. When she took it out and opened it, a folded sheet of paper fell out onto her lap.

Lydia,
He is still here. Here inside me. The only way for me to destroy him would be to destroy her, and I cannot do that. I cannot tell her what he really was, nor will she see what I really am. There are structures in us, set into the foundations of our souls, and nothing can unmake them.
Dearest Lydia, I have crippled the thing that kept me living. Without it, I do not have the power to fight against the dead. You have seen how it is; even with it, I did not have that power. They are all around me; they outnumber me and are greater than me. There is only one way to be equal to them.
Dearest Lydia, I know I led you to believe that you were the thing that kept me living. That ought to be true; it really ought, by all that is just. But as much as I love you, you are not strong enough. Nobody is, not even my mother. Do not show her this. She would ask questions you could not answer. She would do to you what she has done to me.
I can hear you in the next room, drying yourself after your bath. I shall stop now. I shall come to you and embrace you. I shall tell you how much I love you.
And believe me, it shall be true.
Your Salvador.

The Hem Puffer

There is a photograph in my mother's family album that used to bother me. It was taken in 1966, at my cousin Jeffrey's christening. All the matriarchs and matriettes are there, standing in a row outside Auntie Beattie's house: Jeffrey's mother cradling a cascading bundle of lace; my mother (though she isn't my nor anyone's mother here); two grand-mothers; and five assorted elder sisters and great aunts. They look happy enough, but the Sixties certainly aren't swinging in this photograph. All are wearing skirts (of course) and although there is a degree of free expression in colour and fabric (imaginative variations on muddy tweediness), *all the skirts are EXACTLY the same length.* One centimetre above the lower edge of the knee. If you lay a ruler across the gathered ladies at knee height, there is NO deviation. *Not a single millimetre!*

My grandmother (or Nana, to give her her right name) was a home dressmaker. In her sewing room (spare bedroom/my visiting bedroom) was a peculiar device. It had a wooden base, from which protruded a vertical one-metre rule, also of wood. Attached to this was a sort of sliding nozzle with a pink rubber hose, on the end of which was a squeezy rubber bulb. Its innocent purpose was to blow powdered chalk. You put the half-made skirt on a model/mannequin/yourself and proceeded to puff a line of chalk around the desired hemline. Then fold and sew: result, a perfectly horizontal hem.

Taken in conjunction with the geometric evidence of the photo-graph, the chalk-puffing device took on a mysterious, sinister magni-tude in my child mind, like some item of equipment that might lurk in the *cabinets noirs* of the Spanish Inquisition, perhaps even the Gestapo, brought out to monitor the lengths of girls' skirts when they reached adulthood (especially Auntie age). If they were inappropri-ately long or (God forbid) too short, dreadful punishments might await them (possibly connected with those knobbly, suspiciously rigid-looking hats). Nana, too severe and Chapel for the Women's Institute, was a member of the Inner Wheel (a cabalistic, heeby-jeebyish-sounding name for an organisation if ever I heard one), and I used to picture her and her fellow inquisitors descending unexpectedly in the night on newly grown-up and improperly skirted women, armed with their chalk puffer. (Ha-ha! *Nobody* expects the Inner Wheel!)

At what age could I expect to have to forsake my hot-pants and succumb to this draconian A-line regulation? Visiting Nana and sharing the room with that silent device of persecution, I would lie awake at night worrying about it.

I didn't realise then that the Hem Puffer was just the overture to the nightmare.

Half in a daze, Beth wandered across the courtyard, following a set of deep tyre-ruts in the snow. *Somebody* had been out today. The tracks curved in towards the Italian Wing and led away through the rear gatehouse.

She was thinking about Danny. In her lower abdomen, a little pill of warmth glowed where Madame de La Simarde had touched her. The thought of him had ignited the moment the old lady's hand touched. *Yes, I suppose I do . . .* She hadn't thought of him this way in years; whenever unconscious digging unearthed him, she recoiled, scraping him away from her thoughts like clay clinging to a shovel blade.

Yes, I suppose I did . . .

When she thought of the loss Geneviève de La Simarde had endured, she felt a shudder; an ache of shame; sensed the selfishness of abandoning Danny. If she hadn't chosen him in the first place, he couldn't have been cast off like that. She had wanted him, but her affection had been drowned in a froth of distaste and incompetence. And why *Danny*, anyway? Did she *enjoy* torturing herself or something? She had once hoped that Iain would make it all come right, or at least erase the problem somehow, but he hadn't. It wasn't his fault, but every domestic felicity, every desire for unlived-in rooms, made it worse.

When she came to her senses, she found she had wandered right out of the heart of the Château and into a wide yard flanked by stable blocks on two sides and a coach house on the third. She had come up against the vast double door of the coach house, where the tyre tracks she had been semi-consciously following faded out in the feathery fringe of snow and vanished under the door.

Sleety snow had begun falling; heavy and thick and wet, settling on her hair and shoulders. This door was different; impersonal, undomestic, and promising shelter. It pulled open easily, rolling outwards on a little steel castor.

Inside, the light was dimmed by the frosting of cobwebby grime on the high windows, and the atmosphere was thick with oil and petrol and paint, mixed with a cocktail of a dozen other garage scents, the whole brew tinted to sepia by the aroma of age. Parked side by side near the door, their backsides illuminated by the sudden flood of bright, unfiltered light, were the Daimler and a battered, farmery old Land Rover with a cloth canopy. Further in, deep in shadow, were at least three more vehicles, all wrapped like mummies in green canvas shrouds. The one behind the Daimler was thickly coated with oily dust, its shape – high and square, with broad, flared wings – hinting at an ancient vintage. Beside it was a long, low shape, less dusty; one corner of its shroud was carelessly folded back, revealing an elderly meshwork grille and a Mercedes badge. There was also a canvas-draped motorcycle crouching in a corner, and, right at the back of the coach house, near a door which appeared to lead through to some sort of workshop, one more car-shape. This last auto-mummy was small and squat and wrapped parcel-tight in a canvas sheet big enough for a small lorry. Judging by the front-to-back archaeology of vehicles, and the amount of protection afforded it, this must be something truly antique. She was wandering idly around it, looking for a gap in the canvas, when she sensed – perhaps through some tremor in the thick, silent atmosphere of the garage – that she was being watched. She looked up, and found Février standing in the entrance to the workshop.

He had a coil of copper tubing in one hand and a tool that looked like a crude torture implement (perhaps for extracting fingernails) in the other. His usual composure was fractured, and he looked as startled at the sight of Beth as she was by him. His gaze hopped around the garage, as though checking for other intruders, then settled on her again. His eyes narrowed suspiciously, and he walked up to her and stared into her face. She shrank back in terror, but was trapped between a workbench and an oil drum. His eyes darted away again; his fingers, she noticed, were nervously working the jaws of the vicious-looking pincers. Suddenly, he smiled and stepped back to a more respectful distance.

'Apologies, Mademoiselle,' he said. 'I have frightened you. I am not used to . . . visitors, ah, coming to look *behind the stage*, as you say. Please accept my apologies.'

He effaced himself with a deep bow. Beth stared at him, wide-eyed and trembling, and managed a tiny nod.

'You are interested in old cars, Mademoiselle?' he asked.

'Um . . .' she said.

'These are not good examples. They are everyday cars. There are better ones in the old stables next-door. The late Monsieur François – Madame's father-in-law – was an enthusiastic collector.' He inclined his head and assumed a curiously coy expression. 'Would you care to see them?' he asked.

'Um,' said Beth again, reduced to infantile incoherence. 'Er . . .'

Hello, little girl. Do you want to see my puppies?

'They really are most excellent examples,' he persisted, a hint of incipient hurt creeping into his voice. 'Some are quite unique.'

Would you like a sweetie?

'Um, okay,' she murmured.

He put his piping and pincers down on the bench and gave a grateful little bow. 'If you would care to follow me . . .'

A udrey knew she didn't have much time left; she had been warned
once, and so she worked as fast as she could. Sure enough, there
was a chime, and another warning: *No reserve battery power remains. Your
PowerBook will go to sleep within 10 seconds to preserve the contents of memory.*
'Fuck . . .'

Typing as quickly as she could, she rounded off her sentence and hit
Command-S to save it. The hard disk chattered briefly, then the screen
flicked off and the disk spun down with a sad little whine.

Her second battery had given out. Still, she had managed to hack a
pretty good programme proposal out of the material she had memorised. There were a few discrepancies – Yvette Butain had unfortunately become Arlette Putain, and *Einsatzgruppen* had become
Ersatzgroupen – but they had more to do with flaws in Beth's rendition
than lapses in Audrey's memory. She needed more detail, though.
Perhaps if she were to speak to Iain herself.

Fat chance. She sneered at the phone lying mute and useless beside
the dozing computer. She tapped out a rhythm on the dead keyboard,
humming abstractedly, then decided to go and talk to Beth. She might
have recalled some more details.

Beth wasn't in her room. At a loss, Audrey wandered down to the
end of the corridor and looked out of the window. There was no sign
of a thaw; the snow was as thick as it had been that morning, and
clouds were gathering, threatening more.

Beside the window, the corridor turned a corner and ended, forming
a deep alcove. Along one side, placed so that the light from the
window fell full on it, was a tall glass-fronted display cabinet. She
paused to look at it, then wished she hadn't. Like others she had seen
downstairs, it was a selection of specimens of local wildlife. Instead of
being stuffed and mounted in naturalistic poses, however, these

337

animals – rats, mice, voles, frogs, a hare, even a badger – were pinned like crucifixions to the hessian backboard, limbs outstretched in petrified star-jumps. Each had been neatly slit from throat to groin and laid open. Their internal organs were drawn out and pinned: suns and fans of diminutive vitals, all labelled with yellowing card slips written in a minute hand in fading brown ink. Whatever preserving method had been used was obviously being stretched beyond the limits of its powers; bits were beginning to fall off. Detached, decomposing viscera – tiny livers, strands of string-like intestine, a thumb-shaped lung – were accumulating on the baize floor of the cabinet.

Audrey grimaced and stepped back, boggling at a system that gave such wealth and unbearably long leisure to people. It couldn't be good for your mental health if you ended up wanting to pass your time putting together such a collection. What did you *do* with it once it was finished? Show it to your friends at a wine-and-dissection party?

She was about to go back to her room when she noticed the door. It was the key that caught her eye; a heavy iron key sticking out of what looked like just a section of the alcove's dark wood panelling. A secret door! She walked towards it and pressed her hand against the panel. It gave, swinging inwards with just a hint of a squeal, and sighed a breath of sour, metallic air into the dusty atmosphere of the alcove. The carpet and panelling ended, and the short passageway beyond was bare grey stone, slightly glossed, like the colour of the dissected animal intestines. At the end of the passage, a narrow spiral staircase led upwards. Audrey made a little coughing noise and listened to the echoes. It went up a long way. Considering the geography of the castle, she worked out that this must be the upper part of the great corner tower. The twin of the tower in the story in Lydia's diary; the one from which the mad English girl Violina had thrown herself. It was higher than the other towers; almost certainly higher than the paltry hill Audrey had climbed that morning.

She hurried back to her room and collected her phone. One last try; if she couldn't get a signal up there, she would admit defeat and resort to using the castle telephone.

'Surely you must keep records,' Rachel pleaded.

'Not as such.'

They were back at the garage. Tracking Audrey down via her car wasn't made any easier by the fact that none of yesterday's staff were working today. The informality of garage business didn't help, either. Doreen, the Saturday receptionist, was gradually realising that she was not going to get rid of this weird hippie woman without either calling the police or pandering to her strange requests. She decided that, for

338

the moment at least, it would be easiest to comply.

'There might be something in the invoice book,' she said. 'Hold on.' She took a thick, oil-grimed pad down from a shelf and leafed through it, shuffling crumpled carbon sheets and multicoloured duplicate pages. 'Here, this'll be it, I spect. *Recovery, Rose & Hart.* Sixty-two pound forty-eight. Cash paid.' She looked up expectantly, hoping that would suffice.

'Doesn't it say where it was taken?'

'The car? Here, I spect.'

Rachel sighed impatiently. She repeated what she had been told the day before.

'Oh,' said Doreen. 'Then I dunno. Your friend's house, maybe?'

'Not very likely. Would it be possible to speak to the person who drove the truck?'

'That'd be Jeff. He don't normally work Sat'days.'

'Oh. Could you tell me how to get in touch with him? It is important.'

Calling the police was starting to look more attractive by the minute. 'I could try im at ome,' said Doreen doubtfully. 'He won't like it.'

'Could you? I'd be very grateful.'

Reluctantly, Doreen picked up the phone and consulted her flip-up address book.

She waited a long time for an answer. 'Hello, Jeff. It's Doreen here, from CJ. Did you do a recovery at the Rose & Hart yest'day? . . . I've got a lady here wants to know where you dropped it off . . . No, she ain't the owner.'

While Doreen listened, Rachel tried to read the customer's name at the top of the invoice: three lines of barely decipherable scrawl, none of which looked like Audrey's name. The last three words, though, she did just about recognise: *De Le Semard.*

'. . . Thanks, Jeff. Cheerio.' Doreen put the phone down. 'He took it over to B&M,' she said.

'B&M?'

'B&M Autos in Newton Abbot. The ignition system had to be replaced. We can't do that here. We subcontract to B&M sometimes.'

Rachel wrote the name and address down. 'Thank you,' she said. 'I'm sorry to have caused such trouble.'

'Don't mention it,' said Doreen. As Rachel turned away, she added: 'They'll be closed now, mind. You'll ave to wait till Monday.'

For Other People's Use

Pampered, cosseted, preened, worried over, stuffed, mounted and displayed. And yet what use are breasts to their owner? Arms, legs, hands, feet; they move us from place to place, let us dance, write, work, pick things up. They have a thousand uses; look how hard life is without them. Likewise eyes, ears, nose and mouth. Even buttocks make sitting more comfortable. Penises enable their owners to wee standing up without a pulling down of pants. But breasts? What practical benefits do they confer on their bearers? ABSOLUTELY NONE. Only WOMEN have them, and they are the ONLY HUMAN BODY PART designed *entirely and exclusively* for OTHER PEOPLE'S USE. There to be gawped at, gripped, fondled, grappled, licked, rubbed and nibbled and, finally, to provide a pillow for the exhausted lover's head. And, of course, there is their 'true' function: mobile milk bottle stroke squalling baby udderblobs. A range of uses, then, none of material benefit to the poor sod who has to carry them about all her life and worry over their size, shape, state of droop and so on. And speaking of droop, they are the only human body part (aside from the extremely useful and deserving hands and feet) for which we have to expend precious cash on special items of garmentry. A bra doesn't keep you warm, doesn't keep the rain off, doesn't protect you from splinters or brambles or broken glass. It merely serves to support these parasites. Why can't the lazy buggers support themselves?

Added to all of this, these boulders of fatty tissue, dedicated to helping us serve other people's needs and desires, are the body part most likely to kill us.

Hardly surprising, is it, that in culture's metonymic language, BREASTS is so often sufficient to signify WOMAN. They pretty much sum up our status.

340

I never wanted them. When I was a blissfully smooth-torsoed child, I dreaded the day when great gazoombahs like Mummy's would begin to sprout from my chest. I thought they would be rigid, like balloons, and therefore interfere with climbing trees, wrestling boys (HA!) and watching telly lying on my tummy. So I devised a plan to inhibit their growth. Every night (I was convinced they would sprout furtively during the hours of darkness), I went to sleep lying on my front. I would choke the swines to nothing before they had a chance to establish themselves. This regime went on for years. In the end, though, I was betrayed by my own susceptibility to peer pressure. By the time my hormones began to nudge out my very own budding set of fleshy nodules, I had succumbed to the notion that BOOBS ARE GOOD FOR YOU. Boy magnets: the bigger the better. As they grew (and boy, did they grow), my approval rating at school inflated with them, and I was lost. Condemned to a life of straps, lace, underwiring and worry, and enslavement to other people's needs.

In short, I allowed myself to be conned into becoming a woman.

Leaving Danny

1

I allowed myself to be conned into becoming a woman.

Beth closed the little notebook and stroked its tomato-red cover, then opened it again at the title page.

Thoughts and Commonplaces
or
What I Believed When I Was A Child

Bethany Glaister
Christmas 1988

She had bought it while shopping for last-minute wrapping paper in the newsagent's at the bottom of the hill. It still had its fading yellow 49p price label on the back. It had been her first Christmas as an undergraduate, returning to Llanyrafon stuffed with new learning and self-importance; with a whole Cambridge term under her belt, she looked down like a colossus on the ignorant inhabitants of this suddenly very hickish town. She was changing, growing up, and she had conceived the idea of recording her thoughts as she moved through this most important rite of passage. What a charlie. Over Christmas, she filled two-thirds of the notebook, then got bored and put it away in a drawer. This was the first time she had looked at it since, and she was startled by the eighteen-year-old self she found there. Had she really been that angry, that scathing? It wasn't how she remembered herself at all; she had had so little to be angry about; plenty, she had believed, to be aloof and smug about, but no cause for ill will or bitterness. Now that she had plenty of cause for both, all she felt was sadness; some tearful despair sometimes, but mostly just the long sadness of failure. Alone between the closing-in walls of her tiny bedroom, she longed to be back at 3 Ainsworth Cottages with her friends – snooty Audrey, joyful Lydia, shy Rachel – but knew somehow that she would never see any of them again. They were dispersed now, and the little cottage at the end of the muddy, crumbly lane would be occupied by some new crop of Wolfburne's grown-up children. Lydia had moved on to a life unknowable and unimaginable. Rachel had written from York, where she was teaching music at a girls' boarding school. That was months ago; Beth hadn't replied and had heard no further word. From Audrey there had come only silence since the day of the Lit Crit exam. She had presumably shed her old friends as easily as exfoliating dead skin.

Beth heard the garden gate squeal, and she swung off the bed, flinging the notebook to the floor. She was down the stairs and in the hall before her mother had a chance to get her key in the lock. She yanked the front door open and stared at her mother's startled face.

'Did you see him?' she demanded anxiously.

'For goodness sake, Beth, let me get in the house first.'

Beth stood back, closing the door and waiting while her mother – with what seemed like deliberately bloody-minded slowness – came in and began taking off her coat.

'Well?' she blurted, unable to contain herself. 'Did you see him?'

Rosie hung up her coat in the utility room and came back into the hall. She glanced expressionlessly at her daughter, then walked past her into the living room. 'I'm surprised you're so bothered,' she said. 'You didn't want to *know* last time.'

Beth followed her. 'Did you SEE him?'

'Yes, I saw him.'

They faced each other across the middle of the room, each struggling inside with a turmoil of unsayable things. Beth cracked first.

'Is he . . .' she began, tiny-voiced. 'Is he . . . *okay?*'

Her mother snorted. 'As if you care,' she muttered, and went out to the kitchen.

'I DO care!' Beth cried, but her mother ignored her.

Rosie expended her half-hearted anger on the kettle, cups and spoons. When she looked through the window at the back garden, she found her vision blurred by tears. *What might you have done in her situation . . .* She wiped the tears away with a tissue, blew her nose, and went back into the living room. Her daughter was still standing there, exactly as she had left her, staring sightlessly at nothing.

343

'He's fine,' Rosie said softly. 'Happy and healthy.'

Beth forced a smile. 'Really?'

'He said his second word, right while I was there.'

'What did he say?'

Rosie smiled. '*Grandma* . . . Well, it was more like *Gamma* really.'

Beth didn't ask what the first word had been; she could guess, and could imagine to whom he would have said it.

Rosie hesitated; she would do anything to avoid a repeat of the scenes they had had before, but the matter had to be raised. She broached it delicately, trying hard to smooth any wrinkle of disapproval out of her voice. 'You could go and see him yourself,' she said softly. 'If you liked,' she added carefully.

Beth shook her head. 'I couldn't.'

Offer, don't try to persuade. You know how she'll react to cajoling. 'Evie wouldn't mind. She'd like you to see him. In fact, she was asking . . .' She hesitated on the edge of dangerous territory.

Beth frowned at the hesitation. 'What?' she asked suspiciously.

'Well, she'd like to know when – if you're going to take him back.'

Beth's eyes narrowed further. 'You haven't told her, have you?'

'Told her what? There's nothing to tell. It's only a matter of time, isn't it?'

Beth shook her head impatiently, anger rubbed up and beginning to bleed. 'No, no, no! No, Mum. You saw what it was like. I can't cope, I couldn't. I'm not cut out for it – I never will be.'

In the kitchen, the kettle rumbled loudly; its switch clicked, and the boiling sounds subsided, draining away into the gutter of silence between the two women.

'It's not natural,' said Rosie at last. 'It's hard for all of us, but we all cope somehow. He's your *son*, Beth, your own flesh and blood. And mine . . . Go and see him, sweetheart. I'm sure you'd change your mind.'

Beth hesitated for a moment, her face fearful, as though having her mind changed by seeing him were what she was afraid of. Then her mouth set in an uneven line, and she shook her head resolutely. 'No,' she said. 'I can't.'

Rosie couldn't help herself. '*I* coped,' she insisted. 'It was bloody hard sometimes – Christ, it was – but I coped with you.'

'Well, pardon me for not being perfect! I'm *not* you, am I? *I CAN'T* cope!'

'No, you're not me. It's your father you get it from. He was weak as well. Wouldn't face up to his responsibilities. Well, you're going to have to. If you're planning on abandoning him forever, you'll have to tell Evie yourself. I'm not going to, and that's an end to it.'

Beth licked the lip of the envelope and pressed it down with the heel of her hand, then took it downstairs. She was hunting for stamps in the bureau drawer when she found the birth certificate. She paused in her search and gazed at the strange document. Birth certificates, in her experience, were elderly and yellowing, ruffled soft along their edges, grubbied and coming apart at their folds. This one was new and stiff, with clean, sharp corners and bright, fresh type. She had seen it before, of course, but had given it only the most cursory glance before passing it over to the care of her mother. (To Rosie and cousin Evie, she had probably seemed to treat its owner in much the same offhand way.) Now she studied it, feeling oddly detached. The name just didn't relate; not to her, not to any human person. Daniel Rufus Glaister. She had grown so used to suppressing it – referring to the child, even in her mind, as *him* – that it evoked no image, elicited no tug. Her own name in the column headed 'Mother' gave her a jolt, as did the word Unknown under 'Father'. Rosie had remarked once, in a fit of temper, that the names ought to be the other way round: *Daniel* under 'Father' and *Unknown* in place of the child's name.

She found a book of stamps at the bottom of the drawer, where it had slipped down between a stapler and a roll of sellotape. She tore one out and stuck it to the envelope, glancing once more at the address: *Dr V.L. Roy, Senior Tutor, Wolfburne College, Cambridge CB2 3XL.* She still had the birth certificate in one hand; she glanced from the letter to the certificate and back again, as though weighing them against each other, then put the certificate back and closed the drawer.

If the birth had been a vale of horror, then the aftermath was the very pit of despair. Why had he needed to *cry* so much?

Nobody had told her about this; but then, no telling could have prepared her. You had to experience it to understand.

She had wanted to love him; had expected to, prepared herself to, tried to make it come true, but she couldn't. Instead of a child, an object of love, she got a writhing mass of grimacing pink that sucked in milk and slush at one end and ejected it, stinking, at both. She could have stood that; she really could. It was the crying that did for her sanity. It's meant to sound awful, her mother told her, so you do something about it. But there was nothing she *could* do about it. Feeding, winding, changing soiled nappies; nothing seemed to make the relentless racket abate. It screeched and squalled and howled round her ears and rattled inside her skull, so that she heard it even when the demon was asleep or had its mouth temporarily stoppered by a teat or tit or spoonful of glop. The echoes faded briefly during the short afternoon hours of sleep (hers, not his), only to redouble for the night-time shift. Twenty-four hours dragged out to forty-eight, seventy-two, a week, a fortnight, a month, two months, and her cheeks were hollowed out and her eyes lined with red and shadowed with grey. Even with her mother's help, she was going slowly out of her mind.

The crisis came in the middle of the night. Rosie woke, as she often did, to the sound of Daniel crying in the next room. But it wasn't quite his usual caterwaul; it was muted, and she could hear another voice – Beth's – mumbling in the erratic pauses for breath. It was something in Beth's tone – a sort of gaiety – that made Rosie get out of bed and go to investigate. She went to the back bedroom and opened the door. *Beth?* she said, peering into the darkness. There was no reply; just continued muffled crying and Beth's voice slurring *Rock-a-bye baby . . .* Rosie switched the light on, and gasped at what she saw. The duvet and pillows were twisted together and heaped up in the middle of the abandoned bed. Beth was lying, curled up tight, knees drawn up to her chest, in the baby's cot. Her eyes were shut and streaming tears, and she had the baby-bottle clamped in her mouth, burbling her lullaby round its rubber teat. Rosie ran to the cot and leaned in, unhooking the side-gate and letting it down. *Where's Daniel?* she demanded. *Be sleepy-bye-byes in a minute,* Beth mumbled happily. Rosie shook her by the shoulder. *Where IS he?* she shouted, but Beth wouldn't answer. She listened out for the muted crying, and ran to the bed, throwing off the pillows and duvet. The screaming burst out full-voice, and there he was, his rage-fed face beginning to turn blue. She swept him up in her arms and walked him around the room, jigging him up and down and stroking his tiny, heaving back. Beth stopped chanting and stared resentfully at her mother. *You've woken it up,* she complained. Rosie looked at her furiously over the baby's shoulder. *What on earth are you doing in there?* she demanded. *He could have suffocated.* Beth looked anguished. *This is MY bed,* she said. *That's my bear.* She pointed at the pink teddy bear her father had painted for her on the elderly cot's wooden headboard. *I told it it could have my bed, and I tucked it in nice and tight and the crying went away.* Rosie didn't say anything; leaving Beth coiled up and weeping in the cot, she took Daniel back to her own room and cradled him for the rest of the night.

From that moment on, it was hopeless; no amount of persuasion or browbeating could make Beth take care of the baby. She wouldn't even look at him. Eventually, she refused even to be in the same room with him. Rosie considered giving up her job to look after him full-time, but she couldn't afford to. Another solution had to be found. It arrived in the shape of her young cousin Evie, who was comfortably off and lived for the care of her children.

Beth didn't see Evie the day she came to collect Daniel; didn't say goodbye to her son. She just sat in her room with the empty cot and stared at the wall and cried.

The University welcomed her back; if not with open arms, then at least with a reasonably cordial handshake. She posted off a cheque for the requisite fee, and was advised of a date the following summer when she would be permitted to resit Part II of the English Tripos. In the meantime, she continued with her part-time job as a dentist's receptionist on Pontnewydd, saving up her money for the move.

One Saturday in spring, she finally screwed up her courage and decided to visit cousin Evie. She would soon be leaving Wales, possibly for good, and might not get another chance. In Cwmbran, she bought a velveteen rabbit with tall ears and a blue waistcoat, then set off on the long relay of bus journeys: up to Pontypool, then across the heads of the valleys to Hafodrynys and down to Pontllanfraith. It was lunch time when she arrived, hot and out of breath, at the top of the steep rise of Manor Road. Clutching the grinning rabbit against her fluttering chest, she walked resolutely down the drive and rang the doorbell.

There was no reply. They were out. She hadn't phoned in advance (in case she chickened out on the way) and this was the result: a wasted journey. She walked round to the back garden, but there was no sign of Evie or Michael or any of the kids, and the car wasn't in the garage. Carrying the rabbit and a confusing hybrid of relief, guilt and disappointment, she walked back up the drive, crossed the road, and sat down on a garden wall in the shade of a high privet hedge.

Ten minutes later, she was still trying to decide whether to wait or flee when she saw Evie, struggling up the hill with Cerys and Owen trailing behind. Half hidden in an old-fashioned pushchair laden with shopping bags was Daniel. Beth shrank back behind the end of the hedge and watched while, with a great deal of manoeuvring and good-natured scolding, the rowdy troupe disappeared inside the house and the door closed behind them.

Daniel had looked so big, compared with the last time she had seen him. He must be toddling by now. He was changing forever, uttering his first words and taking his first steps, and she wasn't there to witness any of it. She had to see him properly, and it had to be now.

She came out of her hiding place and crossed the road. Then, half-way down the drive, she was seized by a convulsion of terror, suddenly seeing herself as Evie might see her; as Daniel might see her one day. A stranger. Coming bearing her pathetically inadequate gift: a cheap ticket to a day of playing mother before abandoning him once more. She froze, staring at the front door, then ran back across the road and sat down again on the wall, trembling and trying to shrink back into the hedge.

When she had regained control, she took a pen and a slip of paper from her bag and wrote *To Daniel, with love.* Tucking the note in the rabbit's waistcoat, she went back down the drive and sat him on the doorstep; to one side, so he wouldn't get trodden on. Then she rang the doorbell and fled.

She didn't look back, and so didn't see Evie come to the door and look in bewilderment at the empty drive. She walked to the top of the drive and looked up and down the street, not recognising or even particularly noticing the woman walking away down the hill on the far side of the road. As she was going back indoors, she noticed the rabbit. She picked it up and took the note from its waistcoat. Then, with a sad look in her eyes, she went inside and closed the door.

A week later, Beth was back in Cambridge. Instead of waiting until May and staying in bed and breakfast, she went up two months early and took a rented room in Bateman Street. To her astonishment, she found that Wolfburne's lodgings officer had stored all the belongings she had left behind at Ainsworth Cottages, and so she was able to recreate a semblance of her old student room. She put up her Pixies and Ride posters, hung her skew-wiff rattan blind in the window and got out all her old lecture notes and essays. For the next eight weeks, she studied furiously, poring over the notebooks and files by evening and haunting the college library by day, too busy to take much notice of how bleak Cambridge had become now that it had been emptied of friends. Even Salvador had gone. She inquired after him, and learned that he had relinquished his fellowship and moved on, taking Lydia with him.

She sat her exams – most of them in the same hall she had walked out of two years ago – and was awarded her degree. A lower Second; not as good as she might once have hoped for, but a Cambridge degree nonetheless. She stayed on in the town, registering with a recruitment agency on Regent Street and taking a succession of temporary jobs in banks and offices. One day, the agency's manager, who had taken a liking to her (she was a good worker, popular with the clients), told her of a vacancy for a consultant at the agency's Peterborough branch. Beth was tiring of Cambridge – it held too many ghosts – so she applied. To her surprise, she was offered the job. Two weeks later, she left the ghost-place behind forever.

She rented a one-bedroom flat in Peterborough, and within a year was earning enough in commissions to buy a similar one in the same block. The working days were long, and in the small domestic hours between cooking, cleaning, washing and ironing, she started to write. She began with letters to Daniel, in which she tried to explain why she had had to give him into somebody else's care. She never posted the letters; he couldn't read them anyway, and would probably never understand her explanations. Later, she gave up letter-writing and tried her hand at children's stories. At least they were meant to be for children. What came out of her pen were unpleasant tales that even Roald Dahl would have balked at. She tried to make them nicer, but couldn't. She enrolled in a creative-writing course at the local adult education college, and showed her stories to the teacher, a published but only sparsely successful writer called Iain Urbanski. He enjoyed them and asked to see more, although what he really wanted was to see more of their creator. He asked her out for a drink. Over a matching pair of lagers in the Shield & Dragon, he suggested that the reason he liked her stories might be to do with the fact that he detested children so much. Didn't she? She forced a chuckle and said, Yes, she supposed she did. She kept quiet about Daniel. It became even harder to mention him when, three months later, Iain moved into her flat. She stopped writing stories soon after that, excusing herself from the unhappy task by telling herself that one struggling writer was quite enough for one household.

Then it came: a gust of cold wind; a fistful of icy fingers groping up from the past and seizing hold of her heart. One Saturday afternoon, while leafing through the back pages of the *Guardian*, she came across Salvador's obituary. She stared at it, her insides freezing. She had to read it three times over before believing it. Killed in a car crash, it said, and hinted darkly at suicide. It preyed on her mind for weeks after. She thought of writing to Lydia, but couldn't be sure that Lydia had still been with him; the obituary mentioned his mother, but not his widow. Beth got over it eventually; she had stopped truly believing that Salvador and Lydia and all the others had ever *really* existed. Her life had shrunk too small to accommodate people who belonged in another incarnation.

The news of Lydia came as a big jolt, though. It came from Gabriel in an envelope that bore on its front a palimpsest of forwarding addresses – c/o Wolfburne; Llanyrafon; Peterborough – and Lydia had been dead three weeks by the time Beth received the letter. She phoned Gabriel to offer condolences and apologies for missing the funeral. She hadn't missed it. There had been an inquest, and the funeral was to take place at a church in Devon near the Simarde estate.

She caught the train before dawn. Iain dropped her off at the dark station and kissed her goodbye on the ice-blown platform. As the train pulled away, she wondered whether she ought to have tried to contact Audrey and Rachel (Gabriel's attempts to track them down had so far failed, apparently), but consoled herself with the thought that she would rather not see either of them. It would be too disturbing. Besides, she, not they, had been Lydia's closest friend.

1997

DIMANCHE 22 JUIN
She knows. I'm sure she knows.
Still at Gondecourt. I long to be back in England. It's beautiful here, but I don't know if I can stand it much longer. Whenever I mention it to her (God, how timidly – she still has the power to frighten me, even after all this time) she says 'soon'. Always 'soon', but soon never seems to arrive. I'd leave tomorrow, if I could. But I just sit and wait, sit and wait, sit and wait. Sometimes I write, sometimes I think about Salvador. Mostly I just think about home, wherever that is. Gabriel sends me letters – not postcards, just letters from all over the world. The first one said he'd split up with Helen and taken up his old job. The second said he'd got back with her. I stopped opening them after that.

I know she's got to mourn, be near him, and so do I. But it has to stop some time. She doesn't cry. She doesn't even look sad, she just goes around all the time with her lips squeezed tight and her cheeks sucked in, looking even more formidable than when I first met her. (Did I really find her sweet and charming?) It's been over two years now, but still she mourns.

How cruelly selfish can a person be?
She *must* know it wasn't how they said it was.

MERCREDI 30 JUILLET
I once wrote something in my notebook:-"There are times when the pleasure of being out in the world is so intense that I yearn to be home." I wrote that when I first knew Salvador. I didn't realise that there are other times when the pain of being in a strange place so dulls me that I can't leave.

Bought another postcard today. A view of the river at Confolens.

351

Madame said this morning that she was sick of seeing my moping face about the house, so she ordered Février to drive me somewhere. I chose Confolens, and I was so glad I had. I left Février to find himself a bar (horrid man, he gives me the creeps) and went for a walk through the town. There's a carnival or a festival there next week, and the town was being prepared. Normally, it seems such a sleepy, dead-and-alive place, but today it was bustling. It's so strange – people come from all over the world to this little town once a year to dress up in national costume and parade through the streets. They have a big market and in the evening there's a fireworks display. It was a good place to be in my present state of mind. I so yearn for a bit of warm human contact. Something strange happened, though. I felt so uplifted, but lonely at the same time, so I bought the postcard from the little tabac on the corner by the bridge. Then, clutching it excitedly, I went and had a coffee at the Hôtel de Vienne. I sat under the rattan shade on the terrace overlooking the river (lunchtime was long past, so it was very quiet). I realised then that I didn't know who on earth I wanted to write to, so I just watched the workmen putting up all the different countries' flags along the parapet of the bridge. There were some English people a couple of tables away, a woman and two men. It was weird – the sound of their voices made me more homesick than ever, but at that moment I wouldn't have spoken to them for the world. I even tried to hide, turning my chair as far round as I could so my back was to them, but I couldn't take my ears off their conversation. The men kept calling the woman 'Mother', but she couldn't have been more than a couple of years older than them. It was sweet, in a way. For some reason (I still can't think why) I started thinking about the last time I saw Beth, and how unpleasant she was to me, and how much I hated her for it even though she was right, that thing she said. I always wished I'd made it up with her, but she vanished. Anyway, I got the card out again and started writing. I wrote out the whole address, including the post code (I was amazed I remembered it – I hope her mum hasn't moved). I don't care anymore about what she said or what Salvador said. This time I'm going to send it. I've put it on the mantelpiece in my room (I can see it from here) ready for the morning. I shan't give it to Avril – I shall walk to the village with it myself.

LUNDI 4 AOÛT

It's still there. Still propped up on the mantelpiece. I feel like it's mocking me. Four times – FOUR TIMES I've tried to send it, and I just can't do it. It's like with those people the other day. Why can't I?

There – I've taken it down and put it in the box with the others. I shan't buy any more.

Anyway, Beth would only know she was right and think I was even more of a fool.

MERCREDI 6 AOÛT
I still haven't asked about the Confolens festival. I would have liked to go, but think perhaps I'll leave it. Perhaps I'm better off just staying put, keeping to myself. Anyway, I can barely bring myself to look at her, never mind ask her favours.

1998

DIMANCHE 8 FÉVRIER
It's next week. I bumped into her on the stairs this evening, looking even more grave and frightening than ever, and she told me. As if I could have forgotten, but I *had*. How could I?

Next week. I don't think I can stand it.

VENDREDI 13 FÉVRIER
Today has been the worst day of my life. I can't even begin to describe it, and I'm not sure that I would even want to. I don't know how I managed to keep my mouth shut when she started saying those things. Perhaps it was fear that she might say something even worse. Everyone is a failure, everyone has *let her down*. She becomes stranger as every month passes. She isn't all that old, but I think she may be losing her grip on things. Becoming confused. Like Salvador's birthday. She kept referring to today as a commemoration of his birthday. I don't understand. Today is not his birthday – today is the third anniversary of his death.

She worries me. Besides, she kept looking at me over dinner in a way I can't quite describe – sort of expectantly, as though she was waiting for me to say something. Or do something? Whatever it was, I was too distraught to fathom her meaning. And then she started

Perhaps I should speak to Avril. She's always been much kinder to me than her mistress – or her brother, for that matter.

SAMEDI 14 FÉVRIER
She *is* getting confused. The birthday – it's so obvious – it was there all the time, on the tomb. Why didn't I realise before? I understand now. The poor woman. For the first time ever, I actually feel sympathy – I pity her. Not only to have had a thing like that happen, but the coincidence of it. It explains a lot. I'm surprised she's stayed as sane as she has. And I thought *I'd* suffered. Really, they destroyed *each other*.

353

Perhaps I should try and talk to her.

Salvador, you *did* have the power, if only you had recognised it. And I *was* strong enough.

Perhaps I should take

That was it. The diary ended there, interrupted in mid-sentence. Just as Lydia herself had ended.

Beth leafed back and forth, searching through both volumes for other entries – anything: isolated phrases, single words, marked dates – but there was nothing to illuminate what had really been going on in Lydia's head. The diaries began two years after Salvador's death and continued intermittently until about six months ago. The Lydia talking through their pages was so unhappy. Beth tried to console herself with the thought that she might have resorted to her diary when she was most depressed, and perhaps the blank spaces indicated periods of relative happiness.

Maybe. Whatever. None of this could distract Beth from her disappointment. Expecting to unmask intrigue and conspiracy, she had found only the adventitious conspiracy of circumstance; and she herself as the sole victim: the heartbreaking loneliness of Lydia's life, the alien eeriness of this place, the mysterious key, and finally the hidden chest. Beth had anticipated some reason for such secrecy, but there was none. No *real* reason, anyway; no reason outside of Lydia's imagination. From the sketchy description in her notebook, it seemed that this was the same room – or rather the twin of the room – in the ruined château; the one where Lydia first found the box. She seemed so entranced by the myth associated with it that perhaps she had chosen this room quite deliberately. Lydia had always had a propensity for punishing herself; it was entirely possible that she had imagined herself a prisoner like the poor little English girl who had preceded her. Even in the manner of her death, she had followed Violina.

The whole thing reminded Beth of Lit Crit seminars: meanings unfolding, layer upon layer, until all you were left with was a hollow centre. Quite literally in this case: the hollow centre was the dark, dark box. It had been empty when Lydia had first found it, and all she had put into it amounted to a few fragments of autobiographical bric-à-brac. Nothing important, nothing secret, nothing that would *explain why* she had had to die.

She hadn't even taken it back to France with her. According to Geneviève, they had stayed here through most of the spring and summer, and returned to Gondecourt in late September. Meanwhile, the chest had probably been put in its hiding place shortly after the last diary entry, and had remained there, disregarded, forgotten, quietly growing a skin of soot. If it had had any real importance beyond its imagined associations, then surely Lydia would have taken it with her wherever she went.

Or would she? The chest was heavy and bulky; not very convenient to carry from place to place. That wouldn't prevent Lydia taking something *from* it; something that would still be at Gondecourt, where she had died. Another diary, a second notebook, a letter, some telling artefact . . .

Beth stopped herself right away. The diaries, the postcards and the commonplace book told enough of the story: a sad life of masochistic loneliness, topped and tailed by tragedy. Beth, Audrey, Rachel and Geneviève de La Simarde had all helped to bring it about; and Salvador too.

She gathered the postcards together and laid them, along with the notebook and diaries, back in the chest. She took out the tortoiseshell plectrum and held it to her eye like a lens. For a moment, she considered pocketing it as a keepsake, but then put it back in the box and closed the lid.

She had succumbed to solitude again. Audrey would cheer her up. She went across the corridor and tapped on her door. There was no answer, so she turned the handle and went in. Audrey wasn't there. The lights were off, and the room was lowering into afternoon gloom, illuminated by the glow of the dying fire and the pulse of green light from the sleeping computer. At a loss, Beth sat down on the bed and stared into the darkness.

When Audrey showed no sign of returning, she went back to her own room. She folded back the eiderdown, kicked off her shoes, and climbed into bed.

It was on an unmemorable stretch of the A 420, approaching a roundabout somewhere near Swindon, that Iain suddenly noticed that he was enjoying himself far more than was consistent with the mood in which he had left Peterborough. The realisation surprised him so much he almost ran the car right up the rear end of a lorry-load of

Norwegian swivel chairs on their way to Chippenham.

Then, with the engine stalled, as he stared open-mouthed at the lorry's fluorescent tail-stripes, came the secondary realisation: the gaping-arsehole idiocy of what he was doing. Secret nostalgic shag-ins on Dartmoor? *Beth?* He reviewed the evidence, and felt a prickly wave of heat rising up his neck at the thought of his foolishness. What in the name of holy twisted shit had he been thinking of?

The stripes began to recede as the lorry pulled onto the roundabout. Mechanically, he restarted the engine and followed.

He had been cooped up too long, that was the trouble. Thinking back, he estimated that the blur of righteous anger had carried him about as far as Northampton. After that, he had gradually succumbed to the rushing road. He had even been humming along with the radio, tapping rhythms on the gearstick and clutch. He was having more fun than he had had since . . . Well, since before the Book had begun the long, slow process of ossifying his brain.

He drove round the roundabout three times, wondering what to do with his new-found uncooped state and the clear thinking that came with it. The sensible thing, of course, would be to head for home, lesson learned, and no more nonsense. The fun thing, on the other hand, would be to seize the moment; drive on to Devon and give Beth the surprise (as opposed to the confrontation) of her life.

He chose the fun thing.

Meanwhile, back in Peterborough, the telephone was ringing to an empty room.

Audrey whooped triumphantly and slapped the rough stone wall. The soft *prrrp*ing of the ringing tone was like sweet music in her ear.

She had climbed up the spiral staircase, past doorways and dark side passages, round and round, until the steps finally came to an end, opening out suddenly on the rim of a great circular room under a web of radiating roof-beams. You couldn't go any higher than this without climbing out of a window and shimmying up over the fishscale tiles to the very peak. From the tiny slit window near the top of the stairs, she could look down on the roof of the Italian Wing and the ornamental gardens and outbuildings beyond. At last, her phone had enough of a leg-up to catch a firm hold on the tenuous net. At *last*.

. . . If anyone ever answered. Some people, it seemed, had never heard of answering machines. She gave up on Iain – regretfully, because she would now lose his number from the redial memory – and tried Suzi instead. If the ringing tone was like music, the sound of Suzi's voice was a song of angels. Audrey waited impatiently while pen and paper were fetched (Suzi was so *inefficient*), then dictated names, dates, places and brief accounts of wreckers and *Einsatzgruppen*.

'I want you on this first thing on Monday. Sooner. See if you can come up with an NCA slant. I want to see a summary and notes on my desk by the end of Tuesday. Got that?'

'Where are you?' Suzi asked. 'You're breaking up.'

'Shit. Did you hear me?'

'Yeah, yeah. End of Wednesday.'

'*Tuesday*. That's *end of TUESDAY*. Okay, have you got all that? Read it back.'

Suzi's voice crackled and spat. '—ry? D-n't tch that.'

'Doesn't matter. I'll trust you. Remember, I'm at Diamond all day Monday. Did you fax through the figures I gave you?'

All she heard in reply was a bramble hedge of crackles and sputters, rolling away and receding to silence. She looked at the LCD display – scratched from its collision with the chiffonier – as it faded out. Another dead battery. Perhaps she should have bought Motorola after all. Still, she had got her message through at last. She had no more need for it now.

She paused to look at the view once more – it was snowing again – then began the long, winding descent. Past the little lancet doors and semi-opaque leaded windows, past the barred arrow-slits, past the narrow, darkened passageways. At the bottom, she strode along the stone passage and grasped the handle of the secret alcove door.

Strange; it hadn't been stiff when she had entered. She pulled again, then tried pushing . . . No, it *must* pull inwards; it was a *secret* door – there was no handle on the other side. She pulled again, hauling with all her strength. It still didn't budge. A little flutter of panic sprang up in her chest; she crouched down and put an eye to the keyhole. She could see the alcove, the corridor beyond, and the edge of the glass cabinet; an uninterrupted view. There was no key in the lock.

Shit. Now, which would be more humiliating: to break the door down and apologise for it later, or pound her fists on it and scream for help? No contest. She gripped the handle again and hauled at it, wedging one foot against the architrave and throwing all her weight backwards. The door flexed slightly along its top edge, but still refused to open. She tried again, and again; each time, her strength drained away a little more, until she couldn't even make the door bend.

After pausing for breath, she hammered on the wood and screamed for help.

His memory wasn't what it had once been; he might not look his age, but inside, invisibly, his mind was ageing. It was lucky she had noticed before Madame. It wouldn't be good to point this out to him, though. He'd get angry. It wasn't wise to make him angry.

Checking she was alone in the pantry (she could hear him on the telephone in his room next-door), Avril slipped the big iron key from her apron pocket and hung it back on the rack. She would pretend nothing had happened. There was no point making life miserable for herself. Besides his hurt pride, if he knew that she knew about his oversight, it would catalyse suspicion of *disloyalty*. She might *tell Madame*. (As if she would dream of it.) He would take steps to make sure she didn't, and . . . It was better to play blind. See nothing, say nothing.

She began unloading the remains of Madame's afternoon tea from her tray, lining up the china and silver separately, ready for washing. While she worked, she listened, and while she listened, she made just enough noise to warn him that she was there but not *really* listening.

'. . . was said? . . . Yes. Do you know who she was? . . . It doesn't matter. Thank you for— . . . No, Mr Lewis, I do not think that would be right . . . I think the amount you have already got is sufficient . . . You may do that with my blessing, Mr Lewis. It no longer matters. And I shall do likewise . . . Yes, precisely. Do we understand each other? Thank you for your information. Goodbye.'

Février came through from his inner sanctum, muttering to himself but looking smug. 'Where is Madame?' he asked.

Avril stopped swirling suds. 'In her boudoir. She's just had her tea.'

'Alone?'

'Yes. She had one of her headaches. She didn't want company.'

He nodded and headed for the door which led to the back stairs. Avril went back to her washing up, but not before noticing that, as he passed the rack of keys, he paused and stared at it. He turned back, frowning, and seemed about to say something. Avril tensed and concentrated on scouring out a teacup, but he just shook his head and left.

Madame appeared to have recovered from her headache. Février found her in her boudoir, listening to one of Master Salvador's records and reading a book. She seemed in a good mood, which was just as well.

'What is it, Février?' she said, not raising her eyes from the page as he came in.

'News, Madame. I have just received a telephone call from Mr Lewis.'

'Who is Mr Lewis?'

'The tow-truck driver.' She looked up then. 'He reports that a young lady has been looking for your guests.'

'Ah, that would be their friend.' She nodded. 'I have heard them talk of her; they do not seem excessively fond friends. I think we need not concern ourselves about her.'

'Very well, Madame.'

She gazed at him. 'Is that all?'

'I found Mademoiselle Glaister in the garage, looking around.'

Madame frowned. 'Oh. She must have taken my invitation to explore rather literally. Did anything occur?'

'I showed her the collection, Madame.'

'I see. And did she see anything . . . out of the ordinary?'

'She admired the Citroën *Traction* and the Bentley, but saw nothing else to take her interest.'

'Nothing at all?'

'Nothing, Madame. I do not think she has Madame's eye for craftsmanship.'

Madame smiled. 'Quite. A pleasant young lady, none the less. I was quite correct in my estimation of her. Have you seen anything of Madame Quintard?'

'No, Madame. I have been busy. I have not seen the lady since lunch.'

'Find her. Present my compliments and say that I wish to see her.'

'Her alone?'

'Yes. And Février, make sure the outbuildings are securely locked. Lock the rear gate also. I cannot have guests wandering outside the Château into places where they may come to harm.'

'Certainly, Madame. I apologise for my negligence. I shall do it immediately.'

'No. Bring Madame Quintard to me first. It is important. Go now.'

Iain stopped having fun shortly after passing through Exeter. In the last few miles, the roads became worse and worse; rutted with scraped and gritted snow. (Shucks.) He took a couple of time-consuming wrong turns in the deepening country-lane darkness, and by the time he drove into Wheddend, it was six o'clock. This was as close to his destination as his road atlas could take him, so he had no choice but to stop and ask for directions to the Château.

The Post Office had been closed for hours (days, possibly), and the Spar was staffed by an educationally subnormal adolescent who had never heard of any château or any family called Simarde. His last resort was the pub. What the hell, he thought, he might as well have a pint and a pie while he was here.

The bar was already filling up with Saturday evening drinkers. They started early in this village. Most of the customers were men with hard-bitten faces; a few had soft floral wives in tow, some had wives who looked harder than their husbands, but most had wives who had stayed at home. Apart from a few suicidally apathetic teenagers with dull eyes and fruit-machine frowns, that was the limit of the clientele; there was nothing newer than a D-reg in the car park, and not a stitch of Racing Green knitwear in the place. Not holiday-home country, then.

The landlady was friendlier and cheerier than her customers would lead you to expect, and Iain hit gold straight away. She not only knew where the Château was, she even sketched him a little map. Then, while she was pulling his pint, she remarked that he wasn't the only person who'd been asking about them Simmards. Two young women in here yesterday lunchtime. From London by the sound of em. Down for the funeral.

'Really? They didn't happen to mention where they were going?'

361

'Went off with the Simmards' butler.'

'I see. Er, did they have a car?'

'Oh, don't ask me – I just serve em, I don't watch ow they get ere.' She giggled. 'That's five-twenty-eight, my lover. I'll bring your food over when it's ready.'

He steered his glass across the room to a vacant corner near the window. At the next table was an old man: he caught Iain's eye because he was the only other solitary customer. Every pub had one: the mismatched, hermitish old regular no one wanted to talk to. He had a half-pint of beer and a folded newspaper on the table in front of him, and he was gazing about the room, studying the other customers as though they were aliens. Poking out from under his newspaper was the pink binding of an Ordnance Survey map. Perhaps not a local after all. Closer now, Iain noticed that the headlines on the newspaper appeared to be in French. Now *that* was interesting.

Iain leaned across. 'Excuse me,' he said. The old man turned his sad, watery eyes to him. 'Pardon me for asking, but do you know the de La Simarde family?'

'Excuse me?' The old man's voice was low and husky, drizzled with a syrup of French.

'I couldn't help noticing...' He indicated the newspaper. 'I just wondered if you knew the French family who live near here. The de La Simardes?' No sign of comprehension. '... Er, *Parlez-vous anglais?*'

'Yes,' said the old man. 'A little.' He smiled thinly. 'To both questions.'

Iain spent a moment figuring this out, then nodded. 'You're not actually *one* of the family, then?'

'No.'

'But you know them?'

The old man nodded reluctantly. 'I am sorry,' he said. 'You, er...' His eyes narrowed, as though he was searching hard for his words. 'Ah, I think you have the ... *avantage?* Of me.'

'Oh, sorry. Of course.' He offered his hand. 'Iain Urbanski.'

The old man took the hand and squeezed it softly, briefly. 'Jean-Baptiste Duprée.' He gazed into Iain's face. 'Urbanski... You are, er, *polonais?*'

'Sorry?'

'Er, *Pole?*'

'Well, part Polish. My grandfather was a Polish soldier. He came to England to fight in the War.' Well, that was the shortest version of *that* story so far.

'And you are a friend of this family?' There seemed to be a hint of incredulity in his voice as he asked this.

'No, I've never met them.' Iain explained the circumstances of his association, leaving out the jealous rage that had brought him here.

Monsieur Duprée shook his head sadly over Lydia. 'I have not heard about this young lady. It is *tragique* that I come here now.'

He was reluctant to tell the story behind his visit, but Iain was good at probing, and it emerged gradually. Arriving in Britain, he had spent a few days travelling, seeing the sights. Eventually, he ended up in a cheap hotel in Bristol, near the railway station. He stayed for three days. Returning to his room one evening after a day's sightseeing, he found that all his money – most of his life savings, by the sound of it, in cash – had been stolen. The police were called: staff and guests were questioned, searches were carried out, but not a trace of the money was found, nor any clue as to the culprit. The money left in his wallet once he had paid his hotel bill – even with a generous discount by way of notional compensation – was insufficient to get him home. He didn't own a credit card; he didn't even have a bank account. He tried calling the French Embassy, but they weren't helpful. They had queues out into the street; Christmas was coming, and many of their staff were on leave. They would lend him the money he needed, provided he came to London and presented his credentials. No, they could not make him a special case. He told them he couldn't afford to come; did they know how much London hotels cost? They told him they were sorry. He made some inquiries, and found that he had enough money for a single train fare to Devon, plus a little left over for sundry expenses. That little had carried him this far, and was now exhausted.

'There is one family,' he told Iain, 'which helps me, I think. I know them since many years. It was my honour as *vendeur* to sell all the necessaries of music for Salvador. *Tous les deux.*' He sipped his beer. 'They owe me still a little money from long ago, so . . .' He shrugged.

With a sort of smug inevitability, Iain's food arrived at that moment. He felt shamefully greedy as the huge oval plate of steak and kidney pie and lumber-heap of chips was laid in front of him. He hadn't eaten since his late-morning breakfast, and his stomach was griping and growling painfully. He forked a thick chip; it was half-way to his open mouth when he noticed the old man's eyes following it. He put the chip down again, and the eyes looked away.

'You haven't eaten, have you?' Iain said.

'Me? I am fine.' He shook his head, but couldn't help glancing covetously at the pie.

Iain gazed dismally at his plate for a moment, then lifted it up, cutlery and all. 'Here,' he said, putting it in front of the old man. 'You have it.'

'No. Please. I have not enough money to—'

'Exactly. It's yours. I'll go and order another.'

Monsieur Duprée looked as though he was ready to weep, caught between humiliation and hunger. Iain went to the bar and ordered a second meal. While he was there, he bought the old man another half of beer. When he returned to his table, the pie and chips were almost half-eaten. Monsieur Duprée looked up and smiled sheepishly, but his eyes showed a trace of defiance: the resentment of the victim of charity.

'I did not know how hungry I am,' he said as Iain sat down. 'Hungry is terrible. I have seen people . . . *comme des bêtes* from hungriness. It shames us. Two things: hunger and women – men will be animals from them.'

Iain lit a cigarette and drank some beer. 'Well, civilisation is just a thin veneer. Not even that – more a varnish than a veneer.' He took another mouthful of beer and chewed over his next words. It was a long shot, but worth a try. 'You say you've known the de La Simarde family a long time,' he began tentatively. 'Do you know anything about the Black . . . I mean the *Château Noir*? Or *Einsatzgruppen*?'

Monsieur Duprée laid down his knife and fork, and stared at Iain, chewing slowly. At last, he swallowed and spoke: 'The *Château Noir*?'

'The Château de La Simarde was known as—'

'I know. How do *you* know this?'

'I read about it in a book. I'm very interested in all that stuff. My grandfather—'

'Interested?'

'Yes. Do you know anything about it?'

Monsieur Duprée drank some beer and pulled a face. 'Your *grandpère* was soldier?'

'Polish cavalry. He escaped when the Germans invaded.'

'Many did. Many did not. Your *grandpère* – you ask him these questions, like you ask me?'

'He's dead now. Yes, I did. I always wanted to know about the War.'

'Hmm. Does he answer you?'

'Eventually. He didn't like to talk about it much. You see, he was very badly—'

'Then there is your answer.' Monsieur Duprée paused. 'Some people . . . Things were done which were very bad. After it was finished, I accuse you and you accuse her and she accuse me. Many were accused who have done only little bad things or nothing. There were some also who were . . . *soupçonnés*, but not accused to their face.' He put his knife down and patted his chest. 'I was one of those. The *famille* de La Simarde also.'

'Two of them were put on trial,' Iain pointed out.

'True. For long time after, many people had no business with them. I did, because I know what it is to be *méprisé*. I do not believe the stories.' He smiled wanly. 'I have thought sometimes, maybe I am wrong. But you see I need the business.' He screwed up his paper napkin and dropped it onto his half-empty plate. 'You have been good to me. In a little while, we will go see this family together. You have a *voiture*?'

'A car? Yes.'

'Good. I have not. Do me this other kindness, and perhaps I may talk to you of war things.' He looked up. 'Here is your food. Eat, and tell me about your *grandpère*.'

'She is not in her room, Madame.'
      'Then where is she?'
   'I do not know, Madame. I have looked in most of the ground floor public rooms and in the Italian Wing. I think she must have been gone for some time. The fire in her room has not been stoked.'
   'Did you ask Mademoiselle Glaister?'
   Février hesitated. 'Yes, Madame. She had not seen her either.'
   'I see.' Madame de La Simarde looked out of the window at the deep blue darkness. 'You shall seek for her. It is dark. She may have wandered outside. If she has become lost in the snow . . . Well, we do not want a *second* corpse to deal with.' She stared accusingly at Février, and he blanched.
   'Certainly not, Madame,' he said.
   'Fine her. Take the dogs and search outside. Has Joseph gone home?'
   'Yes, Madame.'
   'Perhaps that is just as well. Take Avril with you instead.'
   Février bowed. 'Madame, I trust this will not . . . be inconvenient for you?'
   She considered for a moment. 'I do not think so. Madame Quintard is more of an inconvenience when present. As she has chosen to absent herself, you had better request that Mademoiselle Glaister come to me now. Do it before you begin your search. Do not tell her our concerns for her friend's safety. We do not want to alarm her.'

Rachel and Clifford had agreed to a compromise. As a result, they ended up wasting what remained of the afternoon, and half the evening as well. After the promising lead of the Simarde name on the garage invoice, Clifford had agreed to stay on in Devon for a while.

Strictly on the condition, though, that they establish the state of affairs back home. This meant finding a phone box and calling the only person they knew who owned a telephone: a journalist called Mike who lived in Norwich and was sympathetic to the protest. He hadn't heard any news that day, but agreed to drive down to the construction site and take a look. They then spent four hours waiting by the phone box for him to call back. When he finally did, it was dark and they were stiff with cold. The news was no news: the bailiffs had cleared some of the trees and lock-ins, but the tunnellers were still holding out quite comfortably. There had been some TV coverage, and a few locals had come out in support of the protesters.

They agreed to check in again the next morning. If the situation had deteriorated at all, there would be no argument: they would forget about Rachel's friends and head back. She could always get in touch with them again if she really wanted to. She had waited this long, after all.

Clifford started the engine and switched on the heater. 'So?' he said as warm air began to seep into the camper. 'Do we go to this place or what?'

'We'll have to find out where it is first.'

'Fine. And what if they're not there?'

Rachel shrugged. 'I don't see where else they *could* be. We'll go back to that pub and get directions.'

He snorted. 'Are you kidding? That guy'd tar and feather us as soon as look at us. I'm buggered if I'm going in there again.'

'Have you got any better ideas? I'll talk to him. He might not be there, anyway.'

Clifford gazed sulkily through the windscreen. 'Fair enough,' he said. He put the VW in gear, and they headed back towards the other end of the village.

Février didn't like England much. Despite what Madame said, he saw in the people no greater substance or cause for respect than in his fellow Frenchmen, and he hated their insane weather, their heavy beer and their flabby food. Only two things made the country bearable: the honour of serving in a true château, and his dogs. Like everything else, they were owned nominally by the estate, but really they were Février's. He hadn't been allowed dogs at Gondecourt since an incident thirty years ago, when an animal in his care had got loose and gone digging amongst the ruins of the Old Château. The thing it unearthed there and brought back as a trophy – a memento of the *Château Noir* – had been severely decomposed, but sufficiently recognisable to send Madame into a purple fit when she found it deposited on the lawn outside the house. That was it: dogs were banned from the estate. He could only keep them in England, and he missed them sorely when the household went back to Gondecourt.

At one time, he had kept as many as a dozen, but now there were only three: two Dobermanns and a beagle. He was growing too old to exercise more than that. Too old for a lot of things, he reflected as he and Avril walked across the yard. Like thinking and remembering. If he wasn't careful, he would forget his own identity. He sometimes tried to do exercises to keep his mind and memory healthy, but he was finding that he had to lie to Madame more and more often, to cover up oversights and errors. Luckily, his lie about Mademoiselle Glaister hadn't betrayed him; he had found her in her room (in bed with her clothes on, strange woman). But what if she had gone off somewhere *with* Madame Quintard? The oversight and the lie would have been discovered. He had to be more careful. He had to whip up the weary remnants of his brain and *think*.

The two Dobermanns were first at the gate. As he clanged back the bolt and pushed the gate open, they swarmed round it, barking excitedly, twitching their docked tail-stumps and hurling their forepaws up at his chest.

'Janvier, down!' he ordered. 'Down, Mars!' They stopped leaping immediately, and began circling his legs, crouching and grinning. 'No food yet. Work first.' He handed a collar and lead to Avril. 'I'll take these two – you take Juin and look around here and the Château. I'll go across by the lake, round the woods and back to the gatehouse. Meet me on the Music Room Terrace in about twenty minutes.'

They collared and leashed the three dogs, then Février produced a square of material he had cut from the inside of the Quintard woman's coat. 'Here, sniff it up, boys and girls,' he said, letting them snuffle at the black fabric. He was enjoying himself; he didn't object at all to the obvious futility of the hunt (the fact that the woman had left her coat in her room suggested she hadn't gone outside). At least he was *doing* something. He turned to Avril. 'Got your torch?'

She held it up and switched it on. 'Yes, Février.'

'Then let's go!'

He switched on his own torch and, with the dogs straining ahead of him, set out across the yard.

368

Iain got back into the car and slammed the door. 'It's no use,' he said. 'I buzzed three times, but no one's answering.'

Monsieur Duprée gazed through the windscreen at the squat, headlamp-lit bulk of the gatehouse and the fierce iron spikes across the top of the bolted, chained and padlocked gates. So near; it was the story of his life. He sighed. 'There is perhaps another way, you think?'

Iain switched on the courtesy light and studied the map. 'I don't think so. See, the road goes off that way and that way. This line seems to be the estate boundary . . . The road doesn't go anywhere near it except here. There isn't even a track.'

'M-hm. We wait, perhaps? You try again?'

Iain shrugged. 'It doesn't look like we've got much choice. We'll give it ten minutes, then I'll buzz again.' He switched off the lights and settled down in his seat.

Monsieur Duprée unfastened his seatbelt and drew his thick coat tighter. With the engine off and the heater dead, the car was quickly succumbing to the frigid night. Their breath, thick as smoke, met and mingled and settled on the windows, fogging out the last dark vestige of the skulking gatehouse.

'This story of your *grandpère*,' said Monsieur Duprée. 'It make you very angry, yes?'

'Of course it does. He was betrayed from beginning to end.'

'He was . . .' Monsieur Duprée nodded. 'A man says a thing to me which I think was very wise. *I fear not to be betrayed — it is liberation in other clothes.*' He seemed to sense that Iain was staring uncomprehendingly at him in the darkness. 'Perhaps I do not make it good into English. I always think it was very wise.'

'It sounds like self-justification to me,' said Iain. 'Who said it? Pétain?'

'A man named Didier. He was a Resistance leader.'

'Oh.' Iain picked at the steering wheel with a thumbnail. 'Did you,' he began, and faltered. It was a hard question to ask, in any language. 'I mean, these rumours you mentioned . . . Was there any truth in them?'

Monsieur Duprée sighed. 'You have seen me. Does it seem so?'

'Well, no . . .'

'Listen, half my country was collaborator. My government was collaborator. England would be collaborator too if the *allemands* have come here. It is not *who* is a collaborator, but *how* did you collaborate. Willing or not willing, in a big way or a little way? If your hair cut away, or are you hanged, or is there little whispers about you?'

That was one way of looking at it. 'Which were you?'

Monsieur Duprée didn't answer. His eyes were fixed on the wing mirror, where a hazy white light was growing. 'Look,' he said. 'Perhaps the family comes home?'

Iain twisted round in his seat. The light grew and resolved into two headlamp spots. 'Maybe,' he said, and turned back to his passenger. 'We had a bargain. You said you'd tell me your story. Did you collaborate?'

The old man sighed and gazed into the growing light. 'Yes,' he said.

Chapter 3: The Ways of War

There. It is said. Let anyone who reads this suspend judgement until
they have heard the rest.

Antoine Lefèbvre and I joined the Battalion in the same week, along
with four others from the village. His experience was somewhat different from ours. We had evaded conscription, but were caught and
coerced into service; but Antoine – proud, courageous Antoine – why,
he volunteered right away. Anyone who knew him as I had known him
would have predicted this. He was a bully, and given to fits of violent
temper, so one might say that he was ideal material for military service.
The rest of us, not so; especially me. I had a temper, too – call it artistic
temperament if you like – but no stomach for fighting. The training was
very hard; violent field exercises with live ammunition. I barely came out
of it with my life. But then I got lucky: while Antoine and the others
went off to the front, I was drafted into the regimental orchestra. The
food was good, and my most arduous duty was blowing my *cor* in
parades. The rest of the time, we played for officers' dances in the cities
near where we were stationed.

That lasted two whole years. We moved about, following the regiment, but never came within ten miles of the front. I became soft and
flabby in my backside, and hard in my heart. My shame – which had
never been a very robust thing – shrivelled to bitter self-justification and
contempt for my countrymen's cravenness. All I did was blow my horn
and march; was I really any worse than the café owner back home who
served beer to the soldiers on his terrace? Some little part of me said
yes, but I did not listen to it. Had I listened, I should have gone mad. I
should have had to admit that the blackness of my uniform made me
worse (being a bandsman, I was the only one of our little group ever to
wear that infamous colour), the little thunderflash runes on my collar

371

made me worse. It made no difference that I had been forced to wear them in the face of alternatives that were too horrible to contemplate. I wore them, and that made me worse than the café owner. What was more, I wore my badges right down to my skin. At the end of training, a group of my noble comrades held me down and had the insignia tattooed on my shoulder: a death's head and those familiar crooked thunderflash letters: SS. It is still there. I see it whenever I bathe. I suppose I could have had it obliterated, but I have kept it. It is both my private admission of guilt and my punishment: I never married, lest my bride see it and know me for what I was. And dare I admit it? I guess so: it cannot harm me now. When I see this tattoo, there is a tiny place, somewhere deep inside me, that feels . . . not pride exactly – call it a *frisson*. I cannot explain it, and even if I could, you would not understand.

I am digressing. At the time, I played by ear. I mimed. In truth, I never believed in the ideology they drummed into us. Antoine did. He claimed to be Germanic; of Aryan extraction. The second happiest day in his life, he said, was the day the Germans rolled across the border. The first happiest was the day he was inducted into the Battalion. They recognised his devotion, and made him *Stabsunteroffizier* in pretty short order.

And so things went on. We did not see much of each other, although I heard tales of Antoine's heroism. He proved adept at infiltrating enemy lines, and his handiness with pistol and dagger was a byword; in a regiment noted within the Division for its dervish fighting, Antoine was marked out by a peculiar degree of pitiless savagery.

Then, in the autumn of 1943, everything changed. The entire Division was pulled out of the Italian front and sent back to France for rest and refitting. The rumour among the ranks was that we were destined for the Eastern Front again. There was another rumour that, this time, the orchestra would be disbanded and sent into battle. I do not need to describe how horrified I was by both these rumours.

They never came to pass though; neither for me nor for Antoine.

On its way north, the Battalion was diverted and stopped for two days at a small village in Limousin. While there, Antoine got talking with a soldier from a Wehrmacht unit heading out east. *Come to join the rest of your lads, have you?* said the soldier. *You won't be popular round here.* Antoine laughed. *We're not popular anywhere,* he said. It was true; even in Germany people feared us. *Oh, they've got extra special reason to hate you here,* said the soldier. Antoine asked what he meant, and was told this tale. A few weeks ago, a train carrying a consignment of French gold to Germany had been attacked and liberated near here by a group of local Resistance fighters. After the raid, both the Resistance and the gold vanished into

372

thin air. The Gestapo failed to track them down, and so a company of SS was brought in. They went to the village nearest the site of the robbery, and demanded that all terrorists harboured there be brought out immediately. No one else would be harmed. Needless to say, nobody was brought out. The company split into four groups: one started at one end of the village, one started at the other end, and two covered the fields on either side. You probably know enough history to imagine what happened next. It was not the first, last or only time this was done. When the soldiers left, three hours after their arrival, not one human soul, not a single man, woman or child, remained living; not a single house or shop or barn was left unburned. The gold was not found, but at least the ungrateful natives had received proxy justice for their treachery.

As we continued north, Antoine dwelt more and more upon this tale (I did, too, but for different reasons). He became obsessed with the vanished gold. His temper became shorter as his soul was stretched between loyalty to the Reich and his private lust for riches. When it was confirmed that our destination was indeed Russia, he finally snapped. He broke out at midnight. I happened to be on sentry duty that night, and I caught him sneaking out of the encampment without his uniform. He was a hardened combat soldier, whereas I was a flabby *cor anglais* player. He had a dagger at my neck before I could even blink. He offered me a choice: a slit throat or a long march back down south. The choice was no choice: especially when you consider the dark thoughts I had been having about death in the Russian snow for an ideology that was alien to me. Desertion seemed like a beacon.

I have never understood why Antoine didn't just kill me. When I asked him, he said he needed someone to help him carry the gold when he found it. *Who else should I trust,* he said, *other than my old school friend?* He also repeated something he had said the day he saw me marched into barracks following my recruitment. *The ways of war are fixed, my friend. Our ways obviously lie together.* I have remembered those words vividly all of my life.

I shall spare you the details of our journey south; it is sufficient to record that it was long and hard and perilous. We arrived in Limousin in December, back at the village we had visited the previous month. It now transpired that Antoine, for all his consuming lust and all his cunning, had no idea how to go about finding the gold. We had no papers, so we had to live in hiding in the forests, feeding ourselves off the land and sleeping in makeshift shelters. This went on for two winter months. I did not dare press him about his intentions or the precariousness of our situation: I depended upon him for my survival. Then, one morning, when we least expected it, we toppled out of the frying pan and right into the heart of the fire.

We awoke to find our shelter surrounded by armed men. Six of them, I think. A couple had German MP 40s, but most were armed with British sub-machine guns – Stens. They looked even rougher than us. They did not need to introduce themselves; we could guess who – or rather what – they were. With no more than a few grunted orders, they blindfolded us and marched us for miles through the forest. We ended up in a firelit cave, where we were interrogated for two days. They accepted that we were French, but were suspicious of our northern accents. Antoine astonished me by reeling off the most extraordinary tale. I suppose he must have been concocting it for some time. I would never have credited him with such imagination, or such skill in acting. We had been soldiers in Blanchard's 1st Army, taken prisoner near Lille in May 1940. He described our last battle and even quoted a unit number and the name of our company commander. (I have since learned that these details, including his description of 'our' capture, were entirely accurate. God alone knows how he came by such knowledge.) Our time as prisoners of war lasted three years, apparently. We were moved about a few times, ending up at Stalag Offenburg. Six months ago, the camp was accidentally bombed by the British, who were after the aero-engine factories nearby. (This had not, in fact, happened. I know, though, how he knew of Offenburg: it was quite close to the concentration camp at Natzweiler, where Antoine had served a convalescent tour as a guard after being wounded the previous year.) In the chaos of the raid, he said, we escaped. We made our way back to France, and headed south towards the Vichy zone, unaware until we arrived that Vichy no longer existed. Since then, we had been hoping to make contact with the Resistance, and join them in their fight for the liberation of France.

He told his tale well – he even managed to produce a tear or two of shame when he described our surrender to the filthy Boche. It was a desperate gamble, and – what can I say? – it worked. They questioned us some more, but I could tell they believed us. Some were suspicious still, but one – a boyish, gutsy young girl called Louise – embraced Antoine. I could scarcely believe my eyes as *Stabsunteroffizier* Lefèbvre, formerly of the Waffen SS, veteran of operations in France, North Africa and Italy, holder of the Iron Cross 2nd Class, was seized and kissed on both cheeks by this patriotic freedom fighter who had probably seen friends murdered by men just like him. She was moved by his tale. Perhaps she also fancied him (he was a handsome devil, Antoine, and full of manly fighting spirit). What do I know? Whatever; her gesture was like a sort of signal. From that moment, we were part of the Maquis.

Antoine was pleased with himself; he was one step closer to the gleam of gold (convinced as he was that it would still be in the Maquis's

374

possession). I was ... well, not exactly pleased. I was less ashamed of myself, now I was no longer a traitor. That had all been a bad dream, and I was determined to become the most ferocious resister ever to have bled for France.

We continued living in hiding, and learned the techniques of guerrilla warfare. I took part in raids and ambushes. I personally shot three German soldiers and blew up countless others. I laid explosives, I hid in hedgerows, I smuggled radios. When my knowledge of German was discovered (Antoine, who was less good at languages, managed to keep his secret), I became involved in intelligence gathering. I did great things, and I witnessed terrible things. I was there at Oradour-sur-Glane, in the aftermath (another tale of stolen gold, if you believe the wilder stories; otherwise simple, brutal reprisal). I helped to carry the bodies of women and children out of the church where they had been blasted and burned by men for whom I had once played waltzes and martial airs. Men just like me, some of them; Frenchmen pressed into those pretty camouflage smocks and pitched into committing bestial horrors that should not even be conceivable on God's earth. I could not imagine the experience of those women and children as they saw the grenades come flying in through the windows, so I tried to imagine the minds of those who had tossed them in; after all, I could have been one of them. What did they feel as the explosions and screams echoed inside the church? Pride? Shame? Anger? A sense of justice done? A little of all these things, I think, but mostly contempt: the certainty that any being who would succumb to this deserved to suffer it. That was the kind of perverted reasoning that kept men like Antoine Lefèbvre going. Make of it what you can. I can imagine it, because it had once kept me going for a little while.

After four months, Antoine's frustration was growing unbearable; he was no closer to the gold, and the Allied armies were eating up the north of France. I suppose he must have figured that he needed to increase his vigorish, as gamblers call it. I can think of no other explanation for what happened next.

Word went out that there was to be a meeting. I left my hideout and reached the meeting place – a forest glade – before anybody else. When the allotted hour came and passed and nobody else showed up, I began to grow nervous. I noticed a movement in some bushes away to my right. I crouched down and cocked my Sten, staring fixedly at the bushes. I was about to make my way forward to investigate when I heard a voice speak behind me, in German: *Put down the gun, comrade.* I froze. *Put it down, now, and don't be foolish.* I lowered my gun to the ground and put my hands up. As I did so, several figures rose from the bushes ahead. To my astonishment, I recognised them as my fellow Maquis. For one moment, I thought this was some terrible joke, but the looks on their faces told me it was not. I turned round to face the person who had addressed me. It was Didier, the leader of the group. *You understand German very well, comrade*, he said, reverting to French. Without pause, he gestured with his Sten and ordered: *Take off your shirt.* (It had been very hot lately, and I was the only one still wearing a thick winter shirt. The others were all in short sleeves or singlets.) There was no sense prevaricating: I knew immediately what was going on. But how had they guessed? I unbuttoned my shirt and took it off. Didier looked as though he did not know whether to spit or puke. The others gathered round me, staring at my shoulder. André, Didier's deputy, prodded my tattoo with the muzzle of his gun. *They give these out in the 1st Army, did they?* He said, and slashed me across the face. I staggered back, tripped and fell. Then they all began to lay into me – fists, gun stocks, boots – all except Didier, who just stood and watched. Just before I lost consciousness, I thought I saw Antoine standing behind him. The two of them turned and walked away. The last I saw, I swear Didier had his arm around Antoine's shoulders, as though comforting him.

And that was that. My War was finished. That my life was not, I have only God to thank.

The terrace was exactly the wrong place to be when the wind was in the west. Avril hugged herself and stamped her feet. Juin, sniffing busily around the base of a rhododendron bush, looked up briefly at the sudden noise, then went back to exploring the faint scent of fox.

Février was taking longer than he had promised. Neither of them should be out in the cold like this at their age, missing guest or no missing guest. They had searched outside once already, then inside, and now outside again more thoroughly, and still not a trace of Madame Quintard. How long now before frostbite set in? Wretched woman.

She looked up at the Old Wing. Aside from a faint glow behind the Music Room curtains, the only lights visible were at the far end of the third floor, where Madame had her apartments. How bleak and unin-habited it looked . . . No, she was wrong; there was a dim light high up in the great tower. Somehow, that made it seem all the more bleak. That was the only place they hadn't searched. Avril had suggested it, but Février had insisted it was pointless; it had been securely locked before the woman had vanished. Hmmm. She *had* to be up there. If she were, then there might be trouble before dawn broke. But how in the world could Février be persuaded that this was the place to look without making him aware of his dereliction of duty? Perhaps she should admit what had happened, but somehow take the blame for herself.

She turned away from the Château. Thank God; here he came at last; a finger of torchlight hopping amongst the distant trees. If only they could go back indoors, she would take the blame for *anything*.

'Come along, Juin,' she said, and shook the dog's lead. 'Here comes your master.'

Then, as if her words had conjured the anticipated relief out of existence, the light suddenly veered away and vanished.

'What's happening here?' said Rachel.

As they came down the last slope, the VW's headlamps washed over the front of the gatehouse and illuminated a Ford Escort parked in front of it, lights out and windows fogged.

Clifford glanced at her and smiled. He loved her for these little fresh-as-grass patches of innocence. 'Bit of a long way to come for a shag,' he commented. 'Secluded, though. I wonder what the noble family would make of it.'

As they pulled up, a hand wiped a hole in the fog frosting, and a man's face peered out. He didn't look as though he had been inter-rupted mid-fumble; actually, he looked rather old for that sort of thing. The driver's door opened, and a younger man got out. He appeared to be more or less shevelled as well.

Clifford wound his window down a few inches. 'Evening,' he called.

The man nodded. 'Are you visiting?' he asked.

'Yeah. You the security?'

The man snorted a cloud of steam and came closer. Clifford left the engine running and the clutch down, stick in reverse, ready to back off quickly. When the man was a yard or two away from the window, he asked: 'What's going down, then?' implying (hopefully) *don't come any closer.* He'd had a few bad experiences with people coming up to his window at blocked roads.

The man missed the tone of voice and came closer, until he was within arm's reach. He glanced doubtfully at the psychedelic camper and the grungey dog-man in the driving seat. 'Are you really visiting?' he asked again.

Clifford didn't answer; he didn't like the look of this guy. Rachel, trusting as ever, leaned over and answered for him. 'Yes,' she said. 'We've got friends staying here.'

'Friends?' The man peered in through the window. 'You wouldn't by any chance know a Beth Glaister?'

Rachel squirmed in her seat. 'Yes! I'm Rachel.'

He peered closer. 'Rachel? I've heard of you. Beth said you were a teacher.' She didn't look like any teacher he had ever seen.

'I used to be,' she said. 'I kind of dropped out a couple of years ago. Are you a friend of hers too?'

'I'm Iain.' Rachel's face didn't seem to register any reaction, but it was difficult to tell in the leakage from the headlamps. 'She's my girlfriend,' he explained. 'She lives with me.'

That got a reaction. 'Oh, that's wonderful!' Rachel squealed.

'She didn't mention me, then?'

'Well, we didn't get much of a chance to talk yesterday. Not much more than a hello, really, before she went off with Audrey.' She rattled off a sketch of events since the funeral. 'Have you only just arrived?'

'Mmm. I've come down to collect her. I heard about the car and everything.'

'Have you come far?'

'Peterborough.'

'Peterborough! And you've come all this way just to take her home? That's lovely. She must be thrilled.'

'Well, she doesn't actually know. I sort of came on an impulse.' He nodded at the gatehouse. 'Big mistake. The place is locked up, and there's no way to let her know I'm here. There's an intercom thing, but no one's answering it.'

'Oh. That's disappointing.' Rachel thought for a moment. 'Tell you what, why don't you come in with us and wait, and we can work out what to do. Have you got someone with you?'

'He's a friend of the family. We met in the pub in Wheddend.'

'Bring him. It's freezing out there. We'll get some tea going. We can all fit in, can't we, Clifford?'

Clifford shrugged. 'Why not?'

While Iain went to get Monsieur Duprée (his joints had stiffened, and he needed a lot of assistance to climb out of the car), Rachel rummaged about in the back of the camper, hunting down spare mugs and arranging makeshift seats. Clifford set up the primus and filled the kettle, grumbling irritably.

'This is Jean-Baptiste Duprée,' said Iain, appearing at the back door with the old man on his arm. 'He and the de La Simardes go way back.'

Monsieur Duprée peered uncertainly into the interior of the dormobile, eyeing its gypsy-looking denizens with a degree of suspicion that fortunately went unnoticed in the dim light. He allowed himself to be helped up, and was offered the best seat; a built-in affair padded with foam and draped with beaded rugs. The others sat on camping stools and tin boxes, and waited for the kettle to boil. While the gas hissed and the water chugged, stories were exchanged and recent histories illuminated; Rachel was particularly eager to be filled in on Beth's life since university.

After the first round of tea, Iain went and tried the intercom buzzer again. There was still no answer. What if it was broken? They might be here all night, pressing a dead button. He looked at his watch, tilting it to catch the emerging moonlight. It was nearly half-past eight. He would stay until nine, he decided; after that, the others could do what they wanted, but he was going to find a bed for the night. The Rose & Hart, he had noticed, had a couple of rooms.

He pressed the buzzer once more and counted slowly to ten. Picturing a butler walking Chigley-slow down a long corridor, he counted to ten again. When there was still no answer, he turned away. Instead of going back to the dormobile, though, he walked up to the gate and looked through the railings, hoping to catch a glimpse of the Château. All he could see were the black silhouettes of trees against the pale grey of the snow... And something moving. Staring hard, pressing his face to the railings, he saw it move again: ear-shapes and a pair of forelegs, much too big for a fox. And yes, there was a lead arcing up from its neck, and part of a human silhouette merging with the thick bole of a tree.

'Hello?' he called.

His voice burst the silence like a balloon. The dog, which he now realised had been staring right at him, barked furiously. It was joined by its twin, which had been lurking in the shadow of the tree. Their chain leads rattled and cracked, and a man's voice whipped them to grumbling quiet.

'Hello?' Iain repeated. 'Do you work here?'

The man walked forward, the dogs straining ahead of him like a two-headed Cerberus. As he came, a torch flicked on in his free hand and shone full in Iain's face. 'Who are you?' he demanded.

Iain's eyeballs ached in the flood of torchlight; he tried to shade them and simultaneously peer around the light at the man behind it. 'My name's Urbanski. Iain Urbanski. I believe my girlfriend is staying at the Château? Bethany Glaister?'

The torchlight jumped momentarily over his shoulder, then settled on his face again. 'Who are those people?' the voice asked.

'I'm a friend of Beth's as well,' said Rachel, appearing at Iain's side. 'Beth Glaister and Audrey Shufflebotham?' she prompted.

'The Château is closed,' said the voice. 'Madame is not receiving visitors. You will have to come again in the morning.'

'You don't understand,' said Rachel. 'I arranged to meet them, but I missed them. They came here.'

'There is no one of those names here,' said the voice. The dogs, seeming to catch the hostility in their master's manner, growled louder.

'There must be,' Iain protested. 'They stayed last night. Beth phoned me from here this morning.'

There was a pause, filled with the deep growling of the dogs, then the man spoke again: 'The young ladies departed here earlier today.'

'*What?*' Iain gripped the bars of the gate; one of the dogs hurled a furious bark at him, and he took a step back. 'You're joking! Where did they go?'

He sensed the non-committal shrug in the disembodied answer: 'I do not know. Home, perhaps.'

'What time was this?'

A pause. 'Near lunch. Noon, maybe.'

'But that's—'

'Sorry. Your friends are not here, and the Château is closed. I must ask you to leave the premises.'

'Wait a minute! I—'

'Leave now, please.'

The torch shut off, leaving Rachel and Iain staring blindly into a well of darkness flashing with splotches and clouds of phosphorescent light. Iain stumbled back to the gate and called through it, but there was no reply. When the coloured lights had stopped swirling in his eyes, the gatekeeper had vanished.

Rachel felt a tap on her shoulder. 'You'd better come,' said Clifford. 'The old geezer's having a bit of a turn.'

'A turn?' said Iain. 'You mean he's ill?' Visions of heart attacks and strokes filled his head.

'I don't know. He just went apeshit.'

They found Monsieur Duprée struggling to get out of his seat. He was wedged in behind the picnic table, and some of the rug drapes had tangled themselves round his legs. Rachel clambered in and started trying to help him free himself.

'We were listening in on what was going on out there,' said Clifford, 'and he suddenly started going all fidgety. Saying things in French and panicking. I thought he was going to peg it on me.'

The old man was still muttering under his breath in French; what sounded like a stream of imprecations against the squid-grip of the dormobile's innards. Rachel finally succeeded in freeing his legs and making him sit back, murmuring calming words in his ear.

'Are you ill?' she asked when he had stopped struggling. His face was white, blotched with bruise-red, and he certainly didn't look well. He stared back at her in uncomprehending alarm. 'Are you ill?' she repeated, raising her voice and stilting the words. 'He doesn't understand,' she said. 'Does anyone speak French?'

'It's all right,' said Iain. 'He understands English. He's just in a state.' He squatted beside Rachel and took the old man's hand. 'Jean-Baptiste,' he said. 'It's me – Iain. Do you feel unwell?'

Monsieur Duprée's eyes looked through Iain's face and beyond; an expression of unspeakable horror. He shook his head. 'Go away,' he whispered. 'We go away from here now. Please, we must leave.'

A udrey heard the dogs barking first, faint and distant. She looked through an arrow-slot and saw a torchlight needle sewing its way through the trees near the main gate. They *must* be looking for her, surely?

She was back at the top of the tower, restlessly pacing from embrasure to embrasure. She had been up and down the spiral stairs countless times, until she knew every groove and crack in every stone. She had hammered on the secret door and shouted until her fists were grazed and her throat was sore, but nobody came. (Where the hell was Beth? In her room, mooning over those bloody diaries? Why didn't she hear?) She had examined every window and door in every little passageway, but none would open, and none could be forced. As it grew darker, the search became more desperate. She had watched from the windows as lights went on and off along both wings of the Château, and had waited in vain for them to look in the tower. Now they were hunting outside. What was the matter with them?

'*I'm up here, you useless bastards!*' she shouted, but the wind coiling round the turret-top whipped the words away and flung them to the moor. She sat down on the boards, no longer concerned about the risk of splinter-damage to her skirt, and looked at her watch in the moonlight. Eighty-thirty. Nearly *four hours* she had been in this wretched prison, and nobody had thought to look here. It had occurred to her more than once that she had been deliberately shut in, but she had dismissed the thought as the beginnings of derangement. This was exactly the sort of place to bring on madness. Once or twice, as she went up and down the stairs, she had thought she heard a noise: a little like an animal whimpering, but too indistinct to identify for certain. In the darkening echo-curves of the stair shaft, it had been impossible to locate the source of the sound; it could easily

382

have been no more than the wind humming in the lips of the unglazed arrow-loops. An invitation to paranoid insanity.

She didn't stay sitting on the floor for long; aside from nicotine restlessness (she hadn't had a cigarette in five hours), the air dribbling in through the slot and down the back of her unprotected neck was sub-zero. She looked through the slot again, but the torchlight had gone. Tears of frustration began to come now, and she grasped the solitary iron bar guarding the narrow gap and heaved at it. '*I'm up HERE! Up here! Pleeeaase! Come and le*—...' She stopped crying and looked at the iron bar. She could have sworn she had felt it move. She pulled it again, and sure enough, it was rusted through and loose at the bottom. Even better, the stone at the top into which it was set was cracked and crumbly. She grasped the bar with both hands and pulled. It came away easily, bringing down a shower of mortar shards and grit.

At last! A helping hand! She hefted the bar; apart from the rusty end, it was good solid iron; the next best thing to a crowbar. Almost whooping with joy, she scampered across to the head of the stairs. A few feet down, the air was velvet black, and she had to take the steps carefully one by one. Eventually, after what seemed an interminable descent, she reached the bottom and groped her way to the door. She slotted the bar through the handle and wedged its tip against the jamb. Deep breath . . . and *pull*. There was a noise of splintering wood, and something gave way. Her heart leapt up momentarily, then slumped again as the handle slithered off the bar and clattered to the floor. The door was still shut fast, and now she didn't even have any means of gripping it.

She spent some breath swearing at it, then turned away; she was angry, but not yet defeated. She knew the tower well now, and on her way down the stairs had formulated a shortlist of potentially feasible plans. Second on the list was two floors up.

Climbing the stairs was easier than coming down. She felt her way around the outer wall of the shaft until she came to the second void. Here, a side corridor led away to the left, a narrow passage built within the thickness of the tower's wall. In her earlier exploration, she had found two doors leading off the passage, both locked. One was on the right, just inside the threshold of the passage. The second was beside a window near the far end, and on the *left*; that meant it led back into the body of the Château. She had looked through the window – another open arrow-slot – and estimated that the door would lead into the attic space below the eaves of the Old Wing. Not an ideal route, but probably the best she could hope for. The best thing about it was that the open window faced north-west, yawning down the brunt of nearly two centuries' worth of Dartmoor weather. The sandstone mouldings were eroded by wind and rain, wet green slime coated the walls and floor around the window, and a thin dusting of drifted snow clung to the stones. Decades of perpetual creeping damp had slowly rotted the adjacent door. It had looked potentially breakable, given the right tool.

There was just enough moonlight from the window to illuminate the door. It was even better than she remembered; actually crumbling and holed in places. She slid the tip of the bar between the softened wood and the stone architrave, adjusted her grip, and began steadily applying leverage. The wood groaned and wept a trickle of moisture where the bar pressed on it, and she felt it beginning to give. She pulled harder and harder, leaning all her weight on the bar, and finally, with a loud, damp bang and a chorus of tearing, the door popped open, trailing splintered streamers.

She looked through into the pitch darkness, expecting to find a vast, dusty attic filled with great heaps of cobweb-strewn relics. But her hearing sensed the space, bat-like, in the echoes of her breathing, telling her that she had found a small room. A tiny room filled with old air, heavy with the stench of rot and mould. Holding her breath, she felt her way in, flinching as her fingers touched wet, slimy walls and unidentifiable shapes of furniture with edges softened by furzes of fungus. The ceiling sloped in sharply, and she yelped in alarm as her forehead brushed against a beam covered with a cowl of derelict, grit-impregnated spiderweb. She crouched, drawing her limbs tightly into her body, and took an experimental breath. What rushed into her sinuses was one part air, three parts stinking decay; an oil-thick cocktail of decomposition with a distinctly animal taint to it. Wood wasn't the only thing rotting in here. She snorted the breath back out and decided not to sample any more. She backed up a step, aiming for the doorway, but instead came up against something hard. She yelped down another involuntary lungful and twisted round, flailing at her assailant with the iron bar. There was a loud clang of iron on iron, and the bar jumped out of her hand, landing on the floor with an ominously soft squelch.

Locating the door and nudging it wider with her foot so that a little glimmer of moonlight could struggle in, she found herself peering at what looked like the indistinct outline of a ladder. She touched it. It *was* a ladder; fixed to the wall and leading upwards. Being iron, it was the one thing in the room that hadn't been colonised by whatever vile fungal species lived here. She considered it a moment, then set a foot on a corroded rung. Deciding it would take her weight, she began to climb. The iron bar was left to lie where it had fallen; the furniture was evil enough; she wasn't about to go groping about amongst whatever invisible horrors lay on the floor.

It was a relief to climb up out of that room, even if it was into absolute, unimaginable darkness; at least the smell fell away as she went

384

up. The ladder didn't go very high; about one storey, she estimated. It ended in a confined space, not very much wider than a ventilation duct; too small for a service tunnel. Perhaps a secret hidey-hole of some sort. Those old castle-dwellers loved things like that. There was just enough room to scuffle along in a semi-crawl. Strangely, although there seemed to be no windows, there was a faint tint of light in the air; just enough to tell that the shaft curved to the left. She was still inside the wall of the tower. The light wasn't the only thing in the air; there was also a faint sound: the same weak, unidentifiable whimpering she had heard before. Now, though, it was coming from a distinct direction: beyond the bend in the shaft.

She shuffled awkwardly towards it, cursing as her hair and clothes snagged on the rough stone. The light grew gradually until it was strong enough to pick out the individual stones in the sides of the shaft. The little, animal-like sounds grew as well; a distinct, tearful song of weeping. Or laughing? She listened carefully; yes, it could as easily be laughter as weeping. She shuffled onwards, and came to the end of the tunnel, where it was transfixed by what appeared to be a ventilation shaft: there was a branch leading to the right through which she could see blue-black sky and stars, and another to the left, where she could see a glow of yellow candlelight. This shaft was even narrower. Deciding that her clothes were half-ruined anyway, she got down on her stomach and crawled into the left-hand shaft.

It went along for about three feet, and ended in a wall of crudely fixed timber. She put an eye to a crack and peeped through. Below her was a semicircular room. The floor was of bare, splintery-looking boards and the plaster on the walls was yellowed and cracked, crumbling away from the stone in places. There was a basic fireplace with a mean little fire burning behind a mesh guard. She could make out one side of a small, stained table with a pair of thick white candles in brass holders and a plate bearing the remains of food. To the left was one corner of a narrow bed, and on it, only just peeping into view, was a single bare foot.

The Dormant Hormone

There is a hormone that exists in all women's bodies. Nobody knows what it is called, because medical science has never got around to researching it. Nevertheless, it is there. If you are a woman, then you have it. Don't be complacent; there are some exceptions, but so few as to be statistically insignificant.

What does it do, this hormone? Well, it controls your hair. But *not yet*. It lies dormant in your body until you reach a certain age (somewhere between fifty-five and sixty-five), then it wakes up and comes stamping out, kicking all the other hair hormones out of the way and yelling *I'M IN CHARGE!* For some it sneaks out gradually, but for most it seems to leap out as soon as the menopause is under way.

It has three principal effects.

i) It turns your hair GREY

We all know this, and are more or less prepared for it psychologically. More alarming are the rarer blue, violet and pink tints that sometimes come with the grey. Even worse are the ugly boot-polish shades the hormone often secretes in order to camouflage the act of greying you.

ii) It STOPS your hair GROWING

Not exactly stops it growing, as such, but it *inhibits length*. Once the secret hair hormone swings into action, your hair will never grow past the nape of your neck or (at most) your collar. If it tries, it will fall out, like pubes.

iii) It makes your hair GO CURLY

This is the most puzzling effect of all. I mean, why? Is the comparison with pubic hair not so facetious after all? Does the association with the menopause imply that the secret hormone has some genital connection? *Why is there no research on this?* Because it doesn't matter what colour your hair is now; nor how long or thick or rich it is; nor how STRAIGHT it is. When that horror hormone kicks in, you will find yourself living under a hat-shaped nest of OLD LADY HAIR!

Of course, I may be wrong about the hormone. It may be just an Old Lady STYLE. This possibility, however, rests on the assumption that ALL WOMEN (virtually), when they become OLD LADIES, succumb to a crypto-Nazi HAIR REGULATION (we have a parallel with skirt-length here). If so, who enforces the rule?

I think we should be told.

Audrey was back in her room, working at her computer. Avril was in the kitchen, cutting vegetables. Février was somewhere about, servanting unseen reaches of the castle. Iain was coiled in his armchair, scribbling black lines of story. Rachel was up a tree, shouting at yellow-jacketed beetles swarming below. Lydia was in the soil, trickling slowly up to Heaven. And Salvador was etched into a disc of black plastic, rotating on the turntable of a 1964 Magnavox stereo. Beth was in a cabriole chair that was comfortable for about the first twenty minutes, gazing at Geneviève de La Simarde and thinking about where all the others would be.

Madame's apartments were furnished with an opulence that made the rest of the Château look impoverished. The boudoir was the hub. Its floor was thick with carpets and rugs from every exotic reach of the world, crowded with leggy chairs and voluptuous sofas laden with silk-tasselled cushions. Where the walls were not covered with silk drapery, they were painted, panel by panel, from floor to coving, with landscapes and châteaux and palaces, and where they were not painted, they were hung with gold-framed portraits: a gallery of a century and a half of Mesdames de La Simarde. There were a few there who had been immortalised young and had a milksoppish look of romantic youth about them, but most were older, crisp-edged and aloof. One or two looked even more formidable than the present Madame de La Simarde; as though they would have you flayed for an impertinent glance as soon as look at you. On one side of the room was an enormous carved marble fireplace with an enormous fire rolling and sweltering in it; on the other, between two doors which presumably led to the bedroom and bathroom, was an ancient, frail-looking keyboard instrument (Beth couldn't decide whether it was a harpsichord, a clavichord or a pianoforte). Incongruous beside it, somehow managing to seem like the oldest thing in the room, stood the industrial bulk of the Magnavox, seeping Salvador's liquid guitar from its kiosk speakers.

Geneviève had her eyes closed, communing with the music, and Beth was studying her. She wasn't the sort of woman you gazed at under normal circumstances unless you were as bold as she, and this was the first opportunity Beth had had to look at her properly. She wasn't like any old lady Beth had ever known. If time had abraded Geneviève, it was mostly on the inside. Marrying in 1944 must make her over seventy, unless she had been a child bride, yet her ballet-dancer hair was the colour of dusty tar, and her face had the texture of a pocket-crushed tissue flattened out; lined and dry, without the melted wax look that would normally go with her age. Her hands, though, hooked over the elbows of her chair, were elderly: brown and liver-spotted, curled like claws, skin retreating into the crevices between the bones. Beth remembered that touch, and felt again the odd splinter of warmth.

Madame requests the pleasure of your company. She couldn't get used to the formality; the castle protocol, developed for a family that had lived more like neighbours, that didn't spend the evening watching television in one room. Expecting an audience, she hadn't been prepared for light conversation and music appreciation.

The record finished, and the tonearm, with an old-fashioned rhythm of clicks, clunks and whirrs, lifted itself out of the last groove, swept back and parked itself.

Geneviève kept her eyes closed for a few moments, then raised her head and looked at Beth. 'My son,' she said. 'At the very peak of his powers.'

'It was lovely,' Beth agreed.

'The *Grand Solo*. This piece was playing in my soul the night I knew I had conceived him. It was my father's favourite music. It came again the night he returned to me, and I knew what it meant.'

Beth puzzled over this for a moment. 'Do you mean the two Salvadors?' She had read about Salvador's precursor in Lydia's diary.

'Two?' Geneviève shook her head. 'There was only one Salvador. He came to me twice, the same angel boy. When he was born and I held him in my arms for the first time, I could see he was the same soul; closer than a twin.'

It was a sweet belief, and Beth didn't question it. Instead, she asked a different question. 'Did you really know, or were you just guessing? About me, I mean.'

'Of course I knew. And was I not right?'

Righter than you think, Beth thought. 'But how?'

Geneviève gazed at her and smiled. 'You wish some crude biological

389

answer? That I saw it in the breadth of your hips or the girth of your thighs or the hang of your dugs? No. I am not talking about some capacity for whelping brats like a brood sow. Look at me; do I have a child-bearing body? Not now, certainly, but do I look as though I ever did? I am referring to a calling much higher: a mothering that is beyond mere child-bearing. I am talking of a vocation for fertility that comes to only a few; the gift of nurturing special souls. This gift shows – if one is able to recognise it – in the eyes; it reveals itself in an ability to commune with spirits. I saw this in you yesterday. I remarked it again when we spoke in the chapel this afternoon. Improbable as it may seem, I noticed it the first time we met, at Wolfburne College.'

'Commune with spirits?' said Beth. 'I wouldn't be too sure about that.'

'I do not mean like some fairground charlatan. Deny me if you can that a portion of your soul seems just outside your grasp, receding into shadows, offering up strange thoughts and sights that seem to come from nowhere. Can you deny me this?'

'Well . . .'

'Sometimes you think you see things that are not of this world.'

Beth remembered last night, and the funeral; the shapeless shape, translucent as a rainbow, rising up out of the grave. 'I see . . .' she began. 'Sometimes . . .'

'And these visions,' Geneviève went on, 'turn about each other, perpetually returning to one thought: the knowledge of the Child.'

Beth looked up, startled. 'Which child?'

Geneviève herself looked slightly taken aback. 'There is more than one?'

'No . . . I mean there isn't . . .' She looked down at her lap. 'No, there's only one.'

'I knew it. And he – I take it the child is a boy? – he comes to you in your dreams?'

'. . . Yes.' Mouse-quiet, almost a whisper. 'Except—'

'And he emanates a warmth that enfolds you, so that nothing that is of this world seems quite worthy of your thoughts?'

'Yes.'

'You see? We are the same. This is precisely how Salvador came to me; first and second. And I knew he would be a child of extraordinary, unearthly powers.'

'Except . . .'

'Except what?'

Beth shook her head. 'My child . . . My child doesn't . . . wouldn't have that.'

'Would not have what?'

'Those things you said. Unearthly powers.'

'Of course he does. He shall. I understand your modesty. You believe that such a phenomenon may not occur unless one has a great ancestral lineage to invest the future with its greatness. Do not believe it for a moment. It is true that people such as you and I occur more frequently in great families – the careful selection and refinement of blood-lines encourages it, and this, one concludes, is how they become and remain great families – but the hand of God does not work so simply nor so conveniently for the comfort of mortals. Do you mark what I say?'

'I do,' said Beth obediently.

Geneviève nodded, satisfied. 'The first time we met, you told me a lie. Do you remember it? You told me that my Salvador was not engaged in any illicit relationship with any of your friends. This you knew absolutely to be untrue. Is that not so?' She looked into Beth's eyes, seeing sudden panic there, and smiled. 'Do not alarm yourself. I do not reproach you for it. I believe I understand the motive for the lie. I believe I understood it even then.'

'Sorry?'

'Do not apologise,' said Geneviève, misunderstanding. 'I repeat: I do not begrudge you the lie.'

She gazed for a moment at the framed photographs arranged on a low table beside her chair, then picked one up and looked at it. Beth had noticed it earlier: it showed Salvador and Lydia standing side by side; a wedding picture, judging by the composition. Beth had been itching for a closer look at it.

'All I ask,' said Geneviève, not taking her eyes off the photograph, 'is that you do not lie to me now. I am going to say something that you may find hurtful and harsh. I want you to listen with an open heart and tell me your thoughts honestly. When I remarked in you this gift I have spoken of, when I watched you at the graveside yesterday, I could not prevent myself from wishing that Salvador had chosen you, not Lydia, to be his wife. My daughter-in-law. This seems a cruel thought, I know. I share it with you only because, deep in your soul, I believe you have also thought it. Consider; do not answer me right away; look inside yourself and do not lie. You have thought this, have you not?'

Beth could have answered right away if only she could find her voice; it was hiding somewhere in the back of her throat while her eyes dredged up tears. Instead, she nodded, and the movement spilled the tears over onto her cheeks.

Geneviève's face softened. 'Do not upset yourself, Bethany. It is not such a wicked thing to think. Only tell me why the thought did not come true.'

When Beth's voice came, it came stuttered with sobs. 'He – he was in love with Lydia.'

'I see. While you were in love with him, and also a little in love with her?'

'Not like *that* . . .'

'I did not mean *like that*. None the less, you could not bear to take him from her?'

Beth wiped her eyes on a tissue. 'I didn't want to take him from her. I couldn't have. He was hers, right from the start, before she even wanted him.'

'Then what . . .?'

'I don't know. Sometimes . . . I had a boyfriend. Danny. He was nice, but sometimes I wished he could be . . . When we were – you know – I'd be imagining he was Salvador. I'd never known any man like him. I never have since.'

'They are few. So rare, it is unlikely a person will encounter more than one in a single lifetime. Even I have known only two: my husband and my son. To love such a man from a distance must, I imagine, be a terribly hard thing to endure.'

Beth nodded and sighed.

'And to be possessed by such a man,' Geneviève added, 'I know well what it is.' Her eyes closed briefly, as though hearing the music again. 'To bear his child; that is a glory surpassing all others.'

Beth took a deep breath and released it in a long sigh. She was thinking of the way Lydia had spoken to Salvador in her diary, as though he were still there. 'Yes,' she said. 'I imagine . . . Can we hear another of his records?'

Geneviève beamed. 'Why, of course. Do you have a particular preference?'

'Sorry. I don't know much classical music.'

'Then we shall hear mine.' She walked over to the Magnavox and sleeved the last record. 'This is a recording he made in England when he was fourteen,' she said, selecting a new one. 'It is a collection of early Spanish pieces. I persuaded him to make this record. Some of the works were composed by one of my ancestors. Salvador inherited his gift of composition, but did not have the chance to develop it.' She set the needle in the opening groove and went back to her chair. 'Please let me ask this: why do you not have children already?'

Beth's toes curled inside her shoes. 'I . . .' She picked at her finger-nails. 'Lots of reasons. Iain – my partner – doesn't like them much. Even if I'd persuaded him, how could I have expected him to take responsibility for looking after them? I couldn't give up my job to do it myself.'

Geneviève didn't notice the transition from conditional to past tense. 'Are nannies so difficult to find? I can provide you with the name of a reputable agency.'

Beth smiled. 'Some nannies earn almost as much as I do.'

'I see. Your family would help, perhaps?'

'My mother lives in Wales, and she's got a job of her own. Iain's parents are well into their fifties.'

'Look at me. I am over seventy. Age means nothing.'

Beth smiled at her. 'I don't mean any disrespect, but I think they've probably had a harder life than you have. Physically, they're older than you.'

'You think so? I cannot imagine that anyone has experienced more hardship than I.'

They fell silent for the space of two short Spanish lullabies. 'This is the very best,' said Geneviève softly in the interlude, and the room shimmered suddenly with long, plaintive notes heavy with vibrato, sculpted out of the air by Salvador's adolescent fingers. 'There is nothing I would not give, nor anything I would not do to have him back again. I believe I shall. One day, he shall return.'

'Do you really believe in reincarnation?' asked Beth.

'Resurrection. What occurred with Salvador was more than reincarnation. It was a reconstitution of the body as well as the soul. He shall come again . . . Shall I tell you something? Yes, I shall. This is a story I have never told to a living soul. I think not even Salvador guessed what happened, even though he was the subject of it.' She gazed into the fire for a long while, until Beth thought she had lost track of the conversation. Then, she suddenly asked, 'Tell me, Bethany, have you ever pleasured yourself?'

'Pardon?'

'Have you ever been inclined to sensuality when there is no one to share it with?'

Beth frowned. 'You mean . . .?' She *did* mean . . . 'Well, doesn't everyone, sometimes?' She gave an embarrassed little laugh.

Geneviève shook her head. 'I do not know. In my whole life, I have indulged only once. The consequences were such that I never dared do it again. When I needed to do it once more, it was too late.'

'I'm sorry,' said Beth. 'I don't understand.'

Geneviève stood up and walked across to the windows. Between the two deep bays hung a portrait of the late Philippe de La Simarde. Below it was a simple, elegant rosewood cabinet on slender legs. Geneviève looked up at the portrait, then unlocked the cabinet. 'Quite early in our marriage,' she said, 'my husband gave me a gift. I believe he had it made by a silversmith in Paris. He called it *le soldat argenté*. He intended it as a joke; he was that manner of man. However, I took it very seriously indeed. I was not angry or offended; quite the opposite. I recognised the power of it, and had a box specially made to keep it in.' She reached into the cabinet and took out a small box, about the size of a house brick, and brought it with her back to her seat. She sat with it on her lap for a few moments, then, with an effort, held it out. 'Here,' she said. 'Take it . . . Quickly, it is very heavy.'

Startled, Beth jumped up from her chair and took the box from Geneviève's hands, which were trembling with the strain of holding it. It wasn't actually that heavy; again, about the weight of a brick. She sat down and studied it. What she had first taken for wood was actually worked leather, and it had an elaborate japanned clasp.

'Open it,' said Geneviève.

The clasp gave with a soft click, and the lid hinged up to reveal a long object moulded in polished, glimmering silver. She already had a shrewd notion of what might be inside, but the sight of it still took her by surprise. It was a silver cock. Not a phallus – that implied some degree of stylisation – but a cock to the very life, minutely detailed with subtle veins and even a wrinkled crown and slitted eye at the tip. And what a cock. Mesmerised, she lifted it out and held it up by the light of the fire. It was about seven inches long and . . . well, not actually as thick as her wrist, but probably competing in the same class.

'Lydia saw it once,' said Geneviève. 'Quite by accident. It is not a thing I display. She questioned me about it rather anxiously, because' – she smiled – 'Well, take note of the slight kink in the shaft. Very distinctive. It seems Salvador inherited more than just blood from his father. She thought she recognised the *soldat.*'

Lucky old Lydia, thought Beth. The men she had known could have slipped into the mould that made this without touching the sides; perhaps even brought luggage with them and still have room to turn around and admire the decor. All but one, and he was a memory so distant she sometimes wondered if he had happened at all.

'After Philippe died,' said Geneviève, 'I became very lonely. I had Salvador, of course, who was my life, but there are lonelinesses which cannot be cured by a son, however gifted he is. There came a night when my loneliness became so swollen and painful that I went and fetched Philippe's *soldat* from his box, and took him to my bed. It felt so heavy, it was as though some essence of him inhabited it. As the cold silver grew hot from my body, it seemed to grow heavier still. I had been right to sense the power of the thing. For one night, I had Philippe back with me, just as it had been when we were first married. The morning after, I put the *soldat* away and thought no more of it. Until, that is, a few weeks later. Salvador and I were due to depart for our first tour of

394

North America. On the eve of our departure, he was struck down by illness. He complained of headaches and stomach cramps. The family physician, Dr Giraud, was summoned. He examined Salvador, but was unable to make a diagnosis. Other doctors were brought, and they argued at length over his symptoms and the best way to treat them. By this time, Salvador was growing weaker and weaker. He was unable to lift himself out of bed, even to go to the lavatory, and a virulent rash began to break out on his body. The doctors became even more concerned and even more voluble in their disagreements. They argued their way through every malady in their textbooks, from scarlet fever to meningitis, and ranged far and wide over rare diseases I had never heard of. Specialists were called in, and one by one were defeated. Meanwhile, I watched my son become sicker and sicker . . . He had been ill for a week when other matters intervened and made the circumstance even worse. I discovered that I was pregnant.'

Beth stared. 'Pregnant?'

'It is true, absolutely true. I was carrying a child, and there could be no shade of doubt in my mind as to how the seed had entered my womb.' She looked at the curved column of silver in Beth's hands, its cold metal warming through.

'I did not know what to do, nor what to think. How could I bear another child when my beloved boy was slipping away before my eyes? It dragged on, week after week, and all the time he grew worse, until nothing was left of his body but bones covered with pustulated skin, and his mind was reduced to gibbering, groaning delirium. In the end, I could stand it no more. I dismissed the doctors, and began to prepare for Salvador's imminent death. With Avril's assistance, I nursed him myself, trying to make his last days as comfortable as possible, all the while shutting my mind against the new life growing inside me. Then, just as there seemed only hours to go, something happened.

'I was walking up the stairs, carrying a bowl of the hot, fragranced water we used to ease the air in his room. I was not concentrating, and I tripped. I remember the sensation of falling backwards, and the noise of the bowl smashing. The next thing I was aware of – at least, the next conscious thing – was waking up in my bed with my arm in plaster and a bandage around my head. Dr Giraud had been recalled and had attended to my injuries. He had also . . . he had noticed some bleeding, and so he carried out a thorough examination. Had I been aware, he asked me, that I was pregnant? I demanded to know if the child was harmed, because I felt a worrying pain, and he looked very grave. I demanded to know how Salvador was, and he looked graver still.

'That evening, the pains I had been having in my abdomen grew worse and worse. In the middle of the night, the doctor was called again, but it was too late. Nothing could be done. I writhed and gasped in a bed filled with agony and blood. The child was lost. I had not realised until then how much the knowledge of this new child had blunted the pain I felt at Salvador's inevitable death. Now I was being robbed of them both, and I fell into utter despair.

'I was terribly tired – utterly exhausted – and I slept. I awoke in the dawn to a sight I had never thought to see again. Salvador was standing by my bedside. His eyes were alive again, and he was gazing at me with love. Thinking he was a ghost, I reached out to touch him, and found that he was real. His body was still weak, but the vile corruption had vanished from his skin.

'As he and I regained our strength together during the weeks that followed, Dr Giraud came regularly to examine him. After each examination, he would pronounce Salvador many degrees improved, and shake his head in puzzlement at the miracle *I*, though, *I* knew now what had happened.'

She paused and gazed at the *soldat*. 'When, in my loneliness, I brought his father back to me, I drew forth the nub of Salvador's spirit and implanted it in myself. His body declined and almost died because his soul was slowly trickling out of him and back into my womb. When the child miscarried, his spirit was returned to him whole and he lived again.'

The record had finished some time ago, and the room breathed silence, interrupted only by the crackling of the fire and a slow wind whispering up the castle walls. Geneviève gazed into the flames, then raised her eyes to Beth.

'Well,' Beth said. 'What an extraordinary story.'

'I see you do not believe it.'

'I do. I do believe it.' Here, on a night such as this, she believed it. Holding this in her hands. She glanced down at its firelit lustre and could believe it had magical properties.

'Logic is wisdom,' said Geneviève, 'but it is also a chimera. Truth, ultimately, rests upon belief and subverts logic.'

'Sorry?'

Geneviève pondered a moment. 'Have you ever heard of the Rain Queen of the Lovedu? No, I imagine not. The Lovedu are – or were – an ancient African tribe. Savages, one would call them, though a little less savage than many of their kind. They were ruled by a woman who was called the Rain Queen; I do not know why they called her that, but they did. Always a queen, never a king. In spite of being ruled by a queen, they believed, according to the natural order of things, that the male is the dominant sex. The Rain Queen, although she was always a woman, was in every social sense considered to be male. A man in the being of a woman. The Queen kept a harem of wives, and she lay with them as their husband. From these conjugal rites of union, children were born, and the Queen was their father. Now, you and I may ask how this is possible. We know it is not. On the plane of wisdom inhabited by our species of logic, we suspect immediately that the Queen's wives were impregnated by other means than copulating with their "husband". They must undoubtedly have had intercourse with male lovers. This, however, had no bearing upon what they knew to be an incontrovertible truth: that it was the Queen who fathered their children. She was, after all, the Rain Queen, and the Rain Queen was male in her soul. Which truths are the truer? Primitive as these people may have been, how can you be sure that your truths are any less dependent upon the beliefs you have been taught to accept? Have you ever *seen* a chromosome, other than in a picture? Have you ever *seen* with your own eyes, a sperm fertilising an ovum? But you know this is the way it occurs, because people you trust have told you so and it seems logical.'

Beth followed the argument with difficulty. There was something rather more involved than straightforward cultural relativism. She *sort of* understood the point Geneviève was making; it seemed rather elegant and plausible. However, she *sort of* sensed vaguely that it was leading somewhere. Looking down, she realised that she was gripping the silver shaft unnecessarily tightly. She relaxed her fingers, and the white knuckles blushed pink. One part of her wanted to put it back in its box, but another, stronger part didn't. It was Salvador (or so it seemed, in the light of Geneviève's reasoning), and holding it gave her an odd feeling of comfort, like a pistol on a sinister street.

Without staring openly, Geneviève watched her handling the *soldat*, and her eyes warmed with approval. 'You may return it to its box now,' she said. 'I wish to show you something in the next room. Will you come?'

With a pang of regret, Beth laid the silver cock back in its bed of burgundy velvet and closed the lid. Geneviève was on her feet and beckoning her towards the left-hand door; the one Beth assumed would lead to the bedroom. It was held open for her, and she was ushered through. Instead of a bedroom, she found herself in a small ante-chamber with another door opposite. There was only one window, and the furniture – consisting of a bolster-ended sofa, an armless chair and a simple mahogany bureau – left only just enough space for them both to stand. The room was heated only by overflow from the boudoir, and Beth realised how hot she had become sitting by the fire; this room seemed blissfully cool.

'My inner sanctum,' said Geneviève, gesturing for Beth to sit on the sofa. 'In here, I am able to feel utterly alone, utterly severed from the stresses of the world.'

Beth, sitting down on the delightfully comfortable sofa (so soft after the stiff, formal cabriole), looked up at this tiny, frail woman, and wondered how she could ever have been nervous of her. She tried to recall the impression of almost combustible power, but it was gone.

'I don't know how you cope with having so many rooms,' she said. 'I couldn't.'

'Really? Why not?'

'I don't know really. I just have this phobia about rooms not being used.'

The moment she said it, its meaning slammed into her brain. It was so obvious. Geneviève grasped it immediately.

'I think we both know why that is,' she said.

Beth nodded. 'Yes.' *Do you, though? Do you really?* 'Er . . . You said you wanted to show me something . . .' What curio could possibly top the *soldat?* Platinum testes? Gold pudenda?

'Indeed.' Geneviève opened the bureau and reached inside. The object she brought out was indeed gold, and required two hands and all her strength to lift.

Beth received it, startled by its immense weight. This stick of precious metal bore no resemblance to any body part. It was a plain ingot; its surface seemed to bloom soft light, and was completely featureless except for some crude gouges and scratches on one face, like crossings-out; as though someone had tried to obliterate something.

'It is yours,' said Geneviève simply.

Beth didn't goggle or splutter; she just laughed. 'If only,' she said.

'No,' said Geneviève. 'I tell you it is yours, and so it is.'

'*What?*'

'At current market values, I estimate it to be worth approximately . . .' Her brow wrinkled. 'One hundred and forty-nine thousand pounds sterling.'

'One hundred . . .' Now Beth goggled. The sensation of riches was giddying: far greater than she would imagine could come from holding the same amount of currency, with its mere abstract equivalence value; this was a house and a car and a string of luxuries condensed into an *essence absolue*; actual, embodied, and dreadfully heavy. Thirty, forty pounds? About the weight of a half-grown child. 'This is mad,' she said. 'You can't give me this. I mean, why?'

'Is it mad? It is mine to give, and I am giving it to you. There are many more. When I die, they shall be divided among that pack of worthless mongrels who call themselves relations of the de La Simarde line, along with everything else; things I value more highly than any quantity of gold.'

'But I *can't* take it!'

'You can. And you shall. I shall tolerate no argument.' Geneviève sat on the sofa beside her and touched her arm. 'Bethany, I never thought to meet such a person as yourself again. Our kind has died in this family. I am the only one, and it is too late for me. It breaks my heart to think that you were there in the beginning; that my son might have chosen you to be his wife. I hold myself responsible for his failure. Had he chosen better, there would have been an heir. I am certain that he would himself still be with us.'

'So might Lydia,' said Beth. 'I'm sure she loved him. I know she did. But he was no good for her.'

Geneviève paused. 'Well, quite,' she said.

'Is there no way you can save the estates?' Beth asked. 'Surely there must be.'

'I have asked myself that many, many times. There is a way, but . . .'

'What is it?'

'Well, it . . . There is a way, Bethany; one that is closed to me. A locked door stands in my way. You, Bethany, have it in your power to unlock it.'

'*Me?* What could I possibly do? I'm just . . .' She faltered; the gleam of the gold tugged at the corner of her eye, and she stared down at it. It weighed heavily on her fingers, pressing them down into her thighs. 'No,' she whispered. 'You're not serious . . .'

'I am *absolutely* serious.'

'It's insane! You're suggesting I . . . It doesn't even make sense! It's impossible.'

'Have you not listened to a word I have said to you? Belief is truth; it supersedes logic. Of *course* we would need assistance, but truth shall not recognise it.'

'*Assistance?* What are you talking about?'

'Assistance necessary for belief. It can be anybody you desire. It is not important. It is the spirit of Salvador that shall suffuse you, shall make you a whole woman, *shall give this line the heir it must have!*'

Beth, staring incredulously, was backing slowly along the sofa. At Geneviève's final exhortation, she rose to her feet. The gold ingot fell from her lap and whammed against the carpet. The noise finally jolted her brain away from the last of the hypnotic weeds that had coiled around it. She spluttered and stammered, but no coherent words came out.

'Think of it, Bethany!'

'I don't want to. I—'

'You shall never be poor again. You shall live here with me: you and I and our Salvador. You shall mother him, and I shall teach him to be one of his class.'

Beth put her hands over her face and let out a muffled scream. '*NO!*'

That shut Geneviève up at last. In the tingling silence, Beth tried to speak calmly. 'This is my fault,' she said. 'I've misled you. I didn't mean to; I had no idea what was going through your mind. You see, it's impossible, whatever you believe. I've already—'

'I do not want your excuses,' said Geneviève bitterly. 'You have been offered an opportunity for which you should kneel and give gratitude. If you will not do this thing willingly, then that is the end of it.' She gazed calmly at Beth's face and added, incomprehensibly: 'Not the full amount, remember.'

'Pardon?'

The first thing she felt was a tiny bee-sting on the bulb of her shoulder; before she could even flinch, an arm was around her waist, pinning her arms to her sides. There was a sensation of sinking into dark water, and she thought her blood was rushing up from the ends of her limbs, crowding into her brain. The water closed like a camera shutter around her eyes; the last thing she saw was Geneviève de La Simarde's face, in the centre of the darkness. Her expression hadn't altered; she just gazed and gazed and gazed, and then vanished.

'What do you think?' said Rachel.

Nobody answered: Monsieur Duprée was picking nervously at the rim of the table and staring at his misted reflection in the window; Iain was staring at Monsieur Duprée; Clifford was staring into space, wondering what he was doing here.

'I said, what do you think?' she repeated.

'Who?' said Clifford.

'Any of you. I mean, *are* they still in there? Iain?'

'Hm? I don't know. He said they left about mid-day, but I spoke to Beth about half-one, two, and she was still here.' That was what she had claimed, at least. But a mobile phone could be anywhere, and right or wrong, something in that conversation had alerted suspicion. He leaned close to Monsieur Duprée. 'What is it?' he asked gently. 'What's the matter?'

The old man turned his watery eyes on him. He munched his lips as though he were about to spit. 'This man,' he said at last. 'Do you see his face?'

'The man out there? No, he had a light in my eyes. Why, do you know him?'

Slowly, the old man nodded his head. 'I think . . . Yes, I know him.'

'Who is he?'

'I do not know who now. I know only who he was.'

The girl slumped in Février's arms like a sack of coal; she wasn't lightweight, and he was thankful for the proximity of the sofa. He lowered her gently onto it, arranging the cushions to support her head and making sure she could breathe properly. His shoe butted against the bar of gold, and he glanced down at it curiously.

'She did not prove susceptible to persuasion,' said Madame. 'She seemed so at first, and I was quite convinced of my choice. She appears to have an hysterical element in her personality that I had not previously noted.' She waited for Février to stand up. 'Have you found the other?'

'No, Madame. I am sorry. We have searched everywhere.'

'Outside and in?'

'Yes, Madame. Twice outside. Indeed, such has been the thoroughness of the search, it was only by good fortune that I was present to hear your ring.'

'You need not reproach yourself. I rang only as a precaution. I had not truly expected her to respond so irrationally to my proposition.' She looked down at the girl. 'This will not do. She shall have to be moved.'

'Yes, Madame.'

'Do it now, then search the Château again. That woman must be found. She cannot have gone far.'

'Bloody hell,' Audrey murmured. 'Bloody bloody hell.' What she was peering down on was unmistakable: it was a prison cell. She called out: 'Hello?', but there was no response; the foot didn't even stir. She called several times, but the weeping chuckling sound just kept on bubbling up to the shaft.

She tried pushing at the wooden slats, but couldn't budge them. She backed out of the shaft, turned around and went in feet-first. Three good both-feet kicks cleared the obstruction, sending it clattering down into the room. She twisted onto her front and began reversing out of the hole, lowering herself cautiously, kicking plaster off the wall as she scrabbled for a toe-hold. The words *breech-birth* wandered inconsequentially across her mind, and she slithered out of the shaft and landed with a gasping *whumph!* on the floor.

She clambered to her feet and looked at the bed. Beth's account of her dream crashed into her brain. Lying there, curled into a foetal crouch, face to the wall, was the running girl, exactly as Beth had described her, right down to the clumsily cropped blonde hair and the white nightdress, which in this light was noticeably stained and grubby. Audrey stepped closer and leaned over her. 'Hello?' she said again, quite uselessly; if the girl hadn't been roused by that Die Hard entrance, she was hardly likely to notice someone murmuring hello. The skin on her arms and neck was wax-white, with blotches of pink. In places, it looked distinctly sore. Audrey reached out and tugged gently at her shoulder. She came quite easily, rolling onto her back, and Audrey found herself looking into the face, staring at the rolling white eyes and scab-rimmed lips.

'Oh Jesus,' she whispered, and her hand leapt away from the girl's shoulder. 'Oh Jesus fucking Christ.' Without thinking, she stood up straight and screamed out at the top of her voice: '*BETH!*'

The girl twitched at that, and her eyes opened. Audrey leaned closer again, searching the face. Gazing in stupefaction, she struggled to find her voice. When it came, it croaked the word out weakly, as though it couldn't believe what it was saying: '. . . Lydia?'

The oxygenating bubbles gulped and fluttered up the walls of her jar. She was conscious of them, even though she couldn't see or hear them. The convoluted layers of the visual and auditory zones sparked and flared intermittently with echoes from memory, but were otherwise dormant. As were all the other sensory areas. Throughout most of the land, the ridges and valleys were silent. In the front's dense city, though, the lights were on and the streets were choked with traffic. She tried to order the flow, but couldn't; there was just too much going on. So she retreated to a hillside on the outer reaches and just watched the fireworks fly in the black, feeling the bubbles and waiting for something to happen. Somewhere else . . .

Somewhere else, all connections severed, there was another place as stunned and dying as this. Something . . . a terrible thing was happening there; a trauma; something like an earthquake, but silent . . .

She knew nothing of that. Even less. Suddenly, the fireworks stopped, belches and screeches puttering away, and a chain of terrific subterranean explosions burst behind her, turning the ground luminous with great washes of red and purple. The somatic zone; something huge was happening in the somatic zone. The explosions came symmetrically in dense clusters on both sides of the land; this side, that side, this side, that side; purple, red, purple-purple, red-red. Burst upon burst, like an underground battlefield. Then came a flurry of furious detonations – orange, green, yellow – right in the centre. Beyond, the city froze and the streets miraculously cleared, and she saw the bubbles.

Great glooping chains of bubbles and the concavity of the jar's inner face. Beyond was diffuse light; indistinct, shifting. Shapes moving to the silent explosions. By force of will, she pushed herself forward, contracting her lobes and squeezing fluid behind. Through the bubbles, at the glass wall, all she could see was a stationary blur. There was a movement, and a tiny hand materialised in the blue; it twisted, spread its fingers, and then vanished. There was another chain of blasts behind her, and a crooked leg appeared, stretching away from her like a suspension bridge climbing into fog. It twitched and flexed, then it too vanished.

She was pushing herself forward too forcefully; she was pressed hard against the glass, flattened on it, could feel it about to give way. Then, just as she thought it would shatter, it melted over her face and flowed away. The big blur dissolved into a dance of smaller blurs, which gradually began to coalesce into defined forms.

There was a view along a steep-sided, pale valley. There was darkness at the end of it, spanned by an ornate, flat bridge set with shimmering suns. And a face, hovering.

The mouth opened. 'Another,' it said. 'Now.'

There was a yelp of bright pain on the left, and she was back in the jar.

'Do we know exactly what was wrong with the car?' asked Clifford, trying to bring the discussion back to earth.

'The ignition,' said Rachel.

'What about it?'

'The ignition system was broken. That's why they had to take it to another garage; they didn't have the facilities.'

'Facilities?' said Clifford. 'You don't need facilities to fix an electronic ignition system. You just hoik the old unit out and put a new one in. Any garage can do it.' Everyone turned curious eyes on him. 'Why didn't you tell me that earlier?' he demanded.

Rachel flushed. 'You didn't ask. What do I know about cars? If you'd come *in* with me . . .'

'Hold on,' said Iain. 'Are you saying it's not true? The story about the car?'

Clifford shrugged. 'All I'm saying is, if they took it somewhere else, it wasn't because of what was wrong with it.'

'And where did it go to?'

'Another garage,' said Rachel vaguely, gazing at Clifford. 'Are you thinking what I'm thinking?'

'I guess.' He glanced at Iain. 'We didn't know it at the time. It was heading in this direction.'

Iain was beginning to put things together in his brain, but couldn't make them add up. Only one thing seemed certain. 'They *are* in there, aren't they? But why?' He turned to Monsieur Duprée. 'Are you sure you knew that guy?'

'His voice,' he mumbled. 'I know his voice. I not forget this. Never.'

'Who is he? How do you know him?'

The old man glanced at Iain, then went back to staring at his reflection. All of a sudden, his face seemed to be catching up with his

405

age. 'The two of us,' he said, 'we were Nazis together.'

Clifford snorted, and received a sharp look from Rachel. He'd had a bit of experience with Nazis: they came in uniforms or with shaven heads and DMs; he couldn't conceive of them as fluffy-edged grandads with drooping eyes and woolly scarves.

'Nazis?' said Iain. 'What d'you mean?'

'I mean Nazis. Not all have a choice in this. Some were willing, but most were made . . . After the War, I heard he was in prison. I did not know what happens with him. I never saw him again until now.'

Février looked back before closing the door. He chewed at his lower lip and frowned, then closed the door quietly. As he went down the back stairs, he met Avril coming up. She had some thick white towels and some sort of cotton garment folded over her arm. He stopped her.

'Madame wants to see you,' he said.

'I know. I heard the bell.'

'She's in her apartments.'

'I know, Février. I heard the bell.'

He stared at her as though she had said something grossly insulting, and gripped her upper arm. 'Tell me, Avril; how do you see me?'

She smiled nervously. 'I don't know what you mean.'

His grip tightened, and she yelped. 'Precisely. You think I'm stupid, perhaps?'

'Of course not, Février.'

'Senile, then? Losing my mind?'

'Février, you're hurting me. I don't understand what you're talking about.'

He frowned at her with Vulcanian eyebrows, and she half expected to see smoke trickling from his nostrils. 'Don't act innocent with me. I know you, remember.'

'Février, please . . . Madame . . .'

Invoking Madame's call fractured his attention. He let go of her arm. Before she could turn and hurry on up the stairs, he pointed a finger at her face. 'Remember, *my* part in this isn't finished yet. I am needed more than you are . . . Now, stop standing there like an imbecile and hurry up! You'll catch a rocket if you keep Madame waiting. Go!'

He carried on down the stairs. At the bottom, he turned left into the kitchens, walked through to the pantry, and stood before the key rack. On the end hook, simplest in design yet most significant in purpose, was the iron key that unlocked the tower door. Damn it and damn Avril's trickery; he was sure he hadn't put it there.

Glancing over his shoulder (as though there could possibly be anyone observing him down here), he seized the key and headed for the back stairs again. On the way, he stopped off at the boot room and retrieved his torch.

By the time Monsieur Duprée had finished telling his story, Iain was utterly convinced that Beth was still in the castle. Some dormant officer-gene handed down through Jan Urbanski kicked in, and he assumed command of the situation. He quickly dismissed going to the police; they had no evidence, and their appearance would hardly inspire respect. They would have to go in themselves. Before he could outline his plan, though, Clifford interrupted.

'Go in?' he said incredulously. 'Who the fuck d'you think you are, the SAS?'

'Clifford,' said Rachel, 'my friends are in there.'

'So? What's this guy gonna do to them?' He looked at Monsieur Duprée. 'No disrespect intended,' he added, 'but he must be ancient.'

'Come on, Clifford, you love infiltrating. It's what you do best.' She smiled at Iain. 'He *would* have been in the SAS, in another life.'

'Bollocks,' said Clifford. 'Did you get the size of those dogs? They're *attack* dogs, Rache. They'll have your arm off before you even see them coming. And that place is gonna be *stiff* with security measures. You won't get half-way.'

'We'll just have to be careful, then,' said Iain. 'Look, I'm going, even if I have to go on my own. Who's coming?'

Rachel, inspired by Iain's chivalrous courage, counted herself in, leaving Clifford no choice but to acquiesce. Monsieur Duprée, despite Iain's suggestion that he stay behind and keep watch, insisted on coming too. He had his own business beyond those walls.

A quick search through the boot of Iain's car provided him with a pair of walking shoes left there from a summer trip to the Lakes, and a small torch, which he pocketed for emergency use only. He also took a small screwdriver and a large wrench from his toolbox. In case they were being watched, they drove their vehicles half a mile up the road and left them parked in a farm track, then returned on foot.

The gatehouse was flanked by high brick walls. The one on the left looked to be in a slightly poorer state of repair, so they followed it, looking for a breach. After about a quarter of a mile, road and wall parted company, and they had to trump through beds of snow-filled undergrowth. Iain was considering giving the order to simply scale the wall (they'd think of some way to get Monsieur Duprée over), when they found exactly what they were looking for. A great oak, growing hard up against the wall, had pushed its thick thighs up through the soil, lifting the wall off its foundations. The bricks, held together by mouldering old mortar and lichen, had tumbled down, leaving a gap which had been haphazardly filled with planks lashed together with fencing wire. This makeshift barricade surrendered quickly and quietly to a few concerted shoves, and they were through.

Iain paused under the parkland trees and inhaled the air, sensing and savouring the malevolent calm that existed behind enemy lines. The spirit of Sergeant Urbanski was with him. He divided his raiding squad into two units: he and Monsieur Duprée would make a southerly circuit of the estate, establishing possible lines of approach, while Rachel and Clifford did the same to the north. They would meet up on the far side and decide on a plan of attack. If they had trouble locating each other, the guide signal was an owl call.

Clifford listened to all this with mounting disbelief, but agreed to it for Rachel's sake. All he cared about was avoiding those dogs. Not quite all; he also knew that the kind of people who lived in places like this usually kept fearsome arsenals of firearms. He'd got on the wrong end of them a few times. Trespass was half his trade; the Mantraps Act was his charter, and he knew every clause backwards, but he was uncomfortably aware that, in practice, it didn't do much to protect the likes of him from the likes of them. The best protection would be for him and Rachel to keep as far away as possible from this dangerous loon and his military fantasies.

Plan of attack? he thought as they parted. What the fuck was there to attack?

It took a painfully long time for the fog to clear. Had she been drugged? Audrey picked up the plate and examined the remains of the meal. It was some sort of stew, made from what appeared to be the leftovers of last night's dinner and today's lunch. There were some bony bits of pheasant and chunks of beef, all mixed together in a kind of broth with chopped carrot and potato. She put it to her nose and inhaled, but all she could smell was pheasant, beef and vegetable stew. As if she would know how to identify a narcotic vapour anyway.

She put the plate back on the table and tried the connecting door. The next room was identical, except that, in place of a second door, it had a barred arched window. It was also lit by candles and had some scraps of tatty old furniture. She closed the door and returned to the bed. The girl was at least sitting up now, but she still seemed only vaguely aware that someone was in the room with her. She glanced at Audrey from time to time, but with blank, misty eyes. A couple of times, she convulsed and stared at the door with terrified eyes. The interludes lasted several seconds, then she would relax again.

The girl? Audrey sat down on the edge of the thin mattress and took one of the thin hands in hers. Emaciated, she thought, but realised that the word sprang from the surroundings rather than the face or the hands. She had always been as thin as this.

'Don't you know me?' she said, but the eyes kept sliding past, not making contact.

At least, thankfully, the terrified convulsions seemed to have stopped. The first time she did that, Audrey had almost wet herself with fright. It made her realise the full magnitude of her discovery and the danger she was probably in. What the hell was going on? . . . And who the fuck had they buried out there on the moor?

'Lydia,' she said, 'we've got to do something. *Please* try to understand. It's me – Aud. Audrey. Cambridge. Wolfburne. Rachel and Beth and Audrey. Do you understand?'

Lydia's ghost floated her eyes up and down Audrey's face, then settled. At last, they cleared and seemed to fixate, as though in recognition. 'I know you,' she slurred, and Audrey's heart leapt joyfully. 'I didn't recognise you for a minute. You look so much younger than you did before.'

'Younger? Look, Lydia, we've got to get you out of here. Just tell me what's happening.'

Lydia laughed drowsily. 'I keep asking *you* that.'

'What?'

'I wonder . . . *this is so funny* . . . If you're like this, is Salvador a little boy? He can't be my husband then, can he . . .' Her eyes grew wider. 'Is this before he's even *born?*'

Audrey stared at her. 'Oh Christ,' she murmured. 'What the hell have they done to you, Lydia?'

With a lot of coaxing and pulling, she managed to get Lydia to her feet. Then she hauled off the bedclothes and wrapped a thick grey blanket around her.

'Can I go home now?'

Audrey hesitated. 'Yes, I'm taking you home. Tell me now, is there a way out? You were out last night, weren't you?' She saw abject fear on Lydia's face. 'Don't worry. You aren't in trouble. Everything's going to be all right.'

'Look. I found something. It was in his room, where he works.'

Lydia walked over to the table. She was unsteady on her feet, and Audrey had to follow her to stop the blanket falling off. She pulled open a slim drawer and took out a sheet of paper covered on both sides with a dense scrawl in French. 'I can't read it,' she said. 'His handwriting's terrible. Can you?'

Audrey glanced abstractedly at it. Was that the sound of a footstep she just heard? 'No,' she said. 'No, I can't. Lydia, we've got to hurry. How do you get out of here?'

'I think it's orders. He talks about orders all the time. *Orders and duty, orders and duty.*' Her slow attention wandered back to Audrey. 'Don't you know how I did it? You *do* know. You said you guessed.'

Audrey cocked her head and listened. There *were* footsteps. 'What? Did I guess right? What did I say?'

'You must know what you said!'

'*Lydia!* We haven't got time for this!' She seized her by the shoulders and shook her. 'How do we—'

The footsteps scraped suddenly on stone, right outside the door. Audrey spun Lydia round and propelled her towards the connecting door, opening it and pushing her through in one movement. She closed it quietly behind her (there was no lock or bolt), then rushed around the room, blowing out the candles. When the only light left was window-dimmed moonlight, she pulled Lydia towards a rickety chest of drawers in the far corner. She made her crouch down between the chest and the wall, then huddled in with her.

They were only just in time. Just as she managed to still Lydia's excited gabbling, there was a distinct unlocking noise and the sound of a door opening. With a bit of luck, whoever it was would see the broken bits of wood on the floor and think Lydia had escaped through the ventilation shaft. They might not think to look in here.

The footsteps changed tone: from the scrape of soles on stone to the clonk of heels on wood. They paused a moment, then came marching – *clonk, clonk, clonk* – closer and closer. Unconsciously, Audrey slipped her arms around Lydia and began to pray . . . *Clonk, clonk* . . . Pause. Then two more steps, receding, and another pause. Audrey stopped breathing, willing the steps to resume and fade away. Instead, there was a sudden rending and crashing, as though the door was being torn from its hinges. Lydia yelped out loud, and Audrey shut her eyes.

Once they were positioned and checked for stability, Février stepped up onto the chair, then onto the table. Stretching up on his toes, he could just about peer into the shaft. He could see starlight at the far end, and he swore softly to himself. He *knew* they should have had bars put in. He glanced down at the sheets strewn on the floor by the bed. No, it was pure fantasy; even if you knotted together every sheet in the room, you couldn't get even half-way to the ground. No one would even try. On the other hand, though, who could guess what a madwoman might attempt? They had already had one . . .

He shone his torch into the shaft, just to give it a last once-over; it was then he noticed the tunnel leading away to the right. Aah. He thought about it for a moment, and reckoned he could guess where it would lead.

He climbed down again and went back out into the corridor. Sure enough, the door at the end – which to his knowledge had never been opened during the whole time he had served the family – was standing ajar. What was more, it had been forced. The lunatic must be loose in the tower. So now he had *two* of them to ... Hold on.

He examined the edge of the door more closely. It had been forced from the *outside*. That meant ... *Think!* ... He decided to go back for another look in the chamber.

Audrey was half-way across the dark room when she heard the footsteps coming back. With a lurch of horror, she tried to hustle Lydia back to the hiding place, but she wouldn't move. She just stood there in the middle of the room, in a pool of moonlight, and said one single, astonishing word:

'Audrey?'

Before Audrey could even gasp, the door flew open and dazzling torchlight leapt at her face. 'Madame Quintard?' said Février's voice. 'It *is* you.'

Audrey didn't plan what she did next; she was barely even conscious of it as she did it. She grabbed the trailing edge of Lydia's blanket and tugged at it. As Lydia spun away and toppled to the floor, Audrey leapt forward like a demented matador, carrying the blanket before her; she hurtled into the heart of the light and collided with Février like a flail, flinging her arms and the blanket around his body. As he went down, falling backwards through the open doorway, she went with him, landing on top of him and slamming the breath out of his body. He struggled feebly, spluttering and gasping, but only succeeded in entangling himself more tightly in the blanket. Audrey scuttled across the floor, seized the sheets, and coiled them around his legs and body, rolling him over and over until he was wrapped as tight as a mummy. Then, when she was absolutely sure he couldn't move so much as a little finger, she went back for Lydia.

She found her crouched on the floor, gazing through the doorway at the bound, twitching body. As Audrey helped her up, she grinned. 'That was *fun!*' she exclaimed. 'Just like Rachel!'

'You recognise me ...'

Lydia's eyes clouded with doubt, but then she said: 'Beth says you slept with Salvador. I asked him ... We didn't invite you to the wedding. I'm so sorry, Audrey.'

'It doesn't matter. Listen—'

'Madame got so angry about the baby. She brought Salvador back to life to make one, but it didn't work. He was silver ... Did you?'

'What?' Audrey was barely listening; she was down on her knees, ferreting amongst the folds of the sheets, looking for keys. While she was at it, she secured him more firmly by knotting together any loose corners she could find. Février kept up a breathless stream of imprecations and pleas, which she ignored.

'Did you sleep with him?' Lydia asked. 'He says you didn't.'

At last, Audrey found the key to the secret door, and stood up triumphantly. 'Got it! . . . He said we didn't?' Lydia nodded. 'Well, then, that's the truth. Now, let's get out of here and get you some clothes.'

Lydia was reluctant to move. She kept looking doubtfully at Audrey; whether because she didn't believe her or simply wasn't sure she recognised her, Audrey couldn't tell. She picked up Février's torch, took Lydia's hand and led her away; out of the cell, along the passageway and down the spiral stairs.

The only thing moving in the corridor was the dust in the air; the only sound was the murmur of boards under the carpet.

Audrey pulled down the brass handle slowly and inched the door open. The room was dark; the fire had died down to a faint cherry glow, and the regular green pulse from her PowerBook seemed as bright as fireworks.

'Okay,' she whispered, and led Lydia inside. 'Wait in here. I won't be a minute.'

Leaving Lydia crouched in the darkness in front of the glowing embers, she closed the door behind her and went across to Beth's room. All the way down the stairs, she had been assuming that Beth would be languishing in her room, blissfully unaware of the drama in the tower; she felt a little blip of surprise when she opened the door and found the room as dark and uninhabited as her own. Darker, in fact; the fire in here had gone out completely. Where could she possibly be? Oh well, all in good time: she switched on the torch and started opening drawers. There was no winter clothing; layers would have to suffice. She dragged out an armful of T-shirts and socks. The gap in between would have to go uncovered for the moment; there wasn't one skirt of pair of trousers anywhere. As a last resort, she settled for a pair of thick-rib tights, and carried her haul back to her room.

While Lydia was helped out of the filthy nightdress and into the layers of T-shirts, Audrey tried to find out if there were any servants other than Février and Avril; below-stairs staff whom she might not have encountered. Unfortunately, Lydia didn't seem to understand; she started rambling about some farmer whose grandfather had been a valet.

'She jumped out of a window,' she said suddenly. 'He told me.'

413

Audrey, who was discovering just how hard it was to put socks on someone else's feet in semi-darkness, looked up. 'What? Who did?'

'In the tower. *She* said it was in my room.'

'Lydia, what are you talking about? Is this the person they buried? Everyone thinks it was you; you fell out of a window in France. We came here for your funeral. Lydia, what in the name of Christ has been going on here?'

'Funerals,' Lydia mumbled. 'I've had funerals.'

Audrey gazed at her, wondering what these bastards had been pumping into her veins. She returned her attention to the socks; there would be plenty of time for explanations later. Hopefully. The priority now was to get Lydia away. No; the first priority was to find Beth. Or maybe . . . She couldn't decide; her mind kept wandering back to something Lydia had said; something she hadn't paid much attention to at the time.

'Lydia,' she said, 'earlier, you said *Salvador says*. He . . . he *is* dead, isn't he? I mean, he's not still alive somewhere as well?'

Lydia smiled. 'Oh, Salvador didn't die *really*. Salvador never does. I can't see him, but she can. She tells me all the time, and I believe her. *He* believed her, and he couldn't be wrong, could he?'

'Lydia, please try to understand. Is Salvador alive? Is he here?'

'Yes, he's here. Here with me all the time, waiting to come back to life.'

'Oh, I see.' Definitely dead, then.

With the tights on, Lydia looked like an auditionee for a grunge production of *Hamlet*. Audrey's coat helped, but the lack of any shoes didn't. Still, Audrey thought she knew where she could find some.

Checking that the coast was clear, she ushered Lydia out of the room and down the corridor towards the staircase. She would worry about Beth later.

Février, sealed inside his linen cocoon, lay on the floor and stared frantically around the room, trying to think of a way out. The one sure way, the ring on which he kept the cellar keys, which had a penknife blade built into it, was buried out of reach in his left trouser pocket. His left arm was painfully twisted behind his back, and his right wouldn't reach. There was nothing of any use in the room; it had long ago been cleared of anything that could cut or stab.

The one possibility that did exist gave him the cold sweats. Up on the table, a single candle had survived the sudden drag across the floor. It had burned down to a stub now, so if he was going to try it, he would have to do it quickly.

I would do anything for her . . . Anything. That was what he had written, and it was true.

The table was quite low, but by the time he had snaked and levered his feet up onto its top, his stiff elderly muscles were burning with pain. He paused to let the pain ease, then inched along towards the candle. There was a knot near his left ankle; holding his breath, he nudged the protruding fist of cloth into the flame. It guttered and smoked for a moment, then a thin blue tongue licked around the knot. It blackened and sweated smoke, then flamed yellow. He stared at it as the flame started to creep onto the surface of the sheet; if the knot didn't burn through quickly, he would be in serious trouble. The flame-front grew to an arc four inches in diameter, then five, six, seven, deepening as it ate into the under-layers and began to hum audibly. His trouser-leg was starting to singe, and the flames were searing his skin when the knot finally gave. He kicked and flailed desperately, swinging his legs down to the floor and rolling over and over. The flames sputtered and sparked and gradually died away to striations of scintillating orange on the blackened linen.

The fire had disintegrated and weakened the sheet just enough to allow him to struggle to his knees. The second knot was near his right shoulder. He worked his way back to the table and leaned towards the flame.

They met no one on the stairs or in the hall. Audrey was relieved to find that the wellingtons she had borrowed that morning were still standing in the corner of the vestibule. She helped Lydia squeeze her size sixes into them, then tried the door. It was locked, and the key had been removed. Shit. They would have to climb out of a window. Or . . . They crept back across the hall and down the passageway to the Music Room. For some reason (perhaps this room had Salvado-rian associations), Lydia started getting tense and nervous, and Audrey had to drag her along like a recalcitrant puppy. The french windows were closed, but one still had its key in the lock. One twist and a furtive pull, and they were free; the icy air hit Audrey's face like a slap, and she gasped as she ran out across the terrace, hauling Lydia behind her. She braced herself for the leap down the bank, but then skidded to a halt on the compacted snow at its lip, staring out across the lawn.

Something had moved. Yes; there, near the trees . . . One – no, two figures moving in this direction. There *were* other servants. Or hired hands of some sort. She scanned the possible routes of escape, but none would do: going right would mean skirting the parterre, straight

415

into the path of the two sentries; the other way, they would be silhouetted against the Château wall. She hesitated, and with every moment of indecision, the figures drew closer.

'Shit,' she hissed. 'Go back!'

Pushing Lydia ahead of her this time, she charged across the terrace again and back into the Music Room. Once shut inside, she glanced back through the window. The figures had disappeared. She pressed her nose to the glass, trying to make out where they could have gone. Nowhere, apparently. They had simply vanished into the snow. She glanced over her shoulder to check that Lydia was all right, then turned back for another look. She found herself staring straight at a stubble-bearded, wild-haired profile, less than three feet away. She yelped and stumbled backwards, crashing into Lydia and toppling both of them into a heap on the floor. As fast as a cat, she rolled onto her hands and knees and crawled away into the darkness behind a sofa.

'Lydia!' she whispered hoarsely. 'Over here, quick!' She heard the tiny squeal as the handle of the french window turned down. '*Lydia!*' she hissed, but Lydia just went on staring up stupidly at the opening window.

The two men didn't see her until they were almost on top of her; they were too busy exchanging surreptitious mutters. (It sounded like English, but Audrey was sure she detected a French accent.)

'Hello,' said Lydia brightly. 'Are you the Four Necessary Beliefs?'

They were gratifyingly startled, and Audrey seized the moment. She jumped to her feet, clicked the torch on and aimed it at their faces. She had already been on the wrong end of it, and knew exactly how dazzling it was; it was worth taking the risk. Poker-voiced, she spoke:

'Move a muscle and I'll blow your brains out.'

Both men put their hands up, squinting into the light and cowering quite satisfactorily. Audrey almost laughed at the spectacle. 'Lydia,' she said, 'come here . . . *Lydia! Here!*'

As Lydia scurried across and joined her behind the light, Audrey studied the two men. They didn't look much like servants or security guards. One looked too old, and the younger one – the face she had seen through the window – looked more like a vagrant.

'Did you say *Lydia?*' he asked.

'Never mind what I said. Just keep your hands up. Now, who are you and how many more of you are there?'

He began to gabble. 'Listen, we're really sorry. We didn't mean to come in, we were just passing and saw the window, and . . . well . . .'

'Who are you?'

'Sorry. My name's Iain, and this is . . . this is a friend of mine.'
'Iain?'
'Yes. My girlfriend's staying here, and I . . .'
'*You're* Iain?' Audrey sighed. *God, I hope she never has to depend on him to defend her.*
'Yes.'
She lowered the torch. 'Christ, couldn't you have said that straight away?'
'What?'
'Oh, put your hands down, for fuck's sake. I haven't really got a gun.'
He blinked and screwed up his eyes, peering at her. 'You're not *Audrey*, are you?' He looked from one to the other of them, seeing the state of their clothes and Lydia's mottled, scabbed face. 'This is Lydia? What in hell is going on here? Lydia's supposed to be dead.' He stepped forward, alarm spreading across his face. 'Oh my God, where's Beth?'

He was here; he came dancing off the spooling brown ribbon and made the bedchamber alive with his presence, and she could sense his gladness; he was glad to be amongst his mothers, past and future. The air was full up and laughed with him.

This girl *was* right; Geneviève knew it, had known from the start. The girl knew it also; what a pity she had not embraced the knowledge. Geneviève had watched her handling the *soldat*, saw that she recognised his power. So, his power would be sufficient, with or without the girl's blinkered unreason.

She took her time over the preparation, dimming the lights, adjusting the volume of the music. When everything was clean and ready, she spent a few minutes in contemplation and prayer, summoning up the souls. Then she began.

She applied the grease to the door rather than the ram – persuaded welcome would be more conducive than suave intrusion – working it in and nudging the door ajar with a thumb. It was ready. She put the *soldat* to her lips and kissed his silver crown, blessing belief into him.

In the long moment of elastic tension as he shrugged his way inside, a sigh shivered the still air between the peaks of plucked notes; Salvador's soul rubbed up with procreative lust. Geneviève paused and shared the tremor, feeling its epicentre in the shuttered house of her womb. Salvador was in. She sighed in response, and coaxed him in deeper.

★ ★ ★

417

The glass of the jar grew opaque and turned to bone, fibre and fluid; it closed in, and she saw no more. A neck grew out of the bottom, and limbs unfurled from it like flags.

She opened her eyes and was blinded.

'So where was this light?' Audrey whispered.

'Third floor, that end,' Iain replied. 'How do we get there?'

She glanced back along the passage. 'I don't like this.'

'Neither do I, much, but if there are only two of them left, and they're both old women . . .'

'You haven't met them. Anyway, I don't mean that. I mean Lydia. I'd rather get her right away from here.'

'Nothing can happen to her now. She'll be fine. He'll keep an eye on her.'

Audrey didn't feel very reassured; the old Frenchman had reminded her too much of Février. He had that same shaded look in his eyes, like thick folds of net curtain, as though there was more going on behind them than he wished you to know about.

'All right,' she said reluctantly. 'It's this way.'

They left the mouth of the corridor and began creeping towards the staircase, keeping close to the wall and its drapery of deepest dark.

Lydia closed her eyes; she was so tired. She had been sleeping, and then someone had woken her up. Or had she dreamed that? It had seemed to be someone she knew; someone who couldn't really be there.

She yawned; going to stifle the gape, she found that her hand was full of crumpled, tattered paper. His orders.

She turned to her companion, hardly visible in the darkness. 'Are you French?' she asked.

He seemed to think he was. When she offered him the paper, he took it, and a light came on in his hand. She asked him to read it to her, but he didn't. Perhaps he couldn't make sense of it either. He looked at it; staring as though it made him cross at first, then as though it made him frightened, then as though it made him happy. She didn't see what it made him after that; she was too tired. She climbed up onto the sofa – *so soft!* – and went back to sleep.

'I can't believe this place,' said Clifford. 'It's like a dream.'

They were in the stable yard, and they could hear the snorts and growls of the dogs rolling softly across the crisp snow. They had waited a full fifteen minutes behind the trunk of a thick oak, making owl sounds until the obvious stupidity of it became more than Clifford could bear. Their so-called leader wasn't going to come for them, so they agreed to take unilateral action.

'What do you mean?' Rachel asked.

'I mean security. These people are living in the dark ages. Literally. No security lights, no patrols, no alarms, no CCTV. They've even put their dogs away for the night!' He grinned. 'It's a dream. If those two have managed to get themselves caught here, they're even more dead in the head than they look.'

Rachel didn't like to hear him talk like this. Since they had started looking for her friends, she had begun to see sides to Clifford she had never suspected existed before. A shortness of temper and an insensitivity to her feelings had shown themselves. Also, the way he talked about people. His tongue had always had a contemptuous lick to it, but she had only seen it applied to certain kinds of people: developers, police, bailiffs, politicians, complacent citizens turning a blind eye while nature was raped. Not people like Iain or that poor old Frenchman. It reminded her of the way Audrey used to speak about people. Now, another facet was revealing itself: a quite inappropriate joy in what they were doing, for its own sake. He seemed to be losing track of why they were here.

'*Clifford!*' she hissed. 'What are you doing?'

He had his ear pressed up against a huge double-garage door, and was fiddling with its padlock hasp. He grinned at her and sniffed the air. 'Can't you smell it? It's the scent of too much wealth.'

She inhaled. All she could smell was petrol and old wood.

'And look at the state of this lock. Totally childish.' He took a penknife out of his pocket and applied its blade to the hasp. 'Some people,' he said, 'just don't seem to realise what they've got.'

'Stop it! Remember why we're here.'

'Why *you're* here. Anyway, this won't take a minute. *There!*' He freed the hasp and dragged the great door open. 'Just having a nose.'

Rachel watched him slip inside. When she saw his torch come on, shaded to a narrow pencil beam, she turned away and gazed disconsolately around the yard.

The moment was slow to build, but when it came, it was tumultuous; beyond even Geneviève's imagination. The atmosphere sparked and tingled with arpeggios of light, and Salvador's climax crashed out in a titanic major chord that spanned every octave, from the bottom of the ocean to the peaks of Heaven, glittering with a stratosphere of upper partials. The cosmic release channelled through her buckled and slapped like a gale-whipped sea, and she sank to her knees, breathless and ecstatic as it subsided and ebbed.

419

When she looked up, she saw a fleeting echo of the chord in the sleeping face of Salvador's new mother. The seed was there, she could see; unformed and vague, just requiring the confirmation of faith to bed and grow it.

She left the *soldat* where he was for the moment, and went to search for another.

Avril was in the boudoir, sitting on the edge of a sofa with a damp towel and a bowl of soapy water on her lap. When Madame entered, she got hastily to her feet, a look of fear on her face. Whether the fear was caused by the ritual she had imagined unfolding in the bedchamber, or the simple shock of being caught sitting on the furniture, was impossible to tell. Madame chose to ignore it.

'It is done,' she said. 'You may go now. Your role is played. Tell your brother I wish to see him.'

'Yes, Madame.'

There was a sudden noise out in the corridor; Avril and her mistress looked in alarm at the door as it flung open. Standing there on the threshold, hair all awry, clothes dishevelled, his face a picture of dismay, was a barely recognisable figure.

'Février?' said Madame de La Simarde. 'What in the name of—'

'She has escaped!'

'What? Again? Février, what have you—'

He shook his head at her with shocking, unprecedented impatience. 'It is worse – she has escaped with the other woman! They took me by surprise and tied me up.'

'*What?* How in the name of God has this happened?'

Février glanced at Avril. 'I went up to the tower to check on her. The Quintard woman must have followed me. This must be why we could not find her – she has suspected something and concealed herself from us.' He scraped a hand through his hair in a futile attempt to regain some dignity. 'I shall go at once and find them. They cannot go far.'

'No, Février. I have a more important duty for you. Avril shall go.' She went to her bureau and took a small black object out of a drawer. 'Here,' she said, snicking back the hammer and releasing it before handing it to Avril. 'It is loaded. Try not to use it except to defend yourself.' She noticed Février watching her curiously. 'My late husband taught me more than just conjugal sports,' she explained.

Avril stared at the pistol. 'Madame, I—'

'It is simple. Point and pull the trigger. That woman must not be allowed to escape. Now go.'

Monsieur Duprée finished reading the crumpled words and gazed into the darkness. So he wasn't the only one who felt the urge to try and squeeze it all out of his head. At least his own attempt didn't try so hard at looking creditable. To think, after all this time . . .

The mad girl seemed to have gone to sleep. He shone the torch in her face and brushed the hair out of her eyes, but she didn't flinch. No cause for concern.

Folding the paper and slipping it into his pocket, he stood up and made his way cautiously to the door, feeling more alive than he had in fifty years. The past was coming back in a way he would never have believed possible.

Chapter 4: The Ways of Peace

André, Didier, Louise, Gilbert, François . . . I never learned their surnames. I do not know whether the first names they used were their true ones. I think probably not. *I* did not use my real name. I changed it when I was forced into the SS, and again when I deserted. Antoine did the same. I changed it again afterwards, and I imagine he did too.

I guess he did what he did for two reasons. First, he gambled on their trust in him increasing if he turned me in. Oh, I dare say he spun them a convincing story, and he was a good actor. Second, with me out of the way, he would be in a unique position; the only member of the group who had 'real' military experience. That, at least, is what I imagine he figured, and I did know him pretty well.

As to why they let me live, I am a little surer. Didier was a compassionate man. Once or twice, I saw him spare lives others might have snuffed out. When challenged, he said he was a soldier, not a murderer. And anyway, how could I harm them? I did not know within a hundred square miles where their main hideout was, because I only went there twice, both times blindfolded. I knew their faces but not their true names, and they never emerged from hiding except secretly, to get supplies or carry out an operation. I could have passed on their radio codes, but I could have done that already, and they would have to be changed anyway. So, they beat me unconscious and left me to the Devil and my luck.

I had to stay in hiding for the time being. With no medical treatment, it took me a long time to recover. I was eventually picked up by the Americans. They interrogated me and strip-searched me. When they asked about my tattoo, I confessed all. I guess I was a little hysterical. I was handed over to the French authorities, who tried me and sentenced me to life imprisonment. Had it not been accepted that I had been forced into Nazi service, I might have been executed (as happened to a few of my kind). I served only a few months of my sentence. Since only men from certain parts of France had suffered this particular fate, it seemed unfair that those regions should bear the stigma of it. A debate raged, and the result was that some of us were pardoned.

Free at last, I decided it was time for a little reunion with my old comrade-in-arms. I went back to Limousin under another assumed name and, concealing my accent (after Oradour, it could get you disliked at that time in that area), began asking questions in bars and cafés. I discovered a local fairy tale. The first version I was told was that two German spies had infiltrated the Maquis; both were unmasked and executed. Another version had it that one was shot, the other escaped. A third told that they both escaped. I heard no mention of any gold. Finally, I met a boy who had joined the Maquis in the last month of the Occupation. Not in the same cell, but he had known Didier. Apparently, Didier, André and Louise had been captured by the Gestapo, just after the news of the liberation of Paris had come through. All three were executed. Their betrayer (there was no doubt in this boy's mind that they had been betrayed) was thought to be a northerner who had joined the cell a few months before. Nobody knew what had happened to him. He had disappeared.

Why did he betray them, I wondered, when the War was so nearly over? Had he found a way to his gold, a way barred only by these three? I set about hunting, redoubling my efforts. I picked up a faint scent in Limoges and followed it up the Vienne valley and across to Poitiers. From there, I followed vaguer and vaguer hints back down to Charente. Here, the trail died out utterly. I did hear that he might have become a salesman of some kind, but no clue as to where or what kind.

I came to my senses then. I had no money, and no place to live. I stopped searching for Antoine Lefèbvre and began looking for work. I was very fortunate; I found a good position right away, a position which would allow me to drop out of the world. I met a man who was looking for staff and liked the look of me. I still had some military posture, and I was fitter and leaner than I had been in my orchestra days. He had recently married, and his wife was expecting their first child. Many of their younger members of staff had been lost in the War, he said, and they were really quite desperate for replacements. He thought I didn't recognise him, but I did: like me, he and his father had been tried for collaborating with the invaders (it had been quite a notorious case at the time); but unlike me, they had been acquitted. Knowing this, and feeling that for once in my life I should keep no secrets, I told him my true story. He said it didn't matter, what was past was past. He offered me a position as his valet, and bade me prepare to accompany him to

England, where his wife and family were waiting for him. The young Madame took to me especially well (Antoine was not the only good-looking one at our school), and when her husband inherited full title to the family estates, she made me butler. That was my official title, but of course, I was really *much* more than that.

I had a mostly happy life from then on. I even acquired a sister and, for a while, a lover. I learned a few things about the *famille* de La Simarde, but my loyalty to them was always absolute: after all, knowing what I was, they saved me when others might have spat on me. And Madame; well, for her I would do *anything*. Even ... ah, but that is another chapter; one I may never be ready to write.

Oh, and I might as well mention that I discovered Antoine's gold. How Monsieur de La Simarde came by it I shall never know for certain, but I suspect it had something to do with the alleged crimes for which he was tried. (He had served the British as an agent with the Special Operations Executive, liaising with the Charentais Maquis. When he emerged as the only survivor of a Gestapo purge, he was suspected of treason; suspicion was encouraged by the hospitality given by his father to members of the Vichy government.) He claimed once that the gold was forced upon him by the Maquis; another time, he claimed he found it hidden in the Old Château, secreted away by a renegade Gestapo man. Either way, I am inclined to believe him, and I agree that the country which treated him so shabbily did not deserve its gold back. He used it well, supporting his family and his great line. He was a good master, and I miss him to this day.

The top-floor corridor was dimly lit by shaded wall lamps. Partly the light and partly the knowledge that they were getting closer to their objective made them creep ever more stealthily; each step a ballet of silent care, each carpet-covered floorboard tested for creakiness before being trodden.

They had covered about a third of the passage's length when they heard a commotion at the far end: an opening door and voices.

'Shit!' Audrey seized and twisted the nearest door handle. Thankfully, it opened, and they dived together into the room beyond. Crouching in the darkness, they watched through the hairline crack of the door as Avril walked by.

'That's the maid,' Audrey whispered when she had passed. 'Excellent. That'll leave Madame on her own.'

Iain looked around at the room they had hidden themselves in. 'Good God,' he murmured.

Audrey looked, and looked again. She pushed the door up and switched on the torch. Standing over them like a guard dog was the dappled head of a gorgeously painted rocking-horse with a sable mane. Next to it was a wooden cot, its gate lowered, all made up with blankets. Mobiles and chimes hung from the ceiling, and toys littered the floor around the fireplace. In the centre of the room, arranged as though abandoned by a midget orchestra, was a collection of miniature musical instruments: a piano, a drum and cymbal, a trumpet, and no fewer than three guitars.

Incredible, thought Audrey: Salvador's nursery. She had looked around the room several times before putting her finger on what troubled her about it. It had the eerie air of still being used. The toys in disarray, the cot waiting for a child to be laid in it, and over it all, not a speck of dust, not a whiff of age. She knew for a fact there were no children in the household; Madame de La Simarde had said so. *I so miss the presence of children.* Salvador and Lydia hadn't had any... Other words began to drift like leaves in her mind. Madame de La Simarde's after-dinner discourse on resurrection, that passage in Lydia's notebook, something Lydia had rambled about, barely listened to... *Salvador came back to life to make a baby, but it didn't work*... Something she herself had said, barely thought about... *I always thought Beth was the natural mother.*

She was blind; but for a wash of blurred gold and silver, her only sensations were of her new limbs growing and growing until they stretched out to infinity, and of two voices speaking inside the bones of her skull. They were talking some foreign language she couldn't understand. She tried to shut them out, and concentrated on her limbs instead. They were swelling now, like inflating balloons, and there was another sensation growing somewhere else; somewhere she couldn't locate; like an itch that eludes scratching nails.

'I swore to do anything for you.' He looked away from the bed. 'But what you are asking... I ... I can't do it.'

Geneviève stroked his lapels and spoke gently. 'You must, Février.'

'I can't. I ... I am not... I'm too old for this.'

She smiled. 'Too old? Février, old soldiers are never too old. They do *not* fade away. Certainly not this one. Did your masters teach you nothing? Can you not grasp the importance of this? It is the most important task I have ever offered you. You must do it.'

He stared down at her, and a tone of authority he had never used with her before slipped into his voice. 'I *cannot.*'

'Of course you can. You did it once before.'

'That was not like this!'

'It was exactly like this. When his seed was not working, you helped to confirm my faith. You did your duty then; you must do it now.'

Février gaped at her; he couldn't believe she could remember it that way. 'My *duty?* Madame, the only duty for me was to calm myself, to keep a straight face, while a part of me was dying in agony. The rest was not *duty.*'

'Février, you are bonded to me by blood. You shall obey your mistress in this or suffer for it.' She glanced at the bed. 'See, her eyes are opening. You must do it now! You must be there when she wakes. It is necessary for her belief, Février; without this, the seed may die. The soul of Salvador is in your hands. Look at her. She needs you.'

He looked, and felt the blood seeping out of his face. There was an ooze of white grease coming out of her like saliva, making a dark spot on the sheet. Her head lolled on the pillows, and her eyelids were fluttering.

'Remember, Février, you are inseparable from this. If you imagine it is wrong, do not pretend that you have not done worse.' Her voice dropped and resumed its persuasive lilt. 'You are good and powerful, my Février.' He felt her fingers on his fly buttons. 'You need not enter her,' she whispered. 'You are just the glue. She will feel the memory of the *soldat*, and her soul shall know it is Salvador. All that is necessary is that she should believe she has been penetrated by flesh. She must see you before her when she wakes.'

'I can hear two of them,' Iain whispered. 'A man.'

Audrey pressed her ear to the door beside him. He was right; there were two voices, speaking French. 'He must've got free,' she whispered, and looked at the face hovering next to hers. 'He's an old man, Iain. Don't be frightened. Think of Beth.'

He stared at her; if he hadn't known better, he might think she was actually enjoying this. There was a glimmer of excitement in her eyes, mixed with mockery. 'Frightened?' he said. 'Me?'

Her eyes invited proof. He took a deep breath, laid his hand on the door handle, and hurled it open. As he barged through, with Audrey close behind him, he let out an animal roar. It was slapped out of his mouth as he saw the scene before him. The vast bedchamber was alive with the light of a hundred candles, shimmering on the blue folds of silk drapery suspended from the canopy of the four-poster bed. Beneath, posed as though to give birth or receive a lover, was Beth. Her wrists and ankles were lashed to the bedposts with lengths of silk cord, and she was naked from the waist. He stared at Beth, and he stared at the elderly man and woman standing at the foot of the bed. They stared back at him. He noticed that the old man's trousers were hanging open at the front.

Madame de La Simarde recovered first. 'Who in the name of God,' she said with imperious indignation, 'are you?' She glanced at Audrey. 'Madame Quintard, who is this man?'

Iain looked as though he was about to vomit; his face was white, and his jaw was working slackly up and down. 'I . . . I . . .'

'How dare you intrude in my private chambers!'

Audrey ran to the bed and started untying Beth's wrists. 'What the Jesus Christ have you done to her?' she yelled. 'Beth, can you hear me? What have they done to you?' Chewing at the knots with her teeth, she finally managed to loose all the bonds. She enfolded Beth in her arms and glared at the old couple.

'I demand to know what this man is doing in my home,' insisted Madame de La Simarde.

'He's her husband, you insane old bitch!'

'Husband?' Madame de La Simarde gazed at Iain, her expression altering from indignation to disgust. 'The *Pole?*'

The word seemed to shatter the glaze of petrification that held Iain rooted to the spot. He rushed at them, yelling incoherently. Madame de La Simarde was pushed aside, and he rammed Février, tumbling to the floor with the old man groaning underneath him.

'I did nothing!' Février shouted. 'I did nothing, I swear!'

Iain took him by the throat and squeezed until his protests choked away to unintelligible gurgles. 'He told me about you, you Nazi bastard. Did you know you had a Nazi working for you, hm? Don't you know what cunts like him did to people like me?' Février's face was turning purple; his eyes were screwed up, and his tongue protruded between his teeth. 'Doesn't feel good, does it?' Iain yelled. 'What were you doing to her, eh? What kind of fucking perverts *are* you?'

'*Iain!* Fingers scrabbled at the back of his collar. '*IAIN! Stop it!*'

The man's face was starting to turn blue. Iain relaxed his grip and allowed Audrey to pull him off. He sat on the floor staring venom and breathing flecks of spittle.

Audrey returned to the bed. Beth was starting to wake up; her eyes were opening, and she was mumbling incoherently. 'It's okay, Beth,' she said, putting her arms around her again and pulling up the eiderdown to cover her nakedness. 'It's all right now. You're safe.'

Beth looked up at her with hazy eyes. 'Baby,' she mumbled. 'Wouldn't listen . . .'

'Hush, now. Iain's here. I'm here.'

Beth didn't seem to hear her. 'Baby,' she repeated. 'She wants me . . . have a baby.'

Audrey looked accusingly at Madame de La Simarde, who gazed back with cool defiance.

'Wouldn't let me explain,' Beth went on, slurring drunkenly. 'Can't have a baby again. I's really really ill.' She gazed up at Audrey, and her eyes seemed to focus. Her face crumpled up and tears rolled out. 'Got nothing for a baby to grow in,' she sobbed. 'They took it all away.'

Beth was too weak to walk without help. She was still drowsy, and her legs were stiff and uncoordinated. With Audrey on one side and Iain on the other, she managed to make it as far as the staircase. There, Iain had to pick her up and carry her.

Février walked ahead, also unsteady on his feet. His mistress refused to assist him. Being insulted and placed under an illegitimate arrest in her own château by a member of a contemptibly inferior race vexed her rather less than being disobeyed by her most trusted servant. More than her servant; her confidant and companion; the man who had known her more intimately than her own husband. He had betrayed her, and so she chose to walk with dignity and let him limp.

'How are we going to deal with this?' said Iain, puffing with the effort of carrying Beth and picking his way carefully from step to step by the light of Audrey's torch (they had grown so used to creeping about that it had simply not occurred to them to switch the lights on). Was there no end to these stairs? It hadn't seemed so long on the way up.

'What do you mean?' she asked.

'I mean, do we call the police, or what?'

'Of course we call the police. What d'you imag—... Hey, keep going, you two.'

Février and his mistress had stopped walking. They had reached the bottom of the spiral, and were standing on the crest of the wave of steps above the hall like petrified surfers.

'I said, keep going,' Audrey repeated.

'I think they like to obey me, not you.'

Iain and Audrey glanced at each other. 'Jean-Baptiste?' Iain called. 'Is that you?'

There was a movement in the shadows; the lights flicked on, and they saw what their prisoners had seen: an elderly figure standing in the mouth of the left-hand corridor, as still and poised as the armoured knights. 'Walther P 38,' said Monsieur Duprée, supporting the pistol with both hands and letting its muzzle wander over the group ranged before him. It settled finally on Février, and the voice behind it dropped into French: 'Parabellum,' it said. 'Authentic SS-issue. It's been a very long time since I saw one of these. Rather a powerful weapon for a housemaid to be carrying, don't you think?'

Février stared, and took an involuntary step forward. 'Antoine,' he whispered incredulously. '*Antoine?*'

The pistol twitched. 'Stay exactly where you are.'

Iain didn't understand a word of this exchange, but it clearly didn't concern him. He nodded at Audrey, and they began moving around to get out of the line of sight and join Monsieur Duprée in the hall. 'Its okay, Jean-Baptiste,' said Iain, 'we've got Beth. They won't try—'

'I think you stay where you are,' said Monsieur Duprée. 'Is best nobody moves.'

'What?'

'You do as I say,' he repeated, then switched back to French. 'Who would have thought,' he mused, 'old Marcel Godard would end up a domestic servant? I can't be smug, though; the years haven't been so kind to me, either. Life does nothing but degrade us. But Marcel, you didn't have to write such foul things about me, and after all we went through together. And you; Madame de La Simarde, my honoured patron; what I suffered at your hands. And all the time I was starving because you wouldn't pay my bills, you were living off the gold that should have belonged to me.'

'I beg your pardon?' She glanced at her servant. 'Février, what is he talking about? Do you *know* this man?'

Audrey leaned towards Iain. 'What are they saying?' she whispered.

'Don't know,' said Iain with difficulty; his arms and back were on fire. He longed to lower Beth to her feet, but didn't dare move. 'What's going on?' he asked out loud. 'Jean-Baptiste?'

He was ignored. Février said something, to which Monsieur Duprée replied with an amused, contemptuous sneer. Février swore and took another step forward, then another: the moment his foot touched the hall floor, his right shoulder exploded; there was a pistol-shot layered with panning echoes, and a shower like a bursting fruit pattered across Audrey's face. As she raised her hands and recoiled, Février was twisting and beginning to fall backwards; a second shot missed him, kicked a chunk of marble from the stair and zipped past Audrey's head. Iain dropped Beth and rolled on top of her, cradling her head under his chest, just as a third bullet spat through Février's flailing leg and burrowed into his chest.

In the pause that followed, the echoes seemed to go on and on, hammering off the tiles and vaults in chorus with Beth's half-conscious whimpering and Février's gargling, rattling groans. Audrey coiled herself up against the wall with her arms wrapped around her face. As the echoes died away, she peeped out. Iain was also looking out over a wall made from his arms and Beth's body, as though over a parapet. They both stared in horror at Février, who was writhing like a broken-backed beetle, leaking and smearing his blood on the white marble. Only Madame de La Simarde remained standing; she hadn't moved a muscle. She glanced down at Février, then fixed her gaze on her late husband's pistol, which was now pointing at her.

'You,' she said, 'Monsieur Duprée, or whatever your name is, may care to look at what you have wrought in this household. It is fortuitous that you should appear so, to finish what you started. I have not forgotten: *You* are the one who destroyed my son.'

For a moment, the face behind the gun, gimlet eyes in loose, aged flesh, creased in bewilderment. Then comprehension seemed to dawn: the wrinkles eased, and the eyes narrowed. He drew back the hammer, steadied his aim, and with the full-fist squeeze that was still imprinted in his muscle-memory, touched the trigger.

Madame de La Simarde was ready for death. It had been foretold; it was her final chance. She didn't even flinch as the thundercrack leapt from the barrel. The bullet flew high above her head, flipping a ruby-hilted poniard from the display over the arch. The knife was jolted off its hooks and spun out in a lazy arc, striking point-first on the chessboard tiles at the same moment as the pistol. Monsieur Duprée took a single staggering step forward, and collapsed face-first onto the floor.

When Audrey peeped out again, she saw a second figure – a rag-bag of purple velvet – emerging from the shadows of the corridor, the hall lights glinting on her round glasses, a short, heavy poker in her chubby fists.

Madame de La Simarde stared. 'Who on *earth*,' she demanded indignantly, 'is *this*?'

Rachel gazed down in disbelief at the body crumpled before her feet, then up at the chorus of wide-eyed stares directed at her. 'I've found Lydia,' she said faintly. 'She's alive.'

138 Mount Ave
Sheffield

Thursday p.m.

Dear Bethany,

I hope you are well. Lydia has asked me to write and thank you for your letter. She was pleased to get it, but she does not feel up to writing back yet. She is getting a lot better, the therapy is doing wonders for her. She has had letters and visits from all her friends, and that helps as well I think. She talks more than she ever used to.

The reason I am writing and not Gabriel is that he is away at present, in Australia. This brings me to my point, which is a difficulty. He has been offered the opportunity of a lifetime, a job out there, in Sydney. It is what he has always dreamt of. We would be very happy to take Lydia with us, but we think it might set her back, going so far and being separated from her friends. Lydia says you are buying a bigger house, so you might have a spare room(?). Please write and let us know, it would be a load off Gabriel's mind.

I hope you are better after your ordeal. Wasn't it awful about the old couple? Lydia has got to be a witness, but Gabriel thinks it will be too much for her. Did you know he had to go down for the exhumation? How horrible, that poor girl.

Please write and let us know what you decide. Best wishes from both of us.

Yours sincerely,
Helen Hutton (Mrs)

'Look at that. Do you remember, you called it a *sungel of shrees?*'

'Did I?'

'You know you did.' It was a standing family joke. 'You'd lost two front teeth in a week, and you couldn't pronounce your T's . . . It was somewhere near Chipping Norton, I think.'

'I don't remember.'

'You do!'

'I don't.'

'You remember most things. Better than me, anyway.'

'I wouldn't say that.'

It was just as she had described it. The overhanging trees fell away, and the vale opened up. He steered over to the side of the road and stopped.

And there it was. He got out of the car and walked to the lip of the slope for a better view.

Too much enclosure, he decided; too many verticals crowding in. It made him think of Castle Dracula. There simply wasn't enough natural light in the valley to break down those looming walls. Gifts these people may have had, but architecture wasn't one of them.

She was calling his name. He turned away from the view and went back to the car.

'Danny?'

The red brick on top of the long, flat green one. The archway was all but complete now. He scoured the diminished pile and found his favourite brick: a yellow pyramid, satin smooth, the paint worn away to bare wood along the edges from years of handling and building.

'Danny?'

Frowning, he set the yellow pyramid on top of the red cube,

adjusting it so that their edges were perfectly aligned. Just so. Owen, on the far side of the table, was eyeing the structure with impatient jealousy, his plastic soldiers lined up ready to attack it.

'*Danny.*'

A hand enclosed his shoulder, and he flinched. His finger nudged the green block, skewing the gatehouse out of line. 'Oh, *figgly!*' he muttered.

'That's a nice building. Is it a castle?'

'No,' said Danny, readjusting the bricks. 'It's a palace.'

'A palace?' She knelt down beside him. 'Who lives in it?'

'Darth Vader,' said Owen. 'My soldiers are going to beat him up and chop him in bits.'

She smiled as Danny pointed out the black plastic figure standing defiantly inside his wooden walls. 'I don't want to spoil your game, boys, but it's time for Danny to be getting ready.'

Owen leaned his chair back dangerously, pulled up the fringe of the net curtain and put his head under it. 'I *thought* I heard something,' he said. 'She's here again.'

'She's here? Oh God, come on, Danny – you're not even *dressed.*'

'There's two,' said Owen from behind the curtain. 'She's got the mad one with her.'

'*Owen!* That's a horrible, rude thing to say. Don't you *dare* say that again!'

'She's scary,' he insisted. Suddenly, he flung the curtain down and sprang back from the window. 'She saw me!'

He looked around, expecting attention, but they ignored him. Danny was concentrating on straightening the pillars of his archway, resisting being dragged away to dress.

The doorbell rang at that moment, and he was left alone to perfect his palace walls.

'Where is she?'

'She decided to wait in the car. Evie, don't *stare* . . . Is he ready?'

'He's not dressed yet. You're early.' Evie hesitated, and lowered her voice. 'Did you *have* to bring her?'

'She's okay. She's a lot better now. She doesn't have the panics any more.'

'Thank heaven for Prozac, eh?'

'That's one way of putting it.'

'I'll go and get him dressed. Shoe laces are still a bit of a challenge.' She laughed and turned away. At the lounge door, she paused and turned back. 'Look, I suppose you've got to start somewhere,' she said. 'Do you want to see to him?'

Whoever had made this piece of the world seemed to have run out of hills when they got to this bit. The land rolling past the car window just kept getting flatter and flatter, until it was smaller than the sky. He had never seen that before. Except at the seaside, and then it wasn't really the land, was it?

Beth looked in the mirror. She could just see the top of his sandy-haired head. (Where had he got that from?) 'Are you comfy, Dan? It's not far now.'

He fidgeted in his seatbelt. 'Are there towns here?' he asked. 'I can't see *any*.'

She smiled. 'Yes, Dan, there are towns.'

'Do you live in a town?'

'Yes. A big one, with churches and shops and parks.'

'And a library?'

She glanced in the mirror again. 'Er, yes, it's got a library. Do you like reading, Dan?'

There was a pause from the back seat. 'My name's Danny.'

She ignored the sidelong look from beside her. 'New name, new mummy,' she murmured. 'Don't you like Dan?' she asked out loud. There was no answer. 'I like Dan. It's a nice name. Dan or Daniel.' Still no answer. 'What books do you like?' she asked, adding: 'Danny?'

'Picture books,' he said. 'Biesty books.'

'Beastly?'

'No, *Biesty*. Biesty's Cross Sections. They're best.'

'Oh.' She laughed. 'Iain likes those, too. It must a boy thing.'

'Does Iain write books?'

'He tries to.'

'My grandad wrote books, didn't he?'

'Well, one book. A book of poems. There was a poem about me in it. I was a tiny little girl then. Much littler than you.'

'How did it go?'

'Oh goodness, let me see . . . *Something, something* . . . Yes, I know:

> *Scion sheared out of*
> *Two forms*
> *And laid bare athwart*
> *Her breast.*
> *A bright instant of*
> *Joyous pain's*
> *Sugar spun and coiled*
> *About my soul.*

. . . That was it. He called it a small poem for a small person. What do you think?'

Danny liked it, even though it didn't rhyme and he didn't know what a *thwart* was. 'It sounds like candy floss,' he said.

'*Sugar spun and coiled?* Yes, I suppose it does . . . Would you like to write books when you grow up?'

'No, I want to be an architect.'

She choked back her incredulity. 'Really? That's impressive. Will you design a house for me?'

He considered for a moment. 'Yes,' he said. 'A big one, with a big bedroom for me in it.' He paused, then went on tentatively: 'You can call me Dan if you like.'

'Do I have to, Dan? I really don't want to see it.'

She had always spared him the details, and so he didn't understand. He coaxed her out of the car and over to the furzed lip of the road.

'Yes,' she murmured, looking down into the valley. 'That's how I remember it. It hasn't changed at all.' She shivered in the dappled sunshine.

He nodded. 'She still lives there, apparently. She must be ancient . . . D'you think we ought to . . .?'

'No,' she said sharply. 'I don't imagine she'd be too pleased to see us. Nor I her.'

She noticed he had his hand inside his shirt, toying with something. He drew it out, and she saw that it was the small, shiny russet sliver she had given him last summer, on the eve of his going away to university. She had told him the story that attached to it several years before.

He noticed her watching him. 'I wanted to wear it,' he said. 'D'you mind?'

He had had it pierced and suspended from a thin silver chain which he wore around his neck.

'It's yours,' she said. 'Of course I don't mind.'

'D'you think Auntie Lyd ever knew?'

She gazed down at the castle. She was remembering, and seemed not to have heard. Eventually, she spoke. 'I don't know . . . She might have guessed, I suppose. Shrewdness was never her strongest point, though.'

'No . . . Look, are you sure we shouldn't . . .?'

She glanced up at him, then back down at the valley. She had looked enough. 'Maybe tomorrow,' she said, and walked back to the car.

He lingered a while, fingering his little home-made pendant. It was so light that, most of the time, he never noticed it was there. He would always wear it. It was real tortoiseshell, from Tahiti: not fantastically

438

valuable, but it was the only thing he had; the only thing – apart from the seed that had made him – ever given to his mother by his father.

'Dan? Are you going to keep me here all day?'

He tucked the plectrum back inside his shirt and turned away from the Château. 'Coming, Mum.'